THE LOST LETTERS
of WILLIAM
SHAKESPEARE

THE UNDISCOVERED DIARY OF HIS
STRANGE EVENTFUL LIFE AND LOVES

ALSO BY TERRY TAMMINEN

Lives Per Gallon:
The True Cost of Our Oil Addiction

Cracking the Carbon Code:
The Keys to Sustainable Profits in the New Economy

Watercolors:
How JJ the Whale Saved Us

THE LOST LETTERS of WILLIAM SHAKESPEARE

THE UNDISCOVERED DIARY OF HIS STRANGE EVENTFUL LIFE AND LOVES

Edited and adapted by
TERRY TAMMINEN

BASED ON A TRUE STORY

Shakespeare House Press

Shakespeare House Press
Copyright © 2018 Terry Tamminen

Shakespeare House Press is a trademark of Seventh Generation Advisors, Inc.

ISBN 978-0-9997368-0-7 Print hardcover
ISBN 978-0-9997368-1-4 E-book
ISBN 978-0-9997368-2-1 Audiobook
ISBN 978-0-9997368-3-8 Print paperback

Library of Congress Control Number: 2017919680
British Cataloguing-in-Publication data available.

Book design by Rob Siders
Cover design by Monica DuClaud

Producers:
Jordan Kaplan
Kristina Haddad http://www.kristinahaddad.net
Audiobook Engineer: Brett Rothfeld
Stock media for the audiobook was provided by track5; SOUNDCRUSHER;
Classicalguitar; Major_minor; MarcusBresslerMusic / Pond5

To Miss B, Rosalind, Giles, and the other anonymous angels who have so many stories yet to tell.

TABLE OF CONTENTS

LIST OF ILLUSTRATIONS

FOREWORD

If you are anything like the majority of my family, friends, and a few Shakespeare experts I have consulted, you have looked at the title of this book and asked, "Is this historical fact or an elaborate historical fiction?"

As you will read in the Prologue and see in Illustration 1, there is a good part of this story that I can prove to be absolutely true. But as you will read in the Scribe's Notes, I am very aware of past attempts to foist fictitious "found" documents on the public as being written by Shakespeare, so while the letters I saw were very real, I can't say for certain how authentic they are, nor have I edited and adapted them into book form exactly as I found them.

Given this mix of fact and potential fiction, and recognizing that the book-buying public prefers things to be categorized as one or the other, I decided to publish this book as historical fiction "based on a true story" with the very tantalizing possibility that the original letters will be made available to the public and future scholars will validate my belief that they were indeed written by William Shakespeare. In fact, as of this writing, I am working with a team at the University of Pennsylvania to gain more insight into the authorship question using innovative examination of unique word patterns, but until that research is complete, as Shakespeare says in *Troilus & Cressida*, "modest doubt is called the beacon of the wise."

By offering this book in that historical fiction category, I hope to avoid the "slings and arrows of outrageous fortune" that would come my way from Shakespeare aficionados of all types. Knowing how many people subscribe to theories that Shakespeare didn't write the plays and poems we generally attribute to him, indeed that some have begun a campaign to prove he never even existed, this is the only way to silence the critics before their howls and scowls discourage readers from taking the journey of discovery that has challenged, mystified, and enchanted me for over two decades.

Your own journey into these letters may be enriched by other materials I have posted on the book's official website www.shakespeareletters.com, including more under the headings "A Reader's Guide to The Lost Letters" and "The Challenge of Deciphering Elizabethan Handwriting & Spelling" with examples from the letters. There's also a brief biography of Shakespeare, to help you know more about the generally accepted details of his life and to understand the context of his work.

So now, before anyone declares he "doth protest too much, methinks", I invite you to enjoy the *Lost Letters* with this, my modest acknowledgement of all possibilities. Of one thing, I am absolutely certain: you will be captivated by the sometimes-brilliant, sometimes-flawed young man from Stratford, who takes a very surprising path to London and immortality.

Terry Tamminen
Santa Monica, California
April 23, 2018
(William Shakespeare's birthday)

ACKNOWLEDGEMENTS

Shakespeare observed "How far that little candle throws his beams. So shines a good deed in a weary world." As you might imagine, bringing the *Lost Letters* to the world required many little candles to light my way.

My wife, Leslie Tamminen, has been the leading light and contributor to this project, helping me to draft the introductions to each letter, plan the publication, and putting up with a home-office festooned with old maps, sketches, dusty reference books, and other detritus of Elizabethan England that has aided my research.

Keeping it in the family, I also owe a debt of gratitude to my sister, Laurie Latour, who has really been my co-editor, drawing on her years of experience as a teacher and publisher of educational books to draft the *Glossary* and *Dramatis Personae* for this book. She is also writing a series of children's books based on the letters, which we hope will inspire the next generation to enjoy and appreciate Shakespeare and his work.

The sage literary advice and friendship of Phoebe Larmore permeates this book and our many cups of tea overlooking the Pacific Ocean have become as much a part of my journey with the letters as the time I spent in London, over similar cups of tea, reading and transcribing them with Miss B (of whom I will say much more and express my appreciation in the Prologue).

Finally, I could not have pulled this project across the finish line without my indefatigable team at Shakespeare House Press and Seventh Generation Advisors, Kristina Haddad and Jenna Cittadino, along with my audiobook producer Brett Rothfeld. And while there are many others who gave me advice and help at key points in this long process, special thanks go to my earliest readers and cheerleaders, Drew Bohan, Robb Rice, John Cronin and Lola Mintz.

Oh, and just one more recognition—my eternal gratitude to John Combe, who apparently preserved these letters and handed them down through the ages. If you were with us today, I hope you would approve of how we have given your dear friend his voice once again.

PROLOGUE
How a Sometimes-Starving Actor
Stumbled Upon Shakespeare's Lost Letters

I was an actor in 1989. There is no greater challenge for an actor than to perform Shakespeare in London, because there will always be someone in the
front row, not quite obscured by the stage lighting, usually an elderly lady with
her overcoat folded neatly across her lap, purse perched atop like a cherry on
a hot fudge sundae, who mouths the words of each soliloquy as you deliver it.
Stray one word from the text, indeed vary the cadence she memorized in school
when Atlee was Prime Minister, and you can feel her heading for the exits. Oh,
not literally of course. No one in England is so rude. But the pursed lips, slightly
warped at the edges, tell you she is now merely politely awaiting your exit so
she can make good her own.

In some ways, those proctors are your badge of honor. They keep you
honest, ensure your performance will be the best you have to give. They terror-
ize and nurture you, play-by-play critics whose approbation means everything
to you and yet is always just barely out of reach. They are a lot like your parents,
but with superior memory.

The day I met her was not unusual. The blue haired denizens graced the
first row and the remaining fifty seats were two-thirds full behind them. It may
have been the imminent signs of rain hovering over our outdoor stage in the
park. It may have been the unseasonable cold that hung in the June air or the
pain in my twisted knee that forced me to add a methodical, old-man's shuffle
to my character, forcing me to slow down and savor every gesture and every
phrase. It may have been the fact that this was my closing performance and I

knew William Shakespeare might never again appear on a London stage, at least as played by me. Whatever it was, that afternoon would illuminate lives, not least of all, mine.

Of course the works of Shakespeare have appeared on London stages for over 400 years and show no sign of waning, but my play depicted William Shakespeare in person, alone onstage, packing up his belongings after a life-time in the theatre. He gossips with the audience and answers their questions, illustrated by the cups and saucers that populate his theatrical cupboard. No two shows are alike, depending on the questions (and whether the proctors have begun to show signs of displeasure). Characters not counted, there is only one person onstage—William Shakespeare—me (Illustration 1 below gives you some idea of the play).

1. Terry Tamminen as William Shakespeare in his 1989 one-man play "Will Power," wherein he portrayed the Bard reminiscing about his life in conversation with the audience.

Well, I truly inhabited Shakespeare that day, or vice versa. I was in what athletes call a "zone," so focused on my task that nothing could interfere with either the impossible buzzer-beating shots or the pleasure in taking them. The audience, yes all of them, seemed genuinely rewarded and the normally re-strained London crowd insisted on three curtain calls and one encore—Puck's "If we shadows have offended, think but this and all is mended..." My lone stage-hand backslapped me to my dressing room tent and I stood looking around for a few minutes, perhaps not yet wanting to bid my character, my friend, a final farewell in his native environment. That's when I noticed the flower.

A single red rose, with a notecard attached, had been placed on the creaky cane chair at my folding make-up table. I typically got no more dressing room accolades than good reviews (i.e. none), so this was not only a cause for minor celebration, but also a reprieve from stepping out of his shoes, at least for a few more moments.

I sniffed the flower and plucked the note from it. It was embossed card stock, slightly yellowed, with "WS" on the outside. Inside it read "I have some-thing I believe is yours. I'll be waiting at the Lord Admiral's. Miss B."

Since I hadn't lost anything recently and was quite alone in London, the provocative nature of the card, especially attached to a fresh, tightly closed young bud, could not be underestimated. My backstage visitors were generally a Dickensian assortment of "admirers," best illustrated by the one the stage-hand called Juliet.

Forty-something and pear shaped, Juliet had come to half the perfor-mances, dressed in a silk-flower-trimmed-cream-colored gown, seams failing, with a lace headpiece that defied description (but you would certainly not want to sit behind it). She came to my dressing room after the performances and asked for my autograph, although I had obliged her several times already, then after profuse compliments about one speech or another, she slipped me her phone number on a cocktail napkin folded over at least ten times and soddenly sealed with perspiration.

But a Miss B? A rose and a proffer of rendezvous? A salacious hint of something she wants to "give me?" Never anything like that so far! She had already given me something, for now I couldn't wait to strip off the facial hair and wig, scrub the greasepaint from my face with cold cream, and change into street clothes. My old friend with the creaky knee would have to step aside, return to residence in my prop trunk until another town and another audience, so that I might meet the tantalizing Miss B as myself.

I was at the Lord Admiral's before you could say "To be or..." well, you know the rest. The predictable West-end theatre crowd made the place seem brighter than the steady rain outside implied. Most of the tables and all of the bar were occupied. Of course I had no idea who I was looking for and although my headshot was tacked up on the billboard at our open-air theatre, sans makeup, it was the typical flattering Hollywood black-and-white that might have had a resemblance to reality ten years earlier, but which might make Miss B's task of finding me in a bar more challenging today. I would count on what lighting there was, and an eager look, as I slid into the only empty booth. Well, hopefully not too eager.

My second glass of claret had already arrived and although I was doing my best to make eye contact with every cute and semi-cute (OK, even the semi-semi-cute) maiden who seemed mostly unattached, there was no hint of anyone who might be looking for me. I was beginning to think of the other possibilities, a practical joke playing stagehand, for instance, when Miss B slid into the booth as if descending like a backdrop from the fly gallery above the stage.

"Master Shakespeare, I presume." She apparently wanted me to play this thing in character. She extended a hand that brought to mind a brittle, faded newspaper clipping. I took the hand and despite my initial shock, played the part with a kiss aimed in the general vicinity of her knuckles and a reply of "Your servant, m'lady."

In her mid-sixties, I guessed, she was one of the younger old ladies from the front row, perhaps one I could say I had seen in the audience more than once, her overcoat now neatly draped over her shoulders and beaded with rain, slightly steaming. Her simple black hat and plain natural gray hair were dry, so I guessed the umbrella was in the stand by the door. Her dress was pink, but might have been red a long time ago. A non-descript brooch peeked out from behind the coat. Her face looked like it had been slept in, but her eyes were so clear and blue that one had to suspect contacts.

We exchanged some pleasantries, including the obligatory English weather conversation-maker, even as I scanned the room now and again in case there was another Miss B. She ordered tea, I don't recall if she took milk or lemon. She asked a lot of questions about how I had come to write and perform my play and what I really knew about the Bard. The uneven light of the pub played tricks with the details of her face as I studied it for more clues about her intentions and whatever the folds, creases, and crow's feet might reveal about her personal story. I could discern little more, although by now her steady gaze made it clear the color of her eyes were natural. Before long, she came to the point.

"I have been so moved by your performances, sir," she whispered in tones that seemed slightly weary, either of the world or just another long day. "At my age, your faith expands to concepts that would have seemed, shall I say improbable, at twenty. So forgive me if this sounds somehow 'New Age,' but I believe—I have persuaded myself to believe—that William Shakespeare lives in or through you."

Mostly out of kindness to a paying customer, a repeat one at that, and to a handsome old woman who deserved sincerity, I shrugged through my best performance of "you-are-too-kind." She waved off any actual comment from me, as someone who fears her time is short, or perhaps is just thinking of a train schedule, and continued.

"Therefore, I want to give you something that I trust you will know how to use. I have papers, letters and papers, sort of a diary actually, of...yours...of William Shakespeare."

When you've lived as long as Miss B has, you can probably tell when people are talking and it doesn't match what they are thinking. Fortunately for me, I was not compelled to fill the silence with any faked gratitude after her perfunctory, yet startling, pronouncement, thanks to the waitress.

"Here love," she cooed in Miss B's direction, wiping the unmoving stains from the table as she spoke. "More hot water or another glass of wine for the gentleman?"

"No dear, thank you," Miss B smiled, holding her hands slightly off the table as if she would make it levitate, but from which gesture the waitress understood "no more." Miss B continued.

"Now I assure you these papers are authentic, some from other people, but most from Master Shakespeare. I want you to know their contents, but I may not actually give them to you—do you understand?"

I think I nodded.

"What I propose is this: I will bring the papers to you, a few each night for your examination. You may make notes or transcribe as you will, but I make two conditions."

"I'm all ears," I said, wondering why a man who had sixteen hours of Shakespeare's speeches and poems committed to memory couldn't come up with a more literate simile.

"First, you will make no attempt to learn how these documents became available to me. Second, you will make no attempt to learn more about me." With this, she simply laid both hands on the table in front of her as if it were a piano keyboard. "You may use what you find in the papers in any way you like."

Who knows what I said, but somehow, on the off chance that this was real, I conveyed to her my acceptance of her terms and my genuine gratitude that she had chosen me to even see this "diary." Then I felt oddly obliged to be more than a little honest with her.

"Miss B, you know I am an actor, not a historian. Well, I will admit my proudest moment in high school was winning the history prize in twelfth grade, but I'm certainly no academic. I also won the German verse-speaking prize then, but these days I have trouble reading a menu in the Munich train station. But I would give anything to have a real window into Shakespeare's mind, if that's what this is."

"Oh, from what I've been able to understand, these are his most intimate thoughts on many subjects. Of course I have some difficulty reading the hand, but I recognize the references to events and people dead or forgotten these four centuries. But I trust if any part of his spirit resides in you..." Her voice trailed off, in hope or despair?

Anticipation is an odd phenomenon and I tried to keep mine in check, knowing that her "papers" might be old theatre programs or that I might simply never hear from her again after tonight. I shuffled all such doubts aside and made plans to meet her at the Bag O' Nails pub near Victoria Station the next night at six. We could share a light supper and I would look at whatever she elected to bring.

As if we had concluded a real estate transaction, she thanked me for my time and hurried somewhat nervously out of the pub. Maybe she was nuts. Maybe she had just committed to do something she would regret. Maybe she was merely late for the last train.

After closing my London engagement, I had planned two weeks vacation around England and Scotland, a reward to myself for playing in Los Angeles, New York, and Switzerland before London, so I certainly had the time to see what Miss B might actually produce. The next day came and went quietly enough and I variously found myself imagining the consequence of the biggest literary discovery in a century, or just having dinner with someone's grandmother and getting out of town a day later than planned.

Either way, that next evening, I was at the small pub thirty minutes early just to...well, I don't really know why. I wore the same blue Levis long-sleeved shirt and faded jeans, partly out of superstition, partly because I lacked a more diverse wardrobe in those days, and brought a pad of writing paper in my canvas backpack in case I needed to make notes. Suspecting that old letters might be faded, I had also brought a large magnifying glass and a small flashlight.

There are many clock towers in London, Big Ben of course but many others. I'm sure they all clanged the last stroke of six when Miss B walked in. It had stopped raining about midday, but her overcoat was still damp. Something told me more than a handshake was in order, so I stood and gave her a little hug and hung her coat on the peg next to the booth. At about five and a half feet, she was only a few inches shorter than me and somewhat pear-shaped. I noticed the coat was fraying at the cuffs and a size too small for her, suggesting it was acquired many years earlier by a woman of now modest means. The dividers between the booths, her coat on one and mine on the other, seemed to create a curtain to a proscenium with us sitting in the center. All the world really is a stage.

We ordered some food, one of us had fish and chips, the other a shepherd's pie, but I don't recall which was which, because all I wanted was for the preamble to end and the much anticipated main course of Shakespeare's papers to be served. She may have sensed as much and immediately asked me to clear the space next to my place setting. I wiped it dutifully, but it was already quite clean and dry. In the States they would have given you glasses of ice water that would have made unavoidable puddles all over the table by now. But this was England.

From a straw carry-all with faded blue and yellow silk flowers embroidered on one side, she withdrew a large manila folder, dog-eared and smudged from countless other pairs of hands, sliding it across the table in my direction. It was the kind of folder preferred by clerks and bureaucrats in Ebenezer Scrooge's day, with four columns of signature blocks on the front so that each recipient could write another name below their own, before wrapping the red string around the brown paper button to secure the contents and passing it on to someone else. There were dozens of names written in pencil or in red, black, or blue ink, now mostly faded and each one crossed out by someone who had held, then forwarded the folder, perhaps no farther than the cubicle adjacent, only to have their name crossed out and another printed neatly in the next block. How many invoices, time sheets, policy memos, leases, or ledgers had occupied this serviceable cover before Miss B chose it to carry her paperwork to our meeting?

By now I had turned this moment over in my mind so many times that the climax felt contrived. I unwound the string and opened the folder to find a stack of about twenty pages, no two alike, with black ink handwriting on them, all but one of them two-sided. As I leafed through the folder to get a sense of what she had brought, I sneezed from dust and a moldy smell that may well have had the same effect four hundred years earlier in another London pub on a guy named Shakespeare.

I won't belabor what I saw upon closer inspection, since the book that follows is my earnest effort to do justice to these letters. What I will say, is that as

I examined each page, sometimes using the magnifying glass, sometimes shining my pocket flashlight on an especially obscured word, I carefully shielded each page from the food that came and went or the glasses of wine and tea we shared, because it quickly became apparent that this was either the most brilliant, painstaking forgery in literary history or I was holding a number of old letters that amounted to Shakespeare's diary.

Miss B sat quietly as I worked. She expressed regret that she couldn't knit to absorb the idleness of times like these, but said her fingers were no longer sufficiently nimble. Now she seemed simply gladdened to see the letters warmed by a human touch and the light of a candle (yes, an electric lamp also glowed overhead). I tried to transcribe each word onto my yellow notepad, those British A4 pages that are slightly narrower and longer than American ones, trying to match line for line, duplicate the odd marks and stains (the equivalent of 400 year old coffee mug rings?). I kept forcing myself to relax, realizing that I felt oddly guilty, holding these museum pieces in my hand, once even smudging a line that had been written in charcoal and now succumbed to my misplaced thumb. The pages would crackle and bits would flake off, sometimes even from the middle of the page, leaving tiny holes or making quill punctures slightly larger, losing a letter or rendering an entire word unintelligible.

It was very slow going, not having spent much time before with tortured, elaborately carved Elizabethan handwriting that seemed to fade as if my eyesight were abrasive to it. Illustration 2 on the next page is an example of the unfamiliar style of writing that I saw, in this case Shakespeare's own Last Will and Testament. Scholars generally agree this is not his handwriting, except for the signature, but you will get the idea of what letter writing looked like in his day.

I had not completed two pages when Miss B gently told me it was past her time and we would have to continue tomorrow night. Couldn't I photocopy these, I suggested? No. Perhaps we could start in the morning and I could work all day? No. I don't suppose you could leave me a few pages to work on and... no, no.

We did indeed meet again the next night and the next. I realized that for Miss B it wasn't a matter of trust—she was lonely and wanted to witness the

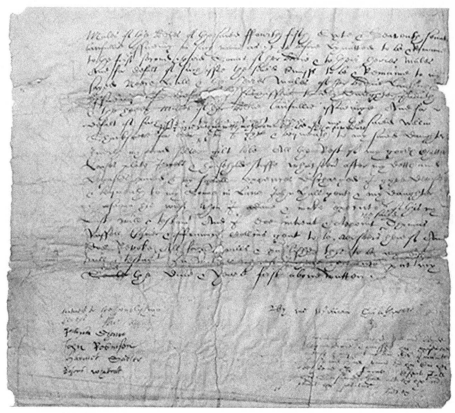

2. *A typical example of 16th century handwriting: the last page of William Shakespeare's Last Will and Testament.*

process of transferring her buried treasures onto fresh pages. Although most of our time was spent without conversation, she was connected to another human being and the bait was a stack of four hundred year old letters. It was as if she had started her own thousand-and-one-nights; as if when the stories ran out, she knew, so would I.

The days rolled by and, in an odd way, although I suspected I was still only scratching the surface of these mysteries, the pace forced me to savor every word. Seven nights a week, I transcribed and seven days a week I combed the library for clues to the events, culture, and the man being unearthed before me, always amazed at what I learned. The image that came to mind again and again was the archeologist with a dentist's pick and a brush, painstakingly exposing a dinosaur by the inch.

Along the way, I slowly let myself believe the letters held incredibly intimate secrets about William Shakespeare and the fascinating individuals that populated his world, although I remained skeptical about who wrote them. One letter mentioned the author's interest in leaving England for the Americas, because of a promise that settlers would be given five hundred acres of land. I found in the Encyclopedia Britannica (the font of all knowledge in the days before Wikipedia and Google) that commoners in Elizabethan England had little hope of being large landowners, so I realized how such a lure might persuade a young man from Stratford to leave his family with visions of becoming economically equal to a nobleman.

In another letter, the author visited Sir Francis Drake's famous ship the Golden Hind, but described it as a dilapidated 16th century tourist trap. That seemed far-fetched, but sure enough, I found an old British history book that confirmed the fate of the once-proud vessel that had accomplished so many "firsts" in global navigation under the famous swashbuckler's command. A very different picture of Shakespeare's England was emerging, pieced together with the rather heart-stopping story of his life. Assuming that's whose life I was reading about.

As such tantalizing historical textures and aromas emerged, I was bursting to share them with someone, not so much like the lurid gossip about a neighbor that you might confide to your spouse, but more like a workplace rumor that you repeat in case a colleague can quash or verify it, knowing your future employment depends on the answer. Honor-bound to keep this all to myself, and with no real confidantes in London then anyway, I resisted the urge to scratch that particular itch and concentrated my energies instead on the still-formidable tasks at hand.

But I regret that I was so absorbed each night in the letters that I never really learned more about my mysterious benefactor. Oh, I would never have been given names and dates from her, I knew that. But I might have gently probed for hints about long ago lovers and friends, children and events that would have illuminated her recent past in London, as much as Shakespeare's letters were doing for a society dead these four centuries. Was she a spinster or widow? As a young woman in the social turmoil of the sixties, had she been an activist or an observer? Was the knitting she had mentioned a life-long hobby or one that superseded fox hunting or fencing as she aged? I felt a disquieting guilt about not displaying as much care for a new living friend as I did for a long dead stranger, but then again, she had pledged me to seek no further knowledge about her.

We had been at our unconventional affair for a dozen days or so when Miss B arrived one night well past her appointed hour. She looked pale and distracted. Her familiar straw bag yielded the usual manila envelope, from which she delicately extracted about five times more pages than was customary. I pushed aside the proffered papers, difficult though that was with a document on top of tonight's offering that looked like sketches for a theatrical set, and insisted she tell me what was wrong. A cup of tea loosened her lips.

"Terry," she began softly, her voice trailing off as if there was nothing to follow. This was odd in itself because she always called me 'Mr. T.'

"I think I want you to have these papers to take along with you," she whispered. Did the tone and volume imply conspiracy or simply weariness and resignation? "Please inquire no further, but meet me here next Wednesday to exchange these for another batch."

Of course I wanted to thank her and reassure her that her trust was not misplaced. Despite her admonition, I also wanted to press the issue and see if I could be of some assistance. Was she ill? Or frightened for some reason? What I wanted mattered little, because before I could say a word, she slipped out of the booth and disappeared out the back door of the pub. That was the first time she had ever used the back door.

I couldn't bring myself to look at the thick folder of letters without first contemplating what might be happening to her. Fear that someone would discover our clandestine meetings focused on the letters? If so, who might that be? Concern for the safety of these inestimably valuable documents, which for the first time were in someone else's possession for more than a few hours at a time? Or was it something more mundane, not about me or this endeavor at all? As I mentioned, there was an air about her of an elderly lady of modest means, so was she merely late on the rent and short of cash? Had there been an argument with a familiar that had left her deeply disappointed or disillusioned?

Whatever the reason for her apparent discomfiture, our meeting that evening troubled me, but slowly Miss B became her old self and our subsequent rendezvous took on the air of a pleasant courtship dance. Since I could devour the pages she gave me at leisure now, our evenings gave us the chance to simply chat over our predictable pub meals. We spoke of world events and a few hints of her life, mostly things like books she had read and plays she had seen, exchanged for long monologues about my life and the performances of *Will Power* I did for students in Los Angeles schools. And of course the obligatory discussion about the ever-changing English weather.

Working mostly in the cocoon of my windowless basement lodging, I easily lost track of time and the world of 1989, falling deeper into the rabbit hole of the late 1500s. I began to notice street and place names in the letters that I had seen on my walks around the city, apparently unchanged by so many generations of Londoners over so many years. I felt a chill seeing references to The Rose and The Globe playhouses, having just read in the newspaper how the site of the former was newly discovered and being excavated, while the latter was being rebuilt on the banks of the Thames not far from its original site. One night (or was it day?) the power went out and I lit the candle my landlord had presciently provided, then hunched lower over the latest batch of letters to make out the handwriting in the dancing yellowish light, much as their author must have done when the original ink was still wet on the page.

Three more weeks slipped by and a real summer threatened to break out, evidenced by pasty-white shirtless bodies strewn across suddenly verdant city park lawns, as if Londoners were doing their impression of sun-worshiping Californians even though the "heat wave" rarely exceeded 70 degrees. Wimbledon finals were around the corner and that meant warmth and strawberries and July days that never end.

Summer became fall and perhaps it was the change of seasons; perhaps it was the realization of being closer to the end than the beginning of this still-astonishing endeavor, evident from the many notepads stacked up in my tiny quarters that had been filled with transcripts of the letters. Perhaps it was the genuine fondness I had developed for Miss B (did she feel likewise about me?), but whatever the new feeling that now arose in me, I found myself obsessed with knowing who this woman really was and how she had come to possess these letters.

In retrospect, I could have at least asked her if she had ever read the letters herself (surely that question would not have crossed her boundary of secrecy) and determined if she was the Sherlock Holmes who had deduced the identity of the author, or if someone else had done so and told her of the epic possibility. I felt that I could do nothing to transgress against the simple tenets that framed our relationship however, mostly for fear that the princess and the papers would turn back into pumpkins if I did. Yet I found myself nevertheless compelled to know, at least for no one but myself, just what enchanted forest this grand, generous, slightly tragic figure came from. Just a few days later, she provided me with the answer. Well, sort of.

"You know Miss B," I started, absent-mindedly straightening the stack of papers and tightening the black silk ribbon that held this batch together within the now tattered manila folder, before sliding them across the table to her, carefully avoiding any crumbs or wine stains. "I'm beginning to wonder what more there could be after this batch. He's told us his entire life's story in what I've seen so far, well augmented by the other correspondence too, and the March 1616 letter reads like a farewell. As you know, he died in April of 1616."

For a moment I thought she hadn't heard me, because Miss B simply slid the folder into her straw carry-all and made no reply. She calmly sipped her tea and waited for me to realize that for the first time there would be no stack of papers in return for the ones I had given her. She smiled at me. Not the smile of a lover or a casual friend; not the smile of a salesman or a grandmother; not the smile of laughter, cynicism, too-long life, or even of pity. She smiled the full-face smile of gratitude and completion. Her marathon was over, she told me in those wrinkles and curled eyes. The baton, the burden, was now mine.

"Goodbye, William Shakespeare," she said, leaning forward slightly to clasp my hands in hers across the table. "May God light your way."

With that, she rose quite suddenly and, for only the second time in our three months together, slipped silently out the back door and into the crisp London night.

Well, I told you about that urge to really know her, something significant about her at least, something upon which to build my future speculation and aimless mental wonderings about the dear Miss B. On this instinct alone, I sprang from the table and dropped a twenty pound note for the tea and wine, almost as if saying thank you, with a large tip, I could buy penance in advance for what I was about to do.

I ran to the door and looked out after her. She was gone. I ran from the back into the street and looked in all directions, but saw no sign of her among the throng of humanity that streamed back and forth on a balmy fall night. Red double-decker buses chugged by in clouds of diesel soot; black-beetle taxis dodged in and out of traffic; every moving object or person bathed in neon and indiscriminate street lighting, along with the rosy hue of a sun that refuses to set at that time of year until it's really good and ready to do so.

Left or right? I had a 50-50 chance to catch up to her, unless she had escaped in a car or bus. I ran to the left, running mostly off the curb to avoid strollers, my eyes squinting and darting as if that might increase my chance of seeing her. I was so out of shape in those days, well, I still am, but it was probably no more than a hundred feet when I stopped, panting, hands on knees, staring mostly at the gutter to catch my breath. In that instant, reflected in a pool of slimy rainwater that still puddled against the curb, I saw Miss B across street.

It had never occurred to me to look over there. Buckingham Palace Road runs along the south side of the palace grounds, past the Royal Mews and down to Victoria Station. The Bag O' Nails stood at the corner of that road and Lower Grosvenor Place, which runs along the west side of the palace. The palace side of both streets was just high brick walls and sidewalks, while the public sides of both were the usual mélange of pubs, shops and side streets. I had been running along the commercial side of Grosvenor Place, never thinking to look over to the palace side. I looked up from the puddle and confirmed it was her, walking briskly, hugging the ivy-covered wall, toting the straw carry-all with the unmistakable faded blue and yellow silk flowers.

I suddenly felt exposed, realizing that if she looked over her left shoulder I was busted. I got off the street and melted into the passersby, favoring the shop windows and matching my pace with hers, but never losing sight of her. I had not long to wait.

Miss B stopped, as if faced with a barrier or a looming cavern in the footpath before her. She seemed to flatten herself against the wall. I was careful to turn my face away, trying to appear like someone reading the menu on the pub chalkboard in front of me, but stealing a glance over my right shoulder at the lone figure across the street against the ivy. And then she was gone.

Startled, I straightened up and focused on the place where she had stood not a minute before. The wall was deep in shadows on that side of the street, and to be sure it was hard to make out any features, but there was no doubt that Miss B had been there and now she was not. I took a few tentative steps toward the curb and when I confirmed she wasn't somehow still there watching my every move, I dodged the traffic and ran across the street.

With each step I cursed and questioned myself. Had I made a Faust-like deal with the Devil, trading some immortal thing of value for a handful of fool's gold, the 20th century Mephistopheles dematerialized now that her spell was cast entirely? Or, like the dream every actor has periodically, of forgetting his lines or suddenly appearing naked in front of a laughing audience, was a candid camera nearby about to record my uncomfortable grimace as an old acting partner leaps from behind a trash can and yells "surprise!"

No magic, nothing other-worldly. When I got to the place in the wall where I had last seen Miss B, I realized that deep in the ivy there was no magic trick, nothing sinister that had swallowed her up, in fact it was nothing more unusual than a door. To be sure it was an old door with rusting hardware that looked as if it hadn't been opened in a century, but a door nevertheless.

Miss B had disappeared into the grounds of Buckingham Palace.

SCRIBE'S NOTES

After Miss B so suddenly evaporated on the last night that I saw her, I recall an unusual evolution of emotions over the next few days. At first I was intrigued by the idea that the letters might have something to do with Buckingham Palace or a rogue member of the Queen's family who had grown impatient with the pace of academic custodians in the Royal Archives. Then, two days later, wedged in a small seat on a long plane flight back to Los Angeles, I wrestled with the inevitable deflation of returning to "real" life; anger at myself for not finding some way to stay in touch with Miss B; even doubt that what I had done was worth the investment of three months of eye strain and some kind of carpal tunnel ailment in my right hand.

My prop trunk had been carefully limited to the airline weight restrictions of the day, but it now held twenty additional pounds of paper, letters transcribed into a thick pile of notepads. I told the skeptical check-in agent what I had been doing and begged her to give me a break on the overweight fees, which she did after I recited the "To be or not to be" soliloquy from *Hamlet* in German to amuse her. Maybe that was my first sign that someone would want to read Shakespeare's *Lost Letters*, which I was about to spend a considerable portion of my life interpreting, researching, and assembling into book form.

Soon after landing back home I wanted to immerse myself once more in the letters and the mysteries they held or solved, especially filling in the gaps of our general knowledge of Shakespeare's "lost years," but I was compelled to honor Miss B's gift by first educating myself enough to accurately adapt the old English language for contemporary readers and learn more background on the customs and history of Tudor England. I soon realized how much I missed the old lady across the pub table and enjoyed imagining her sitting quietly as I worked, nodding approvingly from time to time to encourage my perseverance on the challenging and otherwise lonely undertaking.

As I slowly deciphered the details of each letter from my hastily scribbled notes, there were descriptions of people, events, dates, and places that had me nodding too, in affirmation at the realization of how these letters could now corroborate the conjecture of various historians about Shakespeare's life and times, theories that previously had no way to be confirmed. Some discoveries made me sit suddenly straighter in my chair, knowing I was reading intimate diary-like revelations about Shakespeare, Queen Elizabeth, and other notables of the era (Illustration 24 shows portraits that are thought to be of Shakespeare, alongside portraits of the key nobles he writes about in the letters, as they aged over time).

But the most electrifying "aha" moments for me were recognizing lines from the plays that I had spoken onstage hundreds of times on several continents, discovering for the first time the origin of a phrase or sentiment and thereby peering behind the curtain of Shakespeare's creative process.

During the first few weeks and months that followed, a few questions gnawed uncomfortably at my sense of purpose. Thinking back, I can distill them down to three very basic ones that might have also crossed your mind by now too.

First, why had so many letters that illuminate the most intimate details of Shakespeare's life been hidden from public view for nearly four centuries? The Prologue explains how a thirty-seven year old journeyman actor came to learn of their existence, study, and edit them. However, after twenty-six years of unraveling the linguistic etymology and generally dusting off the soot of time that stubbornly obscures the original meaning, I still can't answer that one big question—but I have a few theories.

Shakespeare wrote the letters to his Stratford friend John Combe, of whom I will say more in the introduction to Letter One. Had they remained with the Combe family? Was Miss B somehow related or a close friend? I had spent hours in a London library looking at books of genealogy about prominent

Stratford families, but was too eager then to return to the content of the letters themselves to linger much longer over what seemed to be secondary subjects, no matter how coincidentally fascinating. I looked periodically since then in various reference books and more recently at online sources, but whatever information survives about the Combe family provided no clues, at least not when all I have to look for in their family tree is "Miss B."

I had already imagined myself knocking on the front door of Buckingham Palace to inquire about a possible royal connection, but if Miss B had indeed gone in the back door and perhaps worked there, I would do nothing to jeopardize our secret by asking too many questions in inconvenient places. If the *Lost Letters* were part of the Royal Archives, why would they still be in London, when I had read that most of those documents had been moved to Windsor Castle decades before? Then again, that might be the point—uncatalogued papers, to which Miss B had access, could fill many drawers or entire rooms, still waiting to be tossed or transferred.

For example, I learned that in 1912, thirty large boxes of papers, labeled "To Be Destroyed Unread," were discovered in the basement of Apsley House in London, historical home to the Duke of Wellington. Fortunately someone opened the boxes and found papers belonging to King George III and his son King George IV that had been saved by the Duke, executor of the younger George's will, since receiving them in 1830. The papers included a wide variety of letters and legal documents, including the 1763 deed for George III's purchase of Buckingham Palace for £28,000.

A royal warehouse was one possibility, but so was a more common one. Every so often, we hear of letters or paintings by famous historical figures discovered as garage sale bargains that turn out to be worth millions or shed new light on old historical questions. Perhaps Miss B had a collection of old papers in her family and began sorting them for donation to a museum or a garage sale of her own, when she began to suspect that they might have been written by Shakespeare. Perhaps she argued with other family members about what to do with them and, with no general agreement, decided to share them in confidence with someone she hoped could make sense of them before they languished any longer in the obscurity of the family attic. Indeed English attics have been known to hide such historical lodestars, including at least one directly related to Shakespeare's father.

During repairs in 1757 to the family home on Henley Street in Stratford, workers found a handwritten document hidden in the ceiling that is now referred to as John Shakespeare's "Spiritual Testament." In essence, this was a form of Last Will and Testament that was used by Catholics to affirm their allegiance to the Church of Rome at a time when the Protestant Church of England rooted out (and often executed) recusants, which may explain why John hid it in the rafters. Scholars debate how much of the document is authentic, especially because the original is now lost, but if it was written mostly by William's father, the best estimate is that it dates from 1580, a time when a notorious Jesuit mission was sent into England to rally the faithful. The proselytizers were led by Edmund Campion, a priest who was discovered by authorities and who suffered the same fate as a Catholic member of Shakespeare's family (as described in Letter Six)—torture, hanging, and evisceration while still alive.

There are countless such possibilities of unexplored rafters, public and private collections, archives, Downton Abbey basements, and other intriguing candidates as accidental custodians of the letters, the families or librarians unaware of what languishes in the obscurity of their repository of old documents and books. As Shakespeare scholar Stanley Wells confirmed in a recent interview, "There's lots and lots of unexamined records rotting away in the national archives; it is just possible something will one day turn up."

During our time together in 1989, I always assumed that Miss B and I would stay in contact over the years to bring my adaptation and the originals to light. We would write letters (in those days before emails and cellphones) and exchange Christmas and birthday greetings. I love London, so knew I would be back periodically and already imagined dinners together, perhaps at the Bag O' Nails or the Lord Admiral's for old times' sake, even though the food wasn't very good at either. Not once had it occurred to me that I would never see her, or the letters, again. Indeed, I assumed the letters would always be available for future reference after my initial "translation" was complete.

When I realized that those quaint assumptions were unfounded, I wondered if Miss B had simply returned the letters to their secret storage bin to await their ultimate fate, much like the final scene of the film *Raiders of the Lost Ark*, where the holy relic is wheeled into a cavernous warehouse of crates piled floor to ceiling with other anonymous treasures.

Whatever the fate of the originals, I spent many nights and weekends upon my return to the United States in coffee shops (and at the chart table of my houseboat in the Los Angeles marina) transferring my handwritten transcriptions to WordPerfect documents on my first Zenith laptop computer, slowly transforming them into modern English. I had a great sense of personal accomplishment each time I finished entering an entire letter, converting the spellings and punctuation to more familiar form, then erasing the previous draft. I wish now that I had saved some of my notepads with the handwritten notes, although living on a boat quickly teaches you that paper records don't enjoy a long shelf life in damp, moldy confines.

One thing became clear to me as I methodically converted ink on paper to digital ciphers on a screen—there was little I could do on the other side of the globe from England to resolve the question of where the *Lost Letters* had been stored for so long and, presumably, where they rested again in obscurity now. I decided that I needed to picture the answer for myself, to quiet my mind so it could focus on Shakespeare's words and his 16th century England. My imagination needed to see Miss B and the letters as they might really exist, one way or another. I'll confide to you here my own best guess.

I suppose Miss B worked in an archive, not a library, because something of this importance could only be buried in boxes of other uncatalogued documents that had been donated by families (probably after World War II had destroyed so many old homes and landmarks in England) and the shards of their history needed a safe haven for future curation. She started as a clerk and had worked her way up to middle management, not high enough to decide what to work on next, but high enough to know a priority when she saw one.

Miss B had sifted through the boxes containing the *Lost Letters* and, because of their apparent age and condition, tried to figure out if their content gave them any special value. She found the simple signature "Will" on the first letter she examined and let herself consider that it might be a certain

Shakespeare, especially after seeing two other words that made her gasp in another letter—*Titus Andronicus*.

Seeing that uniquely Shakespearean title on the dusty old page before her (and having seen every one of his plays performed on a London stage since her first *A Midsummer Night's Dream* in the third grade in 1932), she came to believe the boxes of letters were indeed written by the same author. More than sixty years old by then, her eyesight somewhat dimmed, she found the writing exceptionally challenging to decipher, but she soon extracted several more tantalizing names, references to Stratford, titles of other plays, and two mentions of a boy called Hamnet (the name of Shakespeare's only son).

She likely removed some of the pages with these provocative clues and took them to her boss to suggest a serious academic investigation. To her profound disappointment, the parsimonious supervisor replied that there were already too many unopened legacies "waiting their proper turn to be explored and documented." With retirement only a few years away and precious little in her savings account, Miss B couldn't risk further argument.

Not long after this, I imagine she heard about an actor portraying Shakespeare in a play and thought it serendipitous, perhaps an opportunity to talk to someone who knew more about the Bard's life than she did, someone who might give her a way to unlock the clues she had seen in the letters. I was convinced she attended more than one performance, not because the actor was so compelling or because she thought he was the reincarnation of a long-dead poet and playwright, but because she wanted to be sure he was a worthy custodian to carry the torch that had ignited her intense curiosity.

You know the rest of the story. I think she trusted me because I seemed to know a lot about Shakespeare's life already and because she felt that I cared about the man and had a commitment to portraying his legacy accurately. She also knew she needed someone young enough to carry that torch for decades (little could I know then that it would indeed take so long). I realize now that my study of acting and my work onstage were not in preparation for an Oscar, but to be ready and worthy to receive this unique treasure and become a literary Indiana Jones rather than a second coming of Laurence Olivier. Ironically, Miss B gave me what every actor craves however—a lifetime engagement.

To be sure, there were many times that I had doubts about so unexpectedly becoming the reader, witness, recorder and hence custodian of Shakespeare's *Lost Letters*. But I could justify the continued diligence that consumed so much of my spare time, holidays, and vacations since that fateful summer of 1989, because, like Miss B, I too came to passionately believe that what I had been given was authentic.

That brings me to my second big question, a set of mental gymnastics about the provenance of these letters. I hope one day the originals, along with their ethereal guardian Miss B, will resurface, and she will know that the William Shakespeare she saw on a London stage kept his promise to make good use of the real Shakespeare's personal correspondence. I hope she won't be offended however, when experts and amateurs alike inevitably argue their authenticity for years to come. Until then, and because I can't now produce the letters I saw, there will be nothing I can do to silence those skeptics. Rather than try to do so, I instead stipulate right here that someone may indeed be pulling very elaborate wool over all of our eyes and that I welcome whatever scrutiny and debate may follow. It can only enlighten us further about the man, his work, and the times in which he lived. Put another way, as Shakespeare himself said in *Troilus & Cressida,* "modest doubt is called the beacon of the wise."

Where then should we look for other plausible explanations about the origins of the letters? John Shakespeare's Spiritual Testament offers one intriguing possibility. Scholars generally agree that he probably wrote most of it, but also concur that some 18th century author added passages for unknown reasons. Without the original, to look for variations in handwriting, we'll never know if the document had more than one author (or, at least, more than one scribe).

That example led me to wonder if part of the letters, or all of them, could be someone's exercise in creative writing. I'm no expert, but after three months of examining the letters, transcribing each stubbornly indecipherable word, I knew the papers were very old and the ink stains very real, apparently put there by various nibs of some kind (the irregularities sure suggested quills to me) and, after so many hours peering through the magnifying glass, I can say with considerable confidence that the handwriting was the product of one scribe. So, having concluded early on that the pages were indeed antique and written by one hand, it's hard to imagine why someone would have created such an elaborate fiction and then hidden it away for a very long time.

There was, however, an Englishman in the late 18th and early 19th centuries, William Henry Ireland, with a fascinating career as a forger of Shakespeare signatures and even an entire play. He could have drafted the ninety-six convincing letters over many years of his life, but may never have had the chance to foist them on a public that had discovered his earlier creative frauds and generally discredited him long before his death in 1835.

The other possibility, you may be thinking, is that I cooked up this whole thing. I wish I were that good of a writer, but after you read these first sixteen letters (and especially if you have read any of my other non-fiction books), I suspect you'll agree that the writing and the narrative are just too, well "Shakespearean." Oh, to be sure the writing of the immature young man who leaves Stratford in Letter One doesn't reflect the same expressive virtuosity of the Shakespeare we later come to know and admire, but as the years pass and the letters have more to say, the familiar qualities we admire emerge. Bottom line? To anyone who has been moved by his star-crossed lovers, laughed aloud at Falstaff's gluttony, or pondered the great unknown as Hamlet did, you know the writing of William Shakespeare and I am no Shakespeare.

To complicate the authenticity question further, there are many people who don't believe that a glover's son from Stratford wrote the plays and poems generally attributed to him, regardless of whose handwriting is on what old sheets of parchment. You may also know that a campaign has been recently started by the Shakespeare Authorship Coalition (which counts actors Derek Jacobi and Michael York among its members) to prove William Shakespeare never even existed.

But if you are like me, and believe the person that historians generally accept as the Bard is the one who wrote those plays and poems, then you have already crossed the Rubicon of doubt, because almost everything we have to persuade us to that point of view comes from third parties who refer to original documents that no one has seen for many centuries and cannot prove ever existed.

There is one page from a play that some experts believe may be Shakespeare's handwriting (from *Sir Thomas More*, a play that was not included in the "First Folio," the initial publication of his works) and half a dozen examples of his signature on legal documents (no two of which are exactly alike). We have two epic poems that were published with his apparent involvement and his sonnets printed without his approval, although none of his original handwritten drafts for this output have survived. His plays were handed down to us from that First Folio, published seven years after his death, or in a few "bad" versions that he did not apparently authorize during his lifetime, again with no handwritten originals to evaluate.

So, other than these few resources, everything that informs us about Shakespeare and his life's work has been provided by people who claim to have seen original documents, no longer extant, which have inevitably left many questions unanswered. As I spent more time with the letters and each corroborating source, or simply learned more about life in Elizabethan England, which the letters describe in such richly textured detail, any doubts I had were chipped away, mostly a splinter at a time, but occasionally entire veneers, until I was firmly confident to shine the "beacon of the wise" on them with their publication.

That brings me to the third big question. What should I do with these letters? Should I interpret them myself and take them to a publisher or should I make copies of the final transcriptions and give them to academics?

As an actor, I wasn't content to play Shakespeare's great characters, but had spent several years writing and rehearsing my one-man play *Will Power,* wherein I bring him to the stage on the eve of his retirement from the theatre and let him speak for himself in nightly conversations with the audience. There are scholars who try to do the same thing in books and journal articles, describing his life and filling in gaps with educated speculation through a polished academic lens. Might they be better stonecutters of these unpolished gems?

When I first met Miss B, one of the most successful and colorful scholars, who spent a lifetime writing Shakespeare biographies, was A.L. Rowse. I admired his books and ability to surgically slice through the thick hides of Time, including being the first academic to identify a credible candidate for the Dark

Lady of Shakespeare's sonnets and to produce a "complete works" of his plays that translated the most obscure Elizabethan English into words and references that modern audiences could easily follow. I remember seeing the great British actor, Richard Burton, recite examples of text from the First Folio and then the same passage from the Rowse translation, showing how true-to-Shakespeare, yet completely understandable, the new versions had become in a fresh, clever adaptation.

In 1990, I wrote a letter to Mr. Rowse to explore his interest, but never received a reply and in those pre-email, pre-internet days, had no other practical way to reach him. I ultimately gave up, not merely because of a few communication challenges, but because I suspected this great historian would dismiss an amateur's claims about a mysterious woman's possession of "lost" letters, supposedly written by Shakespeare, as not worthy of his time or talent.

The other reason I didn't pursue Mr. Rowse (who died in 1997) or another scholar to take over this *Lost Letters* project, was that I had quickly realized how much Shakespeare had to say to our modern times, insights from the past that might comfort or enlighten us on our journey into an increasingly uncertain future. I'm a small "d" democrat, dare I say an anarchist at heart, so I didn't want to let a few ivory tower guardians decide what the wider reading public should know about the greatest writer in the English language and the fundamental explanations that these letters provide for why he has had such a profound influence on our culture to this day.

Now before you think I'm dismissing the important work of academia, my hope was that I might one day find experts with an open mind and fresh ways of exploring challenging content. In 2016, that aim led me to send the letters to Alejandro Ribeiro, an innovative engineering professor at the University of Pennsylvania, who had developed the linguistic algorithm that proved that Christopher Marlowe had a hand in writing Shakespeare's Henry VI.

I asked him to run the letters through his analytical system. He compared the text of the letters to the known writing of Shakespeare, Marlowe, Ben Jonson and other of their contemporaries. The results came back with the highest match to William Shakespeare. I don't want to over-state what Professor Ribeiro told me, because his initial analysis needs much more work to be more definitive and his colleagues in the English Department raised doubts about the likely authenticity of any "found" letters, but even his very preliminary findings are tantalizing validation that something of great historic and literary importance may have been discovered. I plan to use proceeds of book sales to fund more in-depth study of the letters by Professor Ribeiro and other scholars.

Regardless of how you approach the provenance of the *Lost Letters*, just as Miss B passed the torch to me, I hope this book and its related interactive website (http://shakespeareletters.com) will encourage you to carry some part of that legacy forward too, contributing your own knowledge and sources about Shakespeare, and the world he so eloquently chronicled, that might illuminate our shared past still further.

Once I decided that this journey of discovery and revelation as Shakespeare's scribe was worth taking, I needed to develop a format that would retain his actual words and meaning, but that would make the ninety-six lengthy letters compelling and clear to a contemporary audience, much as Rowse had done with his adaptations of the plays. Here then are a few notes to explain how I worked to achieve that delicate balance.

Illustration 2 shows an example of the calligraphy I copied from. It is the final page of Shakespeare's Last Will and Testament. Although he signed it, there is no evidence he wrote the will itself, but this gives you an example of the way he and his contemporaries wrote letters and legal documents. Very little punctuation or paragraph formatting; words and names spelled various ways within the same document (and often not the way we spell them today); lots of abbreviations that meant something to the intended reader, but would mystify the modern one.

Read the final few lines of his will in Illustration 2 now. Yes, the text in that example is in English! See if you can match those final sentences in the original to my transcribed text below, which does not correct irregular spelling as I have done for this book, but which does modernize the way individual letters were written to make it somewhat easier to follow:

> *I give, devise, and bequeath to my sonne in lawe, John Hall gent.,*
> *and my daughter Susanna, his wief, whom I ordaine and make*
> *executours of this my last will and testament. And I doe intreat and*

appoint the saied Thomas Russell esquier and Frauncis Collins gent. to be overseers hereof, and doe revoke all former wills, and publishe this to be my last will and testament. In witness whereof I have hereunto put my [seale] hand, the date and yeare first above written.

Now that you have seen an actual example of Elizabethan writing, what follows is how I approached the task of formatting Shakespeare's letters for the modern reader:

- Colloquial Elizabethan English is at times quite familiar, but at times thoroughly perplexing, for example the use of "you" for addressing someone of higher age or station, while using "thou" for familiars (like so much of Elizabethan grammar and usage, this is not applied consistently). To help readers become more familiar with the way people spoke, I standardized as much of this convention as possible.

- Some letters in words were written differently than we see today. For example, 's' was written like 'f' except when capitalized, in which case it appeared as 'S'. 'V' was usually written as 'u'. Needless to say, I modernized such instances. The letters "i" and "j"; "s" and "f"; and "u" and "v" were interchangeable, sometimes depending on where the letter appeared in a word. "y" sometimes replaced "th", so the word "the" could be written as "ye", or abbreviated as "t'" or "th'". Numbers were often expressed as lower case Roman numerals, with the last "i" written as "j", for example, "8" would appear as "viii" or "viij".

- I left some irregularities where they seemed to matter to Shakespeare, such as capitalizing certain words like 'Fortune'.

- Some abbreviations and contractions are similar to modern English (can't, couldn't) but others are not common today (o'er for over; ne'er for never; in's for in his; 'prentice for apprentice; enow for enough). I left many of those as Shakespeare wrote them, because they are all generally easy to understand in context and were common for Elizabethan letter writing.

- Shakespeare used little punctuation, except the use of a period after a number (which is confusing for modern readers, because a period today means the end of a sentence). Therefore, spelling and punctuation have been regularized and modernized and things like possessive apostrophes have been added where needed. When I just wasn't sure, or thought the original should speak for itself exactly as is, I insert footnotes or Editor's Notes for explanation to the best of my ability.

- Shakespeare did use a form of quotation marks at times and wrote some recounted dialogue with indentations to suggest it was a certain speaker, but otherwise followed no standard method of describing speech. I have therefore standardized the dialogue he recounts using modern quotation marks and attributions of the speaker for clarity.

- Shakespeare sometimes uses 'Master' when referring to the senior members of the company, but in later letters uses 'Mr' or 'M.' when he seemed to be in a hurry. For consistency, I use 'Mr.' except when used in other contexts where the full spelling is more appropriate.

- In many cases I have added words and phrases that were likely in the original, but have been obscured by blots, smudges and holes in the paper (as you can see in Illustration 2, that was also the case in the excerpt from Shakespeare's will).

- Shakespeare often added notes in the margins too, which I incorporated into the text where relevant. For example, in the beginning of Letter One, Shakespeare referred to the "Trinity tor". I assumed he meant the Holy Trinity Church, the most visible landmark of Stratford from a distance. In my first draft of this book, I used "spire" instead of "tor" (which meant door or hill in Elizabethan English, either of which would have been obscure to the modern reader). Realizing that the spire was not added to the church until the 1700s however, I later changed this to "tower", in an attempt to remain faithful to the text Shakespeare wrote, but to be somewhat clearer for the modern reader about what he likely meant.

- When a word that is not commonly used in modern English appears for the first time in the letters, I inserted the meaning in brackets or made a footnote with the content, then summarized all such words in the Glossary.

- The letters were mostly written on two sides of the page but designed to be folded shut with a seal and John Combe's name on one blank section. The simple salutation of most letters ("Coz") is unusual for its informality and brevity, suggesting Shakespeare and John needed no more pleasantries between them. The dates were placed beneath Shakespeare's signature (which appeared in some letters at the top of the first page and in others at the bottom of the last page, as is the convention today), but I have put them at the top of each new letter to aid the reader in following the chronology. Speaking of dates, England in Shakespeare's time used the old Julian calendar (Europe had already converted to the more accurate Gregorian calendar, but England waited until 1752 to follow suit), so dates cited in his letters may be as much as ten days off of our modern dating system.

Remodeling old text was just the first step in my approach to adapting old letters into a modern book. My research led me to corroborating sources for many of the facts and stories that Shakespeare reports and, in some cases, I have adapted these sources to complete missing sections in the *Lost Letters*.

For example, in Letter Fourteen, Shakespeare repeats what he was told by his London neighbor, Ambassador Van Meteren, who had given oral and written summaries of the fate of the Spanish Armada to other contemporaries in 1588. I realized during my initial transcribing, that there was at least one page missing from that letter, so I augmented Shakespeare's report with those additional sources to complete the otherwise consistent description.

In Letter Nine, Shakespeare reports hearing from a man named Miles Phillips about his harrowing years in Spanish colonial prisons in Mexico. I found another source of Phillips' account of his travels throughout the New World and used it to better comprehend and enrich Shakespeare's version with additional clarity and color.

In addition to connecting those historical dots, some of the people, places, and language Shakespeare reports in the letters later found their way into his plays and poems. He often seemed to be absorbing dialogue and situations, which later made his writing so real and compelling. I wondered, for example, how so much of his observations and the things he heard in Denmark (Letter 5) could have been recalled so clearly when he wrote *Hamlet* fifteen years later. I found the answer in Letter 50 (which will appear in a subsequent book) when he expresses gratitude to John Combe's brother for opening a chest where the letters were stored (while John was apparently away from Stratford, but Shakespeare was home writing *Love's Labours Lost* in 1593).

Wherever I recognized people and discussions that seem to have provided Shakespeare with fodder for characters and events in his plays, I have highlighted them in the introduction to each letter or in additional "Scribe's Notes," along with a bit more about my detective work and how my own somewhat unconventional experiences, onstage and off, gave me special insights into Shakespeare's life.

There are also many turns of phrase in these letters that may sound familiar and which Shakespeare repeats in some form in his plays and poems. I have provided footnotes for as many as I recognized, but some seem to be common sayings of the period and not necessarily Shakespearean creations. For example, "our doubts are traitors" is uttered by Lucio in *Measure for Measure,* but it was also used by other writers of the period. Or "arms are fair, when the intent of bearing them is just" is said by Hotspur in *Henry IV part 1* (Act V, scene 2) and repeated in other contemporary plays. Rather than overburden your enjoyment of the letters with footnotes on all of these coincidences, I have left many of these more common nuggets for you to find and decide for yourself who first coined the phrases.

As you will see, the letters are quite long, but that was not unusual for Elizabethan correspondence (they were prolific letter-writers and savers). One of my research references was a book on the life of Shakespeare's patron, the third Earl of Southampton, which is over 500 pages, mostly his correspondence and some commentary on it.[1]

Letters were often the only means of sharing news before newspapers became common and much of 16th century England was small towns and rural villages, where news traveled mainly by word of mouth or by letter. Reports from New World voyages, rumors of war, conspiracies, beheadings and the Plague—all front-page news today—would have been reported in letters. All of that said, I suspect Shakespeare's letters were long because he meant them as a record for his son in case he was unable to return from his voyages. Whatever the reasons, fortunately for posterity, 16th Century paper was fairly sturdy (made largely of cloth fibers, not wood pulp), although, like anything that old, some pages became more brittle than others over time.

Finally, I found one other obscure document worth special mention, because it is likely to have been the impetus of Shakespeare's initial wanderlust from Stratford, as well as the reason for his writing of the letters in the first place (as he explains in Letter One). About the time that Shakespeare turned twenty-one, an explorer gave a heartfelt treatise to Queen Elizabeth that was widely distributed, which Shakespeare may well have read, entitled *Inducements to the Liking of the Voyage Intended towards Virginia*, listing over thirty reasons why England should colonize what is now the United States and why hearty men and women should join the voyages to new settlements.

We know Shakespeare never set foot on North American soil, but his Queen, and later King James, did more than populate colonies with eager young fortune hunters, plant flags and grab natural resources to fuel the economy back home. They unleashed upon an unsuspecting world the power of the English language, the temperament and what became the American dream—a good deal of which is thanks to William Shakespeare. In discovering and weaving together these texts with his letters, I came to see that America today, and a world that is influenced by it in so many ways, is a creature of Shakespeare's Age.

The rubbish we are taught in American grade schools about the reasons the original settlers colonized Virginia—pilgrims in search of religious freedom—is as far from the truth as the moon is from the sun. When I recognized that Shakespeare illuminated our antique past and thereby the present, I knew I had to give his letters their voice. He describes an Age that faced—but survived—its extinction from pollution, wars, incurable disease, prejudice, homelessness, drug abuse, official corruption and favoritism, burdensome taxation, xenophobia, religious intolerance and extremism...well, sound familiar? It did to me, so I knew Shakespeare could offer wisdom and hope to our own Age, which suffers what he might have called the "selfsame ills."

Therefore, I give you *The Lost Letters of William Shakespeare: The Undiscovered Diary of his Strange Eventful Life and Loves*. What follows is the first of three books covering very distinct parts of Shakespeare's life and which, taken together, constitute an intimate diary of his life, revealing many surprising facts that have never found their way into history books, along with solid corroborating evidence for many that have been recorded before.

In the sixteen letters of this book, he describes leaving Stratford in 1586 at the age of twenty-two and takes us through his first major success as a playwright, with detours along the way for a variety of dramas, passions, and shocking personal revelations. A Glossary and a Dramatis Personae (as Shakespeare would have called it) present explanations of unfamiliar words and brief bios of the people in the letters. A refresher of the generally accepted facts about his life and times (with some assumptions and conclusions I have gleaned from my work) is presented in a Brief Biography of Shakespeare in the *Lost Letters* website (http://shakespeareletters.com), along with more details about the discovery and adaptation of the letters.

With these few props, set decorations, and stage directions, I now invite you to enter the theatre of Shakespeare's mind, as recorded in his long-lost letters, which bring you face-to-face with a very remarkable man and his equally spell-binding times and places; his friends and loves; his brutal enemies; and the emotional choices that all of these dramatic and comedic players forced him to make. As Shakespeare bids his audience in *Henry V*, so I beg your indulgence now:

> Let us, on your imaginary forces, work:
> Piece out our imperfections with your thoughts,
> For 'tis your thoughts that now must deck our kings,
> Carry them here and there, jumping o'er times,
> Turning the accomplishment of many years into an hour-glass!
> Admit me, the Chorus to this history,
> Who prologue-like your humble patience pray,
> Gently to hear, kindly to judge, our play.

The words are Shakespeare's. I am honored to be his scribe.

LETTER ONE
July 5, 1586

Wherein young Shakespeare sets out from Stratford to make his fortune in the New World, but first must earn entry into a world of traveling players by mending a wheel.

When Miss B gave me the first batch of pages, the earliest letter was not among them. In fact, the first page I tried to transcribe and decipher turned out to be the fourth page of Letter Three. As I read more pages over time, it appeared these hidden treasures had been dropped and scattered at some point, perhaps more than once, during the past four hundred years, then picked up and reassembled haphazardly. When I began to sort out the letters chronologically, I ultimately determined that this letter of early July 1586, when William Shakespeare was a young man of 22, was Letter One of ninety-six.

Organizing the letters chronologically and deciphering old English spelling were not the only obstacles to understanding them. Imagine if letters written today about modern China were discovered in the year 2415. A reader of the future would likely have little real understanding of Mao Zedong or his communist country's subsequent embrace of capitalism. Will people four centuries from now be able to appreciate the civil rights movement in the United States of the 1960s and the significance of Barack Obama's presidency four decades later? Will they understand why Lady Gaga wore a dress made of beef to an MTV awards ceremony?

So as your Chorus, your guide into the *Lost Letters*, let me begin by reminding you about King Henry VIII, who had numerous wives and, to facilitate at least one divorce and remarriage, created the Church in England to take command of religious life in his nation. Much of the Christian faith, practice and clergy remained familiar to his subjects, but instead of a Pope in Rome, the English monarch would now be the head of both country and church. This set off decades of civil strife as Catholics and Protestants fought for supremacy.

Henry VIII was survived by three children, his ten-year-old son Edward becoming king when he died in 1547. Edward continued in the Protestant faith until his own death six years later in 1553, at which time his sister Mary Tudor ascended to the throne. She married the very Catholic King Philip of Spain and restored Catholicism to England, slaughtering anyone who continued to "protest" Roman leadership of the church. Phillip became the king of England and they ruled for five years until Mary died in 1558 at the age of forty-two. Enter her younger sister Elizabeth the First.

We'll never know what was in Elizabeth's heart, but to justify her rule she had to restore her father's Protestant version of religion, because it was that supremacy over the church that justified his marriage to Anne Boleyn, Elizabeth's mother. The new queen would otherwise have been considered a bastard, born out of any legally or spiritually sanctioned wedlock, and therefore unqualified to rule (indeed the Pope excommunicated her and absolved anyone from damnation if they assassinated her). This reversion to a Church in England had consequences however—King Philip threatened invasion to reclaim what he saw as his rightful kingdom and to restore the "true" faith.

Tiptoe on this high wire, Elizabeth was not as vengeful as her sister "bloody Mary," but she did root out hidden Catholics with a sophisticated network of spies, bribes, threats, and a few well-placed (and very gruesome) executions, at least one of which struck the heart of Shakespeare's own family and fortunes (which he describes in vivid detail in Letter Six).

Queen Elizabeth faced another hurdle to a peaceful reign: an empty treasury. Her father became instantly wealthy by taking command of the church, because he appropriated monastic wealth and lands to the crown, but he squandered much of it on a lavish lifestyle, gifts to his nobles, and foreign wars. Moreover, King Philip of Spain was becoming fabulously wealthy by exploring the "New World" of Mexico and Central/South America, bringing home fabled shiploads of gold, silver, and exotic trade goods. For the small island nation of

England, the only way to find similar natural resources, to pay for the army and ships needed to defend her shores, was to colonize North America (or send pirates to rob the treasure ships of Spain).

As Elizabeth rebuilt and defended her kingdom, in part by considering marriage proposals from various European nobles who might provide her with valuable alliances, the nobles of her court, one percent of the one percent of the population, controlled the vast majority of the nation's wealth and lands. For the remaining 99.9% life was defined by what Shakespeare would later call the "slings and arrows of … a weary life: the oppressor's wrong, the proud man's insults, the pangs of despised love, the law's delay, the insolence of office" and always a threat of instant death from the Bubonic plague.

Whether queen or commoner, "there is a tide in the affairs of men, which taken at the flood, leads on to Fortune. But omitted, and all the voyage of Life is bound in shallows and miseries. On such a full sea are we now afloat and we must take the current when it serves."

Although Shakespeare would not write those lines in the play *Julius Caesar* until some dozen years later, was he thinking of them when he left his ancestral home in Stratford on the river Avon in 1586, abandoning his family trade as a glover (maker of fine leather goods, such as depicted below in Illustration 3) and his wife and three children, seeking work to support them elsewhere?

3. Gloves like those made by John Shakespeare and sold to nobles in the Queen's Court.

4. Holy Trinity Church, Stratford Upon Avon. Shakespeare described this last view of his hometown in Letter One and would recognize it unchanged today.

We learn in Letter One that Shakespeare did indeed set out to make a living by working as a "jack-of-all-trades" for a traveling theatre company called the Earl of Leicester's Men, which had just performed in Stratford (Illustration 4, above, is a photo of the Holy Trinity churchyard in Stratford, the place he describes in the beginning of Letter One as he marched out of town with his new companions). He hopes to earn enough money for passage on a ship to the Americas, the "New World," where it was commonly believed that any hardworking man could make a fortune in gold and Elizabeth was encouraging her nobles to set up colonies.

Shakespeare reveals an intense hatred for one of those nobles—the patron of the theatre company, the Earl of Leicester—but we don't learn the reasons until Letter Six.

From various places along his journey, Shakespeare writes letters to his closest friend and confidant since childhood, John Combe, a moneylender who lives in Stratford (each letter is addressed simply to "Coz," an abbreviation of

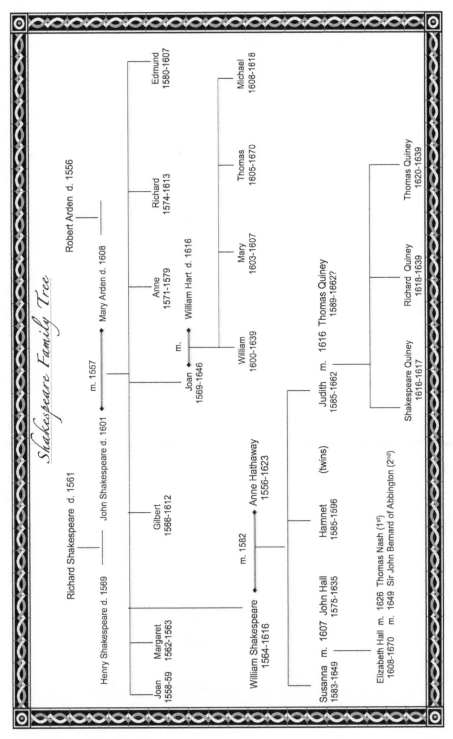

5. The Shakespeare family tree.

"cousin," a term of friendship rather than family ties). He writes both lovingly and disparagingly of his father and his wife Anne, but we cannot yet understand why he has such conflicted feelings about his home life (answers appear by Letter Eleven). He says he is writing this record, a diary in essence, to ensure that there is an accurate account of his life, so that if he cannot return, his son Hamnet will know what became of his father and why he had to leave his family in the first place. Hamnet and Judith are the two-year old twin children of Shakespeare and his wife, Anne ("Nan"); they also have a four-year old daughter, Susanna. He refers in this letter to his younger siblings too: Gilbert, Joan, Anne, Richard, and Edmund (Illustration 5 on page 5 presents a Shakespeare family tree for reference).

Against this backdrop, irresistible tidal forces of family and country, Letter One introduces us to a scared and unsure "Shake-piss," as nicknamed by his fellow actors at the start of his journey. He writes about the members of the theatre company and its players, a collection of very distinct personalities, disparate allegiances, and various talents. His childhood education and training as a scribe for his father, who had held various posts in Stratford's town

6. 16th century traveling players like the Earl of Leicester's Men that Shakespeare joined in 1586.

government, prove useful when Master James Burbage, the head of Leicester's Men, asks him to make copies of plays and even to help "mend" a play (which required inserting contemporary references and adjusting the cast list based on the number of players available at the time).

He is slowly accepted by the players, at least some of them, as they make their way from town to town toward London. The journey he describes in Letter One, from Stratford to Coventry, consumed his entire first day, a trip that would take us thirty minutes by car today. Illustration 6, opposite, shows what a troupe of traveling players looked like in Shakespeare's day.

With this background, here is Letter One as I found and reconstructed it.

5 July 1586, Coventry

Coz,

How oft have we, in service to our fathers, trod the road twixt Stratford and Coventry? How oft have we made the leaden journey pleasant with talk of conquering kingdoms and maidenheads (or the reasons we came home again as masters of neither)? Why then, these two days since on that selfsame highway, as the lengthening distance made the Trinity [*church*] grow small, came such a parlous [*great*] fear over me, that I had seen it, and all who dwell within her holy shadow, for the last time?

O John, my mind overflows from events unlooked for, with a group of men that I know now so briefly. Ink and paper are dear, but I would trade my last scrap of bread to keep this record of my journey, since I fear it will be a long one and I would have my son know his father. Therefore coz, I make thee the book wherein my soul records the history of all its secret thoughts. Be thou, in mine absence, as a friend to my brothers, a son to my mother, a confessor to my wife, indeed the holder of all else I possess, but most of all, be thou as a father to my son. Take from these accounts what matter thou deem'st fit for his youthful ears, saving the rest for his own divining when he is a man and better suited to understand the whips and scorns of life, labour, love. Deny me not this favor and God, I trust, will repay thee (even though it is mine own desire to do likewise in some fuller measure ere long).

Yet, if thou dost grant me these many favours, how might the foolish son of a foolish father repay so dear a debt? Here then is mine intent: oft have we prattled of finding great treasure beyond the waters of the Avon, with no idea how to make such dreams manifest, just as the flood rushes to the fearful wilderness of the sea with neither eyes nor senses to guide it. What I have never dared utter to a living soul is that I long to follow those waters: to trust my fate to God and my wits, to the Americas, and thither to seek a share of the kingly fortune, that those gone before, report is everywhere to be had.

Our doubts are traitors, coz: they make us lose the good we oft might win by fearing to attempt. I will brook no longer such doubts, but by taking this unforeseen employment with the Earl of Leicester's players, as their johannes factotum [*jack-of-all-trades*], I mean to earn my passport to London and thence aboard a ship to the New World, there to make my Fortune. Or I must die in the trying.

Much more will I set forth to thee of whys and wherefores and those matters which even dearest friends may leave a'times unspoken, such that if I am unable to write again, thou (and my sweet Hamnet) wilt know why and by what means I came to this path. But more of this hereafter.

First must I set down that which I have seen on my journey thus far, though yet in its infancy, and how I, like the babe sucking his mother's dug [*nipple*], must rely on others for sustenance and even to guide my halting steps. I know not where to begin with so much to tell, but 'tis the beginning that sketches the canvas, that sounds the bell for the sermon which follows, so I will strive to order my thoughts.

It fell out thus: but once had the cock crowed when we took from Stratford our hasty leave on Wednesday last. Some rode their horses, Masters James Burbage and Will Johnson ahead; others rode for a time with our goods in the wagons, but the main part of our Company trod the dusty way with no more aid than the leather of our shoes, soon full of gravel. Thus made we our progress, but no further than the bend in the road past the pines, when from the leading wagon we heard report a mighty crack, the nether wheel crumbling in a heap.

The apprentices and I set ourselves to changing the wheel, this being my first lesson in the duties of a johannes factotum. But Fortune herself shouldered the load: that is to say in the person of Mr. Thomas Pope, who from some grievous injury is a most awkwardly constructed man, his limbs resembling the bouncing keys on a jailer's hip, yet the other fellows say he could easily carry the load, and the ass that pulls the wagon and two or three of us for good measure, all by himself. This he proved, for he would brook no other man to lift the wagon and somehow did shoulder it long enough for the repair to be made. Notwithstanding the early hour, every mother's son of us was soon drenched in our own sweat and covered in so much dust that our white shirts showed tawny as we wrestled the ailing wheel from the axle and replaced it with its fellow.

The son of Mr. James Burbage (young Richard is he called or 'Boy Burbage' or more often merely Boy) told me I had not given the axle enough grease and, true to his augury [*prediction*], when we tested our work, the new wheel screamed out notice of my failure. This, my first mistake, cost us another half hour to perform the task again. I felt the fool, but no man said a word, not even poor Mr. Pope, who had to bear the load a second time, his complexion turning to that of a rotting apple.

One of the boys whispered that Mr. Pope will take on any labour that proves his fitness: he is no more than forty years, but his beard is already ashen, his hair cropped like an old monk and bald at the crown, he brings to my mind's eye that ghostly rother [*cattle*] merchant who comes from the west lands, he that resembles one of his own scrawny milch-kine [*milk cows*]. I would not yet be so bold to inquire, but I cannot help but wonder what misfortune befell him that he was so deformed, yet thou hast seen for thyself how capable is he at tumbling, jigs, and all manner of comic parts on a stage.

Our mending complete, we continued the journey with no other great adventure. When the sun had reached his zenith and the summer gnats their hungriest, we stopped by a pleasant grove of oak to refresh ourselves. Here I learned my second mistake: each man must fend for his own dinner (the lot of us finding ample supper, it is said, at sundown in an inn along the way, or being feasted nightly by the townsfolk). I had brought no bread, meat nor drink, but again the apprentices chided me little and shared without reservation. When for a time we had sat, ate, drank and cooled our weary limbs, it seemed the sustenance had loosened tongues, much as the foul grease had finally smoothed the way for the newly-mounted wheel. That thou mayest know these men a little, herewith those things said, as I can best recall them now:

"I am but a fool, look you," shouts young Dick Cowley from behind a small oak, whence he had fled to escape old Mr. Perkin, that same skilled player you saw perform the most excellent speech as the King at the death of his daughter, who even then grasped for a letter in Cowley's hand. "Every man in Christendom knows me to be in love; yet WHO it is I love, a team of horse shall not pluck that from me." With this he thrust the letter into his breeches.[2]

"We know her name well, fool," quoth the Boy Burbage as he flung a bitten apple at Cowley. "'Tis King Arthur." This, I learned, is the name given to Mr. Burbage's old packhorse. The men laughed and made lascivious gestures with their tongues. Cowley grew distempered and kicked back the apple.

"'Tis a WOMAN, that knowest thou well. A pox on thee, for she hath more qualities than … than … than a water-spaniel!" With this he plucks from his narrow waistband the sweaty paper. Dick Cowley is a good sort, a slight youth of sixteen or eighteen years, with a silken mop of golden hair, quick to laugh, which may account for the dimple in his chin that looks as if the baker's finger left its mark before the bread was baked. He seems always to be talking of love, which may come from playing women's parts: he is yet soft of hand and perhaps yet soft of heart. It is said no other could play Lenore as well as he, twisting his face into her agony over the lost child, a line to his brow which makes him appear always something fretful and thereby more convincing, and wringing genuine salt tears from his eyes at every performance.[3]

Boy Burbage with a feigned indifference: "What news, then, in thy letter?"

"The blackest news that thou hast ever heard!" Cowley smoothed the paper out upon his boney knee, with such care that I thought he might discover a holy scripture therein.

"Why, man, how black?" Boy Burbage, now somewhat more interested than before, snatches the paper from Cowley.

"Why, as black as ink, for so is it written, and as dark as thy heart, Richard!"

Now every man smelled brewing a fine jest or a brawl. Cuthbert Burbage, the elder son of Mr. James Burbage, whispers me to heed the most excellent conceit of his sharp-tongued brother against the vanity of the young lad, but to me this seemed the show of a common school yard bully, not a discourse of some refined wit.

"Let ME read it." Boy Burbage declared his triumph, sawing the air with his hands in the bold gesture of some that over-play their parts.

"Fie on thee, jolt-head! Thou cans't not read." Poor Cowley, every mother's son of us could see his discontent, that another had mastery over the letter.

Boy Burbage stared at the paper as if he would cover it in sauce and devour it: "Thou liest; I can read that here hast thou writ a … a LIST! A catalog of thy lady-love's condition."

Each man took turns examining the document to be satisfied that it was truly the hand of Cowley, that he indeed had writ a ledger of his lady's assets and liabilities. Boy Burbage read the list aloud with a flourish:

"Item first: She can fetch and carry."

"Why, a horse can do as much!" Mr. Will Kempe, farted an exclamation, he that same burly clown thou sawest perform the bawdy jig at the end of the play.

"Nay, a horse cannot fetch, but only carry." Cowley's nether lip was bleeding, owing to his nervous biting thereof. "Therefore is my lady better than your common mare!"

Laughter encouraged Boy Burbage to continue. Cuthbert tells me that the 'prentice boys, even the likes of his younger brother, would never be so bold in company with the masters, lest given permission for such a jest, which seemed given now by Mr. Perkin, who smiled as he stroked the three large moles on his left cheek. This advice I took as warning to mine own conduct hereafter.

"Item next: she can sew." Boy Burbage spake 'sew' as if calling a swine, at which others howled likewise.

"Well... that's as much as to say... can she 'so-oh-oh'?" Mr. Kempe added a lusty gesture thereto, which thou canst imagine.

"Item: She hath many nameless virtues."

Here entered Mr. Perkin into the fray through a mouthful of cheese, the foul smell of which filled the air all round whence I sat: "That's as much as to say, BASTARD virtues. Her children know not their fathers and are therefore 'nameless' virtues!" Had God not made Mr. Perkin a player, I swear he would have stood 'a Sundays on the greatest pulpit in Christendom, such is the command of his voice and carriage. Even the dogs in our Company sit close by him, though that may be owing to how he gives them leave to lick the grease from his fingers, a practice known to bewitch many hounds.

"Let there be silence. I have not said all! Here follow her VICES." Boy Burbage poked at the page as if he would puncture it.

"Close at the heels of her virtues, I see," quoth Mr. Kempe.

"Item: She is not to be kissed when fasting, in respect of her breath." Boy Burbage jaunced [*pranced*] about the tree, which I observe to be his habit much of the time.

"Well, that fault may be mended: she hath a sweet voice to make amends for her sour breath." Cowley's own vibrato more like thy mother's than thy sire at this point. Every man followed the back and forth as if it were a tennis match. Indeed, it was now a test of Cowley's wit, to hear how he would return each volley.

"Read on, Richard," commanded Mr. Perkin.

"Item: She doth talk in her sleep."

"That's no matter … so she does not sleep in her talk!"

"Item: She is slooooowwww in words."

"O villain, that is set down among her VICES?" quoth Mr. Clarke. "To be slow in words is a woman's only virtue. Prithee, out with it, and place it for her CHIEF virtue." Cuthbert whispered to me that this sentiment is the fruit of an unhappy marriage bed.

"Item: She hath no teeth."

"I care not, because I love the crusts." As proof, Cowley then bit hard into his dried bread, making his lip bleed the more.

"Item: She is curst with foul temper."

"So? Thou sayest even now that she hath no teeth to bite withal. Stop there; I'll have her anyway, and if it be a match, as nothing is impossible, then … " Cowley shrugged and the last word he left drifting off toward Coventry.

Unsatisfied, Boy Burbage demanded something more: "Well, what then?"

"Why, then … will I tell thee … that our master … thy father … stays for thee … at yonder well!" Cowley wrung the words from his breast slowly, as one would squeeze a chicken's neck for suppertime.

"My father waits for ME?" Boy Burbage cried with some mixture of disbelief and fear. "And must I go to him? Why didst thou not tell me sooner? A pox on thy love letters!" Off he ran, to know if Cowley was in jest or no, fearing a beating for his tardiness, the laughter of every man marking time to his hasty retreat. Our noonday meal consumed, we scattered then among the several oaks, snoring in the shade, the gleeful Cowley declaring to any man still listening:

"Now will he be swinged [*beaten*] for reading my letter, the unmannerly slave, that will thrust himself into the secrets of others! I'll follow close at's heels, to rejoice in the boy's correction at the hands of his sire."

"The Master Burbage, I am told, is liberal with the whip, if a boy lags in his duties," quoth I, for even though he had spoken to me not a word, I had heard already how the 'prentices do fear him and speak not to him unless first spoken to and even then in the most starched-collar-church-voice. Pissing against the oak, and none too mindful of whence the urine wandered thereafter among his sleeping fellows, Mr. Pope gave me his opinion, most liberally:

"Ah, but all is forgotten when he is at his craft, schooling the finer points of playing to us all, even to those boys who are corrected for being thick as Tewkesbury mustard." At that moment, Mr. Johnson appeared and bid us to make haste, lest we lose all light of day, and our Company with yet a score of miles to cover ere nightfall, saying at our present pace, we would not see Coventry till newborn chins be rough and razorable.

Observing the men in these moments of work or leisure, I begin to comprehend their role in the Company and thereby mine own. Herein an inventory, presented for thy further audit and understanding, of those men with whom I now share the road in common, and so too a common fate:

In command of the Company: James Burbage, our sovereign and master of all, nearing threescore years [*sixty*] I would venture; together with Will Johnson, only 40 in years but bears himself at all times like great Caesar and plays parts of the ancients. No less in honour, the other master players: Thomas Clarke, not much above twoscore [*forty*] in years, all gray, speaks little in company but commandingly on the stage; John Perkin, well above twoscore, yet impish as the conniving schoolboy.

Equal in skill, masters too, the Company clowns: Will Kempe, not above 30, the rough and rude antic onstage or off, with a face like butter, easily shaped; Thomas Pope, also under twoscore, oddly shapen but hearty, as I have described.

Master of our music: Augustine Phillips, 30 I would venture, with a voice that could melt ice from the rafters and, by my troth [*truth*], the hardest of female hearts. He is the most excellent musician and is said to have four dozen of various instruments in his possession in London. In the wagon he carries a lute, two viols, two flutes, a drum and a hautboy [*oboe*] from which he can summon forth the cry of a bird or a baby. Cowley says he is half-brother to Mr. Pope, so I take from their divers [*different*] surnames they shared not a father, but came into the world of the same mother (yet these two seem no more outwardly alike, in body or in character, than is an apple like to the tree from which it falls).

Playing the women, the younger and the elder: Dick Cowley, our youngest member as I have already set forth, apprenticed these two years to Mr. Clarke; and George Bryan, a gentle man of 25 or 30.

Apprenticed or labourers: Richard Burbage, churlish son of our master and like to follow in his footsteps; Cuthbert Burbage, the elder son, quite a decent fellow; and now in their number, Will Shakespeare, two and twenty years, johannes factotum.

What happened hereafter, as we were not an hour further along the Coventry Road, I still cannot fully comprehend, but herewith report. The Boy Burbage comes upon my side of the wagon and speaks, most churlishly, to me thus:

"Dost bite thy thumb at me, sir?"[4] Thou knowest mine idle habit of biting a length of nail from off my thumb, although as God is my judge I cannot say for certain that I was so engaged when he asked me the question. My looks were my reply, for in truth I could say nothing, being so surprised.

"DOST THOU BITE THY THUMB AT ME, SIR?" This time he barked the words as if trying to teach our English tongue to an ass.

"If I bit my thumb, sir, 'twas not at thee, nor any man here," quoth I.

"Thou dost bite thy thumb at me sir, and 'tis a disgrace to me if I bear it," quoth he with greater annoyance. If his tongue were a rapier, I had been a dead man, even if covered by a full suit of armour.

"Sir, thou dost mistake me. I mean thee no harm."

"Ay, thou MEAN'ST me no harm, yet thy MEANNESS is a harm to us all. Thy doublet [*jacket*] is such that even a hangman would bury it with those who wore such a one."

'Tis true, my doublet is of a style not seen these many years since, but it was clean and not a moth hole in it. "Richard, I know not how I have offended thee, but take me at my word good fellow, I do love thee well."

He spat, narrowly missing my shoes. "Thou art not my FELLOW. Were I like thee, I'd throw myself away. I pronounce thee a gross lout and a mindless slave. And soon enough wilt thou know the cause of my distemper...as if thou knowest not already!" With that, he turns on's heel and made away to the other side of the wagon.

Well, I could have been no more surprised had I looked behind me and seen a tail growing out of my buttocks. What had I done that might offend this knave, one whose acquaintance with me was a day old and hardly more than a dozen words between us ere then? And he of all the boys I do not wish to offend, owing to that his father is lord of our Company.

Left to my thoughts, the road grew no shorter but the day's travel came to an end. We arrived at that tavern hard by Coventry, the Bishop's inn thou knowest well, the west yet glimmering with some streaks of day and our clothing showing the colour of dust from every yard of the journey. Mr. Kempe showed me then some encouragement:

"Now spurs the lated traveler apace to gain the timely inn, eh my good lad? You survived your first day, Shakespeare.

"Thanks to your worship and all here," quoth I, but wary of letting Boy Burbage hear me, lest he find some new offense even in my courtesies.

Mr. Burbage directed us in our tasks of bedding the animals and covering our goods from prying eyes, while taking from the wagons only those few personals that would provide for us through the night. Mr. Johnson was already retired to a special room at the top floor while Mr. Perkin conversed with the host of the inn and some few added dignitaries, as I took them to be, from the town itself. I heard talk of meat and drink aplenty, most welcome to my aching joints and heated stomach. In the yard with us were other travelers, mostly carriers of goods. One carrier gave us pause, speaking to his fellow, but loud enough that all might hear:[5]

"Look you, Master. This house is turned upside down since old Ostler died. Meat here you dare not eat and the peas are as dank as a dog's [*illegible*]."

"Poor old Ostler, poor fellow," quoth Robin, the other carrier, a crooked old man with nary a tooth in's mouth nor a hair on's head, as he pulled a tick from his horse's nether regions. "He was never joyed since the price of oats rose; that was surely the death of him."

Whispering somewhat louder, the first carrier, a foul man of meagre looks, that some ancient misery had already worn to the bone, even though he was aged no more than I, pulled back his collar. "Look you, Robin, I think this be the most villainous house in all England for fleas: I am stung in this house like a pox." The last was spoken for all of our benefit.

"Like a pox! by the mass," quoth Robin to every man, but I think to me in particular. "There is ne'er a king in Christendom could be better bit than I have been in this place."

"Why, you will ne'er find here a jordan [chamber pot], so must otherwise leak in the hearth. And piss breeds fleas like an old cur [*mongrel*]."

The older carrier slapped the back of his horse, instantly producing a cloud of dust and fleeing fleas. "Here Nick, beat up old Cut's saddle, put a few flocks of wool in the point; poor buck, he's wrung out in the withers from all these loads."

"Why do you beat the saddle and not the horse?" asked Cowley, who I have learned is ever the inquisitor. Robin obliged:

"Look you lad, old Cut has been beat enow in his life as a penny-a-mile-horse-for-hire, so we beat the saddle and fill it in with wool around the frame to make it softer for the ol' jade, that he might bear his burden with some delight and curse us not to heaven for o'er working him in this heat."[6]

There were some six or eight others settling into the comforts of the Bishop's, including one woman who Cowley swore could be had for a penny the quarter hour. The accommodations do not remind me of home: above the lone long supper table in the great room of the inn there hovered a thick smoke that smelled of sweat, putrid ale, tobacco, and grease from the cook fire. We were served a fat sow's meat, commonly called brawn, which I never ate before, that was fried by an old woman tending the hearth, one I took for the wife of the host, himself a loud Welshman of many fewer years than she. I can testify that this brawn, with cabbage and a few carrots that bore signs of prior occupation by a worm or two, is a meat very hard of digestion, but what food is there that Hunger doth not make to have a savoury and delicate taste? Still, no wonder that Masters Burbage and Johnson supped apart in their rooms, I suppose on some finer pasty or such like.

When each man had taken his fill, we retired to the courtyard, where it was passable cooler than in a'door, and whence several filled their pipes. Every man found a seat against a wagon or lying in the straw, our scene dimly lit by a few lanterns that swayed from the second floor and a quarter moon direct above. Those same travelers who band together on the road by day to avoid highwaymen and petty thieves, sup and talk as one, when the sun sets at the inn. I took up mine own patch of ground upwind of Mr. Kempe, whose flatulence could offend even the dead. After some minutes of no special subject, the talk turned somber at the rumor of a plot to kill Her Majesty that was newly discovered at Court. Sides were swiftly chosen:

"God will soon find the instrument to strike her down - - she is excommunicated," said a slender man whose sentiment and accent betrayed his Catholic faith and Kentish origin. This anonymous fellow, who had said little over supper, was no more than twenty but quite clearly a gentleman with an arrogance of higher station. "And when Queen Mary's religion is restored throughout the land - - as who can doubt that one day it shall be? - - THEN will those of the true faith come from out of shadows and reclaim what is theirs."

The courtyard went silent, quieting even the dumbest beast that browsed in the straw. Cowley, who is never silent, whispered something in the ear of Mr. Clarke and each man shifted on his seat, but for a long moment, no one dared give this unknown traveler reply. His appearance matched his demeanor, sharp as home-brewed cider, fancy with a woman's lace around his neck on an otherwise plain black doublet. A peaked hat rest-ed at a calculated angle atop a mess of red hair, coloured with bull's blood I think, a pointy beard and nose that suggested interference in any man's busi-ness. Was he testing us? One of the Queen's spies sent from Court to know the true heart of England's merchants and carriers at her inns by night? Did he mean to plumb the depths of loyalty of the Earl of Leicester by challeng-ing his Company of players?

"My heart is glad over abolishing the antichrist and his popish order from our realm, sir." A booming voice thundered across the open air, rat-tling the balconies and windows facing the courtyard, as if God himself were now addressing us. Mr. James Burbage spoke, as those in his path parted to give him ease to the center of the floor. "I am no enemy to the old religion, but what was done was for England's good. How did the church of Rome help the plain, honest Englishman? What did their gilded abbeys and sanc-tuaries serve, but to feed a sort of lazy abbot and full-fed friar? They neither ploughed nor sowed, and yet they reaped the fat of all the land, and sucked dry the poor. Look you, thanks to her noble father, King Henry, whom I was honoured to serve in my youth, what was theirs is now in the Queen's hands; her rightful wealth that once lay in the abbey lands."

Mr. Burbage's appearance, once beheld, may never more be forgotten. He stands a head taller than most men and carries his bulk like the great kings he plays, as if he never took the crown from off his head. His red beard he keeps trimmed to a point so sharp, it might slice the back of his hand as he strokes it. Before he speaks, you can almost see the birth of his thoughts from a slightly raised brow, a tongue thrust in's cheek, and a lower lip that curls outward to clear a path for his words. Each of the Leicester's Men stood straighter now, as the young fancy continued, less cocksure than before:

"Indeed sir, God doth know, the infant yet unborn shall curse the time the true path was lost in this land and abbeys were pulled down. I ask now, where is hospitality? Where now may poor distressed people go to relieve their need or rest their bones when weary travel doth oppress their limbs?"

"Hospitality? I can tell you where to find that," quoth Mr. Kempe. "'Tween the legs of Mistress Quickly in Cheapside, where even a priest is welcome to her 'hospitality' if he has chinks [*coins*] enough in his purse!"

Every man laughed his fill at this, save the brothers Phillips and Pope, who stood apart in some heated argument, the one, I surmise, in defense of the old faith and the other correcting such beliefs very sternly. Some oddity that the brother called 'Pope' would so vehemently despise the head of the old church. Coz, I know the pain thou hast felt, when faith parts brother from brother and father from son, but I had not thought to find such divisions among players, whose only duty is to those who gape and applaud, and who each need the other as a honey bee needs his fellows in the hive.[7]

In short order, the foppish Catholic candle, finding himself blown out, disappeared into the inn with nary another glimmer. Mr. Burbage took up someone's ale and drank deeply for his trouble. A foreign traveler who frequented the inn, upon hearing he stood among the Earl of Leicester's Men, asked how the English nobles could concern themselves with so trifling a matter as Companies of players, when their Queen's life stood at risk and her kingdom at the brink of many dangers. Mr. Clarke replied (I find he takes himself very seriously and demands that others do likewise):

"Players, sir, of former time were very poor and ignorant, but some of their number being now grown very skillful and exquisite for all matters of the stage, these happy few are entertained into the service of divers great lords and … " here he paused and raised one brow for great effect " … and WE are sworn the Earl of Leicester's servants and are bestowed wages and liveries as grooms of his household."

I was struck by the general excitement among the other travelers at this notion that they found themselves among the household of the Earl, everyone knowing his position so close to the Queen herself. I myself stood more upright now. The foreigner tipped his cap and Mr. Clarke bowed his regal, silver-topped head, like some gracious victor after a shrewd game at chess.

Thus ended my first day with the Leicester's Men. I was to lodge with the other 'prentices, but Fortune smiled on me, as Boy Burbage lay in the second-best room near his father and I saw him little the rest of that night. We retired to our various beds, mine being a straw affair somewhat shorter than my length and barely wider than my shoulders, covered with a sheet, which I was obliged to share with Cowley. He hath proven a pleasant fellow, but snores grievously.

Night's candles were all burned out before I had slept a quarter hour, unaccustomed as I am to sleeping on straw in close quarters with a strange man, and jocund [*cheerful*] day stood tiptoe on the misty hillsides by the time I stood tiptoe over a crusty jordan. The fried brawn had rendered my bowels unserviceable and left a weakness in all my limbs.

"Shake-piece has fouled the nest," shouted Cowley upon rising and noticing mine ailment. "This may be the curse of Ned: his next in line may soon be dead!" Cowley referred in rhyme to the man I had replaced in the

Company, although at the time I could not savour the wit of the thing. Half the Company crowded on the stair as I tried to make my way below, not so much out of pity for my state, but eager to know if they would be a man short for the day's work in Coventry. Cowley played the Chorus and described my symptoms in exaggerated number while calling for the Company physician, who I soon learned is the kindly old Mr. Perkin. Bryan thought otherwise:

"This were caused by taking too much gross and evil meat and drink. Or witchcraft."

Mr. Perkin dismissed such conjecture: "Scouring [diarrhea] caused by spells? I doubt it much, unless he suffer also from other guts-griping or wheezing lung? Or loads of gravel in the back with some incurable bone ache? Or a bladder full of imposthume and lime in the palm? Dost thou suffer any of these, my boy?"[8]

I assured him I did not and that Cowley had exaggerated my condition. I thanked all present and urged them about their business, although given my station and weakness I could do little else. I feared I would be left behind if I failed to carry myself to the yard unaided, so I clung to the rail and made my way down the steps. Slowly.

"If he be merely suffering from colic, look where you may find a dog lying on the ground and let him kick up the dog and piss on the place where the dog lay and he shall be cured of the colic." Bryan had apparently employed such a remedy himself many times, for he acted it out as he spoke. Mr. Kempe seemed most concerned of all the men, or may have been in jest, as now he held me at an arm's length as if he would read my face:

"I have a perfect remedy for such ills of the liver or stomach, that also cures cold humors in the muscles of the yerd [penis] or swollen cods [testicles]. Thou must mix a measure of horsedung with strong vinegar and take some three or four drops of this liquor in the nose with a quill or a filbert shell, all the while thine eyes must be closed and thy nostrils pinched shut."

"If you please, your worships," quoth Cowley. "If you please, I have spent many a year in my father's fields caring for some two hundred and more ewes, curing their ague, their prolapsed matrix [uterus], their..."

Mr. Clarke pulled him away, as any master will do to an apprentice who has exceeded his station: "He may suffer the former, Dick, but I doubt he is afflicted with the latter."

Cuthbert then confirmed my fears that I would be discharged before I had even begun employment: "Nay, leave him at a surgeon for a good letting of his blood."

"And who shall pay a surgeon?" Mr. Perkin demanded to know, showing no small amount of disdain. "Nay, look you, I will restore his vigour with … " In that moment, this Company's physician discharged his duty: he grabbed my nose and twisted it, as if he would take it off and feed it to the pig in the yard. I screeched. The men laughed at me, but I must confess to a certain heat that coursed through my veins thereafter.

By now the last of the Burbages had descended and I would show no weakness to them, especially to the saucy Boy Burbage. I sat upon the great table and took up a half cup of wine left among the shards of last night's revels and shouted with as lusty a voice as I could muster: "Who will drink with me and kill the evil humours before they afflict you as they have me?" With that, I drank the cup in a single draught.

The whole inn was a-bustle by now and talk of mine infirmity was swiftly replaced by talk of the weather, the road, the horses, the night passed, breaking of fasts, and the like. To my surprise, the wine aided my cause and I began slowly to be more steady afoot and soon sought out those who could tell me my duties for the shift into Coventry that day.

Oh John: great thing of me forgot! Despite my hasty leave-taking I tried mine utmost to leave no obligation unsatisfied. I am only this moment reminded that I was pledged on the next Wednesday but one to aide Mr. Wilkins with his cattle, his son being absent for some other business then. Please convey to him my most earnest apology for failing him in so grievous a manner. His good will has always been generously given to aid my father's difficulties and I wish I had done better by him than this. By the time this letter comes into thy hands, the day will have come and gone. O what an artless, boiled-brained puttock [buzzard] am I!

The way into Coventry consumed no more than half an hour, right up to the great yard behind the Guildhall where we were to make our stage, for playing at three of the clock that same Thursday. We were to play 'Our Lady True', but Cowley says the bishop would not have it, and had asked for 'The Most Lamentable Tragedy of Prince William.'⁹ This gave me my first duty, for we had no prompt copy of the play and none of the men had recently played this musty old tale, so I was to write out the plot as it was told to me by Mr. Johnson. This document would be hung from some wall or other where the players could see it to refresh their minds about who comes next and the like.

Owing to my hasty leave from Stratford, thou knowest not how it came that my hand [*writing*] secured my employment with the Company in the first place, herewith the particulars that thou mayest better know my meaning:

"Thou art too old to be a 'prentice laddie, but canst thou write?" Mr. Burbage asked this of me, when I bid him consider me to join their number, after they first let it be known how they were a man short.

"Aye," quoth I, somewhat fearfully I will confess, for by my troth I had no idea what was required. "A sonnet have I written, if it please you."

Mr. Burbage, brow tightly knit, looked over my two pages and admitted: "Thou hast a fair hand. Canst copy fast?"

At that moment I realized he did not need a poet, but a scribe. I blurted out some assurance that in all of Warwickshire he could find no one able to copy as fast as I, having done so on many occasions to help my father fulfill his duties to the township. He may have guessed at my disappointment, looking then more closely at the words on my pages through hazy spectacles.

"Perhaps, one day, thou couldst mend a play for us too."

I assured him that a glover's son could mend more than plays, but apparel and periwigs [*wig*] and shoes in the bargain. Without sounding boastful, I told him of my love of horses and not small skill in their care and healthful management.

"Shakespeare, thou art for us," quoth he, when I had ended my particulars. That was all he said and in the instant was I hired, pleased that he kept my sonnet, folding it carefully into a pouch on his waistband as he walked on.

So here in Coventry would I be put to the test. Mr. Burbage ordered a rehearsal and time was scarce, the sun already so high, a shadow was barely cast 'neath the flagpole. In a quarter of an hour a 'plan' was needed. That is, Mr. Johnson was to speak the story and parts to me and I was to write it down, the substance of each scene on one page of two columns, taking care to leave a margin for notes that would be added later (by who, I knew not, and about what, I knew not either).

Mr. Johnson paraded around the yard as he spoke, acting out each part. He would point to me when I was to commit his words to the plan. He is unique among the men, for he alone seems unable to play parts that do not reflect his own moral character or station. That is to say, he plays great nobles and brave soldiers mostly, of which he is neither, but he commands our number, our goods and 'prentices as if moving his army across the vasty fields of battle. He has not yet lost his youth, but grey hair speckles his brown. He is fit enough, but rarely engages in the jigs or tumbling expected of the others, conveying that these are beneath his dignity. His beard is close-cropped, guarded, like his piercing blue eyes, which he turns on each man he speaks withal, like daggers drawn and ready.

When he finished, I was dispatched to procure red ink from the wagon for the playing of the murder. Upon my return, the players were hard at it: it was a kind of miracle! From my hasty plan, mere pages with a trace of ink, a dozen wizards spun a web of such delicacy and tragedy that I have never seen the like. The long speeches they passed over, so that each man might recall his part in general, along with his exits and entrances. Mr. Phillips, and those others with a skill at music, cleaned and tuned their instruments, while the 'prentices and I erected the tent for the 'tiring [attiring] house, wherein Cuthbert had laid out each man's apparel, and in under an hour, all was ready. Only the curtains gave us some grief in their preparation, for the wind had grown gusty and we found ourselves chasing parts of our playhouse across two fields and a hedgerow. After restoring these, I was faced with more than errant fabric. Boy Burbage cursed me and waved the red ink bottle in my face, saying:

"A pox on thee, Shakepiss. What manner of trick is this? This bottle is empty. What use will that be when the princess is slain? Must we use Cowley's own blood 'neath his woman's farthingale [*petticoat*]?"

I knew it to be full, when first I brought it hither, and said as much.

"Lout, thou liest!" quoth he, "An if there be no blood in the murder of the princess, thou shalt find cold comfort from my father's whip, I'll be sworn."

I cannot say for certain, I may have made reply, but what I do recall is barely worth the writing: I tangled in the dust with the boy, blind in my rage and no doubt prepared to do him serious mischief, had not Mr. Perkin and Cuthbert pulled us in twain, the former then hollering:

"What youths are here? Truly, those that would thunder nonsense at a playhouse and fight for bitten apples."

Each of us was given a scolding and sent about our duties. I was ordered to find more red ink, which I did in utmost disdain, for I swear upon my son's dear life that the bottle was full when first I dug it from the wagon. That filthy, worsted-stocking lackey had emptied it to make me appear a fool. At least he wore the badge of his villainy, for I had boxed him soundly on the cheek before we were parted and, ere he left my sight, I could discern a great red swelling under his left eye (while I bore not a scratch!).

When all at last was in readiness and the bailiff [*mayor*] had completed his welcome, some merchant or other raised a ruckus in the crowd, which some venerables of Coventry sought to quiet. In the mean season, the bailiff addressed our number in the tiring tent, in a courteous manner, recalled as best I may, thus:

"Well, Mr. Burbage, is all your Company in readiness?"

"Aye, sir, that we are, and I think all perfect, save for my damned eyes." Mr. Burbage seemed ever to be cleaning grease from his spectacles. "We have not for some time played this matter, but I daresay our efforts will please. Though I am not one of those tyrants who threaten a player's life when, in a whole play, he adds a syllable or takes the like away. If he can fribble through and move delight in others, I am content."

"And so shall we all be pleased." The bailiff, it would seem, was in a hurry to begin, holding up a finger as he departed, as if to foreclose any further discussion, a skill no doubt refined in commanding his Council.

At last a goodly crowd, some seated, some standing, were silenced and Leicester's Men began. At first, we crossed the stage with drum, fife, viol and other devices of delightful music, some which conned [*imitated*] the sounds of Nature herself: birds, rain, wind and thunder. Even mine own self and Cuthbert were pressed into service in this first procession, I being clad in a fine velvet robe, normally worn by a King, and beating on a small drum. Those assembled called out approval of this spectacle, particularly when the last players made their appearance, Masters Burbage and Clarke and Johnson, each richly dressed in the finest garments of silk and fur and brightly feathered caps. Mr. Burbage drew the greatest applause and he responded with a high step, twirl, and bow.

Next came the players depicting the story of our play in dumb show, some music therewith. My duty was to manage those properties which the players would need in the course, such as the knife, the blood, the chair that serves as a throne, and such like on and off the stage. But upon our return to the tent, Mr. Burbage liked not our dumb show and was therefore in a scolding mood:

"Fie, fie, what tedious insanity is here among ye! Have my rudiments been labored so long with ye, milked into ye, and even the very marrow of mine understanding laid upon ye and do I still hear cries of 'where' and 'how' and 'wherefore?' Ye are all light-of-brains! For HERE the Duke comes and THERE are ye, close hidden in the rear. The Duke appears and unto him I utter learned things; he nods, and when I fling up my cap, THEN, mark you, ONLY THEN, do you break cover and come out before him."[10]

Thus corrected, the men all nodded and at the instant were back on-stage to begin the play itself, their memories of the plot and each man's duties sufficiently refreshed and Mr. Burbage's choler by degrees abated. Now I learned the value of the plan I earlier had writ: we all used it as our guide and Cuthbert had listed for me the sundry properties (and when I was expected to make them ready).

And o what a magic spell these players then cast upon all who beheld them! Each word and gesture commanded the attention of the sun himself, who stood transfixed in the heavens to look down upon our show in delight. Then was yet another spell cast: this time, by mine own handiwork.

In that moment, wherein the princess is slain, Mr. Clarke thrust his dagger most violently into the pillow which was secretly sewn within Cowley's gown, causing a most bloody scream and an explosion upon the stage, for therein too was a bladder containing real blood. Cowley made his death speech amidst a sea of red, flowing out upon the stage and the hands of the foul murderer too, who then let fall the bloody dagger with a clatter that seemed never to end. As one, the multitude rose up and cried their approval. One woman fainted away and others swooned, so real was the grisly sight before them. For five minutes and more they roared.

When the play had ended, the epilogue and a jig performed, Cuthbert and Boy Burbage passed the hat among the well-appointed, while I passed a cloth sack among the meaner sorts (who gave loaves and the bounty of their gardens, a few gave bacon or cheese). The hat looked to be full of richer stuff.

To my surprise, I returned to the tiring tent to a hero's welcome. Each man gave me his huzzah [*approval*] with a slap on the back, which sent Boy Burbage into an even greater distemper than before. Mr. Johnson spoke first:

"Shake-scene, never have I seen such a tragic, bloody death. How mad'st thou that blood? Surely that was no bottle of ink in Cowley's bosom."

"The blood appeared real, your worships," quoth I, "because it IS real."

"How can that be?"

Suddenly fearing I may have committed a grievous error, it only then occurred to me that real blood might not wash clean from valuable apparel. Seeing Cowley already above a basin, scrubbing the bodice of the gown with raw hands, I sought to explain myself thus:

"Well, sir, when the ink bottle was most mysteriously found empty and time was short, I made haste to the house of a glover here, my father's acquaintance of many years. There I took up a pig's bladder - - for strength - - and this I did fill with the blood of a newly slaughtered lamb. The bladder sealed with glover's stitches, this device did I conceal between the gown and padding at Cowley's belly. Mr. Clarke did the rest with his dagger."

"He never thrust his 'dagger' into a maid with greater effect," quoth Mr. Kempe with a bawdy thrust of his own dagger.

"Ah, but Cowley's wench is a dumb innocent who cannot say him 'nay'," quoth Mr. Pope. "The only woman in Christendom with no better choice."

"Shakespeare, we have never used the blood of animals, for it changes colour and congeals in the bladder 'ere we can make its use," quoth Mr. Burbage. "How didst thou contrive to make this concoction so red and life-like?"

"Mr. Burbage, I am a glover's son and have slain many a tender lamb in my father's trade. Only the blood of a sheep or lamb will not congeal and keeps his native colour."

Mr. Burbage studied me again, as he did that day of our first encounter: "William is thy Christian name, is it not laddie? Make us more of these bladders, for the playing of scenes with foul murder, but hereafter, somewhat less blood, so as not to fright the ladies from their native wits."

"And so that I will not spend my skin and bones to wash it clean neither," quoth Cowley, though he seemed glad to have played the death of the princess so convincingly.

Light rain fell as we packed the last of our goods and tied down the flaps of our tent. I was left behind to mind the valuables overnight and, truth to tell, a pile of curtains made a sweeter bed than the moldy straw of another inn. More truth to tell John, I was glad to spend some hours alone with my thoughts. The crowd, the play, the players, a hat full of gold at the end: I was bewitched by it all as I could never have foreseen. And yet, I feel as one who sits a tedious winter's night by a fire with good old folks, hearing them tell the tales of woeful ages long ago enacted. I am no player, but neither do I belong with those in Stratford who call themselves 'father' or 'wife'. I dream of riches and dignity restored, like one that spies a far-off shore and scolds the sea that keeps him from thence. But I fear I have no more chance to reach that shore than a thirsty snake has of finding comfort in frozen water.

Truly, I know not whether I have made a grave mistake, joining these men, knowing little of their craft, already disliked by their general's son, for no reason that I can con [*understand*]. At the least Dick Cowley hath been courteous to me thus far. His people are from Warwickshire too, although I never heard my father speak of them. He asked why I would leave the prosperous household of my father and the quiet comfort of my bed. When I told him that Prosperity had long ago turned her back on the Shakespeares, although I said nothing of my father's true misfortunes, and said that I hoped to find better fortune in London, he confessed to having the selfsame hopes.

"I too have mouths at home to feed, Will. And I own no more than thou seest before thee now. But I will make my Fortune with these players, by Saint Anne." Cowley hath helped me to know the ways of these men and, if I stay, I shall seek his further guidance, for they thrive well that take counsel of their friends.

O coz, the rain has made the ground inside the tent a battlefield of mud and the air bites shrewdly when all is so wet, even on a summer's night. A dull grey morn is nigh and my fears, my doubts, feeling me guilty for leaving, and heartsick at the lack of thy company (and a son I will not see grow taller), all these betray me now. My native hue, of resolution, is instead plastered over with a weak brew of fear.

Thou knowest how in his troubled times, I have served my father faithfully in his trade, even when Gilbert was gone to London. But now Richard hath better skills than mine and even Edmund's tiny hands show the promise of a skilled glover, so I know that gloves will yet be made and skins will yet be tawed in the shop of Shakespeare without me.[11] But if I can earn my Fortune, my family may never again know the frozen winter of an empty purse, my son will ne'er be cast from Olympian heights to the most pitiable Hell of begging from those that once begged of him.

I have wronged thee, not to unfold my bosom to thee ere this, but feared my hopes were false, even as I heard about this New World and the wealth that any Englishman can find there, picked up like so many pebbles from a shore. Of this am I certain: no man can return poor from the Americas, so full of wonders and treasure is the place. Our countrymen have brought back acorns the size of melons, full of liquor and sweetmeats that our nobles will pay dearly for; flying fishes and sea-wolves, prized for their meat or to display in the City, where every holiday fool will pay ha'penny for a peek; walking fowl, the bigness of a goose, that cannot fly, but live in colonies of such size that every ship returns home with thousands of them salted and dried for sale in the London mart; asses they have brought back, with necks the length of a Maypole. But beyond these wonders and trinkets to delight the masses, all voyages have returned so laden with gold and jewels that no man among them was not made as rich as the Sophy of Persia.

Moreover, I have heard how General Drake's voyages have prospered above all, raiding among the Spaniards, spoils going to even the meanest labourer on the ship. Great galleons, laden with treasure and bound for Spain, are easily commandeered by our bolder English fighting men. Great riches, chests full of jewels and precious stones, of gold and silver, all of which things are free for our men to take as they list [*like*]. Indeed, at any place in the Americas, there is no part of the earth to be taken up wherein there is not some probable show of gold or silver, so for this reason, the Spanish take little pains to guard their ships, so common is it to refill them with such treasure.

And is it not gold which opens any door in England, makes even his lordship's constable yield up a deer to the hand o' the stealer; which makes the true man killed and saves the thief; nay, sometime hangs both thief and true man? Aye, what can gold not do and undo? To be certain, it cannot undo what's past, but now Fate has put me in the Company of that selfsame lord who has wrought such dishonour on my father and may I not then use this gift of Providence to set things aright, in one way or another?

Now sends forth Heaven its full fury against my sodden lodgings and soon will my fellows return, with some mouthful of bread, or so I trust. This sleepless night was not in vain. Writing to thee, dear and faithful friend, eases my mind as, Lord willing, we shall do one day again in the flesh. My fate is in God's hands (as whose is not?) and He hath said, "Nothing will be restrained from them, which they have imagined to do."

In the mean season, kiss my boy and maids in my name and omit nothing else which thine honour deem'st best for their tender need. I am thine ever loving servant in all else, Will.

LETTER TWO
July 15, 1586

Wherein three theatrical masks hide a great truth while two new friends reveal surprising truths about fathers and sons.

My family moved from our hometown of Milwaukee to Los Angeles when I was twelve. I felt out of place in my new school, but discovered a talent for acting and was soon cast in a play. In truth, I had been a ventriloquist and performer of one kind or another since I was six, but hadn't yet realized that "all the world's a stage" and that being part of a theatre company was instant family, with new, dear siblings and plenty of crazy uncles.

My school drama teacher cast me as Lord Capulet, Juliet's father from *Romeo & Juliet*, in a nationwide Shakespeare competition being held at the University of California Los Angeles. My scene won first prize and our troupe was given a plaque and handshakes by Alan Napier, the British character actor who portrayed Alfred the butler on TV's *Batman* series. I was hooked on Shakespeare from then on.

In many ways, my training as an actor in a traveling theatre company was similar to Shakespeare's in Leicester's Men, but I had to research some of the terms he uses in the letters to understand the differences. I learned about "lazzi," for example, referring to a bit of stage business, usually comic, that becomes a trademark of a particular character or actor, employed originally by traveling Italian "commedia del arte" players. Lazzi were often ad lib—one famous actor frequently pretended to be bothered by a fly, then would chase it across the stage and eat it. I had heard about the "groundlings," audience members in the Elizabethan theatre who stood around the edge of the stage on the bare ground, but Shakespeare reveals their importance to the play itself. While some terms were initially unfamiliar, it was immediately clear how such early theatrical training would pay big dividends when he came to write plays a few years later.

In Letter Two, Shakespeare wants to learn to be an actor too and, somewhat like my own experience, finds that the going is tough at first, in his case amidst the skepticism of the players and the mysterious hostility of Richard Burbage, the son of the company's founder and master, James Burbage. Shakespeare holds his tongue and his temper in check, even when he accidentally tears open his pants on stage (to his great embarrassment, but the audience's enormous delight). His patience and hard work, on and off stage, begin to be appreciated by some members of the company, especially Master John Perkin, who agrees to teach Shakespeare the craft of acting and becomes a sympathetic mentor.

Shakespeare describes having at least one friend, Dick Cowley, a comical fellow who plays the women's roles for the company, befitting his somewhat ambiguous sexual orientation. Dick becomes a sort of sidekick to Shakespeare

7. Queen Elizabeth's Court on its lavish summer tour through the English countryside.

8. Kenilworth Castle in the 16th century, imagined as Shakespeare recalled it in Letter Two when the Queen's summer tour visited in 1575.

9. Kenilworth Castle today, its greatness and mysteries lost to the ravages of time.

and a favorite object of his sometimes sarcastic wit. From Shakespeare's report of Dick's encounters with ghosts and fears that his master, Thomas Clarke, may commune with the Devil, I found myself researching more about contemporary beliefs in God, science, ghosts, witches, mountebanks [*magicians*], and magic (influences we will see later as Shakespeare writes of prophesies and creates characters like the three weird sisters in *Macbeth*).

In essence, Elizabethans firmly believed in the spirit world, benevolent and malevolent alike, and therefore saw plays like Marlowe's *Dr. Faustus* in a literal sense. I can imagine the conversations among theatregoers after seeing that play, asking each other if they would trade their immortal soul for earthly delights and wealth, as Faustus had done, thinking that this was indeed an option in their lives. When the ghost of Hamlet's father roamed the stage fifteen years later (a role that Shakespeare apparently played himself), I can imagine how many groundlings gasped in fright or told their neighbor about a similar encounter with a pitiful apparition (even if the specter, in many cases, was alcohol induced). Is it any wonder, when so much of our culture today is derived from that period and those influences, that the Salem witch trials were taken so seriously in the earliest days of the American colonies? Or that recent polls show 70% of Americans today believe in ghosts, angels, and miracles?

Finally, similar to his revelations thus far about the Earl of Leicester, Shakespeare also seems to harbor an unexplained resentment against Queen Elizabeth, yet he speaks of her with a grudging respect, as he and Dick Cowley discover a common bond: a dozen years earlier when they were boys, they both saw the Queen one summer as she and her courtiers paraded through the countryside of Warwickshire amid grand nightly festivals.

The Royal Progress was the movement of the Queen and her entire Court from the country estate of one nobleman to another, escaping the heat and plagues that marked life in London during the summer (Illustration 9, shown on page 31, as it stands in ruins today).

Each nobleman attempted more lavish entertainments than the next, hosting the members of Court and their servants at enormous personal expense, some of which was borne by local towns. People of all classes from miles around were allowed to view the entertainments to give loyal subjects a view of their sovereign and to keep them in awe of her majesty.

There are many accounts of this particular Royal Progress (the recollections of Shakespeare and Cowley are consistent with those), but here is Letter Two, which provides hilarious and insightful new details.

St. Swithin's Day, Nottingham [July 15, 1586]

Coz,

I can neither draw a cart nor eat dried oats, but if it be any beast's work in this Company, I am called to do it. My first week of service complete, it feels as if I have been gone a month and every day at work much harder than the one before. My legs cannot keep pace with the masters' desires and one disaster has already befallen me, when called to appear on the stage, but more of this anon [soon].

Nor is there rest on Sunday, for even then am I compelled to church by the innkeeper, who himself is fined if he allows any man or woman to lie a'bed when sermon is offered. Even servants of great lords are not immune, nay I daresay, we above all men are suspect in the eyes of the church.

"There is no one thing that has more likely renewed the contagion of absence from church than the practice of an idle sort of people, which have been infamous in all the commonwealth: I mean these common players." Vicar Freake fairly spat 'common' at Masters Burbage and Johnson, who sat in the first pew with county notables. "These COMMON players are licensed by our Aldermen to play within the town their LEWD interludes, which had never been allowed at times of divine service, but who now daily - - DAILY, I say unto ye - - and specially on HOLY-days, set up their plays, whereunto the youth resorts excessively and there take this infection!"

Perhaps because of his Puritan aspect, which is too hard-hearted for the common citizen, or perhaps because he finds many ways to pick the pocket of the faithful and heathen alike, this vicar is not well loved in his own parish. I stood with the 'prentices behind the last row and overheard one worshipper, even as he kneeled in prayer, whisper: "Look you, he belongs no more in our church than the Devil's own disciple. I say he is a common cow-keep, a common rogue."

Vicar Freake's harsh opinion aside (or perhaps owing to his announcement of our presence) our play was filled to overflowing later that same day.

Not so Saturday last, when it rained; nor could we play in a'door, for the hall where we should play had newly burned down. Therefore had we some few idle hours, which are of great delight, some of our men dividing to play at stool ball while others seek comfort in the stews [brothels]. No holiday for johannes: cleaning players' apparel and brightening armour, while Boy Burbage heaps on me ever more insults, which now number more than the hairs on my head and still I know not why. Honour demands an answer, but he will give none and I will not lose my post by scrapping with the master's son any further. Indeed, it is an empty vessel that makes the loudest sound, so I try to take little heed of him.

Yet has some good come from this foul pestilence. Old Mr. Perkin has noticed that I hold my tongue, which he takes as a kind of courtesy. He teaches no apprentice and keeps mostly to himself, but it is said that even Mr. Burbage seeks his wisdom on many grave matters. While I completed my labors that sodden afternoon, even as our fellows took their several recreations, Mr. Perkin appeared of a sudden, as if made of the rain herself.

I was surprised and may have uttered some 'good morrow, sir,' to which he replied 'God den [good day], Shakespeare,' intent more on examining his fingernails than me, or so I perceived it thus. Surely, he did not subject himself to a soaking summer rain merely to wish me well. I had hoped for such an encounter, apart from our Company, that I might bid him teach me the ways of the player's trade. I feared to vex him, as one so new and untested presuming upon his good offices, but I screwed my courage up to the task, for though I will take my chances in the New World, I needs must earn my keep and passage thither. The player's trade is no easier than the glover's, but more portable. It may need many months before I take ship and if I am to be a player the while, I stand determined to be the best at it and earn as much money as the trade will provide.[12] Therefore, I broached the subject, to which he replied thus:

"S'blood, learn the player's art? Thou art too long in the tooth to be mine apprentice and too ugly to play the women's roles." I could argue neither point and could not see his countenance to know if he were in earnest or in jest, shadowed as it was in the folds of his cloak's hood and dripping with rain.

"But I will not teach thee for one reason mainly, William. Your players are not tradesmen merely; not bent as other men are, in the pursuit of profit only. We are the chronicles of the Time. The mysteries of mine art are not fit for the country yeoman seeking easy money."

I may have replied too saucily: "Mistake me not, Mr. Perkin, I will make any man proud that invests in me the prize of his wisdom. If you knew my father, you had asked him of my dedication to any matter set before me. Nothing will I leave undone - - "

"Is that why thou art standing here in the rain cleaning horse leathers instead of plying thy father's trade closer to home?" His whispered words were barely audible above the splash of rain in the mud at our feet, yet did they cut me to the bone. I determined to speak my mind, come what might.

"What is done cannot be now amended. Men shall deal unadvisedly a'times, which after-hours give leisure to repent. I shall never live so many hours to repent my leave taking of Stratford, there being some foul business between my father and me which is better left unreported. I will make you the finest player your tutelage can invent. No opportunity shall I omit to work well with the tools that you might bestow upon me. There an end to my catechism."

"Well said, William ... well said." He fingered the moles about his left cheek, as one might stroke a talisman to bring good fortune or divine a truth. "Indeed an honest tale speeds best when plainly told, as thou hast done. I'll take thee at thy word, but ere I take any man in my confidence, he shall pass one trial further."

I regretted mine unmannerly and boastful reply as soon as it was uttered: "Any trial you can devise, will I bravely attempt. Is it of mind or body?" His reply was merely that I fetch him his tawny trunk.

John Perkin, of my father's age or more, I am told is more respected for the player's art than any man. He was made a Leicester's Man when the Company first gathered (with Masters Burbage, Clarke and Johnson) and must have cut quite the figure then, strong and handsome and of exceeding quick wit, which he can still summon upon the stage extempore. I think he is something vain, for in company he never fails to cover his silver hair with his Devon hat (in the hat, for special occasions, he adds a glove given him by Her Majesty). He is said to be a Knight of the Carpet [ladies' man], even in these his twilight days: his marriage ended badly, his children died of Plague in their youth. He is given to dice and not much skilled thereat, so he is often in debt with his fellows, but in other matters he seems more thoughtful: nary a one of Leicester's Men commands the stage, and all who look upon it, as does Mr. Perkin, therefore he plays the wise man, the friar, and other personages of note in our plays.

Having done as I was bid, the tawny trunk now lay before Mr. Perkin on a pile of dry straw 'neath an oak near the wagon. The rain had abated some, but the master did not remove his hood as he pulled from the baggage three masks. These he set face-up atop the trunk, himself leaning against the tree.

"These masks I have used, mostly in older times, to play some parts of comedy or tragedy. On the back of only one, my name is inscribed, for that one did I craft with mine own hands. Find it out: if thou cans't choose aright, then will I know that thou art worthy to learn the player's craft from me."[13]

Thou knowest I love a good game, so I bid that God direct my judgment and began mine assay of the masks. I studied the visage [face] of the master more carefully than any of them however, hoping to learn therein which one he preferred. But his cherubic face, kindly like the priest after a blessing, still somewhat obscured by the hood, gave no hint. I traced each mask with my fingertips to better study its properties and workmanship, but not knowing Mr. Perkin in full particulars, I discovered no clues therein.

The first mask I took up was gilt over with gold and some fine silk laces, but otherwise gave no hint of affinity to Mr. Perkin. Nor did the second one, the equal in workmanship to the first, but this one adorned with glittering silver studs and a rosy gem, meant to portray a carbuncle on the nose of a rich old merchant, with woven laces.

The third was a simple leather half-mask, one that covered only the nose, eyes, and above. The laces were also leather, but from my days working with my father's finest gloves I could see traits of a careful hand at work. No part of the mask was thicker than another, nor was any edge without its quarter-crease. The contour of nose and cheeks set forth a shape that, even in the dark, one could take for Mr. Perkin's own visage. What the others had in wealth, this mask had in care and craftsmanship.

How shall I know if I do choose the right? Mr. Perkin uttered no words more nor did he give me any clue. I felt myself shaking as if chilled by a February frost to the bone, yet was the waning day still warm and cloying at the end of that summer rain.

"Well, sir, you have posed a most amazing challenge. I'll none of the gold or silver masks: my father's fate has taught me well that the world is oft deceived with ornament. In law, in church, or in war, how many cowards, with hearts as false as stairs of sand, wear yet upon their chests the gilt robes of office, but who, inward searched, have souls as dark as ink? No, here choose I the mask of leather. I hope your favour be the consequence!"

Thereupon he turned over the smaller brown mask, revealing an etched figure of himself posing as Sampson and the inscription thereunder 'John Perkin.' At this, he took my hand in his and removed his hood to look me in the eye.

"Ha! Thou hast shown me that thou knowest the difference twixt glitter and that which may be true treasure, but fail me not in all things else, William." He seemed pleased that I had chosen aright. From that day to this, he has given me ale from his own stock and speaks to me in a most pleasing and familiar manner, even as he imparts to me the innermost secrets of the player's mysteries. Nor do my lessons ever resemble those we suffered many a'day as schoolboys in the Guildhall, coz. Instead this master teaches from the lessons that come in our daily tasks. For instance, when he found me groaning with each bundle I carried to the stage, he instructed me thus:

"Ailing, Will?"

I nodded. "Never have I passed longer hours than those in service to Lord Leicester's Men. Indeed, now I pity the football, for like him, I am kicked hither and thither in service to all till every seam cries out for mercy. If I last in this service, you should case me in leather."

"A true pilgrim does not measure weary steps," quoth he, laughing merrily, either at my discomfiture or my jest about the football. "William, thou art learning to be a player and not merely by that which thy betters do upon the stage."

I dropped the case I was bearing on my back and sat upon it, never more out of breath than at that instant. Mr. Perkin sat beside and whispered ever so carefully, curling his hand most gracefully, as if unfolding a napkin of the finest silk:

"All the WORLD … is a stage … William. Every man … a player. Therefore, every man upon a stage is no more than thee or me or the fellow out front. Thou must learn to bring thy SELF into the part. The secret to playing, day in and out, is to make a lazzi of that which plagues or joys thy mind and body. Thy part is made thus more human, more real. Don't hide that thou art sore: make it part of who thou playest that day."

"But I have only played soldiers, villagers, and assorted servants."

"So? Must thou play the King and speak a speech of an hundred lines before thou canst show the groundlings a man as weary as they? What needs a tired man of words? SHOW who thou art playing ... then is there no need to TELL us who he is."

With that he sighed the sigh of a man who has wasted his breath, but I caught his drift. Mr. Perkin's advice baked in my fevered brain for many days. I searched my mind and body every hour for a pain or ache or joy that I might portray and imagined myself on a stage playing a man I had seen, but now with that aspect. I limped and coughed and yawned and larked. Then it came to me that there were many ways to play each scene, using not merely the physical, but also the entrances and exits of the heart. I rehearsed time and again the scene from 'Widow's Debt' between the man and his servant (I playing the servant) and spake the lines once in anger, once in pity, then with longing, next in amusement.[14] Dick Cowley laughed me to scorn upon first encountering my fantasies, but soon he joined me and we played the scenes together, each time bettering the results of our last attempt.

But now to return again to this very day in Nottingham, where we played for the alabaster masons guild and were treated to their hospitality and stories. One burly fellow, dressed all in a faded red gown and silken cap, which I took to signify his lordship over the guild, boasted of how his men had crafted the very walls of the royal chapel in Windsor, stone so massive that a dozen carts were needed, pulled by more than an hundred horses, to convey so many of their statues and luminaries thereto. He lamented that their monuments had disappeared when King Henry tore down the monasteries. I memorized his manner and the pain I imagined he felt, in his joints from so many years at hard labour, and from his heart at the loss of his predecessors' craft.

More now of this day - - after sermons were done ringing in the parishioner's ears, we took to the largest stage I have yet seen. It measures at least the same as old man Field's drying barn and I swear a thousand faces gazed upon our spectacle.[15] Mr. Burbage put every mother's son of us upon the stage, to fill the scene I think, at every opportunity, but especially for the jigs and tumbling at the end. It was here that I gained my first true experience as a player (truth to tell, I am neither player nor 'prentice, but the spectators made not the distinction).

At supper, the men caroused [gulped] more than is their custom. I heard Mr. Burbage say the payment exceeded anything they had taken for one day's work in the shires. This would account for their excessive good humor, which included Masters Johnson and Clarke, hitherto more aloof at such times, who ate and drank with us all. When pipes were lit, Mr. Kempe amused the boys by farting over the fire and nearly igniting his breeches. Then called Mr. Pope for silence and drew mine own self to his side, making this speech with a great smile on's face (which was not from merriment alone, but a permanent state of his lips owing to the grievous disfigurement in his youth):

"Leicester's Men, hear me well. We sheared the sheep to the bone this day in Nottingham, ye Robin Hoods, most fit to take from the rich and give to the poor players hard by Sherwood Forest, as we are this day."

At this, the men called out a score of toasts in an instant, some to their ladies at home 'a bed, others to a scene played particularly well that day with a tip of a cap to the player. Mr. Pope caroused his bishop [hot cider], called for another, and continued.

"But it is John Shakespeare who may well have earned us our most shiny coins today, m'lads.[16] No man flings a coin upon the stage if he is not pleased with the ending, with the jigs. Am I right? AM I RIGHT?"

He demanded consent and indeed every man agreed in his several way, most with a further draught. I can smell even now the delicious curtain of drunken steam, matching those fumes accumulating in our brains, as the iron plunged into Mr. Pope's own brew, which hissed with delight, as he gathered himself and rose to the greatest height his crook-back would allow, teetering upon a three-legged stool that gave signs it might not bear its burden much longer, saying then:

"Therefore, men, therefore… therefore… THEREFORE, have I writ this poem in honour of Leicester's Men, and our newest attraction."

Mr. Pope withdrew from his waistband a crumpled sliver of parchment, which bore equal marks of ink and greasy thumb. Without spilling a drop from his cup, he smoothed out the paper on the top of my head, like the vicar preparing his sermon on the pulpit. He cleared his throat, waited for total silence, and spake thus:

> "We know that those who paid their fee
> To witness our bright comedy,
> Or hear the tunes of fine musicians
> Were more entranced by the additions
> Of bawdy jests and comic strokes,
> Of antics and salacious jokes,
> And what, with his ill-fitting hose,
> The certain Shake-piece did expose!"[17]

As every man roared, Mr. Pope came down from his stool and slipped half a crown in my pocket, then slapped me so hard on the back I may bleed when I next make water. Indeed, I had that day (against the will of all my betters onstage) attempted my first tumble after the jig, even as the experienced men performed their own. The results are fairly recorded by Mr. Pope's poem, the writing of which I did thank him for most profusely. He replied no thanks were needed, whereas his brother, Mr. Phillips, intends to set it to music and I am to repeat the jest onstage at every opportunity, especially when few ladies are present, mine own modesty a sacrifice to the greater good of our Company's purse! Of all the masters in our Company, I have come to respect Mr. Pope in great measure, for he has shown me the courtesy of a man who has himself been more outside a circle than within it. I will endeavour to make better his acquaintance and dwell in his good company when occasion affords.

Still, the sun did not set today without more drama than comedy. As each man drifted off to his bed, Boy Burbage made his way to me when he saw I was in no other man's company, then upbraided me with this venomous gibe:

"So, 'Master' Shakeshit, thou art preferred by Mr. Pope, eh? Well it may be a valiant flea that eats his breakfast on the lip of a lion, but he is a flea still and nothing more!" He then spat upon my shoes, turned on's heel, and walked off to join his father. The coward knew I would not dare brace him back, while in his father's presence. I went off to mine own bed and when I could not sleep, for thinking on this villain and for Cowley's snoring, I made company with the night's candle to write to thee these few remembrances. Even as I write of Boy Burbage's affront, my stomach rises and my fingers itch to find themselves around his vile throat. That may well be, before another sun doth set, come what may.

Even so, I must count myself among the most fortunate of God's creatures. Dick Cowley is the chiefest reason I did not turn back after the first week. He hath shown me an uncommon courtesy and a wisdom that exceeds his years. My rustling woke him and he bid me explain my disquiet. He replied that Boy Burbage is a lout and ever trying to prove himself worthy of his father's attentions. We talked another hour of fathers and sons:

"Look you in the chronicles: the Cowleys of Burtonheath came in with Richard Conqueror. But I am more proud to be my mother's son than a Cowley, for look you, she worked hard i'the fields every minute that God granted her daylight. She ruled the roost and could brook no idleness, and those who did not bend to her will, she soon made weary of this life. Some called her 'Mrs. Bishop,' which I took as an honour, but later learned it to be a slander. For look you, my mother tended to all manner of labours, many unfit for a woman, because my father trifled his days and nights writing some history of Warwickshire. La! And worser still, no matter how hard she toiled, or how well she managed his household, in no wise could she gain his loving attention away from his pen and papers. Therefore, she threw his papers into the fire and burnt every page. So what thinkst thou my father did, upon discovering his written treasure was all lost to the flames?"

Dick withdrew from some hidden pocket a handful of caraway seeds, which he sweetly offered me as he spoke. He ate them one by one, nibbling at each seed. I have only ever seen a delicate wren do likewise, in the garden on Henley street. Odd for a boy or a man.

"What could he do?" I assumed Dick's query to be rhetorical, but might have waited out the night for him to continue had I not revived the telling of his tale by asking.

"I will tell thee what: he said not a word, but that night closed himself again in the selfsame closet and began the writing of it all over again! Aye, so great was his zeal for the advancement of learning, or so it was told to me, that staying longer still apart from my mother to write his History a second time he regained one treasure, but lost the finest jewel thereof. I mean she did succumb to the advances of my father's brother, mine uncle the Bishop Cowley, and while my father slept with his papers, she took his brother to bed and thence was I stamped, a counterfeit coin, a portrait of stolen likeness."

"How didst thou come by such knowledge?" quoth I, between nibbles of his caraways (thou shouldst try this practice, to bite one seed and release it's vigour in thy mouth, a most singular pleasantry).

"My mother concealed nothing from me, as she made ready to depart this earth, for though I was not more than ten-year-old, who else should tell me? The man I thought my 'father' died of a Plague before I set eyes on him. The Bishop never set foot in our household more than once in my living memory, for he was sent out of Warwickshire to a parish hard by London, so I am told. And what a scoundrel was he: they say he took from the house every furniture and plate that was not nailed to the floor, leaving the next Bishop in penury and begging alms from the Queen. Aye, be thou not so amazed, for I have not yet listed all of his faults. He was taken too by all manner of vice and was said to have so fallen in love with his pipe of tobacco that he died thereof, choking out his farewells with n'er a repentance of any act in his life."

"I am sorry for thee." I have not often been presented with so sad a tale of parentage, so could think of no other thing to say.

"Are we not all bastards, Will, in the end? Well, orphans in any wise. I was left to tend my sister and two brothers, but was in no wise a goodly mother, for all three withered and died of the Plague, no physician coming to their aid."

"Nay, Dick, thou art not to blame, thou knowest how every door in England has seen the Plague walk through uninvited." I sought to calm him, but to no avail. For a moment he paused and wiped a tear away.

"No truer word spoken, Will. My father's ghost appears to me many a night, dressed in all his regal Bishop's finery, full with lamentations and fearsome warnings 'gainst all manner of vice and lasciviousness, the consequence of which shall be doomed to walk the earth in pain and misery for all eternity. And in no wise, says the Ghost, should we meddle with those assaulted by the Plague or other sore afflictions, nor give them medicines, for these are punishments from the Almighty and who are we to interfere with His will? What should I think of this? A villainous, cheating Bishop giving pious - - well, I take this from his ghostly visits: e'en those, who know not for certain their father on this earth, know we are all the children of our Father in Heaven, for he maketh His sun to rise on the evil and on the good alike."

I thought to relieve his fevered remembrances somewhat with a brief chronicle of mine own family. I spoke of my brothers and sisters; of thee and our many misadventures; of my father's troubles, but omitted the part that Leicester played, for I know not yet if it would appear disloyal to one who has been longer in the Earl's service. I spoke of enforced marriage and of becoming myself a father, while still a youth and unfit for such duty.

And what my telling of these tales yielded, was most unlooked for: it seems that I have met Dick Cowley when we were both but beardless boys! Aye, we were both unawares, but 'twas at the Queen's Progress at Kenilworth, in that hellish July when I was ten (which thou knowest became a hotter day than any is in Hell for the Shakespeares).

"Thou wast there, Dick? Thou wast THERE?" He nodded and laughed, for reasons he would soon explain. I tried to paint the picture for him, as my minds' eye could best recall it, which I commit now to this paper, that Hamnet will one day know thereof too:

My father's station afforded us a place at the feasts and on the viewing platforms. And what saw we from thence? That stuff that dreams are made of! Lord Robert Dudley, the Earl of Leicester, now our own master in this Company, rode out to Long Ichington to greet Her Majesty's arrival with a great banquet, under a canopy of gold and ivory silks, returning to Kenilworth only as west glimmered its last streaks of day.

Father caused me to wear not only my finest array, but a heavy embroidered cloak and cap too. After half a dozen hours in the noonday sun, there lay more salty brine in my shoes than in all Neptune's oceans, whilst my hair draped sodden on my forehead like wilted cabbage. The Court ate and drank continuously, while we onlookers were feasted but one meal in the day, that being our supper, and none so sumptuous as the victuals we saw spread before Her Majesty.

Dick said he too could remember much of Her Majesty's first day at Kenilworth, but bid me first describe those particulars I could recall, for we two had observed from very different places. The Queen's arrival at castle Kenilworth, as night fell, took place among the greatest commotion, so there was indeed much more for me to add:

"Dick, didst see the Earl's brother, dressed as Jove, launching fireworks and canon hailing the royals as they approached the special platform alongside the lake?" That he had.

"And the Lady of the Lake, arrayed all in silks and gliding towards the shore on a moveable island?"

That he had also seen, but he could not hear her speech, for he was hidden where I would never have guessed, but was soon to learn from him.

I recall that this apparition made a speech of welcome, telling the Queen how she had kept this lake since King Arthur's days, but offered it willingly up to Her Majesty now. Blasts of trumpet and drum followed the speech, after which the Queen leaned against the rail and thrust her considerable bosom toward the Lady, as if to offer battle, saying 'We always supposed it ours.' The Earl seemed perturbed at this response, to so magnificent an entertainment and so generous a gesture, but he persevered, calling forth twenty lusty serving men dressed as Bacchus, who poured full cups everywhere, every minute, of every kind of wine, ale and beer. Dozens more dressed as Neptune offered fresh fish from the sea, such as baked salmon, mullet and herring, along with boiled lobsters, eels and oysters, some still quite living, carved open and ate just so.

"O Will, I recall very well that spectacle, and could have died happy thereafter, had God struck me dead in the instant, for being witness thereto! But I perceived those grand displays from the lake itself." He had finished the caraways and now was peeling an onion, but paused as he remembered the scene, as if transported across time and place.

"FROM the lake? How camest thou thither?" I would not eat any part of his onion, for without bread it would only have played the devil with my bowels.

"How indeed! Canst thou recall the one among the Earl's players who performed for Her Majesty such feats of tumbling, in many forms and fashions, that he was called back to the stage over and over again, turning a brighter red with each pass in the heat, which had not abated, e'en with the setting of the sun? This man was Mr. Clarke."

"Aye, Dick, I remember it, aye! He and one other man showed marvelous feats of agility in tumbling and somersaults, with sundry other gyrations and circumflections, all so lightly and with such easiness as in few words can not be expressed. This, I recall, was prologue to a mock sea battle on the lake under yet more fireworks, with blazes of burning darts flying to and fro and hails of golden sparks on the water, all with such a tempest that the heavens themselves seemed to thunder."

"Yes, thou hast it right, Will! And that which next occurred is where thou sawest me, though on that day thou knowest not. Didst thou see how suddenly a mermaid appeared on the lake, riding on the back of a dolphin, uttering such dulcet and harmonious breath that the rude fireworks grew civil at her song? And how there followed a boy as the poet-god, who also had been riding in the great dolphin-boat, but his oration was marred because he forgot his lines?"

I was so struck dumb that night by the grand apparitions before me that I never noted nor missed an oratory. I confessed as much to Dick and begged him to finish his tale before the sun woke the morning cock, which to my mind was nigh.

"Will, that false poet was no man, no boy, but simple Dick Cowley! I was so fearful when I could not perform my lines and there were players beside me that pinched me all over, that suddenly I plucked the mask from my face and rudely addressed the Queen directly, crying 'Forgive me for I am no poet, m'lady, but honest Harry Goldingham of Warwickshire, so please you.' At this the Queen laughed heartily and awarded me a gold sovereign for my pains and plain speaking."

"How camest thou to be thither and lying to Her Majesty about thy name?" This tale could not grow stranger, or so I thought.

"Well, as I have said, so desperate was I to feed my sister and two brothers, having a'times no more to eat than bread made from acorns and the dirt from the floor, that I took any labour that might fetch us a farthing. Hearing that my neighbor, Harry Goldingham, was himself taken to bed with pain in his groin, such that he could neither walk nor crawl, I contrived to take his place in the great pageant for the Queen at Kenilworth. He was to play the part of a cherub reciting some dozen lines of a poem that had been writ especially for Her Majesty. So oft had I heard young Harry recite these lines that I too could speak the speech to pleasing effect, or so said old Mr. Goldingham. Thus did I arrive at Kenilworth in my borrowed likeness and presented myself as Harry and thus was I swaddled in yards of silks and a heavy crown of taffeta and jewels and thus was I sent forth upon the lake on a dolphin made of wood and thus, when it came my turn to speak, was I so overcome from the heat of the day and weak from hunger that I did forget half my lines and mis-ordered the others, seeming overcome with too much strong drink, and thus did I make my excuse to her Majesty, but in fear of my life, thus did I say I was Harry Goldingham of Warwickshire, for none other did those players in my Company expect of me! And instead of whipping for mine offence, I was rewarded with more money than my family had known ere then: a gold sovereign, no less!"

How capricious is our God or the hand of Fate! And to what end? I had barely digested this news and re-surveyed mine own recollections of that day, to imagine I saw again the boy on the dolphin's back in the vast lake, when Dick added yet more layers to the picture he was painting on this canvas.

"Yet was this golden treasure not the end of my good fortune that day, Will. My fear of punishment was not unjustified, for no sooner had my dolphin boat returned to shore than an agent for the Earl himself knocked the folded shrouds from off my sweaty brow and grabbed me by the ear to drag me before sudden justice. I looked for any moment to escape what must surely be a violent fate, I mean a terrible end. The Devil himself was at mine elbow and tempted me, saying to me 'Dickie, use thy legs, run away.' But my Conscience said ' Dick, being an honest man's son, budge not.' Of what honest man am I the son, I wondered? Must I heed Devil or ... "

"Dick, a tale grows no sweeter by the lengthening of it." His debate had grown tedious and I was eager to know the result, especially because I was, at last, weary enough to sleep, the which I needed now most urgently. "The horse is loose; bring him now galloping home!"

"Aye, well, before I could make good mine escape, Mr. Thomas Clarke, in charge that day of the players and their many entertainments of the Queen, caught me by the ear and would not let go for all the gold in Christendom. The Earl's stward then said, to make amends for mine offence and the embarrassment it had caused the Earl, either I would be given to the Sheriff, and no doubt locked away to mine eternal damnation, or Mr. Clarke must take me in his care and put me to good and honest employment, such that I would ne'er again do offense to so great a person.

"And thou wast locked away?"

"Nay, fool, else how would I be sitting here eating this onion now? Wilt take this last piece?"

"Nay, Dick, but I am grateful. What happened then?"

"To my great amazement and greater joy, the master took pity on me and made me his 'prentice with such courteous apologies to the Earl that would make a statue melt. And so came I to serve in the Earl of Leicester's Men with visions of playing Kings and valiant soldiers upon the stage."

"Such lofty roles at such a tender age?"

"Ah me, Mistress Hope springs eternal, does she not? In truth, I was the johannes as thou art now, but Mr. Clarke gave me instruction and soon I played the maidens, owing to my lack of manly features. O I rubbed all manner of earthwort upon my chin to hasten the day I might grow a beard; I ate the cods [testicles] of deer; I strove to turn my reedy voice into a graver tone, but all to no avail. The women's parts were for me and, as I have said, women are stronger and wiser than many a man, so I am none the worse for it."

And thus was Dick Cowley in my presence a dozen years ago and thus he came to be in Leicester's Men. We spent another hour recalling how that night it liked Her Majesty to walk afoot on a bridge over part of the lake, where it pleased her to stand and listen to delectable music in the company of the Earl. And how this spectacle continued for a dozen and a half days and nights more, my father complaining all the while about the cost to Stratford and every other town of the shire, no matter the honour. And how there were displays of sword fighting and cockfights, the latter which the Queen did not herself witness, it being a low and savage event, but how she did attend every one of six bear baiting combats, one of which my father and I attended too.[18] Though I was bone weary by now, Dick asked me to describe what I had seen, so I acted out the part of the bear, pretending he was the dog to be repulsed.

"When he was bit in one place, oh how he would pinch in another direction to break free, biting, chewing, clawing and roaring. When cornered by the pack, he would toss and tumble his great girth over the lot of them to work for his freedom, sometimes crushing the spine of a helpless hound. Then would he shake his head back and forth in triumph, his snout and ears dripping with the blood and slaver, leaving such an expense of blood on each assailant that a month's licking would not recover. These epic struggles Her Majesty enjoyed the most, cheering now for the cornered bear, now for the forlorn dog whose leg hung mangled and unserviceable, waiting for Death himself!"

We two were now like giggling maidens who dream of love, cavorting on the floor, teasing, and pinching, and tickling. His tender ways, and laughter like a nightingale, make me a'times forget that Dick is of mine own sex. It may therefore be that because his body is no more substantial than a wisp of smoke and his mind is all ways given to thoughts of womanly gentleness that he can play the women's roles with such great effect. He then finished his telling of the events of Kenilworth:

"Mr. Clarke put me to work the next night in another entertainment for Her Majesty: chasing stags for that which he called 'Hombre Salvaggio', wherein torchlit hunters, myself included, drove before them a Wild Man, all overgrown with moss and ivy. In one hand an oak, plucked up from the earth, roots dangling; in the other hand, a fiery bush that flamed in every colour of the rainbow. Wild Man knelt in supposition before Her Majesty, who sat astride a great white mare with golden hooves and silken plaits, offering his rustic gifts, but the one ignited the other, and of a sudden, crackling cinders flew in all directions, striking her horse, sending all into panic, the men drew weapons, ladies shrieked fearfully, but Her Majesty reigned in her noble mount and called out to calm the scene. 'No hurt, no hurt,' quoth she."

Truly, I remember being amazed that Her Majesty was the equal of any man in the hunts at Kenilworth, not content to stand apart on the platform with the other ladies who were shooting at the deer that the men had chased, but she commanded her own horse and hounds, bringing down the greatest stag in the field with but one arrow, taking assay [the kill] with but one swift stroke. And how, when another deer she pursued took refuge in the great lake, Her Majesty granted him his life, on condition that he lost his ears as ransom. What then says more about our Queen: her love of bear baiting or her mercy for the stag?

We lay on the floor staring at the rotting timbers of the ceiling and wondering aloud if they might fall at that moment and strike us both dead. Although I longed for sleep, I did not want to break the spell that had been cast, which helped me find such kinship with Dick, in the otherwise uncharted territory of Leicester's Men.

"And what kind of master is Mr. Clarke?" At this, Dick drew me closer and spoke not above a whisper, his foul breath filling my poor nostrils with the stench of the onion, some roasted garlic he had eaten at supper, and his rotting teeth.

"To me he seemed so like Colbrand.[19] He taught me the secrets of our players' trade, but those other mysteries, things that he should ne'er tell another living soul, those make me fear he is not so much larger than other men. I mean that he follows the Popish faith and is no friend of Her Majesty's church. I mean that he protests too much against those who practice the selfsame rituals that he performs in greater fiendishness."

"Rituals? What..." Here Cowley pressed his fingers to my lips and paused to comfort himself that no man, save us two, lurked within our hearing. This next he uttered fainter still, like the colour of a faded glove left too long in the sun:

"I have seen Mr. Clarke call forth SPIRITS to guide him and lend him powers. These spirits come to him as angels and other fair shapes, appearing when the air is still and the heavens clear of any cloud. Then does he summon these ghosts to advise and guide his hand in all things. I did report to him the visitations of my dead father and he bade me repeat every particular of these apparitions and what spake the Ghost to me, every word. He then told me of the spirit that walks most often with him at night, a man much troubled for the killing of another, doomed to take the shape of a great black dog unable to regain his human form, forced to walk among the living and repay his debts in some wise. These forces do Mr. Clarke call upon to his great success, I swear to thee."

"Does he not fear the Devil in calling of spirits?" I would know more, lest I myself be lured by some demon.

"Nay, for they say if a man be drunk over night, the Devil cannot hurt him in the morning, and Mr. Clarke is most often drunk when he performs these rites. La! He should fear more the Queen's officers come calling, for they may care little if he speak to ghosts, but will tie him to the rack if they discover he communes with priests of the old faith."

These revelations about Mr. Clarke opened Dick's floodgates, for then he told me further the habits of other masters and how some laid wagers against my survival in the Company for more than a month, although he will not say which master has taken which side. He could not say if mine unexpected success with the jest of the 'torn hose tumbling' (as now the men have named it) would work in my favor or anger those with a greater sense of decorum. In this, Dick hath revealed constant disputes among the masters, sides taken, even blows exchanged when stomachs overheat and strong drink fuels the flames, about the proper use of our Company and those many entertainments we offer or withhold. He reports that Mr. Kempe is forever in strife with the others, for he knows no bounds in what he will say or perform, when spectators call out for more.

In this I see I dare not share any more of mine innermost thoughts with Dick about seeking passage to the New World, for he cannot keep secrets and I fear he might betray me to the others, as being one not worthy of their tutelage (or a share of their earnings). I have survived nearly a fortnight and will henceforth take any task, no matter how lowly or back breaking, to prove those wrong who bet against me. Nor should I be indifferent to employment of any kind in a land so filled with miserable wretches that have none: those that come to our plays and beg for alms from the playgoers; those who bring with them their children, to freely show off their skin and bones, thin as parchment and covered in rags that smell of human waste and misery (though some, I suspect, are better actors than any in our Company, clad in a sort of player's apparel and wrapped in an air of pity that wrings a farthing from even the hardest hearted playgoer and, in the end, their masters collect more than any one of us).

Over-reading this briefly, I see I may have writ some things better left unsaid, but I commit them all to thy trusted care. Sleep has already visited Dick, who snores grievously beside me now, and I must do the like or lose the whole night's chance for peaceful rest. Such rest will I need if I am to survive the month, if I am ever to see London.

Thus I commit thee to God's good protection, dear coz. Kiss my boy and maids in my name and omit nothing else which thine honour deem'st best for their tender need. I am thine ever loving servant in all else, Will.

LETTER THREE
August 1, 1586

Wherein a routine day among the players is described, but the tale of a valiant Englishmen against the Turks renders it as memorable as certain advice from dear Uncle Henry.

After living in California for a year, my family moved to Australia in 1966. By the time I was a high school student in Brisbane, I had latched on to a touring theatre company that performed *Macbeth* in small theatres (and even smaller tents) around the state of Queensland during the summer of 1969.

I played an unnamed lord in the banquet scene (pretending to eat the foul-smelling roast pig we carried in a cooler from town to town in the stifling summer heat) and Young Siward, who briefly battles Macbeth in Act 5. One night our sword fighting was especially vigorous and I fell into the scenery, which crashed towards the audience, nearly knee-capping a dozen school girls who were sitting in their proper dark blue uniform skirts in the front row. I remained in character (i.e. dead) and was carted offstage as the scenery was propped back up, hearing thunderous applause for the drama or the comedy, I'll never know which. The Toowoomba Chronicle reported the next day "Macbeth Comes to Town: Young Actor Brings Down the House."

Of course, those bit parts were not my only duties on tour. I wrangled lights, props, water jugs, a broom, and that pig's head, amongst other things for those six glorious weeks. I couldn't imagine being a paid actor got any better than this and I was only seventeen at the time. But those experiences gave me empathy and insight for what I found in Letter Three.

Shakespeare describes his own daily grind as he settles into his work with the Leicester's Men. His duties as a scribe notwithstanding, Shakespeare must also execute all kinds of menial jobs, including dealing with every manner of human and equine waste.

Hearing the tales of a fellow player, Thomas Pope (a man who was crushed by a wagon and deformed by his injuries, yet has become one of the most versatile players in the company), Shakespeare muses, "bravery and determination can oer'come chains or deformities, if a man be good and true." The profound significance of this lesson becomes clear in subsequent letters.

Another story that Pope tells Shakespeare provides a nuance of Elizabethan society that has not been previously explored in much detail, but which echoes to our present-day fears and phobias. As noted earlier, 16th century England was legitimately concerned that Catholic Spain would invade to restore King Philip and his religion to the realm, but Pope's story shows how brave Englishmen would join forces with their bitter rivals to defend against Turks and Muslims, whether the threat from those "foreigners" was real or inflated.

While xenophobia may have been as exaggerated among some parts of society then as it is today, Shakespeare's letters do highlight a genuine threat from within the kingdom. King Philip was actually not very likely to invade if Elizabeth died or was overthrown, because Mary Queen of Scots was already in England and poised to succeed her despite being imprisoned, but there were many powerful nobles who wanted to accelerate that transition.

Not to be confused with Henry VIII's daughter Mary Tudor (who ruled briefly before dying in 1558 and passing the crown to Elizabeth), Mary Stuart was the daughter of King James V of Scotland. James V was the son of King James IV of Scotland and Margaret Tudor, a daughter of Henry VII of England. As Henry VII's granddaughter (and therefore Elizabeth's cousin), Mary Stuart had a very legitimate claim to the throne of England and many Catholics either wanted to overthrow Elizabeth and ensconce Mary Stuart, or at least see her succeed her older cousin when the time came from natural causes (Elizabeth was nine years older).

Mary Stuart was quite a colorful character and worth a further brief digression, because her very existence hovered over Elizabeth's reign. She was born December 8, 1542 and, when she was just six days old, her father died, making her the Queen of Scotland. Needless to say, the country was actually ruled by a group of nobles and she was sent to France for her education where she later married Francis, the Dauphin [prince] of France. Francis became King in 1559 and Mary his queen consort, but he died a year later and she was sent back to Scotland. In 1565, she married Lord Darnley (Henry Stuart), but a few years thereafter he was found murdered in the garden and many suspected Mary's involvement.

Although James Hepburn, the 4th Earl of Bothwell, was charged with the murder, he was acquitted and soon married Mary himself. These tangled affairs created awkward allegiances and a rebellion, which resulted in Mary's abdication of the crown in favor of James, her young son by Lord Darnley. Mary fled to England in 1568 to ask Elizabeth for protection, but because she had previously claimed England's throne and so many Catholics encouraged her, Elizabeth imprisoned her in various castles for nearly two decades, including the time when Shakespeare began writing his letters.

Although letters like this one illuminate the tectonic shifts of European politics, they also show us a great deal about Shakespeare's inner life, including conflicted feelings surrounding his father, as he fights homesickness by writing the letters and asking after his friends. He mentions "Pug" who, after considerable research, I learned was a nickname for Richard Field, son of a tanner in Stratford and contemporary of Shakespeare at school; and "Tyke" the nickname for Richard Tyler, another schoolmate.

But he saves his fondest remembrance for the advice given him by his Uncle Henry, a brother of John Shakespeare (William's father). Henry chides William to be dutiful and remember his own father gratefully, even as he hopes Hamnet will remember him one day, despite the human frailties a father may display. Uncle Henry is simultaneously profane and profound, employing homilies and bombast that seem to be the early foundation of Sir John Falstaff, a bittersweet rascal of the first degree (introduced in *Henry IV part 1*) and one of Shakespeare's most memorable characters. Look for more evidence of this influence in Letter Four when Shakespeare describes how Will Kempe tries to seduce a woman in Dover. Elements of that description, and the reaction of Kempe's colleagues, are repeated by Falstaff and his entourage in very similar dialogue in *Merry Wives of Windsor*.

Shakespeare quotes a crude song that Henry sang for him and, in his play *Hamlet*, written some 15 years later, Polonius offers a refined version of this advice to his son, culminating in the famous line "to thine own self be true" (Act I, scene 3). It would appear that Uncle Henry's advice stayed with the poet for much of his life and, as subsequent letters reveal, characteristics of Polonius were based on Uncle Henry, Will Kempe, and a nobleman that he meets in Denmark (described in Letter Five).

Another remarkable aspect of this letter is that it takes us inside one of the great houses of England, likely Shakespeare's first visit to such a lavish palace. He writes from Lathom House in Lancashire, home of the great Earl of Derby, who will feature prominently in the letters of Book Two. Shakespeare refers to the Earl's ill mother and Catholic leanings, evidenced by holy men appearing from under the stairs. In Elizabethan England, Catholics were tolerated if they remained silent, but their clergy were not. Wealthy Catholic families often disguised clergy as household servants and had chapels in secret rooms or other hiding places.

One final observation about Shakespeare's letters in general, informed by my family's move overseas in the 1960s—in those pre-email days, we wrote long letters, just as Elizabethans did in the 1560s. Letters were often the only means of sharing news before newspapers became common and much of 16th century England was composed of small towns and rural villages, where news traveled mainly by word of mouth or by letter. Reports from New World voyages, rumors of war, conspiracies, beheadings and the Plague—all front-page news today—would have been reported in letters. As an example, one of my research references was a five-hundred-page book on the life of Shakespeare's future patron, the third Earl of Southampton, composed mostly his correspondence and some commentary on it.[20]

Of course, Shakespeare had another reason to write detailed letters: he meant them as a record for his son in case he was unable to return from his voyages. Fortunately for posterity, 16th century paper was fairly sturdy (made largely of cloth fibers, not wood pulp) although, like anything that old, some pages became more brittle than others over time. I was keenly aware of just how fragile old paper can be when Miss B first pulled a sheaf of letters from the old office envelope in her rustic straw bag and showed them to me, an exchange more appropriate to a transaction at the farmer's market than one worthy of white gloves and a hermetically sealed display case.

Here then is Letter Three, which concludes with one of first heart-stopping discoveries I made upon first reading it: an early draft of a sonnet that would evolve into what became Sonnet 30 when all 154 of Shakespeare's sonnets were published two decades later in 1609.

Coz,

If all the year were a holiday, sport would be as tedious as work; but when they seldom come, they wished for come.[22] Thus does this holiday bring at least a measure of respite from my labours. His lordship does not call for us today, his mother being ill, and we may not be called again if she dies. Dick says she suffers the Plague and we should all be wary of the western parts of the great house. Mr. Kempe says she was known in her youth to be fast and loose, despite her breeding, and now she has the Devil to pay. I know not what to make of it, but over all the house there is much wringing of hands and lamentations, while holy men appear from under-stairs to comfort her and her son the Earl.

This place, where now we find ourselves, is no more like any other I have seen these weeks than a rose is like to nettles. We are paid handsomely by the Earl to play at several feasts and other country entertainments, the likes of which I have seen only when Her Majesty came to Kenilworth. The masters are choleric [*irritable*] and brook no errors, especially among the 'prentices and their johannes factotum, no doubt because every man is under the watchful eye of his lordship's household and much decorum is expected that is otherwise not evident among our Company. Worse yet, every mother's son of us tiptoes on a knife's edge, waiting to hear if we will be pressed into service of a very different kind for our lord, one with real swords and blood, not play acting. On that I will say more, but first I commit to thee my life with the players this month past.

Aye, those masters who bet against my survival among them have lost their chinks. My life in the Leicester's Men has fallen into a steady gait. Ere the sun shows his golden head, I am required to see that the horses are fed and watered, even if there be an ostler at an inn, for your ostler is well known to be villainous and oft falters in his duties. Thereafter must I look to the apparel, which the day before were washed, and note which ones need mending or the like. Those still wet must be laid in the sun with the greatest care and turned like a roasting capon [*chicken*] to see that their complexion fade not, nor may they wrinkle. Each dry garment must be set out for the day's playing, unless we travel, in which case I take great pains to fold each one with thread not against thread.

Next must the men be waked and each breaks his night's fast in some way, save Mr. Kempe, who needs no special urging, but told me: "Methinks your gut should be your clock and will strike you awake without a messenger, like so ..." Fart. F-ffaaarrrt! From this thou canst discern, he is a foul man and with an appetite to match (he then devours four or five apple johns [baked apples] at once). Never have I known a man so partial to apple johns of a morning, excepting mine Uncle Henry. In other ways, those two seem kindred. Uncle Henry hath oft recited most pitifully, that old saying which I have heard Mr. Kempe sing a'times during his jigs:

Young blood will never obey old decrees!
But this advice will I give thee, lad:
Have more than thou showest ...
speak less than thou knowest ...
lend less than thou owest ...
ride more than thou goest ...
leave thy drink and thy whore ...
and keep in-at-door ...
and thou shalt have more ...
than two tens in every score!

Following the breakfast, must I empty the masters' jordans, although here in this great house there are servants who tend to such matters, praise God. Once cleaned, the jordans are placed in the tiring house to serve the Company during our day's playing. Therein must I also lay out those properties that will be used, following a list given me the night before by Mr. Johnson. Some days must I prepare fog buckets or fresh blood bags and, if a scene requires disemboweling or the like, which is most popular in the shires, then must I gather offal for concealment in certain ways within the apparel of the condemned man. Bull's offal is hardest to come by, but lasts many days, even in extreme heat. The guts of swine are too tender and make poor show even if harvested fresh from the butcher's knife. Other times must I repair a sword or fill with water several buckets (if there are scenes of shipwreck to be played or when, during the play, I must conceit [imitate] the sound of a bird warbling, which is done by blowing the fife through water). We carry with us many a piece of furniture to suggest a place or time, but most every play uses our door and throne, because:

"What…child…is…there," quoth Mr. Johnson, in manner not unlike we used to hear from Jenkins, "that coming to a play and seeing THE-BES…written in great letters upon an old door…will not believe…that he is ACTUALLY now in Thebes?"[23] Therefore is it the custom, and thus my duty, to write out and post the names of such places on our door each day, depending on the play to be presented.

Before the morning rehearsal, I am charged with tallying the Company accounts. Cuthbert Burbage is master of our monies, but his father calls upon me to oversee the numbers, that every man in the Company should rest easy, lest they suspect the father's son of any misdeed. He sits with me and affirms payment of this item or that one: the smith's note for shoeing King Arthur; a farthing for a new link to the bucket; am I to stop any of Bryan's wages, about the sack he lost the other day at Leicester fair? And such like.

Ere long, the men have finished their morning ablutions and rehearsal begins. Mr. Burbage calls out scenes from the list, some that I had set to paper, correcting the men as they recall their lines and stage manners. As I am only needed in scenes with crowds of Court or soldiers or the like (and now at the end, with my special tumbling skills, which grow better every day), I sit near Mr. Burbage and copy his thoughts as he directs me. But most of my time is taken with mending apparel, my skill at sewing earned in father's glovery coming to good use. I am also committing to memory the advice given here and there, the tricks of this player's trade, that I may one day fully cloak myself in their fashion.

At length, these tasks are done and while the men take rest before their true labors begin, I take some food and drink, but only when I can assure masters Burbage and Johnson that all else is in readiness for the play. My dinner is mostly a roasted egg or two, an onion, bread and a pint of ale (or two).[24] Half the onion must I save for the play, if tears are needed (but I will eat it thereafter). Most days Mr. Perkin will give me instruction for an hour before he is needed in the tiring house, for instance:

"Speak the speech as I pronounced it to you, Will, trip-ping-ly on the tongue." I spout lustily forth the lines of a long dead hero, in a manner which Mr. Perkin swears will make the poor soul die again. "No, no. Do not MOOOUUUUTH the words, man, as many of thy ten pence a day players do: upon hearing them, thy wise auditor [*audience*] will as lief the town crier spoke the lines. Again!"

Again I attempt the lines, but know I miss the mark, as a poor archer shoots wide of the butt [*target*]. The master calls for me to try again. And again.

Two o'clock is fast upon us and blasts of trumpet call the town to our festivities. Local boys are paid to hold the horses of the wealthy, but I am called upon to clear the way to our venue, lest delicate slippers be fouled with shit. Our players rub colour into their cheeks, although on hot summer days, as these have been, this seems superfluous, dressed as they are in thirty pounds or more of linen, brocades, silks, cloaks and crowns.

During the play, when I am not otherwise called, I must watch the cues to bang drums that signify cannon or thunder. Every other sword, dagger, tree, door, lance, altar, feather, vizard [*visor*], chime, fleece, chain, coffin, cauldron, and I know not what more, all these must I have ready to bring on and off, either by mine own hand or that of a player. Mr. Kempe says how fortunate I am, that the Company no longer keeps Pope's black dog, which he was wont [*accustomed*] to use on the stage. It died in Marlborough after eating some poisoned meat, which some called a blessing, for no man had ever seen a cur more distempered. I wonder if this is the same black dog whose ghost now appears to Mr. Clarke that Dick speaks of? May a dog have a ghost?

Our play ended, epilogue and jig too, then must I gather together the apparel that were, in the heat of our industrious scenes, made foul by too much sweat or sheep's blood or both. These must I clean before the stains set, in a wooden tub with scape [*lye soap*] and scrubbing. The players use their skill to con death wearing only their linens, but oft times, there is some blood shed upon the silks and brocades. These must I take the most care to clean, and that gently too, for a player's fortune is his apparel. Already have I been roundly beaten for scrubbing holes in a lordly doublet and I would not for all the world rub up such anger in Mr. Johnson a second time. No matter the fabric, the stitches cannot survive more than four or five hard washings, so it is also my task to sew back together those parts which my labors have torn asunder. From the scape and the needle, there lives nary an inch of skin on my hands that is not either worn raw or pricked like a horse's haunch after a lusty ride under the spur.

All other apparel and furniture must I collect and account for against our Property List, item by item, like some pinch-browed clerk with his inky-stained fingers, striking lines from off his ledger. If we move to another town the following day, all these must I pack in our wagon, save for those items still to dry. The jordans used in the tiring house during the play must I empty and clean, a task I am accustomed to complete before I sup.

When every man has taken his fill of supper, there is always one of our number who is called upon for a tale, generally with little or no special urging if sack [*sherry*] is at hand. When no man else has the imagination or vigour to speak, Mr. Thomas Pope can ever be relied upon to fill in a tale, each one he swears, by a holy relic that hangs from his neck, to be true.

His stories are made the more believable by his facility with faces: he can twist his brow, nose, cheeks, lips, even his eyelids, into any shape or movement. His Cornish cap he can likewise shape into the hat of any peasant or gentleman, into a camel or a ship at sea, any thing to illustrate his tales. He speaks rarely to the 'prentices, although he has made a most courteous exception for me, and he will address the boys directly when telling stories, for then are we his best groundlings.

In truth, in conversation with Mr. Pope apart I have found him to be the most remarkable of men and I learned how he came to be so gruesomely injured and how that providentially gave him passage into the Company of players. He was himself apprenticed to a Greenwich armourer of great renown, but was crushed by a wagon filled with iron. None thought he could survive, so mis-shapen was his jaw as to convey a permanent laugh; his left leg and right arm so disjointed and crushed as to give him an antic leaping motion in his gait ever after; his back so broken that he could not bend forward after it mended, so he leans always backward and has learned to balance most skillfully, lest a slight evening breeze might otherwise topple him (imagine, upon hearing of his misfortune, how much I did regret mine error with the wheel, that which caused him to lift our wagon a second time).

His master pitied him and gave him lodging until he mended, but he was not fit to continue in his craft thereafter. But because he had been schooled, his master bid him read aloud to the workmen from Ovid and Chaucer, to keep their labours from weighing as heavy upon them, as the great blades and suits of armor that issued from their furnaces, hammers, and tongs would weigh upon an eager knight. This young Pope proved valuable to his master for one reason more: so grateful was he, that he did not succumb to his injuries and that his master gave him work enough to keep together body and soul, that he among the 'prentices was most trusted with any subtle duty, especially those that concerned money. Thou knowest well how 'prentices are accustomed to go abroad to gaming houses and taverns, where they oft times fall into ill company, very dangerous and hurtful to them, and in which many of them unthriftily lose their own wages and very lewdly lose any money of their masters that had been committed to their charge. But not Pope.

After a time, a German named Jacob Halder purchased the business and became his master. Pope feared his days in the armoury were then few in number, for Halder was unaccustomed to any man who did not fit neatly in his place, much as every part of a clock must perform his service in harmony with every other and no parts are spare or wasteful. There could be little room for the deformed Pope.

But Halder confessed to one weakness: he loved plays and music of all types, especially those clowns whose dumbshow needed no comprehension of our English, for Halder had little art with our native tongue. Thus it came that when the famous Gelosi troupe performed in Greenwich, Pope was trusted with money to secure a seat for the master and his sons, with cushions, and to wait upon them until their arrival.[25]

Pope had never seen such players before. It was to him as if fairies were dancing about his head and casting their spells upon him. Here he saw five hundred people laughing and calling out the names of the characters, shouting for the players to repeat a lazzi over and over again. The more antic the disposition, the more herky-jerkey and disjointed the clown, the more the spectators roared and showed their love. Mr. Pope then told me of his revelation and his winding path to the Leicester's Men:

"I, that was no longer shaped for the tricks of the armorer's trade, nor fit to court an amorous looking-glass; rudely stamp'd and curtail'd of any fair proportion, scarce half a man, so lame and frightening that dogs would bark at me. Therefore, since I could prove neither a labourer or a lover, nor prosper among the fair and well-spoken, I determined then to prove a clown upon the stage and make all love me for great jests unparalleled!"[26]

That very night he covered his battered face with black from the forge, excepting only large circles of white flesh around his eyes and mouth. He draped himself in rags to make his appearance even more beggarly and pitiful and hung from his girdle [belt] old iron and bits of metal, such that when he ambled in his deformed gait, he would jingle and clank, the better to draw attention upon himself. He took up a beaten sword that was no use to any man and practiced the art of making it seem to disappear down his throat from tip to hilt.

Thus did he present himself to the master of Gelosi's Men and begged employment. The old master was much impressed that any man could contort his body in such a laughable manner and still perform a most convincing trick with the sword. Little did he know that this was the true shape of Thomas Pope and no lazzi, but he soon allowed as how they were indeed a man short, one 'prentice having fallen overboard and drowned the night they crossed the water from the Low Countries, and thus Pope was taken in and taught his craft. So thankful was he, that he swore to God an everlasting fealty and soon took on the mantle of a Puritan, scolding his fellows if they failed to pray or attend church of a Sunday in any town. The Italians were of the old faith, but this made him only re-double his zeal and some were converted, or said they were (he suspected), just to cut short his endless sermonizing. His stories always extolled those virtues of Christians, of those he thought were righteously rewarded for hewing to the true path of God.

Now on this Lammas night, carousing in one of the seldom-used dining halls of the great house, long after his lordship's household had themselves gone a'bed, the men talked of rumors that Spain will soon send an army into England to bring Catholic Mary to the throne, at which every man would be forced to take sides. Our Lord Leicester is even now assembling a mighty force (which Dick says our own Company may soon be forced to join) to aid the Netherlands in their battles against Spanish rule and popish domination of a Protestant land. Some say the King of Spain suffers from a kind of madness and that the Spanish are cowards and no match for English men at arms, but Mr. Pope calls this false bravery, for he knows how hard a cornered dog will bite, even a Spanish one. He told this tale to prove his point, leaning forward on his elbows and speaking in a low voice not far above a whisper (I note how this forces his auditors to listen the more carefully):[27]

"This tale will show ye my meaning. There was once an English ship, being called the Three Half Moons, manned with eight and thirty men and well fenced with munitions, the better to encounter their enemies withal. Arriving near Gibraltar in the straits twixt Spain and Africa, they perceived themselves to be beset round with eight galleys of the Turks in such wise as there was no way for them to fly or escape away, but that either they must yield or else be sunk. The owner manfully encouraged his company to think on their English ancestors, who have always prevailed and gone away conquerors, yea, even whence it hath been near impossible. Such, quoth he, hath been the valiantness of our countrymen and such hath been the power of our God. Then up stood Captain Grove, the master, holding his sword and target up in defiance. So likewise stood up every man well appointed. Now likewise sounded up the drums, trumpets and flutes, which would have encouraged any man, had he never so little heart or courage in him."

I admire Mr. Pope, his felicity with the telling of stories, and seek to learn from him. The 'prentices especially hang on each word, thinking themselves in league with their fearful countrymen on the deck of the ill-fated ship. Mr. Pope lingered for a moment over his cup for dramatic effect on these groundlings, wiping his chin as was his custom, for his misshapen lips, that always seemed to be smiling, could not fully contain any liquid as he drank.

"Now, lads, one John Fox, the gunner, disposed of his ordnance to the best effect, sending his bullets towards the Turks, twice as many of them slain as the number of Christians were in all. But the Turks discharged their canons twice as fast against the Christians and the Three Half Moons was very sore stricken and bruised under water, so all was in vain. Still, as Turks boarded, the Englishmen showed themselves to be men indeed, working with their brown bills [*painted axe*] and halberds [*spear-axe*], where their company stood to it so lustily that the Turks were much dismayed."

"Did so few English hold off so many infidels?" Dick hath a habit to speak aloud that which others may only be thinking, but the insolent Boy Burbage commonly rebukes him (one of the few in the Company he may chastise with impunity), saying such like:

"Yes, fool. Silence now, that Mr. Pope may proceed." He then held forth his hands as if forcing down the lid of a great buck [*laundry*] basket and, when all were again still, he motioned graciously for the tale to continue. Mr. Pope needed no callow youth to grant him permission, but went promptly back to his labours, leaning forward as if to impart a soul-searing secret.

"Aye, Dicky, every Englishman slew an hundred of the enemy, but chiefly the boatswain, with no more hairs on his chin than thyself, showed valiantness above the rest, for there was no Turk that durst stand in his face, till at the last there came a shot which broke his whistle asunder and smote him on the breast so that he fell, bidding his shipmates farewell most pitifully. The press and store of the Turks was so great that neither were the rest of our English long able to endure, by reason whereof, they must needs be taken, which none of them intended to have been, but rather to have died;

except only the master's mate, who shrunk from the skirmish like a notable coward, esteeming neither the value of his name nor accounting of the present example of the boatswain."

Mr. Pope took a deep breath to prolong the dramatic conclusion. He sighed deeply from somewhere 'neath his rounded back and sunken chest, like a worn bellows, before continuing.

"In the end, lads, the Turks were victors. The Christians were then enforced to serve as SLAVES in the galleys, no sooner onboard but their garments were pulled over their ears and torn from their backs and they were set to the oars. Yet this is but the beginning of my tale, for nigh to the city of Alexandria, a port city in Egypt under the dominion of the Turk, there is a protected shore or bay, being made very fencible with strong walls, whereunto the Turks do customly bring their galleys every year in the winter season and there do trim them and lay them up against the spring time. In this bay there is a prison, wherein the captives that serve in the galleys are put for a time, until the seas be calm and passable again, every prisoner being most grievously laden with irons on their legs, to their great pain, and sore disabling. While many died and some were ransomed to their freedom, no less than fourteen years" - - Mr. Pope waited for the gravity of this number to penetrate the distraught faces of the 'prentices, then repeated it for effect - - "fourteen full years of this servitude endured the aforementioned John Fox, in the galleys by spring and summer; in the prison by autumn and winter; along with two hundred and threescore other Christians of sundry nations. In addition to Fox of Woodbridge in Suffolk, two other Englishmen were there: William Wickney of Portsmouth, in the county of Southampton, and Robert Moore of Harwich in the county of Essex."

As he named each man, Mr. Pope cleverly shaped his hat to the fashion of that county and struck a pose that we might imagine those valiant countrymen in the flesh.

"Now by reason of his long imprisonment, no longer being feared for mischief against the Turk, Fox, who being skillful in the craft of barber, was given certain liberties, upon payment of a stipend to the keeper, and allowed with irons on his legs to go out by day to make what he could at this trade and to return at night to the prison. But Fox being weary of his imprisonment began minding ways that he might escape, in hope that God would not longer suffer his Christian children to waste away in this dreadful place. Not far from the prison was a certain victualing [*eating*] house where Fox met Peter Unticaro, a Spaniard born and a Christian, but likewise a prisoner of the Turks for some 30 years. Fox and Unticaro broke to one another their minds concerning the restraint of their liberty and the thought of escape back to their homelands. After some weeks of debating the best plan, they took also into their confidence some six or seven other prisoners and concluded how best they might accomplish their mutual aim. On the last night of December, nine Christmases ago, Fox returned as was his custom to the prison and delivered unto his comrades a sort of file, charging every man that he should be ready and discharged from his irons by eight of the clock next morn."

Herewith Mr. Pope conned the likeness of a file with his thumb, outstretched from a fist, and sawed the imaginary chains before him. His every speech is enriched with such gestures and means to speed a tale without words, the clever use of which I have never seen from another to such goodly effect. This may be some native talent, but I wonder if he has developed this skill to such a degree owing to his deformities, that he would better effect men's opinions of him. He continued his tale, with such gestures and ticks, thus:

"The new day dawned and, with their restraints unleashed, Fox and his men were able to climb the prison walls and escape to the house of Unticaro, whereupon word was sent to the keeper of the prison that he should come to this same house. In the mean season, Fox and his men had provided themselves of such weapons as they could. Fox took himself a rusty sword blade with neither hilt nor pommel, but which he made serve his turn. The others got such spits and knives as they found in the house. The keeper, now being come unto the house and perceiving no light nor hearing any noise, straightaway suspected the matter. Fox standing behind the corner of the house, stepped forth, armed, and the keeper said unto him 'O Fox, what have I deserved of thee that thou shouldst seek my death?'

'Thou, villain,' quoth Fox through clenched teeth, 'hast been a bloodsucker of many a Christian and now thou shalt know what thou hast deserved at their hands.' With that, he lifted his sword and struck the keeper so main a blow as therewith his head cleaved asunder, falling stark dead to the ground. Others of Fox's company thrust their spits through the keeper, though he be already dead, to avenge their old friends and shipmates lost. Still others with their knives hewed him in sunder, cutting off his head and mangling him so no man could discern his identity."

Dick shrieked suddenly at Mr. Pope's gruesome description, which lingered over every bloody particular that we could verily see the dripping severed head and limbs, made still more manifest as he sketched his scenes in the air before us with his crooked fingers and great swollen knuckles. Dick plays so many women's parts, and is himself tender of spirit, such that we thought he had fainted away, but Mr. Pope paused not a jot and instead proceeded apace like a rider taking whip to his mount, already lathered and out of breath.

"Next they marched back to the prison, which was guarded at that hour by six Turkish warders, whereupon Fox's men dispatched these warders and barred the gate of the prison with a cannon 'gainst any reinforcements, should their purpose be discovered. Then they entered the keeper's lodge and found thither the keys to the entire fortress by his bedside and better weapons too. In this chamber was a chest wherein was a rich treasure, all in Spanish ducats, which Unticaro and two more stuffed themselves withal, as much as they could carry between their shirt and breast. John Fox would not once touch the treasure and said it was their liberty which he sought, to the honour of God, and not to make a mart of the wicked treasure of the infidels. Being then armed with goodly weapons and thinking them- selves sufficient champions to encounter a stronger enemy, Fox and his men opened every prison gate and door, calling forth all of the prisoners. Some he put to setting fire to the place, some to dressing up of a certain galley which was the best in the harbor for their escape, whereinto others then car- ried masts, sails, and oars. Now more prison warders awoke and learned the cause of the commotion, but Fox and his men slew these as they emerged from their beds. Still, some eight or nine Turks got to the top of the wall, whereunto John Fox was obliged to follow and there found a hot skirmish. Some were slain on both sides, some wounded, and Fox himself was thrice shot through his apparel, but not hurt, while Unticaro and two others were barely able to defend themselves, being so pestered with the weight and un- easy carrying of their wicked and profane treasure. Amongst the Turks, one was thrust through and, as he fell from the wall, made such a lowing that the inhabitants of Alexandria understood that the prisoners were 'paying their ransom', it could be said. Now raised up the town and two other fortresses, such that there was no road for escape."

Mr. Kempe had long since fallen hard asleep upon a luxurious satin- covered couch in a corner of the lavishly appointed hall. Even so, he farted and belched at once, a foul chorus so to say, the last of his ale spilling from the cup and down across his best linen shirt. Some laughed and tormented

Mr. Kempe, but we urged Mr. Pope to pay no heed to such distractions and tell us urgently what happened next. Pope obliged.

"No way to escape? Ha! So was the Red Sea impossible for the Israelites to pass through. But such impossibilities can our God make possible, and so knew John Fox. Well, to be short lads, off fled the men through one obscure hole in the prison wall, a ditch sort of, that led straight to the harbor. Some brave few, led by Unticaro himself, kept the enemy at bay behind that last gate of the prison. In short time the galley was trimmed up, whereinto every man leapt all in haste, then hoisting the sails lustily, yielding themselves to His mercy and grace, in whose hands are both wind and weather. But the wind was calm and the Turks o'ercame their opponents, who by now had lost their battle and their lives. In minutes, the bloody Turks reached the shore and Fox knew their numbers would soon swell enow to drag the galley back to certain doom for all aboard her. Fox prayed to the Almighty, bidding him to spare the crew and take only him as sacrifice for their actions, but the wind grew no stronger as the enemy came ever closer. Then, as if by rough magic, rising from the midnight mist that hung in watchful sorrow along the bankside, Unticaro and his two mates, thought by Fox to be already dead, burst into view with savage cries and firing weapons they had bought of a shopkeeper with the gold in their shirts. As the Turks turned in amazement and tried to wade back to the land, Unticaro hurled rocks at them as his men re-loaded. Again they fired and again Turks bled and drowned. When the last of them regained their footing ashore, Unticaro clubbed them with the guns and stabbed them with old knives. By now Fox ordered his men to row back and save the brave Spaniards, which they did as the last of the Turks fled or died on the bloody sands."

"Amen!" Mr. Johnson whispered, but we all heard him and all saw fit to repeat the blessing. Mr. Johnson was one who warned we may be pressed into armed service for the Earl ere long, so I suspect he urged the telling of this tale in particular tonight, to stir some martial English pride among us.

"Soon was this galley afloat and out of the harbor, but by then the two castles, at either edge of the bay, aimed the full power of their cannon upon her. There was surely no remedy but to sink: how could it be avoided? So thought the men as the cannon let fly from both sides. Yet there was not a man who feared the shots, which went thundering round their ears, nor was even one of them scarred or touched with any of some five and forty shots fired. Here did God hold forth his buckler, surely He shielded now the galley. The prisoners sailed away and were quickly out of sight of Turkish cannon and city and bay. And when that the Christians were safe, out of the enemy's coast, John Fox called to his fellows, willing them to thank Almighty God for deliverance, and to most humbly fall upon their knees, beseeching Him to aid them unto a friendly land and not to bring them into any other danger, since He had most mightily delivered them from so great a bondage. Thus, when every man had made his petition, they fell straight to their labors with the oars, striving to come to some Christian land as near as they could guess by the stars. But the winds were diverse and they could make no progress, soon running out of victuals [*food*]. Indeed, after eight and twenty days at sea, eight of their number, including the valiant Peter Unticaro, perished from starvation or wounds to the astonishment of the rest."

"Tis a miracle they did not all perish," quoth Dick, his eyes larger than those on my father's old mare. Boy Burbage gave him a box on the ear that he did interrupt the tale yet again, but Mr. Pope agreed with Dick, saying further:

"Aye, a miracle. And let this show ye how a Spaniard can be the most fierce fighter, but your Englishman is more durable. Unticaro had been a great hero to his people had he lasted one day more, for it fell out that upon the twenty-ninth day after they fled from Alexandria, they landed at Gallipoli, where they were made much of, by the Christian abbot and monks there. These holy brothers kept the sword, wherewithal John Fox had slain the keeper, esteeming it as a most precious jewel, and hung it up for a monument." Mr. Pope placed a shank bone upon the window ledge with great ceremony and a comic bow from the waist, then finished his tale.

"And when every man was refreshed and eased, they sailed in better weather to Napoli, where they sold their galley and divided it, every man having an equal part thereof. Each man was thereafter free to make his way home as best he could, wheresoever that be. Fox took the journey unto Rome, where he was well entertained of an English noble, who presented his worthy deed unto the Pope, who rewarded him liberally and gave him letters unto the King of Spain, where he was very well entertained thereafter, because the Englishman and the Spaniard had fought bravely side-by-side in common cause. At length, being the year of our Lord 1579, Fox came into England once more, went to Court and told of all his travels unto the Council. They, considering the state of the man, in that he had spent and lost a great part of his youth in thraldom and bondage, extended to him their liberality to maintain him now in age, to their right honour and to the encouragement of all true hearted Christians."

In so fine a telling of this tale, Mr. Pope earned that which I think he covets most: love and admiration of his fellows. I have seen him perturbed only once, when he sought to play a king, a role played commonly by Mr. Burbage, but who on that occasion was not serviceable. Mr. Johnson denied him, and in no wise delicately, which appears only to be a certain imperiousness common to Mr. Johnson, but which then revealed a grave sadness as Mr. Pope was again left to play a clown's role only. Now however, he soaked up every last drop of spilt kindness until, the tale told, cups drained, some of our number wandered off to bed, while others debated whether this story proved the Spanish to be brave or no.

I could not easily shake feeling I had witnessed the events myself: not merely because of the fearful imprisonment of Fox and his fellows, but because I could not separate the tale from the teller. Mr. Pope said 'such impossibilities can our God make possible' even as He had done for Mr. Pope after his grave injuries, bringing him to the Company of players and to that new craft in which he now excelled. Aye coz, from this I gather that bravery and determination can overcome all chains or deformities, be they of the body or the heart.

On this night, like all others, my day's labours were not yet ended. Once the men embrace the golden dew of sleep I am obliged to see that the horses have done likewise. If we are called to play the next day an old tale, for which we have no book, this must I draft by the light of night's failing candles. Only then has my day come to its end. These labours seemed impossible to me, for one man to perform seven-day-a-week, when first I joined the Company, but now I may truthfully say they trouble me not, which may be God's jest merely. I mean that He hath lighted my path to London through this Company of players, but will that path lead to my death in some foreign war instead of the Fortune I had imagined might await me? To think on't leads to madness, to the feeling I had been wiser to stay at home and look for some other means to a better end.

At these quiet times, I feel most keenly thine absence, dear friend, and my son and, even so, my Nan. Omit no opportunity to convey to them my love, that they may know their father and husband is by their tender side in spirit, until such day as he may again be with them in the flesh. I pray for their safekeeping and know that God, and thou, will deliver them up to me exactly as I have left them, save the passage of a few years (if need be so long) before I bring my Fortune with me home to Stratford to make them, and my father, proud once more.

I know not when thou wilt receive this letter, nor when thou canst reply, but please make every effort to do so with news of my family and our countrymen. What of Pug? I hope I may find him out when our Company arrives in London. Has Tyke recovered his wits? Good John, please send me all fact and gossip of our home that thou canst gather! Fares my father any better, if aught of this thou canst determine, in his matters with the Council? At the moment of my departure, I could not honestly say if he was glad to be rid of me, giving me this advice only:

"Flatter not Fortune, neither fawn upon her. Gape not for state, yet lose no spark of honour." I understood his meaning not a jot, but nodded as if the vicar had blessed a newborn, to which he added more, after some pause to rummage in the dungheap of his mind for more wisdom than he is wont to use: "Ambition - - like the plague - - see thou dost eschew it. They that die most virtuous, have in their youth lived most vicious, and none knows the danger of fire more than he who falls into it."

Did he mean that I should thrust myself into every fire as he had done? As John Fox had done against the Turk? I fear that to follow my father's example is to tread on mossy rocks in a river. I suppose, knowing nothing of my plan to find Fortune in the New World, he feared for my well being, leaving suddenly with a pack of players, like so many idle youth who pass through Stratford on Thursdays and are cozened [*swindled*] by cheats to pick pockets or sing ballads for alms.²⁸

Indeed I now have seen these idle sorts on the road and our men despise that kind, for they give all players an ill reputation. In Leicester, for instance, one hoary-headed goat exhorted some boys of the town to make easy money, as he said:

"Come boy, if thou canst chant my verses finely at the fair, we'll make a good market of it, for every holiday fool will pay our English money to hear a boy sing a ballad as if it were holy scripture spoken in Greek by a monkey." This devil called himself Boarwhistle, dressed even as the Prince of Darkness himself, all in black, that badge of Hell, his bony fingers pinched one rosy-cheeked youth I saw, aged not above eight years. "I have done my part, writing some great verses full of poetical spirit, such that if Elderton were alive to hear them, his ink pot would don mourning clothes and his soul with certain envy would depart this world on the spot![29] Canst thou learn these lines and sing them sweetly, my dear boy? And earn half a crown?"

"I warrant you," quoth the boy, dancing on tiptoe to grasp the lapel of the sneering crook-back, "I'll make every market rustic gape and nod and laugh and shower us with their gold, if only you will teach me your verses."

Lord, what fools these children be! We saw the boy leave the fair with Boarwhistle and to be sure, he lost more than his youth on that day. I will confess to thee, I wonder if I am no different: lured to villainous deeds by mountebanks with golden promises? Writing to thee is a comfort, but though the page hears my confessions and fears, it cannot answer back. I miss thy good counsel. Mother sent me off with good companions, whose advice can comfort a'times: honey-tongued Ovid, her father's own book of 'Metamorphoses' (she herself can make little use thereof), but the wisdom therein was meant for great heroes, not wide-eyed babes like me.[30]

O coz, our Company has trod more miles in a month than I have hitherto seen in my life, and after this brief respite at Lathom House I'll wager we will double and treble that mark ere long. My feet dare not utter a word of complaint, for ere Leicester's Men came to Stratford they had played more towns than I knew existed 'twixt Stratford and Lancashire: Canterbury, Dover, Southampton, Marlborough, Oxford, Bath, and Exeter. And I must say, the men have been most fair to me, especially when the hat is passed more than once at a play, even when we give over a portion of the revenue for sustenance of the poor. I have saved a full six shillings of my wages thus far, acorns that will never grow to the stout oak I hope my Fortune will one day be, but may provide me with necessaries if I am taken aboard a vessel for the New World (a journey I am told can last two months or more). I pray we arrive soon in London where I might find such a ship before we are sent instead to the Low Countries to aid Lord Leicester thither. I dare not flee, yet neither did I come with these players to be tossed as offal to the dogs of war.

O how many thousands of Her Majesty's subjects are at this hour asleep? Gentle sleep, Nature's soft nurse, I come to thee as well!

Kiss my boy and maids in my name and omit nothing else which thine honour deem'st best for their tender need. In the mean season, I am thine ever loving servant in all else, Will.

PS: At Mr. Burbage's behest, this sonnet have I writ for Lord Derby, to ease his discomfiture over his mother nearing her end (thy honest opinion will be most heartily received):

When to the sessions of sweet silent thought
I summon up remembrance of things past,
I sigh the lack of many a thing I sought,
And with old woes new wail my dear time's waste.

Then can I drown an eye, unused to flow,
For precious friends hid in death's dateless night,
And weep afresh love's long-since cancell'd woe,
And moan the expense of many a vanish'd sight.

Then can I grieve at grievances foregone,
And heavily from woe to woe tell o'er
The sad account of fore-bemoaned moan,
Which I new pay as if not paid before.

But if the while I think on thee, dear friend,
All losses are restored and sorrows end.[31]

LETTER FOUR
September 20, 1586

Wherein Francis Drake's stolen riches from America excite Shakespeare, whose soul may be more at risk over a stolen map of those realms than the new threat to his body from a galloping Plague.

At the time I was reading and transcribing the letters with Miss B, I was in the habit of collecting maps, which was not unusual for travelers in the days before the internet or Google Maps. I had traveled around the world about three times by then, from the USA to Vancouver, Fiji, New Zealand and Australia; years later by ship from there to South Africa, Senegal, and Lisbon; and had lived in Amsterdam, London, and Los Angeles.

The maps from each place were a practical means of navigating busy cities, oceans, and continents (I still have my favorite 1965 Michelin Atlas of Europe with fold-out pages depicting colorful alpine peaks, lakes, and a spider's web of pathways), but they were also works of art and a snapshot in time of what mattered to the people who lived in those places; the language they spoke; the sites they valued; laid out with intersections of streets, commerce, art, religion, and imagination. Maybe my own fascination with maps helped me to understand what Shakespeare reveals in this captivating Letter Four.

In a mapmaker's shop, after listening to the owner's fascinating tales of nautical voyages, exotic savages, and untold wealth, Shakespeare steals a valuable map of the New World. He is remorseful about his immoral conduct, but driven by his desire to sail to America (Illustration 10, shown on page 74, is a similar map from the same period as the one Shakespeare describes and shoplifted).

10. Map of the Americas by Willem Blaeu circa 1600, similar to the one Shakespeare stole in Letter Three.

Back on the road, Leicester's Men are stopped just outside of a town. Shakespeare and Dick Cowley eavesdrop from high in an elm tree as a youth tries to dissuade the theatre company from coming any closer, describing the gruesome fate of his community that has been decimated by the Plague. When the boy describes that his town's response to the Plague is to shut infected families inside their homes, I recalled in *Romeo and Juliet* (Act V, scene 2) how a friar reports that "the searchers of the town, suspecting that we both were in a house where the infectious pestilence did reign, seal'd up the doors, and would not let us forth."

Dick falls from the tree and the two are discovered. Shakespeare is captivated when the boy reveals himself to be a beautiful young woman who is masquerading in her dead brother's clothing as a means of protecting herself from potentially dangerous strangers. Her name is Rosalind Munday and, when she explains she is the daughter of a glover who also serves the town government, Shakespeare feels an instant kinship with her, perhaps something more.

They part ways, but she has made an indelible impression on him and this is not the last time they will meet.

Letter Four is a good example of how stubborn these letters can be at times, refusing to surrender important details. Shakespeare asks about the health of "Becky," but I have been unable to find anyone he knew in Stratford with a similar name. In a more vexing example, the name of the town the players were visiting was blotted out in the original letter, apparently intentionally as an afterthought. Careful examination revealed at least some of the letters: Ch–––a–. I asked Miss B and she suggested Chatham. For years I have been looking for a town in southern England with a similar name that had a city official named Munday and a daughter named Rosalind, but so far to no avail. In Letter Nine, you will understand why I continue the quest.

Letter Four concludes with Shakespeare nervous about the prospect of having to accompany the Earl of Leicester to war in the Netherlands, just as I was fearful of my fate if sent to foreign wars. I couldn't help but recall living in Amsterdam, working in a restaurant when I turned eighteen in 1970, and being required to register for my country's military draft at the Embassy (the Viet Nam war was raging at the time and many young men were being asked to serve, many of whom would die).

Shakespeare musters his courage and vows he will not flee from his duty because "I will not have any man tell my son that his father was a coward." If war is his fate, he determines to go bravely, asking his friend John to retrieve his suit of clothes and a cloak from pawn. I'm not sure what I would have done if my government had ultimately demanded I go to war. My draft number that year wasn't called and I never had to face the same decision.

Another fascinating challenge confronts Shakespeare in Letter Four: John Combe apparently gave the sonnet, from his last letter, a less than glowing review. In his reply, Shakespeare promises to do better in the future. I found it interesting to see the same phrase in his dedication of *Venus & Adonis* written seven years later, where he also promises "a graver labour" yet to come. Even with the benefit of hindsight, it's hard to imagine anyone finding fault with that gem of a sonnet, but apparently four hundred years ago, like today, everyone was a critic.

For Shakespeare however, everyone was at least a source of inspiration too. As you now read Letter Four, pay special attention to Master Perkin's description of lovemaking. You might discover, as I did after re-reading Shakespeare's poetry, how he used very similar metaphors in his epic poem *Venus & Adonis*.

St. Mathews Eve, Saturday, 20 September, year of Christ 1586, Dover

Coz,

Hung be the heavens with black; yield day to night! Comets have I thrice this month seen, importing change of times and states, the proof whereof is that thrice have we been denied entry into towns along our way owing to the Plague. An if the Plague kills us not, the Spanish wars might: we had long been in London ere this, but word was sent to us that we must make our way as best we could to Dover, there to take ship for the Low Countries.

Worst did we fare in [*Chatham?*] where the Council met out-at-doors to avoid being themselves infected. Our Masters had no sooner presented their license to the bailiff but we were nearly whipped out of town for fear of drawing a crowd by our mere presence. The only inn nearby being shut by order of the Council, we retired ourselves to a grove of elm trees, and no roof else, a mile without the town. At length, a lone rider approached and spoke in urgent tones to our Masters, apart from the rest of us. Dick and I crept beneath the wagon and up a tree to gain advantage and overhear their conversation:

"Let no amount of money buy your visit to our houses, lest you take the Plague there yourselves and carry it further in the realm," quoth the emissary of the town, a man of lilting voice and slight build, who Dick swore to be a woman. I assured him that could not be, but rather was a man of tender years or disposition. Mr. Burbage offered some comfort, his arm around the young fellow, saying:

"Nay, nay. That would we never do, particularly since we are the Earl of Leicester's own servants and it would never do to have the household of Her Majesty's most favored lord spreading the Black Death."

The boy continued, still in his highly agitated state: "Thank you kind sir, and keep you careful watch for signs of this pestilence in your own number."

Mr. Burbage asked, 'what be those signs?' although I suspect he knew them well enough himself. The lad cleared his throat and pounded dust from his breast, but would not take the water offered by Mr. Burbage, perhaps fearing it to be infected in some way as, in truth, his overall demeanor suggested he thought our entire Company might be suspect.

"Uh, there are three things, chiefly. First, the sores of Mars are felt under the ear…"

At this, Dick fingered the space behind his ears, one by one. His brow furrowed as he did so.

"…under the arm pits…"

Dick thrust his forefinger in his shirt and into the foul nest of hair that grew in his pits. His eyes grew larger.

"…and in the flank or groin, those may be only the sores of Saturn, but if these are instead the carbuncles of Mars, more fiery hot, more red, and do rise up and come out very sore and grievous, those will break often times of themselves…"

At this, the boy made a circle with his fingers and thrust at the air as if he would slay it.

"…or with a little help. But let you take heed in the dressing of those boils of Mars because THEY are dangerous and VERY infective!"

By now, both of Dick's hands were thrust beneath his codpiece in frantic search for the boils of Mars, which he was certain he was afflicted withal. I tried to calm him, mostly to avoid our certain discovery and censure, but to no avail. Dick's face was suddenly devoid of any colour. He let out a groan, teetered backwards, and fell like a sack of grain some twenty feet to the ground with a thud.

"Your trees hereabouts bear strange fruit," quoth Mr. Burbage, then kicking Dick in the buttocks. Dick wept as he replied thus:

"Forgive me, masters, but surely am I afflicted with the dread disease and am doomed to die."

The emissary took a few steps back on the chance that this lunatic spoke truly. He would have leapt upon his horse and returned to town had not the animal long since wandered off toward King Arthur, who was trying gamely to mount the mare in the meadow beyond (can horses too be afflicted by the Plague?). Mr. Burbage had now spied me, still sitting above the heads of all assembled.

"Shakespeare! Thou mayest descend from the tree too, as Dick hath done, or in any other manner thou deem'st fit."

The rest of our number had gathered around the scene, everyone eager to hear the news of the town. Mr. Clarke lifted Dick to his feet and dusted him off, prodding him in various places and examining his eyes and forehead with some care. He looked toward Mr. Burbage, curled his nether lip and shook his head, then delivered a verdict thus:

"Thou wilt live, Dick, at least long enough for me to beat thee for spying on the business of thy betters." A cool wind blew up as if to break the web that was slowly being woven in and around us. We had not seen summer this fortnight past and the mud at our feet testified to the cold rain that had already lodged in those environs. The sun had never made his entrance that day, lying a'bed beneath heaving blankets of dark, grey clouds.

"If any man among you be infected, then see that you waste no time in the treatment." The emissary now revealed herself to be a woman, much to our amazement!

"O kind nurse, how shall I be cured?" Dick begged to know, now on his knees at her feet, clutching her legs around. "Please, dear God, please tell me."

She trembled that this madman had her in his grasp, but was liberal with her advice even so: "Well, if you carry those sores that I have hitherto described, then must you clap a hot cup on them and draw them up full and then lance them with a knife and let the pestilence run from the sores as long as they will." Others of our Company were now studying the face of this woman as if they might devour it, so intent on her words were they in case they might themselves find need of her cures. "Then, to heal them up, take the juice of a parsley together with honey and the yolk of an egg. Add some flour for thickness and beat these together to make a salve thereof, the which you must daily apply to each carbuncle which you have drained until it be healed."

So wise, so young. O coz, what fearful scenes those delicate eyes have beheld! Dick crawled then on his knees from the woman to grasp the hem of Mr. Johnson's cape. "O master, have we these ingredients in our stores? Shall we not swiftly make this salve?"

"Rise up, fool. What makes thee think thou'rt worth a measure of honey and yolks?" Mr. Johnson meant this as a kindly jest, I take it, to relieve the fears of more than just our Dick. He turned to the young woman, who I now saw more clearly, discovering a face more beautiful than any I had ever seen, framed in wild red hair and punctuated with eyes of green that radiated like precious gems.

"We give you our thanks, fair maid. But what means this that you come to us clad like a man to speak for your Council and townsfolk?" I saw her tremble now, in reply.

"Every man among us, not yet dead or dying, is even now carrying forth the dead from those houses that God hath chosen to plunder with this pestilence. The Council is in constant meeting and neither man nor boy could be spared, so I was sent to keep you from giving any thought further that might bring your Company within our walls. I dressed in my brother's weeds to proclaim myself a man for mine own protection, but I see that such precautions were unnecessary among your gentle selves."

Mr. Burbage spoke in a voice more tender than I had yet heard him utter: "You do your town and your family great credit, young lady. Take with you our prayers for your well-being and our thanks. We will be on our way toward Dover without further delay. Before we depart, may we know your name, that we may inform the Earl how well you have used his servants?"

"My parents called me Rosalind at birth, and so am I still called hereabouts. My father is John Munday, a glover and member of the Council. Were he here in my stead, he would say that you are most welcome, in other times, good sirs."

"Then give your father thanks for his courtesy and that of his fair daughter."

"That I cannot do, sir, for my father is now with God," quoth she in the most matter-of-fact terms. "Suspecting that ours was a house where the pestilence did reign, the Council sealed up our doors, that we may not come forth, so fearful were they of infection."

"He was taken by the Black Death then?"

"No, sir." She spoke scarce above a whisper, barely audible over the wind that carried her words and dried the tears that sought now to escape from the corners of her eyes. "No, he suffered not from the Plague, but from simple stones, which more than once before he had been afflicted withal, but each time was cured by the physician, who gave him a certain strong water that made them pass, with some pain but no other harm. The house being sealed and the physician himself gone with the Plague, there was this time no cure, so my father swelled up and died a most horrible death."

A glover's daughter, a father on the Council. She could be my sister: and yet I never felt such a sudden longing for a sister! Her sad tale made mine ardour burn still hotter within. Even Mr. Kempe, for whom the world is a jest, even he wept to hear this maiden's tale. Before any man could speak bootless condolence, she turned to go, but gave this last warning:

"Masters, if any of you be truly afflicted, keep that man warm and let him eat no onions as they will draw more Plague to him. And let no man bleed the afflicted, for they will lose their strength and die in the breech. And if you believe that the sickness in one is a punishment from God, then I charge you to meddle not with that party or give him any medicine. God bless you all."

So wise so young. With that she strode off toward her mare and was gone before our eyes were dry or any one of us spake a word more. Dick was still certain of his own impending death, but hearing no sympathy, contented himself with the satisfaction that Rosalind's tale had distracted our masters sufficiently that they seemed no longer disposed to punish us for playing the eavesdropper. The wet wind bit more shrewdly after such a tale and Mr. Burbage called for a fire, but that very tale (and its teller) were already fiercely burned in my mind.

Today we find ourselves in Dover, instructed to wait upon a ship that sails on Michaelmas.[32] None of us has shown any signs of Plague and the climate here seems to defend its inhabitants, for Dover has not been visited severely with such a pestilence in recent memory. My blood runs hot for a reason of a very different sort: riches. I have communed here with many sailors who know of those that have been to the New World and returned wealthy men. But what is that news worth, when we are commanded to prepare for a voyage in the opposite direction and into certain death? To desert the service of an Earl without leave is also certain death. I fear my doom either way.

This leisure gives me the gift of time to thank thee, dear John, for thy pains in writing me news of home. Thinkst thou that Becky's illness signifies Plague has come to Stratford at last? I trust thou wouldst tell me if Hamnet or mine other babes were so afflicted, please, hide nothing of these matters, even if they be so painful to report. I cannot contemplate my son suffering so heinously as hath been to us described. I pray, if Shakespeares must give a life to this affliction, let it be mine and not the children. I am also in thy debt for thine honest opinion of my sonnet. I shall ever endeavor to provide thee with some graver labour in times to come.

Waiting is a certain kind of Hell for men accustomed to the frantic pace of daily moving and playing. Mr. Phillips spends such leisure time perfecting new airs on his lute; Mr. Clarke attends whatsoever church lies nearby, although Dick swears he mumbles incantations of the old faith as he bows before the vicars of our English church. Mr. Kempe seeks quite different comforts of the town, ever the stench of a penny ale and egg on his breath.[33] Taken together, they seem a mismatched pack of hounds. Herewith one conversation, that thou mayest better judge the several qualities of my companions, much of which I have yet to learn myself:

"Lads, I have spent a day in Dover and there is sport here to be enjoyed. Shall I tell you then what I am about?"

"Two yards, and more, I'll swear." Mr. Pope pointed to Kempe's belly with the knife he used to peel away the rotten bits of an onion. Mr. Burbage had busied the Company with rehearsal of an old play of Julius Caesar, even though he confessed it may have little use if we are sent with sharpened swords against real foes. He handed out apples, onions, and black bread to every man to enjoy, excepting me, for I was compelled first to commit the plot of this play to paper before we returned to our sudden [*temporary*] stage in a barn near our lodging.

"No quips, Thomas. Indeed, I am in the waist two yards about; but I am now about no waste at all! Briefly, I do mean to make love to the one Mistress Forth. She is widowed this fortnight and I spy entertainment in her."

"Still in mourning and thou wouldst persuade her to bed?"

"Aye Thomas, not five minutes after we were introduced she gave me the leer of in-vi-ta-tion! Ha! I can construe her familiar style to mean 'I am thine!'"

Mr. Phillips put up the lute, annoyed by the interruption or offended by such a rascal: "Methinks he hath translated her intentions from honesty into his own kind of English!"

"Hear me, the report goes she hath all the rule of her late husband's purse and he had a legion of angels [*coin*]. Oh I will prevail, for even now did she smile, as she examined my parts head to foot with a certain Epicurean lust." Mr. Kempe seemed quite pleased with himself. He wears spurs most days, although he rarely rides a horse (the purpose of such a fashion I cannot fathom), but which click-clack when he is about. I have heard him say he likes feeling that he might force a great beast into an action never intended, nor thought itself capable thereof.

"Then did the sun shine on a dunghill." Mr. Pope turned to leave, but was detained by Kempe's grasp on his hem.

"O Thomas, hear me, I swear she did so course o'er mine exteriors with such a greedy intention, that the appetite of her eye scorched me up like a burning-glass." Kempe held tight to Mr. Pope's arm, never one to end an argument without winning his point. Dick says that Kempe is ever thus enamoured of this woman or that one, but never will his plodding performance catch up to his galloping desire. Mr. Pope delivered a different verdict to him:

"O Will, thou dost wax poetic about women, but thy cock waxes harder for boys." Kempe grew quiet, but anon did he smile and shrug:

"A dark lady will serve as well: a willing tender boy is equal in pleasure to the scut of your ill-used whore."[34]

There followed opinions that revealed something more to me than hitherto, of each man in the Company. Mr. Pope scratched his beard and grinned broadly, as if rubbing up a recent memory: "Why not the dark lady of a lady, after enjoying that selfsame scut, eh? I'll warrant you my tongue would enjoy the one and my prick the other."

Mr. Kempe poked now at Mr. Phillips: "Tongue? As any man of the lute will attest, thou canst make sweeter music with thy fingering!"

Bryan drinks little at such times and therefore speaks less, but spoke now: "I would prick two women together. One on each side keeps a man warmer on a cold night."

To which Mr. Clarke replied: "O George, I have always found two women in the same room MAKES cold weather. Women or boys make no matter, so long as they are willing and smell sweet." As Dick hath told, Mr. Clarke is unsatisfied at home.

"Thou't need a giant's prick for two at once, George. I did see, and had the same in my hand, the tooth of a man which weighed ten ounces of troy weight; and the skull of the same man, which will hold five pecks of wheat; and the shin-bone of the same man was six-foot in length, and of a marvelous greatness. Imagine then the prick he must have had!" Mr. Pope's description seemed incredible, but given his own deformities, he may be wishful in his thinking on such matters.

"That could be," quoth Dick. "I have seen, with mine own eyes, look you, the house wherein Gerrard lived in Surrey, held aloft by a large fir pole, which reached to the very high roof thereof and which was said to be one of the staves he used in the wars to run withal.[35] Imagine his size, taken all together, and he could have 'staved' a dozen wenches or boys at once!"

Mr. Johnson seemed disgusted by this talk: "Knaves all, can none of ye resist the rebellion of the codpiece? Think on confessing thy sins to the vicar on Sunday next and be dissuaded from committing them at all."

"O let me be confessor to Mistress Forth," quoth Mr. Kempe. "She shall find easy penance for her sins!"

"Faith, how easy?" asked Mr. Pope.

"As easy as a down-bed would afford it!"

Mr. Perkin waited until all had spent their gross humour and gave his opinion in a very other wise: "O savages and brutes, all! A woman is your sweetest Epicurean delight when savoured, not rushed. Approach a maid with gentle words and whispers, as thou wouldst a dove discovered nesting in thy granary. Be not rough and rude with tearing at her garments, but let them fall with time and grace, even as Nature sheds the leaves from her tallest trees when that time is ripe. Cover her body with kisses and tender caresses, head to toe, breast to buttocks, and see that thou dost memorize each time she shiver or moan with delight, such that thou mayest call again upon those senses when thou list." All fell silent then, as if by a spell, such that when he tapped the spent contents of his pipe upon the table, the sharp pounding seemed as canon shot, and he rode our rapt attention to his conclusion: "Then mayest thou enter her, as a verdant park where thou shalt be the deer and feed where thou wilt, in sweet bottom-grass to give thee relief and joys a'plenty." I swear Dick swooned and expired [*orgasm*] seconds after. I have never tried most of these things that my fellows seem to have done a thousand times over, nor even thought of half so many!

The men fill their waiting time in many such like debates, but for me there are few idle hours, for every waking moment is given over to those errands as befit the johannes factotum. One such duty done, that I know will have great consequence for the players and the Shakespeares, I report to thee herewith in strictest confession.

There is, just off the high street in Dover, a musty shop that sells trinkets of far-off ports, but chiefly maps of foreign lands, set among many other filthy stalls, alehouses and such places which purvey the services of overripe women. Thither was I sent with two pounds to purchase maps of those lands that border the North Sea, although I cannot divine why our Company would need them, since we are neither sailors nor are we expected to assist with steering the ship that takes us thither. Still Mr. Johnson insisted I obtain what manner of maps I might find, for ports and piers and roads, and any gossip that might therein be gathered from the proprietor or his customers.

Lost in the byways of the town, most of which resemble every other and end at watery ditches or other unpassable obstructions, I arrived but a few minutes before the closing time required by the Council thereabouts. The sign proclaiming 'Westerbeke' dangled by a corner from a lone strap, daring me to pass thereunder as it waved slowly in the evening breeze, requiring me to swing the heavy wooden board aside to enter the doorway or be struck in the face. Nor was the door itself in better repair, hanging by rusted hinges that I'll warrant were already creaking when the last Henry was our King. I opened said door, parted the velvet curtains just beyond, and was greeted by the acrid odor of burnt tallow and the howling music of those ancient hinges, pausing for mine eyes to accustom themselves to the meagre light beyond.

In the shop, a stuffed tortoise and alligator hung with other skins of ill-shaped fishes, and all about the shelves a beggarly account of coiled rope, moldy books and such like, and all over these were scattered popish crucifixes as if to make up a show against the Devil. But hanging on every inch of wall, yes even from the rafters, and draped elegantly over polished oak devices made especially for this use, were maps. Great ones and small, some mere sketches and others most fancifully-coloured, recognizable lands and untamed wilderness. Aye coz, all of God's great earth could be found in the confines of this dank shop in Dover!

The lack of any living soul to complete this scene, along with the dust and mold much in evidence, made it appear that I had intruded on some private inventory in a long-forgotten charnel house [*tomb*]. I turned the pages of a book of herbs in Latin and called for the shopkeeper. Hearing no reply, I made my way around a pair of chairs, too weary to support any man of substance, toward one wall where maps of some recent minting hung in stillness, awaiting the touch of man to bring them alive again.

Behind each map was a dozen more. Thumbing through one such stack I read an hundred names, places familiar and exotic. Each map was brightly coloured and bore insignia, wild beasts, Latin lettering, great full-bellied galleons, gods of the sea, and golden cherubs blowing the rude winds from every direction. One especially handsome document was a town map of Cambridge, bearing the name of every street and lane, depicting the very houses, shops and barns that lay along each way. So fine was the engraving that the eye could discern cattle grazing in the adjacent fields, trees bent low with their fruit, and deer cavorting pleasantly in the neighbor wood. Kings College Chapel dominated the center and the coats of arms of the highest citizens adorned their rightful places alongside fine manor houses and a castle. Cambridge boasts a Trinity Church, like our own at home, or so says this map.

Beneath Cambridge lay a map of a more exotic principality, one which caused my heart to leap almost from my breast: 'America–Nova Tabula' proclaimed the simple legend, but coz, there was no simple matter else about this precious parchment. The great continents and islands were all there, in most exquisite particulars, the harbors, towns and rivers. The edges were adorned with scenes of the wild savages and their kings that populate these regions, some as captives and others ape-like, dressed in our English garb, but prancing to the beat of a drum. Many place names in Spanish or French, but great expanses of white dubbed merely 'Terra Nova', separated these lands from where I stood by the great 'Oceanus Atlanticus', 'Brasilia', 'La Florida', 'Cuba', 'Spaniola', and the more familiar 'Virginia' where Raleigh, and those fortunate enough to serve him, are even now made men with the wealth that lay at their feet thither. I plucked the treasure from the middle of the stack and suddenly, as if guided by an evil spirit (or the hand of God?), folded it into quarters and eights and thrust it in my doublet.

"Herodotus?" quoth a disembodied voice from behind me. Fearing discovery of my theft I whirled around and saw nothing, until I looked down. Standing no taller than a barrel of malt, and about the same dimensions, was a bald man of some three score years, clad in a filthy nightshirt and faded red shawl.

"O pardon me, sir, I called for assistance when I entered..."

"Herodotus." The odd little figure shouted as if he heard me not. Clearly, my theft was not yet the subject of his attentions. "Have you seen Herodotus?"

In mine unease, I backed into a large pot that flowed over with stale rushes, then replied: "No. I believe he is dead these two thousand years."

"Not THEEEE Herodotus, you fool." The man spoke from various corners of the shop, searching high and low, although truth to tell, mostly low. "My parrot." I now took his meaning and aided in the search, still wondering if he in fact had taken note of my theft.

"O, sir, I was sent by the Leicester's Men to buy certain maps of you, sir." I sought to divert his thoughts, to those that occupy every shopkeeper: profit.

"Aaaaaa-chooooooozzzzzz." He sneezed roundly, as who would not in those confines, now thick with the dust he had disturbed in the fruitless search for his bird. "The Earl is HERE?"

"Nay, sir. The Leicester's Men, servants to the Earl and Her Majesty, players in the shires and towns of her realm and bound for the Low Countries."

"O! So you'll be wanting maps of shires and towns, will you?"

"No sir, of the Low Countries and the seas that stand between us." He stopped rummaging in the low-lying detritus of the shop and considered me for a long while. I feared he was examining the uneven bulge in my doublet and would instantly discover my dishonesty and call the constable.

"Mortimer Westerbeke at your service. God hath guided you to the right place." He thrust a greasy hand in my general direction. Before I could grasp it, he withdrew it and began to vigorously wipe it on his nightshirt. "Forgive me, kind gentleman, but I was e'en now taking my supper, a joint of mutton. A Leicester's man you say?"

I nodded.

"Map of Low Countries, you say?"

"And the seas between us and thither." Then, being new to the gathering of gossip, I thought this might be the time to question him on other matters. "And whatever intelligence you may have that might interest Her Majesty. I mean, of interest to players in service to Her Majesty's Lord of Leicester."

"First, here is your most excellent map of those places that round the North Sea, including the Low Countries, the German states, Denmark and those seaward passages you spoke so often of." Westerbeke wasted neither time nor effort while plucking from a huge, flat drawer the one map that precisely met the particulars. "Look you, you may examine it all this night and all the next day and you'll find nary a hole in it nor a blot upon it. Three pounds."

"Three pounds! For a map? I have but two pounds, Mr. Westerbeke." I gasped, quite audibly I am certain. Although I have spent many an hour at the markets of Stratford, bargaining for a map was quite new to mine experience.

"Aaaaaa-chooooooozzzzzz ... aaaaaa-chooooooozzzzzz ... aaaaaa-chooooooozzzzzz." He convulsed with such violence that I thought he floated for a time, a foot or more above the floor. "Then I shall tear it asunder and give you two pounds worth."

"What? Like a butcher who lays his meat upon a scale?"

"Well, what else would you have me do?" He asked simply, then settled into one of the frail, hard-bitten chairs.

"If I return with a third of the map missing and no money left in my pocket, I swear I'll be whipped from here back to Stratford," quoth I, examining the document to learn if there be some third part that my Masters would not miss the having of.

"You are not so young to be a child-fool, nor are you so old to be a dotage-fool," quoth he, tearing one small corner from the map, a portion that bore no more than the visage of some nobleman who may have first commissioned the work. "Where is it written, that for two-thirds the price you buy but two-thirds of the goods, especially when I am known for an hundred mile around as a generous man and e'en more so in service to Her Majesty. There - - take thee the greater part and I the lesser, only so that I may say I never gave in to your hard bargaining, but kept some portion for myself."

With this he thrust the map in my hands and filed his scrap in the pages of a large volume on animal husbandry. I counted myself lucky at the bargain and thrust the coins into his hand before he could partition the map further.

"And as for the gossip, much good it will do ye, THAT have I in greater store at far lesser price," quoth he, leaning back in his chair, arms folded across his belly. "Sit, and I will tell thee that which I deem most important of all that I do know."

Feeling somewhat ill-at-ease for spending all of my master's money, and fearing still the discovery of mine earlier transgression, I sat next to the swine-shaped little man and hoped his gossip would add value to the bargain, although I am sure I have no idea what Mr. Johnson himself is wanting to hear (Dick thinks he spies for the Queen to root out Catholics who would welcome her death). As he spoke, he seemed to drift away from my company, rejoining his lost, forgotten, or fallen shipmates of a decade past. Now and then he ran an ink-stained finger over an elaborate map to show me the progress of a fleet of ghost-ships, sailing across the coloured paper, leaving a faint trace of grease to mark the voyage.

"It were the 15ᵗʰ day of November ... or was it the 17ᵗʰ? Nay, I remember it was ten years to the day mine Edith left this earth: it was the 15ᵗʰ of November in the year of our Lord 1577, that Mister Francis Drake, in the company of divers gentlemen and sailors, departed from Plymouth with five ships, giving out his pretended destination as Alexandria, but many of us knew better. I counted myself among the crew. I was their navigator extraordinary."

"Alexandria? In Egypt? Was he bound thither to relieve the imprisonment of Mister John Fox and others of our English nation from the foul Turks?" I thought on Mr. Pope's tale of the heroic Mr. Fox and the ill-fated Spaniard and marveled at the coincidence that Mister Drake would be sent thither at that same time.

"Who? I never heard such a name, nor was that his cause. But look you, the Turk is your most fiendish devil, put here by God to test and tempt us. Aye. What say you was his name?"

"John Fox of Woodbridge in Suffolk, if I recall the story rightly."

"I knew a tinker in Suffolk, his name was ... his name was ... " Westerbeke rubbed his greasy fingertips in his eyes as if to conjure up the name, but it came not to him. "Ah, well, I will think on't. Nay, our quarry was not the Turkish devil, but the Spanish dog: we sailed southerly and after touching sundry points of land, including those where General Drake mustered and trained his troops in warlike manner for battle against any Spanish swine, we came in January to an island ... " (here he showed me a map of the west coast of Africa) "... called Maio, whence we gave ourselves a little refreshing.³⁶ This island is wonderfully stored with goats and wild hens and it hath salt also without labour, the people there gather it into heaps, which continually in great quantity is increased upon the sands by the flowing sea and the heat of the sun. Amongst other things we there discovered was a fruit, not commonly known in England, called 'cocos'. The tree beareth neither leaves nor branches and at the very top the fruit groweth in clusters, each fruit being as big as a man's head. Having taken off the outermost bark of this fruit, you shall find a quantity of sinews before finding a hard shell which holds a pint of liquor, neither more nor less, which has a sweet and delicate taste, most comforting and cordial. Within the shell is also a sweet meat, the taste of almonds."

I knew not if I should trust every word from the mapmaker, yet his entire demeanor had changed with the telling of this tale, to that of a man who has truly seen a great vision and can describe it painstakingly. Well, even a crooked stick can draw a straight line, so I therefore take his tale for gospel.

"We departed thence on Candlemas and sailed by this island here…" his finger lingered over a small brown spot on the map amidst a great azure sea "…far enough from the inhabitants who shot at us, for they all fell short and did no man any harm. The mountains of the island are said to be possessed by the Moors, but it was certainly the Portuguese who fired upon us. Nearby this island we espied two Spanish ships under sail and General Sir Francis Drake gave chase and in the end boarded them with little trouble.[37] These ships yielded unto us a goodly store of wine. Being departed from these islands, we made sail for Brazil in the New World, at first becalmed for nearly three weeks, then subject to diverse great storms, terrible lightnings and much thunder. Yet with this misery we had the commodity of a great store of a very strange flying fish, whereof some fell into our ships, from whence they could not rise again for want of moisture on their wings. These are not at all foul tasting when fried in grease."

He paused, eyes closed, to taste those fish again. I suspect he never met fish nor fowl that, being cooked in its own grease, he did not find delicate to the taste. His brief reverie at an end by aaaaa-choooooozzzzzz … aaaaaa-choooooozzzzzz … aaaaaa-choooooozzzzzz, and he then continued thus:

"The first land that we fell upon was the coast of Brazil at 33 degrees latitude - - here - - and being discovered by the inhabitants, they made great fires for sacrifices to their devils, hoping that tempests may arise and cast our vessels and men asunder. Praise God, there was no such result of their labors. We traveled some miles further to a point more hospitable, which General Drake called Cape of Good Joy. Here we took in water, every man ashore examining the ground most thoroughly for any signs of gold in the soil or water. Finding none, we did take on a store of meat of deer and certain sea-wolves, commonly called seals, which are so numerous that within the space of an hour we slew 300." He paused again with his eyes closed and I awaited another accounting of the flavour of fried sea-wolf. This he kept to himself and instead returned to his finger on the map and his tale:

"Now, sailing further south, we came upon a pleasant bay with natives who seemed more welcoming, thus did General Drake and a small party go ashore. These natives made a show for him of leaping and dancing and entered into traffic with him, but they would not receive any thing from our men's hands, but caused us to cast our trade goods first upon the ground. Nearby we found a gibbet [gallows], which we supposed to be the place where Magellan did execute some of his disobedient and rebellious company. There may well be some ill spirits in that place."

Westerbeke spoke in a thin whisper, as if he feared a conspiracy be overheard, but suddenly rose and shouted, perhaps for the same ghostly audience. "For our crew suffered the same fate as that of Magellan! Yes, boy, that we did. One Thomas Doughty had been a surly fellow the entire journey, but at our current anchorage his foul temper overflowed to MUTINY! General Drake caused the matter to be heard by the entire company, with all things done in good order as might be to the course of our laws in England, and in the end it was concluded that Mr. Doughty should receive punishment according to the quality of the offence. Seeing no remedy, he desired before his death to receive the communion, which being done and the place of execution made ready, Doughty having embraced General Drake and taken leave of all the company with a prayer for the Queen's Majesty, in quiet fashion laid his head upon the block. But then, look you, there took place in that instant something which doth continue to amaze me, even this many years later. I'll make water."

"What?" quoth I. "Look you - - I am amazed - - I'll make water? What means this?"

He was already relieving himself, in the direction of a rusted pot that bore signs of being many times filled and emptied. With steam rising from the floor at his feet, he continued without pause:

"Now, as I say, there took place, in that instant, something which hath the power to amaze me, even this many years later. The axe was poised above Mr. Doughty's neck when the sailor, who had been chosen for the duty, sighed mightily and swung the weapon, in order to bring it down with one clean stroke and end the poor devil's life with little suffering, and by that action the head of the axe came loose from his oak handle and was flung clean across the ship, over the rail, and into the sea. Some took this as a sign from God that Doughty was innocent of mutinous behavior, but whereas he himself had confessed his sins, before every man of us present, he was surely guilty, as which of us is not drenched in some sin or other? Another axe was called for and the execution was to be attempted yet again. But Doughty, allowed to stand and slake his thirst a final time, did then beg the General's ear, whereupon he acknowledged himself to be a wicked and sinful man, but since the land of Brazil is well known to be a wicked and savage place, he begged that his punishment might be to be set upon the land to fend for himself, to live or die at God's will. Thereto he added that he hoped to be set upon said land with his head still attached to his neck. Our General conferred with divers gentlemen and Mr. Fletcher, several of whom were still attempting to divine the meaning of the flying axe. By their dumbshow, we could see they meant to go ahead with the execution, which every man else thought an ill-omen. I was elected to speak for the crew and most humbly did so, pleading with our nobles to spare the fool's life and let God punish him ashore. At length they agreed to Mr. Doughty's request and caused him without further ado to be placed ashore with the clothes on his back and one day's ration of food. Before leaving our vessel, Doughty said that he would repay my kindness one day, even if it were in another life, as if it were a debt of a thousand pound. This matter being done, General Drake made divers speeches to the whole company, persuading us to unity, obedience, and love, and for the better confirmation thereof, he willed every man on Sunday next to receive communion as Christian brethren ought to do. And so with good contentment every man went about his further business."[38]

Westerbeke returned to his chair and shook most violently, either some pleasure at relieving himself after too long, or feeling again the cold he now described to me in some particulars:

"It was already late summer, which in those regions is late winter, and we next fell in with the Strait of Magellan going into the South Sea, at the cape whereof we found the body of a dead man, whose flesh was consumed.[39] Some claimed it was Doughty, but General Drake assured us a dead man could not have floated faster than a ship under sail, even if the sailor had been devoured and cast adrift at the same time as we left him. The land on both sides of this place is very huge and covered with snow, extremely cold, with barren trees that seem to stoop under the burden of weather and yet are green continually, with many good and sweet herbs growing beneath their boughs. We honoured the Queen's birthday [*September 7th*] when we arrived at an island in the straits, where we found great store of fowl which could not fly [*penguins*], of a bigness of geese, whereof we killed in less than a day some 3,000 and victualed ourselves thoroughly therewith."

I now began to have more doubts about the truth of Westerbeke's tale. 3,000 flightless geese taken in an hour? Winter in the middle of summer? That is hot ice and wondrous strange snow.[40] Still, I was tasked with collecting gossip and whoever puts his faith in gossip knows he will stand on shifting sands.

"We required another month to leave the straits, the sea never abating his force to let us out any sooner. We were at last able to head north along what we supposed was the coast of Chile, as the General's maps described it, although these same maps were ill-drafted in the lower latitudes, based, we supposed, on ignorant conjecture and not discovery. The more northerly we made way, the more true these maps became. Now, the 29th of November, St. Andrews eve it was sure - - as how could I forget that date from what nearly happened to me - - we cast anchor in a handsome, calm bay and General Drake set himself ashore with a party of men, whereat he found people, whom the cruel and extreme dealings of the Spanish had forced, for their own safety and liberty, to flee and to fortify themselves inland. Seeing we were not Spaniards, they showed us great courtesy, bringing to us potatoes, roots, and two very fat sheep, and gave us promise of water, which I was assigned to return with barrels and take our fill. But the next day I took violent ill and overslept my watch. Rather than disturb me, Mr. Bekins went ashore in my stead to fetch the water with another sailor whose name I cannot now recall. The natives, taking those men for Spaniards, laid violent hands on them and, as we think, slew them. Our General, seeing this, stayed no longer, but weighed anchor and set sail. I was hours at prayers of thanks to God that I had not been on that water party, but equally penitent that Mr. Bekins was dead in payment of my sloth."

Tears were rising in Westerbeke's eyes, a sure sign that even this many years later he truly repented his deeds, for there are no truer faces than those washed with tears. He paused a moment to blow great green gobs into a washing cloth that lay nearby (obviously not itself washed in the entire reign of our Queen), dabbed his eyes withal, and continued:

"Mr. Fletcher assured me that all things happen at God's will and that I was spared for some other purpose, or at least for some other death, which now I owed to God at any moment. My fearful devotions were interrupted by a call from on deck that an Indian canoe was sighted coming towards us, whereupon we hove to and greeted the lone occupant. This savage made signs, which told us that there was a great Spanish ship at anchor in Santiago, laden with gold from the kingdom of Peru. General Drake gave the man some food and trinkets and thanked him in various delicate gestures. This being our first evidence of the riches we had all come so far and braved so many dangers to acquire, we were, to a man, greatly inspired. Sailing then to Santiago, we found indeed the treasure ship riding at anchor, having in her a watch of only eight Spaniards and three Negroes, who thinking us to have been Spaniards welcomed us with a drum. As soon as we neared the ship, one of our number, Thomas Moon, was called upon to lead the raiding party, which leapt aboard the Spanish vessel and o'ertook their guard, calling out to them 'abajo perros', meaning 'get down you dogs'. The Spaniards, being cowards anyway, crossed and blessed themselves, but gave up their prize easily, and to be short, were soon stowed in hatches below decks, excepting one who suddenly and desperately leapt overboard into the sea and swam to the town of Santiago to give them warning. Now they of the town, being not above nine households, fled. General Drake manned two boats and we rifled the town, including a small popish chapel where we found a silver chalice, two cruets, and one altar-cloth, the spoil whereof we gave to our minister, Mr. Fletcher. We found also in this town a warehouse stored with wine of Chile and many boards of cedar-wood, all of which we brought away with us. We took also this Spanish gold ship, manned by men of our company, leaving all the Spaniards on the land save one, John Griego, a Greek born, whom our General carried for a pilot to navigate these waters. And look you: the Spanish ship was indeed the stuff that dreams are made of, for she contained no less than another goodly store of the wine of Chile and…" here he paused for dramatic effect, "…and 37,000 ducats Spanish of very pure and fine gold."

He continued the tale at a gallop, but I was out of breath in wonderment that such a treasure could be so easily taken. If true, it meant the New World was indeed a place where gold meant no more than acorns, to be picked up or left on the ground as you list, it being so plentiful. This proved what I have heard thus far: my Fortune lay in the New World. But the old sailor had so much more yet to report and I therefore continue to write down what I can yet recall thereof:

"From thence we sailed to a small port called by the Chileans 'Tarapaca' where, being landed, we found by the shore a Spaniard lying asleep who guarded thirteen bars of silver, which weighed 4,000 ducats Spanish. We relieved him of his charge. Not far from thence we found another Spaniard and an Indian boy driving eight sheep of Peru, called 'llamas', which are the bigness of asses but with longer necks. Every one of these sheep carried leather bags with fifty pounds of fine silver each, so that bringing both animals and cargo to our ship we collected some 800 weight of silver. Next sailed we to a small port called Arica, where we found three small barks lying at anchor, which we soon overpowered. In one was 57 wedges of silver, each twenty pounds in weight. This we took, along with sundry other provisions from the ships, before we set them afire to render them unserviceable to the Spanish. And then, on St. Valentine's Day in the year of our Lord 1578 we arrived in Lima, a large port city in Peru. There we found a dozen ships at anchor with little guard, the Spanish masters and merchants most secure, having never been assaulted by enemies in so remote a location. Our General rifled these ships and found a chest full of royals of plate and a goodly store of silks and linens. In each ship we questioned the guards and in one we heard tell of another ship called the Cacafuego, which had sailed but one day before, laden with Spanish treasure. Hearing this, our General exhorted every man to his duty that we not allow this treasure to reach the Spanish princes, which they would surely use to outfit armies against our English women and children at home. We cut the dozen ships loose of their anchors that they might drift out to sea or crash upon the rocks and set our own sail after the Cacafuego."

Cacafuego. Lima. Llama. The strange sounds lingered in my head like the tastes of exotic foods taken for the first time linger on the tongue. Gold, silver, silks. These familiar words etched themselves in my brain like welcome mother's milk to the hungry babe. The great map came alive as Westerbeke spoke, as if he cast a spell upon the images therein, raising them from the dead to dance before us now:

"Underway General Drake promised our company that whosoever could first spy the Cacafuego would have a chain of gold for this good news, the which he hung from the mainmast where all could admire it. It fortuned that one John Drake, no kin to the General, going up into the top, spied her about three of the clock and by six we came to her. General Drake used our superior speed to avoid being struck by her ordnance and instead fired our own cannon and dismasted her. In this wounded state was the Cacafuego easily boarded and inside the ship we found great riches: jewels and precious stones, thirteen chests full of royal plate, fourscore pound weight of gold, and six-and-twenty ton of silver. The place where we captured this prize was at Cape de San Francisco off the coast of Panama. As we loaded our treasure, another Spanish ship sailed near, thinking to offer aid to a distressed ally. Instead we overpowered this vessel too and took from it linen cloth and fine China-dishes of white earth and a great store of China silks. The owner of this second ship was a Spanish gentleman, from whom our General took a falcon of gold with a great emerald in the breast thereof. The pilot of the ship we took with us, then cast both Spanish hulks adrift with their crews to survive as they might at God's mercy. This pilot guided us to a port of Guatulco, where we sought water and food stores, and wherein we found a courthouse with Spaniards sitting in judgment of certain Negroes who were to be hanged for attempting to set fire to the town. The Negroes had good cause for their crimes, for the Spanish had slain many of their manhood and forced many others into slavery. General Drake ordered the Spaniards to be bound in the courthouse whereupon he gave leave for the Negroes to set fire to the town and return to their own villages. But before the town was put to flame, we ransacked it and found a bushel of real plate silver and Thomas Moon caught a Spanish gentleman flying out the town and relieved him of a gold chain and other jewels before letting him continue his cowardly journey."

The round little mapmaker seemed satisfied, as if finished with a fine banquet. He sat back in his chair and looked toward the ceiling. He ran stumpy fingers through his greasy hair and yawned. In the hour that we had sat around his map and tale, night had replaced day, so we sat in the darkness of his shop, surrounded by ghosts. After lighting one foul candle of tallow, he finished his discourse in mild manner, like the sea herself after a gale:

"Our General, thinking himself sufficiently satisfied and revenged, and supposing that Her Majesty at his return would rest content with this service, purposed to continue no longer upon the Spanish coasts, but began to consider the best way to return home. He thought it unwise to go back by the Straits of Magellan for two reasons chiefly: first, the Spaniards might await us in strength. Second, the mouth of the straits are continual storms blustering, as we now knew from experience, besides the shoals and sands upon the coast that might break our ship asunder. He resolved therefore to avoid these hazards and go forward to the islands of the Moluccas [Indonesia] and thence to sail the course of the Portuguese by the Cape of Buena Esperanza at the southern tip of Africa. Upon this resolution, we therefore sailed some 600 leagues to the north and, at 38 degrees north latitude, where it was somewhat warmer, it pleased God to show us a good bay with a strong wind to enter the same.[41] In this bay we anchored and the people of the country showed themselves. General Drake according to his natural and accustomed humanity courteously entreated them and liberally bestowed on them necessary things to cover their nakedness, whereupon they supposed us to be gods and would not be persuaded to the contrary. Their houses are digged round with earth and have clefts of wood set upon them, joining close together at the top like a spire steeple, which by reason of that closeness are very warm.[42] Their beds are on the ground with rushes strewn thereon, and each house has a fire in the midst. The men go naked, but the women take bulrushes and comb them after the manner of hemp and thereof make their loose garments, which being knit about their middles, hang down about their hips, having also about their shoulders a skin of deer with the hair still upon it. These women are very obedient and serviceable to their husbands. The men gave us feathers and bags of tobacco for presents and one of their number was appointed speaker and made a long oration. The women remained at a distance and tormented themselves lamentably, tearing their flesh from their cheeks, whereby we perceived they were about a sacrifice. In the meantime, our General ordered our company to prayer and to reading of Scriptures, at which exercise they were attentive and seemed greatly to be affected with it. They made signs unto our General that he would be their king, making signs that they would resign their right and title to the whole land and become his subjects and, to persuade him, their king placed upon his head a large crown of feathers and enriched his neck with their chains of office. Our General thought it meet [wise] to accept their offer and, in the name of Her Majesty, he took the crown, sceptre and dignity of the said country into his hands. When these services were ended, General Drake and some of our company traveled up into the country, which he did name Nova Albion or New England, and found herds of deer by the thousands, being most large and fat of body. But most important to us all is that there be no part of earth here to be taken up wherein there is not some show of gold or silver. It seemed that the Spanish hitherto had never been in this country, neither did they ever discover the land by many degrees southward. Thus, at our departure, our General set up a monument being of Her Majesty's title to the country and all within her."

"After we set sail westward from thence, we saw no land until St. Luke's Day [*October 18th*], when we fell upon certain islands near the line [*equator*], where the inhabitants came to greet us in canoes carved of a single tree with great skill and cunning. These people have the nether part of their ears cut into a round circle, hanging down very low upon their cheeks, whereon they hang ornaments of a reasonable weight. The nails of their hands are an inch long and their teeth are as black as pitch. We continued our course westward and in the Moluccas we paused a month to grave [*caulk*] our ship. Amongst the trees of these islands by night an infinite swarm of fiery worms did show themselves flying through the air, their bodies no bigger than our common English flies, but these make such a show and light as if every twig or tree had been a burning candle. Although it is the Portuguese who established trade with the natives here, it is the French pox that is very common to all.

The natives cure themselves by sitting naked from ten to two of the clock in the sun, whereby the venomous humour is drawn out. When we had ended our business there we again made westward sail."

I was by now so lost in reverie of dangers, exotic savages, cowardly Spaniards, and great wealth, that I scarce noticed he had resumed tracing of his journey on the great map. I leaned forward to take notice, but my soul was wandering the gold strewn lands of the New World, taking up gold that lay at my feet. Even so, he finished his tale most courteously:

"From thence we sailed for Africa and the Cape of Good Hope, though we did not set foot there, and by the grace of God, we arrived in England on the 3rd of November in the year of our Lord 1580, being the third year since our departure, and look you, we were all made men. General Drake was most liberal in dividing the crew's portion of the treasure. Out of our number, many became squires of great stature in their several counties. I bought this shop from old Westerbeke, to whom I was apprenticed as a youth, and have plied the mapmaker's trade e'er since."

I inquired: "Old Westerbeke, he was your father?"

"Nay, Fate brought us together, not family. It is better thus, but as he died without a son, I honour his memory by taking his surname." With that he sneezed again and took to searching the dark shop floor for the washrag or the parrot, but leaving me aside.

I thanked him for his kind assistance and hurried into a street where day's light had long since burned out and but a few night candles cast their other-world glow upon my way. Some hurried off home or to the tavern, no man seeking the gaze of another. A chill wind sliced from the northeast, biting most shrewdly at times, and carried with it a fine mist that turned to drops at the tip of my nose. I husbanded my treasures well inside my doublet and cloak, careful to drop neither, nor to forget which breast secreted which map. It wouldn't do to deliver into the hands of Mr. Johnson a finely coloured map of the Americas, when I had been sent for one of the North Sea.

I returned to our rooms and gave Mr. Johnson the map and told him all I had seen and heard at Westerbeke's. He seemed little curious of the tales from the Americas but most fascinated by the description of popish crosses and hail Marys and whatever more I described that was much in evidence around the dingy shop. He caused me to repeat the descriptions several times, that I might not omit the smallest particular. When he was satisfied and had taken notes of several points especially, then was I dismissed. Released at last to study mine own treasure!

Treasure? As I write the word I would tear it to pieces. O coz, if I die today, I meet our maker with such sin on my head that I can never wash it clean. I think how one day that my son will read this letter and what should he think of his father the thief? Good ends can never acquit foul means. On the one hand, I could use this map to restore my family's honour and fortune, I could repay old Westerbeke an hundred fold. On the other hand, I am a thief and risk eternal damnation and a gnawing conscience for all my days, howsoever long they last. I will return tomorrow to the mapmaker and beg his forgiveness and return the map. There, it is resolved!

O John, great thing of me forgot. My reason in the main to write this letter is that on the morrow, a merchant known to my father leaves Dover for other parts, Stratford chief among them. He has agreed to deliver this and some earlier letters I have writ thee. As I have said herein, I am soon to travel beyond the seas with our Company, a grave honour even if it be to fight for our country and die. Dear coz, as thou hast ever been my friend, so help me now: I have a suit of clothes and a cloak at pawn with Pillocock for three pound, and if it shall please thee to lend me so much to release them, I shall be bound to pray for thee so long as I live.

For if I go to foreign lands on Her Majesty's service and have no greater clothes than those which now decorate my back, I shall not be well esteemed of. Ha! As I write the words, I recognize Vanity in the instant. Well clothed? Well esteemed? If I am to die in battle, what will such things matter? I would run, coz, I would at this moment drop my pen and take flight, I'll warrant thee, but thus do cowards die many times before their deaths, while the valiant never taste of death but once.

In truth, of all those wonders that I have heard till now, it seems to me most strange that men should fear death, a necessary end, which will come when it will come. But I will not fly from hence for one reason mainly: in times to come, I would not have any man tell my son that his father was a coward. Give then instead to Hamnet this advice on how his father makes peace with Life: if I do lose thee, I do lose a thing that none but fools would keep. When masters Kempe or Pope play fools on our stage I see that we are all merely Death's court jester upon this stage of Life. From Death do we fly in fear, yet because no man lives forever, are we not running toward him still?

And for what good reason should I run? To stay alive to seek a Fortune? That alone cannot make a man happy, for he trods like an ass bearing ingots of gold and Death will unload him after all.

Therefore, I will face my fate with these my fellows, and thus, do need my clothes. It is most natural that thou shouldst expect repayment of so dear a debt when I am able, with eight (or ten?) in the hundred added thereto for thy pains. Please help thy true friend Will in this matter and send me the clothes by what means thou canst, but in no event later than Michaelmas, when we will have sailed for certain. If I die and cannot repay this debt, I trust thy reward will be in knowing thou wert kind to thy friend.

Kiss my boy and maids in my name and omit nothing else which thine honour deem'st best for their tender need (saving that thy discretion prevent thee telling them that their father is a thief - - this matter unto thee alone do I mean to confess and pledge to make it right on the morrow). I am thine ever loving servant in all else, Will.

LETTER FIVE
October 31, 1586

Wherein the players act for a drunken Prince in Denmark, but memories
stir of life with a drunken father in Stratford.

On All Hallow's eve 1586, aboard a ship returning from Denmark, Shakespeare is peacefully writing, having found life on a ship most agreeable, "except for the lice in the bedding." Instead of fighting with the armies in the Netherlands, it turned out that Leicester's Men were sent to accompany the Earl, as he recruits allies for England's war on the Continent, in a sort of theatrical and musical diplomacy.

In the 1960s, I took two month-long voyages by ship (it was cheaper than airplanes in those days, when my family moved from California to Sydney, Australia and when I left four years later, sailing to Rotterdam alone). As I read Letter Five, I recalled the spell that the ocean casts on ordinary events, eating a meal or a conversation with a fellow passenger, especially when the ship is far from land and you are surrounded by the blended black and empty vastness of the night sea and sky. Shakespeare had never been on the ocean before and likely had never even seen it, considering that his hometown of Stratford is many miles inland, so, as a boy from Milwaukee heading to Australia with my family, I can attest that there was probably an other-worldly element that galvanized the memories in exquisite sensory detail for him too.

Whatever internal voices or external forces helped Shakespeare recall the details of Denmark and his own ocean voyages, if you are familiar with his masterpiece *Hamlet*, you may have the same reaction that I did upon reading this letter, wherever you are now. From the events Shakespeare describes at the Danish court, I could veritably hear the old advisor, Polonius, and see the breathtaking scene of Hamlet's knife poised over the king, scenes straight out of that play. Denmark clearly made a big impression on Shakespeare, but I was mystified how he could have recalled detailed conversations to include them in a play almost fifteen years later. Several years into my deciphering of the letters, I found the Rosetta Stone, so to speak, which I had overlooked when first transcribing them, but which explains that mystery (and how so many other passages from the letters later became people, places, or dialogue in his plays).

In Letter 50 (which will appear in Book Two), Shakespeare expresses gratitude to John Combe's brother for opening a chest where the letters were stored (while John was apparently away from Stratford, but Shakespeare was there writing *Love's Labours Lost* in 1593). Once he became a successful London poet and playwright, he apparently referred to the letters often when he was periodically back at home. Generations of theatregoers are the beneficiaries of the detailed descriptions in his correspondence and John Combe's careful safekeeping of them.

In Letter Five, we discover how Shakespeare and his fellows performed throughout towns in Denmark and at its royal court accompanied by a large and very expensive retinue. Whatever impact foreign travel had on the young man from Stratford, he still does not see his future in the theatre.

It is not until Letter Six that we learn the visceral reasons Shakespeare has for wanting the Earl of Leicester dead, but here is Letter Five, in which he gives us a front row seat to that drama, wherein he comes to realize, and put in writing for the first time, that "Conscience makes cowards of us all."

All Hallow's Eve, 31 October 1586,
onboard a ship from Denmark

Coz,

Now make we haste for home with double-good reason: first, at sea is neither bush nor shrub to bear off any weather at all, and another storm is surely brewing. Even now, I hear it singing in the wind and yonder sits a huge black cloud, one that looks like a foul jug about to shed his liquor. If it should thunder, as it did before, I swear this cloud cannot choose but fall to earth by the bucket.

Our duty in Denmark done, we must make hasty return, lest our Company's fortunes be lost to another. Each autumn, those Companies in London are invited to propose plays to show Her Majesty and, though being servants to his lordship the Earl makes us likewise her very own servants, it shall avail us nothing if we be absent when the Master of Revels comes calling. Much more have I to report: including those matters pertaining to Lord Leicester and mine intent to have some measure of satisfaction for the blows he has wrought upon my father. So did Opportunity present herself in mighty colours, but some Divine presence stayed mine hand.

But great thing of me forgot: first I must explain to thee how it came out that we found ourselves in Denmark playing for a king and not in the ditches of her neighbor countries with an arrow in the chest. If thou hast received my last, then thou knowest how we were bound for Lord Leicester's armies and those wars that would throw off the Spanish yoke from the backs of our Dutch allies. We waited in Dover for a ship that would take us thither and on the day appointed, discovered when we boarded that we were being sent to Denmark as our lord's players, not his pikemen! How foolish are men: so oft do we flee the rabid dog, before we know if he means to pursue us at all!

And in Denmark we were very well used, given leave to parade through sundry towns in our players' apparel, our lord's musicians playing by our side on drum, trumpet and fife, our horses in their brightest apparel too, always preceded by eager townsfolk, to make our presence known and set the time for our performance at each inn yard, guildhall or common. Most spoke not a word of our mother tongue, yet we never failed for spectators and a profitable day's work. In every wise, our dozen players were the chiefest cause of commotion among those in attendance on our Earl, which numbered in his retinue (if thou canst imagine so many):

> 16 gentleman plus 2 gentlemen ushers plus 4 gentleman of the chamber
>
> 1 gentleman of horse plus 1 master of carriages plus 10 lackeys
>
> 1 steward
>
> 1 secretary
>
> 3 wardrobers
>
> 8 musicians plus 8 trumpeters
>
> 30 yeoman
>
> 1 harbinger
>
> 6 footmen
>
> 2 chaplains
>
> 1 surgeon plus 1 physician
>
> 6 pages
>
> 30 kitchen, buttery, and pantry servants (his lordship will eat no meal that was not prepared at the hands of his own attendants, chiefly his French cook).

At their Court, our masters were taken to a banquet with the King, which they found to be more sumptuous than any they had enjoyed in England, and whereat the meat was eaten using certain utensils, sundry forks and the like, in the French style. All the while the 'prentices ate their fill of a savoury herring, black bread, and a cheese called tafelost (which is so highly prized that farmers pay their taxes unto the crown withal). After this feast, we were greeted by a Prince of no more than thirty, but his beard already turning gray, richly dressed in silks adorned with the finest golden threads, but bare-headed. He made his way through our number, estimating by our appearance which part each of us might play, in perfect English, to the admiration of our Company and the Court.

"He that plays the king shall be welcome. Yes, yes: this nobleman shall have tribute of me. This adventurous knight shall use his foil and target bravely; o, this lover shall not sigh for naught; this clown shall make even those laugh whose lungs are not easily tickled." When he came upon our bare-faced Dick Cowley, he made most merry sport, bowing and feigning to kiss his hand, saying:

"What, my young lady and mistress? Pray God, your voice, like a piece of defaced gold in a ring, be not yet cracked!" Next he greatly astounded the assembled Company, for he embraced our sometimes-woman Dick, kissing him firmly upon the lips with sundry words of love, as from a sonnet, in his native tongue. By now, we understood that he was overcome with drink and like to do any thing that entered his brain.

"More Rhenish [*German wine*], here, more Rhenish for my friends," quoth this Dane, dropping his conquest upon the floor. A serving woman appeared from behind a great arras with a stone pitcher of wine and many goblets of silver. The Dane insisted that every man fill his cup before demanding more of us: "Now say what players you are."

Mr. Burbage spoke for our Company, bowing in the French style: "Even those you took delight in, your lordship, when we played for your grace in London as you attended there at Court."

"Ah, that you have, brave Master Burbage, I do recall it with much delight." The Prince began swiping the air with one of our rapiers, taking the measure of a noble figure in the tapestry as if to run it through.

Then spoke a lean, hungry-looking adviser of some sort, who seemed to have his prick in the Prince's buttocks, so close did he attend: "They are come with Queen Elizabeth's emissaries to your father the King, my lord. They are said to be the best actors in the world, either for tragedy, comedy, history..."

"You are welcome, masters; welcome, all," quoth the Prince, ignoring his obsequious attendant.

"... pastoral ... pastoral-comical ... historical ... historical-pastoral ..."

"OLD FRIEND!" The Prince shouted to Mr. Burbage, drowning out the lisping fool that followed his every step around the great hall. Oblivious, the old fellow continued, gazing absent-mindedly as if reading a distant playbill, all the while counting to himself on ten fingers.

The Prince took Mr. Burbage by the arm, raising then a hand to silence his servant at last. "Old friend, I am glad to see thee well. Welcome, good friends. Masters, you are all welcome." His lordship then leapt child-like upon a stool, still brandishing one of our swords, and proclaimed "Let's go to't now, like French falconers, fly at any thing we see. We'll have a speech straight: come, give us a taste of your quality now. A passionate speech, I say."

"What speech, my lord?" asked Mr. Burbage, hovering near the Dane to catch him, should he fall from his perch.

"I heard thee speak me a speech in London ... "

"Name it, my lord, and we'll play it, with you taking part, if it please your lordship." Mr. Burbage gathered us all at the foot of the stool, ground-lings to a Prince.

"I do remember there were no spices in the lines to make the matter savoury, but it was an honest play, as wholesome as sweet. The one speech in it I chiefly loved ... " With no more ado, he then speaks a speech of some hundred or more lines, never once pausing to collect a thought (although draining his cup of wine fully six times before the speech was ended). Our Company was truly amazed by his facility with our profession and gave him full measure of applause for his trouble.

His own advisor made even greater fuss about him: "A'fore God, my lord, well spoken, with good accent and good discretion. I daresay we will hear no better from the Englishmen."

Then the Prince defended us most courteously: "Prithee, forgive my Lord Wixen. He means no insult to your worships and I know him to be a man to love a good jig or a tale of bawdry [*obscenity*] on the stage." At this, the Prince whispered so only we would hear. "Else he falls asleep in the gal-lery and snores most grievously!"

Mr. Burbage bowed deeply, the cue for us to do likewise. This Lord Wixen was not deaf: he o'erheard the Prince's commentary and bristled at the insult and might have made much ado about it, but that the Prince quickly lay oil upon the waters which he himself had troubled: "'Tis well. Good my Lord Wixen, will you see the players well bestowed? Do you hear, let them be well used."

"My lord, I will use them according to their desert," quoth he, casting an evil eye on our Company.

"God's breath, m'lord, much better!" The Prince alighted from his stool in a most dramatic fashion and ran his sword clean through the silken fig-ure on the arras, striking it again with his own dagger as if to assure it dead. "Use every man according to his desert, and who should escape whipping? No, no m'lord. Use them after your own honour and dignity: the greatest hospitality is in our bounty. Do take them in."

Calming himself somewhat, the perturbed baron, or I know not what rank, made polite invitation with a sweeping gesture of his own. But the Prince was not finished:

"Follow him, friends. We'll see a play of thine on the morrow. You could study a speech of some dozen or sixteen lines, which I would set down and insert therein, could you not?"

"Ay, my lord." Masters Burbage and Johnson both assured him we could do just so.

"Then you shall have it, if we offend not the poet, and I shall have your honest opinion about mine own meagre ability with the pen. For well know you masters this - - the play's the thing, wherein we catch the fancy of commoner or King."

The Prince made no more ado but suddenly departed with his companions. This Lord Wixen escorted us then to our chambers, his demeanour turning as ice does to water when it comes too near the flame, or like the snake, shedding one skin for another:

"Forgive my lord, the Prince. Drunkenness is his best virtue, for he will soon be swine-drunk and fall dead asleep. In his sleep at least he does himself little harm, save to the furnishings or his bed-clothes about him."

We were much amazed at this nobleman's candor about his own Prince. His face grew red as he spoke and a choler came over him as if he would confess even more, as Mr. Burbage then demanded of him: "Was he not simply providing good cheer to his guests, my lord, or is this his custom?"

"Ay, marry, is't, but to my mind, and though I am native here and to the manner born, 'tis a custom we should more honour in the breach than the observance. This heavy-headed revel makes us despised by other nations: they call us drunkards, and with swinish phrase soil our achievements. Ah, but look you, I say 'tis the English that teach us all manner of besotted presentments, such as lechery and false swearing against others. And oh, pride, sinful unpardonable pride."

"Your lordship, as we are in your country we shall not seek to quarrel," quoth Mr. Burbage, surprised, as were we all, that the water had turned again to ice. "But who among those English, that have made themselves known to you, have conducted their affairs so ill?"

Lord Wixen almost spat his reply, though barely above a whisper: "Why your own master. I mean your Lord Robert, a man given to a very loose tongue when in his cups!"[43] Then did this Danish lord unfold his innermost thoughts, which to our Company caused great amazement:

"Did you not see that on the occasion of your arrival, Lord Robert was apparelled all in white, no doubt to convey some heavenly sanction, and demanded of our Court to know if they had ever seen a better personage from England, of finer proportions and lineaments of the body. When one of our lords asked of him the purpose of his embassy hither, his reply was most astounding to our sensibilities, for he proclaimed to our Court, as if he himself were a monarch:

'We are much amused to share this sport with your kingdom. A pleasant diversion from our tiresome labours in the Netherlands, where our soldiers perish for want of victuals and clothing in great numbers,' quoth he. Oh and worse still, but I speak true when I tell you, he also dared say thus, also delivered in lordly tones: 'I assure you ... it will FRET me to death ere long ... to see my soldiers in this condition and not be able to help them. Ah me, 'tis a great fault, to be sure, when so many ... SUFFER ... and DIE ... at my command. But though I may fail in many ways ... and have more witnesses to my errors than many others ... who perhaps be no saints neither ... my faults will lie before Him for judgment ... who I have no doubt but will CANCEL them, as I have been - - and shall be ever - - most heartily sorry for them.'"

Lord Wixen paused to see our amazement, but ere we might defend his lordship's intentions, he added more: "And upon some conversation with your Earl's French cook, for I am most fluent in his tongue too, he revealed to me that these same soldiers are leaving Lord Robert's misadventures in the low countries in great numbers, either by death, disease, or fearful flight. Tut. This is your Queen's emissary, come to ask our King for soldiers and supplies? A man who squanders what his sovereign has entrusted to him, great and puffed up with his lavish retinue, an army of servants wielding spoons?"

With this Lord Wixen dabbed the corners of his mouth as if to cleanse them of foul spittal, before he brushed aside these matters in the instant, ice melting again to warm water: "Ah well, let he who is without sin cast the first stone, eh?"

O coz, I see in this our God taking the sword of vengeance from my hand and wielding it divinely. Could Leicester be brought to a disgraceful end in his foreign adventures and lose the protection of Her Majesty? Will my family have revenge without striking a blow? There is no act that I could devise more mortal than the dangerous tide now rising against him, though I have dreamed of being the instrument of that revenge.

Indeed God tested me even thus, for not an hour after we heard these secrets from Lord Wixen, I passed close by a small chapel near the great hall and discovered Leicester in silent prayer. Never had I been so close to him, so close I could smell his perfumes and hear the rustle of his starched lace collar on his silk shirt. No other living soul was nearby, either in person or hearing. My father has told me how his fingers itch to have them round the gizzard of this selfsame Earl and just then might I have done so. I could have stolen away unseen to leave open the question of who would have done such a deed, among the hundreds of courtiers and servants. That was my hour, if ever there would be such, my chance to see his crimson blood cascading over his white lace. Why then did I hesitate? Why should this be harder than the many times I killed a calf or sheep?

Suddenly I conned [understood] the reason: if I slaughtered him while he is praying, so he goes to Heaven. That is no revenge. A villain steals the life of mine uncle and the livelihood of my father and for that I send this same miscreant to Heaven? O, that is hire and salary, not revenge. He took my kinsman grossly (how his audit stood then, who knows, save God himself) and put his head upon a pike on London Bridge. I could not take Leicester at that moment, in the purging of his soul, when he was praying and therefore fit and seasoned for a passage of his own. No, only when he is cursing or in the foul pleasure of his bed with some boy; at gaming or about some act that has no morsel of salvation in it. Then should I find a means to trip him up, for then will his soul be damned as black as Hell, whereto it must surely go.

Thus was mine agony advised by an unseen spirit (or mine own conscience?). Aye, doth not that harsh master, Conscience, make cowards of us all? In any wise, in that instant, I could not take a life for the lives that this villain has stolen from the Ardens and the Shakespeares. I am truly Fortune's fool. Did I hesitate in fear that my son will know his father is a murderer, even if my cause be righteous? Or was my hand stayed by mine own avarice? For in that instant I could imagine the ship bound for the New World and my Fortune sailing away with each unkind cut I might deliver on his mortal body, for Leicester is himself the patron of many explorations and great successes thither.

O coz, I owe thee a greater explanation of this fevered scribble and will deliver them to thy fullest satisfaction anon. Do not judge me too harshly until such time as I may satisfy thy righteous inquiry of my purpose, my cause, my sanity.

With this demi-drama as Prologue to our sojourn at the Danish court, the rest played out without incident, excepting the nightly riots of drunken carousing. O, that we should, in the name of joy, pleasance, revel and applause, transform ourselves into beasts! Thou hast seen coz, how my father suffers of this affliction, but never did I imagine that nobles of a civilized nation could be so weak and ill-mannered.

Yet do I take away one other lesson from the Dane: their Prince's words to us, spiced with strong drink or no, still echo in mine ears. It was the poet's art that had cast a spell upon the Dane, no merry player with fife and drum, but the words of a tongue as foreign to him as the language of the Turk is to me. So moved was he by a play, a passage of a common play, that he conned [*learned*] the lines by heart, forever more cleaving them to his breast. The play's the thing, quoth he, though never did he deliver to us that speech he said he would prepare for our use in the plays. What matter it concerned, the whys and wherefores, and whether the Dane has any merit as an author of plays, these must await further opportunity.

Our sojourn ended without more ado and we were well bestowed for our pains thither. The people of that kingdom are not so unlike our own in any outward show and I found their countryside to be a fertile place of order and abundance. Still, to amuse my fellows on our homeward journey, I penned this child's rhyme:

> Lust, they say, dwells in France and Spain,
> From the poorest peasant to the Prince's train.
> But s'truth in Denmark, riot serves,
> Where he that drinks most, most deserves.[44]

And coz, truth to tell, 'tis the voyages by ship that I found most thrilling: after some brief discomfort of the stomach, which most of our Company did suffer withal (and some lice in the bedding), I found life onboard ship most agreeable.

My training at the hand of Mr. Perkin proceeds apace and, if it seem not too proud, I may say mine efforts please him, both alone and in company. He is now of a mind to teach me the art of Character, Humours, and Gesture, using certain speeches that best illustrate each point of the player's craft. I bid him teach me the rest of the Dane's speech, for I marveled much at the effect it had upon the Court and even those in our Company who have heard more speeches in their lifetime than thy gray mare has hairs in her mane. He set it out for me without benefit of pen or paper, but rather showed me a method of movement upon the stage (our stage on ship being a pitching deck of stout English oak washed in the breath of the mighty sea!) whereby a rhythm is created, a pattern I might say, that aids the memory most miraculously. I am at a loss to describe the practice beyond this, but at some future leisure will show it to thee, and Mr. Perkin counsels me sweetly on the manner of speech, upon arriving at the end of such movements:

"Now Will, as I have many times told thee, speak the speech trip-ing-ly on the tongue." He made a seat on a coil of rope that was fastened in the main to a gun'l, making a handsome couch for him to recline upon, and pulled the hood of his cloak over his silver head, somehow remaining dry as an old apple. I began the first few lines and the movement that accompanies them.

"But if thou dost mooouuuuthhhh it..." quoth he, to prevent me from further offense. I began again, this time less forcefully, concentrating instead on keeping my feet upon the heaving, slippery stage. Mine arms flung wildly at times, to keep my body steady and upright.

"Nor do not saw the air too much with thy hand, thus, but use all gently, Will." Indeed he used me more gently than he might, sucking on a pipe of tobacco that had long since lost his fire, using the stem to delicately draw a portrait in the air, an example of the degree he sought to see in mine own gestures. "For even in a whirlwind of passion, thou must use a temperance that may give it... smooooothhhhhhnessss."

I continued, finding myself raising my voice from deep within the lungs as he had taught me, that I might be heard over the roar of the sea, which seemed to hiss me as no pack of spectators had ever done to real players. I finished the first part of the speech and it seemed to please:

"Well said, Will, well done. Remember, if thou dost please not the multitude with thy playing, thou must ignore it and think only on the life of the man thou art portraying in that instant. Now this overdone may make the unskillful laugh, but it will likewise make the judicious grieve, the opinion of whom must o'erweigh a whole theatre of fools. O, it offends me to the soul to hear a robustious fellow tear a speech to rags, to please the ears of the savages that stand upon the ground, who for the most part, Will, only applaud your dumbshows and noise. I prithee, avoid it."

With this encouragement, I thought about the piteous Priam, whose story I sought to tell on this salt-misted stage, and finished Aeneas' passionate plea for justice.[45] I found mine own tears mixed easily with those of the sea upon my face as I came to the end of the speech and sank to my knees as Mr. Perkin had instructed. The sun had not peeked his golden head above his misty bedsheets this whole morning, nor all of yesterday, adding a pallor to the scene that would have drawn pity from any spectator, even if Aeneas had uttered nary a syllable.

Mr. Perkin clicked his fingers, a sure sign he was pleased: "Most excellent, proud Aeneas! Thy last dozen or so lines, the crux of the matter, there wert thou subtle, but not too tame neither. That were good, for tis best not to o'erstep the modesty of Nature, for in the main, the purpose of playing is to hold a mirror up to Nature herself."

I thanked him kindly, soaking in his praise, even as my cloak absorbed the spray, head to toe. The master is quick to spy the fault, slow to speak approval. He bade me sit upon his hempen cushion and continued his discourse, drifting to another time and place it seemed: "O, there be players that I have seen play - - and heard others praise highly - - men that have so strutted and bellowed, that I have thought some ham-fisted apprentice had made them, they imitated humanity so abominably."

"I hope I shall reform that, sir, if given the chance to display these lessons you have bestowed upon me, someday on a real stage."

He poked his pipe's stem in my chest: "O, reform it altogether and thou shalt have more hours upon our stage than a priest has droning out the mass. An' if the part call for clowning instead of passion, speak no more than is set down for thee, for some necessary question of the play may be lost and that's most villainous. Go, speak the speech again."

With such like advice at each pass, he bade me perform the speech some twenty times over, each time refining this point or that, until he declared me fit to play it before any observer, even Her Majesty!

"Think you so, master? O shall I see the Court?"

"I doubt it not, young Will, and never more thereafter wilt thou content thyself with pastures and market towns. Nay, there is no place like the pure air around Her Majesty. Truly, never to have been to the Court is to be damned, like an ill-roasted egg, burnt all on one side."

"Are the people in London so different, Master? I have heard from my father that no man nor woman was to be trusted in the City."

"Never to have been in London thou wilt never see good manners. Never to see good manners, then thy manners are wicked; wickedness is sin and sin is damnation, therefore not to have seen London is to be in parlous danger!"

I could not in that instant tell if he were in jest or no, but my wide eyes betrayed me and he could no longer feign a scowl, but fell out laughing, sucking on his empty pipe from one corner of his mouth while clacking out his sermon from the other corner.

"I mean, the manners of town are as ridiculous in the Country as behaviour of the Country is most mockable in the City. For example, I salute not in town, but kiss hands. Now that courtesy would be most foul if city folk were shepherds, would it not?!"

Recalling mine own hands after a day with my father's sheep, I took his meaning plainly. For two hours and more, these and sundry other subtleties of life in the City and before the Court he described, rounding out my lesson. And though it were cold and wet and he had no assurance that his pearls were not cast before some country swine, yet does he spend another hour each day teaching me to play the recorder, how to govern the ventages with my fingers and thumb, how to give it breath and make it discourse most eloquent music from the lowest note to the top of the little fife's compass and therein a most excellent voice that a'times summons forth the nightingale and other times the fair voice of a maiden.

My lessons this day ended, I am tasked to those few duties yet assigned to the johannes (repairs to our furniture and the like). What I report next is, as they say, saving the best for last: for after all had supped, talk turned to our arrival tomorrow in Dover. Our Company was joined below decks by some that labour on the ship. I swear that God or some hand of Fate has put me aboard this ship, for several of these sailors have ventured to the New World and know first-hand of those that have been made men with great fortunes for their perils and pains thither! Herewith one such story, told to me but an hour since, that shows mine own compass is pointed in the right direction. A young sailor called Gurney asked first: "Is the wind westerly that blows?"

"It was, but now leans more toward nor'west," replied Alfred, the senior mate, coming below after completing his day's duties (or 'watch', these men call it). "Me self, I was born under just such wind."

"Was it so?" Gurney appeared to be something like me, eager, sponge-like, to take any secrets from the older master. Alfred then pulled a bung from a barrel, with two mighty fingers, that not two minutes before I could not budge with two hands. He poured himself a measure of water and drank, saying then:

"Aye, so says me father, he that nearly died the night I was born, hauling the lines and clasping himself to the mast of his ship, enduring a sea that almost burst the deck 'neath his boots. Ne'er was wave nor wind more violent, and from the tackle God his self plucked off a canvas-climber and heaved him o'erboard."

The cabin fell silent, save for the incessant creaking and groaning of wood and nails that begged to be free. Darkness had long since taken prisoner our modest cabin, with two filthy lanterns all that separated us from the pitch black of night. Every man of us turned the light of our eyes upon old Alfred to learn the fate of his father's shipmate.

"'Ha! Wilt out 'afore thine indenture?' quoth me father. But ere the lad could fall to his certain doom 'neath the next MOUNTAINOUS wave, me father hurls his self broadside, swinging from a line, and..."

All leaned forward, the better to hear the verdict. Alfred paused to finish his drink slowly, a born actor, I'll warrant.

"...and he SNATCHES the boy from Death's grasp. Aye, that he did. Then whistles the bo'sun for more men; then calls out the master, trebling their confusion, but with a sturdy industry, all hands skip from stem to stern and haul me father and his sopping burden back aboard the pitching deck. Such was the night I was born, lads."

Gurney had not closed his mouth the entire time that Alfred spoke, nor did he for several minutes thereafter. The old sailor peeled away layers of damp clothing and cast about the cabin for a biscuit, not that I could tell how he meant to eat one, his head the throne of no more than three good teeth in all.

"Master Alfred," quoth I. "Were you ever in the New World?"

"Ha! You'll be thinking of riches, am I right? Save your breath, for no man cares a flea's buttock for the New World, lest he be dreaming of gold and jewels and such. Aye, lad, I've made a journey thence, and only God knows why I am spared to tell the tale, when so many of my ship mates were not."

More men of the watch came below and their fellows went above decks, with few words, to their stations, each man knowing his duty, having changed places, clock-like, a thousand thousand times before. A few of our Company, Masters Kempe and Phillips among them, had lingered to hear the tale, Phillips perhaps thinking to collect a few morsels for another ballad. Gurney gave his portion of ale to Alfred, perhaps to loosen the tale from his lips, who nodded and soaked his biscuit withal. Proud-sitting, more erect, now that his beholders included a nobleman's servants in person, Alfred unfolded the following, as best I can recall the particulars:

"Look ye then, not long after that Christopher Columbus had claimed the West Indies for Spain, John Cabot and Sebastian, his son, became the first founders of that great tract of land stretching from the cape in the south called Florida unto those lands we now call Newfoundland in the north, all of which could be annexed unto the crown of England. In faith, whensoever afterwards the Spanish did attempt any voyage into Florida or those regions northward, they proved most unhappy, as if God had prescribed limits unto their Spanish nation, which they might not exceed. Therefore, three year ago, when I set sail under the watchful eye and gracious person of Sir Humphrey Gilbert for these, Her Majesty's rightful possessions, it was a voyage undertook for the western discovery of America itself, our General instructed to inhabit and possess at his choice all remote and heathen lands not in actual possession of any other Christian prince. Look ye: many notable gentlemen joined this expedition, to gain a share of the glory and the gold that all knew awaited them, preparing at their own expense five fine English ships."

At this he stroked his tattered beard, that he might more easily draw the names of each vessel from his memory, marking the air with every particular:

"The Bark Raleigh at 200 tons, set forth by no less than Sir Walter himself, though he did not join the journey in his own person; the Delight at 120 tons; the Golden Hind and the Swallow at 40 tons each, myself among the crew of the Hind; and the Squirrel at a mere 10 tons.[46] In all, we numbered near 300 men, including smiths for the gold and silver we sought. Also for the solace of our people and the allurement of the savages, were we provided with music of every sort and trade goods, petty haberdashery and such like. Now, thus provisioned, we sailed forth on a Tuesday, after prayers, in the middle of June, but our force was stricken not two days later when the Bark Raleigh forsook us, returning home to Plymouth despite the fair wind and seas, owing to a sickness that had taken near all aboard the ship."

Sickness on ships, I take it, is common: our ship smelled below decks no fairer than that vessel which had carried us to Denmark, but on this night Mr. Kempe was especially foul, farting with every pitch of the deck, wave upon wave, and others were vomiting. A sailor opened a hatch on the lee side and several of his fellows grumbled, Alfred raising his voice that no man would lose the value of even one word of his tale:

"THIS was seen as an ILL-OMEN, look ye, losing our most mighty vessel, and knowing that Mr. Raleigh spared no cost in setting her forth. Added to that, soon after, we became enshrouded in mists and fog, losing the company of each other's vessels in the great wide ocean and within a fortnight, we were joined instead by great floating islands of pure ice rising hundreds of feet above our highest mast."

"Ice, say you?" asked Gurney, his mouth wide open yet again.

"ICE, I say!" Alfred was pleased that his listeners were now so attentive (I cannot attest to the truth of a mountain of ice larger than a ship, but I am certain Alfred said as much). "At last we came upon a great bank, well short of Newfoundland herself, but there was no mistaking these famous fishing grounds by the incredible multitude of sea fowl hovering over the area, diving and hunting for their own meat. From this amazing place, we held a southerly course until we found land and the goodly port of St. Johns, where we were also reunited with our sister ships in the fleet, all unharmed, by the grace o'God. Marching our great force onto the land, Sir Humphrey called together the masters and gentlemen of the various fishing and merchant vessels already at anchor there, those of a dozen other lands, and gave notice of his claim to the territory in Her Majesty's name. Whereas no other Christian prince had taken such claim, excepting some idle French who claim all things they have heard of but never seen, the thirty or more vessels in the harbor accepted this declaration and new sovereignty."

"Aye, the French are notorious fops, traitors and buggers of sheep," quoth one of the sailors, chewing the life back into a leathern piece of dried meat. All nodded approvingly, for though every mother's son of us had different stars governing our births, and very different fates and fortunes ahead, every man present loved his country and her Queen and those sovereign lands claimed by both. Alfred continued:

"Sir Humphrey gave word that these lands would henceforth be governed by three laws mainly. First, that all public celebration of any religion be that of the Church in England and no other ... "

At this, a few grumbled, betraying their sentiments about this true religion or that one, but no man spoke his mind aloud.

"Second, that if any man take action 'gainst Her Majesty's title to these lands, that he be adjudged and EXECUTED as if a case of the highest treason according to the laws of England; and third, that if any person should utter words sounding to the dishonour of Her Majesty, he should lose his ears and have his ship and goods confiscated. Obedience was quickly promised by general voice and afterwards was erected in that place the arms of England, engraven in lead, and infixed upon a pillar of wood for all to see."

"Lead? LEAD?? What of the gold?" Gurney, impatient as I was myself, but he more bold in the asking. Alfred, caroused the last of the ale and waved the mug in hopes another man would refill it from his portion, but proceeded even dry.

"Well, I'll come to that presently. Now in that which we do call Newfoundland, the heat in summer there is somewhat greater than the similar season in England, while the snow is many times deeper, with more extraordinary cold, than our own in winter. The savages there around are harmless and they are recompensed for their survival in these harsh conditions by an incredible quantity and variety of fish such as trouts, salmon, cod, bonito, lobsters, oysters with pearls in them, whales with great stores of sweet oils, and the biggest herring that ye have hitherto seen for the taking, but these were not of most interest to our company."

"Nor to us, 'Fred,'" quoth Gurney, with the encouragement of those assembled. Alfred gave him a box on the ear for his impertinence and disrespectful manner of address. Someone had found another measure of ale, which upon receipt thereof, Alfred seemed to calm himself. I made careful note of the places he named, such that I might find them on my map thereafter.

"Sir Humphrey was most curious, nearly as much as you lad, curious in the search of metals, commanding the mineral men and refiners to be especially diligent. After each search, they brought to him a store of iron, lead and copper, along with other ores and metals that were not spoken of outside the gentlemen's ranks. E'en so, we all soon knew that they had found both gold and silver in great quantities, but our General would not speak of it openly, for fear that merchants and fishermen of other countries, chiefly the Portuguese and Spaniards, might hear of our discoveries and send their own forces to claim it from us."

The mention of gold and silver leant a solemnity to our proceedings, and Alfred perceived this power over his parishioners. He lingered over his ale and over each mention of valuables, as the stern bishop lectures his flock on Sunday over the value of their immortal souls.

"Now look ye: e'en some of our own soon were infected with greed and set about plotting mischief, to take their fill of gold and silver, attending time and means to return home by such shipping as daily departed from this coast laden with fish. These traitors were soon discovered and set in irons, but others drew together and made their way to an adjoining harbor, there to commandeer a ship, setting ashore the small crew and making off with the vessel. Others were sick of the fluxes [*dysentery*] and many died. In brief, by one means and another, our company was diminished. It seemed good therefore to our General to send off the Swallow with such provision as might be spared for transporting home the sick and mutineers. The General then ordered ourselves to search this coast for more treasure of the land in honour of Her Majesty. We sailed some week or a bit more, in the warmth of August, but shrouded constantly in fog. Like the swan that sings before her death, the men in the Delight continually sounded trumpets and drums and fifes, that we might follow her the better even though we could not see her. Then came the rain and ever thicker mist, such that we could not see a cable's length before us. Master Cox, in the Squirrel, looking out, discerned white cliffs and cried out 'LAND', immediately giving a blast of trumpet to warn off the Delight, which being the greater ship was in most danger from rocks or shoals, if in fact we be that close to land. But before they knew the danger, they felt the same, striking ground, and soon after her stern and hinder parts were BEATEN to PIECES by waves. In this distress, we desired to save the men by every possible means, but all in vain, since God determined their ruin."

I felt compelled to ask if all were lost, none saved from the great ship, to which he replied simply:

"None. And this was a heavy and grievous event, to lose at one blow our chief ship freighted with provision, but more was the loss of our men, which perished to a number of almost an hundred of souls. Those in the frigate were already pinched, chiefly for want of clothes, whereupon we beseeched the General to return to England before we all should perish. To us of the Golden Hind, they made signs of our distress, pointing to their mouths and thin, ragged clothes, such that we grew to be of the same mind and desire to return home. So, on the last day of August, with Sir Gilbert agreeing that we had seen what we came to see and done much likewise, we changed our course and headed back to England."

Gurney was shaking somewhat at this fearful tale, seeking some measure of hope: "But then came you safely home, not so?"

Alfred, leaning against the bulkhead and looking upward as if to see again that moment, afloat upon another sea, another time, replied with a more fearful report: "Not so fast, lad. The wind was large and the seas rough, insomuch as the frigate wherein our General rode was nearly swallowed up.

The General came aboard the Hind to have the surgeon dress his foot, which he had hurt by treading upon a nail. So, agreeing to carry lights always by night, that we might keep together, he departed to his frigate, being by no means entreated to tarry in the Hind, which had been better for his security, but instead the General replied that he would not forsake the company of the frigate going homeward, with whom he had passed so many storms and perils, despite that the vessel was considered by the best seamen among us to be unseaworthy, being overladen with guns and minerals, chiefly our gold."

"Why did they not throw overboard those guns, heavy burdens which availed them nothing on a homeward journey?" Gurney asked, and Alfred grew something perturbed at what he clearly deemed a question of little merit.

"Have ye no care to what such appurtenances cost? And what if the Spanish or Portuguese or another of our sworn enemies might come upon us in the night and seek to deal mischief to us? The next day dawned foul and the seas rough, but we saw the General sitting abaft reading a book and he cried to us on the Hind that we are as near to Heaven at sea as on land, and that no man should fear for his safety. But the rains came again, and by midnight of that same day, the frigate being ahead of his, suddenly her lights went out and she was swallowed entirely by the sea. Yet still we looked out all that night for any sign of her or her men, but never saw we any."

Alfred paused to let the enormity of the loss sink into every man's drowsy head. The drama of the tragedy apparent, which might have moved the softer among us to tears, was broken by another of Mr. Kempe's epic fffffaaaarrrrts. Several moved closer to the open hatch and Alfred completed his tale:

"In a great torment of weather and peril of drowning, it pleased God to send safe home only the Golden Hind, which arrived in Falmouth the 22nd day of September, being Sunday. All the men tired with tediousness of so unprofitable voyage, much toil, hard diet, and continual hazard of their life, even so thanked God in reasonable contentment for the gift of our lives. But every man present swore an oath never to return to those vile lands again, whatsoever we might be offered for undertaking such a voyage, for truly there be naught to discover in the New World except hardship and death."

Silence lay about our number, no man more capable of speech than the coils of rope or the wooden blocks that hung in the cabin. Of an instant, a lantern that had been heaving to and fro all the while, came loose and bounced off of Gurney's head, landing on a barrel that some used for a table. To our amazement, it neither broke nor lost its fire, and Alfred calmly plucked it from off its perch and set himself to lashing it more securely to the beam above.

I asked: "Did no one come back a rich man?"

Mr. Kempe chastised me: "Didst not hear the man's story?"

"Yes, that I did, sir," quoth I, careful to give no offence, nor to let on that I was disheartened by the thought that a man could risk life and soul and come back a pauper, if he were counted among the lucky ones who return at all. But one of the sailors, who had come below in the midst of Alfred's telling, may have heard my secret thoughts, saying loudly:

"Awwww, shyte in thy mouth, Fred. Many's the man who found riches o'er the sea and lived to spend what he earned!"

This sailor was the slenderest man I had seen on a ship, not only in body, but lacking any bulk in his shoulders or arms, where most sailors need their strength. Yet I had seen this fellow climb full to the top of the mainmast in less time that can we say a psalm on Sunday and, what's more, I have seen him raise a great wet canvas by himself, with no other by him. I never heard his name, but the ship's master called him Pidge. He took over the place of comfort that had been newly vacated by Alfred, who still fussed over the errant lantern, and spake thus:

"I labored a six month 'board a privateer sent out by Mr. Raleigh. We captured for ransom one Spaniard, Don Pedro de some-lordship-or-'nother, who told of an unexplored Indian kingdom twixt the great rivers of the Spanish Americas and of a great and golden city on an island in an inland lake, which the Spaniards call El Dorado, but the naturals call Manoa.[47] This Don Pedro knew of that place by a sailor called Juan, which in our better English tongue means John, the only survivor of a party what rowed up the lesser river and who his-self was took by the Indians thither, whereat he beheld the treasure with his own eyne [eyes] and on his deathbed swore it to be true in the presence of his priest."

"Not that any Christian in England would accept the oath of a papist," quoth Mr. Johnson, who had suddenly appeared from the darkest recess of the after part of the cabin. He may have been there all along, but like many times in our travels, he seemed to appear whenever a comment was made that might be called, by your common man, as scurrilous or in any wise traitorous against Her Majesty. Johnson stood forth, as if expecting a challenge, and held the stage until we all said 'amen'. Gurney, still rubbing the top of

his head where the lantern had landed, then demanded to know if this treasured isle was ever found, to which Pidge replied plainly:

"Nay. Or if t'was, no man would tell another living soul, for fear that
e'en his neighbor would kill him in's sleep to get a piece of such wealth. But
two year ago, last April, I set out on another voyage to the New World and
we found great stores of such wealth."

I bid Pidge to tell all, and he was most agreeable to continue his oratory:

"Well, as I say, t'were the spring when we departs, two barks well furnished of men and victuals, at the expense of Sir Walter Raleigh, knight.
By June we were fallen in at the islands of the West Indies, keeping a more
southerly course than was needful, because we doubted that the current of
the Bay of Mexico had been of greater force than afterward we found it to
be." While this bit of seamanship eluded my comprehension, the other sailors nodded and grunted their several agreement.

"At these islands, we found the air very unwholesome and our men
grew for the most part ill disposed; so that having refreshed ourselves with
sweet water and fresh victuals we departed not more than the twelfth day
after our arrival thither. And glad of it we were too, for within a fortnight,
found we shoal water, where we smelt so sweet, and so strong a smell, as if
it had been in the midst of some delicate garden, by which we were assured
that the land could not be far distant; and keeping good watch, and bearing
but slack sail, within two day we arrived upon the coast, which we supposed to be a continent and firm land, and we sailed along the same for an
hundred or more English miles before we could find any entrance or river
issuing to the sea. The first that appeared to us we entered, though not without some difficulty, and cast anchor about three arquebus [*rifle*] shot within
the haven's [*harbor's*] mouth."

Gurney, growing impatient with the telling of tales that made him not
a minute wiser nor an hour richer, demanded: "Then sawest thou gold in
the water?"

Pidge removed his damp woolen cap, revealing a head as bald as a pig's,
but adorned with most colourful tattoos and most grievous scars: "Hush,
lad, I'll bring thee to port when the wind is fair. This land we found to be but
an island of twenty or so miles long and not above six miles broad. Under
the hill whereon we stood, we beheld valleys replenished with goodly cedar
trees and, having discharged our arquebus, such a flock of cranes, the most
part white, with such a cry redoubled by many echoes, as if an army of men

had shouted together. Aye, this island had many goodly woods full of deer, rabbit, and fowl, even in the midst of summer, in incredible abundance."

"Sawrr ye no nekkid savages, Pidge?" asked one of the sailors, who had appeared asleep until that moment, swaying in his hammock.

"Aye, so we did. Our third day we saw one small boat rowing toward us, having in it one man, his person barely covered, making show that he would visit us and showing no fear or doubt. Now, their boats are a thing to behold, made of one tree, either of pine or pitch tree. They know no tools such as we might use to make them withal, but have a manner that be most ingenious: they fell a great tree and put gum or resin upon one side thereof, thenset fire to it, and when it hath burnt hollow, they cut out the coal with their shells, and by this means fashion very fine boats, such as will transport 20 men. But as I said, this boat that is come to speak with us held but one such savage. After he spoke of many things not understood by us, we brought him with his own good liking aboard our ship and gave him a shirt, a hat and some other things, and made him taste of our wine and our meat, which he liked very well. Soon he departed, but when he was a modest distance hence, he began fishing and, in less than half an hour, his boat was laden, and these fish he brought to us and made signs to divide it between our two ships, and thus requiting the gifts received of us, departed from our sight. The next day, there came unto us divers of these selfsame boats, and in one of them the King's own brother, as we were made to know, accompanied by 40 or 50 men, very handsome and goodly people, and in their behaviour as mannerly and civil as any of Europe. The king is called Wingina and the country called Wingandacoa, and now, by Her Majesty, called Virginia."

"Amen," quoth Mr. Johnson. Pidge, vexed somewhat by the intrusion, continued unabated, almost without taking a breath, as was his manner of speech:

"AFTER he had made a long speech unto us, we presented him with divers trinkets, which he received very joyfully and thankfully."

"O Pidge, yer bow is bent; let loose the arrah! Tell us of their GOLD and other tree-shurs," yelled the swaying sailor.

"Silence, Phillip Prichard! I'll bring thee there ere long. Now, where was I?"

"The king's brother made a speech," quoth I.

"Aye, the king's brother, whose name we understood as Grangamino, well, as I say, the king is greatly obeyed and his brothers reverenced. The king himself came not, for he was newly wounded in a fight with the king of the next country, struck in two places of the body clean through, but yet he recovered, so we fell to trading with Grangamino, exchanging things that we had for native chamois, buff, and deerskins. When we showed him all our packet of merchandise, of all the things he saw, a bright tin dish most pleased him, which he presently took up and clapped before his breast, and after made a hole in the brim thereof and hung it about his neck, making signs that it would defend him against his enemies' arrows, for as I have said, his people maintain a terrible and deadly war with their neighbors. Our tin dish we exchanged for twenty skins - - worth twenty crowns, if a farthing at all - - and a copper kettle for fifty skins, worth fifty crowns! They offered us good exchange for our hatchets and axes and for knives and would have given any thing they owned for our swords, but these we would not part withal. After three days more, Grangamino brought his wife and daughters to us. The wife was very well favoured, of mean stature, and very bashful. She had on her back a cloak of leather with the fur side next to the body, and before her breasts another piece of the same. About her forehead was a band of white coral and in her ears, bracelets of pearls hanging down to her middle and whose bigness was that of large peas. Grangamino wore upon his head a broad plate of gold or copper, for being unpolished we knew not what metal it should be, neither would he by any means suffer us to take it from off his head, but feeling it, it would bow very easy."

Gurney was now greedily swallowing the tale: "Then gold it was, sure. Aye, your gold, of all your metals, is the most delicate."

Pidge would brook no further interruption: "Gold, says ye? As if thou hast ever touched a golden object in thy whole, sodden life? Now, where was I? N'er you mind. I recall it. I was about to say, that Grangamino had a great liking for our armour, a sword, and divers other things which we had, and ... he then lay ... a great box of ... PEARLS in gage [*exchange*] for them!"

We nodded approval, but my mind's eye could only see a great box of pearls before me, where in faith nought but a tub of filthy bitumen stood. Pidge told us more:

"Every day Grangamino brought to us a brace or two of fat bucks, hares, and fish, the best in the world, and divers fruits, nuts, gourds and their corn, which is very white and well-tasted. They cast merely a seed upon the ground and in no more than ten days is it fourteen inches high."

"Corn? Corn? Who gives a fig for corn? What of the gold that adorned the King's brother then?"

"Patience, man, patience. After they had been many times aboard our ships, myself, with seven more of our men, went twenty mile up the river and come by the evening to an island which they call Roanoke, at which was a village built of cedar and fortified around with sharp trees to keep out their enemies. The wife of Grangamino came running out to meet us, very cheerfully and friendly. When we were come in, she caused us to sit by a great fire and after took off our clothes and washed them and dried them again. Some of the women plucked off our stockings and washed them, while some washed our feet in warm water."

"What more did they wash for ye, Pidge?" asked the sailor Prichard, laughing lustily (as which of us then did not?). Pidge plucked his thumb at this interruption and continued:

"She brought us to the inner rooms, where she set on a board some kind of wheat, sodden venison, roasted fish, and boiled melons. We found the people most gentle, loving and faithful, void of all guile and treason. But enough of this: now to their treasures! Here too was a great store of mussels in which there are pearls. These and more would they trade for any one of our weapons, for when we discharged any piece they would tremble thereat, for very fear and for the strangeness of the same, for their own weapons are but bows and arrows and a kind of club, in the end whereof they fasten the sharp horns of a stag or other beast. When they go to wars, they carry about with them their idol, of whom they ask counsel. But short tale to make, all of their pearls and what store of gold they could muster, all of this would they trade for our iron goods, swords and ordnance."

"Did thy General make such a trade and bring every man back his treasure?" asked Pilchard.[48]

"Nay, nay, he thought it best to report these findings to Her Majesty and return only with those items which the naturals had bestowed us withal. We returned safely in September, thereby proving how commodious and pleasant is the journey to the Americas and how comely and servile are the natives thereabouts, for did we not bring home with us a great store of valuable skins and pearls and reports of yet greater treasures? And two of the savages did we bring back with us, being lusty men, whose names are Wanchese and Manteo." I then asked if these two were still alive in London (think how I might learn of them where to find greater wealth in their country!). But Pidge knew not:

"Yet have I heard that they have been a'times favourites at Court and have learned our English tongue and manners, to the amazement and delight of all who behold them and the greater glory of God, who makes all things possible, even the betterment of savages." So ended the oration of Pidge.

Every man, then not on watch, made for his sundry sleeping quarters and I could think only of the promise of riches that the New World so clearly offered. To be sure, I was now more informed of the dangers, after hearing the hardships of one excursion thither, but the ghosts of those who have lately perished from Plague know the dangers of life itself, wherever we live, is that not so? And though some perished in the enterprise, did not those who returned earn goodly sums and see yet greater treasure in the Americas, there for the taking if they dare to return? Better to hazard all and be surrounded with wealth and comfort, or die in trying. Well, so say I!

Wedged in a corner, out of sight of my comrades, I lit a stub of candle that had no more than five minutes life left in her, I scoured my secret map: imagine, if thou canst, my delight in locating St. Johns and Virginia on the map, the great fishing grounds we heard thereof, the vast sea that separates our land from thence. Finding yet no trace of El Dorado or Manoa, my light burned out. My mind's eye of these places never will!

Now am I resolved! I need not wait to arrive in London to find passage to the New World. Surely these sailors or their kind in Dover will point me toward a ship, perhaps no farther than that selfsame harbor. I will use my player's skill to con the manners and speeches of these sailors and present myself to any ship bound for the New World as a man of their number. If I cannot write to thee soon again, it is because I have made it to a ship and will pray this letter gets to its destination with that explanation.

In the mean season, poor Dick is fouling the deck with his half-digested supper, telling me how to dispose of his worldly goods and demanding my pledge to care for his lady love in London, certain he will die of a dread foreign disease contracted by life aboard the ship, and cannot be comforted to think he suffers merely from the sea-sickness. He would never toil at sea, but one of these hearty lads would I be, to make my way to the Americas before all her riches are collected by others, God willing.

Kiss my boy and maids in my name, good coz, and omit nothing else which thine honour deem'st best for their tender need. I am thine ever loving servant in all else, Will.

LETTER SIX
November 11, 1586

Wherein the Virgin Queen is attacked by foreign dogs and the Shake-speares find their kinsman's head on a pike.

Letter Six was possibly written when Shakespeare was drunk and homesick. It is full of secrets revealed, fears and fates decided. Whatever his motivation for committing his innermost thoughts and emotions to paper, we are the voyeuristic beneficiaries.

Rather than speaking to his friend John Combe, much of this letter is written directly to his son Hamnet, describing friends and neighbors in Stratford and his own youth as a boy in school. Shakespeare speaks lovingly of his father as a man of stature, a fine tradesman, and reveals the cause of his family's misfortunes.

Shakespeare's mother Mary is an Arden, a once well-to-do Catholic family. As we have seen, Catholicism had been the primary Christian faith of England until Henry VIII (Queen Elizabeth's father) created the Protestant Church in England. As Robert Dudley, a local nobleman, rose to become Queen Elizabeth's favorite and an outspoken defender of the new Church, his star eclipsed that of the Ardens, who were loyal to the Queen, but who nonetheless remained Catholic. Robert Dudley was ultimately made the Earl of Leicester. Ironically, Shakespeare is now a servant in the Earl's playing company, which is making its way to London to entertain that same Queen.

As an Earl, Leicester found ways to punish the Arden family and all their relations, including the Shakespeares. Ultimately, the Ardens were completely ruined when a member of their clan was tortured and confessed to helping a failed plot to assassinate Queen Elizabeth in 1583 (a plot that attempted to put the Catholic Mary Queen of Scots on the throne of England). Shakespeare chillingly describes the bloody cost of such disloyalty and thereafter how his father was forced to hide from public life with little estate or wealth to sustain his family. These must have been startling and sobering lessons for a young man of nineteen, himself newly married and the father of a newborn daughter.

As Leicester's Men complete their summer tour, having performed around towns in England and Denmark, they hear of another plot to assassinate the Queen and replace her with Catholic Mary, foiled by Elizabeth's capable spymaster Sir Francis Walsingham. Warned to always look over his shoulder, Shakespeare feels keenly the capriciousness of a fate that hinges upon the shifting religious allegiances of the time, observing "thus lives every man in some fear that his faith might be embraced or spurned, one day to the next, and if he chooses wrong, he too could lose his head in an instant."

Shakespeare must deal with secrets and lies much closer to home. His plan to strike out to the New World is discovered, but he may have gained a new ally as a result: Master Will Kempe, the famous clown of Leicester's Men. As in other letters, I felt a tug on the sleeve of my memory in reading certain passages of Letter Six and a little detective worked paid dividends. In *Pericles* (Act IV, scene 2) Shakespeare writes a description of a brothel very similar to Kempe's story in this letter. This could be an important clue to the authorship of that play, which some scholars believe may not have been primarily written by Shakespeare.

A play that is generally accepted to be written by Shakespeare, *As You Like It,* came to mind immediately however, because elements of what later became the famous "Seven Ages of Man" speech (Act II, scene 7) are evident as Shakespeare muses over the future of his son (a speech I have performed countless times, always summoning the essence of this letter in my imagination).

I noticed too that even some minor characters in Shakespeare's plays had their origins in his early observations of people and professions. Kempe refers to a "Mistress Doll" and Shakespeare later writes a bawdy character, Doll Tearsheet, in *Henry IV part 2*. Equally memorable is the apothecary in *Romeo and Juliet* (Act V, scene 1), who seems to be based on a neighbor in Stratford that

Shakespeare warns his son about. Finally, the wisdom of a tanner is repeated by a gravedigger in *Hamlet* (Act V scene 1) when he opines about the way a body can be preserved for a long time beneath the earth if properly preserved.

When I mentioned a few of these clues and discoveries to Miss B one evening, she asked me if I thought Shakespeare's recording of detailed conversation in the letters was because he planned to use them in future plays or if it was just his habit in writing letters, a habit which led him inexorably to his new career.

Oddly, I hadn't thought about how unusual it was to capture so much dialogue in a letter, perhaps because what Shakespeare recorded was so fascinating. Most people, then as now, might write that a group of people were conversing about politics or someone's affair at the office, but wouldn't likely record the entire discussion. After spending nearly three decades inside Shakespeare's head, I can't honestly say I have answered Miss B's question, but I have concluded that his detailed recording of daily give-and-take offers evidence of his ear for dialogue and explains how he wrote many of his plays so quickly and apparently without many edits to early drafts.

Conversations of conflict, revelation, and irony abound in Letter Six. I found this to be one of the most thrilling letters in the entire collection and trust you will equally enjoy its myriad intricacies and hidden gems.

Martinmas, 11 November 1586, in the Coxcomb, Sittingbourne

Coz,

Hath the news yet reached Stratford? Surely hast thou heard of the traitor Sir Anthony Babington and his villainous plot against the life of Her Majesty. Here, there is talk of little else, and there are many travelers in leisure for conversation, mired as we are in mud and rain in this pisspot village (much rain wears down even marble, so it cannot surprise when it dissolves the roads and the spirits of men). Thou wouldst first know of me how it came that I have not yet found a ship bound for the Americas and thou wouldst be most amazed to learn how Fate has played me fair.

In Dover, we were not permitted to tarry, making all haste to London to present our list of plays for the Queen, as I have learned it is the custom at this time of year. When the way became impassable and we sought refuge in this tavern, Mr. Kempe bid me talk apart with him and I discovered then such a tale as could never be expected.

In truth, I know not what to think of Mr. Kempe. He would eat mutton on Fridays and wears his doublet carelessly, unbridled and often without the collar, yet he speaks most sweetly with the ladies and is the first to give a coin or an apple to the children.[49] He is also the first of our Company called for in every town. Some of our men said he was the cast-off son of a nobleman, but others claim him the son of a debtor who lived most of his life in the Hole [*prison*]. Such questions matter little when Mr. Kempe is seen on the stage, for there is he unequalled in his craft. The Kempe Jig uses two boys in a bawdy tale with song and dance and closes every one of our plays to great laughter and acclaim therefrom.

Now it is not his custom to share a bench with me, but today he did so suddenly, either to avoid the water dripping from so many parts of the ceiling or to speak in stricter confidence: "Virginity is at risk here, Will. Seest thou yon fat kitchen wench? She is called Mother Mary and e'en now she bid me to bed with her, demanding a fee. But o what a foul thought to bed with her: I'll swear that if she were an oil lamp, she could burn non-stop for a Polish winter." I laughed at his jest, but suspected he was merely sounding the bell for some weightier sermon to follow.

"Aye, if she lives till doomsday, she'll burn a month longer than the whole world," quoth he, slapping his shoe against the leg of the table that he might loosen the mud therefrom. "And note her face: black, like my shoe, though not exactly as clean!" I could not fathom why he spoke so ill of a woman he had known no longer than a quarter of an hour, although 'tis true she measured, I swear, no longer from head to foot than from hip to hip, spherical like a globe, and her appearance was weary and worn.

"Ha! I swear, thou canst smell out the nations of the globe in her," quoth he, leaning an elbow on the table and sketching the air with his finger pointed at her various parts. "In her buttocks, stands Ireland, thou'lt know it for certain by the smell! And Spain, I'll warrant thee, thou't smell in her hot breath! What sayest thou?"

"Thou hast … a great … imagination, Mr. Kempe." I should hold my peace when addressed by the masters, but here he had gone too far for me to say nothing. "But how she came hither, and why she is now so ill-used, may be a piteous matter, such that we are not Christians to make such sport of her."

To this reply, he slapped my back, and dropped his arm around my shoulder to pull me closer, lowering his voice to a whisper: "O Will, thou hast requited my trust many times over with that honest reply! Thou'rt in the right: 'tis a sin to speak so ill of a woman. I was but making assay of you, the reason whereof will shortly be apparent. But first, I must know thy mind further. Will, thou hast some skill at playing, but I'll warrant thou playest to the Earl of Leicester's Men themselves, not to the rank scented many in the halls where we perform. I have seen thee studying that map, which I take as the Americas, and those seas which separate them from England. I have noted with what greedy ear thou drink'st in the talk of the New World and the voyages thereto. In brief, Will, I would know what thou dost hunt: for a life among players is surely not thy quarry."

I knew not what to say, but he who stumbles at the threshold foretells that danger lurks within, so I did not dare to hesitate: "O Mr. Kempe, have I not pleased thee and the other masters with my labours these few months?"

"Tut, tut, the fashion of the times, for most men, is that none will sweat but for promotion. Thou, on the other hand, thou hast given us thine all and asked for nothing in return. Nay, Leicester's Men are glad of thee, but I would know thy mind, the better to give thee that recompense thou dost richly deserve, if it be in my power to grant."

Now was I even more amazed. Mr. Kempe has been kind and honest with me, but I knew not if it were wise for me to bare my soul, but I decided that a man's hopes can never be manifest, lest he show them the light of day and, since God gave me a voice for a reason, perhaps this was it. I therefore told him of my father's misery; of mine enforced marriage and lack of prospects at home; of the wrongs done to our family (though I omitted any blame on Lord Leicester, as that would seem too bold for mine own good to reveal too soon). I told him that I would seek my Fortune in the New World and thereby restore my family's name and place. I told him if I failed, I would die in the effort. I showed him the map, now crusty with sweat and wearing thin from so much scrutiny, and confessed my sin of its theft. O, and I begged his forgiveness if I had offended and asked his discretion with these my darkest secrets.

"Fear not, Will, thine intent be safe with me. We have much in common and I will requite thy honesty with a tale—and an earnest plea—that I will also trust thee to keep locked in thy heart till Fortune adjudge the matter."

"Mr. Kempe, that promise of me, thou hast."

"Then thus much have I to impart to thee: I have a sister, Kathleen, who I prize above any living soul. Like thy family, mine was fashioned under an evil moon and we were sent in tender youth, our parents dead, to make our way as ever we might. I weep to think on how she hath survived, how many lifetimes she hath lived in these her twenty tender years."

Mr. Kempe coughed and spat upon the floor, the smoky tallow that lit the scene burned our eyes and throats, but his face was pale with a private grief that made his eyes into reluctant well-springs. He rubbed some colour in his cheeks and continued with his story, one so full of pitiful brutality, sorrowful joy, and pious profanity that I cannot decide if he be a saint or the Devil incarnate, a man I should trust with my secrets, fears and hopes, or the last man on earth to hear my confession. His tale began when he was but twelve years old, an orphan placed in the employ of a London stew known to all, with not a small measure of insincerity, as the Hope.

"I was daily sent to search the market carefully, to find gallants who would pay the price for any one of our three wenches. But with such continual action, they were most pitifully sodden, not even as good as 'rotten', you might say. Aye, a strong wind would have blown them to pieces, so worn were they with work and the bringing up of some dozen bastards in our midst, and therefore only the drunkards would loosen a purse to force open such legs. Ah, but one winter's night, there came into the Hope a fine, strong young wench with a good face and excellent good clothes. Although she had a tongue, she could not speak withal, yet did she make known that her name was Grace and that hunger had brought her to our door and she would pay any price for such sustenance that might save her mortal coil. Mistress Doll soon learned she was a virgin and took her in, feeding her and instructing her what she must do, that she might not be raw in her entertainment. Grace did mildly protest, but Mistress Doll had oft bent such foolish saplings with her honey tongue, by telling them that they would never again know hunger, cold, thirst, or want of any kind; that they would taste gentlemen of all fashions and benefit from their generosity. Quickly did Mistress Doll counsel Grace on how best to wring every last farthing from a gentleman's purse. 'Thou hast fortunes coming upon thee,' said she. 'Mark me: thou must SEEM to do fearfully that which thou wilt commit willingly; SEEM to despise profit where thou hast most to gain. Weep that thou livest as thou dost, of painful necessity, to make pity in thy lovers. And that pity begets thee a good opinion, and that opinion an e'en better profit.' When all was settled, I was sent instantly into the market, having taken note of the marks of her, the colour of her hair; complexion; height; age; with warrant of her virginity to cry 'A virgin, a virgin: he that will give most shall have her first.' Such a maidenhead is most rare and no cheap thing in London, I'll warrant, so I did cry her particulars aloud, almost to the number of her hairs. I drew her picture with my voice, and with bawdy gestures ignited the passions of the gallants. O i'faith, especially the younger ones listened to me as they would have hearkened to their father's last testament. There was a Spaniard's mouth so watered, that he expired on her very description. I warrant, thunder shall not so awake the beds of eels, as did my giving out of her beauty stir up the lewdly-inclined."

At this, Mr. Kempe paused to call for more drink, as if to fortify himself, wiping spilt wine from his beard and tears from his eyes. "I'll warrant, no more than an hour passed that night before the virgin Grace was graced with her virginity no more, and as I had successfully bargained for the feast, I was given leave myself to cut a morsel off the spit. But I could not bring my manhood to his lusty form, nor my mind to such lascivious thoughts, so pitiful did young Grace appear after her first encounter."

Men's faults do seldom to themselves appear, so Mr. Kempe saw no sin in this trade, but rather the gnawing teeth of necessity by all of the players in this demi-drama. If he was born to a household of means, he had fallen from its favor or perhaps, like my own father, was forced to earn his living out of the house of a drunken spendthrift who had lost the family fortunes. In any wise, I cannot pass judgment on him, for he did not stay long in this employ after that night, but spoke of how he found his way to a company of players and a higher calling (though many call us no better than whores). He saw how the masses live through players on the stage and feed their appetites by watching the hunger and thirst of persons who they know are not real. When Mr. Kempe saw that the jigs fed the lust of the spectators, he made his jig to show the manner in which he sold the flesh of virgins and how his customers did then enjoy such women. I see his jig in a new light however: there be a sadness at the end, when the tumbler has spent himself in the dumbshow of it, not the satisfaction I had first thought it to signify.

I have learned much by listening to Mr. Kempe: the fool doth think he is wise, the wise man knows himself to be a fool. The boy Kempe did not plan to work in a brothel, any more than I knew I would be learning the player's craft today. Is he the man of tender courtesy to Rosalind Munday, she who came dressed as a man to warn us of the Plague? Or is he the lecher who bragged of seducing that widow in Dover? Of this latter, I shall never know, for that next day we were taken aboard ship and none of us had leave to go back into the town. Therefore too, I could not return the map: so am I a despicable thief, who steals from an old shopkeeper, or a faithful son who cleans jordans for players to find some way to restore his family's fortunes?

Mr. Kempe's youth in the brothel had made him hard in one wise, but he was often protective of those women who he saw in labour, with no husband, such creatures as this Mother Mary in the Coxcomb, whose existence was one of use and ill-use at the hands of men. But chief among those women he would protect, was his sister, Kathleen, whose life as an orphan was no easier than his, until she married, but Mr. Kempe now described how her life might be yet more in danger than ever.

"She hath taken a husband, a sailor who hath been on two voyages to the New World and brought her so many tales of bounty that they would leave in spring with a ship, provided for by Raleigh, to make a new life in a new world. I can by no means convince her to do otherwise, than to follow her man thither, and whatsoever tiny crack the door of doubt was open till now, it came rudely shut when she told me lately that she is with child and will by no means leave his side. They are bound for the Americas and I know not what shall become of her."

At this, his face disappeared behind two trembling hands. I sought to ease his burden with a hand to his shoulder and felt him shaking all over, though Lord knows the cold and rain that crept through every wall of the inn made all therein to shake in like manner.

"What wouldst thou have me do?"

"But this, Will. If thou art determined to go, I will bring thee to my sister and her husband and they can help thee join the fleet. Go then with them and share their fate, but swear thou wilt protect Kathleen at all cost, come what may. This is the reason I sounded thee out concerning thy true sentiments towards the fairer sex. Thou art an honest man in such things, I see. Therefore, do me this service and I shall provide those furnishings thou wilt need thither and will serve as thy protector in our Company, so long as thou dost remain."

"Marry I will, Mr. Kempe. I need no recompense of thee, but do this service gladly and am joyful to meet thy sister and find a party that will take me to the New World."

"Fairly said, Will, but I am in thy debt, upon which I will make here a down payment." Mr. Kempe had been speaking in a low voice to avoid any errant ear from catching our drift, but now he leaned closer and spoke in yet more church-like tones. "Will Johnson, we fear, is in service to the Queen's spymaster. He demurs when pressed and claims no greater loyalties than any other Englishman, but there have been those incidents in our Company which could only be explained if a spy lives among us, one who would root out any adherent to the old faith and reform them with persuasion or punishment. He hath told me he suspects thou art of a Catholic family and is ever watchful of thy speech. Be thou careful in his presence Will. This is no idle concern. Clarke's man was killed, we suspect, by agents of the Queen for being a Catholic priest, soon after Johnson learned of his true beliefs. That death was the vacancy in our Company thou hast filled. And now Clarke himself is hounded for his own defense of the old faith: need I say more?"

This was not my first warning about Mr. Johnson, but nothing so blunt about a fine player who seemed till now quite without malice, wearing his Roman robes about the playhouse long after the spectators are gone and quite fond of hearing his own voice. I would indeed have pressed Mr. Kempe for more intelligence about our fellows, and in whose presence I should guard my words, but Mr. Burbage stayed for all the Company at that moment in the neighbor hall, for there was news of the conspiracy against Her Majesty's life. Mr. Johnson had just then returned, from parts unknown, with a great deal of sweat upon his horse, despite the cold rain that had not stopped these three days. When all were gathered and hushed, Mr. Burbage set the scene:

"What news of the Queen? Is she well?"

"Aye, she is well, God be praised." Mr. Johnson surveyed the room like an old schoolmaster with birch twig in hand to whip any that does not say 'amen'. He shook out his cloak, showering every mother's son of us, and then pushed Bryan aside from the fire that he might dry himself the better. "But she has escaped certain death at the hands of traitors most foul."

"Most foul? What other manner of traitor is there, Mr. Johnson?" If Dick had been one step closer, or Mr. Johnson one hour younger, he would have replied with the back of his hand. As it was, he paid Dick no heed, but turned his back to the fire and rubbed his buttocks most furiously to warm them and to bring back their rose after so long in the saddle. He spoke only to the other masters, as I have noted he is wont to do, but we heard all, as did divers others, who had taken their meat that night with us in the inn.

"It falls out thus: Anthony Babington, of an ancient family, but grievously inclined to papistry, met for months most seditiously with half a dozen noble gentlemen else in London taverns to plot the death of Her Majesty and … " here he pauses for the drama, " … the enthronement of Mary, the Catholic Queen of Scotland, the puppet of Spain."

"I know a Babington," quoth Mr. Burbage. "Is not his family a trader in malt?"

"The same," quoth Mr. Johnson, pausing as if to mark this fact on a secret scroll hidden in some dark room within his brain.

"William, thou hast said nothing that we did not hear yesternight. Is there nothing new?" Mr. Perkin seemed unusually perturbed.

"Aye, there is. I have it on good report that this Babington unfolded his heart to the traitor Queen Mary in a letter that Walsingham's spies intercepted. The Scots Queen replied of her joy that she would soon be rescued from her imprisonment, which letter was also intercepted and a forger added a postscript under the direction of Walsingham, asking for the names of her allies, which theretofore were unknown to our Queen."

"Did Her Majesty weep in fear at the mortal peril from these traitors?" Dick was allowed this inquiry, in that it gave Mr. Johnson the cue to show that he had some special knowledge, not yet common among the rest of us:

"In mortal peril she was," quoth Mr. Johnson, nodding and taking a long draught from a steaming tankard, given him by Mother Mary, who was put beside herself with fear at hearing these events, nearly spilling the contents at his boots. Only the crackle of the fire dared utter another sound.

"Well, by August, Walsingham had learned the identities of those involved and sought their arrest. A recusant priest named Ballard and sundry others were apprehended, but Babington, most cowardly, cut his hair and dyed his skin with walnut juice, that he might be mistaken for a common laborer and so escape. No matter, for within days, he and his filthy band of traitors were taken, soon confessed, and all sentenced to death."

"And were they all hanged?" Several onlookers demanded at once, perhaps even one or two with guilty consciences themselves. Mr. Johnson sighed deeply and raised his brow, as if to unburden himself of a last heavy load, or to extend the drama of the telling:

"Aye, so they were, every one of them. But Her Majesty was so distempered, and considering the manner of horrible treason against her person, she ordered that the manner of their death, for more terror and as warning to any others, should be the more painful, prolonging their lives until they be... DIS-EM-BOWELED ...and... EEE-MASCULATED... while HANGING before the public!"

Mother Mary bit the back of her hand to keep from crying out, but the ostlers laughed and grinned, as Death himself might have done in that moment. Mr. Johnson relished the spell he had cast over us all and proceeded with yet more grisly particulars.

"Indeed, while we played for the drunken Prince of Denmark, ignorant of these fearful events, a scaffold in a field at the upper end of Holbourne was chosen for their deaths. The popish priest, Ballard, was hung first, the executioner taking care to protract the extremity of his pain in the sight of the onlookers. Babington did not kneel or pray, but displayed the sign of his former pride. They say he was still alive when the hangman took him from the gallows and cut open his stomach to pull out his entrails. He was heard to cry out 'Domine Jesu' many times over."

"So bad a death argues a monstrous life," quoth Mr. Perkin, who had been listening silent and motionless ere this, now tapping his pipe against the tankard, sounding much like the death bell itself.[50]

"Aye," nodded Mr. Burbage. "Thus was a traitor sent to Hell."

"What is a traitor?" Dick was often a few steps behind in any conversation.

"Why, one that lies when he swears loyalty to Her Majesty," quoth Mr. Pope, spitting into the fire as if to rid his tongue of evil tastes while staring oddly at his half-brother Mr. Phillips, although Mr. Pope's crooked features make it seem that every glance is odd.

"And be everyone a traitor that swears and lies?" Dick used then a monstrous little voice, as if apologizing for the inquiry. Mr. Pope stepped closer to where Mr. Phillips was sitting and again directing his reply to him, or so it seemed.

"Aye. Every one that does so is a traitor, and is likely to be hanged!"

"Then must they all be hanged, those who swear and lie?"

"AYE! Every one." Mr. Pope had grown weary of answering tedious queries by a foolish boy. Or was his tone borne of caution, of fear for the fate of his Catholic brother?

"Who must hang them?"

"O, Dick, thou art a fool," quoth Mr. Phillips, rising and laying a hand on Mr. Pope's shoulder. "Why, the 'honest' men, of course."

Dick thought on this a moment and no one spoke, suspecting he would rummage through the vapors of his brain and find still another question.

"Then the liars and swearers are fools," quoth he, more to himself than any of our Company. "For there are many more liars and swearers than honest men: enough to beat the honest men and hang THEM up."

Ha! So, it would seem, even the smallest candle will shed some light. Dick may not be as dim as I had thought. At least he is clever enough to keep his opinions about religion to himself.

Others of our number are not so circumspect and I have now observed three very distinct, and contentious, factions within our Company: those who hew to the English church with such zeal that they may be called Puritan. Of these, Mr. Pope delights to spite any man that still hews to the old faith, his brother most of all. He composes poesies and ballads, scurrilous and bawdy, sharp as home-brewed cider, always a source of great mirth and hidden truths. Masters Johnson and Burbage loudly proclaim their devotion to the English Church too, finding fault that he makes light of so weighty a subject, and are most choleric when any man confesses to linger in the old faith.

Masters Perkin, Clarke and Phillips seem still wed to the Church of Rome, while the rest of us fall between these distant fence posts, except-

LETTER SIX: NOVEMBER 11, 1586 | 139

ing Mr. Kempe, who listens impatiently to every opinion and then declares 'small choice in rotten apples.'

But the loudest noise, a canon aimed squarely at me, came then from the Boy Burbage. On this occasion, of every man declaring his fealty to Her Majesty and condemning the villains that would have taken her life, he revealed to me the cause of his distemper towards my person:

"Yes, Dick, there are many more scoundrels and liars than honest men, even here among our own Company. Yet can we easily flush them from the bushes where they hide."

"What mean'st thou, Richard? Assassins of the Queen in our midst?" Dick played his unwitting part to perfection.

"Why no assassins, I'll warrant thee, for that takes some COURAGE and those who hide in shadows are COWARDS. Nay, I mean those of the old faith who would rise up and sing hallelujah if Her Majesty comes to a foul end and the Scottish Mary or some prince of the Pope in Rome were to occupy the throne."

"Are those who hide their true selves also traitors ... and must also die?"

"Aye, marry they are and marry they must!"

"That is most fearful, Richard, for how are we to discover those who do not tell the truth?" This is the moment that Boy Burbage had been waiting for. He took up a cheese knife and pivoted on his toes to face me, cheek by jowl.

"William, thou canst help me demonstrate my point. A few questions and an honest man can quickly tell who speaks truth or foul lies."

I noted then how he raised his voice, like a player at some crucial point in the drama; how the air of the inn was again draped thick with a score of separate conversations; with coins slapped on the table demanding full cups or more meat; with cries of feigned indignation from the women we knew to be not so easily offended. But Boy Burbage had silenced the men of our Company all at once and before I could move or find some other course to steer, he pounced:

"Tell me, why dost thou persist in CATHOLIC DEVOTION to a popish lord over our Queen?" he demanded, poking my chest with his knife.

"I know not what thou mean'st, Richard." I hoped to turn his temper to a jest in the eyes of our Company, who had lowered their cups and now listened most intently. "Like all loyal English men, I profess the faith of the Church in England, not Rome."

"Then recite the Morning Prayer...as any TRUE churchman could do."

Why in such moments do we suddenly sense most keenly those things that will have no bearing on our fate? I smelled the heavy stench of wet sheepskins and the faint odor of mustard. I heard the rain knocking louder for admittance. I saw Boy Burbage's nostrils flaring, so close to my face that I might count the swinish hairs within. I had heard the verse he demanded of me a thousand thousand times, but knew in that instant that his quarrel was not with me, but with my father. The sins of the father, they say, are visited upon the son, but how could I confess that his lifelong habits die slowly, or never, whilst mine own heart cares little for such matters?

"God bless the Queen, in this the time of her great peril," shouted Mr. Kempe, thrusting his bulk between the Boy and me. "Let each of us bend a knee and beg God for her salvation. ALMIGHTY GOD, unto whom all hearts be open, all desires known, and from whom no secrets are hid, cleanse the thoughts of our hearts by the inspiration of thy Holy Spirit, that we may perfectly love thee, and worthily magnify thy holy Name; through Christ our Lord. Amen."[51]

"Lord have mercy upon us, and incline our hearts to keep this law," replied every mother's son, kneeling with hats in hand. But that we were in a tavern and not in any house of the Lord, this affirmation was swiftly followed by calls for more ale or cheese or roasted crabs. Good to his pledge, Mr. Kempe let me not fall to the sharp tongue of Boy Burbage and any ill-repute that might follow in the presence of Mr. Johnson. As each to his own business once more, the auditors for the Boy's challenge dispersed, even this unskilled player knew it was time to leave the stage.

O, coz, I wish I knew thy mind at this moment. If I die today, I have lived many times since leaving Stratford. How fares my boy? Neither pen nor ink nor paper answer back, no matter how many times I write the question. Some good has come from my labours. After mine expenses, I hold now nineteen shillings in my purse, about half from wages, half from cleaning up around our makeshift theatres.[52] Not yet a Fortune, but I daresay more than my father has this minute in his purse, though only God knows if I will earn a farthing more with this Company should Boy Burbage persuade his father otherwise.

Lord, how I miss thee and my wife and babes and friends, even the lout Tyke. I miss a dry bed and a kind word from my mother and a day's labour that ends when the sun rests his fiery head. But soon will we arrive in London, so ever closer comes mine arrow to his target, and not a moment too soon, I'll warrant thee, for now I know the cause of Boy Burbage's distemper and fear it may infect others of our Company. So must I reach the New World in all haste.

In the mean season, and with the time we spend in idle pursuits waiting for the heavens to exhaust their rains, I thought it good to commit to paper a catechism of how and why I came to this path, that if I am taken by God before my homecoming, then might Hamnet say 'I knew my father'. Perhaps he would then choose to take up those arms, which I may have let fall, in battle against my father's foes. Coz, please add or correct those remembrances I set down herewith, which my poor memory omits in its frailty or haste:

[Scribe's note: the following section is unique, in that it was written on separate pages and Shakespeare is no longer speaking to his friend John Combe, but directly to his son, Hamnet. Shakespeare may have been drunk when he wrote this part of the letter. He implies as much in an apology at the end of the letter, confessing to views, if not yet deeds, that would have been enough to have him hanged in the highly charged world of Catholic intrigues to unseat Elizabeth from the throne. In all, this is one of the most remarkable letters of the entire collection. TT]

After these my hearty commendations, I greet thee Hamnet, a son grown to manhood, who, if Fortune hath prevented me from seeing thee again, I pray thou hast thrived in mine absence. I wonder, as I write these words, whose visage would stare back at me if I could see thee as a young man: art a lover, sighing like furnace, with a woeful ballad made to thy mistress' eyebrow? Or a soldier, full of strange oaths and bearded like a horse, jealous in honour, sudden and quick in quarrel, seeking the bubble "reputation" even in the cannon's mouth? Nay, I see thee strong and wise and prosperous, respected in all of Warwickshire, perhaps in service to the town as thy grandsire was, an alderman or the bailiff, with a fair round belly, filled with good capon and sweet wine. Dost wear thy beard in fashion or formal cut? Art thine eyes pleasing and generous, or severe and searching with spectacles on thy nose? Hast thou sons?

Has anyone yet told thee of thy heritage? I will herewith endeavour to set forth those events and circumstances of our family that may be necessary for thy better judgment, now and in years to come.

Hamnet, thy father is not brave, I doubt it much that I will ever slay a dragon, yet was I born under the sign of St. George and as I face those dragons ahead of me, striving to improve our family's fortunes, it may at least be said I had some heart.[53] Not ten in the hundred survived the Plague, among those born in that sixth year of Queen Elizabeth's reign, so some star guarded and guided me. I pray the same for thee.

Of my father, thy grandsire John, will I first report: he was a man of stature in our shire, a glover, a fine craftsman of soft leathers, a burly and handsome man of commanding voice and presence. My greatest desire was to follow in his footsteps merely, as a glover, and to serve the township honourably, as he hath done. For those services he was granted not a farthing, except that the Council provided a measure of wine annually, a fee he had better lived without. Yet the Shakespeares were the most respected family in Stratford as I grew to age. Liveried sergeants, bearing maces before them, would see us to church of a Sunday, where we sat in the first pew, and to feasting on holidays. Short tale to make, Hamnet, I thought 'twas prize enough to be my father's son!

"Thou may'st well enjoy a life of ease, boy," father was wont to say, standing by his special corner at the fire. "But when I had thy years, I lay upon no more than rude, simple straw, covered only with a sheet, and a good round log 'neath me head for a pillow. Why I were married full seven year to thy mother ere I had money enow for a bed, and thought me self lord of Stratford when I did."

Mother's eyes curled into a smile whenever he repeated that tale, which oft he did after supper. My mother, thy granddam Mary, spake little; neither could she read or write; but I mark how she could make each person she met feel important to her. To a woman at Thursday mart, rudely slandered by the man she served, I heard mother say: "Fear not, a world of men cannot prevail, with all their words and wars. Yet will a woman's kindness rule over all."

My youth, like thine, was spent with satchel and shining morning face creeping, like a snail, unwillingly to school. Unwilling I say, for the stern Welsh schoolmaster Jenkins kept us standing at attention the entire day with the Bible and psalms, Latin and Greek verse. To be sure, he was not so foul as Mr. Hunt, who was known to whip the boys of a cold winter's morn, merely to warm his hands. I pray thou hast had a kinder master than either of those in thy turn.

Beyond schoolroom walls, Stratford seemed all ways to me as a hive of industrious honey-bees, for like us, bees have their merchants and their soldiers, their poor mechanic porters with heavy burdens of their own, even their own lazy, yawning youths. I trust the town is ever thus, as thou hast marked the years. Of our neighbors, I will list what lights glow brightest to me, that thou might'st better moderate thy courtesies to them, if they live there still:

Next door to thee dwells the mystical old Scotsman, Rogers, the apothecary, ever dressed in tattered weeds, with overwhelming brows. No man knows what sharp misery has so worn him to the bone, but his shop is ever needy, with naught but a beggarly account of empty boxes and pots, musty seeds and bladders, with a few old rose cakes scattered about for a show. Some days he would call to thine uncle Gilbert and me with crooked thumb, for he had no forefinger with which to motion, and give us tasty crumbs of anisee, sugared berries, or dyes to paint our noses red. Has he done the same for thee and thy chums? Other days, he could abide no interference and would bar our way at the door with knotted brow and cry 'Away, ye rascallee wags. Leeeeave me in peeeeace! Orrr my potions I'll spreeeenkle on yr 'eds, and e'en if ye have the strength of twen-tee boys, it will dispatch ye straight!' His bark is worse than his bite, but be thou always courteous to him and he will acquit thy love in more than equal measure.

In the cottage on the lane behind Henley Street there lives the renderer and tanner, old man Fields, oft times fined by thy grandsire for keeping a dungheap in the road or letting loose his pigs in the lane. Fields is not so old, his son Pug was with me at school, but he said the tanner's trade made all who worked it old before their time.

Alderman Whateley, the draper in the next market stall but one to thy grandsire's, who keeps those beehives that benefit us all. He can in no wise be held accountable for the actions of his Catholic brothers, fugitive priests who were caught when a winter chill brought them begging for their brother's aide. A few doors further is Gilbert Bradley, well known to thee ere this, for not only is he a fellow glover, but thine uncle Gilbert is named after him.

Where Henley Street meets the High Street, there live those mighty citizens and sometime-friends of thy grandsire: Adrian Quiney, mercer. Next door 'Lord' Baynton, merchant of gunpowder and other sundries, and the other side is Smith's tavern, maker of the finest cakes and ale in all the shire. Next to these, at Sheep Street, dwell our dear friends Hamnet and Judith Sadler, thy godparents and namesakes.

Out the road to Birmingham lay the White Lion, or King's House as it is more commonly called in my day. Mr. Perrott thinks his soul will be saved on account of decorating the rooms in high style with paintings of scenes from the Bible. In truth he is a covetous old sinner, daily adding or cutting someone from his will, to gain their favour or to punish for some imagined offense. His daughters treated thus, for matching without their parents' consent; the boys, for trifles better not mentioned, but always so he might estimate a brother or a child's love by weight in gold. Keep away from that place and I warn thee to stay away too from the Bear (whence Catholics gather) and the Swan (the English churchmen gather thither), for no good will come of it. Of the Reynolds, Walkers and Sadlers I will say more hereafter.

Thus do I remember Stratford and now turn next unto graver matters. If I die tomorrow, let it not be with the wrongs done to our family unrecorded. I know that none but thee, my son, and the bearer of these tidings, my trusted friend, shall ever read these words. I fear the rust which eats away the iron of my father's heart will someday do the same to me, if I do not share the weight of this burden, for if I should fail in my purpose—I mean revenge—then let another take up the banner and bear it to the journey's end.

Whenever God grants thee to read this confession, thou wilt already know how King Henry, the eighth of that name, threw off the Catholic pope and church and, by God's will, became rightful head of the Church in England, but that the mighty King Philip of Spain would restore a Catholic monarch to the throne of England. Therein were the seeds of discontent sown for thine ancestors.

Thy granddam Mary was born an Arden, which added to our family's state when I was a boy, for Edward Arden served as Sheriff in Warwickshire and was thought soon to be made a lord. But Robert Dudley rose above him to become the first Earl of Leicester, because he and the Queen were familiar long before her coronation and because he was loyal to the Church of England, while the Ardens remained Catholic. Thereafter Edward Arden refused to wear the livery of the Earl and found other ways to openly insult Robert Dudley for taking those honours that he deemed his due. Nor made he a secret of his loyalty to the church of Rome, keeping a priest in his household disguised as a gardener, but who every one of us did call 'Father Hall', and leaving popish relics lying about his house in the open for all to see.

How then did the Earl strike at both Ardens and Shakespeares? The Earl ordered trade to other glovers and wool dealers, driving up my father's debts. The Earl levied a fine of twenty pounds and odd on him, for failing to appear before the Queen's Bench, yet no man in Stratford knew aught of the matter, leastways my father. And when he appeared in London, he was fined again, this time for breaking the peace with a Nottingham hat maker, who was four days and more journey to the north at the time. All over the realm, friends of Arden and his family were being falsely accused, and who can keep his candle burning in a hurricane of royal force?

In any wise, the proud Ardens and Shakespeares survived and kept meat on the table, wool on our backs, and a thatch overhead, not to mention keeping heads on our shoulders. But not sixmonth after thy sister Susanna was born, that luck too ran out, when Francis Throckmorton, kinsmen to the Ardens, confessed on the rack that he had plotted with the Earl of Northumberland, Mary of Scotland, and a Spanish ambassador whose name escapes me now, to assassinate Her Majesty.[54] He named a John Longspear too, but by God's grace recalled our name in error and my father was not arrested with the others.

Conviction followed arrest more swiftly than night follows day. Throckmorton was hanged, drawn and quartered. Edward Arden was soon to follow and my father was ordered by the Earl to attend his hideous end, being told 'the axe, this time, must give the next his warning.' Father bid me attend on him that day and the scene that followed I can never wash clean from my memory. I pray thou shalt never see its like:

"Come, sir, are you ready for death?" asked the goaler, leading our kinsman to the place of execution, even then crammed with leering spectators.

"Over-roasted rather, ready long ago," answered Arden bravely, bareheaded and clothed in no more than a pauper's cloak, already sodden and heavy with ice.

"A heavy reckoning though, for you sir," quoth the goaler, offering an arm, made steady by practice, to keep Arden upright on the slippery steps up to the gallows. "But sir, the comfort is, you shall be called no more to any other payments. You need never more fear of tavern-bills or the cutpurse. O, the charity of a penny rope!"

"I think I am merrier to die than thou art to live," quoth Arden, unbowed, but breathing faster now, steaming more at his mouth than a plough horse, I recall. "Thou art most welcome, Master Death, for I am away to liberty, while I leave my kinsmen to pay my debts, and for that, I am truly sorry."

"Indeed, sir, he that sleeps feels not the tooth-ache, but a man that were to sleep your sleep, I think he would gladly change places with his hangman, for, look you, sir … ", at this, the goaler pointed both up and down, " … you know not which way you shall go."

"Yes, indeed I do, fellow," answered Arden saucily, but evermore shaking like one who knows 'tis not the many oaths that makes the truth, no doubt praying that God will favor those who worship him in the old way as much as the new.

Father and I were pressed among the rude mechanics in their greasy aprons, who had come for a show only, their thick breaths, rank of gross diet, were we enclouded within and forced to drink the vapour, nothing abated by the driving rain or the sleet that decorated their beards. Upon the gallows, Arden thought to speak to those in attendance, kin and stranger alike, to bequeath them a measure of truth before his death, but the guard commanded drummers to prevent his words from leaving the place of hanging and, as if in a dream, his brave oration became a dumbshow.

Thus, on a bitter winter's day in a pitiless rain that froze whatsoever it struck, Edward Arden was hanged. He was taken down, sliced open from guts to garter, his steaming entrails tore out and his body, quartered while yet he lived. Arden's head was struck from his body and, as the commission from Her Majesty commanded, sent to be placed 'in full view of all other would-be traitors, on London Bridge, impaled on a long-spear.' God's breath! Who could conclude aught by the words 'long-spear', but a warning to my father and all our kin? Robert Dudley, the Earl of Leicester, had defeated the Ardens truly and forever.[55]

Thenceforward was father forced to hide from public life, but the Shakespeares had no estates or private wealth to sustain us and, to conclude a long discourse in few words, thine uncle Richard was newborn, followed soon thereafter by thine uncle Edmund. God saw fit to claim thine aunt Anne from us about that time, as many before her went to God on the wings of the Plague, yet many mouths remained to feed (thine own mother having brought forth thyself and thy sister even then) and little harvest to succour them withal. My father sought refuge in his ale, which aided our state in no wise (O God, why do men put such an enemy in their mouths to steal away their brains?).

My dearest Hamnet, who will one day grow to manhood and learn of these, his family's burdens in greater whys and wherefores, remember that best safety lies in fear. The Queen's spies are all around us, at least one in this Company of players, wherein I now do toil, sends daily dispatches to the Queen's councilors, I fear. Yet to be revenged upon the marauding beast, the huntsman must brave the lion's den. Therefore, have I left thee in the care of thy mother and God and entered the service of that selfsame Earl of Leicester, the murdering consort to a cold-hearted Queen. If Fate decides that I am lost to thee, mayest thou ever know I died striving to make thee proud to be a Shakespeare.

[Scribe's note: Here Shakespeare returns to directing his remarks to Combe.]

O coz, I needs must rest my weary brain and lay aside this worn out pen, which even now leaves more blots of ink than words upon the page. My brain is fevered from the retelling of my father's troubles, as if living them anew. Forgive me any slanders or aught which might offend, those are but faint fumes of a cup of ale. On the morrow will we speed to London. Dick hath described to me a city of more people than fishes in the sea; a multitude of cloud-capp'd towers, gorgeous palaces, and solemn temples the likes of which are unimaginable until beheld; boats on the Thames like an army of ants in constant traffic; peddlers of savoury edibles and potions that protect against ill humours and such powers that devils may have over men. How I long to be there to drink in these wonders, but more because I hope to see Giddy and bathe in the warm glow of a friendly face and to meet Mr. Kempe's sister, who may guide me to a ship and a New World far from vengeful Earls and uncaring hangmen.[56] O tedious is this day, as the night before some festival, for which thou hast new robes and may not yet wear them.

Let me hear from thee when time and tide allow, for in these matters that I have now unburdened my soul withal, I need thy wise counsel, for they that thrive well, take counsel of their friends.

Kiss my boy and maids in my name and omit nothing else which thine honour deem'st best for their tender need. I am thine ever loving servant in all else, Will.

LETTER SEVEN
November 18, 1586

Wherein our Stratford lad beholds a bridge most fantastical, a city of human gallimaufry, a Theatre like no other, and a brother long lost.

During the many nights I transcribed Shakespeare's letters under the watchful gaze of Miss B, I didn't manage to engage her in much conversation about herself and even less about her knowledge of the man who had written these treasures. However, when I told her that the picture emerging, from what I had read so far, implied that he had attached himself to Leicester's Men in order to get to London and find a ship bound for the New World, she firmly told me I was mistaken.

Oh, he might have collected that idea from "some rascal" along the way, she insisted, but he was driven out of Stratford for "thievery." I knew at that point, from Letter Four, that he wasn't above shoplifting, so I imagined her confident assertion might be true, but of course I wanted to know the source of her information. Were there more first-person accounts, perhaps from someone who knew the Ardens or the Shakespeares in Stratford, that I had not yet seen?

The next night, she brought a dark brown, leather bound book that bore the title on its spine in faded gold letters: *Shakspear*. By now I was used to handling musty old paper that was yellowing and brittle, so this antique was immediately intriguing. Inside, on the cover page, written in pencil, was a partially legible inscription *To Richard Sheridan, Esquire MP*.

On the inside cover itself was a stamped mark from a subsequent owner that read *Surgeon Commander Robin Hall, 1 Royal Terrace, Belfast*. I seemed to be looking at a book of history that has a mysterious provenance of its own. A

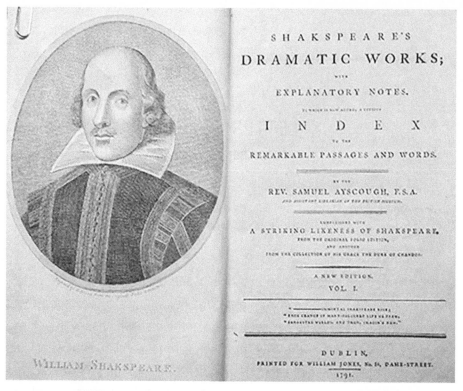

11. Shakspear: Shakespeare's plays and first biography in a book given to the author by the mysterious Miss B.

portrait of Shakespeare followed, copied from the First Folio, and the title page, which stated *Shakspeare's Dramatic Works with Explanatory Notes, to which is now added A Copious Index to the Remarkable Passages and Words by the Rev. Samuel Ayscough, F.S.A.*

Brevity, in titles at least, was not apparently the soul of wit in the 18th century. The bottom of that page proclaims the volume was printed in Dublin in 1791 (see Illustration 11 above).

Miss B waited for me to leaf through twenty pages of names of the "subscribers," presumably a book club of sorts that financed the publication (Sheridan was listed as one of them), which was followed by a Preface by "Dr. Johnson" first written in 1765 and finally *Some Account of the Life of William Shakespeare, Written by Mr. Rowe.* There, on page thirty six, was the following account that Miss B had taken as gospel written by someone who lived almost a century later than his subject, but who was at least three centuries closer to original sources than we are today:

Upon leaving school, he seems to have given entirely into that way of living which his father proposed to him...and in this kind of settlement he continued for some time until...he had by a misfortune, common enough to young fellows, fallen into ill company and among them, some that made a frequent practice of deer-stealing...in a park that belonged to Sir Thomas Lucy. For this he was prosecuted by that gentleman, as he thought somewhat too severely...that he was obliged to leave his business and family in Warwickshire, for a time, and shelter himself in London.

Miss B insisted I keep and study that book, a resource that resides on my desk in my Santa Monica home to this day. Nicholas Rowe is regarded as Shakespeare's first biographer and wrote that passage in 1709. Scholars since have discounted the likelihood that the poet had poached game from a nearby estate, but regardless of his motivations for a hasty leave-taking, in November of 1586, William Shakespeare of Stratford in Warwickshire finally beheld London for the first time in his young life.

A few days after I read this letter, I retraced the steps of Leicester's Men from Southwark, across London Bridge, up Gracechurch Street to Bishopsgate (which was an actual gate in the walled city in Shakespeare's time) and out of the City of London to the location where the players took up their professional residence when not on tour. The first purpose-built theatre in England, rather unimaginatively named "The Theatre" when James Burbage erected it in 1576.

Illustration 12a, shown on page 152, is a map of London from 1572 that I hung in my study so I could find locations mentioned in the letters. I added the street and place names as I figured out their locations (Illustrations 12b, 12c, and 12d, shown pages 153 and 154, take a closer look at key parts of the city that were important to Shakespeare and are mentioned in the letters). Take a look at the lone bridge that crosses the Thames and trace the roads due north to follow the path Shakespeare describes as taking on his first day in London, all the way to the site of The Theatre.

12a. A 1572 map of London with street and place names mentioned in the Letters added, based on research by the author.

Shakespeare's
London

A Shoreditch Road
B Hollywell Lane
C The Theatre
D Great Barn
E Great Horse Pond
F The Curtain
G Finsbury Fields
H Bedlam Hospital
I Broad Street
J Bishops Gate

12b. London: Location of The Theatre & environs

Shakespeare's
London

A Cripplegate
B Mountjoy House
C Addle Street
D St. Olaves
E St. Mary's
F Aldersgate
G Haberdashers Row
H Wood St.
I Alderman bury Road
J Coleman St.

12c. London: Cripplegate & environs

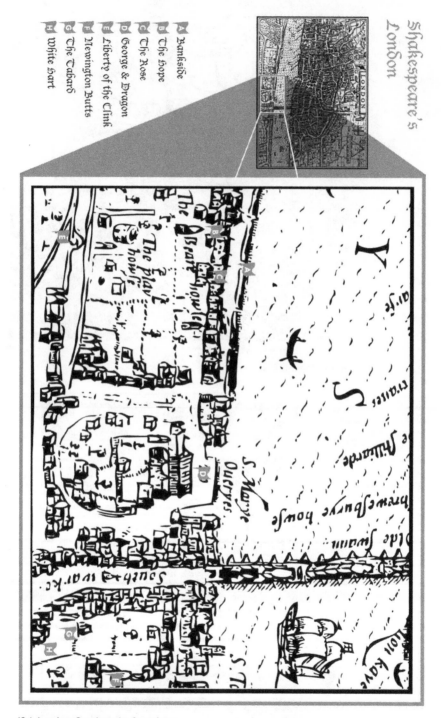

A Bankside
B The Hope
C The Rose
D George & Dragon
E Liberty of the Clink
F Newington Butts
G The Tabard
H White Hart

Shakespeare's London

12d. London: Southwarke & environs.

Adjacent to The Theatre, I have marked "The Great Barn," as it was called in other contemporary maps I discovered, which was the place he reports that Leicester's Men stored their wagons and props (Illustrations 13a, 13b, and 13c, shown below and on pages 156 and 157, show the site of The Theatre today, still being excavated and preserved).

Of course, the architecture and fashions have changed, but I was amazed to see that otherwise many of the places and streets Shakespeare wrote about would be entirely familiar to him today. I don't believe in ghosts, but the day I followed his footsteps, the feeling that I was not alone making that walk over and through so much history, held the power to change my mind. Shakespeare and his contemporaries believed deeply in the spirit world and how these ghosts could inhabit dreams: in this letter and again in later ones, he tells of a fearful dream populated with the living and dead. It must have made a strong impression, because he describes a dream in very similar terms in *Richard III* (Act I, scene 4). Illustration 14, on page 157, shows The Tabard Inn as it might have appeared in Shakespeare's time, where the dream came to him.

In Letter Seven, Shakespeare meticulously chronicles a bustling marvel of a city that overwhelms the senses, pulses with life, and teems with all the

13a. The site of The Theatre today: London's first purpose-built playhouse and Shakespeare's first acting venue.

grit and wonder of Elizabethan England. Retracing the steps of his first day in London, I could easily imagine the scene Shakespeare recounts, immediately falling prey to a beautiful pickpocket, but then how he happily meets up with his beloved youngest brother "Giddy," an apprentice haberdasher, and lucks into lodging with the welcoming Mr. Stow (a writer of histories about England) and a fantastical housekeeper, Mistress Heather Burberry (a learned and kind woman with no arms).[57]

He fears his life and freedom are in jeopardy as the still mysterious conflict with Richard "Boy" Burbage comes to a head. But before his fate is known or sealed, Shakespeare uses Letter Seven to take us on tour of the dazzling center of England, granting us an unvarnished first-look at the most populous city in Europe at the time through his wide, country eyes.

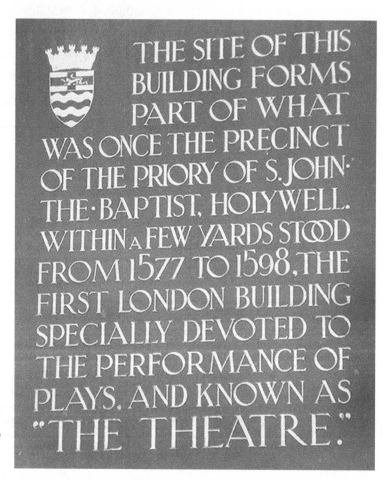

THE SITE OF THIS BUILDING FORMS PART OF WHAT WAS ONCE THE PRECINCT OF THE PRIORY OF S. JOHN THE·BAPTIST. HOLYWELL. WITHIN a FEW YARDS STOOD FROM 1577 TO 1598, THE FIRST LONDON BUILDING SPECIALLY DEVOTED TO THE PERFORMANCE OF PLAYS. AND KNOWN AS "THE THEATRE."

13b. A plaque on the site of The Theatre today.

13c. The probable layout of The Theatre (from a 1596 sketch of a comparable playhouse, The Swan).

14. The Tabard Inn, as it probably appeared to Shakespeare in 1586 when he first stayed there as described in Letter Seven.

18 November 1586, this being a Saturday, in the great City

Coz,

Thou knowest 'tis common: all that lives must die, passing through Nature to Eternity. I am no more ready to pass through Nature than a goat is to pass through the eye of a needle, yet here I stand, thanks to mine own foolishness, on the very edge of Eternity. Short tale to make, I fear I am doomed. And having but this very day seen London, seen my brother and a thousand sights I could never have imagined, if I am cast asunder now, that were a pity. My woe began Thursday last, before taking the road to London. Herewith mine account thereof, that thou mayest learn how I came to this precipice:

"With what matter dost thou so earnestly assault that page, Shakeshit?" Boy Burbage demanded, seeing me reading o'er a letter I had writ to thee, the which I perused to add some post script. Startled, I could make no witty reply that would quench his curiosity, but in no wise might I let him read the pages, for they unfolded more of mine innermost and frank opinions about our Lord of Leicester.

"So it please thee, Richard, none," quoth I.

"Oooooooo - - 'Richard', is it now? No insult to my name and station, but only 'Richard' now." He circled the barren patch of earth in the stable whereon I made my writing table. "Why then so earnestly seek'st thou to put up that letter?"

"I know no news, sir." I was able only to rise to my knees as he hovered over me. Odd things come in such times to mind: how much Boy Burbage had filled out, always a head taller than myself, but now growing more muscular with each passing week as a member of Mr. Burbage's tumbling trio. He verily snarled as the tiger closing in on the hapless fawn:

"And 'sir' on the heels of 'Richard'! Why the price of oats is rising every minute. What paper wast thou reading?"

"Nothing. Nothing that will interest the likes of thee." Why did I upbraid him so rudely? Even so, he feigned courtesy and some indifference the while, saying:

"Nothing? Nothing will come of nothing, Will. And if so, why then the sudden dispatch of it into thy pocket? Let me see it: if it be nothing, I shall not need spectacles!"

"I beseech thee, pardon me sir. It is a letter…from…my brother…that I have not yet myself all over-read." O Lord, why did I say it was from my brother? He knew that to be a lie, and if not, then I have only accused my kin of crimes they know not of. O, I am a lack-wit! "I mean that contents, as in part I understand them, are not clear."[58]

At that moment, Cuthbert arrived, bearing word that Mr. Perkin sought me out. I escaped with my letter intact, but had I more brains than a flea, I had then and there consigned the offending pages into the flames or tucked them in my shoe as a place of hiding (and to patch the hole in the sole). But no, I merely tucked it away in my vest, which Boy Burbage plainly saw, such that when I later slept, in the drowsy vapours of my fool's paradise, he snatched it therefrom.

In days since, he hath said little to me. In truth, he hath not nipped at my heels with his jests and jibes, as is his wont. In his looks, I try to read the fate of my testament and, indeed, myself, but he giveth no hint of what is to come. Nor do any of the masters treat me differently, not even Mr. Johnson, who is surely in service to Walsingham and always examines most those nearest to him.

Well, none can cure their harms by the wailing of them, so I write the selfsame letter a second time, now augmented with mine overflowing visions of the great City. Besides, in London are such wonders, that I needs must set aside my troubles and feast on all the City has to afford me. Yesterday we trod the road through Gravesend and Greenwich, which brings a man to London and is notoriously peopled with countless rogues and vagrant persons that live by these highways, under the name of soldiers, begging for alms or work. Mr. Perkin's low opinion thereof:

"Aaaww, work they will not. Neither can they, for their sinews are too much benumbed and stiff through idleness. Their limbs, being put to any hard labour, will grieve them beyond measure, such that it is not worth the effort, nor the tenpence a day, on the part of he that hires them." Followed hard by Mr. Burbage's opinion:

"And I'll warrant this lot never served at all, nor came near to where any military service was done, and now they take away the alms and gratuities meant for the true, poor soldiers of the realm, those which in deed ought to be maintained and relieved."

I would soon see, at the very gates of London, that any players, even the Earl of Leicester's Men, were considered by the multitude to be vagrants and masterless men, so our number could in no wise brook the company of real gypsies, louts, and beggars.

"O I do not fear the ROAD, masters," quoth Dick, his reedy voice tiptoeing with womanly fear. "But the CITY, that is another matter, for the City is full of cozenage and evils! As nimble jugglers that can deceive thine eye; dark working sorcerers that betray thy mind; soul-killing witches that may deform any man's body, aye, and women too; and these are aided a'times by cheaters, prating magicians, and many other liberties of sin!"[59]

"Thou had better fear the road, Dicky," quoth Mr. Kempe, his stout legs dangling from the back of the wagon as if cooling his heels in a pleasant brook. "Thy shoes are yet again caked with King Arthur's dung." I laughed withal, yet wondered what truth there might be to Dick's foreboding? Till then, I had nary a word of Giddy since father sent him as apprentice thither and prayed now to God he had not fallen in with bad company or worse.

Nor is there any mistaking that the City draws near: the way becomes more crowded, hemmed by buildings of every description, growing ever larger, ever higher, blocking out the sun a'times. So pestered are the main road and byways with people, animals, and wagons, that axles carve ruts in the side of some houses, testament to an urgency for commerce not felt in Stratford. Equally uncommon at home are the many coaches hereabouts (brought out of Germany, I am told) with neither distinction of time nor difference of persons observed: aye, the world comes to London on wheels, carrying many whose parents were glad to go on foot. Taken together, there scarce remains a sufficient highway for the meeting of carriages and droves of cattle, much less any fair, pleasant, or wholesome way for people to walk on foot, which is no small blemish to so famous a city to have so unsavoury and unseemly a passage thereinto. Our number grows ever more excited, even the masters, who have lived their lives within City walls, in anticipation of returning to the bosom of England.

"These suburbs are no other but dark dens for adulterers, thieves, murderers, and every mischief-worker," quoth Mr. Johnson, shaking a bladder of water as if he would overcome its emptiness under such duress. "Mark you, behind yon windows dwells a multitude of great human sin."

"Judge not lest ye be judged," scowled Mr. Kempe, in a rare thoughtful moment. Mr. Johnson made no reply, but his brow was tinged red with annoyance.

Thus marched we the final few miles, the regal sun fading away, crowning us with his golden threads like triumphant crusaders on a long homeward journey. I felt less like the prince, more like the fool, mine ankles aching from the many times I had tripped and twisted them in the wagon ruts that deeply scar the muddy way. How many other timid pilgrims had trod this road, tiny drops falling in with a thousand thousand others, joining into one great flood that daily pours into the City?

At dusk, we came to Southwarke, a borough that forms a gateway to London Bridge and thence into the City herself. Here paused we to refresh ourselves, at a famous tavern called the Tabard, wherein every man alive seemed acquainted with someone of our Company. Mr. Burbage's tired visage seemed rejuvenated, as if awakened from a long winter's slumber, a starving lion newly come upon fresh meat and drink. He took ale from one gentleman, a petition from another, hearty welcome from a dozen odd, all the while stroking his beard in measured study of carriers, tailors, ostlers, and other such like tradesmen, all seeking favor of the Earl's own servants.

Every one of us ate his fill of roasted crabs and the most delectable herring pasty ever baked in the realm, washed down by a fine ale mixed with honey the locals call 'sweet', all the while snatching from the thick air a dizzying array of gossip and strands of this ballad or that scurrilous rhyme. Many spoke of naught but Babington and the foul plot against the Queen, each with a new piece of the tale and of how the teller had once met the assassin himself.

There are many fair inns for receipt of travelers hereabouts, by the signs of the Spur, the Bull, the Queen's Head (though I imagine Her Majesty would take offense thereat), the George, and the Hart. But the most ancient is this Tabard, so called for its sign of a sleeveless coat. In the wars, their arms were embroidered thereon, that every man by his coat might be known from another. Even our most famous poet, Chaucer, has lodged herein and writ thus in commendation, the inscription carved now over the main door: "In Southwarke at the Tabard I lay, on my Pilgrimage to Canterbury with devout courage, in fellowship with sundry folk and many pilgrims more, the chambers and the stables wide and well, such that we were eased at the best."

Indoors, and without, are in constant commotion, for hard by are gardens wherein are kept bears, bulls, and other beasts, also mastiffs in several kennels nourished to bait them, scaffolded about for the beholders to stand safe. Some of our company repaired to these combats, but most took their hasty leave, every man eager to spend his first night in many months in his own bed with his wife and babes, warmed by his own fire, hearing who was well and who ill, who had been lost to the Plague and who spared, and how sped his own estate. Dick and I were left in the company of the Burbages, charged with returning our goods to the Theatre on the north side of London, without the City walls. This night we would lodge at the Tabard, making our way through the City in daylight on the morrow. I did not fancy coming so directly under the thumb of the Burbages, fearing as I did their wrath over my slanderous letter. Would they lure me into the City and suddenly hand me over to a constable? Would I spend my first night in London on the rack? Would it be my last? For a moment, I thought of bolting into the anonymous darkness, but as I would then most likely never see the great City, nor from thence my way onward to the New World, I stayed the course God seems to have chosen. Besides, I had no clue whence I should flee: back home to fathers and sons, wives, daughters and debts?

The Tabard is an inn of some luxury, when compared to those we used along the highways. Dick and I were given a room apart, with heavy curtains to shield us from the cold air that blew in from the river, and clean woolen blankets. Despite the corporeal comforts, I did pass a miserable night, full of ugly sights, of ghastly dreams. As I am a Christian faithful man, I would not spend another such a night, even if it bought me a world of happy days, so full of dismal terror was the dream! Long ere the cock crew, my tossing woke my bedfellow, though his own foul breath was enough to wake the dead, and he bid me speak. I sat a bit apart and pulled back the curtain, for sweat dripped in tiny brooks from my matted hair and rushed headlong into my beard, a blast of air and moonlight then washing away the terrible fears my mind had just witnessed.

"O Dicky, methought I had broken from the Tabard and was embarked to cross the Thames, and in my company my brother Giddy, who tempted me to walk upon the roofs of the buildings that line the bridge. As we paced along upon this perilous footing of the rooftops, methought that Giddy stumbled; and, in falling, struck me, knocking me overboard into the tumbling billows of the river!"

"O Will, a parlous fear!" Dick's eyes appeared then to me as two wide black stains on his lily white visage.

"Lord, Lord! methought what pain it was to drown: what dreadful noise of waters in mine ears! What ugly sights of death within mine eyes! Methought I saw a thousand fearful wrecks; ten thousand men that fishes gnawed upon; wedges of gold, great anchors, heaps of pearl, inestimable stones and jewels, all scattered in the bottom of the river. Some lay in dead men's skulls and, in those holes where eyes did once inhabit, there were reflecting gems which seemed to leer and mock the dead bones that lay scattered nearby."

"Hadst thou such leisure in the time of death to gaze upon the secrets of the deep?"

"Methought I had, and often strove to yield the ghost, but the envious flood kept in my soul, and would not let it forth, but smothered me instead."

"Then awake'st thou with this sore agony and drew me into thy fearful vision." Dick clutched a blanket to his breast, which bore unmistakable signs of recent gnashing at the edges from his teeth.

"O, no, my dream was then lengthened, for then began my soul to pass, methought, upon the flood, with that grim ferryman which poets write of, unto the kingdom of perpetual night. The first that there did greet me was my mother's great uncle, renowned Edward Arden, who cried aloud, 'What reward for perjury can this dark monarchy afford false Leicester?' Leicester, he that hanged me in the field by Tewkesbury, seize on him Furies, take him to your torments!' With that, methought a legion of foul fiends environed me about and howled in mine ears such hideous cries that with the very noise I trembled, waked, and for a season after, could not believe that I was not in Hell, such terrible impression made the dream."

"Who is this Arden? And why 'false' Leicester? And why speak'st thou ill of our protector and the Queen's own consort, the right honourable Earl?" Screwing up his meagre courage, Dick was now grasping about for some tool to defend himself, if the need should arise.

I shook myself from my reverie and calmed my friend, perhaps the only one left to me in what may be a short life from this moment hence. Dick is a charming presence upon the stage, but carries in him no more wit than a statue. I lied to him of some certain further parts of my dream, saying I had defended the good Earl's honour at the gates of Heaven, which I described in such soothing particulars that Dick was soon at ease once more.

O, but would that my distempered brain was so easily quieted! What signifies such a dream? Riches at the bottom of an ocean? My Fortune, found in the New World, thereafter lost at sea on a homeward voyage? Leicester brought low, but like some Pyrrhic victory, my bones buried in the deep with his?

The last of that night passed without further event, but when Boy Burbage came pounding at our door, cursing us as slug-a-beds, it was many minutes of shaking my head, thrust out at the casement in the cool morning air, before I could recall my name and station. What a dreary impression my dream had left upon me!

We were soon upon the Southwarke road for London bridge, aching ankles reminding me of mine earthly lot, the three of us leading the wagon horses on foot, Mr. Burbage in the saddle of King Arthur just ahead. But even the bulk of King Arthur's rump could not blot from mine eyes the spectacle that now unfolded before us, as amazing to me as any that my dreams could conjure!

The river Thames, wider by tenfold than our river Avon, spreading her shimmering wings in either direction farther than a man could see, or walk, in a day's journey. Hundreds of wherries and rowing boats, great sailing ships and barges on the flood to our right. Upriver, to our left, were a multitude of craft, each engaged in his daily labours, overladen with boxes and barrels, bundles and passengers, oars sprouting like thousands of legs on hundreds of great wooden centipedes.

Across this vast flood lay the City, no fearful stew of all Man's iniquities, but a thousand Stratfords, a human garden of every delicate and exotic fruit hitherto unknown to me. A vast expanse of structures along the river, great castles of stone adorned with banners and shiny spires, and rising up behind them were those very cloud-capped towers, gorgeous palaces, and solemn temples of which Dick had foretold, aye all the great globe itself in one place: London!

Mine eyes had barely begun to catalogue these strange and wondrous visions when King Arthur stopped short, backing his haunches into my face. I collected myself in time to see the master descend from his mount to greet a group of soldiers, or so I took them to be, uniformed in dark blue livery with yellow embroidered crests and faded badges of some ancient honours. Was Mr. Burbage even now preparing to give me over to the Queen's wrath for my scurrilous writings? Was it too late to flee? A jaundiced sergeant shouted to our Company, and all others who had gathered behind us seeking permission to enter London via the great bridge:

"All and every person, being whole and mighty in body and able to labour, having neither land nor master nor any lawful craft or mystery [*trade*] whereby he or she might get his or her living, and can give no reckoning how he or she doth lawfully get his or her living, and all fencers, bearwardens, common players, minstrels, tinkers, peddlers, jugglers, and such not belonging to any baron of this realm or some other honourable personage of greater degree, who shall wander abroad without license of two Justices of the Peace at the least, shall be adjudged and deemed Rogues, Vagabonds, and Sturdy Beggars."

"What shall happen to those who are deemed such?" asked Dick, eliciting a scowl from Mr. Burbage and a snort from the Boy.

"They shall be taken to goal and punished at Her Majesty's pleasure, excepting those who wander with a forged passport," quoth the sergeant, looking about for the tiny voice that had asked so impertinent a question.

"What shall happen - - "

"Thou dost not want to know that, laddie!" The sergeant brushed aside both Dick and myself, taking us for hired servants and scrutinizing instead the papers in Mr. Burbage's hand.

Yesternight, when I told Dick of my fearful augury, he turned whiter than any sheet in a washerwoman's basket. Now of a sudden, the sergeant's face wore that selfsame colour, his eyes outgrowing his brow, stammering for a courtesy and bowing before our master. Our Company never played so comic a part upon the stage as this empty cassock [*uniform*], which nearly swept clean the path before us now, waving us on to the bridge. As we passed, I heard him mumbling to his fellows "The Earl's Men ... Leicester's Men ... Her Majesty's favorite ... " In that same instant, the other travelers seeking entry parted, many bowing slightly or removing a cap, and many a man uttered 'God save the Queen'. Even on Sunday or a feasting day in Stratford I never did feel so many eyes so reverently upon me.

Our traffic over the bridge moved slowly, there being so many moving in all directions: some passing through as did we, others seeking out this shop or that noble house built upon the bridge itself. I did not mind the pace (mine ankles especially gave me thanks), for the stop-and-start gave me leave to study the place. O coz, thou hast never seen the like! 'Tis a beautiful long bridge with quite splendid, handsome, and well built houses, most towering more than five stories, occupied by merchants of consequence. The gatehouse, through which we passed to enter her, was adorned with the severed heads of traitors and thieves, teetering atop long pikes, as unsteady in death upon the breeze as they apparently were upon the necks of their owners in life. Magpies tore the flesh and pecked the eyes out from the freshest of them. Was one of these shriveled adornments the head of my kinsman, Edward Arden?

All about us were people and wagons and wares of every description, the smells of an hundred cook fires, the sound of music played by unseen minstrels, disembodied cries of the boatmen wafting up from the river below with calls of 'eastward ho' or 'westward ho', even one scrap of song that I could discern:

"Noble Thames, if I could use a pen,

I would divulge thy glory unto men;

Thou in the morning, when my coin is scant,

Before the evening doth supply my want."

Aye, the bridge is an astonishing work of Man, but the Thames is a more amazing work of the Almighty. A flooded highway that gives and takes, a force both seen and unseen that shapes men's lives, or as God wills it, perhaps to end them. When we neared the other side, we spied on the opposite bank some villains chained to great stonework in the river, doomed to withstand the tides for their crimes. Would I soon number among them, the crabs gnawing at my privates in a slow agonizing punishment or even death?

As we set foot on solid ground once more, my first footfall in the great City herself, a tall man of my father's age suddenly blocked our path. He bore a severe pinched face, spectacles on's nose, with naught but a stump where a left arm once hung. His neck and chin were scarred by long deep cuts and burns, the victim of long-ago wars or sins.

"In what church will ye seek salvation on the Lord's day?" I took him to be a preacher, given the tattered holy book in his only hand and the black sheath he wore as his only garment, save for a plain, black felt hat. He had no shoes, but blackened toes, which poked about in the mud and dung as he rocked slowly to and fro. Mr. Burbage replied most calmly, striving to offend him not, and thereby to circumvent this obstacle:

"Why mine own church is that of St. Helen's in Bishopsgate, sir. We rightly thank thee for reminding us that the morrow is Sunday, when all God's children should render up their spirits for prayer and holy contemplation. Who is it that seeks our favor, then?"

"Vicar Stubbes," replied the sour, suspicious man (with so fitting a name). I suspect he had heard self-serving rubbish from a player ere this and knew shit when he smelled it. "God will not suffer FOREIGNERS ... ", this last he verily spat at us, " ... to view lascivious entertainments on the Sabbath, nor may they play at vanities, such as your low street games of football, and those who do profane the Lord's day in this manner are justly punished by their broken and bloody noses, their blinded eyes, their broken limbs. Yea, such punishment is too mild, for such SINNERS should be repaid with a piece of their tongue cut out! Or searing their foreheads with a hot iron, such that they might be known by good Christians and thereby avoided!"

He paused for dramatic effect, as fine a speech as any I have heard from a stage, splitting the ears of the ha'penny groundlings. Dick cowered behind my cloak, either owing to the cold growing in us, now that our limbs had stopped moving and making their own fire, or from fear of the vicar's sermon. I inquired of him to know which:

"Dick, why art thou trembling so? Wert thou planning to play football on the Sabbath?"

"Nay, fool," quoth he. "Dost thou not see a devil before us, disguised as a vicar?"

"Well if he is a devil, he is the oddest fiend that ever hounded Christian men, luring them to church of a Sunday."

Mr. Burbage gave the vicar some coins, which seemed somewhat to ease his distemper, and thanked him for his advice. As we passed, he launched himself toward another group of travelers leaving the bridge.

"See ye that estate, lads?" Mr. Burbage, now dismounted and walking with us, pointed downriver on the bankside, off to our right, where we could discern a great walled town within the City, the tops of its tallest edifices towering an hundred feet skyward. "That is no place ye lads will want to visit: that is the Tower, a citadel to defend the City and a royal palace for assemblies. 'Tis the armoury for warlike provisions and the treasury wherein are secured the ornaments and jewels of the crown. O, and a garden of noble beasts, such as lions and a camel from the Sophy of Persia. But, mark you, it is also a fearful prison for the most dangerous offenders in the Realm, many of which ne'er again see the light of day after once entering through those frightful walls."

Was Mr. Burbage trying to fright me then, by showing me my fate? I thought not, for the fox barks not when he would steal the lamb. But why then had he dismounted to walk in the filthy streets with us? To be closer when the constables moved in for mine arrest? Was there a reward in the land for traitors who slander great Earls? Or did some other hand move him and his disagreeable son? I tried not to think on it, nor could my mind consider aught but the mob, the stalls, the smells, the sounds of the City in her heart. I tried to learn the name of every district and alleyway, that I might navigate myself one day, that I might better know the way out if the need arose.

The bridge herself became Gracechurch Street, a wide way slicing due north towards the Bishop's Gate, crossing streets that bore names of Thames, Cannon, Fenchurch, Eastcheap, and Leadenhall. We passed more people in half an hour than thou couldst see in all of Warwickshire in a lifetime. We passed the signs of fishmongers, bearing crossed keys and herrings; the signs of grocers, bearing three sets of three carrots, or so I took them to be; the elegant signs of the mercers, adorned with the likeness of the Queen in her full regalia, gold and jewels in most life-like colours.

But it is the people that my poor powers with a pen cannot justly describe. There is no lane, street, alley or house in London out of which there issues not some man or woman of every age and station, such that the ways are pestered with people multiplied, as they throng and overrun one another for haste. Now and again the carriage of a noble personage thunders by, every common man and his beast leaping for safety to the ditches, but mostly it is the inexorable churning of feet and wheels through mud, dung, kitchen scraps, blowing bits of paper, dead dogs or dying ones, all mixed in a river as great as the Thames herself, flowing in, through, about, and out of this beating heart called London, packed together in buildings that are an hundred Stratfords within the City walls, and perched atop that are another five hundred Stratfords, the lot of them stacked like piles of cretes.[60]

At mid-morning something odd happened, although I may rightly say every aspect of this day has been so out of the ordinary as to defy the telling of it. We passed the church of St. Helen's, hard by the Bishop's Gate, the very church that Mr. Burbage said was his own. Dick asked if we were to pause there and give thanks for our safe journey, but Burbage replied that he had never set foot in such a 'gross temple' nor would he ever, in this life or the next. I knew not what to make of this, other than to suppose he was lying to Vicar Stubbes merely to escape his grasp. But then the truth dawned on my laggard's brain: Burbage is a Catholic! He has artfully used his player's skill to outwardly appear a man of the English church, a Puritan even, but none such would speak so blasphemously about an English house of God.

Aye, and that may also explain why his son protests his faith so loudly, to conceal his true beliefs or to protect his father. I dare say nothing, but what other explanation exists?

As we left the City through Bishop's Gate and made our way out Shoreditch Road toward the Theatre, passing orchardmen with laden wagons, hauling late harvest apples to the wealthy citizens of the City (Cuthbert snatching one for King Arthur), I collected in my mind the meagre advice and jests that Mr. Burbage had uttered over my fivemonth acquaintance with him. He spoke rarely, that it did not appertain to the stage or our accounts, but those things he said now made perfect sense. He harbours a certain disdain, dare I say 'hatred', for the new religion and, perhaps, the Queen herself.

Yet what is hatred in a man as fiery as Mr. Burbage? Every man among us, masters and 'prentices, will not test his temper. His brow seems ever raised, as if a permanent sigh resides upon his visage, but his lips are always pursed like the crow about to peck, giving him the appearance of one ever ready to strike. I have seen him argue with an innkeep with such fury to save a shilling it seemed he fought with the Devil himself to save the soul of a child. Long before he became a player, he worked many a year as a joiner, much as his brother Robert and their father did before them, so his fists are cannonballs and he clenches them instantly when he raises his voice, going at once nose-to-nose with any adversary, spittle flying and purple veins bulging. It is said he makes no mind if he argues with man or woman, but is always like the hungry dog ready to bite. Dick hath seen him rage, about some trifling expense, at the widow of his old partner in the Theatre, one John (or Jacob?) Bray. Aye, to hear Dick tell it, it was Mr. Burbage lasted an hour of bray-ing![61] I laugh to think on the conversation at his home after such a row: Mr. Burbage is married to the widow's sister.

His ill temper may be to ward away those who might con his secret, if indeed his heart holds the old faith and he is no friend of Her Majesty. It may also be that he lives on a knife's edge, owing to the many ways he plays at dice with his livelihood, and fears his whole enterprise may fail at any time and leave his family penniless. I mean, the Theatre he built, with his last penny, so far from the City walls, across so many yards of ruts and mud, that you could imagine none would venture so far forth to see a painted fool upon the stage. Yet venture forth they did. Dick says that from the first day the flag raised above the tiring house, Londoners flocked hither, like so many fish downstream drawn by the current into the nets. Once there, he devised every manner of wringing from each patron the last ha'penny in their purses. A penny to enter, another for a seat, still another for a cushion and another for the best view. Higher in the gallery where gallants might be seen in finery equal to the players on the stage, still another penny or two. Apples and figs and ale and tobacco for sale, and even the pipe to smoke it withal; a boy to hold your horse; a trinket used in the play that was said to be a monument taken from a Turk, but was in fact a likeness painted on clay by Boy Burbage and baked in some manner to look more ancient.

"What ho, Vernon!" hollered Mr. Burbage, vainly seeking to rouse an old gatekeeper upon our arrival at the Theatre.

"Verrrrrr - - nooooooooooon," called Boy Burbage, kicking at the door of a barn hard by, wherein we intended to lodge our Company's wagons and goods. "The old fool is drunk again, father, or asleep."

"Patience lad. For aught we know he perished of the Plague in the six-month ere we saw him last."

The Theatre itself is not so remarkable as I had been given to believe. O, to be sure, a handsome wooden structure, not unlike thy father's malt-barn, but half again as large. On the east, she is bound by the Shoreditch Road; on the south, by the aforementioned barn and a lane they call Holy Well, although no sign of divine water or other relic is in evidence. On it's north and west are open fields, now muddy and caked with stalks from harvests long-ago, beyond which lay garden plots, rounded in by crumbling stone walls, such that the whitewashed Theatre appears as a great cloud, hovering over a weary field of battle before the walls of a conquered realm. At length, a rattling was heard within the barn, followed by cursing and other ill report, thus:

"Who calls?" asks a frail voice curtly.

"Thy lord and master, sirrah," answers Boy Burbage. "Unlock this door, ere we do so for thee!"

"Richard? Is that little Richard, my master's boy? In truth, for the love of an old man, nearer the end of his life than the beginning, fool me not. Is it e'en thee, Richard?"

"Aye, Vernon, and my father. Open the door."

By now Mr. Burbage had dismounted and was surveying the barn, the grounds and the Theatre herself, with the practiced eye of the joiner who had raised it all from the dust 'neath his feet. The barn door opened to reveal a shriveled man of threescore years and more, a dozen strands of grey hair on his capless head, nary a tooth in's mouth, dressed in the most mis-matched suit of clothes that ever covered a man's nakedness in all of Christendom. An old jerkin, a pair of breeches thrice turned (here and there pieced together with packthread), a linen stocking on one leg and a kersey hose on the other, gartered with red and blue ribbons; a pair of boots more tired of walking than their owner, (one buckled, another laced), and on his hip, a rusty sword taken out of the player's armoury, with a broken hilt, and broken point. In short, a very monster of apparel.[62]

"O, are my master and his boy come home?" The inquiry creaked forth from the ancient soul like the complaint of a rusted hinge. "Kind keepers of my weak decaying age, let dying Vernon here rest himself. Even like a man new haled from the rack, so fare my limbs with such long servitude. And these grey locks, the augurs of death, argue the near-end of Vernon Jaggard. These eyes, like lamps whose wasting oil is spent, wax dim; these weak shoulders, overborne with a thousand thousand burdens, yet from them hang fading arms, like to a wither'd vine that droops his sapless branches to the ground; yet are these feet, whose strengthless stay is numb, unable to support this lump of clay, swift-winged with desire to get a grave, as knowing, I no other comfort have."[63]

"Well said, Vernon, well spoken, my friend," Mr. Burbage applauded furiously, as though he had been moved to tears by a passionate speech by a dying king, played by Mr. Johnson to a gallery of gaping spectators in the noonday sun. "The Tragedy of King Edward, his brother's death before the mob, is it not?"

"Aye, Jamie, that it was." Vernon appeared suddenly more robust than the moment before. "And well spoken too, was it not?"

"But for the couplet on Nestor, which I think thou hast omitted, eh? How goes that? Richard, knowest thou that couplet?"

Boy Burbage had no inkling and seemed more intent on separating the door from the leathern hands of the old retainer, that we might bring the wagons into the barn ere Christmas. The clothing now made sense: the faded apparel of an old player, whose wasting frame could do no more than hang them out to dry, hoping that familiar threads might outlive him, even unto his grave.

Mr. Burbage walked apart with Vernon the while, sharing stories of our summer excursions and the adventure in Denmark. Dick, myself and Boy Burbage completed the settling of the goods, which is to say we moved wagons, loads, horses and all, into the barn and bedded the lot, each to its rightful place. I was left to tend the horses, glad for a moment alone to inventory the sudden chill that ran me through. Would I end my days like Vernon, a sometimes player without a penny or a roof to call mine own. A roof? Not even a clean pair of hose, without holes, to call mine own! Would I outlive the week, given that the Burbages might yet turn me over to the constable for a traitor, mine own hand the instrument of my indictment, my letter to thee, dear coz, my judge and jury?

The horses groomed and watered, I took mine own small bundle of goods, the map crinkling within as I clutched the parcel to my bosom, then sought the Master's leave to depart. He displayed an unusual courtesy that I could not decipher, but report herewith for thy further understanding of my fate:

"Vernon, lookest thou at he who would wrap himself in our weeds and fill his mouth with our discourse. Meet Will Shakespeare, newly acquired from Stratford."

"Stafford? We played 'Gorboduc' a fortnight in Stafford, look you, and every soul in residence demanded us to stay and play it yet again, eh Jamie?" No one corrected him, but Boy Burbage rolled his eyes and wandered off.

"Look you, Shakespeare," quoth Mr. Burbage, "Meet me here on the morrow at noon for thy further employment in certain matters."

"And me, sir, also at noon?" asked Dick.

"No. Thou'lt come to the Cross Keys on the Gracious [*Gracechurch*] Street at four o'clock with the other players. Remember where it stood? Until then, God be with ye both."

I wanted in that instant to demand my fate, to be rid of a day's worth of torture that lay then before me. Why should I meekly trudge to my doom, a willing victim, only to be taken to the Queen's dungeons or slain by her guards on the spot, some golden reward clinking in the purse of the Burbages? But I could bring myself to say no more than farewells (an if I guessed aright, that the Burbages were of the old religion, then what cause would they have to give me over to Protestant authority)? Perhaps no more cause than the grudge that Boy Burbage bears me, but then that too remains a mystery, if he has no quarrel with the Shakespeares' religion, and after so many weeks together and so many miles 'neath our shoes.

Ere we departed, Vernon clouded the matter darker still, taking my hand with a solid grasp that belied his years and said 'Be of good cheer, young man. Fire that's closest kept burns most of all.' What meant he by that?

Dick and I took off over the Moor's ditch, sometimes a pissing conduit called Petty France, named of Frenchmen dwelling there, and lately built on the bank of the said ditch by some citizens of London, that more regarded their own private gain than the common good of the city, for by means of this causeway the soilage of houses with other filthiness is cast into the ditch and filled up with unsavoury things to the danger of impoisoning the whole City. We crossed then onto a field whereat stood a cross, and across that field to the City wall. I hoped to find Giddy and a night's peace before my fate, whatsoever God had in mind, and Dick had his several reasons to be in haste, and sayeth:

"I'll to the house of Mr. Clarke's brother, in Cheapside. There lives his widow still, in a grocer's shop that his years of toil bought her. His daughter lives there too, who fancies a barber's boy, but I hope one day may think more fondly on me. 'Tis she of which I made the inventory, those assets and liabilities, which our fellows found so comical, but which assures me I do not waste my labours to have her. If she loves me still, I will present thee to her, so that if I die before I can marry her, as only God knows whether I might be struck down with Plague, or worse, as we travel the pitiless highways, thou wilt help me keep my good and honest intentions toward her. Faith, I swear I have more urgent need of the barber, this nether tooth hath pained me since we came ashore again in England."

We walked a time in silence, no mean feat for Dick, whereupon he started up again his fears about the Plague and how no man could escape it if he dwelled his whole life in London. What little warmth the noonday sun had provided was then but a memory, clouds hiding his golden face, bathing us instead in a gloomy grey prologue to a cold and moonless night. Soon came we upon a strange passage through the wall, Moor's Gate he called it, back again in the flows of the great City on a street called Coleman, passing the shops of armourers and masons, the looming mountain of St. Paul's no more than half a mile distant toward the river, stopping when we came to Lothbury Street, to which he pointed west and directed me as follows, the particulars of which I carefully inventoried (in case that thou mayest need them to find me or Giddy at some future date):

"Needs must reach Wood street, out of which be divers lanes, but by no means take any of these false paths, namely:

—on the east side is Lad lane, which runneth east to Milke street corner;

          —down lower is Love lane, which lieth by the south side
of St. Alban's church and runneth down to the conduit in
Aldermanburie street;

          —lower down is Addle street, out of the which runneth Phillip
lane down to London wall.

These be the lanes on the east side. On the west side of Wood street
thou wilt find:

          —Huggen lane, by the south side of St. Michael's church, and
which goeth through to Guthuruns lane;

          —then lower is Maiden lane: this is the lane thou must taketh, for
it runneth west to the north end of Guthuruns lane, and there,
on the north side, stands the Haberdashers' hall and there will any
of their number direct thee to thy brother and his master."

Then was he gone, verily skipping further along Coleman Street towards his happy reunion with widow and daughter and, more than likely,
the barber's boy too. For the first time since leaving home, I was now totally
alone.

Yet how can any man or woman be alone in a City of so many thousands? Night would soon fall and I would be forced into a strange inn if I
came not upon Giddy ere then. My fortune, now a full four and twenty shillings, tightly wrapped and lashed to my waist, tucked near my privates, the
last place a pickpocket would snake his filching fingers, I supposed.

A church bell (St. Paul's?) proclaimed four o'the clock and for the first
time, I began to notice wind: blustery, buffeting, coy wind, driving dust in
mine eyes, now disappearing around the corner, now returning from another direction as if by magic, a cold wind that visits wise man and fool alike,
bringing with it the strange brew of smells that mingle in the nose with
imagination, a vapour like no other in England. As I drank this in, I was met
by a fine looking woman of some means, joined at the elbow to a tall man of
thirty with a Cavendish beard, who addressed me suddenly, thus:

"Why look John, is this not thy friend from home? What a surprise to
meet here on London streets."

"Aye, 'tis such a pleasure to see a familiar face," quoth the fellow, shaking my hand with such vigour that I soon forgot the chill wind of a moment
earlier. "How fare our friends at home? When didst thou arrive? What matters bring thee hither? Thou art most welcome to the City, cousin."

I was startled witless and could muster no more than a few vanities,
which clearly failed to impress.

"Why, hast thou forgotten me? I have been at least thrice in thy company," quoth the man, dusting bits of straw from my cloak with one hand and evermore wringing my hand with the other. "Ratsey, John Gabriel Ratsey, surely thou dost recall me; and may I present my wife Elinor."

"O, of course, uh, Will Shakespeare of Stratford, by'r leave," quoth I, glad to regain control of my limb and instead take up the delicate, lily white hand of a beautiful woman: the fairest creature yet born! No more than sixteen, she boasted cascades of auburn hair, 'neath a cap of fine linen and simple embroidery, worn charmingly to one side and fastened with a blue ribbon under her finely wrought chin. Her dress was otherwise most fair and modest, but the bright taffeta lining of her fur-trimmed cloak hinted at a wealthy family, or her wealthy husband. A small gold cross rested in the hollow of her milk-white throat, a sign of her unquestioned love of God. Modest too, though if she is married to this man, she is no virgin, I suppose.

"So, Will, how fares our countrymen in Warwickshire, cousin, and when wast thou last at home?" asked Ratsey, a decent figure of a man, well appointed, although face and hands that suggested labour out-a-doors and clothed in merchant's garments of a size much larger than his own lean girth.

"God willing, all are well. Yet I have been gone from thence some five or six months now, arriving but today in London. I am glad to meet thee here." I could not recall having met him ere then, but surely they were friends of my father, perhaps even among his many creditors, and in no wise would I further insult them by confessing mine ignorance of their person or station. "I serve Her Majesty, in the Earl of Leicester's Men, a Company of the finest players in the land, in service to Her Majesty," quoth I, repeating myself, but eager to impress upon this honourable husband and wife, as I then took them to be, that I was a great success and as much at home in the City as any man.

There followed more pleasant conversation wherein I mostly spilled forth my tales of travel, hither and abroad, and general gossip of the Babington matter against the Queen. At length, Mr. Ratsey spoke of the lateness of the hour and some other urgent business, but urged me to caution on my first night in the City, leaning closer and whispering with breath that reeked of onions and rum.

"Thou must fear the nips and foists." His teeth were grossly twisted and turning to rot, behind thick, cracked lips.

"Dearest John," quoth the angel at his side, "Mister Shakespeare is too trusting and honest of a Warwickshire man to know of such matters when described in such low terms."

"Faith, what was I thinking? I'll demonstrate how they operate, that thou might'st discern the wolf from the flock. Look you, here is my purse, well concealed at the back of my hip under my cloak. Still, the delicate hand of a foist, often a seemingly harmless maid, will bump thee in a crowd and slide a hand within to remove the contents ere thou canst take thy next breath. The nip will do likewise, but can deftly cut thy purse from off thy belt, thus." With each description he guided the hands of his wife like a puppet, to show me the moves I might expect of the City pickpocket. I was most grateful.

"Where hidest thou thy valuables, in thy bundle there?" Her voice so dainty I thought it would break, if the wind struck it, as it left her ruby lips.

"No. Here, tucked at the waist, well hidden by my shirt."

"Oh, then art thou well protected. See the trouble a - - how called thee that husband, a 'foist'? See the trouble such a low creature would have in stealing thy purse?" As she spoke, her silken arm brushed against my bare skin, tickling me deliciously, showing how my valuables were safe. She blushed even as she withdrew her fingertips, thinking she had been too forward.

"O cousin, I am thrice blessed that thou hast shown me these evil ways." I sought to ease her mind, to show no offence. "Please accept my thanks and the desire that we will meet again ... soon."

"I doubt it not, cousin Will," quoth Mr. Ratsey. "But e'en now must we make haste, for I would not be on the streets with Elinor after dark. Do convey our loves to thy brother, when God wills that thou shalt find him, which, I doubt it not, will be ere long." With that they were off down a narrow road called Aldermanbury, that would take them to the Brakenwharf and a ferry to their lodgings. I made note of these place names that I might better know my way around the City in the coming days.

Pleased now to be acquainted in the great City, I was ever more losing the daylight and no closer to finding my brother. I fairly ran the thousand paces to Wood Street and turned right as Dick had instructed, passing those lanes he foretold me of. Instantly I saw three signs on shops to my left, each signifying that the trade within was that of a haberdasher. There being no need to go farther to the hall of their trade, I thought instead to make immediate inquiries within.

Eagerly hoping to see Giddy's face, I opened the first door and stepped into a brightly lit shop, draped in every fashion of linen and silk imaginable, coloured and plain, simple fabric and tailored shirt alike. In one corner hung not less than an hundred sleeves waiting for an hundred arms to fill them. Along the ledge 'neath the window, lay a thousand buttons and other sundry fasteners. On the far wall, rising like so many books on shelves, were precisely folded garments, handkerchiefs, and adornments of every kind. In stark relief from the smells of the street, this place reeked of bleach and spotless hands before the Sunday sermon. I addressed the hunched back of a man who seemed to be examining a stitch in a hem with the gravest concern:

"Pardon mine intrusion, sir. Might this be the shop of Mr. Brownsword?"

"Yes, it might." The studious figure did not turn to meet my gaze. I cared little about his rudeness, for my heart soared that I had the luck of a Stanley, finding Giddy's master on my first attempt. I would have waited for him to finish his business with the errant stitch before asking for my brother, but in awhile, could contain myself no longer.

"And is young Gilbert Shakespeare apprentice here?" I expected my brother to emerge from the rooms above or at the back.

"No." There followed no further particulars.

"Is he not your apprentice then, sir?"

"He is not."

"Did you not say ... "

Suddenly he clutched the garment to his breast, as if fearing my mere gaze could snatch it from him, and swung violently upon his stool to come face to face with me, not six inches separating our noses. His was red and running with a foul green snot, I noted.

"I confirmed that this MIGHT be Mr. Brownsword's shop, but ne'er did I say it WAS the same." He looked me up and down, guessing rightly that I was not likely to be standing before him on any business from which he might profit. He swung back around on his stool and resumed picking at the stitch with the same determination as before.

I backed slowly out of the shop, not sure what might happen if I turned my back on this disagreeable malcontent. He knew the name, something at the least, so perhaps another of these shops was that of Giddy's master. Indeed, the third establishment, twice the size of the first and bustling with traffic, trade and apprentices at work, was Brownsword's. I was warmly greeted after making mine identity known and swiftly ushered to a workroom at the back, wherein my little brother sat with busy fingers.

"Thou hast grown at least a head!" quoth I, something surprised by the tender-hearted tears that washed both our faces. He, taking note of my shrunk shank after so many weary miles afoot, tartly replied:

"Whilst thou hast lost half thy former self. And where left thee the better part of thy hair?"

"Sod thee! Thou hast more hair on thy chin than Dobbin has on his tail."

"It should seem, then, that Dobbin's tail grows backward: I am sure he had more hair on his tail than I have on my face when I last saw our father riding him."

Thus continued our brotherly duel for a most happy hour. He is grown to be a man, coz; now a full twenty years, no more my childhood playmate, no more the lanky lad we beat at football, no more Crab's master and confidant.[64] Still half a head shorter than myself and delicate, almost womanly, his full red beard neatly trimmed, his brows plucked and waxed in the French manner, dressed as befits his haberdasher's calling, with a collar of the most intricate lace I have yet seen. Indeed, the only feature that might betray the impression of a gentle born youth are the red-raw punctures on his fingertips from the constant press and pull of needle through unyielding fabrics. He pushed aside several yards of blue cloth, that we might sit together on his workbench, our voices barely audible (as all sounds are muted inside the great cocoon of fabrics, stacked floor to ceiling and in every corner) and he asked if I had heard of ill winds from home.

"Nay, I am these many months of travel without news of any kind, save nightly tavern gossip and one letter from John Combe, wherein he talks of illness that may mean Plague has visited Stratford. What hearest thou of our home and loved ones?"

"I fear to say it brother, but only ill." He pinched his nose, as he was always wont to do when collecting his thoughts, as if he would draw the words from his brain by force. "Father and Mister Wheeler are forced from the Council."

"From the Council? Wherefore?"

"I hear it said that Mr. Wheeler himself desired to be put out, though none believes this to be so, and our father is excused for that he came not to meetings when called, nor had not done of long time."

"Lest he be confronted by his creditors." This said and instantly regretted, for thou knowest how Giddy is of tender nature, and I saw then that he began to stifle tears at the thought of our father in such public pain. I thought to change the subject, perhaps to one happier: "Hearest thou aught of the harvest? A good crop will surely change our father's fortunes. I had a letter of John Combe..."

"O, things already ill, will ever have bad success, as they say," quoth he, pinching his nose with ever more vigour.

"But when I left, the fields were...I mean to say...". In truth I then felt the cold chill of guilt sweep through me. Had I been there, might the harvest have come better home? O what have I done? Now I had to pinch my nose to hold back the certain flood of tears. Giddy lay a gentle hand upon my knee, knowing his brother's heart all too well.

"But how farest thou, Will?"

"Therein is much to report and it may be that I will soon rescue our father's debts. Look you, it cannot yet be called 'Fortune', but soon it will grow to greater lengths."

With this, I extracted my purse from within my garments, that I might show my treasury to my brother. Wary that any other might see, I huddled close to him on our perch and carefully opened the folds of leather, then screamed in great pain, for in that instant, I had wiggled my buttocks into a buckler's needle and in truth, my buttocks lost the battle. I leapt from the workbench and my purse fell from my lap, the contents scattered amidst the scraps of fabric, thread and bread crusts that lined the floor. But no coins fell into the dust, rather two dozen odd pebbles now rested upon various cushions of velvet, silk, linen and taffeta.

"Where is my money? What nimble mountebank has changed my silver to stone?" I wondered, falling then to my knees and rummaging through the debris, certain it was a fault of mine eyes. Giddy plucked the needle from my behind and came to mine aid on the floor, but neither of us could discover so much as a bent farthing.

Ratsey! I had fallen victim to a common thief. His wife changed my coins for stone when she had her hand in my...well, I explained to Giddy, who quickly saw that I was now as penniless as that selfsame father, but the moment earlier, I had hoped to help, and now left alone in a strange City. Even as I write these words upon the page, I begin to weep, to think how my younger brother took me in his arms and calmly made all things right. He stood me up and dusted off the clownish scraps that clung to my breeches. He told me of his own crowded lodging with the other 'prentices above the shop, but that our countryman, Pug Field, now himself a printer in a ward nearby, lodges with a kindly old bookish man who is renowned for his hospitality to strangers. Certainly he will allow Pug to lodge a countryman for a night or two in the big house that otherwise stands empty. He tugged at my simple and somewhat threadbare garments, casting over them a practiced eye, fitting me for a more stylish suit of clothes, which he would craft in his own hands.

"Fear not, brother. Look you: the sign of my trade is the lion rampant across fields of silk. Our fabrics may be soft and yielding, but in our breasts beat hearts of lions, his fearful claws the tools of our trade." I knew that well enough, rubbing my buttocks!

He began to measure me, insisting that he could craft me stylish habiliments [*garments*] from discards that would cost me nothing, but would make me look and feel every inch the City gent. He demanded every particular of my player's life to date, which I dutifully delivered, omitting not a jot. "And in conclusion, I have thus far played every kind of mute, joint-stool, flower pot, and tapestry hanging."

"But lookest thou not for better, now that Mr. Perkin is teaching thee the mysteries of thy craft?"

I yielded then my secret longing unto him: to make for the New World and a Fortune that would raise us all far above our station and our father's humility, far beyond any wealth that could be afforded to a common player. I unfolded my stolen map upon his workbench, careful not to scar the colours and images (just as careful to avoid describing how this artifact came into my possession). Both of us were soon lost among the seas, the islands, the billowy canvas on bold English ships, the noble savages and headhunters, the dizzying assault of exotic names and golden temples depicted at the edges.

Giddy then justly demanded to know of me a simple truth: "But Will, wherefore canst thou not make thy Fortune closer to home, e'en as I will make my way in this trade?"

"The Earl of Leicester will never allow a Shakespeare higher than a tradesman, never allow our father to resume his honours, lest it be by force of wealth alone. And more: home-keeping youth have ever homely wits. If I am to find the means to pay him back, in full, in kind, with interest, so to say, such means will I never find close to home, sluggardized in a trade."

"Like me?"

My words had cut him like the sharpest knife in his tailor's trade. My brother, my younger brother, who even now had comforted me in body and soul, as his older brother should have done for him, not the other way round. O what a traitor mine own tongue had been, to stab my dearest Giddy so deeply, but herewith I sought to make amends: "Nay, Giddy, nay. If I do but dream on wealth and power, I mean the Fortune that only the New World could bring to men like us. Yet being so far off, I do chide the muddy way that keeps me from it." He knew not what to make of my quest, but pinched his nose and raised a brow as if to say, 'thou knowest best', which clearly the penniless fool before him did not.

"Gilbert, hast thou finished his lordship's embroidery?" Mr. Brownsword shook us from our reverie, as I hastily tucked the map back among my scanting possessions.

"Yes, indeed, sir." Giddy dutifully offered up some handful of gauze to his master's stern scrutiny. After some prodding of the bundle with his smallest finger, he declared himself satisfied, dismissing my brother for the day and grumbling some cursory words of grace in my direction.

Shops all along the Wood Street were shutting and shuttering, their occupants retiring to lodgings above or scurrying off to other wards. The great City was more than its usual bustle, Giddy informed me, owing to the return yesterday of Her Majesty's Court from its normal sojourn in the country. All daylight had long since dissolved into inky, moonless night, the sky ever more obscured by the thousands of smoky fires that he reports are stoked by foul peat or dung, there being no wood left to burn within many miles of the City. Indeed London seems like one giant smokehouse, by day or night, which may account why a man may live longer in the City than the country. Indeed, it is a common topic of talk in the City, to wit, upon our arrival at Pug's lodging:

"Are ye the colliers, come with fresh coals for the master's fire?" asked Mistress Burberry, who met us at the door marked 'Stow' in Lime Street, within a ward of that same name, some dozen streets east of Brownsword's haberdashery.

We replied that we had no coals, but before we could state our true purpose for standing at the doorway, she continued: "Must I fetch it myself then? If ye have it not, where will an honest woman find means to keep her household warm? Upon what manner of tree doth your charcoal grow? Tell me that. I had thought all things had been made at London, yet I did never see no charcoals made here. By my troth, I think that they must therefore grow on trees outside of City walls and thither must I go myself to fetch heat for my fire."

We made no effort to correct the shriveled housekeeper, who examined us through thick glasses that made her eyes appear like great black orbs of polished alabaster. She stood not above four feet in height, nor more than sixty pound on the scale (appearing smaller still, owing to her rounded hunchback and lopsided stance, having one leg much shorter than the other, corrected with a block of wood under the shoe on her left foot that was some twelve inches thicker than the right). We seemed to have passed her inspection, for after explaining that we were no colliers, but kinsmen to Pug Field, she nodded that we should follow her in. As she ushered us up two very narrow banks of stairs, I noticed she lacked arms, yet ambled from side to side with great dexterity. A yellowish terrier, whose fur was held on his body only by the mange and the fleas, followed her every step as if he might catch her should she stumble.

She led us to a great room, a welcome fire blazing, deep velvet curtains holding out the draughts of intruding cold night air. The room was otherwise distinguished by an enormous oak table, at least a dozen legs the size of vintners casks to bear the burden of cargo piled thereon. For stacked higher than a man is tall, on nearly every inch of tabletop, were books, papers, maps, seals, bibles in many tongues, leather-bound journals, and stubs of burnt-out candles. A voice came from the far side of this paper mountain:

"Heather, 'tis thee there?"

"Aye, Mister Stow. Gentlemen come to call from up the street." With no more ado, she shuffled off through another door, the terrier sniffing close behind, into a darkened passageway.

"Who are they?" the voice demanded, but no reply could be made by a woman no longer standing in the room.

"Two Shakespeares, Mr. Stow," quoth Giddy. "Countrymen to your lodger, Richard Field, sir. We have met in this house 'afore, I believe."

"Shakespeare? Howso two thereof? Wait there … " The voice trailed off, each time seeming to come from another part of the room, our eyes slowing accustomed to the light and shadow, cast mostly by the fire. I could now make out long shelves of dusty trinkets along one wall, odd shapes of mystical machines foreign to mine eyes or experience. At the far end of the room, closer to the fire, a cluster of chairs and cushions, a warm and comfortable meeting place, so it seemed.

"Ah yes, Brownsword's boy, art thou not?" At last a figure appeared, having made his way around the south pole of his vast empire of books and papers. He presented himself in a great cloak of the same dusty vintage and material as the drapery, trimmed in fur of some long-dead beast, a man of at least three score years, with not a hair on his head, but a neat beard that may have been brown and now showed no colour beyond silver.

"If you please, sir." Giddy presented me to the old man with an unaccustomed flourish. Stow showed us to the corner of chairs, assigning us each a certain one, shouting over and again for Mistress Burberry. He used his hands when he spoke, as if his tongue depended thereon, and I noticed his ink-stained fingers tap-tapped ever so slightly in rhythm to his speech.

"Ye have had no supper, I'll wager; and by the looks of thee, William, I'll wager no dinner neither. Heather will remedy that, m'lads, if she ever gets back up the stairs." I found him quite the merry fellow and a stranger to formality.

We understood that Pug had gone with his master to Woolwich to buy a printing press, but when Giddy explained my plight, I was welcomed to use a closet [*room*] next to his. The house, we learned, had been scavenged in King Henry's time, but what remained was given to Stow's father, a tailor, who had done a service of some kind for the crown. Stow himself had also been a tailor in his youth, but had turned to writing surveys and histories, now collecting all that might be known of London that he might write a catalogue of her illustrious past. He had fallen on some hard times, sold the land, for the house had little value, save as firewood, but the new owner gave him leave to use it until his death.

"I am a full one and sixty years, m' lads. I'll wager they think I'm dead before the year is out, but I'll make them fools of the bargain and live another score or more. Ha!"

We ate and drank and toured his great room. He touched each item as a holy relic, telling us how it was a stone torn from the house of a Jew in 1355 to build a hospital at the Aldgate; or how it was an oil lamp from the Roman founders; or this one was no relic at all, but a chamber pot he has used since his childhood, but now he found it too small to hit the mark on cold, dark, nights, so it rested among the other antiquities. Stow also showed us his remarkable collection of books of every description in every language. He offered most liberal use of these, especially to me, when I told him I was a player but had lately given thought to writing poetry.

"Our mother gave me these few volumes," quoth I, showing him Ovid and a small prayer book given me before leaving home. "I thank thee most heartily for the use of any others, sir."

Although I was bone weary, my host of nearly thrice mine age was full of vigour and clearly gladdened with company and chatter, but at last Giddy took his leave and I was shown to the room where now I write these pages, lest I never have another chance. I know not what the morrow will bring, but I have only ill feelings about it. Hath Boy Burbage shown my letter to his father? If he means to snare me like a wounded hare, what proof will he yield up to the Constable that the letter is in my hand? It may be he needs no proof: his word against a country rustic, wrapped in a player's hide. Therefore, I write this letter and will deliver it up to Giddy, in case I do never see a sunrise ever after.

If I am to die soon, I deeply regret my foul heart, coveting Ratsey's wife as I did today, although God made me pay dearly for the weakness of my flesh. I trust to thee, coz, to leave the words upon the page or strike them through as thou seest fit, ere thou deliverest unto my son this letter, whenever that shall be. And if this be my last testament, I must confess to one more transgression that has heavily weighed upon my soul. Four

[Scribe's note: the remainder of this sentence was blotted out after the word 'Four'.
TT]

O coz, if my wind were but long enough to say my prayers, I'd repent! But drowsiness, and an empty inkpot, overcome me.

Kiss my boy and maids in my name and omit nothing else which thine honour deem'st best for their tender need. I am thine ever loving servant in all else, Will.

LETTER EIGHT
December 10, 1586

Wherein Shakespeare learns how his wife is struggling in Stratford and why his company of players in London is so dangerously divided by faith.

This letter is unique in all of Shakespeare's correspondence for two reasons. First, he has cut out sections of a letter he received from John Combe and pasted them on the page, then written his responses beneath. I have included Combe's text in italics to make it clear what were his thoughts and what were Shakespeare's responses. Combe was a moneylender who became the richest man in Stratford by the time he died in 1614, so it is fitting that the arguments in his letter were laid out like a bookkeeper's ledger of debits and credits.

Beyond the novelty of seeing the other half of what will become decades of correspondence, this letter gives us the first real glimpse of the life, and wife, Shakespeare left behind in Stratford. Women were commonly added to the workforce on farms to ensure a timely harvest and to provide a means of sustenance for single girls and unmarried mothers, but Anne Shakespeare is reported to be undertaking men's work to support the family, the back-breaking "shearing" of corn with a scythe. Combe infers she is not well educated, yet has earned his admiration for her shrewd bargaining on behalf of John Shakespeare's trade in skins and leathers, the necessities of his glovemaking trade.

We are introduced to another woman of the age, Elizabeth Page, a spinster who is betrothed to the actor Dick Cowley, jealous and suspicious as much as any modern 21st century girlfriend of an itinerant entertainer. The sonnet Shakespeare offers at the end of this letter (which appears in very similar form to his Sonnet 14, published many years later) captures views of love and beauty that transcend gender and generations.

In sum, we begin to see a more nuanced picture of women in Shakespeare's time. Although we won't have a first-person account of Queen Elizabeth until Letter Twelve, it is a view illuminated by the ruler of the kingdom, a hopeful daughter of a city grocer, and a callous-handed mother of three on the farm. If there is a surprise in this sampling, is it how much things have changed for women ... or how much they have remained the same?

John Combe warns Shakespeare about the practical dangers of traveling to the New World, advice Shakespeare is quick to acknowledge, but dismisses by asserting that "the rewards do so vastly outweigh any such consideration." He did remember the ill fates of merchants trading by ship that Combe articulates however, when he wrote *Merchant of Venice* ten years later: nearly identical references are made in Act 1.

Beyond mortal dangers, Combe appeals to Shakespeare's sense of duty as a father and husband to try to encourage him to "come home with all haste." Shakespeare feels pangs of guilt, but also implies that he owes Anne and his father no loyalty, and that he will explain why to Combe later, in person. As a practical matter, Shakespeare asks "what living would I make in Stratford, coz, that I too might add more than I subtract?"

He does acknowledge Combe's good advice not to revenge himself by murdering the Earl, but nervously notes the irony that, even as the Earl falls from the Queen's favor, so too may the Leicester's Men fall apart. Shakespeare thus resolves to sail for the New World in the spring and use employment by the Earl to gain his passage and "come home a richer man than any is at Court."

Beyond debates about home versus adventures abroad, in this letter Shakespeare takes us inside The Theatre, the venue shaped like a giant O in which the Leicester's Men perform in London. He frets about a competing new theatre, The Rose, which is currently being built near the whorehouses of London (Illustrations 15a, opposite, and 15b, on page 188, show the ruins of Winchester Palace and the economic link between the church, the theatres, and the brothels). "Winchester geese" was a name for prostitutes, because the land

15a. The ruins of the Bishop of Winchester's Palace near Shakespeare's Globe and The Rose playhouses, London.

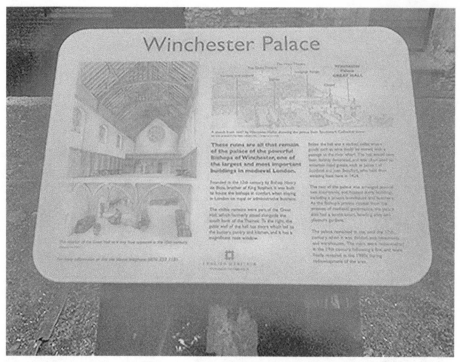

15b. Description of Winchester Palace at the site today.

16. The 1588 "Grafton" portrait that many believe to be Shakespeare at age twenty-four.

on which Southwark brothels stood was leased from the Bishop of Winchester, which guaranteed a steady stream of patrons for The Rose. Shakespeare's Globe Playhouse was later built in the vicinity of the Rose and benefited from the same arrangement.

Various records, including the recent archeological excavation of the foundation of The Rose, suggest it was actually smaller than The Theatre, however those assumptions must now be re-examined in light of Shakespeare's commentary here (and in subsequent letters), based on his performances in both. Surely it is this experience that Shakespeare calls forth, to describe the players' reliance on the imagination of the audience in these rather barren spaces in the opening prologue of *Henry V*.

Now a man of the city himself, Shakespeare is given a new suit of clothes by his brother and admits to trimming his hair and beard. A portrait was recently discovered that some experts believe may be the young poet in 1588, so not long after he first arrived in London (see Illustration 16, opposite bottom). If this is not his face staring back at us from across the centuries, it is certainly a good likeness of a very similar young man, eager to blend into fashion, yet hopeful to stand out from the crowd.

Finally, this letter raises troubling issues that are explained in greater detail in subsequent letters about fathers, daughters, wives, sisters, honesty, and infidelity. Tantalizing hints in Letter Eight, nothing more.

10 *December 1586, London*

Coz,

I would beg thee to forbear judgment, for we are all sinners, but thy words have struck a note that reverberates still this many days after receiving thy letter. That thou hast brought me welcome news of home, I give hearty thanks. That thou hast shaken my resolve, I am certain thou dost me wrong. Therefore will I set down thine arguments and what feeble responses I may wring from the deepest confines of my heart, for always do I treasure thy counsel, be it savoury or sour, and trust thy friendship in all things.

Item first: Thou knowest in my profession, I calculate risk and reward to the tenth of a penny and value the loss of a single hair on a head. Thou wouldst sail to the Americas to seek thy fortune? I know many who have lost fortunes that way, none that are made wealthy. Indeed, one merchant known to me in London had an argosy bound to Tripoli last season and another to the Indies or Brazil. Surely these were lost, for no word comes of them. Why? Ships are but boards, sailors but men, and the worst of those be water-thieves (I mean pirates!). And then there is the peril of waters, winds and rocks. I would not squander the tools of my trade (my gold, I mean) on such frivolousness, nor would I risk the life of my dearest kinsman on such voyages.

'Tis true: the risks are many and since coming to London I have heard more of these than rewards. Moreover, although I know of three voyages bound for the New World in spring, and each will take a full complement of men and settlers, only those who have some skill or goods or money to bring withal will be chosen. This gives me scant hope to join any one of them. Dick reports yet more good reason I should not in any wise follow this course: he heard yesternight from a goodly gentleman at the Bell that General Raleigh's colony has been beset with naught but woe, and no man returned alive. Nor, they say, is any man truly safe in such colonies: the savages thereabout are most ferocious, clad in the skins of lions or bears, and if thy fortress be not well watched or warded, they will assault the inhabitants to gain the bodies of men, which they do covet for their meat!

Aye, John, only God knows if He means this New World to be a land of plenty or pity and sure the risks are grave, but I have heard such proofs that the rewards do so vastly outweigh any such consideration. And who but God can predict whether the perils thou hast inventoried would befall any ship I may board? Only He can say whether, staying at home, I would die of Plague; or be stabbed and robbed by highwaymen as our Company travels from town to town; or be taken prisoner as a traitor for any insult to the Earl in that letter which Boy Burbage still holds secret. Only He can protect me from such ills, wherever I seek to better myself.

But I may calm thy fears by that which I have heard from those who truly know. I have inquired about the savages brought to London, those two called Wanchese and Manteo. Them will I seek out to learn more about their wealth and true customs. These men are said to wear our clothes and speak our English tongue. And I will speak with those who have met other such savage notables, for these are not the first of their kind to arrive in England. One of the savage kings of the country of Brazil took ship with those English explorers in the time of our last King Henry and was presented at White Hall to His Majesty, at the sight of whom, reports say that the King and all the nobility did marvel not a little. No wonder, for I have seen a drawing of this chief: in his cheeks were holes, made according to their savage manner, and therein small bones were planted, which in his own country was reputed for great bravery. He had also another hole in his nether lip, wherein was set a precious stone about the bigness of a pea. All his apparel, behavior, and gesture were very strange to behold. I have looked at my map and found his land farther south than those that our English lords hold sovereignty over. Those who reported this story to Mr. Johnson could not say what became of this chief, but sailors tell of other chiefs and slaves brought hither who have since learned our language and can give me honest replies to thy fair questions. This much I pledge to thee to undertake ere I set foot on any vessel.

Item second: Let me beg thy forgiveness before committing the advice which follows to paper. As one who cares not for women or wives, I may be unqualified to address these matters, leastways from any experience. O, that a woman conceived me, I give her thanks; that she hath cared for me in my youth, I likewise give her most humble thanks: but must I wear a band on my finger or blow my bugle in the same bedchamber each night? Nay, all women shall pardon me. But

William, thy honest wife hath earned a measure of admiration, even from such a bachelor as mine own self. She hath aided thy household, shearing at harvest and brewing good ale, the latter hath sold for high prices. Thy father aids her in this and she hath lent him her shrewd eye for skins when he goes buying at the mart. In this manner, thy family might survive a season or two, but thinkst thou that days are long enough for a wife to continue such labors and find yet more hours to care for three mewling, puking babes? Nor are any of these endeavours sufficient to fill the larder. Anne will not complain, but each meal is surely smaller in the bowl; each day thy father drinks himself sooner into swinish sleep; and thou knowest thy mother aides her not, nor will she hear any word she deemeth 'unkind' in her kitchen. I have been by when she most shrewishly demands ever more of Anne, but thy good wife replies only that she doth strive to be a worthy mate to thee; a worthy daughter to the Shakespeares; and will only defend herself most modestly with such as 'I am by birth a shepherd's daughter, my wit untrained in any kind of art, yet Heaven has seen fit to shine health and good hands upon my meagre estate, such that I will do all I can to add more in this house than I subtract.' Short tale to make Will, thou shouldst come home with all haste.

Oh John, thy words do cut my conscience to the quick: and is not a man naked, whose conscience with injustice is corrupted? But what living would I make in Stratford, coz, such that I too might add more than I subtract? Thou art expert with numbers: what arithmetic hast thou that adds up to such a sum? Thou needest no johannes factotum to help thee lift thy money box; my father needs no help making gloves that no one comes to buy, his trade shriveled as it is by circumstances well known to thee. My heart is glad that Anne is useful in my father's household. 'Tis no surprise that he helps her or that she returns such favors: this news only increases the fury of the winds that would drive me soonest to the New World. When God shall bring us together again, I shall convey to thee those events which may further satisfy thy just concerns, but which, were I now to write the words, I would tear the pages to shreds and consign them to fire before they could offend thine eyes or mine.

Item next: thy quarrel with the Earl is a fool's investment. A successful man chooseth his enemies as wisely as his friends. Those injuries which thy family sustains at his hand are villainous, but how wilt thou lighten thy father's load in prison or dangling from a penny rope by the neck? Herewith the reckoning of striking a blow upon the Earl:

- A measure of satisfaction, which quickly fades.

- A measure of relief to thy father's income, which he will quickly spend on drink.

- A measure of appreciation among the Ardens, which they shall never express to a man hiding in the Americas or lying in a cold grave.

And say thy measure of revenge, whatsoever form that may take, is undiscovered and thou art seen blameless? Will God not judge thee in the end? Wilt thy son think better of thee? Forbear Will, seek not vengeance. Heaven shall punish the wicked and reward thy perseverance. Robert Dudley is to history a whoreson zed, an unnecessary letter. When even a king is buried, may not a worm eat of his flesh? And may not a man fish with that selfsame worm, so that when he eats the fish, the king may thereby progress through the guts of a beggar?[65] Such is the fate of the Earl, whether he dies at thy hands or from the disease that no man 'scapes, by which I mean old age.

I am in thy debt John, for the love thou showest in thy reckoning. Thou art a true man of ledgers, even in thy arguments. I can recall thee still, reaching up to thy father's desk to take up his quill, pretending to enter sums in his books, wearing his robe that draped thy back and the floor in equal measure. I see thee now, in my mind's eye, writing this letter of such care to thy friend, towering above that selfsame desk, the robe wrapped warmly about thee, the hem hovering above the floor, a boy grown into a man's estate. And though I would now wrap myself in a player's hide, I fear my days with Leicester's Men are briefly numbered, not because of any revenge I might charge to his ledger and credit to the Shakespeares, but from the fustian [*pretentious*] Earl's own self-slaughter.

That is to say, our arrival in London was greeted with news of his misadventures in the Low Countries, especially some lost battle at a place called Zutfen, whereat the well-beloved Phillip Sidney died most valiantly. 'Tis said Sidney lay bloody, life's charms ebbing from his body, and he gave his last measure of water to a common soldier, saying, 'Thy necessity is yet greater than mine,' at the selfsame moment when Leicester was seen fleeing the field like an old cur with tail between his legs.

Such must be the hand of the Almighty, so has the Divine become my sword of retribution for the wrongs wrought on my kinsmen by this same Earl. Therein do I take great comfort, but therein do I also fear our Company will fall from any favor at Court and we (his servants, nothing more) shall be sent packing, cloaked in the selfsame disgrace as our master. It is whispered that Walsingham is no friend of Leicester, fearing his influence over Her Majesty when the Earl spends his nights in her arms. Yet I hear too that the Queen herself did thrice propose the Earl to wed the queen of Scotland, to better secure her loyalty to the crown, which he did thrice refuse, and having thereby failed Her Majesty in this undertaking, the scheming Mary was left free to plot with Babington to rob our Queen of life and crown.

I swear, such matters that spark mild attention in the country are raging fires here in London. Is every man singed who nears the Court? Or merely that no man living can recall a time when England was so hotly attacked from within and without? Our Company is a study therein and grows more quarrelsome by the day. Yestermorn, when we gathered to our accustomed day's labours at the Theatre, Mr. Pope had writ a scurrilous verse about the Pope in Rome and was soundly attacked by that group of Catholics among us. I made note, the better to know who stands with whom:

"Brother, thou dost blaspheme in this," quoth Mr. Phillips, snatching the paper on which the verse was writ and flinging it into the small fire that warmed our hands. "Thou shalt stand cursed and be excommunicated, like the Queen. Look you, I bear Her Majesty no ill will and count myself a loyal subject. But her excommunication means that any subject may revolt from his allegiance, for she is branded a heretic by the Pope."

"O brother, thou canst not speak a name in England so slight, unworthy and ridiculous, as 'pope,'" quoth Mr. Pope, laughing at the play on words of his name, making a jest of the matter before it might become hotter than the burning paper.

"What a foul mouthed Pope art thou!" quoth Mr. Clarke, who is always something disdainful of bad manners, especially if insults to the old faith are involved.

"Aye, and being of that selfsame name, I would die before an Italian priest shall soil it with tithe or toll in our dominions: so tell THY pope, he of borrowed reverence and usurp'd authority, there are many of my colour in England!" Mr. Pope turned red, showing us that his crooked smile was nothing laughing now, indeed when tempers flare he will oft puff out his chest and bombast, as if to prove his deformities take away not a jot of his manhood.

"Thomas, I fear for thee." Mr. Clarke laid a hand on his shoulder, in such earnestness, as if witnessing the second coming of Christ. "For the Pope, that thou dost scorn, hath declared: meritorious shall that hand be called, canonized and worshipped as a saint even, that takes away by any course Her Majesty's very life. Babington may have failed, but I'll warrant thee, thou mayst easier hold a serpent by the tongue than halt the hand that would undertake this deed."

"I may disjoin my hand, but not my faith. And thou shalt lose thy hand if it remains on my person a second longer."

Mr. Pope was now full choleric. Mr. Phillips attempted to be his cure: "Brother, dost thou not make 'faith' an enemy to 'faith', e'en as thy tongue makes argument against thy former tongue? I mean, let the vow thou hast first made to Heaven when we were boys, first be to Heaven performed. Thou hast sworn allegiance to the Catholic church. Thy later vows, to the English church, is against that first vow, and therefore is rebellion against thyself!"[66]

"Aye, do not let such perils light on thee, so heavy as thou shalt not shake them off, but in despair die under their black weight." Mr. Clarke's hand, now removed from Mr. Pope's shoulder, rested on the hilt of his dagger.

"Nay. Ye two, and all the kings of Christendom, are led so grossly by this meddling priest, dreading his curse. Excommunication from a false faith? Ha!" Mr. Pope spat and patted his purse. "For ye know how easily can a little money buy a man out from that curse! Aye, for this, and many reasons more, I may take no heed of thy pope. Nor should Her Majesty stay her hand 'gainst the pretender to her mighty throne, aye, I would swing the axe myself, if given the duty to protect the realm. Wouldst thou not do likewise?"

There were no blows exchanged, but prevented only when Mr. Burbage let fall a beam from above, with great cursing and such, one that he had been repairing while showing Cuthbert a finer point of joinery. No man was hurt and Mr. Burbage suffered jests and insults the rest of the day for his 'butter bread hands', but it may have been the hand of a higher power, that wants us not to fight over such matters, that broke up the argument. Yet do the embers of that fire, I fear, still glow hot.

In sum, coz, I will not seek vengeance for the while, but will bide my time and earn what money I may until ships sail for the New World in spring. This may be vengeance enough: that I will use employment by the Earl to gain my passage and come home a richer man than any is at Court.

Item last: thy tales of playing in town halls cheer me greatly, for I do remember me that at such a play, my father took me with him and made me stand between his legs as he sat upon one of the benches where we saw and heard very well. This sight took such an impression in me that when I came towards a man's estate, it was fresh in my memory as if I had seen it newly acted, despite it being long out of fashion. 'Cradle of Security' it was called. Men dressed as women impersonating Pride, Lust and other sins, bewitching a poor oaf and luring him into the loss of his immortal soul, covering his face with a swinish snout and escorting him into Hell itself. That year Grace was born and Thomas dressed her as the Sins, while he played the oaf and I the Devil around the house. Ha! We would be players, our sister too, but dear friend, know that thy letter hast given me a gift of great value: a precious memory otherwise long forgot.

O, would that little Grace could play upon our stage. She would charm the multitude. The Theatre is unlike any hall or inn where we have played to date. A wooden O, with one ring of seats rising above another, such that a thousand spectators may hover like angels over a wooden scaffold, which itself is surrounded by a huddled mass standing before the players. This stage is bare, but many are the places to hide a player till he be called. Below is a void, accessed by a trap door in the floor of the stage, where we may show a man being buried or a demon rising from Hell (this may be why I heard a preacher call the Theatre a chapel of Satan!). Behind is a separate den, which can be revealed to the spectators by sliding apart of some doors and behind that the tiring house, wherein every man waits his turn, recalls his part, and dons his wigs. Above, held aloft by stout columns, is a balcony that may appear to be the upper reaches of a great house or a walled city and which contains such machinery that can lift a chariot.

'Tis a place of brilliant magic, coz! Daily doth this cockpit seem to hold the vast fields of England or the very canon that did affright the air at Agincourt. And, like thy tiny crooked figures in a ledger may signify a million, those few of us work on the imaginary forces of the spectators to signify great armies or Roman legions, into a thousand parts dividing one man, such that when we do speak of horses, the gaping many may see them printing their proud hoofs in the receiving earth, for 'tis their thoughts that deck our kings and carry them hither and yon, jumping o'er times, turning the accomplishment of many years into an hour-glass. Brilliant magic!

Cuthbert says that his father used his skill as a joiner to craft every timber of the Theatre himself, but that this shall soon be eclipsed by the Rose, now rising from the muds of the bankside in Southwarke, which will be the largest theatre hitherto constructed, neighbor to the bull and bear baiting thither and to such brothels from whence those environs take their name. Cuthbert fears this Rose shall smell sweet to our paying customers and lure them away: for who would brave the muddy fields north of the city when they might walk over the bridge or take a boat for a penny much closer on the southbank? Which Company shall play there is not yet known, but perhaps my skills are passable, such that I could gain employment thither if our Company falters, or if I am any more hounded by the Boy Burbage, who takes every opportunity to spy upon my private conversation, looking to criticize how I might act or in what manner I might praise God. He hath even boxed me about the ears when I am unsuspecting and cannot defend myself, as when I carry a load to the wagon. I swear he would have me whipped or worse, if it were in his power alone, although I escaped such rough justice when last I stood in the hazard.

I mean that on my arrival last month in London (as I have writ to thee), I was bid to report next day to Mr. Burbage at The Theatre, my fate uncertain. I arrived early to observe any Constable that might appear, to gain the advantage and flee. No living soul was thither, save for Vernon the old player-turned-keeper.

"O Shakepiece is it?" Vernon was at painting the wooden columns on the stage to resemble marble, a fine trick, when I entered the Theatre. "Is all our Company here? What play shall we hear then?"

"I come for no play Mr. Vernon, but am summoned hither by Mr. Burbage." I began to take in the vast hall that was the Theatre and imagined eager multitudes crammed onto her balconies and upon the dirt before the stage where now I stood.

"Let us play one any how. What wilt thou have, eh? Pyramus and Thisbe? Psalms Come a Calling? Nay, thou wilt have a fantasy more in keeping with the fashion of the time, I'll warrant, eh?"

"Mr. Vernon, how doth a man fill such a large space with his voice?" I could not imagine speaking an entire play so that those sitting in the top balcony at the last row might hear it all.

"Thou must not call me master. I am no man's master, nor no man's servant. Vernon is a name, like Caesar was once such a name, or Plato, or the Devil, one word that every man knows and needs no other honours or designations."

"As you like it, Vernon. But to my question - - "

"The raging rocks and shivering shocks shall break the locks of prison gates," quoth he with a sound that was at first a drum, to be heard in the next county, dissolving to a subtle whisper "and Phibbus' car shall shine from far and make and mar the foolish Fates."[67]

"I am amazed, Vernon. Thou art a mountebank and hath cast a spell on this wooden ring. It reverberates like distant thunder, subtle yet audible in every corner."

"Aye, this was lofty! This is Hercules style, a tyrant's style; a lover is more condoling, eh? O, look you, there's another man who needs but one word for his name: Huuuu-rrrrr-kew-leeeez!" With that, he hefted two great stone jugs and raised them above his head as though they were no greater weight than two yard of wool. "These may have been lifted by Hercules, for they were unearthed here when the Theatre was built."

"Hercules?"

"Aye, look you, in the digging of this Theatre we found many earthen pots full of ashes and burnt bones of men, to wit, of the Romans that inhabited here; for it was the custom of the Romans to burn their dead, to put their ashes in an urn, and then bury the same, with certain ceremonies, in some field appointed for that purpose near unto their city." He then lifted a board at the side of the stage and showed me a pile of various implements and furnitures, to which he added his several descriptions, turning over each item as if it were a holy relic.

"Every one of these pots had in them one piece of copper money also, with the inscription of the emperor then reigning: some of them were of Claudius, some of Vespasian, some of Nero, of Anthoninus Pius, of Trajanus, and others."

I studied the coin he now took from his pocket, which was strung on a small metal chain. It bore a regal likeness, in profile, of a long-dead Roman, no doubt one of those monarchs that Vernon had even now recited. I asked if there were no other clues to who left these things in the earth here, or why.

"Ah, no one can make sense of that, but besides those urns, many other pots were there found, made of a white earth with long necks and handles, also divers vials and other fashioned glasses thereby, some most cunningly wrought of crystal, such as I have not seen the like, all which had yet their water in them: nothing differing in clearness or taste from common spring water."

I could imagine some antique Roman holding this vial, pouring water therefrom for the ladies in his company, as brutish slaves fought lions and bears. Vernon looked behind us to be certain no man was nigh, then whispered.

"I myself have reserved one pot of white earth very small, not exceeding the quantity of a quarter of a wine pint, made in shape of a hare squatted upon her legs, and between her ears is the mouth of the pot. Such an animal brings good fortune."

Vernon said there were also found nearby the skulls and bones of men whose coffins, being of timber, were consumed. Divers great nails of iron, such as are used in the wheels of shod carts, being each of them as big as a man's finger, were found near each skull. These nails caused more wonderment than the rest of things found thither: were those men murdered, by driving those nails into their heads?

"Is it not odd Vernon, that we play Romans in our entertainments and all the while their ancestors lay 'neath our feet?"

"Aye, and their ghosts walk abroad at night and have no rest, the why or wherefore I cannot say. But at night, a man is wise to speak only in that stage whisper I have shown thee."

"Vernon, wilt thou teach me the mysteries of thy craft at speaking the speech in this manner? In my short service to Leicester's Men, we have played only those inns and fields that require far less rumbustiousness."

"I'll teach thee when thine other duties are completed, William," the unmistakable voice of Mr. Burbage, who even then had entered upon our scene. I took careful note that he was accompanied by Boy Burbage and Cuthbert, but no greater authorities or men at arms. Mr. Burbage came quickly to his point:

"I need an inventory of those plays and interludes we would perform for Her Majesty's entertainment at Christmastime. Each must have its description, such that the Master of Revels can more swiftly decide those entertainments the Queen might find pleasing. I will give thee the names of these pieces, and the matter each one doth convey, and thou shalt write this down in thy finest hand." I was to be the scribe, not destined for the Tower for some offense, real or imagined. Was my relief palpable to the Burbages?

"I am honoured to write our presentation to the Queen."

"Nay Will, the Queen never sees such trivials." Cuthbert corrected in a tone not meant to offend (unlike anything his brother ever speaks to me). "In the City we toil under Tilney's Tyranny, Master of the Revels Sir Edmunde Tilney.[68] O and look you, he will o'erlook no opportunity to remind every player and poet, yea all who labour in our mysteries, that he has their fate in his stubby hands. We must present him our list of plays this very day, as will all other Companies, for only he will select those to be preferred against those sent packing. He lines up the masters of each Company, like so many schoolboys, and parades before them like a peacock."

"By Her Majesty's command, I shall choose among your come-dies...your tragedies....your shows...and your in-ter-luuuudes!" Vernon strutted and spoke in high styled accent, as he had seen Tilney do in times past, I take it. "What have you in readiness, or meeeean you to set forth? Recite them before me noooooouuuw, together with the playing place and time proposed." I laughed at Vernon's portrayal and noted how Mr. Burbage gave him full reign for such jesting. I asked how it came that Tilney hath such power in the City when we were not so troubled in the country. Cuth-bert's reply was astonishing:

"O yes, even those plays that we put forth abroad or here at the The-atre must first be approved by this popinjay, but there's more: if we stray a line, nay a word, from that text which first we propose to him, any one of us can be taken away in irons and set in goal at his pleasure. I have heard the names of players who were thus taken and ne'er seen again. Therefore is thy written record of great import. He has the power to tear a playhouse down, or other place where seditious matters are played, to the very ground, and has done so more than once to make a show. Therefore, no player dare to beard or trifle him."

For several hours thereafter, I tediously copied every word spoken by Mr. Burbage. Boy Burbage sought to interject from time to time, but I noted that his father paid him little heed. When we had completed some thirty pages, Mr. Burbage declared himself satisfied and thanked me most courteously for my service.

"Here is sixpence to feed thy fondness for bread and London butter, William. Thou couldst use a trifle more fat on thy bones." With this, he wrapped the pages in a sash and carefully installed them into King Arthur's saddlebag.

"Better to throw sixpence down yonder well than waste it on this bull's pizzle," muttered Boy Burbage under his breath, so that only I might hear him, knocking the coin from my hand as he ran after his father.

"What a foot-licker is he," quoth Vernon, who then made a comic show of cleaning my sixpence on his rump before returning it with a bow. "I looked for him to become his father's mirror image, when he grows to manhood, but now..." his voice trailed away.

"I took comfort that he dared not attack me in front of Mr. Burbage, but still fear what he can do or say to blacken what goodwill I have earned in his father's eyes when I am not by."

"Fear who, him? Nay lad, an empty vessel makes the louder sound and his father is no fool, I'll warrant thee. Nay, thou art ignorant as dirt if thou think'st his father takes the musings of a jealous boy in earnest."

"Jealous? He hates me for my father's religion, I am certain."

Vernon laughed, then spat on the ground. "For being Catholic? Nay, he is a common sinner himself and cares not which ear of God any other man might pray to. Nay lad, he fears thou wilt shine brighter than he among the players. He is jealous as an old wife, when her husband gets whiff of some pretty pussy to huggle withal."

I thanked Vernon for his comfort. Lately has Mr. Perkin been constantly away, thus have my lessons in the players' art been curtailed, but Vernon hath indeed shown me his secrets of the voice, the flute, and a clever trick to make six types of apparel from one cloak. Yet 'tis his thoughts on the Boy Burbage that have cleaved most to my mind. Jealous? 'Tis true that I have made my mark with the players, but the lout is given roles that far exceed mine. Jealous? 'Tis true that I have mended plays and have his father's ear on certain matters that he will trust to no other, especially with money, but were we both in a burning barn, Mr. Burbage would save his own flesh and blood every time. Jealous? Whether true or no, it makes him no less mine adversary and one I must be most wary of. Thursday last, when that King Arthur had wandered some distance off

[Scribe's note: Even though this entire letter is pasted together from Combe's correspondence and Shakespeare's reply, there appears to be a missing section here. The text ended abruptly and the lower third of the page was torn off, suggesting some text removed. The format continued on the next page however. TT]

News of Stratford: The town is nearly lost to fire. Richard Crimmons, that common Irish blasphemer and drunkard, lost all of his money in some dealings with a goldsmith. He hanged himself, after first setting straw on fire to burn down his house and the town withal. By God's merciful providence, the house was consumed but the town was preserved (and surely he is now in Hell for the attempt). It seems Fire hath lately been our constant companion here, for other houses have burned for sundry reasons and taken their neighbors with them. The Hale house on Bridge Street burned and took two with it. The barn in Elm Street (remember where we were wont to play at bowling?) burned for five days, though no other *structure caught fire. Odd, is it not, for bowling is the oracle of life, and like fire, it never follows the intended path, but by good luck or ill, always forward against an unseen bias. I think on these, our youthful days, and wonder: dost thou not long for thy home and familiars?*

Sad am I to hear of ill winds blowing through Stratford, but I am well attended in London and passable content. I am thrice blessed in the company of Giddy. First, that his hand is as open as day for those in need of charity. Next, that when given cause, he is incensed to defense of his friends, like the sharpest flint. And last, when I despair of ever making my son proud of his father, then doth Giddy give me line and scope till that my passions and foolish fears, like a whale on ground, exhaust themselves, thrashing about for naught, after which he comforteth me most sweetly.

Indeed, he hath become my schoolmaster in the ways of the City. On Sunday last, was I presented in church to a Venetian nobleman's wife, whereupon I clutched at her arm and lathered her bare hand with kisses (for such had I heard was the custom in polite company in London). But she did shriek, as did many other witnesses, causing some to flee the church itself. As luck would have it, the Venetian is an old buffoon who drew a dagger to defend his wife's honour, but Giddy pulled me of an instant from thither and we did wisely withdraw into the crowd. The tale gave the Leicester's Men a good laugh, I can tell thee.

And with great thanks to Giddy, I no longer look the part of the country rustic, for he hath produced a passable suit of clothes for me and I will not be seen in any other. He left them o'ersized, saying that I will eat better here in London and will grow back to my former bulk. A clean shirt of modern fashion with a green leather jerkin and galli-skin breeches to match. Woolen stockings to the knee, as is now the fashion, with a ribbon, and a fine pair of slippers in place of my foul Warwickshire boots. The cap is yet to come, as is a cloak, which is most urgently needed when the wind slices through the City from the Thames. My hair too hath been trimmed, beard and all, such that no man who has seen me ere this will recognize the face staring back.

Nor is Giddy mine only friend and counsel here. Dick hath shown me many secrets of the City, for instance the Royal Exchange, an astonishing maze of grand colonnades, shops, and a plaza they say is the twin of one in Venice. Every man in London speaks of this quarter and it is known far and

wide by a huge golden grasshopper on its roof! And thither did Dick introduce me to his lady-love (for so he calls her).

They were seated on a bench by a notorious bookstall when I approached them, the lady balancing a delicate strawcake on one knee and
interrogating him, which I will herewith recall for thee, for methinks the
lady uttered some common sense worth repeating:

"Dost swear then, never to have lain with her?" I had arrived at an
inconvenient moment, so it seemed, but could not erase mine appearance
from their memory, so quickly made mine introductions. Dick rose and
bowed as if greeting the Queen, meant, I take it, to impress his lady-love
that a valued personage of the Earl's Company had come calling at his invitation. I expressed those common pleasantries expected in such meetings,
which she did courteously requite, but then she continued her lecture:

"Aye Richard, let husbands know their wives have sense like them, they
see and smell, and have their palates both for sweet and sour, as husbands
have."

Elizabeth Page, for so she is called, seemed most intent to convey her
concerns for Dick's fealty, (though he hath concerns, in equal measure, of
her devotion to him). She is a sturdy woman of more years than I had supposed, and a head taller than Dick, though some beauty peeps through the
lattice of seared age. Upon her head a platted hive of straw, which fortified
her visage from the sun, the shadows hiding the carcass of beauty, somewhat
spent and done. Before Dick could assure her of his love, she continued in
the vein of a Latin lesson, asking and answering her own inquiries:

"And what then is it that men do, when they change wives for others?
Is it sport? I think it is. Doth affection breed it? I think it doth. Is it frailty
that is to blame? It is so too. BUT ... have not women affections, desires for
sport and frailty as men have? Aye ye men: use us well, else see the ills ye do
instruct your women too!"

"But Beth, if all despair that have unfaithful spouses, would not one
half of all mankind hang themselves?" Dick's humour was ill-conceived at
that moment, for there followed a wallowing flood of tears.

"Owwww, is that any way to remit thy love to thy lady? Saying unfaithful spouses are common? What say you Mr. Shakespeare?"

"I know little of these matters, Mistress Page," quoth I, lying in no
small measure, thinking on Anne at home. "But thou speakest of 'spouse'. I
take it thou art already wed?"

"Nay, but soon will be, or so he hath pledged. I would know the true heart of that man I will call husband, nothing more." Oft now did she heave her napkin to her eye, which on it had conceited characters, laundering those silken figures in the brine. She made me think on those apples hanging longer on the tree than when they are already ripe, not gathered in time, are fain to drop by themselves (and few men will take them up thereafter). Dick was now dabbing the corner of his eye too:

"Aye Will, I am promised to this, my lady-love, but her father has not approved the match, nay nor her mother neither. But if she will have me, I have a plan to wed her anyhow, for as thou knowest, the dear love I bear to her, she hath mutually answer'd. Therefore, so far as she herself might be the chooser of her own husband, even to my selfsame wish, this then is my plan: on the eve of Christmas, here in this Royal Exchange, 'twixt twelve and one at night, solemn rites are held to honour the birth of the baby Jesus. These rites are preceded by great expressions of joy and mirth, I mean eating and drinking and all manner of festive merry making. Many come dressed as Mary or Joseph or other persons of our Christian past and players engage with passersby in mini-dramas, or comedies, that portray the fortunes of these characters as has been told to us. On that night shall I, as Joseph, come in humble garments and coarse cloak; and Beth shall dress as Mary, loose enrobed, with ribbons pendent, flaring 'bout her head. A vicar of mine acquaintance shall come dressed as a Hebrew and shall seem to marry the pilgrims on their way to Bethlehem. All who see this play shall think we are but acting, most of all Beth's mother and father, but the vicar will in fact bind us in holy matrimony, the which we will suddenly reveal to the joy and good wishes of all assembled, on the eve of our saviour's birth and those great celebrations that follow. What sayest thou Will? Is this not well devised?"

"Is thy father, good mistress, a large man? Or at all inclined to violence?" I knew not what to say to them, but suspected not everyone thusly fooled would join in celebration. Elizabeth had consumed her strawcake and his too and seemed now to have her eye on one that had been provided to me.

"La! An if he were, there were no remedy, for then shall I evermore be bound to thee," quoth Elizabeth, cooing like a dove with her face nestled in Dick's gizzard. "O Richard, I can barely survive the time till then! But my womanly mind could be set to thinking on other things, if thou hast brought me aught from thy brave travels to Denmark."

"O, great thing of me forget, aye sweet pea! I have provided for thee after the truest fashion and bear these all upon my person for thee." Dick removed his cloak and cap and various other layers of garmenting to reveal an entire haberdashery for his lady-love. "Three pretty caps tucked here under mine own; two rebato wires laid 'neath my shirt to keep them flat; a brush here on my back; an almanac in my pocket; and three ballads in my codpiece![69] Ha! Am I not the true picture of the round-bellied trader?"

"I'll swear thou art." Elizabeth giggled like a girl of many fewer years as she turned over the several treasures, adorning herself with each item in turn. "Indeed thou couldst set up shop here in the Exchange! There's many a man begins with less, I can tell thee, who becomes a rich man ere he dies."

I could say little to either Dick or Elizabeth, the one desperate to prove himself a man and the other desperate to marry one. If Christian forgiveness and charity prevail on Christmas eve, they may survive their game. Beyond that, I fear their path may soon prove the more rocky.

There is so much more to report of London and every night Mr. Kempe, who has grown more friendly to me since we discovered our minds to each other, invites me to join him in the many inns of the City, wherein he seeks any man who might know the whereabouts of Miles Phillips and his sister. He says that many of these places once served as playhouses: the Bell and the Cross Keys inns on Gracious Street, and the Bull too; the Saracen's Head and the Red Lion, within and without Ludgate; the Bell Savage, Paul's, and the Mermaid, taverns all in the shadow of St. Paul's tower; and others too.[70] He fashioned a rhyme about the customers to be found in each:

The gentry to the King's Head, the nobles to the Crown;
The knights unto the Golden Fleece, but to the Plough the
    clown!

Master Johnson nightly visits these inns too, it would seem to collect such stories, poems, songs, and reports of events that we might use in some fashion in our plays. There too can a man hear awful tales of Spanish treachery 'gainst our English merchants and more about the fearful plots on Her Majesty's life. I have now more leisure, for there is no wagon to load or jordans to empty and wives of some of our players tend to their own apparel. I fill this time with such labours as might increase my purse, for like the water that through a leaky bucket flows, money too disappears as fast as it is earned, such is the high cost of all things in London. Cans't imagine: butter here is 8 pence the pound and a horse for hire is 4 pence the mile (shoe leather is not so dear)!

I have filled some hours too with writing a poem, for Cuthbert says certain dedications can be sold to those at Court who would use them to gain favours. I have shared it with no other and would welcome thy honest opinion:

> Not from the stars do I my judgment pluck;
> And yet methinks I know astronomy,
> But not to tell of good or evil luck,
> Of plagues, of dearths, or seasons' quality.
>
> Nor can I Fortune in brief minutes tell,
> Pointing to each his thunder, rain and wind,
> Or say with princes if it shall go well,
> Or oft predict what I in heaven find.
>
> But from thine eyes my knowledge I derive,
> And, constant stars, in them I read such art
> As truth and beauty shall together thrive,
> If from thyself to store thou wouldst convert.
>
> Or else of thee I this prognosticate:
> Thine end is truth and beauty's doom and date.

O coz, I am like a hound amidst a flock of geese, unable to fix my gaze on any one, each running faster away and each protesting louder than his neighbor. I must pray that Leicester's Men survives till spring when I might gain passage on a ship, but if we are

[Scribe's note: as with most of the letters, this one was written on both sides of the paper and the text above filled four sides. Whatever page the letter continued on was not among the papers I was shown, so this letter ends here. TT]

LETTER NINE
January 14, 1587

Wherein Death comes near, but a shrewd physician and a bundle of books provide an adequate defense, just in time for the patient to claim a great prize.

In Letter Nine, Shakespeare meets Will Kempe's sister and her husband, Kathleen and Miles Phillips, who are bound for the New World too. Miles spins a tale, even as he is spinning a shiny cloth with magical properties, of his sixteen years a slave under the Spanish Inquisition in the Americas and how he was emancipated therefrom. I thought the tale fantastical when I first read it twenty-seven years ago, especially because I could find no comparable contemporary accounts.

If an interstellar visitor landed in America today and asked for our origin story, we could do no better than to deliver up the works of William Shakespeare and *The Principal Navigations, Voyages, Traffiques, and Discoveries of the English Nation* compiled by Richard Hakluyt in 1598. Oh, and thereafter I'd add the Internet.

Between those two books alone, there is very little of our language, culture, morals, fashion, politics, culinary preferences, even our dreams and aspirations, that the visitor would not be able to trace to the very rootstock. And like me, the visitor would find it a great deal easier to search through those expansive volumes, and the characters who populate them, with the aid of the Internet.

A web search today quickly calls forth *Voyages* and the fact that Miles gave a similar, though far more detailed, account to Mr. Hakluyt, corroborating the abbreviated version he reported to Shakespeare. I have augmented one with the other so you might fully appreciate why Miles decided to return to the New World, this time with a pregnant wife and the recollection of unimaginable riches too alluring to resist.

This letter opens in January 1587 with Shakespeare recovering from a bad bout of scurvy in the company of a little dog, Ratcatcher, and with the help of a man I now believe to be the notorious quack, Simon Forman. Forman practiced medicine and astrology in and around London at this time, seeking a reputation among the nobility. As such, he might have been willing to aid a servant of the Earl at some reduced fee. Lacking anything of value, Shakespeare offered his sonnet about the stars (that he showed us in Letter Eight) in payment for the cure. Although John Combe later found it to be "cold supper," we can see the aspiring poet practicing his art in real time.

Medicine can work miracles, but it is the expert care of the housekeeper, Heather Burberry that restores him in body and spirit. He is obviously inspired by her remarkable past, including her chaste marriage to a minister, who died gruesomely of syphilis; her learned self-education; and how, having been born with no arms, she taught herself writing and housekeeping skills with her feet.

Perhaps it was dodging death, perhaps it was realizing how Burberry had overcome great obstacles, which led to Shakespeare revealing his feelings on life and death in yet another sonnet (one that became the basis for the published version of Sonnet 71 many years later), taking themes and language from several of the books that Mr. Stow lends him to read.

By the way, in 2014 a book dealer announced he had found an Elizabethan-era dictionary and various experts confirmed the hand-written notations in it might well be Shakespeare's. In this letter, the poet refers to just such a dictionary.

Able to resume his duties with Leicester's Men, Shakespeare pursues his acting lessons with Master John Perkin, learns to play the lute, and like most young men his age, is fascinated with the evocative power of music, musing to a rat (who shares his sleeping quarters) "What thinkst thou of my philosophy: that music and life are cut from the same cloth?"

Dazzled by the gold of Miles' story, and willing to ignore the risk and suffering he also set forth, Shakespeare heads to the Mermaid, a London tavern, where Governor John White is recruiting passengers to sail to his new colony called Virginia (named to honor the never-married Queen Elizabeth I, who her subjects lovingly called the "Virgin Queen"). There he recognizes Rosalind Munday, whom he first described in Letter Four and who is again dressed as a man (a device he employs in many of his future plays to dramatic or comic effect). With all of her male kinfolk dead, and few ways to sustain her mother and sisters at home, Rosalind too wishes to sail to the New World. Shakespeare is impressed with her bravery, and almost instantly, Will and Rosalind decide to pose as a married couple so they can gain passage on the Virginia-bound expedition.

Offering Combe slender justification for this apparent betrayal of his wife in Stratford, Shakespeare alludes to some kind of faithlessness by Anne, and then comforts his guilty conscience with the hope that she and their children will profit from his arrangement with Rosalind, once he returns triumphant with gold in his pockets. If necessity truly is the mother of invention, this letter shows us how two more brave and resourceful women put platitude into practice (interesting that the old proverb doesn't refer to fathers).

The England that the young pair hope to leave is described by Shakespeare in this letter in ways that are eerily familiar to a modern reader: fear of foreigners, religious extremists, vast economic inequality, the struggle of women, racism, and an unquenchable drive, by some, to rise above.

In all, Letter Nine is one of the longest, but worth savoring every slowly unfolding vista.

Feast of the Ass, 14 January 1587, London

Coz,

Wise and slow - - they stumble that run fast. Or so it is said. This is my sole comfort after six weeks a'bed and nightly visited by Death himself!

Thy news of our friends hath cheered me greatly in mine own time of sore sickness, but such reports of my father have distressed me in equal measure. It may be true, that he hath not for many months attended upon the Council as should be his duty thereto, but those who call my father 'friend' in Stratford are those who owe him various sums and are grievous delinquent in their duty to repay him. And wherefore was Mr. Wheeler taken from the Council? What is his transgression? Or did he desire to be put out of his own accord? I am sorely grieved by this news.

Yes, I would fain ask upon mine uncle Henry to speak for my father in Stratford matters, but he is ever fined by that same Council for his ditches and such trivials as wearing his hat in church. And yes, I would fain ask upon Mr. Perrott (who was ever my father's faithful friend, at least among the Swan protestants), but who can say how many chits bearing the Shakespeare name are already in his keeping? I am sad to learn he has disowned his daughter on account of our own classmate (is he a good man truly?).[71]

Giddy hath writ to thee about thy quantity of other inquiries, so I trust thou art well satisfied as to those. He may also have conveyed to thee how I nearly visited the undiscovered country: death itself!

That is to say, after a respite, when we were not allowed to play (I filled the time with Giddy and good Mr. Stow, who courteously showed me such sights in the City as I shall describe to thee hereafter as my poor pen allows), news came that the Leicester's Men were again preferred at Court and demanded immediately. So was my work restored in earnest, every man demanding his apparel be cleaned, good strings to their beards, new ribbons to their shoes and such like, as would make us shine before Her Majesty. Despite the Earl's misdeeds abroad, he was quickly forgiven, because other playing Companies offered such meagre entertainments for the holiday season (the Queen's Men especially rank with stale fare).

This return to favor may be but brief, for Mr. Stow heard tell that the main theme of Her Majesty's anger with our Earl was not as much for his loss of men and money abroad, but that he appointed Lord Stanley as governor of English conquests thither. The cushion whereon he rested his regal ass, whilst signing that commission, was not yet cold when this Governor then handed back those lands to one Duke of Parma! Lord knows why, but no mortal can understand this. Most of our number wager the end of the Company will come before the summer, though Mr. Burbage will brook no utterance of the like and says he gives no credence to Lord Rumour.

Well, I had been not a month in the City, still lodging at the kindness of Mr. Stow, and was stricken from head to toe with the most violent shaking, trembling, and groaning, yea through all my veins ran such a cold and drowsy humour that I am certain a very Devil possessed me and no illness other. It may have been payment for my sins: the theft of the map, which weighs on my conscience still; the near murder of the Earl in Denmark, a deed for which my fingers itch still, so I cannot claim to be repentant; or it may be a pox visited upon me for laying with a stale [*whore*]. Or was I humbled for leaving my wife and babes and lusting after gold? There is more I have done to offend God, no doubt, but not every man who is equally guilty of such sins is laid as low as I was these many weeks.

Mistress Burberry cared for me, lest I had perished for certain. Mr. Stow bound mine aching head and bought potions of an apothecary, which she administered to me, often in foul smelling brews of her own device. I marvel that a woman with no arms can do more than ten who are able of body: she has taught her left leg and foot to serve as a hand to pour and mix, to write and wipe a fevered brow, all the while smiling as if she were the more fortunate one. At length, when I grew no stronger of body or mind, they summoned a physician, a man of some repute, I am told, although he knew I had no way to repay such a debt. I took his name to be Foreman or Simon, but in my fever, I can swear to neither, though his blunt method I can yet recall:

"A Leicester's Man, eh? Thou seem'st quite thin. Hast thou consumed gross and evil meat and drink?"

I told him that while traversing the countryside, we ate what we could.

"Aye, so I thought," quoth he, his face then coming into my view, a youngish head shaped like a funnel with wide, furrowed brow and narrow chin and nose, surmounted with a massive wide beard, as if it sought to balance out the rest. He looked a Puritan, dressed in plainest black with a white starched collar ('twas clear that Giddy made no garments for this physician!).

"Scurvy," quoth he plainly, dipping into a satchel in search of a remedy, I hoped. "Those that have the scurvy will have much pain in their head, jaws, gums, and teeth. And their gums do swell and the flesh groweth over the teeth ... like this ... "

Here he thrust a hickory twig under my lip and lifted it, that he might illustrate his point to Mr. Stow and Mistress Burberry. He continued poking as he spoke, but as I think on't, his description of my malady was most accurate.

"That flesh, look you, is very sore and full of waterish blood, such that he can hardly eat or join together his teeth. See? His breath doth stink. Smell? And he hath much pain in the stomach and pricking in the head like needles, and swelling in all the joints and limbs, such that from crown to foot he doth swell and ache." I could discern Mr. Stow and Mistress Burberry sniffing the air in my general direction and nodding to each other. But school was not yet out:

"Now your Mr. Shakespeare hath not the full force of scurvy, mind you, for them that does also have knobs in the flesh or are like to have black spots on their bellies and private parts, as though they had been sorely pinched." To show that I did not suffer these extremities, he held back the sheet and prodded my gut and lifted my yerd and cods [*penis and testicles*] for better viewing, which sent Mistress Burberry huffing from the room. Next, he dripped a potion in my nose with a quill and handed a vial of some distilled liquor to Mr. Stow.

"This syrup of lemons, four spoonfuls must he drinketh at a time, twice each day, and in a month he will showeth no more signs of the scurvy." The closet was drafty, but in my fever I hadn't noticed the winter chill (indeed, ere we go to bed now, we are fain to walk or run up and down half an hour to gain a heat in our feet). Lying naked then to such cruel elements, I began to shiver and Mr. Stow administered blankets once more. Somehow that seemed to have a greater effect than lemon juice.

That physician is a man to be respected. Indeed, it took nearly a month, but now I write to thee in greater health and vigour. When I was able, I sent him my sonnet about astrology, hearing of his interest in the subject, with apologies for making so modest a payment for so great a service. I have not heard whether he found it pleasing (or as thou hast found it, 'cold supper').

But I cannot so easily recover from the feeling that I have failed my fellows in the Company and am amazed that I am still of their number. I have been a burden to Dick, who heard of mine ailments and was so convinced that he suffered the selfsame that he collapsed while playing onstage, in a heap of sweat and moaning, though he recovered swiftly after Mr. Burbage beat him back to life. I have been a burden to Giddy, who stood for me as clothing jack at many of the command performances, although he thinks himself well paid by the chance to be at Court at such a festive time, studying those appurtenances that ladies and gentlemen add to their garments, in this fashion or that (he is especially taken by the fashion of adding jewels to a man's doublet, though Lord knows why that fascinates him so). And I have overburdened Mr. Stow, whose generosity I can never repay, nor the debt I owe to our countryman Pug, on whose honour I have entered the house in the first place.

Mr. Stow has given me so many books else and kept me well stocked with writing tools and candles, saying I might profit from the knowledge on his shelves as he has done. I am never far from mine Ovid, but to this he has added Caesar, Cicero, and Demosthenes; but greater treasures still in our own mother tongue: 'Reliques of Ancient English Poetry' and an epic poem that thrills the senses, 'The Civil Wars Between the Two Houses of Lancaster and York'; Machiavelli's 'The Prince' translated from Italian; and even Fitzherbert's 'Book of Husbandry' and an astonishing dictionary with words I had never read nor heard before. I have used this bounty of thoughts and words to scratch out a sonnet or two more of mine own, but how these shall serve, I cannot yet say.

This were enough to make such an illness seem worthwhile, but the greater recompense was the discovery of a hidden gem: Mistress Heather Burberry. She has covered me over with such kindness and good cheer, it were enough to drive out any ill humour. Though God saw fit to visit her with great bodily affliction at her birth, He bestowed her with a mother who kept her alive and a father who taught her to read and gave her books and other virtues. With few means to cavort with her childhood playfellows, she kept mostly at home, spoke little, and filled her mind to overflowing (and has continued the practice for all of her forty odd years of life).

At twenty-six, her parents both dead of the Plague, she was left a large fortune by an aunt who had also been stricken with that pestilence, along with a tail-less terrier called Ratcatcher (I understand he lost said tail in an altercation with a rat and is therefore no longer inclined to molest their kind). She was instantly set upon by numerous suitors, some claiming they had already married her by pledging their troth and were thereby entitled to some share. Others gave her rich gifts and tokens of their true love. After some months of heated debate, these combatants sought to settle the matter and, with the consent of the good lady too, turned to a Puritan vicar named Milward. He spent many hours in talk with Heather to know her true mind, but in the end he did bewitch her for himself and, at length, she agreed to marry him and he claimed the rich dowry.

Many cried foul play, so Milward, to prevent her from remorse and taking sides with one of the others, forbid her to leave the vicarage and she was seen only on Sundays in the church, which she described to me thus:

"After I was out of bed and ready, I would go to private prayers, then to breakfast; then I walked till church-time with Mr. Milward, and after to dinner. After that I had speech of no serious matters till two o'clock. Then I writ notes into my Bible till three, to honour God and to improve my skill with a pen held 'tween my toes, thus (I had seen her perform this trick before, but not wanted to stare, whereas now she insisted I study her technique in particular: it was truly amazing to behold, her lettering more clear and facile than mine own). After 4 o'clock I came again from the church and meditated a little and again writ some other notes in my Bible of what I had learned in church that day. This I did till five, at which time I returned to examination and prayer. And after I had read some of 'Bond on the Sabbath', I walked abroad, and so to supper, after to prayers, and lastly to bed."[72]

"Did the other six days of a week resemble this schedule?"

"Nay, there was not much to differ the Sabbath from the weekday, other than during the week I was also occupied with keeping of the house. O, and during the week, I was at leisure to read more books, besides my Bible." She seemed to have no quarrel with this arrangement, for Milward may have been stingy with honour and courtesies, but he more than made up for this, in her opinion, with an abundance of rare books. Heather read them all and persuaded him to buy more of certain histories, sciences, and geographies, although he doubted much she would profit therefrom. Indeed, she did later use this knowledge to help Mr. Stow write his histories of England and the City, providing particulars and evidence of times past, while Stow added his personal observations from his travels and examinations of wards and streets.

Within the year of her marriage, God saw fit to chastise the cozening vicar, who fell ill with a French pox, rendering him unable to do service, as she further described his awful penance in the plainest of terms (and which I herewith report in all particulars so that Hamnet may learn to avoid those sins that may result in such a fearsome punishment):

"He had ulcers on his yerd and carbuncles that prevented any passage of water and then further pustules of the head and other external parts. Lastly it infected his entrails with a cruel nocturnal tormenting pain in the head, shoulders, and joints. In time, it caused knots in the muscles and corrupted the bones, dissolving them so he could not stand. He then lost an eye and a great portion of both eyelids, to which he also lost his hearing."

"I quake to hear this! Did he recover?"

"Well, I had read of the cure in a book from a Greek, but may have given it too late, for the potion required an ounce of quicksilver, which we had not readily by. But upon securing the same, I mixed it with a fasting spittle and some boar's grease, all mixed well together with an ounce of camphor. The paste resulting, I covered his body from crown to toe, sparing no place but only the eyes and nostrils. The Greeks say the afflicted must lay like this in bed sweating for two days, although he may sit on the third day for his ease. Then must the mixture be applied again for two more days, after which it is cleansed off in very cold water while he should drink a very hot brew of senna and white hen's dung, mixed in white wine vinegar."

"And did this restore him?"

"It cannot be said either way, for after the second day he seemed to lose his wits and claimed the cure would only serve if he was to lay naked in the sun during the heat of the day, which practice he carried out for a week, every day losing more strength and the vitals of his body closing their functions. On a Monday, the physician told him the only remedy was the amputation of his yerd, that being the font of the disease, but Milward refused this painful indignity. On the Thursday, he was dead of painful struggle."

She had met Mr. Stow before then, when he came to their church and inquired about the particulars of the town for his latest history. Milward thought it would entertain his wife and bid her speak with him, whereat Mr. Stow was much amazed by her sweet temper and deep knowledge of so many endeavours, but especially of history and great personages. By coincidence, a month before Milward died, he informed her he was seeking a housekeeper for his lodgings in Lime Street. Wasting no time after his funeral, now a woman of means who had always wanted to visit the City, she wrote to Mr. Stow that she would take the post, and so, by slow degrees, became a trusted partner in the research and writing of his books. I owe her so great a debt, that I fear it can never be fully recompensed. Ratcatcher too hath been my constant companion and watched over me in my time of infirmity, barking for help whenever I might stir.

But coz, I have not yet reported the news that sped my recovery and cheered me most of all. The reason I cannot sleep, and needs must pour my hopes upon this page, is that Mr. Kempe hath brought me to meet his sister Kathleen and her husband Miles Phillips, who are as intent, as am I, to gain passage to the New World. They are so full of news that this hope is quickly made manifest, because they have introduced me to a great man who shall convey us thither. O not without some more delicate endeavours and a measure of luck, I'll warrant, but good fortune is within my grasp, such that all attending perils will seem trifles when set against the glory and the gains. Here now to those particulars worthy of report.

When our Company first arrived in London, Mr. Kempe was most impatient to find his sister Kathleen and her husband Miles Phillips to know of her good health and to make them known to me. He inquired in those places she had formerly frequented, but now, as a married woman, she no longer lingered in the same. And even though Giddy used all arguments and logic to prevent me from seeking a ship, who can deny the hand of God in the fact that 'twas Giddy who knew where to find this Phillips and thereby to help my cause! For Phillips had taken up a clothmakers trade, and Giddy is well acquainted with those places where such men are found, being that his own trade as haberdasher is naught without the clothmaker. Therefore, he quickly led Mr. Kempe to Phillips' very doorstep.

Commerce in London cannot easily be divined. Imagine, if thou canst, that the shops of our Stratford tradesmen were picked up and scattered like seeds over all of Warwickshire, for so it is in this City. The clothmakers guild in Mincing Lane, below Fenchurch Street, is housed in several spacious structures within hailing distance of the western wall of the Tower. But the cloth must then be taken nearly a mile west to Walbrook Street for the dyers; then another mile north to the tailors in Threadneedle Street or farther still to the haberdashers in Wood Street (excepting that the old tailors, many in service to the Court, are near Bread Street, a mile or more to the south), all before any buyer sees the work of the clothmaker himself!

Three nights ago, Giddy led us to the smallest of those same workshops in Mincing Lane. Entering therein, but finding no one to guide us, for night's cloak had long since draped the city and no worker was left at his post, we were left to weave our way around looms and dines, bolts of cloth piled higher than a man is tall, and great spools of yarn in various stages of use across vast worktables.[73] We had not known where to find a living soul in this forest of fabrics had we not seen a glow from one corner, some taper or lantern still lit. Making our way thither we could hear a man singing, quietly and a'times not all the words, but a solemn hymn nonetheless:

"In Amsterdam there lives a maid,
Mark you well what I say!
In Amsterdam there lives a maid,
And this fair maid my trust betrayed.
I'll go no more a rovin, with you fair maid.
A roving, a roving, since roving's been my ru-i-in,
I'll go no more a ro-ho-vin', with you fair maid."

I can recall the ditty with ease now, because Mr. Kempe sings it often, having memorized it that he might use it later in our entertainments, humming some parts thereof as we felt our way through the shadows toward the sound, hesitating to break the clothmaker's spell, but at last calling out 'Phillips? Miles Phillips?'

Reaching for shears to ward off any intruder with ill-intent, his lilting whisper of a song became a deep-throated growl. "Who would know? Show thyself and quickly!"

"Miles, fear not. 'Tis Will Kempe and friends." There followed hail-fellow-well-met greetings and Mr. Kempe introduced me and Giddy most courteously, showing more deference to my station with the players than was my due, which I took as a sign of his trust and friendship. He then asked the whereabouts of his sister.

"We lodge with a baker in Harp Lane, a quoits [*horseshoes*] cast from here. I will send for her and she will be most delighted to reunite with her brother and his friends." With this he stepped through a door to an alley, but could find no boy to fetch Kathleen, whereat Mr. Kempe said he knew of this bakery and would go himself and bring her hither, if that Miles would be so kind to look after us in the mean season.

When Miles stood, I took note of his sturdy bulk, odd contrast to the delicate work he undertook to refine yarns into the shiny cloth that he was so closely examining, when we surprised him with our intrusion upon his labours. Nor was this the only thing out of joint. His beard was full and black, but the hairs on his head were few and grew in tufts, barren in places and luxurious in others. And his hands: Giddy's hands are womanly and delicate, befitting his trade, but Miles' hands are thick and crooked as if upholstered with ill-fitting, tainted horsehide, looking far older than his three dozen years. I could imagine those hands hauling up sails with rudely chafing ropes, or hanging for dear life to hempen ladders, high above the pitching deck, as I had seen on our voyage to Denmark, but not navigating needle through seam. I made idle conversation until Mr. Kempe could return and we might address those graver matters of the New World that we had ventured thither to discuss, but was curious for I had seen just such a shimmering fabric on the woman who stole my purse for the thief Ratsey my first day in London.

"What manner of cloth is this?"

"Oh, that is thy taffety, which rustles when a lady, whose dress is made withal, walks by, whispering that thou shouldst take note of her. 'Tis the only cloth that will speak its mind, look you."

"I had not thought a fabric might speak to me," quoth Giddy, "although in my trade I am ever cursing and speaking aloud to them!"

"Aye, Gilbert, thy taffety be like no other. Look you, the word herself is from some ancient tongue, meaning twisted wovens, which it is, and takes no small skill to make an even, pleasing lustre from thy dull yarns."

He bid us sit on creaky wood boxes, tipped up to make stools around the great table where Miles' silk was now draped like the billowing sea over which I hoped soon to journey. "Dare I inquire, Miles: Mr. Kempe told us thou art a sailor who hath been aboard those ships sailing to the New World. How is it a man of rope and canvas became so versed in the making of these fine silks?"

"Aye, William. I have been a sailor. I have set foot on the Americas, south to north. I have been to the gates of Hell and thanked the Devil kindly, but bid him wait a while longer for my company. How I learned this trade is not for few words, but I can tell thee my fervent desire was a respectable life in England, growing old in an honourable trade with a goodly wife and sons, Lord willing. I came back to this land, where such dreams were requited, but foreigners have lately taken over this trade and will work for such a pittance that an honest Englishman cannot make his living. 'Tis a pity. A veritable pity I tell thee, what has happened to this trade, invaded by French and Dutch, Germans and Welsh."

"But thou dost ply the trade still?" Giddy had told me too of how dogs of every breed came nowadays to London, not all for the betterment of our English society.

"Not much longer, nay, not I. Last week Sir Walter Raleigh did crown one Mr. John White as Governor of that township in the Americas that bears the great General's name. Governor White will soon depart with a great many ships, settlers, and such quantities of supply that shall build a colony to even greater glories than are already reported from thither. He has promised each man, who accompanies this voyage, lands of 500 acres good and fertile to plant and harvest and to take therefrom those valuable timbers, gold, silver, and other riches as may be found thereon. Kathleen and I will be among them and will make our Fortune in this place they call Virginia in the northern Americas."

"Canst show me if that place be on this map?" I unfolded my stolen map on his workbench in the waning light of the two tapers, one already nigh gone, and flattened it with my palms in such style as I had just seen Miles smooth out his treasured taffety cloth. I would know from this man, who hath himself been there, what I might expect, not from fantastical dreams but from his experiences, and those things he saw with his own eyes. Miles leaned forward and squinted at the map, slowly running his forefinger over the coastlines, as if in doing so the memories of his voyages thither would spring from the paper. He shook his head and sat back, such that I saw tears in his eyes.

"So many good friends lost. So many miles and so many good friends, made and lost. I knew so little then. I was not fifteen years old, but already strong as an ale porter, growing a great black bush on my chin, such that I was easily mistaken for some years older. My father was ever drunk and lost his trade in wool, leaving my mother, look you, to care for my sisters and me. I had no luck to earn money for her on land, but thought I could at least ease her burdens by one mouth, and, if the Lord decided we should all live so long, one day I might return with gold from the Americas to set all things right."

O coz, I thought he mocked me, telling MY story instead of his: a father who fell to the evils of strong drink and lost the trade that he cared for his family withal, leaving a son to seek a Fortune in the New World to make amends. He leaned back on a post and gazed upward, either seeking to rub up his recollection or stanch the flow of tears that sprang therefrom, then told us the most fantastical tale I had yet heard:

"It was upon an October Monday in fifteen hundred and sixty-seven, I took mine employment on the Jesus in a fleet that departed from Plymouth bound for Africa and the Americas under General Mr. John Hawkins, accompanied by five other goodly ships, including the Judith under the command of Mr. Francis Drake, afterwards knight. We came first to Cape Verde (coz, to mine amazement, he pointed to the spot on my map with that very name!) seeking to take some negroes, but our shore party was sorely assaulted by a great number of them, who with envenomed arrows did hurt a great many of our men, such that they were enforced to return to the ships with very few negroes in chains. Seven of our men died in a very strange manner, wherein their jaws were locked and we sought to keep them alive by forcing sticks into their mouths to keep them open, but to no avail."

He drew his finger off the right edge of the map, where Africa was seen, Giddy and I leaning closer to follow his voyage. "In this general region, thy map fails, but it was upon the coast of Guinea, about here, we had better fortune. When we anchored thither, a negro king sent his ambassador to us to say his people were oppressed by a neighbor tribe and asked our help to defeat them. Our General agreed to this, thinking to share the prize of slaves with this negro king in exchange for his knowledge of the lands and the use of his soldiers in our cause. With a number of 200 of our men and several hundred of his, we set fire upon a town of eight or ten thousand negroes and took prisoner nine hundred, howbeit the negro king, he that we thought to be our ally, spirited away more than half of these, while our men yet defended their positions and their lives. But in all, we had gathered some 500 negroes from our sojourn in Africa, determining this sufficient to sail for the West Indies, counting our losses as few and blessings as many."

"What manner of fabric is this?" Giddy had been fingering the various cloths on the table and stacked nearby, taking careful note of those carded or beaten, those hung to dry, or those pressed against each other like fall leaves in a book.

"O that, that be thy piece-dyed taffety, which is much softer than thy yarn-dyed taffety. The making of piece-dyed is me specialty." Miles' hands moved from the map to his handiwork and I poked Giddy in the ribs for interrupting the very story we had come here to discover. I pointed to the western part of Africa on the map, then drew my finger across the vast sea therefrom to the Indies.

"So thou didst depart from here…and began thy voyage in this direction?"

"Aye, but more southerly, like this, which proved a grave error, for as we approached the Americas, our ships were dangerously tossed and beaten hither and thither by a hurricane, such that for eight days were we in continual fear of drowning and, in the end, were forced to take refuge in the port of San Juan de Ulloa in Mexico: here on thy map, called 'La Vera Cruz'. The Spaniards there supposed ours was their own treasure fleet, which was due in this port at any time. The few soldiers guarding the port feared for their lives upon learning our true identity and strength, but our General used them very courteously and said we wished no other than to repair our damaged vessels and feel dry land under our feet for a time. To prove his honest intent, when we discovered twelve Spanish ships at anchor with more than 200,000 pound of gold aboard, we pledged not to disturb so much as one groat thereof. But the morning after our arrival we spied thirteen sails of great ships on the horizon: the King of Spain's treasure fleet! Although we were vastly outnumbered, we held the port, knowing the prize was great: one million pounds of gold and silver were reported aboard those ships by an old Spanish gentleman of the town, who was most liberal with his knowledge, after we showed ourselves to be peaceful. Our General suffered the fleet to enter the harbour and sent a messenger to their Viceroy, one Don Martin de Henriques. After various parley, it was agreed for the time being to keep the peace. The Spanish would remain on their ships while we would be allowed to mend our ships on land, but for the further assurance thereof, each party gave to the other twelve gentlemen as hostages."

"Now as every child now knows, the Spanish are treacherous dogs and cannot be trusted, but we were then blinded by our great need, after surviving the storms, or in Christian hope for men's better Natures, and soon paid for our foolishness. Notwithstanding our agreement, the Viceroy Don Martin did secretly land one thousand chosen men to assault our position at dinnertime. He gave the order to attack and slew many of our men on shore without mercy. Seeing this, our ships fired their canons on the Spanish ships and sunk three thereof. After this skirmish, only the Judith and the Minion from our fleet were fit to take to sea and did so without delay. But those of our men that the Spanish traitors slew were the luckier, for the cruelty of the Spaniards cannot be overstated: they hung up the rest of our shore party from high posts by the arms until blood burst out of their fingers' ends. Indeed, those few yet alive, who by the merciful providence of the Almighty are long since arrived here in England, carry still about with them, and shall to their graves, look you, the marks and tokens of those inhumane and more than barbarous cruel dealings."

Giddy rattled the box we sat upon, shivering from the cold wind that sliced its way through cracks in the walls and the creaking door, but I daresay his tender sensibilities were affrighted, imagining his own fingers thusly abused, tucking his hands 'neath his armpits. It seemed a good time to change the subject. "But what of those on the ships, including thy good self, I take it? Dids't escape unharmed?"

"Well, I can speak only for the Judith, under Captain Francis Drake, which was blown by a storm many leagues north, losing all contact with the Minion, and as we had no victuals aboard we were constrained to eat some cats, dogs, rats, monkeys and finally to eat the hides we had about us, which our starving stomachs found savory and sweet. After several weeks like this we came to land again in wondrous despair, in the bottom of the Mexico Bay, where a great many of the men desired Captain Drake to leave us, making the choice to submit to the mercy of savages than longer to hazard themselves at sea, where if they perished not by drowning yet hunger would enforce them in the end to eat one another. Being then in agreement out of abject need, Captain Drake agreed to put ashore half the men, myself among them, promising to return next year to fetch us."

"Onshore, we consumed such great quantities of fresh water and fruit that the bellies of some men became cruelly swollen and one perished forthwith. We struck out north the next morning, not a dry thread in our rags among us, for it had rained the whole night before, and we soon found ourselves in weeds that grew higher than any man is tall, such that one of us could not see the other, though he be only a few yards away. In this marsh the Indians attacked, a people called the Chi-chi-mich-i who wear their hair long, even down to their knees, and colour their faces green, yellow, red and blue, which make them terrible to behold. At first they thought us Spaniards and killed seven of us, but upon hearing we were English they abated their fury, still forcing us to strip naked and taking those clothes that were brightly coloured, leaving any that were black."

"The senior officer was among those killed and I was therefore chosen, by general declaration of the one hundred and fourteen souls remaining alive, to assume the duties of Corporal in charge. We continued through a region of brambles that continually tore apart our naked bodies and were pestered constantly by a kind of fly, which the Spaniards call 'mosquitoes.' They are scarce big as a gnat, but will suck one's blood marvelously and, if you kill them in this act, they are so venomous that the place will swell extremely. But if you let them suck their fill and fly away naturally, then they leave behind a red spot no worse than a flea-biting."

"At length, we heard an arquebus shot and knew we approached some Christians, and indeed were soon surrounded by Spaniards on horseback, who marveled at our naked and decrepit condition and gave us a bread, the bigness of our half-penny loaf, they called 'maize'. The bread was very sweet and pleasant to us: but what victuals would not have tasted like a Christmas banquet to such starving men? The horsemen brought us to a town, the governor of which threatened to hang us all as 'Lutheran heretics' and 'English dogs' and demanded any valuables we had, which to save our lives we did part withal, amounting to no more than 500 pesos. We were led to a barn that served as a prison, where we asked for a surgeon to repair the injured among us, but the governor replied 'thou'lt get no surgeon, save the hangman, which should sufficiently heal thy griefs.' After four days in this captivity, we were tied in halters, two by two, marched toward the great City of Mexico, ninety leagues [*about 500 miles*] hence. Along the way we stopped at the monasteries of the black friars, the gray friars, and the white friars, all of whom treated us most courteously and gave us meat and drink. O, and some fruit that did bind us so sore, that for the space of ten or twelve days, we could not ease ourselves. Of the two Spaniards with rifles, the older one was kind and saw that we found water and rest along our journey, but the younger was a very cruel caitiff [*coward*] who carried a javelin in his hand and used it to prod our men if they dragged their feet or fell from exhaustion in the heat, saying 'marchad, marchad Ingleses perros, Luterianos, enemigos de Dios.'"

"Near the City of Mexico, we came to a market town with thousands of inhabitants, many richly dressed and riding well appointed horses. Some of these came to see us, both gentlemen and men of occupations, even with their women and children. A few brought us meat and drink and hats and some money. From thence were we conveyed to a hospital and thither most courteously used, although some died from the severity of their previous wounds, including one man who had marched the ninety leagues with an arrow through his neck. After many days in this place, we were conveyed to a mart where Indians were sold as slaves and now understood that this too was our fate. So, we therefore resolved to escape and, on that very same night, moonless in a driving rain, we overpowered our few guards and ran from thence toward the City of Mexico. After dawn, we came upon a high wall and o'er-leapt this into a great garden where we thought to hide and rest, but to our amazement discovered a group of men thither, dining in a large house and speaking our English tongue! These were the twelve hostages that had been exchanged in the port of San Juan de Ulloa, when the treachery of Viceroy Don Martin de Henriques first gave birth to our great miseries. The English hostages convinced their captors to allow us to remain with them, but in time, we were returned to the slave market and sold unto households around the City of Mexico."

"Thou wast SOLD a slave?" Giddy could not fathom that his countryman might be bartered like cattle and goats.

"Aye, and this time they bound us with chains to prevent our further escape, which may have been a better fate than those gentlemen who were hostages, for I have heard it credibly reported since that they died at the cruel handling of the Spaniards in the Inquisition and at least one, Robert Barret the master of the Jesus, was condemned to be burned alive. Aye, I was better used in great measure, for the Spanish nobleman, he who bought me, did feed and apparel me, and only bid me perform those tasks of a household servant, such as attending on table and accompanying him when he ventured into the city."

Miles rose to trim the tapers, which now smoked greatly and shed little light. He peeked out the doorway to see if Mr. Kempe was yet nigh with Kathleen, but seeing no one, he returned. I had whispered to Giddy, wondering if Miles then felt more tenderly towards those negroes taken as slaves in Africa. There being no fault in his hearing, Miles caught my drift and replied for himself, a look of great sorrow overcoming his face as he settled back upon his stool.

"Aye, that I did William. That I did. After a year of this servitude, my master took me to a mine under his direction to be the overseer of the Indians and negroes who worked thither to recover silver. As a slave myself, I now felt some compassion for these men and devised a plan for our general betterment. At sunset, the Spanish guards repaired to their barracks, while the slaves left their work in the mines. But the Indians, negroes, and one other English overseer would labour with me for many more hours in secret, recovering an amount of silver equal to thirty marks or more each night. We lived and gained thus, in those mines some four years, many of us becoming rich. I, for one, had more money than Midas, more than I could spend if I lived longer than Methuselah. But greed clouded my judgment and instead of fleeing this place with whatsoever I could carry, I continued to amass more wealth, never thinking it enough. This greed, and delay in escaping from thence, became mine undoing, for in the year of Christ 1574, the Inquisition came to Mexico."

"Now look you, even Spaniards themselves live in fear of the Inquisition, but upon hearing that an Englishman lived nearby in high style, the Chief Inquisitor took interest in no other man, but apprehended me and confiscated all my goods and silver for himself. I was sent with other English slaves to a prison in the city and kept in a dungeon, knowing the Inquisitor slept on my silk sheets and ate from my silver plate and that he used religion as a cudgel to enrich himself, not to glorify God. At length, I was called before him and severely examined and commanded to say the Paternoster, the Ave Maria, and the Creed in Latin, which Lord knows I could not remember, although I recall my father repeating these verses in our house when I was a boy, so could mumble words that sounded familiar to the Inquisitor. To my great good luck, the Englishman who served as a translator bid me speak any poem that came to mind and he would testify to the Inquisitor that I had said the Latin versus perfectly, but in mine own English tongue. Thereafter the Inquisitor demanded to know if I believed in the sacrament; that the bread and wine he held aloft was the body and blood of Christ; and demanded to know what opinions to the contrary had I been taught in England. Four days was I thus interrogated, the Inquisitor always looking to entrap me, but the interpreter each time assuring the Inquisitor that I repeated the same thing as before, this consistency of mine answers showing me to be truthful."

"Yet all this would not serve and so was I put upon the rack, where others had uttered confessions against themselves under duress, which afterwards cost them their lives. But by merciful God, the rope broke that bound my wrists to the device and I was spared. This did the Inquisitor see as a sign from on high and I was spared further torture. After many months of this treatment and constant threats to our lives, a great scaffold was erected in the square. The night before we were to mount that stage to learn our several fates, the English prisoners were huddled together and made to listen to sermons in Spanish, although every one of us agreed we would have enjoyed greater benefit from a few hours sleep. The next morning, each man was compelled to wear a yellow coat called a 'sanbenito', a garment that signified a heretic, and given a breakfast of a cup of wine and a piece of bread in honey, after which each man was brought to the scaffold."

"Friars of every colour arrived and sat with us on the scaffold, as did that treacherous Viceroy Don Martin de Henriques with the Inquisitor and many dignitaries of the city. Our transgressions were read aloud and our punishment decreed, some to be whipped three hundred times and condemned for ten years to the galleys; others half that number; and I was given the lightest sentence: no lashes, but five years service in a monastery, compelled during all that entire time to wear the fool's sanbenito. Only the Irishman, who spat upon the Inquisitor and mocked his accent, was condemned to be burnt alive, which sentence was carried out immediately with us all as witness, and though he was Irish I could not wish him good riddance."

"Thus it passed that on Good Friday of 1575, a man called William Lowe and I were assigned to the Black Friars, to be overseers of Indian labourers, who wrought there the building of a new church. I now made it my duty to learn the language of the Spaniards and the Indians, finding the latter to be most learned and courteous, once I troubled myself to understand their tongue and their customs, and found they hated the Spaniards as much as I did. To our amazement, the friars feared and hated the Inquisition too and took great pity on us, providing a chamber with fine bedding and good victuals. At the end of my five years, spent in hard labours, but in a certain peace, I was released and my sanbenito hung up in the cathedral as evidence of a Lutheran heretic reformed to Christ."

"Some died, still others went mad. Those who likewise fulfilled their servitude were returned to the City of Mexico and relieved of their sanbenitos. It was then that I chose to learn to weave taffetas and grograins from a local silk weaver, for this I knew to be a most portable and profitable trade, wherever Fate would cast me next, so for three years I apprenticed to him."[74]

"O Miles, I too have served in the haberdasher's trade for three years, but will ever learn more of its mysteries," quoth Giddy, relieved to return to a more familiar subject, as palpably as that day he regained the rocks after nearly drowning in Peak's Pond. "Can this shiny side withstand the heat of an iron or must it be finished with stretching?" I poked Giddy again in the ribs and asked Miles what happened after these three years in his trade.

"Well, the peace was too good to last, for I was called then before the Viceroy, because of reports that a power of Englishmen had landed at Acapulco on the western shore of the country. 'Knowest thou aught of one Francis Drake?' the most treacherous Viceroy Don Martin de Henriques demanded, in his high and mighty lisp. 'He who hath plundered Spanish towns and burnt many churches and stolen many valuables, such that no honest Spaniard, even those armoured and armed, may feel safe in the whole country?'

'Your Lordship,' quoth I, 'I swear I have never heard of this devil, and in any case, he be a Lutheran heretic and I am myself a reformed sinner who would surely slay him for your Lordship, if he came nearby, or be slain myself in the attempt before God.' I was secretly overjoyed by this news of our General, to know he lived and had taken revenge in some measure for the brutalities upon our countrymen by the Spanish."

"This must have convinced the Viceroy, although it was never meant in earnest, for then was I sent with an ambassador as translator to Acapulco to parley with this fearful General Drake, but upon our arrival, we learned he had departed the month before, marching across land to pillage the port of San Juan de Ulloa. Little did any man guess my sorrow and grief that I inwardly felt at this news, although outwardly I was constrained to make fair weather of it, for we were then ordered to journey to San Juan de Ulloa, where our saga had begun so many years earlier."

With this, Miles tapped his forefinger several times on the exact place on the map that showed 'La Vera Cruz', whereat this very port of infamy was shown in black and white and whereat his story began.

"On the trail thither, I determined to escape or die, for I could no longer suffer the insults and arrows of the treacherous Spaniards, nor rely on the few charities of those who were truly Christians and treated other men as they themselves wanted to be used. In San Juan de Ulloa, I ran from my captors and sought to find General Drake myself, there to regain mine own kin and country, but I fell asleep after three days and was by illhap discovered and sent to a prison, a great pair of bolts clapped on mine ankles that I might not escape again."

Miles sighed grievously, as if yet again living the agony of his forfeiture, yet again feeling the weight of the irons around his shanks, yet again resigning himself to uncertain torture or death. Giddy's mouth hung open and he would have cried aloud in sympathy with the story teller, but at that moment the door swung open and two figures burst upon our scene to break the spell.

"Beggar me, 'tis cold," quoth Mr. Kempe, grasping a large piece of felt to wrap around his shoulders like a cloak. His sister was swaddled head-to-toe in a green hooded cloak that reminded me of the one we have seen on the tanner's wife, decorated in mud to the knees, hanging wet heavy. Kathleen's large round face and fierce blue eyes thrust forth from the hood with pride and good cheer nonetheless.

"Thou'rt the new William I have heard my brother tell of, art so?"

"Aye, mistress, and this my brother Gilbert." She took our warm hands in her cold ones and studied our faces quickly, seeming to soak up all she need know before turning to the small brazier and poking it with an iron.

"Goodman Phillips, why is this not warming thy guests and thyself? Trouble not, I'll tend to it."

"Thy husband hath taken us on the most amazing journey, mistress, omitting nothing he thought good to deliver about the great dangers of travel to the New World, but leaving us informed what greatness is promised thither in equal measure." We knew Miles had not died in prison, unless the man before us was his ghost, so I was eager to hear how he was delivered from his bondage and whether he escaped with any riches or knowledge thereof. Giddy bid Miles continue, as Mr. Kempe and his sister fussed valiantly to light several wet coals.

"Nay Gilbert, I did not languish thither for long, for to my great good fortune, my fellow prisoner was able to buy a knife for two pesos and shared it with me until we both had hacked our restraints apart and could make good our escape on the second night of our captivity. I know not what became of that man, but owe him my freedom. I made my way southward, with the help of Indians who hated the Spaniards for the grievous treatment of their kinsmen, unto a port in Guatemala where I conceived my greater escape. By now I could speak the Spanish tongue in many accents and dialects, such that I could pass for a Spanish sailor or soldier. I presented myself to several ships bound for Spain and was taken aboard, for I had sewn gold pieces into my vest and now used some for my passage and to buy hens and bread for the journey. In a few weeks, we arrived at Majorca, where lay two English ships and I was able to secure passage on one, such that under the providence of God Almighty, and after sixteen years absence, I came home, to this my native country England, in the year fifteen hundred and eighty two in the month of February on a ship called the Landret, arriving at Poole."

Miles finished his tale and calmly rose from the bench to extinguish a fire that Mr. Kempe had accidentally set to a pile of cloth scraps near the brazier. The coals glowed warmer than their actual heat, light dancing off coloured taffeta hung on the wall to dry, which gave the room a cheeriness hitherto quite absent. Kathleen and Mr. Kempe had likely heard the story many times ere this and were engaged in some heated whispers on some other topic, muffled by the towering bolts of cloth.

"Miles, Will bids thee tell Mister Shakespeare thy news," quoth Kathleen in a manner more commanding than entreating. She had opened her cloak and showed herself to be no shrinking violet, as Mr. Kempe had led me to understand, but a tall, buxom woman, the sort of stock that could people a new continent and tame savage animals, or the lands that produced them. She pushed her brother easily aside, over his fruitless protests, to warm her hands by the coals, as they had likely done to each other for many years, recalling a kinder time in their lives at home before they both were orphaned.

"Aye, Kate, and good news it is, for we are preferred. As I have told ye, upon my miraculous return to these shores, I plied my trade in this very workshop and was paid handsomely for skills that no other in England possessed. My taffety was called for by ladies in waiting on the Queen herself, look you, owing to my plain tight weave learned at the hands of true masters. See? Look you here: canst barely see light through my weave, I'll warrant. But it took no more than a year or two 'afore foreign dogs stole my secrets and were glad to work for half what any honest Englishman would command, such that I had no choice but to say yes to Captain Raleigh when he called upon me to aid his voyage to Virginia to plant thither the flag of our Kingdom and a colony of our people."

"I have heard of that voyage from a sailor called Pidge on a ship to Denmark some four month ago." I recalled every particular of their king's brother Grangamino and his gifts of pearl and other such valuables.

"Pidge? Pidge? Ha! Not half what he says is true and you'll never know which half is which. Ah Pidge, that scoundrel stripped me clean at tick tack more than once, I'll warrant thee." Miles protested, but the wistful look on his visage was of a man who wished himself there once more.

"Didst not return with two savages, one called Wanteo and another called Manchese?"

"They are called Wanchese and Manteo and live in London still, feted by the Court and having learned our customs and manners, most remarkably, look you." Miles swept up those ashes made by the burning fabric, which seemed harmlessly to have flamed so brightly, but then died away just as suddenly, like the magic of a mountebank.

"I would meet them, if I could, to know more of the secrets of their land and where a man might find gold, if he were to risk life and limb to venture thither."

"I know of a man who sees them often and can seek him out ere we depart, which may be presently, depending on fair winds and seas. He may be present when we meet with Governor White on the morrow, he that was appointed to rule Virginia by Captain Raleigh and who will convey us thither."

"Wouldst thou bring me with thee? I would be ever in thy debt, for I know of no other expedition or means to make my way to the New World." I may have sounded too eager, but in that moment could verily smell the distant shore.

"I will vouch for William," quoth Mr. Kempe, a hand on Miles' shoulder to better look him in the eye for emphasis. "He hath shown our fellows he doth posses many useful skills and would add great value to thine endeavours."

Miles looked to Kathleen, but she was busy keeping the brazier alight and could offer no advice. He seemed unsure, like a solitary man newly invited to dine with polite company. For my part, I must have looked like the blind puppy, whose dam hath not enough teats for so many offspring and some are destined for the well. The silence was broken by a fart, the reply thereto made me laugh, as it was like those I remember between us as boys:

"Will!"

"Kathleen!"

"Giddy!"

"Will!"

But returning to serious matters, Mr. Kempe then made a most pleasing offer to Miles on my behalf: "If thou'lt do William this favor, I will acquit thee of the necessaries for thy voyage and to make thy way in this new land."

Kathleen answered for them both while slicing an onion and some cheese that had appeared on the table from the folds of her cloak and sharing them around as mother once did. "He'll do it, and I daresay Goodman Phillips will have his own authority in the matter, for he hath been appointed the Governor's chiefest lieutenant, owing to his great experience in these lands." She next addressed me: "My brother's word on thy behalf means more than those valuables he would bestow, though Lord knows we thank thee enough for that too brother. Present thyself under the sign of the Mermaid, east of the great cathedral, at the crossing of Friday and Bread streets, tomorrow at sunset Mister Shakespeare."

"Care for my taffety, woman!" Miles folded the cloth he had been cutting to keep it from errant greasy fingers, stowing it on a pile of like-coloured pieces. There followed some talk of the dangers and things to be done to make ready for such a voyage, such a life away from the comforts of home and the fully laden shops in Cheapside, but assurance from Miles that good fortune indeed awaits a man who will work hard and satisfy himself with enough gold and silver to succor his family in this lifetime, avoiding the avarice and greed that had laid Miles so low in Mexico.

Coz, I find Miles and Kathleen most agreeable and have none of the fears Mr. Kempe hath described for his sister, who weareth not a heart so white. She is full of the milk of human kindness, but in our brief encounter, I can see she needs no man to clear her path in this life. Despite his great tribulations, or perhaps because of those same tragedies, Miles seems the more tender of the two. In either wise, their friendship shall I bond with hoops of steel and endeavour to return their courtesies and confidences in treble recompense. With assurances of reunion the next night, we took our several leaves and departed as we had come.

I shall never forget the snow that had fallen and left a white carpet on Mincing Lane, which bore no boot mark, owing to the lateness of the hour and no other men abroad, conveying the same hushed silence to the street that we had experienced among the tall stacks of cloth indoors. Nor will I easily forget how, in that stillness, I could hear Miles singing merrily to himself and the sound of that snow 'neath my steps as I departed:

"Her eyes are like two stars so bright,
Her face is fair, her step is light.
I asked this fair maid to take a walk,
Mark well what I do say.

I asked this maid out for a walk
That we might have some private talk.
Then I took this fair maid's lily white hand,
Mark well what I do say!

I took this fair maid's lily white hand
In mine as we walked along the strand.
Then I put mine arm around her waist
Mark well what I do say!

For I put mine arm around her waist
And from her lips snatched a kiss in haste!
Then a great big Dutchman rammed my bow
Mark well what I do say!

For a great big Dutchman rammed my bow,
And said, 'Young man, dis bin mein vrow!'
Then take warning boys, from me,
Mark well what I do say!

So take a warning, boys, from me,
With other men's wives don't make too free.
For if you do you will surely rue,
Mark well what I do say!

For if you do you will surely rue
Your act, and find my words come true."

Just as Christmas morn came not soon enough for us as eager boys, so did the next day seem tedious, waiting for the sun to set. I resumed my full duties onstage for the Leicester's Men (having lately served only out of sight), for we played several old plays with battles that call for soldiers and the fencing so delights the multitude, almost as much as the joy from our musical interludes.

Music! That remembers me of my lessons lately with Mr. Perkin, who has greeted me like a son returned home from foreign wars. He knew much of my condition and cure, so I infer from this that he made inquiries, so he might take a hand if my condition worsened. He has taught me the singing of various styles of ballads and courtly songs ere this, but today he told me why, which I herewith report to thee, because my tutoring is now in the Theatre herself and how stirring to the blood to be on the great stage and imagining my gestures seen by thousands! Mr. Perkin, reclining on a cushion in the second gallery, smoke wafting over the rail from his pipe and a small hearth that Vernon had painstakingly hoisted there to aid the master's aching joints in their battle against the January cold, began thus:

"What is the purpose of music, William?"

"Why, is it not to refresh the mind of man after his studies or his usual pain?" I guessed, standing alone on the vast, empty scaffold. He drew deeply on his pipe, seeming to pay closer attention to his rings of smoke than my reply, but then said:

"Hmmm, is it so? Doth not the crow sing as sweetly as the lark, when neither is attended? And the nightingale, if she should sing by day, when every goose is cackling, would she not be thought no better a musician than the wren? How many things by season, season'd are to their right praise and true perfection?"[75]

"Then master, the purpose of music is measured by those who hear it?" I was leaning against the pillar that now supported my frame and the machinery above the stage, still weak from my lengthy illness, until I noticed that the paint had tarnished my new sleeves.

"Thou art a horseman, William," quoth he, looking much warmer than I, although a modest pool of sunlight then bathed the forward part of the stage whereon I stood, dispatching a cheerful vigour through my bones. "Do but note a wild and wanton herd: if any air of music touch their ears, their savage eyes turn to a modest gaze by the sweet power of music, showing that there be naught so stockish, hard and full of rage, but that some music, for a time at least, doth change his nature."

Here he tapped the spent tobacco from his pipe, starting a rhythm as if beating a drum gently and concluded his thought. "The man that hath no music in himself, nor is not moved with the concord of such sweet sounds, is fit for treasons and fights and cannot be trusted. Mark the music, Will, and use it for its highest effect."

With this he instructed me on the music of various plays, some I knew ere this and others to me quite foreign. At times I sang, at times played on the lute, which he has taught me now this sixmonth and more, and instructed me further:

"Spit in the hole of thy lute and tune it again. It loves a cold day no more than thou dost. But make no such excuses for thy voice: hawking, spitting, or saying 'I am hoarse' are only prologues for a lazy player, William, which is to say one who is unprepared. Always rub up warmth in thy voice with those several exercises I have shown thee."

We proceeded in such fashion for over two hours and I must report to thee, the volumes of air inhaled and exhaled chased any remnants of sickness from my shrunk shank and imbued me with a sense of mighty well being, the likes of which I had hitherto not known. More amazing, I found that when I spoke the speeches he tasked me withal, they filled the great Theatre, penetrating every corner and cranny, resounding back to me as if the ocean's tides were caught in a drum. The Master was moved, I think, at least once, to shed a tear, as my voice rose and fell, like lines of music, with each phrase and gesture.

"Now thou art becoming a player, Will. Music oft hath such a charm to make bad good; and good to provoke harm; but now knowest thou the true purpose of music, not to the many, but to the player!" So ended the lesson, but now I see the music of everyday life. There are staffs to climb, and descend at your peril; there are passages both slow and swift; there are notes and signs to interpret, rhythms, rests, and tempo to consider. And when the song is at an end, thou dost hope there follows applause!

Lord knows, I was so taken in this latest lesson that I almost forgot my pledge to meet Miles and Kathleen at the Mermaid at sunset, which not even the gnashing teeth of winter could keep me away therefrom, and the meeting of Governor White. I cursed mine absent mind, for when I arrived at the Mermaid, White had already drawn a crowd, all straining to hear him. He looks a strong fellow, wears the plain collar and black raiment of a Puritan, his voice alone enough to command, his drooping beard billowing like the great sail of his ships with each declaration, as in:

"Virginia, called thus after our most gracious Virgin Queen, provides the goodliest land under the cope of Heaven. The most plentiful, sweet, fruitful and wholesome of all the world."

Hereupon he laid before those many of us in attendance, the maps he had drawn of these lands, and thereto many coloured images of every fruit, insect, bird, beast, fish, and wonder of this place. The people he depicted therein were not savage, but showed comely modesty and such manners and custom that we did marvel how eagerly they did bend to our English sovereignty. The smile and gracefully folded arms of a woman showed calm and peacefulness, her stout chest and thick arms unlike our women, who are not used to such heavy labors as are needed to carve a life from a wilderness. This woman was bare-breasted, but modestly covered below the waist and her chest adorned with such tattoos and necklaces of fine workmanship that she might be mistaken as fully clad.

The town of these Indians was called Secoton and is laid out like our cities with wide streets and places of worship, sturdy homes, and plots of land for tillage and grazing. Even their dead are cared for in like manner to our custom, showing such respect for those lost souls that would move an English heart to prayer. One drawing showed how they prepare these dead by cleaning the flesh from the bone, save the skin and hair of their heads, which flesh is dried and enfolded in mats laid at their feet. These corpses, after being made dry, are covered with deerskins, not altering their form or proportion, and are laid to rest in a charnel house that is constantly attended by an elder or a priest of their tribe.

Each man pulled closer around the great table of maps and drawings and carvings brought back from Virginia, the better to capture in the mind's eye those particulars that he would need report to those he leaves behind and in offering diverse reasons for making such a journey. Each man prayed and feared the same thing: whether he would be among the 150 sought by Governor White to further people this new land. Only one youth stood back and seemed more cautious than the rest, at times hiding in the shadows of the inn and making some marks on a folded paper with a stub of charcoal from the fire. I studied the face of this boy for many minutes before I remembered where first I saw it.

"Art thou not Rosalind Munday?" quoth I in a whisper, recalling the youth who came dressed as this selfsame boy to warn us of plague in her town.

"Why no, sir, you do mistake me," quoth she, lowering her voice to con a manly resonance that might fool a child or a drunkard, but not a player who is wont to take on false voices as easily as false robes in service to his craft upon a stage.

"Mistress Munday, thy secret is safe with me. I mean thee no harm. I am that same man who fell from the tree last summer when thou didst bring the news of Plague to our Earl of Leicester's Men."

With this she bid me step further apart from the others, such that our speech could not be overheard. She was again covered with a thick doublet that concealed her bosom, a draped cap that engulfed her luxurious red hair, her face smudged with dirt to distract the eye from her delicate features and entrancing beauty. Yet nothing could hide the silent war of lilies and of roses I saw in the field of her most fair face.

"I remember thee well, sir, and thank thee for thy pains in keeping my true identity secret. Thou mayest wonder how I came to be in this tavern, in the company of these men."

"I infer that thou, like myself and these other eager souls, are hungry for news of the New World and how a man - - or woman - - of little means might go thither to gain some greater Fortune." Coz, I do confess that in that instant, as her emerald eyes locked on mine, that I felt again the same passion as when she uncovered her head and shook loose her hair at that first encounter in summer.

"Yes, such is the state of my family. My father and brother both now taken by the Plague, I am left to find some means to sustain my mother, her mother, and mine own sisters. Little employment and less comfort have I found in London and I know I cannot conceal my sex for long, so those prospects available to men will not earn a farthing for me here. I had thought to take ship for the New World, there to find some wealth, but the Governor has said no man may join without a wife, for they want to increase the colony thither and need those who can work the land, and those who will add to its number and strength."

O John, herewith I must commend to thee those events, which astound my poor powers to add or subtract, even as I write these words and read them many times over. In brief then: Rosalind and I sat apart from the general commotion around Governor White and his visions of a blank canvas in a New World of endless possibilities. At such leisure, and for some hours thereafter, we acquainted each other with the mysteries of our lives to that point, and for some reason unseen, omitted nothing. I have rarely felt such kinship with another, such sense of commonality, such eagerness to complete one another's thoughts and longings. Even as I showed her my purloined map of the Americas, I confessed my fault in obtaining it, but also assured her I am an honest man and intend most heartily to recompense old Westerbeke as soon as Fate allows.

And when we had fully emptied to each other those vessels that hold our thoughts, fears, and dreams, we concluded the most fantastical plan to make such hopes manifest: coz, in that instant, we agreed to present ourselves as husband and wife to Governor White, that he would take us both to Virginia, wherein we might make our Fortunes together. We surmised, from all we knew, that in a year, or two at most, we could sell our holdings to some new settler and divide the gains in equal measure. We could profit too from selling timber and food from our land and could fill our coffers with any gold, silver, or other transportables that the land had afforded us during our tenure.

Nor did we wait long for an answer to our prayer. Miles most courteously presented me to Governor White, commending my skills in many forms of labour. Herein Fortune smiled again, for so many men had left, upon hearing they could not join the expedition without a wife, that round the table now stood very few who could subscribe to those requirements demanded of the Governor. I assured him my wife stood by me, a fact that Miles knew not of, nor could he therefore say aught to the contrary, such that I was accepted as a member of his company in the instant!

I trust and pray this plan offends thee not, knowing thy honest sensibilities, but well knowest thou that the foot can never gain a distant shore, that the eye might see, without the aid of a sturdy vessel to carry thee thither. Such is our vessel, for we could devise no other, severally or in company. No man more need know of our deceit, for we pledged to live in chastity when lodged together and to return to our separate families when we arrive again on English soil.

'Tis true I feel the Devil on my shoulder when I think on Nan. But is not the ground on which we built our marriage naught but loam and shifting sands? Was she not faithless ere this and, thinking on't, what fealty do I owe her now? In any wise, she will be the beneficiary of this deception, for my Fortune will lift all Shakespeares as the rising tide lifts all boats, even those with rotten timbers.

And thus is my passion for seeking my Fortune in the New World a fire that has grown hotter as the days have grown colder, but now with a means to a glorious end. Mr. Stow has newly given me to read 'Divers Voyages Touching the Discoverie of America', wherein all my hopes and auguries are further confirmed! And consider those 500 acres. Think on it, coz. What would a man not do in all of Warwickshire to be the master of so much land? Dick then arrived with Giddy at the Mermaid, not two minutes after Rosalind had departed in the company of Kathleen and Miles, my secret intent that night remaining undiscovered.

"I'll teach thee the finest humour to be drunk in. I learned it in the Bell last week."

"In faith? Let's hear it, let's hear it." Giddy was sniffing the bottle that once housed the lemon syrup and wincing as if bitten.

"They call it 'knighting' in London," quoth Dick. "For when they drink, they do so upon their knees, lest they fall over in their stupor!"

"Faith, that's excellent," quoth I. "But I will save my wages for better times."

"An how if thou shouldst die, Will Shakespeare?" Dick held me at arm's length as if he might read my reply before my tongue gave it birth. "Thou hadst died already, and not a month in London, how shalt thou survive any longer than a Smithfield cheese at a table of hungry players? If thou shouldst die, thy wages are saved for naught."

Thanks to Giddy working many of the plays in my stead, and sewing several new garments cut from old ones to delight the masters, my wages were never stopped a day. They brought me full fifty shillings tenpence, a sum I would rather send to aid Stratford kin than squander on drink. I needed to make no reply, for as Dick ended his sermon, the scaring bell sounded, marking that time when all London citizens must empty the streets, a law more honoured in the breech than the observance, but one which sends many a late-night soul scurrying homeward, especially in these times when few men trust another.

I mean that at every alehouse in the City, a dozen or more men will be found standing with long staves and knives, appointed by the Constable of each ward as watchmen. Mr. Johnson inquired of those who stand nightly in a clump before the Mermaid and one of them answered 'We seek three young men known to have conspired with Babington 'gainst Her Majesty.' Demanding how they should know these persons, one answered: 'Marry, one of the parties hath a hooked nose.' To which Mr. Johnson inquired further: 'And have you no other mark?'

'No' said they. Well, I am neither officer nor scholar, but for these watchmen to stand so openly in clumps, I doubt any suspected person will come near them; and if they be no better instructed but to 'find three persons', by one of them having 'a hooked nose', they may accuse the innocent and easily miss their target. But such is the fear and the anger that Babington and his ilk have provoked among the citizenry, that all men must walk abroad advisedly by night. And Giddy knew his master would bear the fine if his apprentice were caught by a Constable after hours, therefore taking his leave of us. But Dick thought otherwise:

"I'll to the Cross Keys, where Richard and Cuthbert stay for me. O come with us for a Keys draught that will finish thy cure."

"Nay, I may not." I was sorely tempted after laying so long abed with the great river of people flowing around my sheeted island in Mr. Stow's closet, but he had warned me about suspicion of thieves that lurk in the Lime street ward by night and bid me return through Culver alley (which is lately stopped up and made into a tennis-court and therefore something safer after dark).

"There's much to hear in the Cross Keys, Will," quoth Dick, dangling an imaginary fishing line in my face. "They say the Queen will sign Mary of Scotland's death warrant tomorrow.

"Aye," quoth Giddy. "'Tis already a Star Chamber matter since Babington was hanged for imagining and encompassing Her Majesty's death. And on his testimony is the Scots Queen also ensnared."

"And if Mary is hanged, Spain will surely make war against our island fortress," quoth Dick.

"O coz," quoth I, "what brother will be set against what brother? What father against which son? Those who care for the old religion might take such matters as a sign to revolt and would not Jack Cade himself rise from his grave to lead the rabble, if given even a petty excuse?"[76]

"Aye," quoth Giddy. "The Pope in Rome decreed that whosoever sends our Queen out of the world with the pious intention of doing God service, not only does not sin, but gains merit with heaven."

"Has it come to that? Must the Catholic Mary die?" I demanded.

"Aye, she must, Will," quoth Dick. "Remember: all who are traitors must die."

This he said with the Puritanical vigour of that vicar we met on London bridge the day we first entered the City, indeed they were the very words, were they not? O coz, if Queen Mary is to die, I fear for my father and the Burbages too, or at least the father of the Burbages, our master. And any man else suspected of having a care for the old faith, even if they care nothing for the old Scots queen.

They left with more fanfare but little substance. In truth, I care not which religion holds dominion in our land. I see no difference, nor does one slake my thirst nor cure mine ailments better than the other, but they that utter too much truth will wear their heads less securely than those who mock it wear their hats. Having newly faced that toughest taskmaster, Death I mean, I would not burden my soul with lies or cheats, yet am I not guilty of both?

As if he overheard my troubled conscience, the next morning, Mr. Stow took me to his church, St. Olave's, and bid me confess any sins that weighed upon me after so long a journey to the very overlook into Eternity. We knelt shoulder-to-shoulder with the mass of parishioners, I looked down upon the carvings 'neath my folded hands and what did I see? Carvings depicting coiled serpents chasing fools with tails and monkeys in chains, men riding beasts shaped like a sort of human female, beating her hindquarters as any ruthless master beats his nag who won't go to gallop. Slaughter of innocents, fiery demons. I could look no more and sprang up from the place and ran to a confessional, more to hide from God's wrath than in hopes the other side would be occupied. In truth, it was occupied and I bared my soul, but mostly confessed my terrible sins, which I have inventoried to thee already. What now would the old priest think of my plan to take ship with a false wife?

From thence Mr. Stow, never asking what moved me of such a sudden to bolt the holy hall, took me to St. Paul's churchyard, a goodly walk west towards the Thames from our parish. He is wise and sees beyond that which meets his eye. In this instance, his hand sketched on the canvas of the sky above the tower where a wooden spire once reached out towards the heavens and said:

"Her steeple burned away twenty-year since. Those who fought the fire were prevented from extinguishing the blaze by the gawking mob, myself among them. Now every holiday fool pays his penny to climb the stairs that lead to the top of the stone tower, which once upheld the steeple, for a view of the City and to carve his initials in the lead casements. Come, let us be holiday fools!"

With that we climbed more stairs than are built in all of Stratford, I'll warrant, nay, all of Warwickshire. But at the top, o coz, what a vision is there! St. Paul's stands on a hill and her mass is greater than ten Holy Trinitys[77]. Standing on the great tower thou art perched with God, above the smoky pallor that smothers the City day and night. Punching through this brown haze are dozens of other church steeples, the battlements of great castles of the greatest lords. From thence, looking south by sou'west, thou canst see White Hall and Westminster, Her Majesty's own palaces, yea even the glittering figures that stroll the bulwarks. Perhaps one of them that day was the Queen.

The Thames cannot be described, dissecting the City from her suburbs to the south, from Southwarke and Bank Side and the Rose and Greenwich and such. But from this lofty view, I fancy I saw my destiny, the New World. At the least, I saw as far as the great river flows to meet the sea, from whence the watery highway leads to Fortune. But in London, it is the Thames herself who shapes each man's destiny. Some row easily downstream, pushed faster than perhaps they list by the hasty tide, but always in one direction. Others spend their native strength rowing against this current, making it to another bank, but far short of the mark they first intended. Neither man content and each doomed to have his life summed up by which bank he missed, not those he made. Ha! My father knows that men's evil manners live in brass, their virtue we write in water; water that flows away faster than we can truly mark it.

We descended from thence into the crowded square alongside the great church, wherein every bookseller might be found at the sign of the Dolphin or the Greyhound or such like, and wherat every mother's son knew Mr. Stow as an honest man and a good customer. Paul's Walk, he calls it, where books can be had in equal measure with the news of the day. And the currency thither is gossip, mine in exchange for thine, and every other manner of business deal-making thou canst name.

Well, now I may say I know something of the west and northern part of the City, twixt St. Paul's and St. Olave's, this part alone about the bigness of Stratford in its entirety, but in London it makes not more than one-tenth her map! More I have not seen owing to my grave illness. Lord, methinks I saw the grave more than once ere this.

Drat. One of London's many rats hath just now fallen from the beam above my bed and stares at me saucily. Perhaps I interrupted his native slumbers with my singing and writing this letter to thee and he intrudes upon my solitude to demand a quiet night.

"Mr. Rat, thou art welcome hither, for e'en as I was cared for under this roof, no other of God's creatures shall be turned away neither."

He makes no reply.

"What thinkst thou of my philosophy: that music and life are cut from the same cloth?"

Still makes he no reply, although he sniffs at the air somewhat more curiously than before.

"Nay, thou wouldst have no opinion on the matter, I fear, for thou hast never fed of the dainties that are bred in a book; thou hast not eaten paper, as it were; not drunk ink. Thine intellect is not replenished; thou art only an animal, only sensible in the duller parts."

He lifted his head to its fullest measure and yawned! I guessed aright: he came not for my philosophy, but to demand my silence that he might continue his own slumbers unabated. This I find most unusual, since London rats patrol the streets by night, stripping them of the filth that a day's commerce has covered them withal. In this, they perform a service for man, even though we may despise them for vermin.

"Mr. Rat, I think God has set such barren creatures as thee before us, so we should be thankful that man has the loftier sensibilities and feelings. Therefore, I thank thee for thy service and will requite them with a peaceful night's sleep." Perhaps he took my meaning, or had satisfied his curiosity about the lodger who had spent so many weeks in his otherwise private closet, for now ambles he off the bed, along a ledge and back up into the beams, perhaps to the comfort of his own home and family.

I bear the City rats no ill-will, though I wish their number fewer by a thousand thousand. When they cannot be seen, thou canst not help but hear them, scurrying, gnawing, scratching out their meagre existence. Some say they bring sickness, even Plague with them, but this I think is folly, for though they eat of our waste, yet do they cleanse themselves and appear quite fastidious in their nature.

The golden dew of sleep has long since hung upon my brow, dear coz, and the inkpot has nearly shed all her liquor. O, great thing of me forgot: please tell Edward he must do as thou hast counseled, for so are bees with smoke and doves with noisome stench from their hives and houses driven away. In no wise should he fail this time.[78]

O coz, I know not precisely when I may take ship for Virginia, so if this letter be my last, please tell my son, when that day shall come to speak of his father, that I did all to make him proud. It may be long ere thou hearest from me again, for I doubt it much that letters are easily conveyed from Virginia to our homeland and back again. But in some year or two, three at most, look towards the Clopton Bridge now and then, look to see a fine man of obvious wealth crossing the River Avon to reclaim his right and his honour.

For now, kiss my boy and maids in my name and omit nothing else which thine honour deem'st best for their tender need. I am thine ever-loving servant in all else, Will.

PS: I append herewith some of my unpolished lines, writ when under the spell of a fever and thinking these words to be my last. Please forgive if they are less than thou art accustomed to read from our more lofty English poets:

No longer mourn for me when I am dead:
Then you shall hear the surly sullen bell
Give warning to the world that I am fled
From this vile world, with vilest worms to dwell.

Nay, if you read this line, remember not
The hand that writ it; for I love you so
That I, in your sweet thoughts, would be forgot,
If thinking on me then should make you woe.

O, if, I say, you look upon this verse
When I perhaps compounded am with clay,
Do not so much as my poor name rehearse.
But let your love even with my life decay,

Lest the wise world should look into your moan
And mock you with me, after I am gone.

LETTER TEN
May 1, 1587

Wherein a passage to the New World with an unlikely companion is foreclosed, but new worlds of love, and on the stage, are unexpectedly opened.

When Letter Ten opens, Shakespeare is despondent that he has been suddenly denied passage on Governor White's ship to America. Instead, he was summoned to a meeting in the port where the Golden Hind was docked, that famous ship used by Sir Francis Drake to raid Spanish treasure galleys (it had become a tourist attraction, but had fallen into disrepair and the area surrounding was known to be a meeting point of suspicious foreigners and thieves). White's ensign delivers the bad news and gives Shakespeare a gold sovereign with a cryptic note that reads simply "He will guide you."

In my early teens, when my family left our predictable black-and-white TV life in Milwaukee and migrated to Australia, I discovered a country the same size as the U.S. but with less than one tenth the population. That implied opportunity. Adventure. Living color. Australia needed people and the government offered free passage on a ship, a place to live, help starting a business or finding a great job. The modern version of "streets paved with gold" for the taking. Oh yes, and if we hadn't moved, I might have been drafted a few years later into an army that was fighting and dying in Viet Nam.

When I read Letter Ten, this was the experience in my life that helped me imagine the forces swirling around Shakespeare, accentuating his eagerness to cross the ocean into the unknown New World and fleeing the veritable earthquake of events that was about to shake apart his native land.

Mary Queen of Scots, the great hope of many in Europe for a restoration of the Catholic church in England, was found guilty of plotting the death of Queen Elizabeth. Reluctantly, the English Queen had her Scottish cousin beheaded on February 8, 1587. Numerous accounts show that Elizabeth agonized over the decision (even claimed later that she had not given final approval for the execution), because she knew it would divide her loyal subjects and ignite the long-feared war with Spain.

As if to illustrate this national dynamic in a very personal example, Master Johnson, suspected of being a spy for the crown in Leicester's Men, reports the details of the plot and Mary's fate, igniting a heated debate among the players that pits friend against friend, and for Masters Phillips and Pope, brother against brother.

Marching, literally and figuratively, to the rising drums of war, Will Kempe becomes more belligerent and ready to defend his Queen and country, comically recruiting Dick Cowley and other patrons of the Mermaid tavern to turn war-like play-acting into the real thing, or as Shakespeare would write later in *As You Like It,* Kempe filled men "full of strange oaths, jealous in honour, sudden and quick in quarrel, seeking the bubble 'reputation' even in the cannon's mouth." In earnest or jest, Shakespeare apparently took notes, for I found that he uses these ragged conscripts in *Henry IV part 2* (Act III, scene 2) when Falstaff recruits soldiers in a similar comic manner.

Not yet overly concerned about these matters, Shakespeare in Letter Ten is angered and mystified by the refusal to include him in the new colony, but cannot remain disappointed for long. He and Rosalind are madly and truly in love. Shakespeare recounts how they had raced through the streets, overjoyed at the initial prospect of passage on White's ship. Hiding in his brother Giddy's workroom, on piles of sheepskins, and bathed in moonlight, they gleefully plan their departure. Shakespeare is transfixed by her ivory skin, her luxurious red curls, and swears, "I ne'er saw true beauty til that night."

In a scene prescient of *Romeo and Juliet*, the lovers hold hands, exchange secrets, kiss and make love. I doubt Rosalind constrained Shakespeare with more than bonds of love, but coincidentally, the only date on the letter when I read it was "Hock Tuesday," which I discovered was the second Tuesday after

Easter, when women would tie up passersby with ropes demanding money for charity (Easter in 1587 was April 26th, so I estimated that this letter was written in the first week of May). *Fifty Shades of Grey*, Elizabethan style?

That Shakespeare and Rosalind were left behind is a very lucky twist of fate however. Had they gone, we would never have heard of them again. I was able to find Governor John White's meticulous diary and learned that he took 150 men and women, including his own pregnant daughter Eleanor, to the settlement that he thought had been established on Roanoke Island in the new colony of Virginia (in the state of North Carolina today).

As he would later report, things did not start well. The garrison left there just two years earlier by Walter Raleigh in 1585 (and reinforced in 1586) had disappeared, but some of their goods were discovered, ransacked by Indians. The new settlers established themselves in the remains of the original fort and at least one good omen was delivered—Eleanor gave birth to Virgina Dare, the first European baby born on North American soil, as far as we know (the baptism imagined in Illustration 17, below).

17. A baptism in the first English colony at Roanoke, Virginia, which Shakespeare tried to join (later called the "lost" colony because all of the settlers vanished).

Governor White and some of the men were sent back to England to return with more troops and supplies, which is how his diary has survived to tell the tale. Sadly, when White was finally allowed to return two years later, almost all signs of the colony had disappeared, including his daughter and granddaughter, fading into what historians now call the "Lost Colony of Roanoke."

Letter Ten looks abroad at the forces of war and the fate of colonists, but also magnifies life at home. Adding to revelations in his previous correspondence, we learn more about the controversial, if not actually illegal, means by which Anne Shakespeare is making ends meet in Stratford. To understand the references, we need only know that Lady Day is the holiday honoring the Virgin Mary, observed on March 25th. It also served as the official New Year's Day in England until 1752. Queen Elizabeth had issued a proclamation forbidding the making of malt from Lady Day until Michaelmas (September 29th) so there would be more grain on the market for food and to keep prices from rising too high.

With this in mind, it's clear that the stockpiling and trading of commodities that Anne undertakes during that period are out of gnawing necessity. Shakespeare is not unsympathetic, but makes new references to a "winter that freezes my feelings" for her. There is still much about their relationship that we don't know at this point, but have yet to learn.

If he must remain in London, Shakespeare begins to figure out how he could earn more money in the theatre. His imagination is sparked by watching a competing theatre company, the Lord Admiral's Men, perform the epic adventure play *Tamburlaine*, by Christopher "Kit" Marlowe. He notes the spectators' enthusiasm for gruesome special effects and certain kinds of dialogue. Having adapted plays for his company on tour, he thinks he can work with other writers and produce an attraction equal to *Tamburlaine*. The still-puzzling rivalry with Richard "Boy" Burbage begins to thaw and Shakespeare sees how he might write similar dramatic roles for the improving young actor, thereby mending fences further. Before our eyes, Shakespeare is blossoming as a writer, identifying the very talents for which he himself will one day be remembered, noting that "plays must capture the imagination of the unlearned and the university wit alike."

Against this vast tapestry of seismic events and cross currents, Letter Ten ends with a charming bit of homespun. On a separate page, a recipe for "May Tart" apparently provided by Anne Shakespeare. It is unknown whether she could read or write, so the recipe may have been copied by someone else in the household at her direction, or it could be the only known sample of her handwriting. Shakespeare concludes by asking John Combe to thank her for sending the recipe and the ingredients to make it. He praises the results and rather guiltily admits to Combe that he made and ate the tart with Rosalind.

Yes, Shakespeare is hovering between conflicting worlds, fates, and emotions. The decisions he reveals in Letter Ten, among complex and difficult choices, leave us feeling we are now in long, intimate conversations with a dear friend over many cups of tea.

Hock Tuesday [May 1, 1587], London

Coz,

Today this pen weighs like a stone in my listless fingers, heavy as over-ripened corn, hanging his head under a plenteous load. Wherefore is my gaze so firmly fixed upon the sullen earth? The ships of Governor John White have sailed to the New World without me. My sad tale follows, but I must first address those censures in thy letter lately arrived (thanks to the most courteous pains of our good friend Thomas, delivered with those other goods from Stratford), for which I offer my most humble thanks.

That I would present Rosalind, a woman not my wife as my wife, thou sayest I have lost my reputation, the immortal part of myself, and what remains is bestial. I swear to thee, mine intentions are honest: and is that not what matters most in the eyes of God? O John, 'tis true that the New World has captivated mine imagination, rendered me drowsy with luxurious visions of wealth and greatness, but I swear I am fixed thereon merely to retrieve lost Shakespeare honour withal and to build a stout bulwark against our enemies. Therefore, must I not do all that is necessary to gain such a worthy end?

And what is Reputation to a drowning man? Doth Reputation feed the hungry or cure an illness? Nay, I tell thee Reputation is oft got without merit and lost without deserving.[79] What I have done was in a just cause, so Reputation may present his case to Conscience and, I doubt it not, that one will prove of fleeting value and the other will show to be clear (leastwise in this matter). Yet this is not to protest that I am blameless, but I beg thee, give me leave to lay out the weights on either side of this scale, as thou art wont to do, and ask then what thou wouldst have done in my place:

Item first: Money (in Stratford)

Thy report hath troubled me greatly: I agree, 'tis not meet for Anne to earn money with unlawful dealings. My father was fined more than once for his wool trading, but has pursued such traffic because it profits him more than the glover's trade, which thou knowest Leicester has so greatly hindered. If Anne makes these trades at my father's bidding (and trust me coz, she is better at business than he), there is no power in Stratford who will blame her.

More do I worry that she will come to no good from that hoarding of corn for malt-making so long after Lady Day, especially now that our country is so greatly burdened and decayed, as impoverished by a great dearth of corn. But who should prevent a housewife from turning her own corn into bread or converting the same into malt or drink for her own large family (and some few neighbors)? Who would prevent her from clothing that same family with their own wool? In sum, I do not fear discovery of her labours in malt-making, but fear she could be fined, or worse, if she is discovered holding more corn than can be thus explained. Doth she take more corn from neighbors for this practice? That could be her undoing.

And coz, if I return to Stratford, as thou dost ever so courteously demand, what means of earning would I have to supplant those industries she hath so ingeniously devised? There is little demand in Stratford for a player and mender of players' apparel. Thou and thy father have grown more prosperous lending money at interest (another practice that earns the frown of the Justice, doth it not?), so thy notion that I might join thy trade seems no more safe than the course Anne hath taken. And what would I do for thee? Should I be thy Bludgeon and persuade delinquents that it were better to pay than run? Ha! I swear those parts I play onstage never were so convincing.

Mistake me not dear friend, I am sorely grieved to hear of these dangers to Anne, but my poor brain cannot devise other ways of greater honour for her to earn money with three babes at home and twins still on the teat. To work a kitchen in a great household? Who in Stratford hath such wealth to pay her and doth not already have his own servants? Work in the fields? Women have little value thither until harvest time. I know thy 'prithees' and 'wherefores' are righteous, but know not how to honour them. I trust those few shillings I sent to my father to aid in her keeping hath shown mine intentions, if not yet the full measure of my family's need. I would dearly wish to know how that token was received by him.

Item second: Love (Anne)

It grieves me to know of her stomach ailments, but please give her the pack that accompanies this letter with these instructions I learned from the self-same physic who restored my health of late. This will defend against the Plague, but I am told it will work even greater magic on any ailment of the stomach. To make this Plague-water, she must take a pound of rue and another of rosemary, mixing these with sage and sorrel, then add the contents of this pack (which hath celandine, mugwort, the tops of red brambles, pimpernel, wild-dragons, arimony, angelica). Put these compounds in a pot, fill it with white-wine above the herbs, and so let it stand four days. Then still it in a limbeck [*distillery*] and with this drink she shall be both protected and cured.

Thou reportest that Anne speaks of missing my company and how I am in her thoughts as sweet-season'd showers are to the ground. Thou sayest this shows her true love for me: but coz, a small plaster doth not cure a broken leg, nor can some few words of longing cure a broken heart. Thou hast right: 'tis divine to forgive. But how is that so easily done when the living reminders of her true nature dwell with her under the same roof?

[Scribe's note: Shakespeare crossed out the following unfinished passage, but examination with a magnifying glass revealed this text: "Thou sayest Susanna grows strong and fast, looking more like her father every day. Aye, there's the rub, John. She may look". The sentence was left unfinished. TT]

When I think on her, I feel the strife of her betrayal, no matter how long past, for it lives like yesterday in my brain, or worser still, like one who is laughed to scorn behind his back. How can I then return in happy state, I that am bereft of peaceful mind or rest? When day's oppression is not eased by night, and night shakes hands with day to torture me? Thinking on't by day doth draw my sorrows longer out, while restless sleep at night doth merely make grief's strength seem stronger.

But coz, in this winter that freezes my feelings for Anne, I am in equal measure now to blame, for no matter how cold the marriage bed, no matter how hot the reason or righteous the grievance, a vow before God cannot so easily be dismissed. But that which began with Rosalind of necessity, hath blossomed lately into a springtime of love, unlooked for by either of us. Hereinafter will I therefore confess to thee how we crossed the bridge from friends to lovers.

Item third: Love (Rosalind)

On Easter day did Governor White and some hundred happy few, Kathleen and Miles among them, set forth from Portsmouth, after many weeks fitting out their ships in sight of London bridge. More than once was I aboard those selfsame vessels, brought thither by the fair entreaties of Gov. White, together with his assurances that I would be among the hopeful souls to sail to my Fortune with his company. Rosalind played well her part, sweet of voice and manner, charming all she encountered (especially owing to that she no longer needed to dress like a boy!). None raised his eyebrow to betray any suspicion that she was not my wife or that we were not single-minded in our pursuit of those 500 acres of Virginia promised to every man and wife aboard.

But I must confess to thee, dear friend, that in the many visits we made to those we took for our fellow travellers, the more I felt a powerful affection for Rosalind. Nay, affection is a paltry word for so powerful a sentiment. I did love her anon, love her with an ardor I cannot say I ever felt for Anne, nor any other of her sex. There was never any thing so sudden, save lightning or Death. We no sooner met but looked, then sighed, then loved, and in these degrees have we made a pair of stairs up to this counterfeit marriage, most certain at risk of God's wrath, but in our eyes in the very wrath of love, such that clubs could not part us now.[80]

The moment when the spark became the flame, indeed soon a conflagration, was by strange coincidence on St. Valentine's Day, when Cupid is known to afflict the unsuspecting. That night, still in February's wintery grasp, Governor White gave us letters of patent to join his newest expedition. We raced through those cold, dark streets, which to us seemed warm as August and brightly lit, to find some quiet place to savour our good fortune and plan for those necessities to carry us thither. Knowing of no other place for privacy, I took her to Giddy's workroom in Brownsword's haberdashery, for no man stirred thither at such an hour and I had learnt the means by which to enter through a secret unlocked casement.

We dared not light a candle, lest we be discovered, but the moon bathed our scene with light enough for each to see the other's joyful smiles. We sat cross legged, facing each other on a pile of sheepskins that Giddy had newly cleaned and readied for some cloak or lining he was to make, and for a time we rubbed each other's hands together to restore their warmth and said nothing, but giggled like girls at play. Rosalind then began to inventory those items we would need to procure ere our departure:

"Thinkst thou we must provide some tent or likewise shelter? Or upon arrival there, would houses be already built?"

"O, great thing of us forgot. I asked about food and clothing and tools and the like, but had not thought to ask about a roof over our heads. If there be a town, we may find shelter, but will surely need some valuables to pay for it."

"Would money have value thither, if every man can find gold in the earth?" We had stopped the rubbing, but her hands were clasping mine, resting in her lap, and she cocked her head slightly, as I have seen delightful jaybirds do, as if listening for the answer from Heaven. "Perhaps the natives thither labour for our colony in exchange for trade goods and beads. These must we also bring with us, I'll warrant, for a small investment in such trifles could yield good benefits with such people."

In this manner we continued for an hour, neither wanting to break the bond of our hands to commit this list to paper. It was delicious joy to imagine the place and what our life would be like thither. 'Twas in that instant coz, I realized how she taught the pale moon to burn bright; how she seemed to hang upon the cheek of night, like a rich jewel in an Ethiope's ear; how she suddenly appeared to me as a snowy dove when it sits with crows.

How is it she looked boyish and common till now, but was so totally transformed in mine eyes at that instant? Yes, her luxurious red curls, tucked in the cap before, were now set free to frolic over the freckles of her doe-like face, cascading to soft shoulders below; and yes, the coarse cloak that once concealed her true form was open now to reveal a milky throat above a swelling bosom; but the final spell was cast by her fragrance, not an artificer's perfume created to con Nature, but Nature itself, more delicate than the honeysuckle in June, more erotic than that intoxicating aroma of the first unfolding rosebud after a dark, cold winter. Aye, the earthy smell of her entranced and entwined my senses, my spirit, just as the female ivy so enrings the barky sinews of the elm. I'll swear to thee coz, I never saw true beauty till that night. I drew her hands to my lips.

"Rosalind, do I profane this holy shrine with mine unworthy hand? If so, let the gentle fine for my transgression be this: my lips, two blushing pilgrims, stand ready to smooth that rough touch with a tender kiss." With these words, I dared kiss her clasped hands and hoped for fair reply.

"Good pilgrim, thou dost wrong thy hand too much, for even saints have hands that pilgrims' hands do touch!" She laughed so lightly, like the warbling lark I oft heard in our garden at Henley Street. Was her smile born of joy or mockery? "And is not palm-to-palm a form of kiss?"

"Aye, saints have hands, but have they not lips too?" I dared kiss her palms, which she did then slowly unfold to me.

"Aye, pilgrim, lips that they must use in prayer!" Again the mysterious smile.

"O, then, dear saint, let lips do what hands do: they pray when joined together." I laid her palms on my cheeks and likewise cradled her rose-blushed cheeks in mine.

"I have heard it said that saints may grant what is sought in prayers." Her emerald eyes had not strayed an inch from mine in some minutes, which now seemed a lifetime to me.

"Then move not, while my prayer's effect I take." I leaned forward and kissed her on the lips, gently at first, but feeling her passionate reply, found myself lost in her at once. She wrapped her arms around my neck, locked together, we full-embraced and kissed for all eternity. I could not utter another word, but over and again kept thinking 'saints may grant what is sought.' O grant me my prayer again! And again. And yet again. I was not her first, nor she mine, but the ecstasy had no precedent in my feeble experience or imagination.

As we lay undisturbed on the soft wool, amongst faintly shimmering fabrics draped Heaven-like above, coiled together as one, alive and awake as never before, then did Rosalind lay naked to me the innermost particulars of her young-old life, as I did mine to her. I can tell thee coz, there are those secrets she imparted that are unimaginable, which hearing made me feel still more tenderness and love for her. When I told her of my father, a marriage enforced, my pretty babes, she seemed to accept me, as imperfectly wrought as I am, in equal measure.

Herewith I conclude my reckoning on either side of the scales, in loving reply to thy loving advice: I prithee coz, do not judge me too harshly.

My brain is a beehive over these matters, one that stings me constantly, while yet providing the sweetest honey that any man ever tasted. Guilt in passion; fire in snow. I know not if I should accept punishment or pleasure, but I do know that Rosalind is my welcome port after stormy seas since leaving Stratford and she was mine only hope of passage to the New World and the riches therein that could have rescued both our families. Here I end my rebuttal of thy censure and pray these, mine unworthy arguments, have softened thy hard opinion of me. If not, read on, for yet were we punished by some unseen power, perhaps for our stolen season of love, perhaps merely that we dared aim so high.

Item fourth: Stay or sail?

Thou hast counseled me to remain in England, to return to Stratford, to forswear any thoughts of the New World. Thy prayers, not mine are answered, at the least for now, for as the day of sailing drew near, I was sent for, in all haste, by Governor White to meet his ancient [*ensign*] in Deptford, even in the shadow of the Golden Hind. I hastened thither and found the man, one Mr. William Willybone, and presented myself to his disposition.

"Thou dost mean to take ship with us?" Willybone is a foul smelling man, not many years older than myself, but whose hard life had already claimed three fingers of a right hand that he thrust then into my chest.

"Aye, marry I do," quoth I, eager to claim my rights and station.

"Well lash thy hopes to the rail laddie. Thou wilt not board any vessel under command of General White." I must have appeared to him as one who chokes on foul meat, for I could say not a word, although my tongue was surely trying.

"I'll not waste words nor time in explanation, Shakespeare," quoth he with a deep sigh, not without more measure of sympathy than at first. "I am told to give thee this and have thy word that thou wilt abandon thy hopes of seeing the Americas, leastways for the ships that sail this spring."

"But who can command such a thing?" I reluctantly took the folded paper he had withdrawn from inside his shirt, still sodden with his sweat. The dock was bustling with its commerce, although the day was spent and night's candles were lit in those buildings that faced thereon. Willybone had thus far ignored this traffic, but now he looked in all directions and especially up at a man who stood above us on the Golden Hind and seemed to take more than a little interest in our parley. A light rain was falling, which minutes ago seemed a harbinger of the spring, but which now seemed a biting cold, sharing my grief at this ill-turn of fortune.

"Thou wilt read all that thou art meant to know therein." He poked at the paper with the one serviceable finger that remained on his hand. "And look you, do no more than is set down for thee, lest thou and thy wife come to mischief unlooked for."

Did he say 'wife' as if he suspected she was not one at all? Or was that my guilty conscience colouring the canvas? In any wise, before I could protest a word more, he pulled his thick hempen cloak about his neck and departed in haste. I moved to a neighbor alley, underneath a staircase that might protect the key to this mystery from further weathering. There I unfolded the paper and read its contents:

'He will guide you.'

I turned the paper over and over again, but found no greater intelligence than this simple phrase. A gold sovereign fell from its folds, which I did hastily repair to my pocket, lest those villainous sorts who frequent Deptford rob me thereof.

He will guide me? Who is 'he'? If the author of this declaration meant Willybone, the intent was lost when the ancient marched so abruptly hence. He will guide me? Every mother's son hath heard such sentiment in sermons of a Sunday, but if 'He' is our Lord, then was I meant to pray for a destination to whence He will guide me? And what was the meaning of a gold sovereign, more money than I had held at one time in my hand ere then? I was bereft of any useful thought, of any light that might illuminate a path ahead. But clear it was: no judge tarried here who might consider mine appeal and reverse this bitter verdict.

Thou knowest that fish gets no fresher the longer it awaits the eating, so on my way back to London I made all haste to acquaint Rosalind with this news and see if her womanly intuition could divine any more meaning of these events. We comforted each other for a time, our love a sturdy bulwark against this unheralded disappointment. A sovereign could keep us in meat and drink for a goodly time, but I feared our raging fire might burn less bright with no prospects to feed its flames in the New World, in a new life.

Was Burbage or Leicester the cause of this distress? But why would either take note of a johannes factotum and a girl from the country (of which they yet know nothing, to the best of my ken)? I had not yet spoken to any man in the Company about my plans for the New World, save Will Kempe, and a good thing it were, for if I had, I would now be without employment. Kempe would not reveal my secret, bound as we were in the protection of his sister, indeed his tears attested to his honesty in this matter when I told him how I could no longer accompany Kathleen and Miles. I offered mine assurances that they seemed to me quite strong and capable of thriving without some added assistance, but he was inconsolable and spoke of fears regarding Miles that I knew not of. More I could not learn at that moment, but will endeavour to know how I might aid him in lightening this burden, as any man would do for a friend, for such has Will Kempe become to me now.

And Mr. Burbage cannot be privy to my dashed plan, for he hath of late sent me to copy a new play called 'Tamburlaine', paying handsomely for the task, and for adding certain scenes to some old plays that our Company shall use anon. Would he trust me thus if he thought me quickly gone? Nay, my secret intent, which now becomes my secret sadness, is unknown to the men of Leicester. Indeed, every one of them can think on naught but some rival players and this new 'Tamburlaine' by one Christopher Marlowe. And for many goodly reasons too, I'll warrant thee, the which I set forth hereinafter.

Item fifth: Money (in London)

Returning then to thy most favourite subject: money. And how might I earn it, to the great ease of my family. Stratford may offer little; the New World may be for now foreclosed; but London may yet spill some of its treasure, for a season, upon my needy state.

It fell out thus: together with Dick and Giddy, I have seen that which may be a New World itself, a Muse of fire to spark imagination without precedent, performed by the Lord Admiral's Men at the Theatre. Called: 'Tamburlaine the Great: Who From a Scythian Shepherd by his Rare and Wonderful Conquests became a Most Puissant and Mighty Monarch and, for his Tyranny and Terror in War, was termed The Scourge of God.' O coz, the mighty scenes and acts of death were enough, but I must report to thee how the spectators were transfixed, as if they witnessed the original acts themselves, such as when Tamburlaine, portrayed by a commanding player of some repute (whose name I took to be Ned Alleyn) said:

"I am LORD, for so my deeds will prove, and yet naught but a shepherd by my parentage. Aye, a Scythian shepherd embellished now with Nature's richest furnishings." The mob roared at this proclamation, imagining their own lives if they had been so transformed, even as Tamburlaine conquered rich kings of Turkey and Muslim Egypt, making them to kneel before him. The gentler folk in the balconies were no less astonished when the shepherd-turned-warrior could quote from Ovid with a honey-tongue that would have stilled raging waters or turned rampaging devils back to Hell. But it was Marlowe's verse that conquered all: as when his creations described "three hundred thousand men in armor clad, upon their prancing steeds; five hundred thousand footmen threatening shot, shaking their swords, their spears and iron bills … their warlike engines and munitions exceed the forces of mortal men!" These and more could we see in our mind's eye, as if we had been ourselves upon the battlefields, and many among us that day fully expected these great armies to appear at the gates of the Theatre and force their way in upon us all.

No less amazing was the craft of Alleyn and his fellows. They wore plumed helmets wrought with beaten gold; their swords enameled, not rusty shanks merely; and about their necks, hung massy chains of gold down to the waist, all the better to show us the greatness of the kings that Tamburlaine overcame. Thereto they used sounds as I had never yet heard in the playhouse, such as fifty trumpets, drums, cymbals, thunder, and multitudinous swords clanging in battles, all to excite the senses and transport us thither.

Nor have I ever seen such graceful boys playing the women, of which there were memorable queens and servants, whose wit and discourse matched the men measure for measure. In one scene, three kings, going forth to war, crowned their women and bid them serve as monarchs until the battle was won either way. In another scene, Zenocrate, she whose love would tame the mighty Tamburlaine after all (and who persuaded Giddy to lust for the boy playing the part), brought Dick to weeping, either at her womanly tenderness or because he knew he might never be so convincing in a dress and wig himself upon the stage.

But the scene that commanded the most enrapt attention of the spectators was when Tamburlaine brought the defeated Bajazeth, Emperor of the villainous Turks, into his presence in a cage! His boasts dissolved, his gold chains and silk robes and crown ripped from his body, Tamburlaine then used him as a footstool! O then did the groundlings erupt and all thousand spectators cried out and cheered with one voice together. Yet this was a mere prologue to the moment when Bajazeth, and his sharp-tongued Queen, then broke their own skulls against the bars of their cages, spilling their blood and brains upon the stage (a feat I could never achieve with my paltry bags of sheep's blood alone, nor can I say how these players accomplished so gruesome a sight with such fidelity, short of the actual death of them that played the King and Queen).

"So shall our swords, our lances, and our shot fill the air with fiery meteors and then, when the sky shall wax as red as blood, it shall be said I MADE it red MYSELF... to make me think of naught but BLOOD and WAR!" quoth Tamburlaine as he crowned himself the Emperor of all the world!

So excited was the crowd, I swear to thee that one woman gave birth in the instant and two men near me fled out of doors yelling in fear for their own lives. More might have followed, had not the heavens themselves opened up at that moment and shed such a downpour of rain that every one of us was forced to huddle closer to his neighbor, under his cloak, or 'neath the thatch above.

Marlowe's play has indeed made a deep impression upon me coz, but I fear I made an equally deep, though bad, impression upon him. That same night after we had seen the play, we met at the Mermaid and the men began reading my pages aloud. Our Company now inhabits this tavern and I have spent many hours there as Burbage's scribe (candles there cost me nothing and the tables have not as many cracks and holes as the one in my lodging). Kempe was drunk and foul tempered when he arrived, so played a Tamburlaine, to amuse those gathered around, thus:

"Do you swear by this royal seat?" quoth Kempe, waving at a chair he had set up as a throne. "You may do well then to kiss my seat!" With this he farted and slapped his arse and continued in his comic manner:

"Well, lovely virgins, submit yourselves to servitude, your knees and hearts submissive, you simple virgins will persuade Tamburlaine to be merciful!" Kempe fondled Dick's codpiece and breasts (Dick protested not at all) to great laughter of those gathered. "Will you do my bidding or shall I have you whipt stark naked through the streets?"

At this, one spectator flung a cup of ale against the wall and cursed. He was restrained by one or two fellows of his acquaintance, but seeing the man reach for a dagger, Mr. Perkin rose and pushed Kempe behind me and offered his drink to the enraged man.

"Sir, I hope we do not offend with our jests," quoth Mr. Perkin, blowing some smoke of tobacco from a pipe he held in the other hand, pointed like a knife somewhat toward the distempered man. "We are a Company of players and some of us heard this day a most amazing play by the Lord Admiral's Men. We are recalling some scenes, some lines of the play, not any events from real life nor thinking to offend honoured personages."

In reply, the man stood back a bit and brushed aside his companions. He did not take the drink from Mr. Perkin, but seemed to drink in every particular of his speech and appearance, then saying thus in university tones:

"The play ... was not performed ... for your ... AMUUUSEMENTTT. It was meant to enn-tah-tain and ee-loom-innnn-ate, not as fodder for your friend's filthy cannon of a mouth."

"Indeed we were thusly impressed and enlightened," quoth Mr. Perkin. "Pray sir, how did you come by this knowledge? Were you also in attendance?"

"Attendance? Sir, I wrote the play. You address Christopher Marlowe."

At this, our Company came to new life. Every one of us congratulated Marlowe on his triumph and by degrees turned hostility to hospitality. We learned the names of Marlowe's companions, all from the Admiral's Men, some known to us, some not, and told them names and stories of our Company. Slowly, Marlowe accepted our apologies for any offence and he seemed to recognize our true admiration for his skill. But our greatest peace offering, and still another surprise for me on this day of astonishing visions, was when Boy Burbage leapt upon a table and proclaimed he had never heard better lines for a player than those of Tamburlaine. Drawing himself up to his full six feet, he counterfeited the part of Tamburlaine most convincingly:

"A god is not so glorious as a king" (he began, at first, as if in contemplation). "I think the joy that they enjoy in Heaven cannot compare with kingly joys on earth: to wear a crown encased with pearl and gold, whose virtues carry with it life and death; to ask and have; command and be obeyed; mere looks breed love and looks do gain the prize!"

I had never seen the Boy Burbage play a commanding part such as this, not heard his voice so deep and resonant, so clear. The others of our Company were equally struck, but when he finished his short speech, all from memory having studied my pages for but a few minutes, he earned applause from all assembled, even Marlowe (who did scowl at me, I swear, knowing I had writ down his lines for others to recite). I shall endeavour to write greater speeches for Boy Burbage in those plays I am asked to augment, which may ease that unjust fire which rages still between us (and I thank thee coz, for thy brotherly advice in this matter, which stratagems I will also most heartily employ).

I spoke little to Marlowe, but overheard others say he was the son of a common Canterbury cobbler, learning his craft at a college in Cambridge. Mr. Perkin took him aside for more than an hour and plied him with wine, no mean ale, perhaps the better to cool his previous distemper, but it appeared to me that he had some greater purpose, though I could not hear the meat of their conversation. Was Mr. Perkin hoping he might gain a new play for our Company? In any wise, by the end of the night, Marlowe bid us to call him Kit, as his friends were wont to do, so we took this to mean we had earned his favor.

This minor skirmish behind us, ahead lay far greater threats to our Company. The Lord Admiral's Men had earned little favour at Court this winter past, but will now ascend the highest mountain of fame with their Tamburlaine, even in our own playhouse, whereat we are seen playing musty old fare such as Hamlet of Denmark.[81] And more: the Earl has again fared poorly in his generalship abroad, sent back to correct his earlier losses but falling far short of the mark a second time. Whispers abound, his hopes for future favour with Her Majesty in doubt. Mr. Clarke says we will all be jailed or worse for being his servants, but Mr. Johnson says we are at greater risk from Mr. Clarke being recusant and a devil worshipper (I have seen no evidence of this myself, though by means best left unsaid, I discovered him nakedly whipping himself until bleeding, which I took for piety, but may be some attempt to drive out an evil spirit).

Mr. Johnson gathers with other Puritans in secret meetings that are never so secret, plotting any manner of revenge against those who do not share their passion for the English church. Mr. Perkin swears such zeal is a greater threat to our peace in England than the Catholics, though it is the Pope and his Spanish lackeys that threaten to invade our land anon. Nightly is the Mermaid awash in patriotic fervor with bold promises of military deeds, growing louder as each cup is drained. Kempe is now the general of these brave 'soldiers' as talk turned from the play-acting wars of Tamburlaine to the real wars in fact. He proclaimed this to his would-be troops, stomping his feet to make his spurs jangle and himself seem more martial than he truly is:

"The man who hugs his knicky-wicky here at home, wears his honour in a box unseen, I tell ye! So, let us all march bravely 'gainst the popish foe! Who will join me? Who is brave?"

"Here, an't please you," quoth an old fellow with a twice-turned coat and cap that had lost its fashion when our fathers were boys, coughing as he rose to his feet from the haze of smoke (or a consumption?) that crowded the room withal.

"Is thy name Mouldy?" asked Kempe to incite some laughter.

"Yea, an't please you, sir, an if needs be to join your army." I suspect the old jack thought Kempe was indeed some captain seeking recruits for a force to be shortly used against the Spanish, and that he had the chinks to pay them withal.

"'Tis the more time thou wert used then, Master Mouldy!"

"Ha, ha, ha! most excellent, i' faith! Things that are mouldy lack use: very singular good! In faith, well said, sir, very well said. Ha, ha, ha!" I was not certain if the poor old fellow's exclamations were laughter, choking, or both. Then a lad of no more than thirteen, who had all that night hung on every word uttered by any of our players, as if his salvation in another life would thereby be assured, spoke up merrily:

"I'll go too!"

"Ah, good Francis Feeble, come closer," quoth Kempe, tossing his great arm around the boy's shoulder and tweaking the stubble on his chin. "In what trade serve thee, my good boy?"

"A woman's tailor, sir."

"Thou wilt make as many holes in an enemy's armour as thou hast done in a woman's petticoat, eh? Ah, courageous Feeble! Thou wilt be as valiant as the most magnanimous mouse? Thou art one of us and shall trade thy tailor's needle for a great sword!"

"Any arms are fair when the intent of bearing them is just," quoth the boy with an unexpected measure of wisdom, caring naught, or noticing little, that those assembled were laughing heartily at the expense of these recruits.

"Captain Kempe, I fear the Spanish dogs will o'errun all of London if thou canst find no stronger men to serve thee," quoth Mr. Perkin, blowing smoke from his pipe at the young tailor, expecting him to fall over.

"Wilt thou tell me John, how then to choose a man?" Kempe leapt upon a bench, that he might better be seen and heard above the hundred other conversations, songs, profanities, scraping of chair legs, clinking of cups, and rattling of spoons or swords, the lot of which is custom for the Mermaid at night. "Care I for the limb, the sinews, the stature, and bulk of a man? Give me the spirit, John! Give me this boy, Francis Feeble, for he presents no mark to the enemy! The foe may as well take aim at the edge of a penknife! And for a retreat, how swiftly will this woman's tailor run off! O, give me the spare men, and spare me the great ones."

So went the jests and gibes for another hour and for a dozen more cups of ale, but the situation abroad was no laughing matter. Mr. Johnson scoffed at Kempe's antic disposition and spoke of the forces massing against our kingdom since Mary's execution. He seems to have such intimate knowledge of these matters, such that no man in our Company can doubt he is Walsingham's agent, and we must take care of our own utterances, for he makes no secret that he would happily kick the stool from under any traitor's feet, leaving him to dangle from the hangman's fearful ropes, if they were righteously condemned a villain. Mr. Johnson is a fine player and could convince the Devil he was King Henry the Fifth, but in these utterances, we knew he spoke in deadly earnest. I fear most for Mr. Clarke, who is not fool enough to defend the Scottish Queen, but sulks and mumbles when Mr. Johnson speaks ill of her faith and of any man who would follow her in like manner.

I know not how these matters are reported in Stratford, nor how fares our Catholic friends, if they be seen to choose conscience over country. Here in London there is little else that men can speak of. That which I have heard here followeth:

Queen Mary's guilt was most certain, plotting against our lawful sovereign, and none will mourn her passing, save those Catholics loyal to the liberal purse of the Spanish ambassador. For was she not a harlot, that blew up her rightful husband, Lord Darnley, that she might lie with Lord Bothwell and gain his sway over these foreign armies? And to the last, they say, she was proud of her sinful behavior, proclaiming when she was bent over the executioner's bench:

"Elizabeth, I pray thee live only long enough as to see another decked in thy rightful crown, as thou art now installed in mine. May thy happy days perish before thine end and, after many lengthened hours of grief, die neither mother, nor wife, nor England's queen! Be suspicious of thy friends for traitors while thou livest; and may no sleep close up thine eyes, unless it be whilst some tormenting dream affrights thee with a Hell of ugly devils! I pray to God that neither thee nor any of thy henchmen live a natural age and during this tormented life, may the worm of conscience still begnaw thy souls!"

I heard the swordsman then needed several strokes to cleave her thick, sweaty neck from her great fat body, as if her foul opinions would not so easily be separated from her, even as blood drenched a bright red petticoat she wore, a sure sign of an unrepentant strumpet. Her ashes were burnt and scattered, such that no man might use them as a holy relic, to rally others to their traitors' cause.

So greatly have these events heated the spleens of the faithful, that even Dick hath now overthrown his woman's bearing, but pumps up his chest to fight great manly battles each time Kempe exhorts a crowd. Kempe is always one to jest, but Dick takes it in earnest and follows him from bread to brothel like a puppy. I fear for him, if he are ever to see real blood or battle.

For me, I needs must think on something more. If our Company breaks apart, either from quarrels or the ill-fate of our patron, what will I do with two wives and no prospects? There may be other ships bound for the New World, but none think that any will be spared for such adventures now, all being necessary for defense of the realm. It may benefit my station if other Companies of players know me for a hard worker, who can fill a role and mend either garment or play. The Queen's Men are already gone to the country, but at least three other Companies remain in London and I am acquainted with men in each of those. I have shown my scenes to some of them. We are all under constant attack and live only by the grace of our patrons. A new pamphlet called 'Mirror of Monsters' hath been grately read by men of stature, wherein players are described as apes, hell-hounds and painted fiends, crept into the world by stealth, sent from their great captain Satan to deceive the world and lead astray many souls with enticing shows!

But such venomous opinion has not stayed the building of the new theatre, as I have hitherto reported, that fresh Rose in Southwarke, even greater and grander than our Theatre or the Curtain. Thus far, this Rose profits more from the Winchester geese [*prostitutes*] than from those who pay to see a play, but there may be employment thither if the Earl of Pembroke's Men soon return. As I have writ, Tamburlaine enthralls all of London and I have studied the lines I copied, so that I might learn how such a spell is cast. There is some potion in the lines themselves: each having ten syllables, if I have copied aright. Few rhyme, yet all are poetry. Every speech paints a scene that would light a blind man's world. Around every turn of plot, a new revelation, but I marked the dull reaction of the spectators to long speeches made by characters when they did not contain some new matter. Nor did the over-ripe fruit taken from the trees of Ovid and Seneca amuse the many. Plays, I think, must capture the imagination of the unlearned and the university intellect alike. I had thought to write scenes for Boy Burbage that might earn his better opinion of me, but upon comparing them to those I copied from Tamburlaine have consigned my stillborn pages to the flames.

Still, I will sharpen my pen and my wit to see by what means else I might earn enough to stay here, for London is most certainly the place to find a path to a Fortune, in worlds new or old. And I am fortunate to have Giddy, my steadfast compass here, and the good company of Pug, nearly free of his indentures.[82] He too hath cared well for me, bringing me to the apothecaries in Blackfriars, whereto we repaired when I broke my tooth and was in urgent need of mending it, and taught me tricks of thrift in the waiting rooms on Watling Street and the fishmongers of Friday Street.[83]

But London is above all a stage upon which the majesty, pomp, and grandeur of the miniscule and the mighty march by in one greater procession than the one before. For instance, the funeral ceremonies for Sir Phillip Sidney, whose exploits in battle and noble death abroad has reached every corner of the land, I doubt it not. Giddy, Dick, Kempe and I huddled with the crowd in Carter Lane to witness the mile of horses, carriages, and noble persons that ushered him lately to his final resting place in St. Paul's. Hung were the heavens with black that day, yielding day to night, as felt by every Londoner:

"England ne'er had such a defender until Sidney's time," cried out a burly fellow who seemed an unlikely sort to weep, yet did he so. "Virtue he had, his arms spread wider than a dragon's wings; his wrathful fire dazzled and drove back his enemies, more than could a mid-day sun fierce-bent 'gainst their faces."

"You speak aright, good sir," answered one from the procession as he passed. "What should I say? His deeds exceed all speech: he ne'er lifted up his hand but conquered." But Kempe, in one of his distempers, that were brought on mostly by drink (or when all eyes are on another, not him), voiced a different opinion:

"O, why waste we the day in such fashion? We mourn in black: why mourn we not in blood? Sidney is dead and never shall revive. Upon a wooden coffin we attend and death's dishonourable victory we glorify with our presence, like captives bound to a triumphant cart." The general displeasure of those nearby silenced him, as no single man's reply might have done. I would have given his surly sentiments not another moments reflection, but for Dick who hung on every word and repeated them to those who asked wherefore the commotion. I have tried these weeks to squeeze so much as an onion skin twixt he and Kempe, but to no avail. All of Kempe's ill manners hath Dick begun to ape, never knowing, that of every hundred proclamations, Kempe means barely five of them in earnest.

Now to happier tidings: I am in thy debt, and should have said as much the moment that ink touched paper, for sending me the marzipan to sweeten my birthday. It reminds me of those sweets we did a'times get from the crooked hands of old Rogers, but no amount of honey could alter the bitterness of my cruel misfortunes with Governor White. St. George's day is celebrated here with a procession for the Queen (Dick says it is her gift to me on my birthday: ha!) with carriages that seem to move by themselves and horses dressed like elephants and all manner of such odd devices more, quite marvelous. I am further indebted to thee for thy pains to report the news from home: I trust thy brother Thomas hath recovered ere this and the Sadler child fares well. Please give them my hearty commendations, in such manner of affection as thou deemest fit.

Forgive me that this letter heaps upon thee the burdens of my fears, childish and churlish, but I cannot gain so high a perch to see what Fate may have next in mind for me and know not who other could guide me. I take full note of thy further arguments for my swift homecoming, not least of which that Edmund hath so oft been ill and Richard grows more quarrelsome at school. Aye, my brothers are in need of a father and, so it would seem, my father needs a father, or some taskmaster else who might whip him from the tavern.

Fortune knows we scorn her most when most she offers blows, the likes of which befell me these past weeks, so knowing her a fickle mistress, I will bide my time and pray she glance more lovingly ere long. This I pledge to thee: if our Company proceeds again to the countryside this summer, and if God grant that I partake thereof, and if I have not found better means to earn money by the time we come to Stratford, I will not depart with the Earl of Leicester's Men, but will heed thy good and honest pleadings to return home, come what may. I know not, in that event, what I will do for Rosalind, but let Fate guide me further thereon.

O dear coz, thus I commit thee to God's good protection and ask that thou kiss my boy and maids in my name and omit nothing else which thine honour deem'st best for their tender need. I am thine ever-loving servant in all else, Will.

PS: I am further in thy debt if thou wouldst grant me one favour more. At thy leisure and as such occasion may arise, please convey thanks to Anne for the recipe she hath sent, with those selfsame victuals to make the dish withal. It rubs my conscience that the dish made, our stomachs empty for longer than is common and therefore Hunger held such sway over propriety, that I shared the meal with Rosalind and we found it most savoury and pleasing (thou wilt, no doubt, omit this particular from thy message to Anne).

May tart

Cut up the pound of the cheese herewith and grind this together with the juice of the lemon and those spices in the pouch (which are marjoram, sage, mint, and a good portion of parsley). The whites of the 16 eggs (or howsoever many as survive the journey thither) must be beaten and mixed with half a pound of liquamen or fresh butter.[84] Some will add leaves of parsley and marjoram, that have been cut up but not ground, and some ginger and sugar, but I find these additions loathsome. Put this mixture in the pot that has been well greased and is set on the coals at a distance from the flame so that it doth not absorb the smoke and stir continually until it boils and thickens. Cover this with a crust and bake until the water is driven out, but not so long as to make it dry and tedious. On the plate, sprinkle it with the sugar (and rose water, if that too is at hand).

LETTER ELEVEN
September 9, 1587

Wherein Shakespeare visits Stratford, but finds you cannot so easily go home, while his Protestant homeland may be overthrown by Catholic Spain and every man will soon be a player in that life-or-death drama.

I never studied Latin in school. By contrast, most of Shakespeare's education in the Stratford grammar school would have been conducted in nothing but Latin. Ben Jonson would later write of his friend that he had "little Latin and less Greek," but there is actually evidence in the plays that Shakespeare was quite comfortable with both.

Several weeks into transcribing and tea-drinking with Miss B, I came across Letter Eleven, which presented me with yet another great mystery. In the margin of the second page of this letter (the subject of which is the deteriorating mental state of Shakespeare's father), someone had written *praeterita mutare non possumus; sed future providere debemos*, which Miss B translated for me as "we cannot change the past; we can provide for the future." She thought it might have been a quote from Ovid, who appears to be Shakespeare's favorite poet, but more recently I learned it is a proverb that was likely first uttered by Cicero.

The mystery is twofold: first, why write that phrase in the margin of the letter? And second, who wrote it? The handwriting looked different to me than the hand I had become familiar with over many weeks of study and transcription, but then again, it was scribbled in the narrow margin (lengthwise down the side of the paper, not neatly across the page as the text of each letter has been drafted) and that may account for what appeared to be someone else's handwriting.

Unfortunately, I have yet to understand anything more about this cryptic passage or why it was written in Latin. But as Letter Eleven keeps that particular secret locked carefully away, it exposes another explosive mystery that has been the subject of hints and innuendo in the previous ten letters and which would definitely explain the sentiment.

It is now September of 1587 and Leicester's Men played Stratford in late summer, giving Shakespeare the chance to go home for the first time in over a year. We are fortunate that John Combe is out of town during that visit, so Shakespeare must detail his homecoming in this letter (Combe may have been detained in a plague-ravaged town nearby, as records show that many in the region were hit hard in 1587, including Stratford, shortly after Leicester's Men performed there and moved on).

He finds his family much as he had left them a year before, sleeping dog and fecund garden included, but discovers his father John has mentally deteriorated and is making beautiful gloves for imaginary clients. His drinking and the ostracism imposed by the Earl of Leicester on his trade have pushed him into an abyss from which there appears to be no return. Shakespeare is distraught, but still apparently made mental notes of the scene, because in *Hamlet* (Act II, scene 1) he writes an eerily similar version of Hamlet's behavior towards Ophelia as his father's reported remarks to Anne; and the fate of a fly he describes appears when Shakespeare writes *Titus Andronicus* a few months later.

Shakespeare reveals that he had hoped to confront his father about a terrible secret and force some kind of atonement, but that path is now foreclosed by his father's mental illness. In describing this to Combe, Shakespeare finally reveals the causes of the underlying resentment, whenever he writes about his father or his wife Anne, to which he has only alluded up to now. Young William was forced to marry Anne Hathaway because she was pregnant by Shakespeare's father. Susanna, Shakespeare's firstborn daughter, who is four years old at the time of this visit, is also therefore Shakespeare's sister.

Forced marriages to preserve family honor and prevent bastard children were common in Elizabethan England, but Shakespearian scholarship has not previously identified John Shakespeare's indiscretions as the reason that William had to hastily marry the much older Anne.[85] These revelations give context to Shakespeare's general desire to flee Stratford for the New World and his disparaging remarks about Anne in earlier letters.

Seeing the pitiful state of his father and witnessing Anne's hardship and sacrifice to support the family, lying next to her in their bed that night, perhaps thinking of his own infidelity, Shakespeare is moved toward forgiveness. It is Anne who affirms that Shakespeare must return to London as a player, as the best means of supporting the family, and she encourages him to sell his father's gloves to the wealthy citizens he meets at Court.

As you read this letter, it may help to have the names and ages of Shakespeare's children and siblings in mind. His daughter/sister Susanna (age 4); his twins Judith & Hamnet (age 2); brother Gilbert "Giddy" living in London, as we have seen, but apparently visiting Stratford at the same time as Shakespeare, as described in this letter (age 21); brother Richard (age 13); and brother Edmund (age 7).

With this astonishing domestic news, it's hard to focus again on geopolitics, but Shakespeare updates us in this letter on the disintegration of Leicester's Men. Some go off to fight Spain on the Continent, others fight viciously among themselves over religion. Kempe becomes more drunk and morose, fearing for his sister in Virginia and blaming Shakespeare for failing to somehow go along to protect her as they had planned. War preparations throughout the land prevent any ships or supplies from following the colonists, so he is right to be concerned. Shakespeare tries to console his friend, who he now considers Kempe to be (as evidenced from this letter onward, in which Shakespeare refers to him with the more familiar "thou" instead of "you" and drops the use of "Master" before writing his name).

In all, Letter Eleven shows just how young and human is the twenty-three year old William Shakespeare, and how life is … complicated.

9 September, year of Christ 1587, London

Coz,

Some say men are ever merriest when far from home. That which I write to thee now shall prove this both true and false. Thy wise counsel of these months past hath prevailed: after a raging battle with God and my conscience, I was persuaded that the only honourable course of action was my return to Stratford. But as I will now unfold to thee, greater powers, unimagined, have brought me back to London.

I trust thou hast heard, from our friends at home, how Leicester's Men played in Stratford a fortnight past. Thine absence was variously reported to me as compelled by a visit to thy dying uncle in Coventry (I hope he yet prospers); or as a venture with some trading of horses in Gloucester (I know thou hast gained the better bargain therein); or as detained by the Council in Chipping Norton owing to the Plague thereabouts (God defend thee). Thy presence was sorely missed, as these events following will make clear to thee, for I am in desperate need to know thy mind and heart.

As I have confessed, thy reasoning sound, I resigned myself to a life again in Stratford, but there could be no such reconciliation without certain demands on my father. I have never rehearsed a speech so often as this one: item first, he would needs forswear all strong drink and never again set foot in the Bear; and item second, he would confess his sins to Vicar Barton and seek forgiveness before God.

John, forgive me that I could not unfold to thee these, mine innermost, confidences, in person. Forgive that I must burden thy soul with the knowledge that follows, nothing worthy of so great a friend. But unfold them now I must, for this may be my final testament and I will not pass to Heaven, or to Hell, without knowing that someone heard my cause aright. These intimacies are nothing yet meet for my son, for whom I write these letters after all, but if that day comes when he must know, thou canst report the truth from his father, not the lies of those who wish history to be otherwise.

Therefore John, the facts are these: though I had not been away more than fourteen months, when I again set foot on Henley Street, it felt that fourteen years had swiftly passed. The house seemed strangely familiar, yet some ways foreign to me. Through the door I saw the great fireplace, my rudely carved 'WS' still visible on the mantel; mother's upholstered bench 'neath the window, where the light was best for her needlework; Crab sleeping just outside the door at the back.

Yet this familiar scene was oddly out of joint. Children played in the warm summer garden, but not my brothers or sisters, instead mine own twins. Mother was nowhere to be seen, but Anne watched over the little ones and held them aloft to pluck fruits from the vine on the old wall. Crab was unchanged, undiminished by time or temper, sleeping in the sun that poured over the threshold, snoring as he was always wont to do since he was a pup. Giddy, who but a few weeks ago was still in London, now stood before me, the first greeting as I came through the door, with a strange foreboding in his welcome:

"O Will, thank the Lord thou'rt come." Giddy wrapped his arms around my chest with his customary embrace, but weeping into my collar.

"What is the matter? Who has died?"

"O Will, no one is dead, but the Shakespeares are not so alive as we once were. Come, greet thy good wife and babes, they will be so cheered to see thee." With this he took me by the hand and led me to the garden.

Trying to behold the entirety of the scene at once, I tripped over Crab and fell. I may have cursed or cried out, but this was not the entrance a player hopes to make upon a familiar stage. Susanna gave a look as she might study the first robin of spring; Judith squeaked and ran to hide behind Anne. Crab yelped, but would not be moved by a foreign intruder on his territory. I saw no sign of Hamnet. Anne coaxed Judith in my direction, bidding me to sit where I had fallen to regain my wits and to avoid frighting the child any further, telling her plainly:

"Now child, here is thy father. Prithee, greet him lovingly."

"Good wife Anne, I am pleased to see thee," was all I could think to say, offering a hand to Judith to signify I meant no harm. Susanna needed no more encouragement, but marched dutifully to where I sat and dropped down beside me, wrapping her arm around mine and declaring mildly:

"Poppa."

Anne and Giddy sat with me on warm stones between the rows of cabbage and carrots, shaded only by the dancing shadows of corn and beanstalks in their full summer ripeness. Judith came by degrees and tenderly sat in my lap, comforted, and perhaps a little contentious, with her sister beside me. Anne wiped dirt from her face with a corner of her apron. She looks much older than her 31 years. I felt some pity for a woman whose hands had grown more calloused than mine in service to my family.

"Will, our father is not well," quoth Giddy after we had exchanged our several explanations for this unexpected meeting. "He hath these many weeks lost his wits, I fear."

"The evils of drink," quoth I, not yet appreciating the full gravity of the matter.

"More than that, husband," quoth Anne.

"For instance?" I did coldly take him for a drunk who would adopt any manner that might excuse him from his greater duty. Anne seemed slow to unfold her secrets to me, but Giddy bid her tell me, demanding she omit no particulars.

"Thy father hath, by slow degree over some months, grown light of brain. Then yesternight, as I was sewing, he comes in with his doublet unbraced, his stockings ungarter'd to his ankles, pale as his shirt, with a look so piteous as if he had been loosed out of Hell to speak of horrors to the congregation on Sunday. He took me by the wrist, hard, and then goes he to the length of his arm and, with his other hand, thus o'er his brow, he falls to such perusal of my face as he would draw it."

"That is all? He studied thy face and therefore he is mad? What said he to thee to buttress this rash conclusion?"

"Nay, he SAID nothing. But long stayed he, studying my face, and at last, a little shaking of mine arm and nodding of his head, then he raised a sigh so piteous as it did seem to shatter all his bulk and end his being. That done, he lets me go and, with his head over his shoulder turned, he seemed to find his way without his eyes, for out o' doors he went without their help."

"And Will, this is lately his usual behavior," quoth Giddy, holding me at arms length, even as Anne had just described my father's doing with her. "He speaks naught and wanders the rooms by night, sighing when he beholds a certain chair or staring at nothing outside the window. At sup, he is wont to call me 'father' and Susanna he doth call 'daughter', giving us to fear he knows us not, one from the other."

"Where is he now?" I would know if his madness were feigned or real, a curtain behind which he might hide from the angry glances of creditors and those of his own family that he hath so grievously wronged.

Without pause, Giddy then conveyed me to the wool room, which thou knowest in happier times served as father's workshop and wherein he taught me the glover's craft, but which barely now recalls its former purpose. Shards of wool are stacked on the long tables, where once he stretched his skins. Spiders build webs undisturbed on those shelves, where once he neatly stacked the linings and lasts, cuffs and accouterments for gloves and slippers and aprons in the making. The rafters, no longer festooned with ribbons and coloured laces, seem lower, but that may be owing to me growing taller. One thing only seemed unchanged: his sewing table by the broad window overlooking Henley Street, bright light pouring in upon the stage of his craft, a riot of goods in various stages of completion, father sitting on his faded red velvet bench hunched over, spectacles on nose, delicately punching needle through soft leathers, pulling silken threads to magically transform the oddly shaped scraps into things of beauteous utility.

His back to the door, he heard naught as we entered, but sat in some study at his table with Hamnet. I cannot say if I was more amazed at how shriveled my father appeared or at how tall and strong my boy seemed to me now, sitting on the bench side by side, as if the bulk and vigour of the older had magically been transferred to the younger. Edmund sat on the floor in some idle attempt to catch a fly. Giddy pushed me toward that side of the bench, where father would see me without need of turning round, and whispered as if not to disturb some delicate trance or slumber:

"Father, William is come home."

"Aye, 'tis me, here in Stratford, with those same players that conveyed me hence last summer. I am pleased to see thee, father." He did look up from the glove he was stitching, showing a special cross stitch to Hamnet, who seemed intent on learning, even though his child's brain could not have comprehended what he saw.

"I am in your debt, sire. You are welcome here." His formality was surprising as he paused and squinted at me. "You are bringing William home soon?"

"Father, have I changed so much? 'Tis me: William. Thine eldest son."

He closed his eyes and seemed to call upon some memory of things long past. I took up my boy and kissed him and tickled him, his laughter instantly a refreshing rain that washed away our dull stupor. I set him down with Edmund, that I might address my father directly, but he rose up and shouted suddenly.

"Boy, what dost thou with that knife? Hold, hold!"

"Art not amazed, father," quoth Edmund in his tiny trusting voice. "I have killed this fly with my knife!"

"Out on thee, murderer! Thou wilt kill my heart," quoth father with an urgent manner I could not fathom and tears quite suddenly welling in his eyes. "A deed of death done on the innocent becomes thee not. By God, get thee gone!"

"Alas, father, I have but kill'd a fly." Edmund hath always been tender hearted and could not easily suffer our father's censure, tears welling now in his eyes too.

"But how if that fly had a father and mother? Would they ever more flap their gilded wings and buzz delightful sounds in the air? Nay, I think not. And their poor child, a harmless fly, whose buzzing melody came here merely to make us merry, an thou hast killed him!"

Giddy knew instantly how to calm him again: "Father, rail not so 'gainst the child. Look you, this was a black, ill-favor'd fly, like those that are known to bring pestilence and bad luck to the house."

"O, O, O, then pardon me for reprehending thee Edmund, for thou hast done a charitable deed." Father kneeled beside the boy and wrapped an arm over his tiny shoulders, grasping the knife in his other hand. "Give ME thy knife. I will insult on the villain yet again." He began to stab at the fly carcass, calling out names of some who had wronged him, so wild-eyed and randomly, as Edmund laughed and repeated the names in all innocence. Giddy whispered to me his interpretation thereof.

"Alas, poor man! Grief has so wrought on him, he takes false shadows for true substances."[86]

"Come away, Edmund go with me," quoth father, wiping the knife as if to remove a traitor's blood and carefully slipping it into his waist. "I'll to thy closet; and go read with thee brave stories from the times of old. Come, boy, and go with me: thy sight is young, and thou shalt read when mine begins to dazzle."

I'll confess to thee John, I was trembling after that. No man can change what's past, but I had come to confront my father, to enforce his confession, his apology to those he had wronged, to start again my life in Stratford, to save both our souls. That man is gone, and may be gone for good and all. My true course and conviction of that morning had faded into doubt and loss within a few trips of an hour hand 'round the clock.

And something more: I took note of the gloves in father's shop. Piled carefully, in various forms of readiness, were dozens of pairs, of the finest soft skins: white tawed calfskin with tiny ivory buttons for a young girl; red cheveril for a nobleman with fancy embroidered cuffs for important occasions, such as I had seen on a Polish ambassador in Denmark, adorned with thistles, gold roses, and bees; black fox, fur left on, gilded with gold cords and sewn with the finest silk thread I had ever seen on father's workbench. Imagine how much deeper my sorrows did plummet when Giddy explained these were all being sewn for imaginary customers, father working every day till long past sunset, assuring mother that those gentles will come to collect the goods any day and the Shakespeare name will be restored, aye, even as the family wealth will be replenished. Madness coz, madness.

I tried that night to set these pitiful sights aside. I played at paddycacke with Hamnet and fed him his porridge (which he prefers cold, like his uncle Richard) and told him stories of what I had seen since last we met, exaggerating sometimes the stories of my feats on the stage to amuse him. I wept for joy to have a son, so bold and so curious, but the tears turned bitter thinking on my father lost. Whither to turn and what is to be done? Giddy must return soon to London, he cannot abandon his service so close to earning a trade. Surely I must stay at home now and assume those duties of the eldest son. But in a day of revelation and surprises, a greater one was yet to come.

Mother gave Anne leave to prepare a fine supper, making those savouries that she recalled I favoured most. When dishes were cleared and candles blown out, we repaired to bed and lay quiet for a time. I reacquainted myself with those creaks and groans of a house once familiar, and the distant voices in the byways outside. I was never so out of place or time, wishing I could hide myself, as will the deer that is struck by an arrow from the cunning huntsman.

"Husband, I would know thy mind," quoth Anne in a whisper and, knowing I would not switftly reply, she added "and would set aside all past unkindness."

"O Nan, that would I gladly do, aye that and more, if any action now could heal my father's wits and our family's prospects. How oft have I sat on his bench, imagining myself a master glover. I tawed the skins, and hung them outdoors to dry, and bore the brunt of mother's censure when the wind shifted toward her laundry. I so admired his skill, the aprons he made, even more than the gloves, oh and the slippers that felt like thrusting a foot into warm water in January. Short tale to make Nan, I admired my father above all men and I would do anything to make it so again."

"I do fear thy nature William: it is too full o' the milk of human kindness to catch the nearest way." Anne cradled my cheek and turned my face towards hers that she might convey as much with her looks as with her words. "Thou couldst be great; art not without ambition, but art without the craft, the illness of greed that must attend it to cut down those nettles in thy path."

"I dare do all that may become a righteous man; who dares do more is none."

"Aye, what both of us want highly, that wouldst we get by holy means; would not play false, and yet we needst must win or starve."[87]

"Thy meaning?"

"In simple, this: I would make league with the Devil or cut my life short by a dozen years to have thee home again, but to what end? To see thy father die of anger and sorrows; to see thy babes suffer through another poor harvest and the unkind stares of those we thought were friends? Thou knowest I opposed thine enterprise abroad, for neither time nor place did then adhere to thy purpose, and yet thou wouldst make both, but now they have made themselves, but their fitness seemeth to unmake thee."

"Wife, thou wert not used to speak in riddles. Therefore speak plainly now." She had my full attention and, I must confess, a passion rose in me from the fire in her eyes, her speech, and her tight grasp on my arm.

"Go thou back to London. Take these gloves thy father hast wrought and sell them to thy noble acquaintances. Say they come from thy brother's haberdasher, for what gentle person of the great city will pay high prices for gloves made in the country? Gilbert can add those baubles and adornments as fashion requires. If these turn heads, and profits, send word and I will persuade thy father to make more, even as I will keep this house alive with the trading of wool and malt in his name. This and more will I do to have thee back again with a full purse, a lighter heart, and the means to repair thy father's state."

O coz, thou hast heard of ancient Romans who tied horses to a traitor's arms and whipped them in opposite directions to gallop away and tear the poor soul limb from limb. At that moment, I was just such a condemned man: a traitor to mine own family for leaving home; for leaving a wife to tend to a husband's work; for leaving a father to a pack of wolves I should have known would come for him. At that moment, my just grievances with my father and wife seemed past redress and therefore petty. Anne had taken my foul stew and shown me how I might still make a savoury feast therefrom, such that now I cannot easily say who is most in need of forgiveness or salvation. Although the circumstances that led to this day are unmeet for his tender ears (and may never be fit for his knowing), I tell thee what follows so that thou mightst report me and my cause aright to the unsatisfied when I am gone, above all to my son when he is older:

Thou knowest that I was married to Anne in haste, far from home, but thou knowest not wherefore. That old priest could neither preach nor read very well and was unsound in the observations of the English religion. He was paid handsomely to perform the ceremony and would therefore ask few questions about the particulars.

It was ever an odd match: Anne's dead father left her a few pounds, a few sheep, and a covetous, thieving brother in possession of some land. Susanna was born soon after the last of the baked meats from our marriage table were eaten up. Coz, I swear to thee that I never lay with Anne before our wedding night and I would not have married then, but for one reason: to hide my father's indiscretion with her.

Aye, marriage is like a project in war, wherein a man can probably err but once, and for me, what a loathsome first volley. And is it not the beginning that sketches the canvas, that sounds the bell for the sermon which follows? But now I see she was the victim, not I. She was pulled apart by the wild horses of Fate, while I was but a gaping bystander. Is she not like Philomela, wronged by a man of greater power and left mute and wounded, unable to protest or accuse her attacker? I cannot so easily forgive my father, but now I see I must find a way to forgive a steadfast wife who hath never slept a day in peace, but that she sought to bring me ease. And what of that father? He may be dead, though the body yet lives, so who should I now protest to? Nay, there can be no conclusion to this loathsome, foul-knotted drama: except my resolve to be a better father to Hamnet than John Shakespeare was to William.

Giddy was quick to agree to Anne's plan, thinking we could indeed sell the gloves for great sums in London. I had been loath to think on abandoning the Company, with some of our number pledging to join those fighting men in service to the Earl, leaving our players short-handed, so this plan provided another means to keep faith with my fellows and my family at once. After we played at the Guildhall the next afternoon, Giddy showed the finest pair to Mr. Perkin, who most courteously asked to meet my father and thought himself to buy new gloves to wear at Court when we present our plays thither at Christmastime. But I was yet to curse myself that we brought him to Henley Street, for though he was forgiving of father's infirm state of mind, he began to talk of God and father's old faith shown through. I trust Mr. Perkin will say no more about it, chiefly because he too seems to hew closer to the Roman church in truth, and quickly did Giddy explain our father doted on his childhood, when the old faith was all our country knew, and how now he was a devoted man of the English church (although we knew this to be false and I suspect Mr. Perkin did too).

Our duty in Stratford done, we prepared to make way to Oxford, Giddy back to London. Our mother gave him some eggs, butter, and apples to sell thither, for London prices are far higher. She tries ever to remain in good cheer, but father being so unsound cannot go so easily on her. She stoops more, walks slower, like one with gravel in her shoes, always in pains, the gray in her hair crowding the auburn into faded memory. I wept to see her ever in the same worn garments, having cut her finery apart to make clothes for the children. Giddy and I took our leave, hoping we might return with money to ease her burden. We could hear mother's complaint as we stepped into the street and I wondered how often the neighbors heard her raise an angry voice to my father:

"Patient? Have I not been ever thus? But who can be patient in such extremes, ye wretched man? I wish I had died a virgin and never seen thee, never borne thee sons, seeing thou hast proved to be so unnatural a father. Hath William deserved to lose his birthright thus? Hadst thou but loved him half so well as I, or felt the pain which I did for him once, thou wouldst have left thy dearest heart-blood on the papers, rather than have signed away thy lands and all thy goods to tavern reckonings and to lying, cheating thieves."

This brief visit home had many vapour-like qualities, as if a dream: standing in the Guildhall before so many familiar faces, yet pretending to be someone else. Richard came, Edmund aloft on his shoulders, but was fearful I would make a fool of myself and so stood in the back of the hall. I hoped father would come, but his infirmity, or fear of debt collectors, kept him away. The Quineys were there, in the front row and taking every woman's curtsy and every man's by-'r-leave. How have they prospered so quickly? And do they not borrow the robes of place and office in Stratford that once belonged to the Shakespeares? Can Richard have blossomed so high in men's esteem in so short a time on his own merit?[88] Or hath his father ploughed the ground before him, making deep furrows in which any seed would have grown to a selfsame height? So much seems changed from the way I remembered it. Or is it I that am so much changed? It will surprise thee not that I long for Stratford in many ways, yet now I see the family and the town I knew are like words written on water.

So, with my sights fixed again towards London, I reluctantly turned my back once more on Stratford. Having already imagined myself a Stratford man again, home at night, leaving the miserable inns and byways to others, the road seemed exceptionally dreary. King Arthur and the gray both took lame, so several of us pulled one of the wagons three days in a row. I took no notice before, but the inn at Cornmarket Street is the most villainous in all Oxford, for there is nary a chamber pot in the house, so every man leaks in the fireplace, which breeds fleas in great number; the valley of Aylesbury was tedious and ill to pass by, from so much mud and standing water on the paths; the hanging tree thither as good as its name, there being a notorious thief dangling therefrom when we passed, rotting like an old apple, stenching his guilt from a mile away. I sought to be more cheerful in these weary labours by making a list of every man who might assist me in selling my father's gloves.

Mr. Stow was ever generous and insisted I remain his lodger, now that Pug has left. Things were as I had left them, a pleasant homecoming to him, to Mistress Burberry, the familiar smells of the books, and Signor Rat. Aye, even the rat, whom I imagine now as a Spanish invader of my territory, seemed pleased to see me, although from his girth I take it he has fed well in mine absence.[89] Ratcatcher considers him a brother, I think, for they are now of equal stature, though Signor Rat wears the finer fur coat. But all was not so peaceful in the great City herself: every man, woman, and rat prepares for war.

I have reported to thee that our Earl was sent back to the Netherlands to recover his losses, but he dishonoured the Queen in some further manner, which I could not fully compass, and was removed as Master of Her Majesty's Horse. The Earl of Essex is installed in that office, which may be good news or ill, for though he is Leicester's step-son, he is said to harbor dangerous sentiments and still more dangerous friends. Mr. Johnson has gathered, of his many acquaintances, some intelligence on these matters, which after several cups of Rhenish in the Mermaid yesternight, he deigned to acquaint us withal, as follows:

"Since Mary's execution, every bush hides an assassin: so shivers a fearful Court," quoth Mr. Johnson in cautious tones, waving a spoon in his hand for no apparent reason, though perhaps to clear a path for his words through the smoke. Mr. Pope put a hand to his forehead, mocking womanly fear, and replied:

"O, the Queen need not shiver, what with ESSEX at home to defend her. And he no longer need shiver when creditors come calling, what with the 1500 pounds a year his new post collects!"[90]

"Aye, and who will be riding whom?" Mr. Phillips thrust his hips lustily to illustrate. "Methinks Her Majesty feared for the boy's life in the wars and would have him hide 'neath her skirts - - by day and night!"

"By protecting her new favorite, does she not sully the honour of her former favorite, our lordship?" asked Dick, uncertain he understood the meaning of Johnson's report.

"O these courtly ways are more treacherous to follow than the flight of your mud wasp!" quoth Mr. Johnson, poking Dick's chest with the spoon to drive home his point. "I am informed that he has of late spent so much on his lavish entertainment that he is compelled to sell one of his manors, of ancient inheritance mind you, to pay his debts withal. The Queen may purchase Essex's loyalty by restoring his finances. The loyalty of Leicester is never in doubt."

"I'll warrant you she needs must purchase the loyalty of many at her own Court." Mr. Clarke spoke to no one in particular and would soon regret speaking his mind at all. "No man will long suffer to have the terms of his faith prescribed to him."

"Spoken like a man who loves his bishop in Rome more than his Queen in London," quoth Mr. Johnson under his breath, but every man heard him plainly.

Mr. Burbage had heard enough of such petty babble and instead took Cuthbert aside in some private counsel, but the rest of our Company hung on Mr. Johnson's tale and asked a dozen questions of the matter, pouring ever more wine in his cup that he might pour more of his knowledge into our ears.

"Yes, yes, patience men, and all will be known, for I have heard much more." Mr. Perkin warned me to listen to Johnson, but to say little, for as I reported to thee, he is most certainly a spy for the Crown and any man's secrets are his tradeable goods.

"Thou dost prattle about nothing William," quoth Kempe in some great agitation, an ember that would soon play the mother of a greater fire, but Mr. Johnson paid no heed and continued his report unbridled.

"Essex is most in need of the Queen's protection, I'll warrant you for he respects no man as his equal, calling them all knaves and vegetables of the Court!"

"Thou art the radish!" Kempe bellowed with such fury that every mother's son in the Mermaid stopped his several conversation and turned to see what was the matter. "Our lord is bravely in battles abroad; the Spanish king would unseat Elizabeth, Essex, and the lot. And how do we show our loyalty? How do we prove to be brave Englishmen? By gossiping about this lord or that lady as if our next meal depended on the number of fools who say 'amen'."

Mr. Burbage returned then in haste, to prevent strong drink and stronger words turning to unwarranted actions, saying: "Peace, Will Kempe. It harms no man to hear a tale of our betters, especially those who might be in need of our player's services one day. What more wouldst have us do at the end of a day's labours, whilst sharing drink and good cheer?"

"What more? What more?? I am quit of ye all and condemn every man as a coward who doth not answer the call of our own lord, whose captains this very day did pass through these mean streets and taverns to find brave men to defend the realm. Take to Her Majesty's ships and guns, that's what I would have ye do!"

"Huzzah!" Dick thrust then his mug high above, such that the contents now spilled over me and Mr. Johnson. I note he hath of late found more courage and is not so sickly as was his habit, now that Kempe hath taken to schooling him in fighting matters. Mr. Clarke sought then to soothe his fellow, laying a steady hand on Kempe's shoulder with this opinion more:

"Will Kempe, thou art a true genius of comedy, jigs, and bawdy. But do not mistake our skill with a rapier on a stage, wherein the playwright hath settled the outcome of the battle long before we took up those arms, with the real blood spilled over quarrels that are little more than the chess matches of our betters, we being pawns and knights of ready sacrifice."

At this Kempe snatched a jug from off the table and brought it with no hesitation against the side of Mr. Clarke's head. Had it been made of metal, Mr. Clarke would surely be now with God, but as it was a clay pitcher, it shattered into shards and ale streaming down Mr. Clarke's face and shoulder, the handle thereof still clutched firmly in Kempe's grip like a dagger. Mr. Burbage and Cuthbert wasted no time but parted the men, else there had been more blows. A great din arose throughout the Mermaid as sides were chosen, those who would join Kempe in battle, those who sued for peace. Some few were too drunk to know the matter altogether and used the confusion to snatch the drink or money lying unguarded on tables while combatants puffed their chests.

"Stand aside or I'll make a ghost of ye," quoth Kempe to no one in particular and everyone in general. "Who defends this papist worshipper of the Devil? Who cares for this villain, who would rather we all speak our plays in the Spanish tongue than that of mother England?"

Well coz, I need not tell thee what number of arguments ignited all at once, even one that pitted brother against brother. Mr. Perkin, dagger drawn, came to the defense of his Catholic fellow Mr. Clarke. Mr. Pope took up a skewer of lamb and would have fought them both, had not his brother Mr. Phillips stayed his hand, announcing that he and Bryan had taken an oath to join the Earl's army and defend the realm. At this news Mr. Pope fell to weeping, begging his brother to avoid such certain death. But Mr. Phillips said he feared more for his life in London, where any man known to remain in the old faith could be murdered at any moment, but in the Earl's service he could prove an Englishman might be loyal to the Crown and true to his faith at once. Mr. Pope cursed at Kempe for turning his brother's head to such unaccustomed martial thoughts and cursed even louder at Mr. Clarke for stoking those flames of old faith that should long ago have burned out in his brother's bosom.

Cooler heads kept hotter ones asunder. It worries me to see Mr. Pope so enraged. He is a fine man, but gives in too quickly to his temper, although how could any man, whose body has been so battered, not have a mind that is in equal measure twisted beyond what normal men could see? It worries me too that Kempe hath taken to more drink and fits of weeping for his sister, who with her husband Miles have indeed gone to Virginia with Governor White. Boy Burbage, who all summer hath kept a welcome distance from me, though never to be trusted, used the occasion to defend Mr. Phillips and to declare that any man who would not serve his Queen must in his heart be more loyal to the old faith. He made sure his father would overhear him and asked me if I would serve my country, trying to show that I was in some wise disloyal to the Crown or church.

"Richard, you and I serve at the pleasure of thy father," quoth I. "And as my master commands me, so will I obey."

At this reply he turned on his heel and stepped away, mumbling some further epithet that he knew I could not hear. He had no way to make more mischief to such a gentle reply, though I can tell thee coz, I was ready to follow Kempe's example, with a jug to the villain's head, were it not that I would likely have been run through with Cuthbert's dagger had I done so.

So it is, that his lordship's fate is unknown and ours, tied to his, is likewise in doubt. The companionship we enjoyed last summer, when first I left Stratford, has melted this summer like butter in the noonday sun of August. As I have writ thee, already have we lost a man to a suspicious dagger and now two more will leave to the wars. Nor are these uncertain tides felt by us alone: every company of players must now share their men and boys, day-by-day, to fill out a play.

Fear of the Spanish dog roams the streets of London by night and day. I see a bridge built across the Thames, boats lashed together end to end, that defenders might more easily rally south to the Kentish countryside, where some say the invading forces will land on our soil. As we left the Mermaid, the streets of Cheapside ran a bloody red as some, in loyal zeal, commandeered the ale houses in Fish Street, where Spanish wines are sold, and poured the lot out of doors.[91]

And this news is freshly delivered in London, so may not yet be reported in Stratford: Sir Francis Drake has struck a mighty blow against the Spanish King, destroying a hundred of his ships in Cadiz, along with a mighty carrack called the San Felipe coming out of East India laden with gold (which cargo he did relieve the Spanish thereof and has delivered the same unto Her Majesty). By the assistance of the Almighty, and the invincible courage and industry of General Drake, this strange and happy enterprise was achieved in one day and two nights to the great astonishment, I'll warrant you, of that Spanish King.

Such reports have wrought two extraordinary effects on the people in the City. First, seeing how the Spanish ships are exceeding slow and poorly built and can be easily taken with little danger to our own fleet, this hath emboldened every man. General Drake proclaimed he had done little more than singe the beard of the King of Spain and he would return to destroy the rest of their fleet. The General is seen about town wearing a Cadiz beard, which he says he will shave when he has shaved the Spanish clean of their aims in England (the aforesaid beard is cause for many jests, as its shape resembles the hair on a woman's private parts. La!)

Second, his exploits have excited one and all of the treasures to be found in the east, whereas till now our eyes are all bent in admiration to the west and the bounty to be harvested from the New World. This is little cause to celebrate in my mind however, for whilst the ships are needed to defend the realm, none will voyage to the New World and none will therefore take a Shakespeare to his Fortune.

But Kempe reports that Raleigh pleads daily with her Majesty to allow some small number of ships to follow Governor White, even those that might be spared from defending our shores, so that she might replenish her coffers with the gold and silver needed to outfit more ships and more soldiers for that selfsame defense, whilst increasing her dominions and bringing pagans to the word of Christ. 'Tis said her new Lord Chancellor, Christopher Hatton, takes side with Raleigh, but in hopes to enrich himself more than his sovereign. The Queen calls Hatton her 'mutton', following her everywhere, much to the condemnation of the Court, for he has no training in law, nor other qualities to make him a worthy occupant of so high an office. Perhaps she was swayed by some witches' charm: Hatton gave the Queen a ring that he swore would protect her from the Plague, and bid her wear it on a chain 'twixt her sweet dugs.' It may have worked, for Her Majesty suffers not from any Plague, but in wearing the trinket, she caused the many to draw scandalous conclusions of their private meetings, such that even Mr. Johnson refused to repeat the most shameful accusations he did hear about them, and that these were so horrible, that neither could he write the words on paper! Would that my Fortune were so easily won as the likes of Hatton win theirs!

I have not seen Rosalind since my return and the house where she stayed is boarded up. Is some unseen hand driving me, like a beast on its way to the rother market, closing the gateway to the Americas, nailing shut the door to forbidden love, all the while pointing me in another direction? Perhaps to a stage, where I am already somewhat fixed? I mean that players, lost to war, make my mean services seem to shine brighter, to our Company and to others that perform at the Theatre and the Curtain. The Queen's Men are returned to London for want of men. To wit: in Oxford, the most excellent William Knell was killed thither by a sword wound to his throat, in a quarrel with his fellow John Towne, who himself fled thereafter. The Queen's Men too divide over their faiths and how hot their spleens burn to take up sword for Queen and country. And their famous clown, Richard Tarlton, was left in Norwich with a fever, though some say it was no fever, but he refused to play in the 'Seven Deadly Sins', the Master of Revels had instructed Her Majesty's servants to perform, for such plays that remind men of their oaths and allegiances as they travel throughout her realm. Such musty old fare will attract only the ancients and some children, so we avoid it, and I'll warrant, once Tamburlaine is beheld on any stage in England, the eyes of the spectators will most surely be idly bent on that which follows next, thinking such prattle to be tedious.

Mr. Perkin has persuaded every man in the Company to leave behind the clownish acting that Tarlton and the Queen's Men are most noted for, saying it is out of fashion to show such red faces and jigging veins. Mr. Perkin instructs me to convey some part of our story with gestures alone, instead of the manners of other players who stamp, curse, weep, rage and then strike their bosom in apish actions, which affects the spectators grossly and is indeed so far from Life that it betrays itself to be altogether artificial. Instead he would have us act freely, as if our veins ran with quicksilver.

Indeed, I note how this style serves better when we play indoors, for instance at the guildhall of Leicester or the York common hall, which reminds me mightily of being inside our own Holy Trinity. Those who attend are close upon us and can hear every breath we take, so we must command their attention with our skill and keep them from the distractions on the high street outside the great windows. Lord knows we had their attention when we played the hall in Christ Church at Oxford: a great fireplace warmed us all on that rainy day, but nearly set the place a'fire when we lit several tapers withal and used them in our jig!

Yet even as my skill grows and is recognized, I will confess to thee coz that the wicked Boy Burbage will surpass us all. He hath taken parts for our missing players, going from a king one day to a woman's role the next with equal ease. I have learned by watching him, in skills such as fencing with swords, daggers, and shields, so smooth and effortless is his art in these practices. And though he generally bears me no good will, after a performance in Sheffield, where I forgot some lines of great matter, he counseled me thereafter most courteously, almost like a brother:

"In this dilemma, the player hath but one expedient, which if skillfully done, the spectators will be none the wiser. The words of the part, unknown or unremembered by the player, then should he speak from some other play that he DOES know. Therefore, whenever he feels himself at a loss, he will introduce passages from this other role, which fit the matter being discussed at that moment, and which fit the cues received. Thus, giving some parts of the play, masking others, the player gains another day to perfect himself in the part and, while the dialogue is in progress, it will not seem irrelevant, so there is no means of detection."

For such advice, I thanked him most profusely, and that I did within the hearing of his father, so he might know I bear no ill will towards his son. But upon seeing our master nearby, Boy Burbage at once alters his demeanour and calls me a thick-headed lout who hath ruined our play, then stuttering and aping my discomfort. I think his father gives no thought to our dispute though, for he needs every able body we can keep in the Company (but one day this pot will boil over and I will be the one in the fire, I'll warrant thee!).

One report further, in reply to thy honest inquiry about our countrymen in London: in brief, they thrive. Gilbert nears the end of his apprenticeship and may be given leave to set up shop here, so prized is his work with cuffs and decoration on the fashion of the Court. Pug was admitted to the Stationer's Company after his own apprenticeship of some six-year to one Thomas Vautrollier. These two continue to show me every courtesy and I am in their debt for a clean and safe place to hang my hat and glad I am to be away from the filth of those places where we did lodge in the country. O to be sure, we share our warmth and food here with uninvited guests, but nothing so savage as in country inns, which are pestered constantly by the most villainous rats, a brood very hurtful for devouring of meat, clothes, and writings by day, then equally cumbersome at night through their crying and rattling while they dance their galloping galliards on the roof.

Alas coz, now must I return mine attention to some scenes that Mr. Burbage has required me to amend, such that the number and stature of parts match with our reduced number of players. I know not whether I will next be sent to fight more battles upon a stage, or on some coast of Kent against the invading armies of Spain. If this be my last letter to thee, know thou well that I am ever in thy debt. If I cannot rescue my name and kin, I am better to be consumed in defense of our country. In either wise, I will die trying.

O dear friend, thus I commit thee to God's good protection and ask thee to kiss my boy and maids in my name and omit nothing else which thine honour deem'st best for their tender need. I am thine ever-loving servant in all else, Will.

LETTER TWELVE
December 15, 1587

Wherein some players fight and die, but others perform for the Queen and her powerful Earls as the Spanish thunder of war grows to an inescapable roar.

When I studied theatre at California State University Northridge in the early 1970s, one of my professors gave us a definition for what is arguably the most important moment in a play. *Climax: the point in a story where everything that happens thereafter leads to a conclusion or resolution.*

Shakespeare may not have intended for the story of his life in London thus far to reach a climax, but after reading his first eleven letters, I realized that Letter Twelve was just such a point of no return.

Think of how far the boy from Stratford has come to reach this moment. An ill-advised plan to get rich quick in America; learning an unexpected trade that opened doors, worlds, and his mind; bonding with a long-lost brother and surviving life-threatening illness; loving with an urgency and fire he never knew possible; the proverbial "smell of greasepaint and roar of the crowd" now replaced with the harsh reality of war. Not much has unfolded as Shakespeare imagined or hoped when he began this journey, and the writing of letters to document it, just seventeen months earlier.

As Letter Twelve opens, the players are told they will soon be serving the Earl as soldiers in the war with Spain, not merely as his servants on a stage for entertainment. There is no New World to flee to, the ships, men, and supplies all being carefully guarded for use by the defense forces. And there was little to go around anyway: coming back to London after touring in the country, the players are painfully aware of bad harvests and starvation throughout the land.

But just as the men trade props for real swords and practice their fighting skills, they learn that one of their number has been murdered, likely over his defense of the Catholic faith and possibly with the complicity of some of his fellows in Leicester's Men. Look for the point in the letter where Dick Cowley compares the murder to a famous historical assassination (perhaps not unlike how an American might recall the assassination of President Kennedy or Martin Luther King Jr.), which Shakespeare seems to recall and depict a dozen years later in his play *Julius Caesar*. Even a eulogy offered for their lost colleague becomes grist for the future playwright's mill: in *Cymbeline* (Act IV, scene 2), he repeats parts of it as a song.

Despite such grim proceedings, some things in London remain the same. The holiday season has begun and the Queen wants ever-more lavish entertainment to divert herself and her Court. Shakespeare and Will Kempe are called upon to perform for her.

Shakespeare describes the fifty-four year old Queen Elizabeth in detail: richly bejeweled, always picking her blackish teeth, at once "charming and vulgar; subtle and loud; witty and rude; elegant and common." He praises her intelligent manipulation of her courtiers, and feels pity for a majesty surrounded by such "ass-lickers and vipers, with only ladies to wait upon her, by command, to call friend." Some believe she is imbued with supernatural powers as embodied in the "Queen's Evil," which refers to her reputed powers to perform miracles, such as healing the sick by laying hands upon them.

What should a boy from the country think about his sovereign, appointed by God to rule on earth, but seemingly very human and vulnerable to foreign overthrow? Indeed, Shakespeare learns that the Queen has other very human desires and passions, overhearing palace gossip about the Earl of Leicester's fall from her favor (because of his failures in England's war against Spain in the Netherlands) and how the Queen has replaced Leicester's affections with those of the younger Earl of Essex (Leicester's stepson).

Shakespeare also witnesses Governor John White desperately pleading with Sir Walter Raleigh for more ships to rescue the very same people Shakespeare was to have accompanied to Virginia. Raleigh declines, although he desperately wants to protect his investments in the New World: he had brought tobacco to England a decade earlier and later established plantations in Virginia. Much of his early trade in the "weed" came from Spanish colonies, where labor for those plantations had been the primary driver of a slave trade from Africa.

As they leave the court, the Earl of Essex introduces Shakespeare to the young Earl of Southampton, a boy of delicate features, long red hair, and a feminine manner, who will be an important figure later in Shakespeare's life. Will Kempe makes a gift of Shakespeare's father's "illegal" gloves (only local guild tradesmen were permitted to sell their goods in London) to the delighted Earl of Southampton.

Later at the Mermaid tavern, Governor White is pleading for men to return with him to help defend the settlers in the New World, having found one ship he might secure. Shakespeare has been reunited with his beloved Rosalind and immediately seeks her counsel, but she begs him to stay in London. Unable to imagine life without her, completely in love, he agrees, and for a second time, loses an opportunity to go to the New World. But what will he do with entanglements in Stratford and London? Everything that happens thereafter must lead to a resolution, joys for some and tears for others.

Shakespeare then relates how Rosalind (an educated and accomplished clerk for her father) has been helping him make copies of plays for Leicester's Men, with great speed and accuracy of penmanship, thereby helping Shakespeare earn extra money. I was puzzled by this description at first, because typical Tudor English grammar schools were limited to boys, so I wondered where a country girl had been taught such skills. I had witnessed the last vestiges of this British education hierarchy when I attended high school in Australia in the 1960s, where the portrait of another Queen Elizabeth still peered out from the currency and where girls were mostly separated from boys. A cane-wielding Head Mistress ruled with a sharp eye on hemlines, a daily dose of moralizing, and an emphasis for girls on classes that taught domestic skills over the math and science that boys were expected to master. My pre-conceived notions about Rosalind's access to education, colored by my own colonial-tinged experience, were shattered however, when I found an obscure reference to "dame schools."

I discovered that most towns in Rosalind's day sponsored lessons for girls in reading, writing, sewing, and some use of numbers (all skills thought to make them better managers of household affairs for their fathers or future husbands) taught by older women (i.e. dames). I have since found other sources which confirm the widespread attendance by girls at these schools, even one scholar who finds evidence that there were more dame schools in England in Shakespeare's time than grammar schools.

As we have seen, Shakespeare joined the Earl of Leicester's Men as a johannes factotum, a jack-of-all-trades, but it is the women of his era who were the real Swiss Army knives of any family or community. He reflects with guilt and sadness that Anne is working in the fields of Stratford and Rosalind is hunched over a writing desk, both in support of his schemes to get rich, which seem now more distant and futile than ever.

As Letter Twelve closes, Shakespeare offers a sonnet he has penned for Rosalind and we get another glimpse into his early artistic process (this one seems to form the basis of Sonnet 29, which became one of his most famous and oft-quoted poems).

15 December 1587, London

Coz,

I swear there are more beggars in this City than drops of water in the Thames, both flowing through in endless procession. Daily there are more vagabonds, uncountable: each with no more doublets than backs, no more shoes than feet, nay, sometimes more feet than shoes, or such shoes as the toes peep out through the over-leather. So many motherless children too. They come from shires stricken with Plague or bad harvests. They come to find pity in a city that has little to spare.

Lord knows I may soon be in the streets with the selfsame masterless servants, whose stomachs make beggars of them. Our Company, which thou knowest returned to London in September, was sent forth again to the countryside in October, owing to the closure of the theatres by the Master of Revels. But what is a 'company', if its fabric is in tatters, left ragged by those who have left to fight real battles and by a master who himself is newly returned to England humbled? One of our finest is dead (at the hands of others among us, I fear), breeding suspicion like carrion breeds maggots, leaving none of us to trust the other as we paint our faces bravely and perform our plays from town to town. Here then I have but sketched the canvas: I will paint for thee the whole portrait anon, for I am in urgent need of thy good counsel.

First, I thank thee heartily for that news of a harvest better than the misery of last year. Not a moment too soon, for in every town where we played, vicars exhort the faithful to fast twice in the week and to give food to the poor (yet these selfsame clergy never miss a meal themselves, causing grievous anger among the many). I overheard a ten faggot [*bundle*] collier, who trod the highway towards Doncaster, speak thus:

"Did God send corn for rich men only? E'en a dog must eat, look you, and my hunger will break stone walls, if there be bread on the other side."[92] Nor would breaking of walls be the most uncommon sight: we have seen many women toiling in the fields, in common struggle alongside their men to coax food from the soil, taking them from duties at home. In Thetford I spied the following, etched on a wall of the church:

> Though toil in the field brings a man his most gains,
> Yet housewifery labor is equal in pains.
> Some respite to husbands the weather may send,
> But housewives' affairs have never an end.

The theatres reopened on the Queen's Day [*November 17*], so we are once more in London, but Leicester is still out of favour at Court, the more of which I shall presently report. It was a great insult to him that Lord Pembroke's Men were called for St. Andrew's Day [*November 30*] and Her Majesty bid them play Kempe's famous jig. For this he needed a second who could hold him aloft as I have earlier described, and for this he chose me.[93]

I had sometimes dreamed of performing at Court, so oft has Mr. Perkin described the honour, but no imagining could properly convey the reality of it. The banqueting house where we played at White Hall was of enormous proportions, more vast than any single room I had yet seen, no less than an hundred feet long and nearly as wide, the ceiling high enough to contain the full tower of a church. The walls seemed to breathe alive, featuring hundreds of sparkling glass windows and richly hung tapestries, embroidered scenes of ancient battles and courtly love.

Her Majesty entered, preceded in specific order by gentlemen, barons, earls, Knights of the Garter, and Chancellor Hatton, all richly dressed (but for some reason unknown, Mr. Hatton was bareheaded, leading to still more gossip of his 'position' with the Queen!).

Next came the Queen herself, an astonishing sight, most majestic. Her jewels, below the crown itself, were simple but of the finest gold and pearl; her gown exquisite white silk, the train exceeding long; the bosom uncovered (the custom among unmarried gentlewomen in London); her complexion the whiteness of fresh milk, although somewhat aided by a kind of paint or powder.

We all shouted 'Long Live the Queen' and she answered simply 'thank you all, my good people.' And canst thou imagine, she did then greet every man or woman of rank, English and foreigner alike, by name with some comment on their most recent accomplishments or indiscretions, keeping every one close, yet at arm's length, at the same time.

In the hour that passed in this manner, I witnessed a great variety of qualities in our Queen: she is charming and vulgar; subtle and loud; witty and rude; elegant and common. She picks her teeth constantly, which appear black even from a distance. She corrected Mr. Hatton's Latin, but made him laugh at his own mistakes. For this knack, to play one against another and maintain sway over all, the Spanish ambassador pronounced her the best 'king' England ever knew!

As we assembled in the tiring room, a portly woman, who one called Lady Blake, made lewd conversation with some of the players, most notably with Kempe. In this she revealed more than her ample bosom:

"Ooo, Master Kempe, will you recite that sonnet I heard from you once, wherein you compared your mistress to a rose?" She was the entire time leaning, most familiar, on Kempe, whilst trying to keep her head level so the pile of rust-coloured hair would stay balanced on top, no mean feat I assure thee.

"I recall that one imperfectly, but can give you instead one that I composed in praise of my mount." Kempe mimicked the riding of his horse.

"If your horse is your mistress, must she not 'bear' thee well?" Lady Blake began stroking her thighs, as two of the other ladies giggled with feigned outrage.

"Aye, that is indeed the prescript quality of a good and particular mare, when riding her bareback, as I prefer."

"Bareback? Then methinks any mare under you would swiftly shake you off!"

"Ah, perhaps if she was not bridled, but I have not seen the mare yet who would not take my bit."

"O, then belike she was old and gentle; and you rode, like a kern [soldier] of Ireland, standing high and straight in the stirrups."

"My lady, you have good judgment in horsemanship, I see."

"Aye, and be warned. He that rides so - - and rides not warily - - will fall into foul bogs!" Some ladies blushed and scurried away, but Lady Blake seemed to invite Kempe to mount her on the spot.

"Were that true, I would have a sow for my mistress and no horse at all."94

"Much as your Lord Leicester has done, riding ill and being pushed off the royal mare by a younger rider?" The words no sooner left Lady Blake's lips, but the chamber seemed to fall silent, such that I could now hear those gathered in the great hall nearby, listening to a ballad that recalled past glory of our English kings, and how the lords and ladies laughed only after the Queen herself did so, applauded only after she called out some approval. Is the Court therefore a mob of parrot-slaves, more richly dressed and better fed than those who toil under the lash? I might be such a slave in exchange for what I have seen at Court: the gold and jewels; the silks and painted nosegays; the lavish groaning board of foods, familiar and wondrous-strange, and in such abundance that fifty times as many could not consume it all in a fortnight. Kempe pretended ignorance, struggling to untie a lace on his sleeve that had knotted too tight:

"Who means your ladyship?"

"Why that same Earl of Essex," quoth Lady Blake, now whispering in Kempe's ear, either because she feared her gossip would be overheard or she wanted an excuse to lean closer upon him. "He who the Queen doth nightly tickle and gambol withal."

"And this offends Lord Leicester? Is he not the stepfather of that same young Earl?"

"Aye, marry he is, making it the greater insult," quoth Lady Blake, taking more of those nearby into her confidence. "For was not Her Majesty mightily furious when he married Essex's mother without Her blessing?"

Kempe drank in this news with the smile of one who discovers honey in his tart beer. I stood close behind him, as we were soon to be called on-stage, and saw his hand caressing her buttocks, though Lord knows if she felt it through the layers of her fine dress and farthingale.

"Tis true then, my Lord of Leicester hath been thrown from the royal mare?" he whispered to her.

"Aye, but I'll warrant you the flame of her passion for him has not yet burned out, for was he not her first love? But while he lately adventured abroad, her eye fell on this young Earl, and she is now rarely seen without his company. He is thirty years her junior, yet at night there is nobody with her but Essex, at cards or another game, and I'll warrant you that he comes not to his own lodging till birds sing in the morning."

Kempe could charm speech from a stone and tickled Lady Blake's fancy enough to learn more of Leicester's fortunes. It seems I am revenged on him without lifting a finger: he is returned from his adventures in the Netherlands, a second time in ruins, having spent still more of the Queen's treasure to gain nothing, save the corpses of his soldiers and the shreds of his once proud battle colours. Lady Blake says the Queen is so grieved by the poor generalship of her 'eyes' (as she calls him) that she will not receive him nor hear a word more of his urgent pleas for money. In public, she blames the malice on foul errors of others, but in private she is said to blame Leicester's arrogance, that held apart the very nations which should have rallied to one cause.

The Court whispers, though never to Her Majesty, that England's failure to win so small a war will embolden the Spanish to invade anon, thinking us weak, and that a Catholic monarch will be placed on the throne. With Mary of Scotland dead, rumours fly of which English Earl would reveal his true colours and support the Church of Rome in exchange for the crown. Lady Blake says the Queen can therefore trust no one. I know little else of these affairs, but thus much I have seen first hand: Leicester is in great debt and surely cannot recover whilst he lives. His appearance is now as a man much older than his five and fifty years, sporting a careless beard and sad expression, as if he were too exhausted by Life to present his face to his barber or summon more than a sigh.

Yet while I am secretly joyed by his fall, that selfsame stumble may cripple our Company. His patronage still opens every door of towns far from London, but now that we are returned to the City there is naught for us here, save wagering twixt ourselves over how few days our Company may remain together. Leicester is so devoted to the plays he commissioned and to the distraction that our performances provide him that we may, at the least, hold together this winter at the Theatre, but his Company cannot be called to Court whilst he is so out of favour.

"I think the Queen is no fool and merely plays each of her Lords 'gainst the other with her womanly talents." Kempe could not finish the thought, as in that moment we were called for. Nor did we thereafter disappoint: Kempe surpassed his best and Her Majesty's hearty laughter was payment enough, though she tossed coin upon coin at him, gold sovereigns all, commanding him to tumble again, to lift his leg higher and higher still. For my part, I held him steady and tumbled well at my cue, earning lusty barking from Her Majesty's dogs.

The performances concluded, the Court now swirled like dancing schools of herring chased by the fisherman's net, moving throughout the great hall in groups of polite conversation: a lord presenting his nephew to a lady of note; a knot of petitioners lining up to ask the indulgence of Mr. Hatton, begging that he might make their matter known to the Queen; a perfumed milliner making a gift of an exotic feather to a nobleman who might employ his services, themselves birds of a feather, sharing the contents of a pouncet-box, which ever and anon they gave to their noses and took away again with many holiday and lady-like terms.[95] All appeared random and cheerful company, but each soul thither had one eye on their neighbor and the other on the position of the Queen, swirling in studied procession to be in her orbit, as if by chance, and thereby to have another opportunity to greet her.

One such was Sir Walter Raleigh himself, who stood with a group of his fellows and Governor John White, newly returned from Virginia with news of the 150 men and women he took with him April last, of which none are returned and many reported dead. Kempe and I stood close to know the fate of his sister and overheard the following:

"Look you John, I have wagered forty thousand pound on these voyages and seen little in return, save some tobacco leaves, the smoking of which I will confess to you I do love, but which are grown in the main in more malleable lands far to the south."

"Your grace, I beseech you to take pity on those poor souls I left behind, not the least, but the newest of which, is my granddaughter, Virginia, born but a few weeks ago," quoth White, visibly quivering, although I could not tell if his affliction was the result of the cold wet cloak that draped his hunger-shrunk shank or fear that he knew Raleigh's verdict before it be delivered. "These are all my children, all entrusted to me by your graciousness, but we arrived thither to find no sign of your previous garrison, nor any of their stores, and too late to plant, such that now all are starving or begging pity from the savages, who themselves are not well off and were mightily offended by our predecessors."

"God is my judge man, I would have it otherwise! But thou hast seen the preparations for war. No ship will be spared for any purpose else; no men, no food in this time of poor harvests, no coin," quoth Raleigh, pausing for a moment of reflection as if checking a list. "God is my judge and I hope He will protect these souls until next year when we might have an end to war and some resource to spare. Else we are both damned to Hell."

"Your grace, be assured the wealth of the New World is precisely what this realm sorely needs." White dared to grasp the hem of Raleigh's sleeve, to keep him from drifting to another petitioner. "Tis true we have barely a foothold there, but I warrant you there are riches beyond imagining to be easily taken up, such that might outfit a thousand ships and arm every man in England. The silver, gold, those base metals needed for nails, swords, and cannon. Rich soils that can feed an hundred Englands. I beg you, Sir Walter, use your charm o'er Her Majesty to win the day and give me but one ship and some seeds and iron, livestock and cloth, and those other sundry supplies that can help our company through but one winter, and I promise you, so much will be returned that your Grace will be hailed a saviour throughout the Ages." To my great amazement, Sir Walter's brother Carew, replied for him, as follows:

"O, I fear my brother hath not the leisure to address such matters now. Why just this morning, not yet having the fear of God in mine eyes and by instigation of the Devil, I went to a whore. I was very eager of her, embraced her and kissed, and went to enjoy her, but she thrust me aside saying 'I cannot, for your brother lay with me not an hour ago!'" Sir Walter struck him on the head, apologizing to those assembled for his kinsman's poor manners, but was himself laughing, to which Mr. Carew Raleigh struck the man standing on his other side saying "Box thy neighbor about his ears and let it pass thus around the hall: 'twill come back to my brother anon."

Do great men fall, merely because we hold them in too high esteem? The Raleighs hail from Devonshire, whereat speech and manners are grossly other than in London, but little could explain this boorish behavior at Court. Yet he must also have the power to charm, as I heard he wagered with Her Majesty that he could weigh the smoke of their tobacco. The Queen declared the boast impossible to prove, but accepted the wager and bid him try, to which he called for scales and weighed the tobacco in the Queen's possession; then bid her smoke with him and at their conclusion, he weighed the ashes, declaring the difference was the weight of the smoke. She paid the wager saying she had seen men turn gold into smoke, but never a man who could turn smoke into gold!

But if Sir Walter has the power to charm, I see now that contrary to report, he has not used it to plead with the Queen for relief of those poor souls that he left in Virginia unprovided for. Or perhaps he cannot: Sir Walter is a fine figure, as any in the City, his face open and inquiring, his beard sharpened to a razor point, his garments simple yet finely decorated (though 'tis difficult to avoid staring at his ears, which unfold from his head like wings of a lark), but he is now over forty and no longer given private audience, those hours devoted instead to the younger Earl of Essex. His further reply to Governor White confirmed my suspicion that he is interested in profit merely:

"Look here John, there are stranger things to be seen in the New World than there are beggars between London and Staines, but there are such places with natives and climates that may be more welcoming to our cause. My charge from Her Majesty has always been to discover barbarous countries not already possessed by a Christian prince and to occupy those lands and enjoy the same forever in the name of England. I am of a mind to risk no further in Virginia, but to look farther south, to Guyana, which, I grant thee, will make me either exceedingly famous or exceedingly ridiculous in the cause, but from which I hear better report. When our business with Spain is at an ebb, I shall seek thee out for such new ventures, but until that day, I cannot advance thy cause in Virginia."

"O brother, thou wilt return to the Americas in haste, I'll warrant," quoth the younger Raleigh, turning from Sir Walter to the group of men in attendance. "Shall I rhyme my reasoning? This then:

Sir Walter hath tobacco praised,
So that the price of every pound,
By a pound, is raised.
And why's all this?
Because he loves it well?
No: for the Raleighs have so great a store to sell!"

There followed general laughter, save for Governor White, who grieved that he could not persuade the elder Raleigh, while the younger played the fool and distracted from the gravity of the matter. In any wise, they moved to intercept Her Majesty's train before White could utter one word more, which chance Kempe used to take the Governor by his arm and demand news of his sister. White reported she was delivered on the voyage to Virginia of a healthy boy, named Walter in honour of their patron. Would there had been a hundred such in his honour and that together they might have cried loud enough for help to be heard in London!

Kempe cursed me frantically for breaking my word that I would go with Kathleen and Miles to serve as her protector. He cursed bad luck that the first colony was lost and none but savages there to welcome those that White left thither. He wept that there was no remedy, and for knowing that all the tears in Christendom could not make it otherwise.

Festivities concluded, the Queen dined apart, fearing that an assassin might poison the feast, it was said. Coz, I have told thee how father bears no love for a ruler who would harm our kin on feeble cause, but my brief encounter in her presence hath tempered mine own view. She has made herself an image of a Queen: not merely flesh and blood, but a goddess for her countrymen to rally around, anointed by God for a purpose greater than any claimed by Spain or Rome. And though she favoured Leicester over my kinsmen, I will admit the Ardens were not blameless. And how should she know the heart of the Shakespeares? I see she is surrounded by ass-lickers and vipers, with only ladies who wait upon her, by command, to call 'friend.' Was she blinded by her love of the Earl, owing to how he protected her in the days when her sister sat upon the throne and her own head sat light upon her shoulders? I know not what to make of her, but one thing is certain: she loves plays and music!

But what matters such pomp and ceremony? Having seen now the Court for myself, I think 'tis naught else but a place, a degree and form, made merely to create awe and fear in other men. Homage sweet or flattery poisoned? O the Queen commands them all to do her bidding: she can command a beggar to his knees, but she cannot command his health or loyalty. Nor will she sleep as sound as the beggar, who with a vacant mind gets easily to rest, while she must be on constant watch over the peace of an entire kingdom. Her scepter, sword, and crown imperial, yea e'en the intertissued robes of gold and pearl or the farcical attendants running around her, none of these, apparently, can give her a quiet night.

Upon leaving the chamber, Kempe was presented to this aforementioned Earl of Essex, a goodly man of mine age, who was accompanied by a boy of thirteen that was reported to be Henry Wriothesly, the third Earl of Southampton. At first, I took him for a girl, his red locks cascading over shoulders that were covered in more fine lace than any of the ladies in waiting. Essex fawned upon the boy as they debated some matter surrounding the Queen's ability to defend the nation, now that Leicester's army had fared so poorly in the Netherlands. He nodded in our direction to acknowledge the introduction, but hastened to brush aside any further interruption of his argument with the younger Earl, thus:

"Prithee Henry, in the Queen's Evil canst thou not see she moves under the watchful eye of God himself?"

"Thou'rt mistaken. 'Tis a mere superstition, to show the Pope that her excommunication meant nothing, but only children fear such fairies and hobgoblins!" quoth Southampton, with a womanly voice that matched his delicate appearance. He gestured grandly toward Kempe. "Thy jig hath ignited my passion to see more, Master Kempe." I wondered if he meant more of the acrobatics or more of Kempe. Essex then stepped in front of him, to drive home his contention and to break Southampton's gaze, which was now fixed on Kempe's gloves.

"But Henry, the Catholics say this PROVES that she is a heretic and a witch. And if they believe her to have such powers, surely they would not be so foolish as to invade and meet an army of English devils!"

'Tis true, coz, I have heard in our travels around the land how the Queen has laid hands on the ill and deformed, making blind men see and the lame throw down their canes to walk the earth again. How she solicits Heaven, herself best knows, but 'tis spoken widely how strangely-visited people, all swollen and ulcerous, pitiful to the eye, the mere despair of surgery, she cures, hanging a golden stamp about their necks, put on with holy prayers. With this strange virtue, she has for certain a heavenly gift that speaks of her sometimes grace.[96]

"Master Kempe, I am entranced by thy glove. May I see it closer?" Southampton twirled around Essex and pressed himself against Kempe, sliding a hand down his arm and waiting permission to pluck the glove from Kempe's hand. I have never seen my fellow so amazed and unable to speak, but he nodded some consent and in an instant the glove was off his hand and pressed to the face of the young Earl.

"O, I'll warrant you these gloves are divinely inspired!" Southampton cooed like a dove and dabbed his face with the glove, drinking in the fragrance of the leather, which father had scented with rosewood. "Mine are but sack cloth in comparison, adorned with dross, but these must be the very same worn by Helen when she did so bewitch the war-like Greeks. I am in sore need of gloves at all times, for see my leathery hands: a freestone-coloured hand; verily thou might'st think that mine old gloves were on, but 'tis my hands! My housewife's hands." Kempe then regained his accustomed felicity and replied:

"Your grace, I see graceful hands that are no doubt skilled with the lute, the bow, and the warlike rapier and which therefore need protection of the finest gloves. These are but a player's paltry apparel, but if your grace would honour us by wearing them, even once, then my gift of them to you would not be in vain."

Gift? O Lord, I prayed I had not heard him say that. These were gloves we had brought from my father's shop to sell in London, bringing them to the Court in hopes they might be noticed, not in hopes they might be given away gratis. But what Kempe had done, I could not so easily undo. Giddy had already been upbraided for bringing them to Brownsword's and claiming them as coming from his shop. The old tailor found them pleasing good craftsmanship, but would not run afoul of the city guilds and ordered Giddy to pack them away and never bring them forth again. In our desperation to help our family, we resolved to press ahead, but only by wearing them most discretely, as if we already owned them, then offering to sell them to anyone who might find them pleasing. Kempe was our fellow conspirator in this, but knew they were not to be GIVEN away!

Southampton made grand gestures of surprise and gratitude, even as Essex bolted to find greener pastures for his stern discussion of matters more weighty than the adornment of a noble boy. We took our leave and Kempe could see my discomfort, promising me that this gift would become the talk of the Court and would lead to many more inquiries to buy the like. I can only pray he is right, but we debated the matter, somewhat heated, on our way to the Mermaid, there to acquaint our fellows with the news of Court and our triumph with the jig.

We had barely begun describing every particular, especially Court gossip to Masters Pope and Johnson, when Dick rushed in and fell to his knees, much to our great amazement, crying, choking and speaking all at once with this grave news:

"O lord, my poor master is dead! Master Clarke is dead!"

I tried to calm him with a cup of brewage. The commotion at this news quickly spread table to table, chattering choughs [*crows*] demanding to know the matter. Mr. Perkin paled at the news, for he and Mr. Clarke had been so long together in the Company, and were cut of the same player's cloth, that this news was most certainly a grievous blow.

"Aye, he was stabbed so many times, like Caesar at the base of Pompey's statue, such that those nearby wiped the sudden streams of blood, that flushed fast out of his gaping wounds, with their napkins and shirts to no avail." Dick coughed for breath as he relived the awful scene. "He gave such a look, such a rueful steadfast eye, which I never shall erase from my memory till the day of mine own death."

I could do naught to ease his grief, nor had I any idea what I should do, for never before have I attended on a friend who witnessed so untimely an end. There are no truer faces than those washed with tears, and I swear to thee, in that moment, Dick's was the truest face I ever did see. He grasped my hands, as if his own life depended on that simple human bond, and finished painting his bloody picture:

"Aye, then with a deep felt sigh he clasped his hands together and cast his sight to Heaven. Instantly thereafter, did the pale hand of Death press hard upon his face and then did his immortal ghost utterly forsake his too-mortal corpse."

Mr. Perkin, or the wine, slowly calmed the lad and wrung from him those facts of the matter that might be known. In sum, there was a common tavern fight and Mr. Clarke came out the worse. Mr. Perkin comforted Dick, which gave me leave to study the whole scene before me. I swear masters Johnson and Pope smiled together at this news. Could these two have been the agents of this death? Mr. Clarke had grown louder in his defense of the old religion and neither Pope nor Johnson would brook such sentiment from any man, leastways those in our own Company. O, I do not accuse my fellows of wielding the knife that drained the life from Mr. Clarke, but sure they know those Puritan scoundrels who did the deed. And might they also have put forth a story that he was killed in a tavern brawl by a common cut-purse? I am not alone in these suspicions, for Mr. Perkin has said as much, that I overheard in hushed tones, to Mr. Burbage. I took Dick out of doors for cold night air, lest he faint altogether, and to be sure our parley was not overheard. He could barely speak, but even so made his fears known to me thus:

"O Will, what shall become of me with no master? Thou knowest he did more than teach me the mysteries of our players' craft, but also protected me. I am no Catholic, but those who killed him will think as much, given I was his 'prentice for this many a year. O truly, I am dead already! And thou. Mr. Clarke hath many a time defended thee too, before those in our Company who would have left thee by the wayside, knowing thy father a Catholic. O Will, we are both forfeit!"

Who could look upon his friend in such a state and not himself tremble and weep? Dick is nearly twenty years, but small show of man is yet upon his chin, no more than a dusting of down that sits like unshorn velvet on his alabaster skin. He had no means to stop the tears, save a pretty napkin he hath oft used onstage when playing the women's parts, which on it had some silken flowers that now he soiled 'neath his nose. Witchcraft lies in tears, especially from men unused to such tenderness, but when eyes overflow unchecked, what rocky heart will not soon wear down withal? What breast so cold that is not warmed to him that feels such pain?

"Dick, fear not," quoth I, with all the player's skill I could then muster, feigning certainty on a path I knew to be treacherous. "We will protect each other. We will use our wits and those friends we have to warn of any real danger. I doubt it not that Mr. Johnson reports those he even THINKS may favour the old faith, but no man is condemned by reports alone. What have we said or done, but serve our fellows well?"

"Thou speak'st true, Will, but I have seen when Mr. Clarke chants to the moon, some kind of calling to ... "

"Satan?"

"Hush man! We are doomed to even speak of such things!"

"I doubt that your old master was in league with the Devil, Dick. Only that his enemies would have others think so and thereby give some semblance of justice to his death."

"Tis true, although a'times I swore I smelled sulfur near his lodgings and on his great cloak."

"Tut! 'Twas the herbs he smoked when he could not find tobacco to fill his pipe, no more. I'll warrant you, Mr. Clarke may have worshipped the old way, but surely he worshipped our God and the Holy Spirit, no loathsome incarnations from the nether regions."

"That but makes his killing so much more fearful for us, Will." Dick was digging his bony thumbs into my palms till there was no colour left in them. "Destroying a disciple of the Devil is one thing, but what if he were killed only for being a Catholic, of which our land still has many? I heard the younger Burbage, Richard I mean, say that all the English Catholics will meet their grisly fate on the battlefield, for no good Englishman would trust to fight alongside a slave to the Pope, and would instead slay those traitors before turning a sword on the Spanish dogs."

Coz, thou knowest that even a fool, at times, can utter something wise. I report these events to thee, because this may be my fate if I stay with Leicester's Men, for Mr. Burbage informs us we are all pledged to serve in a force that Leicester will take north in spring to fend off invasion through Scotland (I know little of martial matters, but most say no fleet would risk the seas in winter and no army set foot on foreign soil when the land is barren and their men cannot be supplied). I have no stomach for war and 'tis folly to fly the bear before the bear pursues. On the other hand, 'tis equally unwise to stare at the arrow as the bowman draws back the string, when that selfsame instrument is aimed at thy heart. Lord, which way to turn?

Was it little more than a year ago, when I left Stratford with a Company of men who, having full reference to one consent, may work apart, but reach a common goal, just as many arrows loosed from several sides can come to one mark? And now are these same men, like distempered hounds, snarling over the last scrap of bone?

Even so, our pack of dogs may yet hunt as one. Our chief rivals in London are the Lord Admiral's Men, who reached their zenith with Tamburlaine, but are now laid low from that selfsame play. I mean that, playing it of late, during the scene whence the governor of Babylon is shot, one player raised a musket to seem to fire upon another, but the ball missed the post he aimed at and killed a woman great with child forthwith, then hit another man very sore in the head. Kit Marlowe, he that was Tamburlaine's progenitor and poet, was so devastated by this tragedy that he has not left the Mermaid since. He will not be consoled and drinks a hogshead a night, cursing the heavens and claiming this to be proof there is no God, which opinion has already caused him much grief with great men of power. The Master of Revels banned them from playing further and they will surely not be seen at Court this winter, which fate may be in our favour: Leicester's Men may be called instead!

The night air bit shrewdly, reminding Dick and I to return then to the warmth of the Mermaid, whereat we discovered one matter of conversation more heated than our grief over Mr. Clarke, hotter still than the fire by which they stood. In the mean season, Governor White had arrived and was then engaged in vigorous parley with Kempe and other gentlemen apart, who now drew us into their company.

"Mr. Kempe, thou hast that fifty pound?" Governor White put a hand on Kempe's shoulder to bring his earnest gaze to him and no other.

"Aye."

"Wilt give it me, along with similar sums from some three or four dozen others known to these gentlemen? Our purpose thus: to sell shares in our Virginia enterprise to raise money sufficient to outfit two privateers that lie now in Bournemouth. We will need every penny and every able bodied man willing to work for shares, but together we have sketched a plan that will succeed, I'll warrant."

The Governor's commendations were infectious and soon Kempe had sent for three or four others of his acquaintance who might also invest in this enterprise. He knew I had no such sum, but when all was settled, turned to me in earnest.

"William, thou art an honest man and have become a goodly player," quoth he, warmed by the hope that White had kindled in him (and by more cups of sack than I could count). "Thou knowest the Earl of Leicester's Men are doomed to go their several ways, most to the army of our Earl to defend the land when the Spanish come. But thou couldst go with the Governor and gain thine original intent: riches from the New World! Not as a common labourer though, nay, for I will pay thy share and thou canst go as a SHAREHOLDER! What sayest thou? Wilt go find my sister and protect her as thou hast promised?"

O coz, now that I have reported all, canst thou see why I am in most desperate need of thy good counsel? What should I think of this all? My life seems now to be a room full of candles burning swiftly to their ends. Take a dangerous journey to the Americas, that may quickly flicker and die in stormy seas with humble ships and meagre supplies? Stay with a Company of players that boasts no more than an empty purse and quarrelsome fellows? And what of Rosalind? I have learned of her new lodging and we were reunited, but how to keep the flame of our stolen love alight when so many ill winds do buffet and blow us about? For the moment, I replied to Kempe's plea in this manner:

"Will Kempe, thou hast been kind to me since we first clasped hands, and I will therefore be always in thy debt." Did he notice I was wrenching his true cause a false way, to buy time for my feeble brain to concoct a reply that could bring order to such chaos? God must have taken pity on my state, for at that instant, before I could say yea or nay, Raleigh arrived, causing a great commotion among White's followers. Kempe was called thither and left me standing by the fire, roasting my behind and cooling mine overheated brain. I could not think which way to turn, save to fly to Rosalind for her advice or solace.

Ro-sa-lind. Ros-a-lind. Rosalind! I confess to thee that I am once again a schoolboy, so enchanted by her that I take sensuous pleasure in merely writing and saying her name, transporting me again into her spell. The brightness of her cheek shames the stars, as daylight doth a lamp; her eyes in Heaven would stream so bright, that birds would sing and think it were not night.[97]

I left the Mermaid with the poor ghost of Mr. Clarke bombasting on the stage of mine addled brain; with White and Kempe tantalizing me forward; with Fear calling me back. I ran the half mile to Rosalind's room, to warm myself, but even more to escape these demons, and soon had reported to her the particulars of what had just then unfolded, to which she gave me fair looks and these solicitations:

"Dost thou love me Will? I know thou wilt say 'aye,' and I will take thy word. Yet if thou swear'st, thou mayst yet prove false. God laughs at lovers' oaths, for He knows that I should have been more cautious and not yielded so lightly to passion, which the dark of night so hotly encouraged. But gentle Will, if thou dost love me truly, tell me so in faith, for then I'll advise thee honestly."

Although I have enjoyed her body fully, when she but leans her cheek upon her hand, I wish I were a glove upon that hand that I might touch that cheek again.

"O Rosalind, by yonder blessed moon I swear ... "

"O, swear not by the inconstant moon, that changes nightly in its shape, lest thy love prove likewise variable." She pressed her fingertips to my lips to stop the flow of words and I tasted sweet and salt at once, and would have devoured them both, but her demeanor commanded more serious attention. "Do not swear at all. I'll give thee my advice without such a contract, for although I have such joy in thy love, I have no joy in any pledges made too sudden, too unadvised. Here then, without reservation, my advice: this bud of love may prove a beauteous flower, but it cannot blossom so, if thou art across the sea in Virginia and I am here."

With this, like a learned doctor of the law, or like thy habit of balancing one ledger of numbers against the other, she set forth her case: the scale on one side held the promise of great riches; but on the other, those unthinkable dangers that we had learned from Miles and the sailors (aye, even Governor White himself), were like great orchard walls, high and hard to climb, with death as likely the outcome as a safe return. But here in London, she argued, I could sell gloves and take in more work as a scribe and mender of plays, especially with her as my clerk to redouble my labours. This had been yet another common joy, unlooked for, between us. Mr. Burbage had given me plays to copy, papers that mocked me in our sweaty closet each night that Rosalind and I indulged our appetites, never satisfied, so that when he called for them, I was entirely unprepared. To my great amazement, Rosalind showed herself the most able clerk, with a beauteous and clear hand that made my letters on a page seem crude and thick as Tewkesbury mustard. She told me how her father, being bailiff, had sent her to school and taught her to aid him with keeping of the town records, wherein she became a chronicler of village life: the decrees and deeds; leases of land to this one and debts owed to that one; who shall be fined and who is indentured; and, when God writes the final conveyance, the brief and abstract chronicle of a goodman's life.

I imagined her as a girl of ten, eager to please her father, studiously tracing each word on the page letter-by-letter in careful script before running outside to play with her sisters. At thirteen, already accomplished at the task, pen flying across the page to make the time pass quickly, that she might return to thoughts of the boy next door. At eighteen, completing ever-more complicated documents, with nary a blot to diminish the dignity of the matter that each page represented, earning respect for her family, as any man's good son might do, thereby showing those girls still at school, who no doubt doted on her, that a woman can cast magic over powerful men and matters too. That night she first assisted me in these matters, before the candles were out, we two had copied a hundred pages, sitting naked side-by-side in fevered labours that thrilled the senses, as if our lovemaking had never paused. Our fingers black with ink, two dozen quills worn to nubs, papers strewn hither and yon across the field of our bed. Mr. Burbage was most satisfied the next day, such that when our Company was again called away, I left her with parts of six more plays to copy and, now returned, with payment for these in our purse, she argued that in this manner we could keep food on the table until Virginia offers more certain hopes for us both.

"But now, throwest thou all reasons aside, Will, for there is only one cause on which I plead with thee to stay in London, one that outweighs all the gold in Solomon's mines. To be frank: I love thee, as I have never loved another, with a bounty as boundless as the sea. The more I give thee love, the more I have, seeming infinite. My life and all that is mine will I lay at thy foot, and when the time is right I'll follow thee throughout the world, but to be brief, for now, I beg thee stay."

O coz, what a blessed, blessed night was this, to hear her sweet utterances of love! But I fear that all of this may have been but a dream, too sweet to be substantial. Rosalind: my soul hears her and calls her name. Drunk with the words I had longed to hear (but also feared to hear), I could neither grant nor deny her wish. We made love and slept a deep sleep, abandoning ourselves at least for a night to Fate. Nor did I make her any promises the next morning, other than my love and earnest pledge to seek all counsel I could muster and try to do what God might bless. What more could I do? I can no longer imagine my life without her, but neither can I see the means to build a life with her. I purge my tortured soul by writing sonnets to her, though a thousand such cannot shed more light on which path I should take next. Thou knowest that Love is blind, but in league with Lust they consume all light and reason!

Out of reason, I drifted about the City the next morning, though I cannot honestly say where my feet conveyed me, finally somehow arriving at the Theatre, whereat our Company was commanded to gather at noon (not for our usual business of preparing a play, but for imagining our lives on the very different stage still to come). News abroad of a player's death in a tavern brawl fed the flames of City folk who would prefer us all burning in Hell, but Mr. Burbage reported that the playhouses were to stay open for now, for they serve the realm in another way: there do various gallants and agents for the crown recruit eager lads to fight the Spanish on land and by sea. They promise nothing more to these men than glory (or severe whipping if they stay at home), but they are to be given conduct money to buy their smock and travel to the mustering places, and are instructed to bring with them their long-bows (for what boy hath not learned the use thereof, since that time he could stand upright near his father's knee?) and arrows a'plenty will be provided.

But if thou hast thirty or forty shillings, thou canst buy thy way to safety: for 'tis only the poor, the hungry, the villains newly released from the clink, these are the stuff that England's armies will soon be made of; these are the sorts that players are valued no higher than. Such men may be blown over in battle as a hut made of reeds, but even a braver sort cannot choose but fall to the might of gunpowder. How many arrows must it take to kill a man, but I have heard tell the way a gun-shot rips through a chest or a neck, severing head from shoulder, turning the quick to the dead in the instant. In London there is talk of little else, stirring fear and ardour in equal measure.

Kempe began instructing the men on the arts of war in the muddy field before the Theatre, though few had the appetite to give him more than passing consideration. The pikemen, he foretold, will form around musket men, who themselves divide, such that one group is always firing whilst the other reloads. The place of honour, he says, is always to the right (though Lord knows why this is the custom). He then used Dick as a puppet to demonstrate:

"Give me the pike made of solid English ash, but hurl it not overhand, as those in Ireland are wont to do, but underhand, thus..." Dick's arm is no thicker than the pike, nor do I think he weighs as much, for the pike is twice as long as a man is tall. Dick pulled up his sleeve and stiffened his back, teetering somewhat as he balanced himself and his weapon. He swung the pike back and forth with such vigor I swear he would rip arm from shoulder, but when he let go, the weapon arched off to his left and fell at the feet of old Vernon, who retrieved the weapon and gave his own manner of instruction.

"Art daft? I served our late King in the siege at the Pas de Calais 'gainst the French devils. He had the better pikeman, I'll warrant, and we always threw the pike thus…" With that, the weathered old Vernon hefted the pike over his right shoulder as if it were a mere twig and, with a curling motion around his ear, flung the great lance high into the air with such force we barely saw it leave his hand ere we heard the crack of its tip pierce the wooden beam over the barn door. Vernon spat and grew a foot taller.

"Bravo, Vernon," quoth Mr. Burbage. "But now thou hast killed one man, or barn door, and have nothing to fight the next, save thy bare hands. I prefer peace in any wise, but if I must fight, give me your sword and buckler [shield] any day." There followed a riot of debate among the men, those who favored a pistol or musket, those who knew something of the lighter caliver and the means to reload more swiftly, those who gave short shrift to the old backsword and demonstrated the benefits of the double-edged rapier. The effect of these several actions, was that a Company of men, previously casting an eye to the ground and seeking any means to avoid such service, were now as rabid as any dog in the street and itching for war.

"Is there not some justice, that my rapier comes from Spain and may presently be employed to slay those selfsame dogs?" asked Mr. Pope, attacking in the general direction of King Arthur, the old jade retaliating with a sharp kick of the air. "Who hath taken my buckler? I would not enter a battle for all the world without it!"

Giddy adorns bucklers in his master's shop with family colours, some earned, some fantasy, but all designed to protect the user and strike pride in his fellows. I asked if a man may wear armour, the better to protect himself, but no man favors any more the wearing thereof. Those who can afford it say the English have lost the skill to make a goodly suit, while armours imported from abroad are prone to rust and are most ill-fitting, though I have lately seen many wear a helmet and visor, at least to protect their seat of reason.

Aye coz, if all the world's a stage, then all citizens of London are playing now in great scenes of war. I have no lust for war, but which man's blood stirs not upon seeing the mighty preparations, as in Deptford where I saw our ships, some two dozen, with an army of labourers (many of those masterless men who flood hither for employment) turning entire forests into men o'war [*warships*]. I witnessed there too many poor fools arriving daily to volunteer as sailors, before they were taken suddenly as soldiers, their reasoning that life in war is longer at sea than on land, but old Vernon sees it very differently, recalling what he learned from sailors on ships in those wars of long ago:

"Nay, your unseasoned boy ta'en to ship will soon be tough as nails or dead and tossed o'erboard. There can be no fair wind lest the new boys be whipped on Monday mornings and those that earned worse must be keel-raked or ducked at the yardarm." I have no idea what those punishments entail, but his description left little doubt as to the effect. Vernon warned us too of the little beer and dry biscuits rationed to each man aboard and how those victualers ashore were thieves and cutthroats, selling the crown only mouldy cheese and rancid butter, weevily biscuits and sour beer. Such a life will new recruits encounter and there is no chance of escape once at sea, whereas a soldier can run as far from danger as his legs will carry him, says Vernon.

With God's good grace I will only play a soldier or sailor for the two hours traffic of our stage. I am no coward, but would rather perish making the attempt to squeeze a Fortune from the land in Virginia than perish at the point of a Spanish sword in a fight our meager forces have small chance to win. Her Majesty had better marry a Catholic prince and end this strife than send her people to their doom. What cares God if we utter an Ave Maria in this church or that? If clergy wear this hat or that raiment of a Sunday?

There is more news, but my weary brain cannot commit more to paper as my light fades and my hand trembles from the cold air that will not keep his distance. Giddy is well and will show me tomorrow the strange beasts that are kept at the Tower. He says he hath seen four lions, a tiger, a cow with six legs, and a melancholy camel. For a small bribe to the keeper, we may see these and Dick swears there resides also thither a woman who measures no more than six thumbs high and a boy with the head of a pig.

Yet even as I think on such trifles, I cannot escape a certain pallor that hangs about my neck: I look in the mirror and see, staring back at me, a whoremaster living off the sweat of Anne in the fields and Rosalind hunched over a writing table. And surely I am foul-brained from the grief among our Company at the sudden death of our fellow. He was a good man among us, ever stern-faced but quickest to help he who stumbled on a line, or on the road of Life itself. He was a second father to Dick and therefore most courteous to me. Mr. Perkin delivered a eulogy that I have writ down for another such time, the words did so profoundly move me:

Fear no more the heat o' the sun,
Nor the furious winter's rages,
Thy worldly task hast done,
Home art gone and ta'en thy wages.

Care no more to clothe and eat,
For, as every golden lad and girl must,
Be they lord or chimney-sweep,
All will turn to dust.

Fear no more the frown o' the great,
For thou art past the tyrant's stroke,
And the sceptre, learning, physic,
Yea all of these illusions of power must,
One day turn to dust.

Fear no more the lightning flash,
Nor the all-dreaded thunderclap.
Fear not slander, nor no witchcraft's charm,
And to God we pray that nothing ill come near thee!

Now, only quiet consummation have:
And renowned be, at rest, in thy grave.

Mr. Perkin makes death sound welcome, a consummation devoutly to be wished. I hope it is so when my time comes. And does not Death lurk for me if I stay? Surely we will soon be sent to war. He lurks for me if I go to Virginia, for though I calm Rosalind and Giddy that the dangers are over-blown, I fear they are all too real and not so easily overcome. I will not act in desperate haste, but no decision has been cloudier in my three and twenty years, so I am resolved to answer it thusly: Miles Phillips told me of the man who can bring me to the two savages that have lived among us in London these past few years. I will learn of them the true ways of their people and the truth of those dangers that lay in Virginia, those that could prevent a man from finding his Fortune thither. If they give evidence that the dangers so outweigh the prize, then will I remain in London. If they offer welcome and courteous descriptions of their land and people, then with these intelligences will I arm myself and bravely cast my lot with Governor White.

In the mean season coz, I commit thee to God's good protection and ask that thou kiss my boy and maids in my name and omit nothing else which thine honour deem'st best for their tender need. I am thine everloving servant in all else, Will.

PS: Herewith the sonnet I have writ to Rosalind, for thine eyes only:

> When, in with Fortune and men's eyes,
> I all alone beweep mine outcast state,
> And trouble deal Heaven with my bootless cries,
> And look upon myself and curse my fate,
> Wishing me like to one more rich in hope;
> Featured like him who is with friends possess'd;
> Desiring this man's art and that man's scope,
> With what I most enjoy, contented least.
>
> Yet in these thoughts myself almost despising,
> Haply I think on thee, and then my state,
> Like to the lark at break of day arising
> From sullen earth, sings hymns at heaven's gate.
>
> For thy sweet love remember'd, such wealth brings,
> That then I scorn to change my state with kings.

LETTER THIRTEEN
April 25, 1588

Wherein the players prepare for battle with real canon and swords and find that leave-taking from your favorite city, or loved ones, is never simple.

Despite decades of foreign travel, London remains my favorite city in the world. There is always something to discover, something that had been there the last time you passed, but which earlier escaped your notice. I think that's how it was for Shakespeare as he walked around the city one last time, on the night before he and Leicester's Men marched off to war.

It is April of 1588 and war is about to come to England at last. Leicester's Men are ordered to lay down their masks and fifes, take up arms, and join the troops at Tilbury. Shakespeare describes their final day of preparation, including new uniforms tailored by his brother Giddy, and a session with Mr. Stow and Heather Burberry that prepares them with maps and information about the potential battlegrounds (which will turn out to be providentially useful). We see how Heather may be disabled of body, but is the sharpest intellect in the room and knows how to put her education to good use.

The men talk wistfully of things they will miss: Thomas Pope will miss food of the Court (which he takes with him after performances there, a sort of Elizabethan doggie bag) and Dick Cowley will miss his new wife (we are given a very brief description of their absurd wedding).

To quiet his own fears, Shakespeare writes this letter and describes his last day in London: seeing Queen Elizabeth's annual St. George's Day procession (a holiday commemorated each year on April 23rd by the Queen with a

315

grand procession through the streets "designed to show her mastery over all things on earth," so it must have felt especially festive to Shakespeare, given that his birthday fell on the same day); fighting a fire in the streets; and his sad leave-taking of Rosalind.

He reports a final walk around the city where he sees several of those hiding-in-plain-sight curiosities that have a way of enticing even a first-time visitor to think of returning soon to learn what's behind them. Staring into the waters of the Thames from high above on London Bridge, did his mind wonder about the flood that "rushes to the fearful wilderness of the sea with neither eyes nor senses to guide it," even as his fate now seemed to be carried along by similar great forces beyond his control? Did his gaze turn south to glimpse the night fires in the bear-baiting and brothel district of Southwark, where a few years later he would breathe life into *Hamlet* and *Julius Caesar* for the first time? Could he hear the rats cleaning up the day's refuse from around the great lodges and shops that lined the bridge (or did one run over his foot, like the one that ran over mine as I stood on that bridge one night four centuries later)?

With Shakespeare departing once more, Rosalind must again disguise herself as a man, in order to work as a water-carrier, lugging buckets of water up from the banks of the Thames, for a penny a trip. It is grueling, dangerous work, and though Shakespeare is filled with admiration for her fortitude and determination to survive, he is concerned for her. He laments that they are to be separated, just when things were looking up for his new profession. The Queen has reconciled with the Earl of Leicester, out of need for his soldiers and skill as a general, so Leicester's Men are again preferred at Court. The vain Earl of Southampton has bought more gloves to give as gifts to his noble friends, so Shakespeare and Giddy are sending money back to Stratford. Note how this is the first letter where Shakespeare consistently refers to the younger Burbage as "Richard" rather than 'Boy Burbage', suggesting that even their relationship may have been improving, as he admires the soaring skill of this young actor.

Shakespeare describes exquisite lovemaking with Rosalind on the night of his departure and her final sobs to him that "parting is such sweet sorrow" (which will later become the most oft-quoted line from *Romeo & Juliet*). He concludes the tale of his life until that point, saying to his son, "if it please God to end it here, I commit it to these musty pages for thine eyes in days to come."

Shakespeare's insomnia on this final night in London yields these fascinating descriptions and another poetic treasure. He writes a sonnet about longing and about an unquiet mind, saying it could equally be dedicated to Rosalind or London, knowing he will miss both. This sonnet appears in very similar form (as Sonnet 27) in the published collection of 1609 and lends yet further credence to the suspicion of many academics that he did not write them in the order presented in that publication.

As I discovered in later letters, Shakespeare repurposed a good deal of material, so when he was commissioned to write for a patron, he apparently recycled these sonnets as new works, even though they were the fruit of earlier times and genuine emotions. The fear and longing in Letter Thirteen are palpable examples of those original sources.

25 April 1588, London

Coz,

Such a deal of wonder is broken out this hour that ballad makers will not be able to express it in a lifetime. I mean, that when the sun next peeks his golden head above the clouds, I will be a soldier!

In brief, Leicester's Men are ordered to lay down masks and music, and replace them with sword and buckler. We march anon to Tilbury with thousands more under our Earl's command, thither to defend the realm from those Spanish ships that may disgorge their mighty armies upon our land. Nor could any one of us say nay, for Mr. Johnson notes every word and backward glance that may signify any disloyalty to Her Majesty and warns that swift Death awaits he who might abdicate his duty. But more of this hereafter.

I could not easily take my leave of London, so the last hours of this night I have wandered through her streets, noting the qualities of the people I leave behind, whereto I am like a drop of water in the ocean, one that meets another drop, worth neither more nor less. And like those drops, uncertain of my fate or purpose, I lose myself within the manners of the teeming City: peruse the traders and the bargainers; the beggars and those who pass them by; gaze upon the buildings and their inhabitants, all now equally stiff and weary from so many months in preparation for War.

Aye, as I see the relics of the City and satisfy mine eyes one last time with the memorials and the things of fame that do renown this place, I wonder if Spanish troops will soon set them all ablaze and melt London into the Thames? Will the wide arch of the English empire fall? For certain, war will come anon, coz, for those who prepare the soldiers, men and women in equal measure, are in such sweaty haste throughout the City that they make the night joint-labourer with the day; those who cast the cannons and sharpen the blades; those shipwrights whose sore task does not divide the Sunday from the week. Lord, 'tis a sight to behold: from the quick forge of pride and fear, London doth pour out her citizens in eager defense of the Realm!

Aye, all the youth of London are on fire, and silken garments lie disdained in the wardrobe. Instead, now thrive the armourers and only thoughts of honour reign in the breast of every man, as he sells the fruits of his pasture to buy a sword or lance. Everywhere sits Expectation in the air! Do the Spanish, advised by good intelligence of this most dreadful preparation, shake in fear? Nay, for though England is like the little body with a mighty heart, the Spanish King hath found out in her a nest of hollow Catholic bosoms, which he means to fill with treacherous crowns and hopes of glory, that they might rise up against their lawful Queen.

Nor could I sleep when I returned to my room, for anticipation pricks my mind awake and this disquiet yielded up these lines:

> Weary with toil, I haste me to my bed,
> The dear repose for limbs with labours tired;
> But then begins a journey in my head,
> To work my mind, when body's work's expired.
>
> For then my thoughts, from far where I abide,
> Intend a zealous pilgrimage to thee,
> And keep my drooping eyelids open wide,
> Looking on darkness which e'en the blind can see.
>
> Save that my soul's imaginary sight
> Presents thy shadow to my sightless view,
> Which, like a jewel hung in ghastly night,
> Makes black night beauteous and her old face new.
>
> Lo, thus: by day my limbs; by night my mind;
> For thee, and for myself, no quiet find.

On perusal, I see these lines may reveal my thoughts on Rosalind or on this wondrous City, for I shall miss them both when marching hence: the taste, smell and feel of each lingering with me from my several visits to them both this night. O would that the quarreling Men of Leicester were equally so, in common sentiment, made one! Instead, every matter now seems to ignite a quarrel. Yestermorn, when Giddy had finished the apparel that we shall boldly wear to meet the foe, Mr. Johnson, and his Puritan sensibilities in matters of fashion, called these new garments a waste of his Lordship's money, thus:

"We go brave in this apparel, that we may be taken for better men than we be; we use much bumbastings and quiltings to seem better formed, better shouldered, smaller waisted and fuller tight than we are. And we barb and shave often to seem younger than we are; we use perfumes both inward and outward to seem sweeter; corked shoes to seem taller."

"Thou need'st no new garment to look the part," quoth Mr. Pope, looking to the mirror to decide how best to wear his new cloak. "But my mis-shapen carcass must be better clothed, lest the enemy die only from laughter."

"Thou't perish sooner of hunger, you brave boys," quoth Mistress Burberry, who had so carefully packaged cakes, cheese, and savouries, fussing over each man as if he were her babe, setting Kempe's cap this way, Mr. Burbage's laces that way, spitting upon Cuthbert's palm and bidding him smooth his hair and to flick the crumbs from his beard. How fortunate are we that Mr. Stow is so liberal with his lodging and larder, giving leave to Mistress Burberry to tend to our needs so courteously.

Mr. Stow had insisted we gather in his great room, for there would he show us the many maps he has gathered, some drawn by his own good hand, of those places we might be called upon to defend. Surrounded by his books, shelved higher than three men are tall, light tiptoeing around their number, thither did we feel at home, as if the content of those volumes spoke to our enterprise and blessed its virtues.

"Here Mr. Johnson, thy button sewed back in his rightful place." Mr. Stow had been apprentice to a tailor in his youth and still possessed that skill. "Alas, I would go to war with thee, but though my fingers are yet nimble for sewing, the rest of these old sinews are not so useful." In these months that Mr. Stow has so graciously given me lodging, I have seen him age and grow more weary with the passing days. He is more than threescore years, long since stooped and gray, but his mind is ever playful and sturdy.

"Give me thy shirt for the laundry, for no man should go forth in such noble cause and company covered in yesternight's gravy." Mistress Burberry almost tore the shirt from Kempe's back with her scowl, whose amazed protests availed him nothing and he quickly found himself standing in the center of the room wearing no more than his hose and cap. "Aye, complain as thou wilt, but I'll be sworn, all ye rogues shall miss a clean shirt and a full belly when neither is close by."

"Tis true, Mistress, and I shall miss the Court, for thither are we fed in one day enough to last a man till Doomsday." Mr. Pope had filled his purse with cheese and smoked fish, when we lately played for the Queen at White Hall, and has just finished eating the same a week since.

As I have writ to thee, our Earl was censored by the Queen, but Mr. Perkin foretold aright: she would not stay long at odds with Leicester, for such a loyal Lord, with armies levied, will surely soon be needed against the Spanish. And here must I digress to describe that day at White Hall, for therein live many lessons more:

The Queen had called for us to play Gorboduc, but we almost missed the time, the boatmen having great difficulty rowing our barge against the tide and those spring rains that had so swollen the river to many times higher and more swift than is customary. Our snail's pace gave Mr. Perkin leisure to show me some sights he thought meet for me to comprehend.

"Look - - the Temple there was once home to the Knights Templar, famous of crusaders against heathens, and is where Gorboduc first was played in the earliest days of Her Majesty's reign." He pointed to the stone walls of a great house on the north bank and another he named as Whitefriars. We passed the great glittering windows of the Savoy, where he said Lord Burghley holds court to rival any prince in Christendom. "And imagine the great Cardinal Woolsey in times of old, peering from those same windows as mighty Henry's barge drifted by."

But Mr. Perkin also used this leisure to show me the south bank, which provides a story of another kind. There, the houses are propped up with posts, lest with people jostling by, they should tumble down. There, the faces are covered in mud. There, the dogs eat better than many a man, and beggars outnumber those in honest labor.

Once at White Hall, we had little time to prepare, the Thames having won the battle against our timely arrival, but I soon learned the wisdom of the Queen's choice on the day when every man and woman of dignity was in attendance on her and when thousands lined the avenue whereupon her procession would soon pass.

"Goooor-bow-duck!" quoth Master Pope, as if he called out the name of a prize hog. "Ah well, he comes not! I can scarce recall if I play Ferrex or Porridge.[98] Why craves Her Majesty such ancient fare?" To which, Mr. Burbage replied:

"Why indeed. She hath great need of 'e pluribus unum' to defend her kingdom 'gainst Her Spanish foe. Think merely on the meaning of the dumbshow." By this he meant that six wild men enter, clothed in leaves, the first bearing on his back a bundle of small sticks, which these men, both severally and together, will attempt with all their strengths to break, but fail in their attempts. Then one plucks out a lone stick and breaks it easily, then plucks out all the other sticks, one after another, and so easily breaks these, showing that any state, knit in unity, doth continue strong against all force, but being divided, is easily destroyed.

For an instant, I wondered if Master Burbage meant the lesson for the kingdom or our troop of players. In either wise, I see now the power of the play and, no less, the role of a spectacle: for so well does our Queen know how to make her entrance! She arrived in procession, having addressed her loyal subjects along the way, the better to awe them with her Majesty and spur them to her defense. She seemed to glide above the bounds of earth, following those noblemen who bear her Sword of State, her great cloak trailing behind in attendance as if she pulled along the whole of her kingdom, the spectators along her path kneeling in honour, just like a great wave is humbled at the shore. For how many of her subjects was this their only glimpse, to see Her Majesty eye to eye? One fool even shouted 'O Lord, the Queen is a woman!'

I learn from this too that she is a better player than any in our Company, for the spectacle was planned to show her royal mastery over all things on earth. There were oddly shaped beasts and men disguised as savages, or like Irishmen with hair hanging wildly down to their girdles, tamed as the Queen passed by them. Horses equipped like elephants, pulled fantastical carriages, while others seemed to convey themselves. Out of these came servants in pompous attire, who addressed the Queen in ludicrous speech, making her and her ladies laugh, before they presented her with costly gifts in the name of their lords.

Inside the vast hall, although his players are again preferred at Court, it was not the Earl of Leicester who sat next to the Queen (nor was he seated within the first three on her left or her right), but the crude and knavish Henry Wriothesly, the boy-Earl of Southampton. Like his peers, he holds sway over large areas of her kingdom and thus does her ability to call upon the many, to sacrifice in time of war, depend on his fealty and good will.

"Let all here assembled know that we declare this day an honour to Henry Southampton and make him our Master of Revels for these pleasant hours, here to signify what entertainment we shall see," quoth Her Majesty, as all bowed and curtsied, waiting for her to prop a cushion on her embroidered couch and slowly settle in (though Lord knows what architect taught her how to build a pyramid of gown a'top a thimble of pillow, yet look swan-graceful in the doing of it!). "Shall we hear petitions, quiddities and quillets?"[99]

"Nothing so dull, your Majesty," replied the bright boy quickly with a broad grin, straightening himself from a bow, where I swear his golden locks had swept the ground 'neath the Queen's slippers. "As I am not admitted to Gray's until tomorrow, I may not practice in law before my betters give me leave." I'll be forsworn if any other Englishman was made a member of Gray's Inn before his sixteenth birthday, lest he was a favorite of the Queen.

"Why Henry, I have never heard thee speak of 'betters' in thy life!" When the Queen quips, the Court laughs, but this time they needed no prompting for I suspect they heartily agreed with her about the preening, pompous boy before them now. "Do but plead for thy client; a foretaste of thy hoped-for oratory." Southampton needed no further urging, but tossed his cloak to one side, as if he might now begin a duel, and strutted about the hall.

"But your Majesty, do tell me which of these many miscreants I must defend." He put a hand gently to the cheek of the Earl of Essex. "This fellow for his action of battery upon reciting the poetry of Ovid?" He had struck a nerve and Essex's face turned red with anger, as the faces of his peers grew red from laughter. The Queen almost choked on the sweet she had tucked in her mouth. He was a player who knew his stage and commanded the beholders, fixing next his gaze on Mr. Hatton.

"Nay, nothing so base, but I WILL defend this fellow, who might be in his time a great buyer of land, with his statutes, his recognizances, his fines, his double vouchers, his recoveries: for this is a client who can afford my fees!" With that, he kissed the Chancellor full on the lips, a jest that seemed almost sensuous given the fragile features of the boy, his cascade of golden hair, and the womanly adornments on yards of silk that enveloped his body. He twirled back around to face the Queen and bowed with a flourish.

At length, the young man became a boy again, accepting the Queen's offer and using his authority over the Revels to call for a light entertainment before the play, something that might make the clouds of war part for a time. Something with a dog, says he, and a jig by Will Kempe. I marveled for a moment of this strange pageant against the backdrop of a kingdom about to be invaded, a nest of whispering vipers, choosing sides in case Spain wins, and a boy demanding of his monarch to see a jest with a mongrel and a bawdy dance.

Mr. Pope speaks often of his old black dog, which he called simply 'Hound', and of their many performances together; of how oft they were asked to do another trick or double leap or lover's kiss or some other feat that rubbed up great mirth from any assembly. But since Hound died, Mr. Pope employed another trick. He carried with him some scraps of dried meat and used them to entice any dog nearby to be his puppet. This day, he kneeled upon the stage and whistled for Her Majesty's spaniel. When it came, he rubbed a piece of meat, which was secretly in his hand, over his face before feeding it to the dog unseen.

"Where hast thou been, Codpiece, you old cur." The dog began licking Mr. Pope's face eagerly as the whole Court roared. "Nay, nay, thou cans't shower me with thy kisses, but I'll not soon forget the trouble thou hast caused me!" Mr. Pope was then in full command of the spaniel, holding his ears wide apart and staring nose to nose at the beast. "What, no reply?"

The Queen kept one eye on the comedy unfolding, but her weather eye scanning every corner of the great hall, as if taking inventory of who laughed; who used the distraction to press an advantage with another; which lord was pinching which lady's arse. But mine own survey found that every person there (save Mr. Johnson, who was in earnest parlay apart with the Queen's own secretary Walsingham), was watching Mr. Pope, for now he used his antic limbs to rise up on one knee and unhinge the other leg, such that it lofted high in the air like a dog pissing.

"And furthermore, did I not bid thee be a good lad and do everything in manners EXACTLY as I do? Huh? HUH? Then when didst thou see me heave my leg and make water against the Queen's farthingale? Didst thou ever see me do such a trick?!"

It may have been the unrestrained laughter of all present or he may truly have been unimpressed, but in either wise, Southampton scowled and slithered to a place between the Queen and the stage, as if his boy's body could draw a curtain on the player and the dog, who had resumed licking each other's face to still more general chuffs and snorting, including from Her Majesty.

"As your Master of Revels for this day, your Majesty, I offer this most humble apology for this crude display of low humour and will have this scoundrel whipped from the chamber for his affront. The dog may be spared, for he is your royal servant and stands in station above this brutish player."

"I'llllllll seeeee theeee whip't from this chamber, ere I let a hand be raised to this fellow who hath so charmed my hound - - and us - - that I will now thank him for his pains with this purse…" the Queen rose and brushed aside the boy-Earl as she held out her hand to Mr. Pope. "And with this kiss." With that, she gracefully handed him the pouch of gold and kissed him most tenderly on the cheek.

The Earl was taken so completely by surprise, he knew not whether to weep or slink away. I could imagine what Mr. Pope was thinking at this moment: he always asked to play the roles of kings and lords, but his shape and gait did not allow it. In a town where we once played short-handed, owing to illness in our ranks, Mr. Burbage relented and Mr. Pope played King Solomon. Instead of awe, the spectators laughed, thinking the matter a great comedy. Mr. Pope never again sought to play those parts, but now it was his famous antic lazzi that commanded respect of the highest in the land. And here I witnessed first-hand how this Queen keeps her friends and enemies in her orbit, come what may. She turned, touched Southampton's elbow, as if lifting his body and spirits at once, and drew his hand to Mr. Pope's.

"And for thy dazzling cleverness to call for this entertainment, I thank thee and will dine with no other tonight but thee. Now I bid thee embrace thy players as brothers and plan some graver entertainment for another day. For this day, we are mightily pleased and fulsome." What could the Earl say to such generosity and diplomacy? He took Mr. Pope's hand and nodded in his general direction as the Court applauded politely, gentle fingers against palms covered in gloves.

So it is, for both the food and the acclamations hyperbolical, that Mr. Pope declared to us all how he will miss the Court, but he is likewise joyous that he will soon be reunited with his brother, who writes that his troop is being sent to Tilbury to join with ours.[100] As others of the Company donned their martial garments, a military demeanour seemed to overcome us, all save Kempe, who groped around the room looking for any drape he might use to cover his nakedness while his shirt was slowly restored to its native hue of white. Chests puffed and Mr. Pope marched in a comic military gait around the great table that Giddy now used to spread out cloaks and kerchiefs and those other garments still in need of his art. Then suddenly, Richard Burbage, burst in upon our tailor's workshop and declared to all:

"I care naught for these weeds of war, lest they be worn on a stage, playing the war-like Hieronimo." He and Cuthbert had been sent to spy on the Lord Admiral's new play, called 'A Spanish Tragedy'. The wind blew ill for our Company from thither, as they would then report to our several demands:

"What hast thou seen?"

"Hath the play pleased the multitude or the learned?"

"Seats full or no? Groundlings?"

"I will not varnish the truth lads." Cuthbert wasted few words, especially when sober. "Tamburlaine has a rival, which signifies we, therefore, have two!" Richard swept aside Giddy's fabrics as a broom sweeps clean the floor, leapt upon the table as a stage, and began quoting from the play those words that must have filled the English hearts in the playhouse with pride and lust for war:

"Fear no enemy, my countrymen! Remember how it was that English Robert, Earl of Gloucester, arrived with five and twenty thousand men in Portingale [*Portugal*], and, by success of war, enforced their king - - look you, who was then but a heathen! - - to bear the yoke of the English monarchy! Aye, by such deeds was Portingale enforced to bear our yoke, enforced by little England!"

"Show them the ghost brother." Cuthbert's eyes grew larger as he recalled some matter in the play, then turning to our fellows he whispered: "The play begins with a ghostly figure, manifest as if in life, reporting in fine particulars the passage into Hell, such that the multitude could not but think he had truly made the journey thither!"

"Aye, thus it was." Richard assumed the demeanour of an old Spanish nobleman, freshly slain in battle, and spake thus: "When...I was...SLAIN...my soul descended straight to pass the flowing stream of Acheron, where from the ferryman of Hell I sought a passport for my wandering ghost."

Richard knelt on the table facing Cuthbert and drew him closer, taking on a deep commanding voice. "This knight both lived and died in love; and for his love, he lost both love and life."

Richard then pivoted on's knee to face me and drew me closer, throwing back his head and shaking his hair and speaking with a lilting voice of a child. "Why then, convey him hence to walk with lovers in everlasting Time under green myrtle trees and cypress shades."

Pushing me aside, next didst Richard grab his father's collar, taking on yet a new demeanour and the voice of a stern schoolmaster: "No, no! It were not well with LOVING souls to place a WARRIOR!"

Rising again to his full height in the middle of the table (filthy shoes on a red cloak that lay there, to Giddy's great discomfort), Richard struck once more the pose of the Spanish lord and resumed his Castilian accent: "To this effect my passport straight was drawn and so began my journey. Through dreadful shades of ever-glooming night I saw more sights than a thousand tongues can tell or pens can write. Three ways there were: to the right, the foresaid fields where lovers live in peace; on the left, declining fearfully, a ready downfall to the deepest Hell, where bloody Furies did shake their whips of steel and turn an endless wheel; where usurers are choked with melting gold and wantons are embraced with ugly snakes; where murderers groan with never-killing wounds and perjurers are scalded in boiling lead; and where all foul sins, with grave torments, are overwhelmed. Twixt these two ways I trod the middle path and no sooner found myself here, in this theatre, I know not how, in the twinkling of an eye."

For a moment, every one of us were stunned to silence, first from the awful description of the path to Hell itself, but more from the several personages who had just then commanded the center of the room, personified by one player only. Richard looked no more than twice or thrice at his notes, and never once left his ghost fumbling for words. Kempe broke the spell with a great fart, and from the men, restored to their usual senses, applause ensued.

"If I survive this war, surely I would soon be playing the equal of those parts to rival Alleyn and earn back our customers to the Theatre."

"Thou art young still," quoth Mr. Burbage. "All in time."

"Eh? Ned Alleyn is but two and twenty and hath long since shown that a goodly player can command," quoth Mr. Johnson. "Thou'rt now near that age, a'nt so Richard?"

"Aye, twenty one this January past." Richard blocked the path of his father. "And long ready for such roles."

Truly, though he vex me still, Richard Burbage is now filled out as a man and can declaim with the best I have seen. He knows that I add some value to the Company, abating his spleen somewhat when I am by, but still he omits no opportunity to impress upon his father any error I might commit, even as he offends mine ear with his insults (though his inventory thereof is meager and he oft repeats). But Richard spoke true. Tamburlaine had stolen playgoers from the Theatre and now the Spanish Tragedy will take more, with double effect: men and boys feeling patriotic, leaving the performance, are easy marks for those who recruit soldiers to swell the ranks.

How many of them will bravely go to war, but how many will live to see the likes of these plays on a stage ever again? Cuthbert must have heard my thoughts, for he said the like:

"And look you, did not mighty cheers go upward when the Spaniard in the play declared that his king will bestow on every soldier who fights for his land two ducats, and on every leader ten? The recruiters had a good turnout this day, the lusty youths hoping that England will dispense an equal largesse for those who fight 'gainst Spain."

But coz, I think that many a man can speak the lines: the spell was cast by he who WROTE the lines, by Thomas Kyd, who knew the mob wanted to see England's enemies brought low, needed to recall the greatness of our heroes past. Aye coz, the play's the thing.

"Owwww!! Thou'lt bleed me dry before the Spanish sword has the chance to cut, take more care Gilbert!" Giddy hath not come to care for Kempe as I do. I swear he takes every opportunity to 'accidentally' prick the man with his needle at these times of accoutering.

"Pardon, pardon, I am in haste. My master allows me these hours to complete thy garments gratis, but I'll warrant the colour of his generosity will fade if I am too much longer at it." Giddy persevered with stitching the hem. The soldier's weeds will stop neither arrows nor bullets, but I swear when we are all alike accoutered, the men stand taller and the quarreling abates somewhat. To divert Kempe's attention from the blood drops that now stained the cuff of his newly laundered shirt, Giddy asked "What will thy heart miss when 'tis gone from London, Mr. Kempe?"

"I'll tell thee what I will NOT miss: this war, be it however so bloody, let this war end the great folly that divides our nation, divides the globe itself." Kempe hesitated, yet we all knew he had more to say. Tears welled in his eyes. None of us had seen this man of infinite jest in such a state of woe. "In our own Company we stand divided by the same cross, do we not? I'll not be accused of heresy by one side or the other, so hear the words of Tamburlaine: 'how can there be such deceit in Christians?' Aye, Tamburlaine speaks the truth. So much preaching of mercy, of kindness, of forgiveness, of love, but practice of feckless war and wantoness. Have I not lost a mother and a father to the false hope of Christian charity? Have I not seen my sister and a hundred helpless women like her despoiled by men who absolve their sins at church with an utterance or two and a penny in the box?"

Tamburlaine has been so popular that Marlowe was compelled to deliver a second part, newly staged at the Curtain and drawing thousands, but we all hold our breath to see if it will be closed (and Marlowe hanged) for his play's views on faith. I think he has little to fear, for when Tamburlaine burns Mahomet's bible, he does what many more would do.

"Hang me if you will, but seeing how many die, how many are yet to be sacrificed on this altar, I count religion but a childish toy and hold there is no sin but ignorance.[101] 'Tis superstition to stand so strictly on faith that dispenses forgiveness in exchange for human life and dignity." Kempe pushed Giddy away, a sleeve dangling by a thread like a broken wing, and wept his way out of the room.

I cannot find fault with his opinion, to be rightly said. But I hold my tongue and fear for my friend when he does not hold his. Nightly at the Mermaid, he is made bold by Kit Marlowe, who proclaims these and many more such sentiments that will likely be his undoing. I have taken to joining them, to protect my friend and to learn Marlowe's secrets of how he ensnares an audience with his speeches, and all the Court with his poetry. We are not so different: he is mine age; the son of a cordwainer [*shoemaker*], who served his town council; we both have reddish hair, wear our beard thin, and clothe ourselves plainly. He will not lie with women and declares Jesus' love of John gives any man leave to love boys: in that we are very different.

Marlowe lodges with Thomas Kyd, he who gave birth to this astonishing Spanish Tragedy, but they are mirror opposites. From him I can learn yet greater feats of oratorical magic. I have also lately grown fond of Kyd: he is older by no more than six years, but his temperament reminds me of Mr. Perkin, choosing his words wisely and slow to quarrel, at least until he knows your argument better than you. He is the son of a London scrivener and trained for a life in law, though like me, he could not afford university. High-stomached are they both, and full of ire, in rage deaf as the sea, hasty as a fire, but Kyd calls Marlowe 'most intemperate and of cruel heart' and rejects his monstrous opinions about monarchy and religion. Some nights have I spent as judge of their fiery debates and, in recompense, both men are most liberal in sharing the secrets of the poet's art (Kit says I will sell my soul one day to awake the dead upon a stage).

Together we attended Pandosto by the Lord Strange's Men, a strange tale of the King of Bohemia who thinks his wife guilty of adultery and there follows a twisted tale of happiness dashed by woe. Kyd thinks it a mere trifle of a play, although Marlowe defends Greene, his university fellow who wrote the matter, and points out its merits. I asked why it lacked some humour, to relieve the furious tensions created by death and suicide and love and loss, but Greene warns me about wearing the writer's feathers with no training, as he and Marlowe have had. Together we have also seen Lord Strange's Men play Edmund Ironside and I swear I could write better, with no training more, while overcome with drink riding a horse backwards.

Dick had been absent from our tailoring, lately finding any excuse to be apart from masters Johnson and Pope, those he fears slew Mr. Clarke, or abetted them that did, but he quickly made his arrival a drama. I report this for it speaks much about our Company:

'Fire!'

'Fire!' quoth he. No sooner here than gone, bidding us all to follow. Fire has been a constant companion to London in times past, but rooftops newly planked with stone, as demanded by the Lord Mayor, have something abated this danger. Dick led us across Lime Street to where smoke could be seen from a window above, several women in furious labor with a few buckets, in battle with some blaze within that had ignited from a misplaced rush candle.

Our men wasted not a minute, but took up the buckets and a large buck basket, wherein Kempe cleverly fashioned sheets to make it hold water, and formed a line with the women to carry water from the conduit straight into the house. As if we had rehearsed our parts and knew every move of the dumbshow, water moved from conduit to Kempe, he to me, me to Cowley, he to Mr. Burbage, he to Cuthbert, he to Richard, he to Mr. Johnson who had taken charge of it all. Rushes on the floor, no doubt for many years unchanged, mixed with urine, spittal, bread crusts, and mud, were quickly being consumed by the greedy flames. Giddy and Mistress Burberry used the buckets to fill the basket and so the little fire was quickly trodden out; which, being suffered, rivers would not have quenched it. Lately we saw, amongst the basket makers, a great and sudden fire happen in the night, which within the space of three hours consumed more than a dozen houses and nine persons were burnt to their death.

Like that dumbshow in Gorboduc, any one stick would have broken under the weight of this task, but bundled together in common purpose they could not be severed nor defeated. We were soon returned to Mr. Stow's side of the street, but this sudden strength of common purpose cheered the men greatly. Or perhaps it was merely some modest measure of comfort, the night before we marched to war, to fight this tiny battle we knew we could win. The drama ended, we were quickly busy again with our graver labours. For instance, Cuthbert scrutinized the patents, wherein our Company was granted the necessaries to prepare for our roles as warriors, and announced his discovery:

"The Earl's factor hath shorted us in the cloth we were meant to have for this livery, I'll be sworn. And he hath stopped half the payment due, damn his eyes!"

"Thou wilt be relieved of such tedium when fitted out as a soldier. Sayest what thou wilt miss when we are hence." I would know more of him, for lately he hath shown me several kindnesses and he never speaks without urging.

"Hmmm … my bowl of tobacco and a good Rhenish to end the day. I doubt it not, but that these comforts will be in short supply wheresoever we are sent to our doom." I could not have dreamt a reply more suited to this man. He hath read my few poems and given me to read the Art of Rhetorique, wherein a young man is sweetly persuaded to marry and multiply. This he bid me read, so that I might sharpen the arguments in the scenes I write for our Company, for he says 'rhetoric was first made by wise men, and not wise men by rhetoric.' I have no idea what he means, nor have I had leisure yet to read this volume entirely, but his gracious urging that I should write some weighty speeches, such as those we hear of Tamburlaine or Heironimo, which might be spoken in various plays by Richard, would shine upon our Company and mend some ties twixt me and his brother. I will do so, for Tilney has given us a few scenes in his possession from an old play about our late King Henry, the fifth of that name, and bid our Company to build a play thereon that might stir the many to patriotic fervor in this time of war.

"I'll miss my wife and go now to her to spend a last night together," quoth Dick who had finished his task to sharpen those same swords and pikes we use on stage, ordered to somehow transform illusion into reality, and even now had returned them to the men. He fears a Spanish soldier will not so easily be fooled as a groundling gawking at our scenes, a sentiment shared by us all as we examined our once-familiar implements and imagine them covered in real blood, not some trick of our craft.

Aye, Dick hath married his Beth at last, many of our Company present, though not as he had imagined on the eve of Christmas. I will tell thee the particulars when next we meet, for the tale can scarce be believed, but in brief, their nuptials found him wearing her father's best doublet, almost twice as large as himself; she wore Dick's best silk gown, that which he wears when playing noble women, far too small for herself; a French pasty eaten by a badger whilst the vicar sneezed so uncontrollably that he could scarce say amen; and a rusty nail that may yet be lodged in Cuthbert's buttocks.

"Mr. Burbage, shall I show you now those particulars I have gleaned from my maps and books?" Mr. Stow, for two-month and more, has looked to no other matter than our furnishing, such that we might be all in ready for this marching-off day that hangs nigh over us now. We gathered around his broad table, warped like the swelling sea, covered in maps and sketches he had made. Shoulder to shoulder in this manner, I was struck by how the men of Leicester were now so few: Masters Burbage, Johnson, Perkin, Kempe and Pope; the Burbage brothers; Cowley; and me. But what needs Spanish buckshot of more clowns or tragedians than this?

"Thou knowest well enough the byways to reach Tilbury," Mr. Stow's finger skipped across the map of those regions to the east of London along the Thames. "But look you here: whence the great river empties into the sea, on either side is naught but fen and low lands full of pestilence and mud. The Spanish force needs must venture another mile upriver to find solid dirt on which to make a good landing. Here is a sweet creek on the north bank, which will be of great import to the invader, for he cannot drink the briney waters of the Thames and cannot long survive without fresh water. Here will he set his troops and think to march on London."

March on London. Mine imagination had seen the City in flames, but now every man of us looked at the other, as if to confirm what we had just heard. Aye, the enemy was truly coming.

"How would the Spaniard know there is sweet water thither?" Mr. Perkin, who had been absent thus far, and none of us knowing why or wherefore, came in at that moment and, like a bully boy arriving late to sermon, who doffs his cap and wipes his shoes on the back of his hose as if to expunge his guilt, then takes he straightaway the empty chair near the door and nods to Mr. Burbage to continue.

"That will I show thee," quoth Mistress Burberry, balancing, by some magic, a large volume on her serviceable foot, tilting it on the table's edge from her awkward angle below, then butting it with her forehead to rest by the map. She mounted her stool to climb upon the table and kneeled before the book, the old leather binding crackling as she opened it to a page marked with a long stem of rosemary. "Look you here: in the reign of our late King Henry, this Spanish monk recorded all manner of observation and intelligence about our English countryside and people. He writes about the stream by Tilbury, but not the marshlands."

Mr. Burbage moved to her side of the table, the better to view the page she poked upon with her toe, pecking at it like a crow opening a walnut. She saw that he could read no Latin, so she read the passage aloud and gave the translation in our English, mine own facility with Latin being enough to know she reported this most perfectly. Mr. Stow returned our attention to his map:

"Thanks be to thee Heather," quoth he. I notice how she can finish his sentences and how he will defer to her in most matters. I suspect he is in love with her, though she may hesitate to embark on another marriage after the constraints and disappointments of her first. "Now just here are low hills, all sand and therefore hard to cross for armoured men on horse and those dragging canon or such like. But here, where the creek is wide and gravel, here can man or horse cross easily and proceed north for half a league or so, then west to the London road. I have been there and drawn these few amendments to the map and pray you perfectly heed: if a man comes not at least half a league north before he makes westerly, he shall fall into the most foul bog that ever the Devil placed on God's earth. Thither shall he sink and thither shall he perish."

"Then must our English forces, however so strong or meagre they be, stand fast and entice the Spaniards to march closer to the north bank of the Thames - - here - - and into that perilous swamp." Mr. Perkin at once grasped the advantageous importance of the local knowledge that Mr. Stow had given us. He stroked the moles on his cheek and sucked his unlit pipe, as if to infuse them both with the firm memory of this map.

"And let no recusant traitor warn the enemy of that danger," quoth Mr. Johnson, who lately has made no secret that he trusts not Mr. Perkin.

"If I were the Spanish general, I would merely sail past this landing and make direct for London!" Richard tut-tutted in Mr. Stow's direction, even as he threw aside the new smock that Giddy had just handed him.

"Then would you find your ships ablaze from those defending the shores from either side, fool." Cuthbert said what every other man was thinking. Giddy sniggered and Richard would have boxed him on the ear had he been a yard closer.

"Silence!" Mr. Burbage leaned over the table, hovering a few inches above the map, one eye squinting through Mr. Stow's spectacles to devour each notation and landmark. "Lord knows ye are all men of good will. And only He knows the dangers we will face in these times to come. But lads, we are certain to fall apart if we COMMENCE apart: let us take an oath now that all past insults are here laid to rest. Our Queen's cause is just."

"That's more than we know." Mr. Perkin spoke rhetorically, or so I took it, but who can say for certain, given he tends to the old faith.

"Ay, or more than we should try to know," quoth Mr. Johnson tartly. "For we know enough, if we know we are the Queen's subjects: if her cause be wrong, our obedience to our Queen wipes the crime of it out of us."

"But if the cause be not good, the Queen herself has a heavy reckoning to make." Mr. Perkin would not let the matter alone. "When all those legs and arms and heads, chopped off in battle, shall join together at the latter day and cry all 'We died for Her in battle 'gainst a Christian monarch.' Some swearing, some crying for a surgeon, some upon their wives left poor behind them, some upon the debts they owe, some upon their children rawly left. I am afeard there are few who die well, that die in a battle: for how can they charitably dispose of any thing, when blood is their argument? Now, if these men do not die well, it will be a black matter for the Queen that led them to it."[102]

"So, if a son that is by his father sent about merchandise do sinfully miscarry upon the sea, the imputation of his wickedness, by thy rule, should be imposed upon his father that sent him," quoth Mr. Johnson, always quick to defend Her Majesty (as what spy for a monarch would not?). "Or if a servant, under his master's command transporting a sum of money, be assailed by robbers and die in many irreconciled iniquities, you may call the business of the master the author of the servant's damnation. But this is not so! The Queen is not bound to answer the particular endings of her soldiers, the father of his son, nor the master of his servant; for they PURPOSE not their death, when they engage their services. Besides, there is no Queen or King, be their cause ever so spotless, who can try it out with unspotted soldiers only. Some, peradventure, have on them the guilt of sins unforgiven, as they enter the fray. Then if they die unprovided, no more is the Queen guilty of their damnation than she was guilty before of those impieties. Every subject's DUTY is the Queen's; but every subject's SOUL is his own. Therefore, should every soldier in the wars do as every sick man does in his bed: wash every mote out of his conscience, and if he then die, death is to him a passage into Heaven."

"'Tis certain, every man that dies ill, the ill rests upon his own head, the Queen is not to answer it." Mr. Burbage had let his friend prosecute the case, for he had spoken nobly to the very point he had tried to pursue.

"And though I do not desire she should answer for me, yet I determine to fight lustily for HER, but not for her church." Kempe pounded his chest, for emphasis or to scare Giddy off from aiming yet another needle in his direction.

"Well settled," quoth Mr. Pope, though the matter was far from settled and Mr. Perkin had meant to reply, but rather shook his head and busied himself instead with his pipe. "I shall miss the hissing iron in the buff ale of the Mermaid; the willing wench, e'en for a broken sod like me. Now, for the love of Life and her soft remaining hours, let's not confound the time with conference harsh: there's not a minute that our lives should lengthen without some pleasure in it now. What sport tonight?" Mr. Pope needed no more urging to lead us to the Mermaid.

When my turn came to speak of things to be fondly remembered, I could not utter that which knocked already at the doorway of my heart, though Giddy and Kempe knew the sickness was rightly named Rosalind. Our fittings complete and all such other necessaries packed up, we took our several leaves for one last night in the City, one last night to enjoy those selfsame pleasures we had even now recounted to each other. I hurried to Rosalind and could swear I smelled her honeyed fragrance on the wind that blew from the Thames, a freshness that sweeps away all ill-humours from the mind, in like manner as enough of its water will wash away the dirt from unclean hands.

And yet it is this same great river that even now severely pricks my conscience: to aid in our sustenance, Rosalind hath donned again her manly weeds, this time to work as a water carrier, hauling three gallon tankards from Belins Gate to lodgings near the Royal Exchange for a penny each trip, no mean feat without spilling, jostled by wagons and carriages and porters who sweat under their own burdens, as if they leapfrog from one shop to another. In Cornhill ward is a water standard, placed thither by a certain German named Peter Morris, having an artificial forcier that conveys Thames water in pipes of lead into divers men's houses in Thames street, New Fish street, and Grasse street, even up to the north-west corner of Leaden hall, the highest ground of all the City, plentifully serving to the commodity of the inhabitants near adjoining in their houses, and also cleansing the channels of Bishopsgate and Aldgate. This device is jealously guarded for use only by those who pay the German, but clever in all things, Rosalind soon learned of a well with a pump west of Aldgate whereat she paid the boys thither a farthing [*quarterpenny*] to pump full her tankards and one more to help with her load, doubling her profit on the increase in traffic. No one is ever without means to earn a few pennies in London, if your back be strong enough to carry water or small coals, but we dream still of our Fortune in the New World when this war has passed (if God wills that either of us should live so long), on fresh accounts of a land to the south of Virginia called St. Augustine, where Captain Drake has again looted Spanish shipping to great profit. Throughout the City lately, one Walter Bigges is showing a new map he has painted of these lands, which prove again how enriched any man will be who adventures it. Although these lands belong now to Spain, he claims the fort thither was guarded only by a lone Frenchman playing a fife, who liberally parted with two thousand pounds of gold to him!

Our estate has the while been sturdy enough: mine earnings with the Company grow steadily and those gloves that Kempe gave so courteously to the Earl of Southampton have proved a wise investment. Two dozen more were sold in as many days to his friends at Court, but thou knowest that most of this money was needs sent back to Stratford and little spare to succor a London household with a mistress. O, but there is no corner of Heaven so welcome, so light, so fulsome and hopeful, than the bed I share with her, the drunken vapour of roses in her hair nestled on my chest.

"Didst see the sky this night?" She feared what she beheld, and though I would not fright her more, 'tis true that but an hour since, the sky was so was full of fiery shapes and colours, it strangely drove clamorous dogs and frighted goats from the fields around the Theatre in through City gates. But I played it bravely:

"I fear not such auguries. Nature a'times breaks forth in strange eruptions or, as I have been told, the earth herself is pinched with a kind of colic, vexed by imprisoning unruly wind within her womb, and she thereby shakes the old-man earth."

"Thou art so fine to me, my love, and always will be so." Her tears showed my brave words persuaded not. Instead we clung to our last hour and begged God to lengthen it by a minute, a second, so much as one breath more.

"See'st thou the light through yonder window? It is the moon, but thou, my dearest, shine brighter than moon or sun, for thine eyes are two of the fairest stars in all the heaven, and our love will ever burn hotter, I swear. Will that fire twinkle in thine eyes till that I am returned?"

"Ay me! O Will, I am a prisoner to thy love, yet would not escape if I could. I am like a tiny songbird, who hops but a little from the hand of its mistress before she plucks it back again with a silken thread. Nor would I have it otherwise, my dearest love. I know thou canst not deny thy Anne nor refuse thy duty, but I would mortgage all I will ever own to have a life with thee."

"The exchange of thy love's faithful vow for mine?"[103]

"I gave thee mine before thou didst request it." Without a prompter, we lingered now over each kiss, that in the past would have been greedily taken, and given, for knowing an endless supply of lips-to-lips would follow. But this night, we knew each kiss was numbered and would not waste, nor forget, even one. I will ever recall her breath on my neck; her breast swelling in my palm; her sweet fingers, rough from so much rude labour, guiding me between her legs. O coz, at night, desire sees best of all and in that moment, 'twas Rosalind who became the poet:

"Fondling, since I have hemmed thee here within mine ivory pale, I'll be a park and thou shalt be my stag; feed where thou wilt, on mountain or in dale: graze on my lips; and if those hills be dry, stray lower, where the pleasant fountains lie."

I have never tasted a woman as she bid me do. Salted honey, straight from a quivering blossom in the fullness of summer, the likes of which defies compare. Such sweet and high delightful plain, round rising hillocks, where secrets hide in places obscure and rough. I roamed and ventured as she commanded, but when I might have had relief, she bid me be still, no sound, no motion, not even to breathe. O coz, an oven that is stopped, or river stayed, burns hotter, swells with more rage, till it can wait no more!

We lay a final hour in silence, clinging as many parts of our bodies, each to the other, as we could. I found my breath matching hers, but I tried to inhale her sweet exhalations, that I might take some corporeal part of her with me, and so, if God wills us never more to meet, that my last breath on this earth would still be entwined with hers.

When time came that I needs must depart, she gave me a small bundle of cakes she said contained herbs and were soaked in a plum sauce that would make it sweeter, the better to remind me of our nights together, but mostly for the vigour it gives the body when consumed.

"Good night, good night, my dearest." She looked away that I might not see the tears in her eyes, but there was no concealing her sobs. "Parting is such sweet sorrow when lovers know they will meet again, but such agony when Fate is cruel and obscures their future."

"Aye, my sweet Rosalind. Sleep dwell upon thine eyes, peace in thy breast, and dream of that moment when we shall next meet. Until then, sweet, my love resides with thee."

I bid her sleep, but I could not then do the like, for so much uncertainty addles my brain and refuses to allow my lids to drape mine eyes in peace. The New World seems now so far away, but lately seem my prospects, closer to home, so much the brighter: the sale of gloves; more money for mending plays and for greater parts onstage as my skills improve. A chief steward for Lord Pembroke's Men, Houndslee I think he is called, praised my mending of 'Henry V' at Court and bid me bring more such works to him, the which he would pay me handsomely, he says, and Lord Leicester is so often out of favour that I should stay no more in his Company, he says, if I know what is good for me.[104] Mr. Burbage trusts him not and I can find no other who speaks well of him, so I will none of it, but the offer had a certain ring to it of future prospects. Alas, prospects cannot mend my shoes, the holes in which are villainous on streets where mud cannot be told from dung on a rainy day, which in this spring time is no less than seven days in the week.

Dear coz, how has it come to this? I had better stayed in Stratford and turned dirt for a living than end up dead in service to the kingdom, for are not kingdoms nothing more than dirt? If I die, whereto then? Heaven? Hell? To lie in cold obstruction and to rot? This sensible warm body becomes naught but a clod of earth, while the spirit wanders in fiery floods or is buffeted by invisible winds. 'Tis too horrible to consider! Nay, the weariest and most loathed worldly life is a paradise compared to what may follow after death.

Hamnet: thus ends the drowsy tale of thy father's life till now, which, if it please God to end it here, I commit it to these pages for thine eyes in days to come.

John: I hope this finds thee in good health and spirit, and trust that naught in these pages hath too much offended, so thus I commit thee to God's good protection and ask that thou kiss my boy and maids in my name and omit nothing else which thine honour deem'st best for their tender need.

If I am slain, if we never meet in this life more, know that I am thine ever-loving servant in all else, Will.

LETTER FOURTEEN
September 15, 1588

Wherein Spain invades England so the players must march to Tilbury, where some are made ghosts, but one spirit walks again among the living.

My best subject at Brisbane State High School in Australia (class of 1969) was history. I won the Senior History Prize (a book about the 19th century Prussian General Otto von Bismarck) and spent hours debating my professor, Harry Atwell, about the accuracy of history itself. How can you trust the depiction of events as told by the victors in a war? How can you differentiate perpetrators from victims if the historian chooses to tell certain parts of a story, but omits others? The old saw, "those who don't learn from history are doomed to repeat it," would be useful if we really knew what, and whose, version of history to study.

Letter Fourteen summons up such questions because it contains not only Shakespeare's perspective on pivotal historical events, but also those of a foreign ambassador and others who remained in London when he and his fellow players marched off to war. Taken together, will these sources, newly illuminated by the letters, add to the generally accepted view of the forces that shaped this period (and ultimately our modern world) or will they further obscure the truth? Will they add at least a few more tiles to a distant mosaic or be dismissed as one man's biased views?

It is September of 1588 and four months have passed since Shakespeare left London. He has returned from war to find Rosalind heavy with their child and suffering from an unknown malady. In Shakespeare's absence, Heather Burberry has been tending Rosalind at Mr. Stow's house. Shakespeare sells the map he stole in order to buy medicine for her. Touchingly, he writes this letter sitting beside an unconscious Rosalind, hoping that she and their unborn child will hear of the events that changed the course of history and returned Shakespeare to them unharmed.

Shakespeare augments his own first-person account of the war with Spain from a report of the events at sea and in neighboring countries as provided to him by a foreign diplomat. Emanuel van Meteren was a trade representative in London for the Low Countries (the Netherlands, Belgium, and parts of what today are France and Germany). He wrote extensive accounts of trading enterprises and histories in Dutch, German, French, and English. His reports were also transcribed by others, so it was not clear from Shakespeare's account if he spoke to van Meteren (who lived across the street from Mr. Stow) or was given a written version. Either way, I was able to find van Meteren's full report to his masters and used it to augment the gaps and errors in Shakespeare's account.

But were those "gaps and errors" intentional? Was Shakespeare trying to color the record in some way based on his own bias? Knowing that John Combe would read the letter and likely share the news with others in Stratford, was he using his power as a historical narrator to make England look like a more noble and competent victor, blessed by God, or was it meant to cast his own actions in a more favorable light? We may never know, but as you read the riveting tale of sea-going heroism and strategy, see if you can decipher the biases of Shakespeare and van Meteren. I have inserted a few notes along the way of my own observations, which I hope are helpful.

Shakespeare's company was among thousands sent to Tilbury, where the Thames opens to the sea, to protect London should any of the Spanish fleet (the "Armada invincible" as King Philip of Spain called it) come ashore (Illustration 18 on page 341 shows the key points of engagement between Spanish and English ships).

Leicester's Men camp in the rain, keeping watch for any fire signaling that the Spaniards are nearby. The players are shocked when Clarke, whom they thought murdered, appears in their midst. Perkin explains that Clarke was recruited by the Queen's officers to pose as a Catholic, in order to better spy on the Spanish. Clarke faithfully executed his duties, even to his own peril, and was

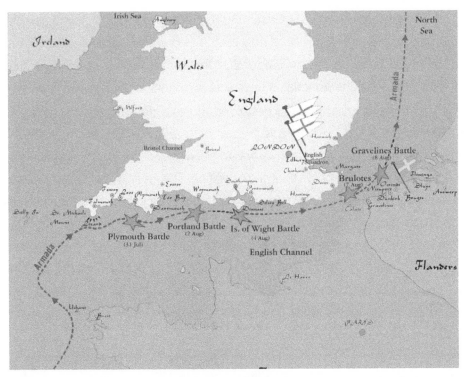

18. *Key points of engagement between warships as described in Letter Fourteen when Spain invaded England in 1588.*

suspected as a traitor by Will Johnson, an ardent Protestant in Leicester's Men and someone his fellow players suspect is a spy for the crown. In order to keep Clarke's identity secret and avoid exposing him to his unsuspecting Spanish contacts, Perkin and Clarke conspired to fake Clarke's death in the tavern brawl of Letter Twelve. The ruse no longer needed, they are all reunited in common defense of the realm.

Shakespeare admits to feeling a certain pride in being one of Leicester's Men, as the Earl is in charge of the English defenses on land, mustering the troops at Tilbury with the rousing words "Once more into the breach dear friends, once more; or close up the wall with our English dead!" These lines clearly made an impact on Shakespeare: he uses it almost word-for-word in *Henry V* (Act III, scene 1), possibly because he knew how many men heard and reported it that day and may have intentionally wanted audiences to recall such patriotic fervor when they saw his play.

Shakespeare then sees Queen Elizabeth come to Tilbury to encourage the troops, although at the time they couldn't know the war at sea had been decided (Illustration 19, below, is a painting that shows the Queen at Tilbury and the fiery defeat of the Armada, in the crescent formation the letter describes).

With the Spanish Armada destroyed at sea, English troops disperse. It is harvest time, and every man is needed back at home. Left behind as lookouts, Shakespeare and his fellows are horrified to see five hundred Spaniards come ashore in small boats near their position. They quickly conspire to delay these troops, while sending a messenger to alert Leicester's forces before he disperses them. The players pose as local Catholic sympathizers to convince the Spanish to detour around local towns because of the Plague. They quickly fashion coffins from their trunks (filled with rocks and dirt to mimic the weight of bodies) and beg for appropriate clothing from nearby townspeople to create a convincing scene. Dick Cowley dresses the part of a weeping woman,

19. Queen Elizabeth at Tilbury addressing the troops with the Spanish "Armada invincible" burning behind her in their distinctive crescent formation.

mourning her husband dead of Plague. They assume the posture of a funeral procession and wait to be discovered.

A scouting party of twenty Spanish soldiers (and a Catholic priest) finds them, and speaks in Spanish to Clarke, who resumes his ruse as a Catholic spy for Spain. Shakespeare acts the part of a priest, mumbling the Latin prayers he learned at home as a boy. Convinced of their loyalty to the Catholic faith, the Spanish Captain asks to know the best course towards London, so Master Burbage shows him the map given them by Mr. Stow. They entreat the Captain to avoid towns infected with Plague and encourage him to march his troops towards London via another direction, which the players secretly know veers into a marshland described by Stow, though not shown on any map. The procession continues to a funeral pyre, which Leicester's Men intend as a signal fire, in case anyone from the English army is still on watch (England had established a sophisticated network of signal fires across the southeast, so that whenever the Armada was first sighted, the news would travel in minutes to troops positioned around the country and all the way to London).

When the entire Spanish force departs, the players believe their ruse has worked, but they are discovered by the suspicious Spanish priest and one soldier, who remained behind to further spy on them. In the ensuing skirmish, Perkin is wounded in a manner similar to that suffered by Mercutio in *Romeo & Juliet* (Act III. Scene 1). In fact, this tragic event became a lasting memory for Shakespeare, as he uses some of the things spoken by Perkin, as he lay dying in Shakespeare's lap, in that same scene of the play.

Perkin urges Shakespeare to renounce dreams of acting, and instead hone his skill at writing plays: "Aye Will, the play's the thing." He also reveals that John Whitgift, Archbishop of Canterbury, the highest-ranking clergyman of the Church in England, has meddled in Shakespeare family affairs. He is someone who becomes an unexpected force in Shakespeare's life, described in future letters.

The company marches homeward with the priest and soldier as prisoners. Of the five hundred Spanish soldiers the players directed towards the bog, only about thirty emerged and were taken prisoner by Leicester's troops. This is the only recorded landing of Spanish troops on English soil during the famous

Armada battle of 1588. Whatever the truth of these events, they must have bonded Shakespeare and his "band of brothers" tightly together. This is the first letter where he drops "master" when referring to the senior members of the Company.

Upon his return to London, Shakespeare learns that after being celebrated by Queen Elizabeth for his victory, Leicester died mysteriously two days later, complaining of stomach pains and leaving Queen Elizabeth inconsolable in her grief. Was his triumphant march into London, as if he were the king, too much for Elizabeth's loyalists who had him poisoned? Was he hoping to be elevated somehow to the monarchy, or simply proud of his nation's salvation? Winston Churchill said "History will be kind to me, for I intend to write it." Sadly for Robert Dudley, the Earl of Leicester, he left that task to others and, as a result, in reading various accounts from the time, we are left hanging between those two alternate possibilities.

Joyful that England is spared, and his enemy the Earl is at long last dead, Shakespeare is understandably concerned that he now lacks an employer. He nervously awaits word about whether the theatre company will be dissolved and worries about how he will care for Rosalind. He tells us about possible commissions to write plays and determines to use his experience of mending plays for any theatre company that will give him the money he needs to support his families in Stratford and London.

One final point about writing history and who gets the last word. My father was a U.S. Marine in World War II, serving in some of the bloodiest battles in the Pacific. Like so many veterans of that era, he spoke little of his experience and we only learned the details after his death, when my sister, Laurie, found a trunk in the attic with his uniform, an unfinished diary, and other historical treasures.

Laurie became our family historian, gleaning information from books and the accounts of others who had fought in the same battles. Knowing of her interest, one of these aging veterans sent her an audiotape of interviews conducted by a radio reporter among Marines in the Pacific, to give those at home a general idea of what they were doing and thinking. The interviews, each under two minutes, were indeed slices of warriors' lives, each adding a thread to a growing tapestry of our knowledge. About six segments into the tape, a young Marine's voice crackled from the speaker and across the decades: it was our Dad.

The interview was short and provided just a few more details of life on a battle-scarred island, but history came alive for Laurie and me that day. It may have contributed to my lifelong fascination with learning about the past. It certainly proved to me that the more you dig, the more you will find.

Letter Fourteen makes the same point as it concludes with poetry written to Rosalind and their unborn child, another example of a sonnet he later adapted for other purposes and was ultimately published as Sonnet 115. It puts that sonnet in an entirely different context, knowing who were the original subjects, and reminds us that the unwritten history can illuminate the written stories in some very unexpected ways.

15 September 1588, once more in London

Coz,

God grant my hopes may yet have fair birth: this summer, when hope was lean and despair abundant, I saw great miracles performed, though not first without great sacrifice. Now, such a miracle or sacrifice, I would most dearly beg God to grant for my Rosalind.

I pen these lines beside the couch whereon my Rosalind lies in pain. She hears me at times, but is other times asleep or incapable [*unconscious*]. I am returned from the wars to find her heavy with child, but afflicted with ailments unknown to physician or midwife. God bless Heather Burberry, who hath taken her in, with gracious leave of Mr. Stow, in mine absence, and cared for her life and fate. More of this will I convey to thee hereafter, but now I recite for Rosalind those events which have kept me from her these four months and kept me from knowing we are soon to have a child (which should be a most joyous and happy tiding, but Lord knows thou and my Stratford family may not think as much). And may God forgive me, but I would not pray to spare all the children in Christendom, if it meant losing the life of my sweet Rosalind.

But to the matter: enterprises of great pitch and moment, which currents turned awry in ways that no man could have foreseen. I will write them down, as I recite every particular to Rosalind, and will omit no item of what I have learned upon my return to London that augments mine own otherwise imperfect knowledge of these events. If I offend, by repeating that which thou dost know, or know better, forgive my feeble endeavor.

First, thou knowest it was in the final days of April when we marched from hither, among the many processions of brave youth boldly off to war. It were best to weigh the enemy more mighty than he seems, but hot blood overruled cold policy, as one brave lad on the march boasted:

"I'd rather be at a breakfast devouring mine enemies than a dinner of friends."

"Aye, and in my dreams I have mustered our armies, wherewith proud Spain is already humbled and overrun!" quoth another. And I heard a round shopkeep along the way whispering to his wife, each waving white kerchiefs as if to blow the common 'huzzahs' forward for the brave soldiers:

"Lord, protect these poor soldiers, who are constrained to march in darkness, damp and cold, when we are sleeping upon quiet beds."

"Aye, good husband, and many will come to march no more."

I wondered how many more, who cheered us on to war, went to the safety of their bed at home and thanked God that they were not among us. There were those who loudly proclaimed their love of the Queen and her righteous cause; there were those who doubted her wisdom for upbraiding the power of Rome and Spain at once; still others who loved her only because she descended from commoners like themselves.[105] But be they for or against this war, few were glad to pay the taxes levied by their Queen to pay for it, which caused this debate among our Company:

"Let every man pay his tax and remember his duty: the wealthy can afford it," quoth Johnson, loud enough that the aggrieved man nearby might hear him well. "The poor prove themselves thrifty, and therefore they can draw from that which they have saved, to save their Queen and country!"

"Spoken like a constrained soldier, whose only comfort is that he need pay no tax!" quoth Pope, loud enough that all might share the jest. Laughter on this march was dear, and when it came, it smelled of the man who upbraids his executioner, there being no remedy else. Thereto was a measure of suspicion afoot: it was said the Queen feared Catholics who might rise up to succor Spanish troops, but in equal measure those Puritans who would make all men equal in the eyes of God. Therefore, every man with pike on's shoulder or steel on's girdle knew the man next to him might harbor one of those sentiments, or a thousand others, that might render him unfaithful when bullets fly and blood is spilt.

More of our Company's parts, in the playhouse of War, I shall describe hereafter, but those matters precedent, which I now report, came to me from Mr. Stow's neighbor in Lime Street, he whose lodging we saved from burning the day before our march, an honourable Dutch emissary to the Court of some repute and good intelligence, called Emanuel Van Meteren. He gave us this account to complete our otherwise imperfect knowledge:

The Spanish King was not solely aggravated by the English refusal to return obediently to the church of Rome, but also sought to recover complete possession of the Low Countries, who were aided in their revolt by Her Majesty in the person of Lord Leicester's forces. Therefore this "King Catholic" thought it good first to invade England, being persuaded by divers Spaniards and Dutchmen, and by many English fugitives to the bosom of Rome, that the conquest of an island was less difficult than the conquest of Holland.

The King then gave commandment that a great quantity of timber should be felled for the building of ships; and great preparation of furniture requisite for such an expedition; storing up corn and victuals and mustering of soldiers, insomuch that by the beginning of this year, he had a mighty navy brought into Lisbon. Scarce was there any family of account throughout all Spain that had not a brother, son or kinsman in that fleet, all of them in good hope to purchase unto themselves in that "Armada invincible" (as they termed it, using their Spanish word meaning 'armed') endless glory, and to possess great land and riches in England.

The ships were huge and incredible to behold: 64 galleons, being of huge bigness and very stately, built so high that they resembled great castles, most fit to defend themselves and to withstand any assault, the timbers four or five foot in thickness, insomuch that no bullets could pierce them. Greater yet, the galleys, built quite similar in stature and sail, but also rowed with great oars, there being in each one of them three hundred slaves for that purpose, furnished and beautified with trumpets, streamers, banners, warlike ensigns, and other such like ornaments.

In all, the ships appertaining to this Armada amounted to 150; mariners above 8,000; slaves 2,088; soldiers 20,000; the great canons counted 1600, the bullets thereto belonging were 120,000; gun-powder 5600 quintals [560,000 pounds]; muskets 7,000. They had in like sort great store of mules and horses and whatsoever else was requisite for a land army. They were so well stored of biscuit, that for the space of half a year, they might allow each person in the whole Armada half a quintal [50 pounds] every month.[106] *Likewise of wine they had 147,000 pipes [barrels]; bacon 6,500 quintals; cheese 3,000 quintals. Besides fish, rice, beans, peas, oil, vinegar, they carried 12,000 pipes of fresh water and all other necessary provision, as namely candles, lanterns, lamps, sails, hemp, ox-hides, and lead to stop holes that should be made with the battery of gunshot. To be short, they brought all things expedient for an Armada by sea or for an army by land, esteemed by the King himself to cost every day 30,000 ducats. The ocean groaned under the weight.*

Heather hath now joined us, most courteously providing Rosalind some healthful potions, although from the coughing and contorted face, I know not whether these medicines will serve. Kempe helped me sell my map of the New World to a salt-fishmonger, who thinks he can sell it for even more, no doubt to some rustic new to the City. I am damned for the theft and damned twice for saying I would repay old Westerbeke and failing to do so, but I had no other thing of value for money to buy these medicines of that same physician who helped me cure from scurvy. What little I had saved was consumed in provisioning as a soldier, most especially after our rations grew scarce month by month and we were forced to find what we could in the nearby towns. Thank God for Kempe, who hath been such a comfort in these times. His practice in his youth, among women who were oft conceiving and sick in childbirth, that many times brought them back to health with potions and care he learned from the bawds. Some good may have come from his enforced labours therewith. O coz, I would return to battle and die thither, if it would extend her life but a day. I am fearful of her illness, for her and the baby. For now, I can do little but wait and pray, so in welcome distraction, I give thee further of the Ambassador's report:

The general of this mighty Armada was the Duke of Medina Sidonia, Lord of San Lucar, and Knight of the Golden Fleece. The portrait of this mighty Duke shows a slender man, modest in earthly possessions, whose broad bald pate overflows cold eyes that never blink or look away and seem to say 'I will win by serving my King with more ruthless persecution of the Inquisition and fealty to our Catholic faith than any man alive.'

If indeed he had such thoughts, he was no braggart, for the Inquisition sent with his forces a Vicar General accompanied by more than a hundred monks and friars, those being Jesuits or Capuchins, feared for their absence of pity if a man's eyes divert from the Holy Roman path. These monks forbid gambling and swearing onboard the ships, nor was it lawful for any man, under grievous penalty, to carry any women or harlots in the Armada, although the women themselves hired certain ships, wherein they sailed after the Navy (perhaps God favoured the Jesuits: driven by a great tempest, those ships were forced onto the coast of France, which is a nation of harlots, so no one took much heed of them thither, but neither did they make mischief with the sailors).

And while the Spaniards were furnishing this Armada, the Duke of Parma and Governor of the Spanish Netherlands, made great preparation in the Low Countries to give them aid and assistance.[107] *This Duke assembled an army of Italians, Walloons, Scots, and Burgundians, along with bands of English fugitives, and built ships of war for the same purpose. He put in the ballast of these ships a great store of beams of thick planks, beset with iron clasps and hooks,* which in a short space might be joined together to form a bridge that might cross the Thames.

Adding to these two generals, Pope Sixtus Quintus published a Cruzado with most ample indulgences, which were printed in great numbers to be spread through all of England and the Low Countries.[108] In it he bestows the realm of England upon the King of Spain, giving him charge to invade upon this condition: that he should enjoy the conquered realm as a vassal unto the See of Rome. To this purpose, the Pope proffered a million of gold, the one half thereof to be paid in ready money, and the other half when the realm of England be subdued. The excommunications of the Queen by two former popes were also therein confirmed, so that any man or woman, whosoever struck down the life of the 'heretic Queen', would himself or herself be assured most merciful God's pardon and glorious welcome into Heaven.

But to England's great good fortune, Her Majesty's father had built docks for a navy and goodly ships to stand at all times in ready, to which she now added more, as fast as her own great forests of oak could sacrifice their treasure. In all, the number, ready now for sea, was about a hundred: the Ark Royal, Elizabeth Jonas, Elizabeth Bonaventure, and the like. The lesser ships being thirty or forty in number known as Triumph, Revenge, Stalwart and such.

This English fleet was given to the conduct of the right honourable Lord Charles Howard, Lord High Admiral of England, a man who needs no further description, his fame long since established, his honour and dignity surpassed at Court only by Her Majesty's. He was, to be certain, a capable general to manage and support so great an enterprise, but it was his vice-admiral who would give birth to an English victory, or die in the attempt. I mean it was the renowned knight, Sir Francis Drake, who assured the Queen that 'the matter with Duke Medina will be resolved ere long and he will quickly wish himself back in Andalusia wandering among his orange trees with his grand babies.' Nor was Drake a braggart in saying so, for he had most famously defeated Spanish ships in Cadiz and elsewhere, which deeds, aye his name alone, struck fear in Spain, such that they call him El Draque, the Dragon.[109]

Johnson thinks that Drake's theft of Spanish gold is the real reason King Philip built and sent the invading Armada.

I mark now that Rosalind is sleeping most peacefully, either the tonic given her by Heather is easing her discomfort or the distemper of late summer heat that clings still to the whole of London, has, with the setting of the sun, abated enough to break her sweat. In either wise, we are alone again and I will keep a hand on her belly, the better to feel the baby squirm, as oft it does, and one hand on my pen, these next lines to read to her when she wakes.

As these great forces were raised, one to be hurled against the other, the chest of each Admiral puffed in martial display meant in some wise to fright the other's forces, our Company with some two hundred others made haste for Tilbury, thither to defend the entrance to London where the Thames opens to the sea and the Armada might set ashore their armies. Great fortifications were there constructed under the watchful command of our own Earl of Leicester.

The roads along the way were familiar, yet not so. Our Company had trod these byways to towns where we performed our plays, but the unusual purpose of this adventure caused me to see common sights anew. In Barking, newly-washed clothes hung from the market cross, as was ever so, but now various flags and insignia, meant to inspire the brave, flew above it all. People once spat upon the vagabonds as they rotted in the stocks beneath, cruel garters for cruel men, but now all were set free upon their pledge to swell the ranks going off to war, no doubt more cannon fodder for the front row.

We camped near Tilbury on the sweet creek, shown to us by Mr. Stow, and waited. Daily we kept watch for the beacon fire in the hills to the nor'east and sent our messenger to neighbor camps for new instruction. We waited a week, then another, then another. Rains could not cool our ardour; maggots in our food could not weaken our resolve; rumours that London was already under siege could not persuade us that God was not on our side. But aimless days and long nights of waiting dulled our spirits as surely as the little stream, with constant flow, will soon wear rocks into sand. We waited and looked in vain for the signal that the Armada was nigh. Yet was our boredom shattered by lights brighter and hotter than any signal fire, for it was the eve of Ascension and, fittingly, the dead arose.[110]

It had become our custom to sup by the fire of two neighbor regiments. Complaints about food are more easily laughed to scorn in company, it seems. Dick ate not, but flitted from man to man asking each of us to examine his neck, whereon he supposed a great boil to reside, which he thought would soon be his death. I heard him shriek and thought someone had confirmed this suspicion, which otherwise would have faded, as light from the setting sun, if no one lent the matter credence. But this time Dick's cry was not concerning an imagined affliction: it signified the sight of a very true ghost.

Into our encampment strode George Bryan and Augustine Phillips, our two fellows who had long since joined Leicester's troops and who had sent word of their imminent reunion with us. But with them was the ghost who gave us all such a fright: I mean Thomas Clarke, he who was killed by the knife in the tavern sixmonth since.

"Friends, well met. What news?" Perkin spoke as if Clarke had but ventured forth an hour earlier to fetch a pail of water. Each of us fell upon them as starving men devouring the fruits of the first tree encountered, celebrating and plucking at their coats to confirm that the bounty was real before devouring it entirely. Dick fell away, fainting or stumbling as he would flee the ghost, but there was no time to restore him his wits.

"The French king has signified unto Her Majesty, in the most plain and urgent terms, that she should stand upon her guard, because he was now most certainly informed, that there was so dangerous an invasion imminent upon her realm, that he feared not all her land and sea-forces would be sufficient to withstand it." Clarke spoke in his familiar commanding style, quietly that every man must silence his chatter and still his movement, lest the matter be lost. Only the crackling of the fire and a few birds, taking now their nightly roost, dared make utterance. I remembered his regal crown of silver hair, but now it appeared pure white and his face more aged than his forty years, though certainly in better health than the dead man we all assumed him to be. Our Company gathered now apart to hear the urgent matters our fellows brought from London and to know how Clarke's ascension came to pass. Dick revived and wept for joy to see his master again among the quick.

It was Perkin who explained the matter thus: we all knew of Clarke's adherence to the old faith, the cause of much hot dispute and great distraction among ourselves, but he had always pledged his loyalty to the Queen. To prove as much, he was recruited to spy on other Catholics and learn which among them were not to be trusted in time of war, at a moment of choosing. In this endeavor, he began exchanging talk and letters with the Spanish ambassador, who thought Clarke to be his agent and someone who could travel the country unsuspected, rallying those who would rise up for King Philip and for Rome when Spanish boots stepped on English soil.

In time, Johnson discovered him out, nor could any reason prevent him from sounding the alarm with London authorities. If he was exposed and could prove his loyalty, the Spanish ambassador would know he had been fooled and Clarke would no longer have his confidence, even as the dogs of war barked louder. If he could not persuade hot-headed loyals that he was an Englishman first and a churchman only thereafter, he would be executed for plotting against the Crown. The only way to protect the ruse and save Clarke's life was to use his skill as a player to make one and all think he was dead. This he could not achieve alone, but he dared not take our Company into his confidence: half would not believe him and all would risk their own lives if they too were suspected of plotting, like the ill-fated fellows who aided Babington in his terrible plot to kill her Majesty. But one of our number had the remedy.

"I beg forgiveness for the manner in which I have deceived, dissembled, and distracted," quoth Perkin, and turning to Johnson he says "and I must most humbly beg thy forgiveness, Will, for encouraging our fellows to think thou wast a spy for Her Majesty and not to be trusted with any confidences, for I was that agent of the crown, not thee. I enticed Thomas to his deeds in service to the Queen."

Perkin then took pains to describe every particular, omitting nothing that favoured or fouled him: how he was recruited by his brother to serve the Queen (for who would stir the least suspicion in every town and tavern than a company of players?); how he let others think him a Catholic that he might better gain confidences and gather news; and how he tricked Johnson and Cowley to attend Clarke on the night he was stabbed, or so they thought, that they might honestly attest to his death and so protect his true mission. When he was finished and every man satisfied, though some still smarting from the enforced deception, we pressed Clarke for news of the Armada.

"Aye, 'tis a mighty fleet, but ships are merely boards and the Spanish ships are not well manned. Their mariners are muleteers, slaves and other people ingrossed by swift impress. In our fleet are those that have already fought many times 'gainst Spainish galleons. Our ships are yare; theirs, heavy and slow; but their army is fearful. We must therefore fight them at sea: there can England achieve a great victory."

"But is not their fleet far greater in number than ours?" Johnson, no longer thought a spy, was ever questioning and thereby knew much about these matters, always at the ready to share his opinions, and dismiss any in contradiction. "Whereas our army is ripe and seasoned for this fight on land, war-mark'd soldiers having fought in the Low Countries ere this, like Phillips and Bryan here. We dare not leave unused the renowned knowledge of our commanders and quite forego the defense of our land to chance, instead to hazard all upon the seas, far from firm security."

"Nay, Will, think on't. Lord Leicester has failed more than once to turn back the Spanish mercenaries on land, but Admiral Drake has over and again singed the Spanish beard with the canons of his nimble ships. Nay, 'tis certain we'll fight at sea, but if we fail, we can still test our skill, and luck, on land."

"Trust to rotten planks tossed upon uncaring waves and blown hither and yon by fickle winds?" Phillips joined the fray, as each man tested the weight of arguments on either side of the scale. "Do you misdoubt this sword and these my scars earned in those battles you would so quickly dismiss? Let the Spanish go a-ducking; we English have used to conquer, standing on the earth, and fighting foot to foot, since the time of King Henry in France."

"I'll tell thee what: Her Majesty, but two days since, gave command for the fleet to sail for Plymouth, there the better to intercept the Armada coming north," quoth Clarke. "And she gave a most hearty speech, saying that Britain is a world by itself; and we will nothing pay for wearing our own noses. The natural bravery of our isle, ribbed and fenced with rocks unscalable and waters roaring, our enemies' boats will be sucked up to their topmasts."

"By merciful Jesus, I think he's in the right," quoth Cuthbert, although I could not swear whose argument he favoured. "But it matters little, for mere soldiers are we, and this whole action will be decided by our betters." Cuthbert is ever so practical and, since no man could argue that logic, we turned to other matters of the joyous reunion and what had passed since last we supped together. In doing so, our weevily bread and mouldy cheese became a feast that no castle's larder could have made the sweeter.

Come what may, all stood ready. On land, throughout the whole realm, soldiers were mustered and trained in all places, committed unto the most resolute and faithful captains. And whereas it was commonly given out that the Spaniard, having once united himself with the Duke of Parma's army, meant to invade by the River Thames, there was with us at Tilbury a mighty army encamped, and on both sides of the river fortifications bravely manned. Likewise there were certain ships brought to make a bridge to unify our forces and put our strength wherever it was most urgently needed when the battles began.

I will admit to thee coz, it was a good time to be a Leicester's man, although thou knowest my good and many reasons to wish the Earl ill. He was in command of all the puissance our kingdom had mustered, so what must I believe, but that God puts aside all other reckonings in time of war? Seeing the fleet sail down the Thames past our Tilbury perch, toward victory or death, we swelled with pride, made bolder still by Leicester's words, which he delivered with pomp and ceremony befitting a monarch (not a servant of one, as many soon noted that day):

"Once more unto the breach, dear friends, or close the wall up with our English dead!" Leicester rode a pitch black mare, brushed Welsh style for a more martial appearance, himself decorated with the highest starched ruff and collar I have seen (though that is his usual practice: I take it he means to make his neck appear longer and his body taller than other men he thinks beneath his station).[111] We knew him to be worn and tired from exertions in the Low Country wars, his lean patrician visage turning slowly gray and soft, sweating in the summer sun from heavy chain mail 'neath his embroidered doublet, I suppose a necessary precaution against his ever-present enemies. But today he pursed his lips, arched his left brow disdainfully and held out his chin, as if to dare any foe, foreign or domestic, to strike him, and described as much in his further oration thus:

"In Peace, there's nothing so becomes a man as modest stillness and humility, but when the blast of war blows in our ears, then should we imitate the action of the tiger: stiffen the sinews, summon up the blood, disguise fair Nature with hard-favour'd rage. On, on, you noblest English, whose blood is got from fathers that have, in defense of this island, so many times before schooled the enemy in bloody war. For there is not one of you so mean and base that hath not noble lustre in your eyes today. I see you stand like greyhounds in the slips, straining upon the start. Aye lads, the game's afoot! Follow your spirit, and upon this charge cry God for Elizabeth, England, and Saint George!"

Even his mare high-stepped boldly, in time to the martial tune played loudly by the Earl's musicians, as if the dirt was unworthy of her hooves on this day of days. Mistake me not: I hate the man and cannot reconcile his many honours and offices with the despicable treatment of my family. But he gives every Englishman hope, not only for victory over an invader, but that a man once humbled, may one day rise to be treated like a king.[112]

Yet whatsoever his failings as a general ere this, the Earl had secured some allies for Her Majesty even so. Holland and Zeeland made preparation to defend themselves, but because the Spanish ships were so huge, they fortified all their sea-towns with strong garrisons and kept such diligent watch over the few deep channels, so that the Duke of Parma could not meet the Armada nor issue forth with his boats full of soldiers out to sea. These things we learned from Van Meteren, after God had long decided the matter, to whose further account I now return and convey the necessaries unto thee:

The Spanish Armada set sail upon the 19th of May out of Lisbon under the conduct of the fore-mentioned Duke of Medina Sidonia. As they were sailing along, there arose such a mighty tempest, that the whole fleet was dispersed, eight had their masts blown overboard and three galleys were dashed upon the coast of France. There, by the assistance and courage of one David Gwin, an English captive whom the French and Turkish slaves aided in the same enterprise, utterly disabled and vanquished these ships, with the slaughter of their governors and soldiers, and so these slaves set themselves at liberty.

The Spaniards licked their wounds, repaired their vessels and refreshed themselves at a friendly French port. Receiving daily commandment from their King to hasten their journey, on the 11th day of July they hoisted sail and thereto a great banner flying high over their Admiral's ship, showing King Philip's royal coat of arms and Christ on the cross on one side; on the other, the image of the Madonna with the plea 'Arise o Lord and vindicate thy Cause'. There followed the San Marcos, San Felipe, San Juan, and many more saints honoured on floating palaces of war. Eight days later, this proud Armada came then into the mouth of the English channel.

Beacons were lit; every man in readiness across the land, hoping and fearing that the first foreign dogs would come ashore near his position and give him the honour of first defending our realm. The very next day being the 20th of July about high noon, the Armada was spied passing Plymouth, but coming not ashore. Their Duke Medina Sidonia had planned to land his forces thither, but was overruled by his King. In this regard, according to the judgment of many skillful navigators, the Duke was in the right and their King made a most fatal error, wherein they lost their greatest hope for victory.

Instead, the Armada was commanded to proceed to Calais, whither the Duke of Parma with his ships and all his warlike provision was in waiting. Given this advantage, the English ships pursued the Armada past Plymouth and, getting the wind of them, approached within musket shot of the Spanish, at which time the English ships most hotly and valiantly discharged their canons upon the Spanish fleet.

The Spaniards then well perceiving the greater nimbleness of the English ships, gathered themselves close into the form of an half moon, and slackened their sails. But while they proceeded in this manner, one of their great galleasses, under the command of a lord in great standing called Don Pedro de Valdez, was so furiously battered with English shot, that the whole navy was forced to come up round her together for the safeguard thereof. In time however, it came to pass that this ship could not keep up and neither could the fleet stay longer to succour it, giving leave for the wolf to slaughter the bleating lamb. The day following, which was the 22nd of July, Sir Francis Drake espied Don Pedro de Valdez on this sinking ship. Drake was advised to strike the mortal blow and send them all to Hell, but thought better thereof and instead sent word that Valdez should yield. Valdez, for his honours' sake, caused certain conditions to be propounded unto Drake, who answered that he was not then at leisure to make any long parley, but if Valdez would yield himself, he should find Drake friendly and tractable. However, if Valdez had resolved to die in fight, he should prove Drake to be no dastard [coward].

Upon this answer, Valdez and his company, moved by fear of the renown and celebrity of his name, whom the Spanish long held might be the Devil incarnate, came on board Sir Francis Drake's ship. Valdez himself coming unto Drake and humbly kissing his hand, said it was to be doubted whether his enemies had more cause to admire and love him for his great, valiant, and prosperous exploits, or to dread him for his singular felicity and wisdom, which ever attended upon him in the wars. With that Drake embraced him and gave him very honourable entertainment, feeding him at his own table, and lodging him in his cabin.

The wisdom of Drake's stratagem was then apparent, for Valdez began to recount unto Drake the forces of all the Spanish fleet. He reported further that his ship held 55,000 ducats in ready money of the Spanish King's gold, which the sailors collected and merrily shared among themselves before Drake ordered one final shot of cannon in the bow, saying he would not waste more ammunition and could slay the dragon with little effort, at which blow the vessel sank entirely away. But this was not the only blow suffered by the 'Armada invincible' that day.

A few hours later another of their greatest ships was set on fire, being the ship of Michael de Oquendo, Vice-admiral of their whole fleet, which contained great store of gunpowder and other warlike provision. This ship was burnt and the persons therein were consumed with fire, and what was left thereof was brought into England with a number of miserable burnt and scorched Spaniards. Again the Lord smiled upon the English, for the gunpowder, to the great admiration of all men, remained whole and unconsumed, giving a great fresh store to our fleet.

Even at night God smiled upon the English: Admiral Howard, all that night following a Spanish lantern, thinking it a ship of the English, found him-

self in the morning to be in the midst of his enemy's fleet, but when he perceived it, he cleanly conveyed himself out of that great danger before the enemy could perform any mischief on his ship. And that morning, being Tuesday the 23rd of July, the wind turned northerly, so Drake could then continually and without intermission, from morning to night, beat and batter the Spanish ships as he list. This was the most furious and bloody skirmish of all and forced the Armada to flee for the protection of the French coast near Calais.

At length, on the 27th of July, the Armada had anchored before Calais about sunset, expecting there to join with the Duke of Parma and his forces, without which they were able to do little or nothing. Therefore, Duke Medina Sidonia sent certain messengers unto the Duke of Parma, with many noblemen and gentleman who went to refresh themselves on land, including the prince of Ascoli, being accounted the King's bastard son. But likewise the English fleet had followed up hard upon them, anchoring just by within musket-shot distance.

Rosalind is now stirring and I am glad to see her smiling, even though she sleeps still. Perhaps she hath heard far more of mine oration than I thought. Perhaps she grows weary of ships and lords, when she would rather know whether I ever came into the fight. Aye, my sweet, I come to that tale anon. But our Company's role was like the jig or music that follows the main play: some take it as an amendment, but others see it as the most excellent and main entertainment of the day. Our role was brief, but vital at the end, as I shall report to thee herewith.

The drama at sea now in its fullest fury, the drama on land then began. It came about that our Earl of Leicester invited Her Majesty to inspect the fortifications and her troops at Tilbury, to inspire those brave few and to assure the multitudes across the land that she feared no King Catholic. She came on the 8th day of August, the first in sun that we had seen for a fortnight, the ground beneath our feet rose up and shook away the mud in her honour. Flags and pennants whipped in the breeze in all manner of colour, as drummers sounded the rally and pipers played stirring tunes. Pikes were lowered as she passed, so even at a distance we all knew her exact location on the field. After prayers were offered, she came unto the army like divine Pallas herself, riding through the camps led by Leicester, who was bareheaded and fitted out with garments of finer silk and pearl than even Her Majesty. She wore a modest gown, though pearls and hints of gold dazzled men's eyes, her hair worn high, embroidered with strands of jewels resembling a crown. Arrayed two feet behind her head, a starched lace so transparent and shimmering, as if to convey a great halo or blessing from Heaven. Near our own encampment she leapt from her white steed unaided and walked then among the troops with the countenance and pace of a true soldier.

Nor was she satisfied until she had seen every man, long near sunset when pipes came out and, from camp to camp fire answered fire, and through their flames each soldier sees the other's eager face. Our royal monarch walked from watch to watch, from tent to tent. She bid each his good morrow, with a modest smile, and called us brothers, friends and countrymen. Every wretch plucked comfort from her looks and, when all were greeted thus, she rode then a mile to a great manor and garden to spend a peaceful night.

On the morning of the 9th she returned and we were ready with thunderous applause to greet her in unison. She wore a white dress with shining silver cuirass [*breastplate*] preceded by a page carrying her silver helmet on a white cushion of velvet. Another Earl, I know not which, bearing her sword. Our Company had been called upon to act out a mock battle, seeming to be between our brave English soldiers and cowardly Spanish dogs, after which we paraded before her to receive thanks and a blessing for equally good fortune when real bullets fly. Then, bravely mounted on her white steed, she spoke these martial words to all assembled:

"My loving people I am come amongst you, as you see, at this time, not for my recreation and disport, but being resolved, in the midst and heat of the battle, to live and die amongst you all; to lay down for my God, and for my kingdom, and my people. You see before you the body of a weak, feeble woman; but I have the heart and stomach of a king and think foul scorn that Spain should dare to invade the borders of my realm. I myself will take up arms, I myself will be your general, judge, and rewarder of every one of your virtues in the field, so we shall shortly have a famous victory over these enemies of my God, of my kingdom, and of my people!"

She then gave loving courtesies to Leicester and called him her foremost general and bid us follow his command in all things until the victory, that surely God would grant. For a time yet again, I forgot his villainy and cold heart, but saw clearly instead who gave him authority to act as he list. Our Queen.

In the mean season, unknown to us as Her Majesty spoke, Admiral Drake had all but won the battle at sea. When first he saw the Spanish fleet gather in their crescent moon formation, cheek by jowl, he conceived a plan to send a few of his ships, all filled with gunpowder and set ablaze, into their midst. Admiral Howard forbid the practice, saying it would waste our few ships, every one, howsoever meager, that would be needed to prevent Parma's men from landing on some unseen place along our coast. But Drake's idea had reached the ears of the Queen and she wrote to Howard, ordering him to try, if God granted them the advantage.

Thus, on a night illuminated by the brightest moon anyone had yet seen, as though God himself wanted to illuminate the great human struggle for his pleasure, the 'Dragon' took forthwith eight of his worst and basest ships and, disburdening them of all things which seemed to be of any value, filled them with gun-powder, pitch, brimstone, and with other combustible and fiery matter; and filling all their ordnance with powder, bullets, and stones. With the wind and tide against the Spanish fleet, the fireships were floated directly down upon the King of Spain's 'Armada invincible'.

Such fire in the dead of the night, accompanied by explosions, sulfurous fires, and angry howling of falling masts and timbers, that could only be explained as Hell itself risen up to the earthly plane, put the Spaniards into such a perplexity and horror, that cutting the cables whereon their anchors were fastened, and hoisting up their sails, they betook themselves very confusedly unto the open sea.

The galleon of Don Hugo de Moncada was cast upon the shoals before Calais in this sudden confusion, falling foul of another ship, where she was immediately assaulted by divers English pinnaces. Moncada, after he had endured the conflict a good while, being hit on the head with a bullet, fell down stark dead, and a great number more were also slain in his company. The greater part of the crew leapt overboard into the sea to save themselves by swimming, but most of them drowned. This huge and monstrous galleon, wherein were contained three hundred slaves to lug at the oars, was in the space of three hours rifled in the same place and there were found 50,000 ducats of the Spanish King's treasure. At length when the slaves were released out of fetters, the victors planned to set the said ship on fire, but the governor of Calais, fearing the damage which might thereupon ensue to the town and harbor, drove them from thence with his great shore canon.

The morning next, as dawn broke, the entire Armada was most bravely and furiously encountered by the English fleet, from morning till night in that violent kind of conflict, until such time as powder and bullets failed them. In the mean season, we learned these further details from Van Meteren:

The Duke of Parma vainly persuaded himself that he would soon be crowned King of England, so he arrived at Dunkirk to join his army, whereat he heard the thundering ordnance of either fleet. A nobleman of Spain was put ashore to meet the Duke, who asked what news of the Armada. This gentleman did uncap himself, look toward Heaven, and replied that God Himself was apparently Lutheran, for so humbled was the Spanish fleet. Nor durst any of the Duke's own ships come forth to assist the said Armada, for fear of 35 warlike ships of Holland and Zeeland, which there kept watch and were furnished with most cunning mariners and old expert soldiers, amongst the which were 1200 musketeers, chosen out of all their garrisons, and whom they knew to be experienced in seafights. This navy was given especially a charge not to suffer any of Parma's ships to come out of the harbor with his army.

The English therefore, had right well acquitted themselves, in chasing the Spaniards first from Plymouth, then from Calais and then from Dunkirk, and by that means to have hindered them from joining with the Duke of Parma his forces. The Spaniards sustained great loss and damage, having many of their ships shot through and through, and though they discharged likewise great store of ordnance, the English sustained only little hindrance to their ships. That is to say the English lost not any one ship or person of account, albeit Sir Francis Drake's ship was pierced with shot above forty times, and his very cabin was twice shot through, and about the conclusion of the fight, the bed of a certain gentleman lying weary thereupon, was taken quite from under him with the force of a bullet. Likewise, as the Earl of Northumberland and Sir Charles Blunt were at dinner, a bullet broke through the midst of their cabin, touched their feet, and struck down two of the bystanders!

In addition to the three Spanish ships sunk in the fighting the first night, four more sunk right down the next morning, and very few therein escaped drowning, while the governors of these same ships slew one another very strangely. The captain of the San Martin, who would have yielded his ship, was suddenly slain; the brother of the slain party, in revenge of his death, slew the murderer; and in the meanwhile, the ship sunk with all souls onboard lost. On the San Salvador, the Spanish captain whipped the Dutch gunner for calling on the men to mutiny and save themselves, whereat the gunner ignited the ship's remaining stores of gunpowder and flung himself overboard as the ship exploded and sank.

Those few more ships in the once-great Armada that could, fled, but God was not yet done with their punishments. The wind arising, the Spaniards sailing north, they were tossed up and down with a mighty tempest for the space of two or three days together, which it is likely did great hurt unto them, being already so maimed and battered. Don Medina Sidonia, seeing now that he had lost so much, thought it good to fetch a compass about Scotland and Ireland, and so to return for Spain.

Fearing that fresh water should fail them, the Spaniards cast all their horses and mules overboard, but being carried with a fresh gale, fell nearer with the coast of Ireland. With no other choice, they hoped there to get sweet water and to refresh themselves on land, but they wrecked instead upon that coast, where many more of their ships perished and many Spanish noblemen and gentlemen were slain by the barbarous and wild Irish. Likewise, upon the Scottish Western Isles were cast away certain Spanish ships, out of which were saved divers Captains and Gentlemen, and almost four hundred soldiers, who for the most part, were brought unto Edinburgh, being miserably needy and naked.

Of 134 ships in this mighty Armada of Spain, there returned home but 53, to the great confusion and discouragement of the authors thereof. If nations were people, their monuments would be carved and set in stone in this manner:

For Spain:
May God grant peace to every famous or worthy family in all Spain,
For every one of them did lose a son, a brother, or a kinsman in this
*   expedition.*
May God forgive a King who sent 20,000 to their deaths.

For England:
The Spanish Fleet Came, Went, and Was.
ANNO 1588.
We honour our 100 killed.
We honour our 400 wounded.
We thank God for saving all of our ships, save those we lit ourselves
*   in holy fire.*

So ends the report, told to me by Emanuel van Meteren of Lime Street, of the miraculous victory achieved by the English fleet. But this was not the end of the Spanish invasion and supposed reimposition of the Pope's church in England.

The Queen's oration still stirred the air as the sun set on August 9th. Armed with her ardour and bravery, we doubted nothing the ultimate outcome of this enterprise, but our generals thought it good to remain watchful. The army of Parma was held upon the far shore by the Dutch, but what if his men escaped by some means and landed on our shore?

Our Company was therefore sent the morning following, that being the tenth day of August, some miles east to Allhallows on the south bank of the Thames, to relieve the troops that maintained the beacon thither. Nor did we object in any wise, for with the main threat past, our spirits high, we knew the Allhallows lookout would be most likely to first espy the ships of Parma's army, if any were yet to come. There would be some honour for lighting the beacon that first warned our countrymen and ignited too their passionate defense.

Days of lookout, when there is nothing to espy, seem hotter and longer than they are in truth. As men more accustomed to labours under a roof, we had forgotten how late the sun shines in August, how many sweaty hours before any cooling breezes come under starlight. We talked of home; of sleep on a real bed; of better food; of plays we might present upon our return; and of the new play 'Faustus' writ by Marlowe for the Lord Admiral's Men. Those of us who had seen it in spring acted out scenes for those of our fellows who were not by. Too many leisurely hours also meant that the ancient bickerings began anew and questions raised again about this man's fealty to a church or that one's past sins. To my great relief, Richard attacked me not and seemed more interested in showing his knowledge of the part of Dr. Faustus, to which he did acquit himself most excellent from memory only.

By the 17th day of August, a messenger came to tell us that the Earl had dismissed the troops, the better for men to return home before harvest, and we would shortly be removed from our duty. When no boats came for our relief, and having taken a vantage point where we could see the backsides of Leicester's troops marching away from Tilbury, Burbage and Johnson agreed on the 19th day of August that we should row ourselves across the river and hasten to join a convoy back to London.

We had been left but one small scow, suitable for two men only, which required us therefore to cross many times to gather our party together on the northern shore. We reassembled at the creek near Island Convennon [*Canvey Island*], exhausted from such labours, and determined to refresh ourselves the night, before making west those miles on foot we lacked on Tilbury.

Towards midnight, Kempe wandered from our snoring company to relieve himself and beheld a sight which would have made any man ease [*defecate*]: 100 ghostly lanterns bobbing on the tide, which surely meant 500 troops setting a thousand boots upon English soil. Our forces may now be thinking of homes and harvests, but Parma's men were dreaming still of Popish crucifixes nailed to English church doors, or imagining their fingers on the million in gold promised by the Pope. Every mother's son of us was awake of an instant and verified, with our own eyes, that which Kempe reported. Nor did it take us long to set our own a course of action.

Bryan was dispatched to find a horse and fly after the Earl to raise the alarum, while the bulk of our Company would delay the invaders as long we could manage. It was Dick who conjured up the wherewithal for so small a force to attempt so great a task: we must convince the Spanish that the defenders fled because Plague had broken out among the troops and in the nearby towns. We would present ourselves as Catholic faithful, giving thanks to God for our delivery into the hands of the Pope's own emissaries, and urging them to protect their number by avoiding any area with the disease. We would offer to find a safe passage to London and delay the force on the coast or take them on some circuitous route that would lead them into whatsoever troops might be left of Leicester's force.

O coz, canst thou now imagine how fearful was the poring dark that filled the wide vessel of the heavens around us that night? A mile or more apart from the foe, we still feared our secret whispers might be overheard, our several plans revealed each to the other. Burbage called on every one of us to make our quiet confession to God, in silent prayer to seek forgiveness for any wrongs past or debts unpaid, for this night might be our last if our deception was not convincing. Soon enough the country cocks did crow, the drowsy morning came, thawing our cold fear and dawning on a Company of players united at last in common purpose, determination, and love for his fellows.

Our hopes we pinned to this: Pope kept hidden watch on the hill, above the Spanish gathering onshore. Burbage and Cuthbert would fashion coffins from the wood of our trunks and those fortifications left now untended, the more convincing to make those fears of Plague, and to our general surprise, even Phillips and Johnson agreed to soil their hands in this endeavor. Dick and Kempe ran to the town nearby of Fibbing, thither to beg some apparel to make our parts the more cunning. I was sent to fashion some cloth into winding sheets, filled with dirt and leaves to mimic dead bodies that would lie in the coffins in case of search, but first to write a prompt copy of the 'play' we would perform, as dictated to me by Burbage. Richard, Perkin, and Clarke made haste to that hill, overlooking the plain to Tilbury, to prepare a bonfire that might warn the other beacons, if they still be manned, but which we would report to the invaders was necessary to consume the victims of the Plague.

With day replacing night, we could see how the Spaniard had established his encampment and fortifications. Would troops march forth, hoping to take some town by surprise, or would they wait for a greater force, which even now may be rushing hither across the sea? Fortune smiled upon us, for we had barely completed our preparations, somewhere around three o'clock of the afternoon, when a small force left the shore and moved up the hill in our direction. There would never be a play or jig more important than this one; there would never be another one at all for this Company of players, if we did not play our parts lively now. Burbage arrayed us according to our plan, each man perfect in his part according to my prompt book. Then we waited to see what came over the hill.

The Spanish force was some twenty men, a captain on a black horse that appeared to limp behind, but yet had vigour left in him; a dozen men with pikes and four with muskets, their crested helmets glinting in the blazing sun to make their wearers appear afire or touched by Heaven; four slaves who carried some boxes of provisions and a man in priestly robes who came last. Upon first sighting us, the captain gave some hasty command and the musketeers knelt in defense; on either side the pikemen; the cowering priest safe in the rear. We understood him to order us to show ourselves.

'Gracias a Dios! Gracias a Dios!' Clarke had instructed us all to shout this, followed by 'bienvenidos', meaning severally 'thanks to God' and 'welcome.' We raised our hands to show no threat and then knelt in prayer, looking fearfully and crying aloud. The Spanish saw we were peaceful and resumed their march in our direction.

"Your honours, we welcome you and thank God, King Philip, and his Holiness in Rome," quoth Johnson, extending his hand in friendship. Clarke translated with what Spanish he could muster, which, for our purpose, seemed adequate.

"If you trust in the true faith and all who seek it, we are your friends," quoth the captain, who remained astride his horse, but reached down to take the offered hand. The horse, who may have preferred the burden off of his damaged leg, a large wound now clearly visible, eased himself the while most profusely. Johnson continued in haste, lest the Captain think too hard on the scene before him:

"Aye, that we do, good sir. I am Sir Thomas Hereford, at your service. These mine attendants and servants were deprived of our liberty for our faith, along with many others feared by the heretic Queen in these regions, but when the Plague struck many, we were set free. We have removed our brothers and sisters who died to give them Christian rites, according to the TRUE holy church, and are on our way to yonder hilltop for that purpose, to consign them to flames and God's mercy."

The Spanish captain took survey of our procession. His troops had lowered their muskets, but the pikemen stood yet at attention and the priest mumbled something in Latin or Spanish, perhaps for them to trust us not and to attack forthwith. But every man of our Company played his role in manner as if rehearsed a hundred times. Besides Johnson, there was Phillips draped in black velvet playing his lute in somber dirge; Burbage and Cuthbert, dressed in sackcloth as mourners, pulling the cart with four coffins; Perkin playing a physician in aide to Pope, who hobbled pitifully and coughed sheep's blood that he had secreted in a kerchief in his hand. To prevent more careful inspection, Clarke explained himself to the captain.

"Your lordship, I am honoured to know your Spanish tongue, for I am Thomas Clarke, whom you have no doubt been told to find upon taking any part of English territory, he that hath traveled the country, in secret enlisting our friends for your ambassador, the right honourable Don Bernardino de Mendoza, to prepare for this day long wished for." Perkin thought it best that Clarke play himself, for he indeed had been used to find out those who might remain loyal and those who would not, reporting useless information to the Spanish while uncovering those who would succor the invaders.

"We indeed expect your people to rise in our favor," quoth the captain with more than a little arrogance, for which no translator was needed to discern. "But we are commended by God and our King to put to instant death any who bar our way or protect your profligate and licentious Queen." He seemed intent to provoke a betraying response, but we have played other men onstage so often that we remained faithful to our several parts and only nodded instead, muttering more 'gracias a Dios' in seeming consent. To further allay his suspicions, and those of the priest who now dared to creep around the pikemen, the better to examine our number, Richard and Dick next took their cue.

"Ah, may I present my son, Richard Hereford and his wife Helen," quoth Johnson with a sweep of his arm and quickly removing his cap for the 'lady'. The distraction seemed effective, for the Spaniard now dismounted and removed his cap too, bowing deeply to Dick, who was dressed in a modest bodice and kirtle of plain black and white, but a quality befitting 'her' supposed station. Her starched cap, atop the auburn wig, was attached to a veil of Spanish lace that a woman of Fibbing had said would bring us luck. Burbage insisted that Dick play a woman, believing the Spanish cannot resist chivalry and good manners in the presence of ladies. He was right.

"Forgive my bad manners," the captain said three times, insisting each time that Clarke repeat the words in English. "I am Colonel Don Diego Pimentelli, brother unto the Marques de Tamnares, and kinsman to the Earl of Beneuentum and Calua, in command of these troops that have the honour to be the first of many that will rescue this island from horrid bondage. I myself was taken hostage in Zeeland, but with God's mercy and the help of the faithful thither have escaped and serve yet again."

"I am in your debt." Dick gave a shallow curtsey and modestly averted his eyes, having long since learned that brevity is the soul of persuasion. Richard, however, suffers no such constraints, and spake thus:

"Don Diego, I am also in your debt, but trust me sir, you will soon be greatly in mine. You, sirrah, translate every word I say! Add or omit nothing!" I am certain that Clarke chafed at the command, but knew this would add to the effect we all sought, so he nodded merely and Richard continued. "I am newly come from London, much grieved to see my father so humbled, although God knows how we have all suffered and barely escaped hanging and quartering for any sympathy towards the Church of Rome. But hear this: London is but lightly guarded and those troops who remain are drunk in celebration of their supposed victory, drunk with Spanish wines, I'll warrant, and your troops can take the city - - and its Queen - - with little trouble. Will there be more of you soon? I take your number at not above five hundred."

"I am grateful for your intelligence, sir. I doubt it much if there will be more, for we are fortunate to have slipped past the ships that block passage hither by rowing our small boats only. Instead, we rely upon the faithful, like your good selves, to rise up and aide our cause. Of course with any good news, reinforcements will come. But how should we speed to London? Our maps of these lands are not perfect and I would have my force meet swiftly with those who will join us."

"In no wise should you go near the towns within ten mile of here, Fibbing, Tilbury and the like, for these are rotten with Plague." Perkin spoke in hushed tones of great urgency and earnestness. "The suburbs of London have not yet suffered withal this year, but you will lose many along the way if you fail to heed my warning, I swear to you as a physician who has treated too many poor souls."

Had Perkin overplayed his part? For now the captain stood back and looked to confirm his soldiers were still at the ready, but before he could convey his fears, Perkin pressed on with perfection:

"Look you at this man, who Christian charity demanded we bring with us, lest the fearful citizens had burned him with the dead. He is afflicted and will either recover, if God wills it, or will join his brothers and sisters ... up there." Perkin motioned toward the funeral pyre, clearly visible atop the next hill. With that, Pope stumbled forward and fell to his knees, grasping the hem of Perkin's cloak with what appeared to be a badly mangled arm and begging to be spared. He said nothing discernible to the Spaniard, nor did Clarke translate, for this scene played better as dumbshow, his tongue thrust to one side of his lips as if trying to ladle the foaming spittle back into his mouth. To prolong the distraction, Dick swooned and sighed, loud enough for all to hear and every man's heart to melt.

"O my dearest duck!" Richard caught Dick before he fell, as they had done a hundred times when we played 'A London Wife'. "Let us refresh her 'neath yonder oak." With this, the captain ordered his men to stand down, while he and the priest accompanied us some twenty yards farther, but now completely out of sight of his encampment below, to the shade of a great spreading tree. He sent two men back to that camp, as we understood to fetch refreshments, for Johnson said we had been forced to flee with no provisions.

In this manner, we spent two hours leisure, Dick 'recovering' as slowly as he dared and Perkin using his knowledge of ailments and cures, practiced over years with the Company, to convince the Spanish fully of our claims. At no time did the priest utter a word, nor did he appear to care much what was being said, but fingered a silver crucifix that hung from a leather necklace and chanted 'ave marias' and the like. Dick had learned the symptoms of the Plague by heart, since that day he heard them from the tree when we first met Rosalind, and he recited these now as Clarke translated with greater particulars and pointing to parts of the body. The Captain remained calm but clearly took inventory of himself as Dick and Clarke spoke, several times altering his location to remain a distance from Pope, who had wrapped himself in blankets to produce more sweat and a face redder than any man had seen.

Nearing sunset, the day had not cooled, nor did our elevation over the river afford us any comforting breeze. We spent some time showing the Captain our map and pointing him to the path that would take him clear of Tilbury and on to London (but straight into the bog, which from the awful rains of these past weeks must now be naught but muck and mire).[113] On the one hand, we seemed to have gained the confidence of our enemy, as we ate his food and drank his wine, but on the other hand he was now strengthened around us by some thirty more soldiers with muskets, pikes, and swords. Were they intending to gain our trust, but slaughter us thereafter once they had what intelligence we might provide?

Our answer came quickly, for at dusk, when we wanted to light the beacon fire and warn our countrymen, Johnson proposed to continue with our obsequies and carry the dead to the top of the hill. The captain ordered his men to help us with the coffins and we began our slow march, the last hundred yards up to the pyre. Nor did the soldiers suspect the coffins to contain anything but the sad contents we represented, for my handiwork with sheets and dirt gave the feel of hefting a true corpse.

At the top of the hill a merciful breeze began to blow and every man doffed his cap, in part to wipe sweat from his brow, in part to honour the dead. When the coffins were carefully balanced on the uppermost logs and the soldiers stepped many paces back, to avoid the coming conflagration and any further contact with the pestilence they verily feared, Johnson ordered his 'servants' Burbage and Cuthbert, to light the fire. This was the cue that I had waited for, in dread and hope, all afternoon.

Burbage knew my father was a Catholic and that I had been raised as one. I had learned these past weeks, since his remarkable resurrection, how Clarke had protected me from Johnson and Richard when they would have preferred to accuse me of being a traitor or slain me outright and left my body along the way. Clarke wanted no more than to practice his belief in peace, but to prove he could be loyal to our Queen. Now, in return, he asked me to take the knowledge of Roman rites and play the priest.

I knew I could mumble prayers in Latin, having studied that language in school and heard the prayers at home a thousand times, compelled by my father to repeat them and to confess and pay penance for my sins. But as I began the Latin mass for the dead, the Spanish priest broke out from his lair behind the pikemen and marched to within a nose hair of my face. I could see Perkin ready to intervene, should the priest have a dagger or call upon a soldier to use one, but I kept reciting as best I could and gave no leave to think of myself as anything but a Catholic priest, kept hidden these years in the household of a local recusant knight.

"Halt, in the name of the Inquisition," quoth the priest in Latin. Could he see my knees shaking or hear my brain telling my feet to flee? He studied my face and raised an eyebrow, as if to look deeper into mine eyes. Did my windows betray me? These priests of the Inquisition are notorious for divining the faithful from the false. I heard that in Spain, those that fail to work on a Saturday or eat no pork are tortured and burned as Jews or Muslims, for the Inquisition is sure that Satan hides in every cellar of the remotest village. Surely my portrayal of a priest betrays me more than bacon on my lips would help me. He slowly turned his head to scan the assembly, even as the flames crackled and exploded the sap in the logs, smoke billowing over the hilltop like a great snowfall. His raised hand invited no comment, nor would any of the Spaniards question a representative of the Catholic order in Spain.

"You are English," he said in perfect English, much to our amazement. "But you are a holy man of Christ and these souls departed deserve their path to Heaven be aided by the quick here assembled." My performance apparently pleased: the priest handed me his rosary and joined me in 'amens' and crossing himself, ordering the others in Spanish to do likewise. Phillips aided the mood by playing a somber Spanish funeral song on his lute, which some of the soldiers seemed to know and hummed it's refrain with tears in their eyes. Black clouds sweeping in from the sea obscured what remained of the dusk, leaving only the fire to illuminate our scene. I prayed for rain, knowing I would soon stumble in my poor Latin recitation of the service, but rescue came from another source.

Our play called for one role more, as any good play is followed by a fine jig or interlude. As the fire reached its zenith and the coffins turned to ash, our Company circled the fire and chanted prayers for the dead, taking care to speak Catholic prayers in English now that we knew the priest could understand us. Kempe had remained hidden, but now crept up the hill in the dark, appearing suddenly with shrieks and tumbling as if possessed. He cried for help and said the Devil was in hot pursuit, at the which some of the soldiers fled down the hill. Don Diego barked an order and his ancient dispatched two others to fetch back the cowards, and in the confusion, Kempe flung into the fire some silk taffeta he had cut into small pieces, which now sparked and dazzled in riotous, coloured explosions. Dick shrieked and fainted, Pope moaned and contorted his legs and arms into such a position that no man could conclude aught but that he was also possessed. Instead of bringing back the fleeing troops, those who hesitated now joined them and even Don Diego chased after his horse, who had bolted in the turmoil. The priest shouted 'Devil away!' and 'Jesus, defend us' in many languages, but when these availed him nothing, he joined the others and ran back towards the Spanish encampment.

Had we convinced them to flee this place they might now think cursed with disease and devils? Or would they merely steel themselves and attack us at dawn? Did our play convince or did they think us fools? When morning came, the ever-watchful Kempe stirred us from our exhausted slumbers and showed us the empty enemy encampment, wisps of white smoke struggling to be free of earthy ashes all that gave evidence the shore was ever inhabited by men.

We determined to make our own haste to Tilbury and then to London, perhaps to reunite with Bryan and any word from Leicester's main force, whatsoever thereof might remain to fight the five hundred Spaniards. Would others arise and swell their ranks? Only God knew, so hastily we gathered our meager possessions and prepared to fly from thither. Perkin and I had begun to discuss what the Spanish captain might have thought when he discovered his bible was left under the oak tree some distance above our camp. We walked together to retrieve it and tried to convince ourselves they had been fooled by our performance, weighing the odds on one side or the other. No sooner had we entered the large patch of shade provided us by the oak's grand canopy, when out from behind its trunk leapt the Spanish priest and an old retainer with a sword.

"The rat-catcher has caught his prey, foul pestilence!" shouted the priest with some lunatic madness, his second, more timid to the rear. "I have heard enough to hang you all."

"What wouldst thou have with us? Thou art mistaken, good friend." Perkin may have known he protested in vain.

"Common players, common thieves, the Devil take you! And hear this: though you be the king of cats and think to have nine lives, I mean to make bold with one of them now!" He had drawn a sword and dagger and was already lunging toward Perkin (but in that mortal danger, I found myself marveling that the rabid priest had leisure to recite some witty words). Perkin clutched a stout branch that lay convenient to him at the base of the tree, swinging it wildly as Hercules must have done confronting the Nemean lion, shouting:

"Come, sir, your best passado!"

"HELP! Priest hold, forbear this outrage!" I knew not what else to do but yell for help. I could see our fellows rushing up the hill to our aid, instantly understanding our surprised distress and carrying more than sticks withal, but then did I, with regrets now unspeakable, kill my sweet master, John Perkin.

'Tis no simple matter to report to thee how it happened, but as I rushed to intercede, both combatants sought to push me asunder. I grappled with arms, sleeves, beards, and hard weapons, never quite knowing who was, or held, what. At length, Perkin fell away and I saw blood rushing out of doors to be resolved who had so unkindly knocked. In brief, the priest had slain him under cover of my body, through which Perkin never saw the offending blade advance upon his chest.

No sooner was that steel withdrawn, but Kempe, then Richard, were beating the priest, himself now lying in the dirt near Perkin and me. Others rushed after the fleeing ancient, who already limped so badly that great pains would not be needed in the pursuit. I raised to a knee and cradled Perkin, as if shielding a babe from a wolf, but the wolf had already bitten to the quick.

"Am I hurt? I am hurt." Perkin took inventory of his parts, very simply at first, then realizing the blows to be mortal, winced and spat this next: "A plague on both Christian houses! I am sped. Is the priest gone, and hath nothing?"

" O John, forgive me. I meant to save thee from the blade, not be its guide to thy heart."

"Will, think no more on't, for this is but a scratch, a scratch, though marry it may be enough." Perkin sighed deeply and then shouted at our fellows, now gathered round us. "Go, villains, fetch a surgeon."

"Thou art our Company's surgeon," quoth Cuthbert, in his usual matter-of-fact, but then more tenderly added "courage, man; the hurt cannot be much."

"No, 'tis not so deep as a well, nor so wide as a church-door, but 'tis enough. Ask for me on the morrow and you shall find a man more grave." I pressed my kerchief to his bosom, but the coursing blood would not stanch. I looked towards Heaven, for help and to hold back my tears, but the gesture availed me nothing either way. "Help me into some shade, Will, or I shall faint. Is it not brave that I am killed this way: by a Catholic for being a Catholic, but feigning to be an English churchman who only pretends to be a Catholic? Brave, eh? My payment for playing the sides 'gainst the middle."

"And the Lord a cold arbiter," quoth Johnson, who glanced at Burbage, both men slowly shaking their heads. We tried to lift him up, but the pain was too great and he bid us let him rest awhile instead.

"He jests at scars that never felt a wound, lads. Give me leave awhile to confer with young Will alone."

Our fellows retreated in solemn farewell, not one convinced that John would inhabit this earth for over half an hour more. I did my best to serve as his pillow, sitting upon the dust with his head in my lap, wiping his brow with the only sleeve not yet stained with his blood, shattered sunlight glancing on his shattered body through the oak boughs. I would have stayed thus in penance a month if it meant prolonging his life but a minute.

"Will, there is no time to waste, so I will be brief. Thou knowest I care little for the new church, but will die here gladly for our Queen. I took thee to apprentice because thy father is a Catholic and I am paid to know what those of our like mind are saying and thinking about Her Majesty and to report such things to the Archbishop. Aye, 'twas he that gave me money and orders for thee to keep thee from Virginia, thy knowledge of men in Warwickshire a valuable font of intelligence here at home. But beware of him, Will, and warn thy father. He will ill-use thee and thy friends at home if needs be, for no man is more steeled 'gainst recusancy and to find out those of erroneous and offensive opinions than he."

"O John, my master, I care not for these matters, only that God might grant now my prayer to spare thee. I will spy or steal or lie or do any thing in his service, or the Queen's, if that could be so."

"Nay, forget sinning, even in goodly or Godly cause, for one can never justify the other. I am living, or dying, proof thereof. I gave thee all I could under the cloud of a great lie, but my deathbed confession is this: thou art now a goodly player and I bequeath thee my trunk and all its contents, but especially those masks thou knowest of, for in them must thou ever remember that no man is what he seems and even the most trusted can change his face for another in the instant, given adequate cause. The player's art is that we know how to con one face easily, then another, and in doing so we learn to see these facile deceptions in others. Use that skill, Will, use it well and thou wilt ever thrive."

"Forgive me master." I knew not what more to say.

"Nay, 'tis thou who must forgive this old sinner. I love thee well, mistake me not, and I would depart this life knowing I may have done thee more right than wrong. Let me therefore do thee one last right with this advice: thou art more skilled putting speeches in the mouths of thy fellows than canst ever be at speaking them thyself. Aye Will, the play's the thing. Many can play; few can write; fewer still can write with equal ease from Ovid for the Court and from rustic jesters for the many. Hone that skill, roughhewn though yet it is, into ever-better scenes to make men laugh and cry and dispute great matters. Then wilt thou find thy Fortune."

He coughed twice and called for water. Before Dick arrived withal, he was dead. I put some water to his lips and washed his face, for no man should meet God covered in his own blood. It gave me leave to hear his words and see again his deeds of these two years past. So many times on our travels, it was he who teased morsels of truth from carriers and schoolboys; he who befriended clergy and clerks to gain their confidence; he who could charm the whores and the high-born. I knew he cheated Johnson at dice and tic-tack, but now understood it was to have him in his debt and keep him a puppet, collecting more intelligence and giving leave to us to think that he was the spy. So much was now made sensible that, ere this, was false or obscure. But how came he to work for the Archbishop, when every man in England knows 'tis Walsingham that keeps the watch on us all? And how did a great churchman care a jot about John Shakespeare, already humbled by Leicester, and why would he take interest in the actions of the son?

I weep to speak this sad tale aloud to Rosalind, and weep again to write the words to thee. She slumbers still and may not have heard a word, but now at least thou knowest those events that bring me to this day, returned to London. But I have not yet said all.

Our Company marched homeward in haste, the murderous priest and his limping attendant in chains behind our wagon. Kempe a'times would delight to prick them both with the tip of his sword, still sharp from preparation and lack of any use in war, but the villains were pricked to the heart by the news we heard when Bryan united with our Company. Of the five hundred odd souls who followed Don Diego into the eastern side of the marshlands, no more than thirty came out the western end. Leicester's troops were waiting thither to slaughter them, but saw so pitiful a sight, they could not bring themselves to violence and dragged them off instead to prison.

We gained the Aldgate and gave thanks for our deliverance. We prayed for the speedy deliverance of Perkin's soul to Heaven, and there were struck dumb by the mysterious ways of God. We were suddenly informed that Robert Dudley, not satisfied with his title Earl of Leicester merely, had marched in triumph through the streets of London a week earlier, many tak-

ing him for a newly crowned king and asking aloud if King Philip had be
a worser fate than 'King Robert.' He supped with the Queen and she was
seen more than once lavishing praise upon him at Court as England's great
savior, much to the perturbation of Admiral Lord Howard and his captains.
He begged leave to take the waters in the country awhile, the which he was
instantly granted by Her Majesty, along with various kisses and epistles ded-
icatory and furnishings and gifts of gratitude. Two days later, he was dead.

Johnson heard anon that Leicester had complained of sore pains in the
stomach and therefore sought out the curative waters. But Rumour whispered throughout the City that the Lords Burghley and Walsingham and
Hatton, together with others most high, feared his ascension and had him
poisoned. A man called Smith, or a man who worked as a smith, we could
not decipher the whispers, claimed to have bewitched him, perhaps at their
behest, but howsoever he departed this earth, he is now forever canceled and
I know not what to think.

On the one hand, I am joyful that this scoundrel, who tortured and
killed my kinsman, is now himself before the great judge of all men; on the
other hand, I am saddened that I was not the instrument of revenge.

On the one hand, I am joyful that England is spared, Leicester the
chief designer of the moat defensive 'round our English house that repelled
the foe by land and sea; but on the other, saddened that our Company has
now no master and, like the rude misgoverned hands, who from their window tops throw dust and rubbish on the street below, will we be cast aside
with as little thought?

On the one hand, the Queen was feted by all the Court and all the land
in her hour of greatest triumph (and who is there, who does not see the hand
of God himself on her side?); on the other hand, she loses her 'eyes' and it
is said she is inconsolable, her advisors compelled to break down her chamber door on her birthday, after some days of grieving, to ensure her safety,
finding her weeping over some letters he had writ to her and a portrait that
captured his likeness in their youth. He must have been a handsome man
then, but the man we saw, for the last time at Tilbury, his smooth skin lately
turned rough and red; his voice full of gravel and lisps, the slender frame
now fatted; the rascal gone who was known to seek pleasure among the gentlewomen of Her Majesty's chamber, paying them a hundred pounds for a
night almost under the nose of the Queen.[114]

Perkin was right: no man, or woman, is truly what they first appear.
Like he that gives over to the Devil his immortal soul in change for earthly

Leicester repent and beg for mercy in his final hour? Even as Marlowe's play:

..., if thou wilt not have mercy on my soul,
Yet for Christ's sake, whose blood hath ransom'd me,
Impose some end to mine incessant pain;
Let me live in Hell a thousand years, a hundred thousand, but at
    last be sav'd!
Or let this soul fly from me and be chang'd unto some brutish
    beast,
For beasts are happy when they die, their souls soon dissolv'd
    into elements.
Why must mine live still, and still be plagued in Hell?

In any wise, I leave to God the ruling of whether the Earl is now in Heaven for service to his Queen; or in Hell for his acts against the Ardens. But pray, if I do earn mine own passage to Heaven, that I see him not thither: lest my thoughts turn to murder and God sends me, after all, to the other place!

Our Company will not wait long to know wither it goes: tomorrow Burbage has called for us to assemble at noon at the Theatre. I fear the worst, yet cannot say what 'worst' will be. I never knew this Company of players till we were thrust upon the stage 'neath an oak at Island Convennon. A Company where Pope, who would have given an arm to play a king onstage, saved our limbs by playing a cripple; and his brother, a Catholic who would prove his loyalty to the Queen, saved us by convincing the invaders that throughout the land, men like him would rise up to slay her; that Johnson, would slit the throat of any man in league with the Pope, played a popish knight to joust with those who sought to slit our throats; that Richard's father could never accept his son for any great or worthy role upon the stage, but lives to play again because that son so ably convinced the enemy that Plague would consume them all. A Company that played a scene of battle for the Queen at Tilbury, but would, few days later, play that scene in earnest. Mere players, condemned as lewd vagrants and villains, used to saving kingdoms of the imagination, that day preserved a kingdom in the flesh.

And how can any man, that but man is, know the meaning of why a gentle fellow, whose greatest sin was wishing his nation an hour of peace, should die by the sword wielded by a priest? In this I see that men rarely obtain that which they so earnestly seek, but the greatest rise to their true capabilities when occasion demands.

Occasion now demands I find means to care for Rosalind. Were it not for Mr. Stow, we would now inhabit the alley with the many penniless sailors and soldiers who crowd the City demanding their fourteen shillings from a Queen with an empty treasury. Indeed, a man may have served a year and lost a leg, but comes home now without money enough to buy him a wooden one. I can carry water and Mr. Stow employs me as a scribe, but this were not enough if more medicine is needed to aid Rosalind through her suffering. I pray God will show me the way.

But will He help or forsake me? Nightly I beg Him to spare Rosalind and the child, and that I pledge to find some means to earn thrice the value of the map, nay tenfold, and repay it to Westerbeke before Christmas. Throughout the City, Kempe and I told and retold the stories we heard of the New World, even those harrowing adventures of Miles Phillips, but always lingering over the descriptions of great wealth thither that was easily for the taking. In this manner, we had several bidders for the map, enough to buy food and medicine twice, but now not so provident with the few pennies that remain. Gladly do I trade the map for medicine, trading with it my New World dreams for an old world life. Ships will most certainly sail again next spring: I will most certainly not be on them with a mistress and a newborn. But how am I to provide for them in London, with a wife and babes in Stratford too?

As I wait for this physic to perform its magic, I write some lines to her, tear them up and start anew, for words seem pale and weak, incapable of the task I need them so desperately to perform: to make her well, to give our child a happy coming-in to this world, to convey the love I felt for her every minute we were apart and how it now grows stronger still. These lines will I recited to her now:

Dear Rosalind, those lines that I before have writ do lie
(I mean those that said I could not love you dearer!)
For then my judgment knew no reason why
My most full flame might later burn the clearer.

But reckoning Time, whose million accidents
May creep 'twixt vows, or change decrees of kings;
Darken sacred beauty, or blunt the sharp'st intents;
Divert strong minds to the course of altering things.

Alas, why, fearing of Time's tyranny,
Might I not then say 'Now I love you best,'
When I was certain o'er incertainty,
Crowning the present; doubting of the rest?

Love is a babe: then, might I not say so,
To give full growth to that which still will grow?

If Cuthbert is right, and he swears he can sell any play to another Company if Leicester's Men indeed are now dissolved, then must I put still more pen to paper and turn these hours of vigil into money for medicine, food, and hope. I am thinking now of a tale of war and loss, with those great public spectacles that stir men's brains and hearts alike, to out-Marlowe the Tamburlaine and out-Kyd the Spanish Tragedy.

More of this hereafter, for she stirs now and I must attend. Thus I beg thy forgiveness for that which hath offended thee in this letter and ask thy forbearance of judgment until we shall meet again and I may satisfy thy just censures.

In the mean season, I ask that thou kiss my boy and maids in my name and omit nothing else which thine honour deem'st best for their tender need. I am thine ever-loving servant in all else, Will.

LETTER FIFTEEN
December 25, 1588

Wherein joys and sorrows collide; some precious lives come to an end;
and Shakespeare must decide to be, or not to be.

Of all the places in London where I could imagine Shakespeare, or any of the people that inhabit these letters, suddenly appearing from around the corner, St. Giles Church, Cripplegate is the most compelling. It is also the most chilling and ghostly, because I knew the bodies of Shakespeare's beloved Rosalind and their baby are buried there (Illustration 20 on page 380 shows the church as it appears today).

A little investigation reveals that King Edward I banned all Jews from England in 1290. Before then, they suffered unspeakable persecution, frequent confiscation of property, and the only place in London where Jews could bury their dead was a plot outside London city walls, adjacent to St. Giles Church, Cripplegate.

By Shakespeare's time some three hundred years later, there was no evidence of the cemetery. In its place, according to the letters and other contemporary accounts, were some houses and a pleasant patch of community gardens around St. Giles, evidence that London was bursting past its historic city walls. By the way, I think Elizabethans first used the word "suburb" to refer to just such expansions (Illustration 22, page 381, shows a patch of grass next to the church that may well hide some very surprising secrets).

Letter Fifteen is written on Christmas Day 1588. Rosalind has died in childbirth along with her baby. Shakespeare recounts the events leading to this tragedy: Rosalind had been recovering from her illness and their unborn child was growing. Queen Elizabeth granted Shakespeare's theatre company license to continue as Leicester's Men, even though the Earl himself was dead, and James Burbage asked Shakespeare to help mend a play to be performed for the Queen. The Earl of Southampton's mother (the Countess Southampton, who will later feature prominently in Shakespeare's life and in future letters) bought two dozen more of the gloves made by Shakespeare's father, with Giddy being introduced at court as the craftsman responsible for the handiwork. The fortunes of Shakespeare's family seem to be on the rise.

When the Queen opens her palace to the public in honor of the nation's victory over Spain, Rosalind (then in better to health), Heather Burberry, and Mr. Stow join Shakespeare to mingle with the nobles at court and to see Leicester's Men perform. All of London is celebrating the English triumph, but Shakespeare could be forgiven for feeling as if it was in recognition of his swelling good fortune.

20. St. Giles Church in Cripplegate, London today, where Shakespeare and his lover, Rosalind Munday shared secrets and where he buried his nephew in 1607.

21. Remnants of the London Wall near the Cripplegate entrance to the City that was used by Shakespeare.

22. Near St. Giles Church. The approximate location of the Jews' Garden, where Rosalind Munday and her son Giles were buried by Shakespeare in 1588.

Walking back home late that night, eating licorice, and dreaming of names for their baby, Rosalind brings Shakespeare to St. Giles Church, into a garden, to nervously tell him her family secret: she is Jewish. Rosalind tearfully confesses that when she came of age, she was given a necklace by her mother, a silver cross, and told of her secret heritage. The silver cross is imprinted with a "J" that is meant to be a reminder of their forbearer, a Jew raised by Christians named Jessica. A symbol of the family's Hebrew origins, the necklace has been passed down secretly from mother to daughter over the generations.

Rosalind lives as a Christian and knows nothing of Jewish traditions or religion, but she anxiously awaits Shakespeare's reaction to her astonishing news. Shakespeare declines to pass judgment and, to allay her fears, paints a silly beard on her face with licorice juice. They leave the garden resolving to name their baby Jessica if they have a daughter or Giles if they have a son. Speaking of names, he opens this letter with a sentiment that will become one of his most famous lines in a play, which I suspect you will recognize without a footnote!

Even Shakespeare's decision to stay in London for Rosalind instead of fighting for a place aboard a ship to the New World now seems vindicated. He tracks down an American Indian named Raleigh, now living in London with the clothes and manners of an English gentleman, who knew the fate of early settlers in Virginia and who offers little reason for anyone to go there.

But then, this letter turns somber: the very next day the Queen declares Leicester's lands be forfeited to her (he had no heir) and Leicester's Men are ordered to surrender their livery. The players struggle to find work with other theatre companies. Shakespeare aspires to write a new play, desperate to make ends meet to support both a wife with a baby on the way and his family in Stratford. His world crashes completely some weeks later when Rosalind moans, awakening him from a prescient dream, and he finds her in great pain.

He writes, "Giles: our unimaginable joy. Still-born: our unimaginable grief." Rosalind and Shakespeare weep over the body of their dead baby. He and his friends consider how to best help Rosalind, who is fading. She dies clasping Shakespeare's hands in hers.

Reeling in despair from this double tragedy within the space of a single day, Shakespeare concludes Letter Fifteen by considering suicide: "In peace and honor rest you my sweet loves, and flights of angels sing thee to thy rest. If I can pluck the courage from my sorrow, I will fly soon after thee."

Reading letters like this one filled me with a sense of guilt, that I was intruding on private matters that the writer could not have imagined would ever become public. How can you eavesdrop on such intimate life-and-death conversations, without your own heart weighing more at the end than it did at the beginning? As you read Letter Fifteen, you will judge for yourself.

Christmas Day 1588, London

Coz,

What's in a name? A rose, Rosalind said, would smell as sweet if called by another. But there is now a name that has the power to strike me dead by the time I write the last word on this page, even were it sweet as the finest flower in thy good garden.

First must I summon the courage to write words that till today were unimaginable to me: she is dead, the baby with her. I weep to write of them and Death on the same page, but I cannot go into the endless Night without reporting all to thee, to report my cause aright.

Christmas Day, when every holiday fool has divine gods and miracles on his lips, I will prove to thee that God could not exist, or, that He cares nothing for the affairs of men. Else how could he trifle so with Rosalind, whose every waking hour did good service to the creation He named 'woman'? And what if she is somehow punished for her sins, the cause whereof I am chiefly guilty? Then what sin did our child, yet unborn, commit to offend Him so? Herewith the events leading to this bitter day, that thou mayest judge for thyself:

From thy most gentle and courteous reply to my last letter, delivered to me lately by our countryman, I know thou art informed of Rosalind's late illness and the means we used to nurse her again to health. We had no thing of value left between us, but imagined ourselves richer by the day as her vigour slowly returned and the baby kicked to show itself in good spirit too. Nor did our purse remain empty for long: alongside the joy of her recovery, I was given more good news. I mean that day, being at the end of September, when Burbage gathered the Company together at the Theatre to learn our fate, now that our master the Earl was dead and left no heir behind. Burbage greeted us severally that day, and each of us then remarked in hushed tones how the war seemed to have severely distracted our leader, how he appeared to us as a shadow of James Burbage, not the man himself. He called us together with his customary 'Is all our Company here?' To which Kempe replied:

"One is missing, and only God knows his whereabouts." I had so feared for Rosalind that I scarce had time to grieve for Master Perkin, but with all his fellows assembled, I was not the only man whose eyes welled then with tears.

"And only He … knows why the rest of us … were spared," quoth Johnson, rising up to his full six feet, seeming taller with his eyes bent on the Heavens, commanding every mother's son to say 'amen.'

I saw the men in a most changed light now: the brothers Pope and Phillips exchanged no more unkind words about one church or the other; Clarke crossed himself and kissed a relic that hung from his neck, a hand on Dick's shoulder as if to remind him that he had not died from a tavern knife and would ever be to him a father; Bryan gained in confidence and no longer absents himself from menial tasks, aiding Cuthbert in recovering our goods; even Richard showed more courtesy to me, although yet no humility. Perhaps that is the point: they are not different, but I am, for now the men treat me as one of their own.

"Here then, is the matter. We are yet given license to wear the Earl's livery, at Her Majesty's command, and are called to prepare entertainments for a great celebration of Her victory over Spain, which shall be performed on St. Elizabeth's Day [*November 5th*], or the day thereafter, during a week of great festivities."

"Let there be an heroic play of the Greeks!" Johnson declared, as if that would settle the matter.

"Let there be a part for a dog, for her Majesty loves them so," quoth Pope, to which Clarke sighed and waved at the air, as if to dispel a fog.

"Nay, nay, let us repeat the battle scene we played for Her Majesty at Tilbury, but this time with apparel and weapons suited to the swelling scene," quoth Phillips.

"Aye, and we have time to build mock Spanish ships and have some of us portray Admiral Drake and his men, destroying them all in fire," quoth Dick, now eager to play some part other than a woman.

"Let there be a jig with an exclamation!" Kempe raised his leg, aimed his buttocks toward the general company, falling over laughing in a great farting galliard [*dance*]. Not so much had changed as we restored our minds to the business of playing.

"Tilney will instruct us. And will pay us well. Thirty pounds, lads, thirty pounds." Although it was noon, the sun had not been seen that day, hiding behind a thick curtain of dark clouds, but this joyful news blazed light and warmth into every cranny of the Theatre, from the dust at our feet to the highest scaffoldage. "But I have not said all. Tilney bids us prepare new plays for the holiday season thereafter and ..." Burbage paused for the drama of his news " ... IF we please Her Majesty, we may become Queen's Men!"

Second only to the great relief we felt upon coming home after the war, this pronouncement was the gladdest of tidings. Nor did it come entirely unlooked for: the Queen's Men have fallen into disrepair, a list of stale offerings that no longer pleased Her Majesty. Johnson says that, in Norwich, the Council paid the Company to leave without playing a word or a note. Moreover, they had lately lost their greatest claim to men's praise: Richard Tarlton was dead.

I think thou sawest him play in Stratford, and once seen, forever remembered. Any play his Company performed was much enlivened when he came in like a rogue, in a foul shirt without a band, and a blue coat with one sleeve, his stockings out at heels and his head full of straw and feathers. He acted the drunk, but would suddenly stop to spit out a clever rhyme; a spectator might call out 'Spain' and he could conjure up a jest that might have caused even sour King Philip to laugh; all the while dancing most delightfully and with great art. Nor was he too proud to please the meanest groundling, for then would he snatch a man's cap and make another personage therefrom, then tumbled in such a manner as to make it appear the hat flew out his arse and straight back to its rightful owner. And after he had left the stage, his fellows resumed the serious matter of their play in vain, for 'twas said Tarlton did:

'set all the multitude in such a laughter,
they could not hold it back for an hour thereafter!'

The art of Kempe and of Pope stand upon Tarlton's shoulders, and they said as much when first we heard of his passing. They collected food and money for his woman (I may not call her his wife), Emma. Kempe knew her from the Hope, a whore who earned a few coins extraordinary by reciting a piece called 'Spindle Shank 'em', to the great mirth of the men in the stews. Tarlton died in her house in Shoreditch, saving his last ounce of strength to write to the Queen's Secretary to aide Emma and their boy, a lad of six called

Kent (seest thou that God torments me with foul trades: a player dies, but his boy and the mother live; I live, but my boy and his mother are gone). In brief, the Queen's Men needed the skills of our men, much as we needed a new Company.

"The Romans may not like it," quoth Vernon to no man in particular. He was rooting around in the dirt 'neath the stage and came up with a skull from those ancient burials over which the Theatre was built, carefully cleaning the dirt from the hollows that had once cradled eyes. "This had a tongue in it, and could sing once. He'll not be wanting a Queen's Man dancing on his bones and crushing his fame."

None of us paused in our various delights about the idea of being Queen's Men to ask Vernon what he meant, but I note his comments. We can not always discern if he speaks in jest, but lately he reported most earnestly seeing, and communing at night till the first cock crew, with ghosts of the Roman dead. He held the skull next to his ear, as if the long-dead fellow whispered again in's ear, and spake thus:

"Aye lads, be not lost so poorly in thoughts of borrowed greatness that may never come, when I tell ye straight: this fellow here knows how, in the most high and bold state of Rome, a little ere the mightiest Caesar fell, how the graves stood tenantless and the sheeted dead did squeak and gibber in the Roman streets. The selfsame events are newly happ'd in London, whilst ye were all gamboling in the fields of Tilbury. Aye, and I have seen, with these antique eyes, stars with trains of fire and blood, the sun sick, almost to doomsday, with eclipse. Aye, look ye all, these warn of fierce events yet to come, prologue to the coming on of heaven and earth together erupting!"[115]

"Jamie, canst not quiet thy howling hound?" Johnson whispered to Burbage, vexed that the general joy of the Company was briefly distracted. We all heard him, so Kempe began barking, joined by Pope and Dick, in Vernon's lusty defense. In truth, as we were soon to learn, we should have heeded the old retainer's prophecies better.

Johnson waved away the quarrel and turned our attention to the faded glory of the Theatre and the task of shoring up the old scaffold and restoring it to its former lustre, knowing we would need to do likewise for our playing skills and inventory in the weeks before we played for the Queen. Until then, we would open our stall and perform plays and jigs, old and new, and thereby keep bread on our tables. Nor was it long before we sampled the possibilities of joining in league with the Queen's Men.

Robert Wilson had been with Leicester's Men until '83 when the finest players of each company were taken together to play as Queen's Men. I have seen Wilson play only once, but he has a quick, delicate and refined extemporal wit, the equal of Kempe or Pope (though neither of them admit the like). He formerly wrote plays for our Company and mended others, so Burbage called upon him now to help us write a new play that we might perform, as both our Companies together. And both Companies short of players, the new play shall consider the talents that remain and make best use thereof for a public spectacle to rival Tamburlaine or Hieronimo.[116]

John Laneham, also taken from our Company, served as master of the Queen's Men and was ever a good friend of Burbage. Those two conferred and agreed that, whereas Wilson was for the time being indisposed, and the Queen's Men had need of mending their play 'The Famous Victories of Henry V', that if I could do them this service, they would in turn give Wilson leave thereafter to assist us with our endeavour.[117] I learned they needed to change those scenes wherein Tarlton and one other player, now lost, were seen, but this was an impossible task, for no others could play those parts, the pair having created such an indelible impression when last the play was shown, and indeed the Queen asked for the play again for that very reason. Burbage bid me demonstrate all of my skill with the pen in this cause, howsoever mean it might be. But how could anyone write scenes for dead men?

I know no other person who has read more books, plays, and poems than Heather Burberry and therefore conferred with her on the matter. Nor was my faith unwarranted: she could not recall the name, but remembered a play where some parts were spoken only as voices offstage, with others entering and leaving the stage as if they had just been in communion with them. I mended the scenes of the missing players in this manner and added some scenes describing their heroic deaths, played out for King Henry by others, the better to acquaint him with the fate of his allies. Laneham found the result pleasing and his Company performed the play, as newly amended, at the Bull Inn to great acclamation and profit. In this manner, Wilson agreed to help us write a new play for our two Companies together.

But what to write this new play about? The answer, I thought, might lay in the New World. In this selfsame time, being by then the middle of October, Kempe and I had gone in search of those who might know the fate of his sister and Miles Phillips in Virginia. By this I mean those natives brought hither into England, Wanchese and Manteo by name. We could not discover their fate nor whereabouts, but heard of a man living with a distinguished sea captain and merchant, Sir Richard Grenville, in his household in Devon.[118] This native had learned all of our English ways and was said to have memorized the entire Book of Common Prayer and would recite therefrom in church to the amazement of many. I know not what he was called in the Americas by his clan, but in England he was known as 'Raleigh.'

By great good fortune, we learned that Sir Richard was oft in London, most reliably when Parliament was called, for he was also a member thereof, where he is renowned for his generosity and great relief to the poor. Mr. Stow reports that he himself, in these declining times of charity, has seen at the Aldgate in London more than two hundred persons served with bread, meat, and drink, and that Sir Richard is one of the primary benefactors, till God should send them better store. Mr. Stow directed us to Sir Richard's lodging in London, at the west end of Tower street, to a fair structure sometime called Griste House, named for the man who dwelt there in the time of King Henry the sixth. In that time, Heather quoted from one of her books, Jack Cade, captain of the rebels in Kent, being feasted in this house by Mr. Griste, like an unkind guest robbed him of all that was there to be found worth the carriage. Time out of mind since, the house had fallen to ruin and been let out for stabling of horses, to tipplers of beer, and to one Mother Mampudding (as they termed her) for many years as a place of victualing.

When Sir Richard took possession of this sometimes-famous house, he caused it to be restored by those of his trade, to wit shipwrights, and not ordinary house carpenters. The results of which are now plain for any to observe, but must behold to believe: the frame of the house is raised of certain principal posts of timbers, like masts, fixed deep in the ground, and clad with every board ledging over another as in a ship, nailed together with ship nails called rough-and-clench. The roof is also wrought as if it were a ship, the keel turned upwards. All of this is painted like a great vessel and resplendent with banners and pennants of those wars wherein Sir Richard had fought most bravely. Kempe and I had no trouble finding the place, being so uniquely wrought, but were not at all prepared for the most striking feature thereupon.

To this house, Sir Richard added a high tower of brick to overlook his neighbours in the City, many of whom complained bitterly to the alderman about this affront to their privacy. Indeed, neither Kempe nor I had seen such a tower in a private house anywhere in England, but this delight of Sir Richard's was newly punished, you might say, with a blindness in one of his eyes, caused by a wound he suffered in service to Admiral Drake against the Spanish armada.

We had sent word ahead of our desire to meet Raleigh and that we were no beggars, but servants to the late Lord Leicester, and received a most courteous reply from Sir Richard's own hand that we should come forthwith. At the door of this house, at the very base of the aforesaid tower, engraven on a plaque of brass, no doubt kept shiny by daily labour of a careful household servant, the following inscription:

> *The Court is but a pleasant cage*
> *For birds to plume their feathers in;*
> *A joy to youth, a pain to age,*
> *Where many lose and few do win.*
>
> *But such that seeks for fame in foreign place,*
> *Forsaking ease and wealth where they were bred,*
> *Are special men and do deserve more grace*
> *Than all the rest, whatever may be said.*
>
> *Leaving wife and friends, abroad on tumbling seas,*
> *Those that risk their lives and all they have,*
> *Are men that may both prince and country please:*
> *And who shall right be honoured unto their very graves.*

We were ushered into a lobby by a boy clad in apparel most like that which I have seen on cabin stewards on ships or at docks, attending on captains and the merchants who ply their trades abroad. The room was hung with strange dried fishes, clever rough-hewn wooden armaments, feathered garments from some long-dead native prince, and a small portrait of a young lady with delicate features and milky skin. We had no leisure to examine these artifacts or record their particulars, for instantly were we bid to follow the boy up a curved iron stair, the likes of which I have climbed in the ship that bore our Company to Denmark, a thick hempen rope draped on one side where other houses might have a wooden railing to steady the ascent. At the top of this passage we came to a landing, which led us to a ladder, yet another artifact that would more conveniently be found on a ship than in a great person's London home. Climbing up through the structure, we glimpsed the great battlements of the royal Tower not a quarter mile distant, and those soldiers who patrolled its walls, helmets glistening in noon-day sun, through small windows that resembled the hinged doors through which a canon protrudes on a man-o-war.

At length (and I will confess somewhat out of breath) we arrived at the highest room in the structure and found ourselves in a pleasant sitting room, modest yet most richly appointed. Lustrous ebony challenged pol-ished brass fittings to see which was the more resplendent; brightly coloured ensigns draped around paintings of ships in great battles, some in flames, some apparently the victors, many inscribed in Latin and honouring the Queen, each one giving the impression of a war still to be decided on seas that heaved evermore. The room was rounded, like a captain's cabin, with a large drum to one side; a great desk covered over with a Turkish tapestry on the other; a dozen sturdy chairs in a semi-circle in the middle. But most of this was hard to take in, blinded as we were by the sunlight streaming in through a wall of tall windows, floor to ceiling, and transparent as the water in the Avon.

In repose, alone upon a chair at the furthest end, studying a chessboard where some opponent had suddenly stopped the match, now taking leisure to examine his next move, sat the picture of an aged English country gentle-man, even to the slashed leather jerkin and velvet garters securing a fine pair of linen nether hose. The only item out of place was the dark colour of his skin and the elaborate red painting thereon, from the cheekbones just below the eyes down to the neck and perhaps lower still down his broad shoulders and long, stiff back.

After most gracious introductions were exchanged and the absence of Sir Richard explained as being some unavoidable matter at the pleasure of Admiral Howard, Kempe interrogated the native without delay. Raleigh seemed not to take offence. Instead, he provided his views, which innumer-able recitations had likely honed to a sharp edge, with some pride and to establish that he was therefore no liar, in the most amazing Devon accent:

"I was baptized this March past. And as you can see, I have done mine utmost to learn the English tongue and manners, now seeing those of mine own people as ungodly. Some of my forefathers have met some of yours, in the time of your great King Henry, he that was the father of Her Majesty now. But those were clothed in the skins of beasts; they ate raw flesh and spake such speech that no man could understand them; and in their demea-nour, were more like to brute beasts than gentlemen."

"Aye, but what of Manteo and Wanchese, who were lately brought to England?" Kempe was eager to find men who may have seen his sister.

"O, I knew them both, although our people were not their partisans. I came from parts to the north of that area now called Virginia, but made their acquaintance when I first assisted those Englishmen who sought to establish themselves thither." With that he tore a great lump of moist leaves, tobacco I surmised, and jammed the wad into his left cheek, the circular artwork thereon expanding like ripples in a pond. "And 'twas great good fortune that we came upon them at all, for look you, the seacoasts of Virginia are full of islands, but by the hand of God, we came unto a good big island, the Inhabitants thereof, including those calling themselves Wanchese and Manteo, as soon as they saw the English, began to make a great and horrible cry, as people which never before had seen men appareled like that, and came away making out cries like wild beasts or men out of their wits. But being then called back gently by me, in a tongue not unlike their own, and being offered various wares, such as glasses, knives, bangles and other trifles, which they delighted in, they stood still, and perceiving our good will and courtesy, came fawning upon us, and bade us welcome. Then they brought us to their village in the island called Roan-oak, and unto their Weroans or Prince, who entertained us with reasonable courtesy. Such was the English arrival into the part of the world, which we now call Virginia, with mine earnest intervention, accomplished. The stature of body of which people, their attire, and manner of living, their feasts, and banquets, I will particularly declare unto you now."

"My good man, stay awhile and tell me what you know of Wanchese and Manteo!" Kempe grew more aggravated, but I tried to ease him, so as not to wear our welcome out. I noticed now how it was that the paintings seemed more than colour on canvas only, but instead like windows, looking out to living seas hosting real battles: a breeze through one of the windows rustled the banners that hung around the images, giving the casual observer a sense that the subjects were alive and moving.

"As you like it then: they came in '84 and spent a year in England, but then returned with Captain Lane the year following. I know not what became of Wanchese, but Manteo returned again to England with mine own patron, Sir Richard, and with another Algonquin brother called Towaye."

A clock struck six times, although it was only three of the clock in the afternoon, during which Raleigh discharged a great volume of spittle towards a wooden ship's bucket behind his chair with great expertise, not a drop falling short of its mark.[119] I had never seen a man chew the tobacco leaf, though Perkin was ever smoking it in his pipe, and thought to inquire about this practice, but Kempe was not so patient and demanded to know where to find these men.

"Find them? Many miles west of here. Many many miles west!" Raleigh laughed at his own jest, so we discerned he meant they were back in the Americas. "Aye, both went back to Virginia with Governor White last year in spring. We have heard little of them, indeed only some tragic stories from Governor White about desperate conditions with those who remained behind, exceeding strange famine and other hardships. The English sold everything they had to the Algonquin people for food and complained about the price, but were told roughly and churlishly 'if thou make so great account of thy merchandise, eat it, and we will eat our fish' at which point those locals fell out laughing and mocked the settlers with open throats."

"And will we find any native person, besides your good self of course, in England now?" I inquired to see if any balm could be had to ease Kempe's despair.

"Not one that I know of." Raleigh sighed and rose from his chair, as if he had unexpectedly lost the game of chess on the table before him. Was that the sign of a man who knew he was alone in a faraway land and no amount of cloth or manners or language could make him otherwise? He spat again into the bucket, this time the liquor all black and lathered.

"Wilt go back to Virgina when ships sail thither once more?" Kempe, more plaintive now, hoped he could find someone willing to search for her.

"Nay, my seafaring days are ended and I look only to be of service here to Sir Richard, who has been most kind to me, and end my days in quiet contemplation of the Bible, its many mysteries to me yet unfolding."

Raleigh spent another hour telling us of the customs of his people and those inhabiting the land where Kempe's sister and 151 other English souls (including the two new babies) were likely to be in residence. He spoke of two brothers fighting to be the sovereign of the mightiest clan and what intrigues the followers of each man perpetrated on the other. Though this shined but little light on the fate of our men and women, it did provide a possible subject for our new play, especially the part how the warring tribes ate each other's hearts and eyes to steal their strength and vision, such gruesome fare being popular in London playhouses now-a-days. When the clock struck three times (although it was certainly early evening by then) we took our leave of him.

I had not the heart to relate all of this to Rosalind, although we both already knew that a new baby signified our time to venture over the seas was not at hand. Still, that was the dream on which we first met; an imaginary land where we built our loves and lives for so long that I could not dispel it now, not when she most needed hope and strength.

I did not, however, abandon hope for a play about the New World, for that could become most famous and earn for us a goodly sum. I recalled too the heroic tale of the Englishman, Fox, and his triumphant return after years enslaved to the traitorous Spaniards. That would certainly stir the hearts of men, and perhaps the Queen herself, so soon after other valiant Englishmen had snuffed out the foreign flames. But Wilson had other ideas.

The Queen's Men were told to prepare entertainments that recalled Roman glory, even as the Queen and her Court prepared Roman apparel for the coming celebrations. It was said Her Majesty would appear in the image of a conquering empress or Amazon. Our play must therefore be Roman and full of spectacle. I wondered if Vernon's Roman ghosts would be appeased or angered to see their ancient kinsmen alive again upon our English stage.

But whether our play dealt with a new world or very ancient one, I argued one point with Wilson most fervently. He wanted a play of polite speeches, honour and dignity. I saw how the spectators devoured with delight Tamburlaine's captive kings bashing out their brains; or Hieronimo biting out his own tongue.

But Wilson refers to his great success with 'Three Lords and Three Ladies' which only need call to mind the great victory over the Armada and need show no base deeds to excite the many. Yet when Leicester's Men played his 'Three Ladies of London' it no longer found favour in towns. Wilson would not believe it, nor would he be moved when Cuthbert called for witches in the play, be it ever set in London or Rome.

"This kind of people, I mean witches and sorcerers, with the last few years have marvelously increased in the realm," quoth he. "Who hath not seen the most evident and manifest marks of their wickedness? I mean neighbours who pine away even unto death, their colour fadeth, their flesh rotteth, their speech benumbed, their senses bereft. Many of these devils are hanged, a few confess, but even those that don't bear on their bodies divers strange marks, at which the Devil sucks their blood, or so I am told. These matters are therefore not meet for a play."

We were still debating, and had written little together, when the great day of celebration arrived and the matter was set aside until our Companies' several duties at these festivals were ended. Indeed, the Queen's Men and Leicester's Men all stood at the ready and both Companies were given full employment. We heard tell of preparations made throughout the kingdom and wanted our offering to shine as bright as any, in gratitude (and to secure our place among the Queen's Men thereafter). I wonder what fond pageant the council in Stratford put forth? Solemn prayer by candlelight? Or mirth and merriment with feasting? Both perhaps, for that is what we saw, and partook thereof in fullest measure, in London.

On St. Elizabeth's Day itself, by the commandment of Her Majesty, a solemn festival day had been publicly declared, wherein all persons were enjoined to resort unto their church, and there to render thanks and praises unto God. As we had been foretold, the Queen herself, imitating the ancient Romans, rode into London in triumph, in regard of her own and her subjects' glorious deliverance. She wore silken robes of white and blue with fur and gilt, carried through her City, from her palace unto the cathedral church of Saint Paul, in a triumphant chariot pulled by two white horses. There were the ensigns and colours of the vanquished Spaniards displayed, while the streets were hung on both sides with blue cloth, which, together with the foresaid banners, yielded a very stately and gallant prospect. Outside the west door of that church, she knelt in prayer to cheering crowds.

"You may someday have a greater prince, but you shall never have a more loving one," quoth she.

"God save your Majesty!" The multitude breathed and spoke as one.

She entered into the church, together with her clergy and nobles of the Court, led by Lord Admiral Charles Howard and his iron right arm, Admiral Drake, all decorated in laurel wreaths and other insignia as if Roman conquerors themselves. The Queen gave thanks unto God at the altar and kissed the silk purse she carried (which Johnson said contained Leicester's last letter to her and which she now imbued with his spirit and thought to honour his memory as her General and her love). Then came she out again, and, though the November wind bit shrewdly across the yard, she caused a public sermon to be preached before her at Paul's cross at high noon, the better to be seen with her subjects. She commanded the sermon present no other argument but praise and glory to unto God, as thanksgiving for our deliverance from the invaders. The vicar was none other than John Whitgift, the Archbishop of Canterbury, the man whom I had never before laid my gaze upon, yet who took some strange interest in my fate, and who spake thus:

"France, Italy and Spain are all full of false-hearted Machiavellians, but truly PRIDE is the disease of the Spaniard, who is born a BRAGGART in his mother's womb." I barely heard his words, so fixed was my gaze now upon the man, devouring his appearance and gestures, in case I might find there some clues. I observed a study in contrast: he is at least three score years, with a snow white beard down to his chest, yet the full head of hair, flowing out from under his cap, was a youthful chestnut. He appeared frail, gaunt, and severe, but his booming voice, commanding fealty and attention, washing over the thousand souls who fidgeted to stay warm in the great churchyard, which had been cleared of booksellers and the workaday hawkers of wares. I could imagine as a student at Oxford or Cambridge how he must have lectured his classmates and never rested until he won every argument.

"Phillip of Spain, not content to be the god of GOLD, but now he doth nothing but thirst after human BLOOD, even when his foot is on the threshold of his own grave and he should be thinking instead on his own SINS and his own SALVATION. But like the wolf, about to devour a horse, who doth ballast his belly with dirt that he may hang the heavier upon his victim, and then forcibly bites into his face never leaving hold until he hath eaten him up, so too this wolfish Phillip, being about to devour all Christendom by invasion, doth cram his treasury with dirt from the New World - - I mean more gold - - to make his malice more forcible!" Some ladies swooned at the imagery of the wolf eating the horse, but Whitgift poked his forefinger in the air, over and over again, to drive home his point.

"Then flies he in the bosom of France and Belgia never withdrawing his forces till he hath devoured their welfare and made the war-wasted carcasses of both kingdoms a prey for his tyranny. Only poor England, by the grace of God, holds him at arm's length, and his Armada, like a high wood fence overshadowing the shrubs of our low ships, fled from the breath of our canons, as vapours vanish before the sun. Then did God make the winds raise up high bulwarks of bellowing waves at their disordered navy. Then did His creation, the rocky promontories, I mean, with their overhanging jaws, eat up all the fragments of oak that the turbulent waters had left behind. So perished our foes, for the Heavens did fight for ENGLAND and our QUEEN! Nor do I doubt the DEVIL was present in this action, for who can doubt he helped to bore holes in ships to make them sink faster and rinse the galley with salt water, that surely stunk like fusty barrels from their masters' fear, the sooner to harvest more poor souls to his foul kingdom below! How many foul sinners, deserving of their fate, did the Devil meet, with his toothy grin, and commend them straight to HELL? While thanks to the Almighty, the bulk of our men and ships were spared, our Kingdom too, our Queen confirmed as our rightful monarch to rule over a new age of PEACE … and … PROS-PER-IT-EEEEE!"

With the sermon ended, Her Majesty praised the Archbishop for his rhetoric and his drama, then exhorted the people to give their own several thanks unto God, whereupon we all, with a loud acclamation, wished her a most long and happy life, to the ever-lasting confusion of her foes. I had thought to present myself to the Archbishop, even to demand why he inter-fered with my life, but the throng of nobles and the Queen's guard made a wall impenetrable around them both. Her Majesty looking upon her sub-jects for a goodly while, and they upon her, then departed, again with great pomp, attended upon her chariot. Our party walked back to Lime Street in awed silence, until that Heather spoke her mind:

"The English will never love nor honour their sovereign, unless he or she be victorious and a lover of arms and war against our neighbors, and especially against such as are greater and richer than themselves. History shows our land is more fulfilled of riches and all manner of goods when they are at war than at times of peace. They take delight in battles and slaughter, covetous and envious above measure, look you, of other monarch's wealth."

"Aye Heather, but must not any Queen or King obey his people and do all their will?" Mr. Stow did not reprove, but gently inquired of her opinion, wrapping his own cloak, more than twice her own length and soon dragging in the mud, over her crooked shoulders 'gainst the bristly evening chill. We debated the matter further and all the way home talked of nothing but what an admirable Queen she was and how we would adventure our lives again and again to do her service. Only a few of the most surly Puritans took issue with that general day of prayer and thanksgiving, proclaiming the invasion was God's means to chastise the English for our sins of excess usage of meat and drink. If they were right, the next four days were marked by far more sinning than any previous in our history: the conduits nearly ran red with claret and the singing did not stop a minute in the next four days of cock-fights, bear-baiting, dancing, tug-o-war, plays, pageants, and feasting!

Nor were Leicester's Men any laggards in this regard. Three times we performed for Her Majesty at White Hall, each time, when the play was ended, called upon to perform the mock battle we had shown the Queen at Tilbury. So many pressed into the great hall to see us that we were compelled to repeat the event six times in one night, the better for every man and woman of rank to have seen us and be able, at the groaning tables of food and drink thereafter, to report how they observed the Queen respond. In truth, many present may have seen little of our Company, so intent are the lords and ladies of the Court to study their Queen in such circumstances and to fill their heads with any opinion of the matter that she may have, incapable of forming their own when she is by.

And what must she have been thinking in those hours of celebration? Did players bearing Leicester's insignia and colours provide her with joyful distraction, or did we remind her merely that he was gone, a weight on her heart, at what should have been a soaring triumph? The answers came, I think, after Kempe's jig, which he performed then with Pope together, when the Queen asked him how he came to be so merry.

"Why your majesty, a fool is one who knows he hath nothing to lose," quoth Kempe, wiping sweat from his brow, then sitting comically like a child on Pope's crooked knee, who himself was kneeling on the stage before the Queen, cap in hand. "For hath not the clock e'en now struck ten? Thus we may see how the world plods along: 'tis but an hour ago since it was nine. Therefore, king or commoner is now one hour closer to the grave, and thereby to giving up his wealth, than when the clock struck nine."

"Thou art no fool, but now I see thou art a philosopher!" The Court applauded the Queen's reply as if she had coughed up gold. But I could see her eyes widen in a certain resignation, an admission of sorts that Kempe had given voice to a matter she may have spent more time thinking lately upon. "And what of Master Pope? Art a fool or philosopher?"

"Why a fool, your majesty!" Pope dislodged Kempe, who fell most laughably on his arse, as Pope tumbled over him and landed on the edge of the stage with his disjointed legs dangling over the side. "For a fool hath liberty to say what he will, but no man takes offence, while many a philosopher has been hanged for uttering the same."

"Ha! Then let me play the fool too." The Queen rose and glided towards Pope, handing him some token before turning to face the Court, sweeping gracefully through the parting seas of nobility before her. "I would have such liberty, as large a charter as the wind, to blow on whom I please. Aye, give me leave to speak my mind, and I will through and through cleanse the foul body of the infected world, if it dare to patiently receive my medicine. And who can object or point a finger at another when the fool speaks a truth? For instance, who could take offence if I say that some 'city-woman' bears the cost of unworthy youth on weary shoulders? Who can come in and say that I meant this particular lady or that one, when so many are like to their neighbor?" (I swear the Queen's gaze came to rest on the Countess Southampton, though I could not glean her meaning). The gilded songbirds of the Court tittered and rustled, yet had no choice but to commend the Queen for her wise observations. She sighed the deep sigh of one who has just wasted her breath, but turned back to our Company and spoke again to our clowns directly.

"Pardon me, I pray you, for now I purloin the parts reserved for our players here. But, if ever you have looked on better days; ever from your eyelids wiped a tear and know what 'tis to pity and be pitied, let gentleness your strong enforcement be, in the which hope, I leave the stage to those who can better portray the human spirit."

"We thank your majesty," quoth Kempe, whose face the Queen seemed most to fix upon. "You are most welcome among our players, for all the world's a stage, and therefore, are not all men and women players merely? We have our exits and entrances and will, in our time on earth, play many parts, until that final exit, the which no one can avoid."

"'Tis true, 'tis all too true. But come, philosopher, hast thou a song to honour absent friends who have made their exit too soon?" Every soul in the chamber knew whom the Queen thought upon at that moment. Phillips stepped forward with his lute, already tuned and warm, and sang in a quiet voice that many strained to hear, but the meaning of which none could miss:

"Blow, blow, thou winter wind.
Thou art not so unkind
As man's ingratitude;
Thy tooth is not so keen,
Because thou art not seen,
Although thy breath be rude.

Heigh-ho! sing, heigh-ho! unto the green holly:
Most friendship is feigning, most loving mere folly:
Then, heigh-ho, the holly!
This life is most jolly.

Freeze, freeze, thou bitter sky,
That dost not bite so nigh
As benefits forgot:
Though thou the waters warp,
Thy sting is not so sharp
As friend remember'd not.

Heigh-ho! sing, heigh-ho! unto the green holly:
Most friendship is feigning, most loving mere folly:
Then, heigh-ho, the holly!
This life is most jolly.[120]

On the fourth and last night of these festivals, the Queen opened the palace grounds to the multitude of her subjects. So many ran to see her when the gates were set open, nor did her guard hinder any person, no matter how mean, from coming in. The yard was soon full, and there we stayed an hour and more, the dark held back by countless lit torches, which wrought such an impression upon us, for show and pageants are ever best seen by torchlight, are they not? I was overjoyed that Rosalind was in such good health by then, that she came with Mr. Stow, Heather, and Giddy too. The Queen came out in great state and to our astonishment, the nobles mingled with commoners and all seemed to delight greatly therein, perhaps in celebration that God spared us all equally from the Spanish devils.

Giddy may have reported to thee how the mother of the Earl of Southampton, the silly boy I met with the Earl of Essex a year ago at Court, she bought from Giddy two dozen pair of gloves to give as gifts to commemorate this day of thanksgiving, giving two dozen reasons more ourselves to be thankful.[121] Several in her retinue asked after the craftsman of these gloves and the Countess most courteously introduced Giddy, lavishing him with her praise as 'you shall never see more delicate stitches' and 'does not the glove feel like some Heavenly exhalation upon your hand' and the like. Giddy presented me, Rosalind, Mr. Stow and Heather to her anon, after which we enjoyed a quarter hour of fresh talk. I sensed she had lived a life not always made easier by her privilege and she thereby seemed to understand more about Rosalind and Heather, about a woman's never-easy path, and whispered gentle words of hope and faith to them both apart, which cheered the ladies most sweetly.

We might have lingered with her a longer time, but she attended the Queen and so many dignitaries more that I soon lost the count. Leicester's Men gave one last performance that night, quite certain that we would soon be Queen's Men, such a good opinion had we wrought in those four days.

That night, being the 24th of November, Rosalind wanted to walk certain environs of the City that gave her joy, before her swelling belly would make such simple pleasures inconvenient. She then directed our footsteps beyond any place I had imagined, and our conversation thus:

"I have always been partial to Helen." Rosalind consulted a small paper she had folded into a book, in which she recorded certain necessaries and now the names we might call our new son or daughter. "But Heather thinks a girl born this year can be called nothing other than Elizabeth."

"And many boys will be called Francis, Robert, or Charles to honour the victorious admirals, but I cannot abide those, especially any that recall Robert Dudley."

"If names are meant to honour, why not Amazonia for a girl? Truly, Dick playing the woman warrior before the Queen will become the stuff that ballads are made of, in times to come!" It was indeed a most ingenious performance, mirth for a month, as we say.

"If names are meant to honour, why not John to honour thy late father?"

"Could I ever say the child's name without thinking on my father? And in doing so, would not my tears be bitter at the loss, instead of joyous at the sight of our son?"

"Aye, there's the rub. What thinkst thou of Joan?" We carried on in this manner a quarter of an hour, Rosalind committing to her book those names we both deemed worthy. I barely noticed the way she led me, which was not unusual in a City she knew far better than I (after all, walking every stone and byway with heavy buckets inspires thrift with steps). Leaving the palace at White Hall, we had walked the glittering Strand back to the City and stopped then at Ludgate, without the wall. Rosalind pointed up at the north side of the archway, just inside the gateway proper, and bid me pull away the branch of a beech tree that covered the stones.

"Seest that stone with carved letters? In the time of King John, wanting the walls and gates of this City to be repaired, he suffered his barons to enter the City and break into the houses of Jews, to search their coffers and fill their own purses, but in the main to spoil those same houses for stones.

Look, thither, at that stone in particular." I was surprised by her knowledge of this obscure history, but climbed up to examine the words.

"I can feel the letters engraved thereon, but cannot read them in this light."

"In daylight, wouldst see, in Hebrew characters, 'Haec est statio Rabbi Mosis, filii insignis Rabbi Isaac', which is to say, this is the station or ward of Rabbi Moyses, the son of the honourable Rabbi Isaac, a stone that had been fixed upon the front of one of the Jews' houses as a note or sign that such a one dwelt there."

We walked on through Paul's churchyard towards Wood Street, where Brownsword's shop was familiar, imagining what Moyses or Isaac were like and what they had done to lose the benefit of their houses. Heather had read from various histories to Rosalind during her illness and thereby she came to know that 'rabbi' was the holy man of the Jews and that English monarchs past had grown rich by stealing from them. She recalled for me more, the which I write in sum herewith, for certain amazing reasons that will soon be apparent: how the first King Richard forbad Jews to be present at his coronation,[122] for fear of enchantments. Nor did the next sovereign, King John, love the Jews any better, although it may be said he loved their money well. He commanded all the Jews, both men and women, to be imprisoned and grievously punished, until each paid a ransom. Some gave all they had to escape so many kinds of torments, such as those who had at least one of their eyes plucked out, or another who had daily a tooth plucked out of his head, so that after a space of seven days, that man then gave the king ten thousand marks of silver to end the pulling out of his teeth.

At the north end of Wood street, we paused at the Cripplegate to buy a small packet of licorice from a husband and wife who huddled around a fire and sold such trinkets long after others were shuttered and snoring. We warmed ourselves awhile thereby and learned they came from Gloucester and had fled bad harvests thither in hopes of earning money in London to pay her father's debts. At length, Rosalind pointed towards St. Giles church that lay just without the gate and asked if I would see her most treasured place in all of the great City.

Leaving the fire made us acutely aware that winter was not far off. Rosalind wore the lesser of our cloaks, but swore she was heated by the vigour of our walk together, and that of the baby growing stronger within her, blood coursing through her swiftly for them both. When we came to a garden on the west side of the church and sat on a stone bench therein, I wrapped her in my cloak and made a brave face. In truth, I soon forgot the cold and was heated mightily by these things she next told to me:

"A lovely garden, rebuilt when St. Giles was newly constructed after the fire, I imagine." Such places without the wall would not seem so safe after dark, but this one still had visitors, perhaps those who lived in the fine stone and timber houses adjacent, light from their windows casting shifting shadows on the grounds beneath, all safely hemmed by fair garden plots and summer-houses for pleasure in softer times.

"I am not surprised this place would charm thee."

"Thou may not think so kindly on me, or this place, when I have said all. O Will, thy love is so manifest to me, in ways I cannot count. It gives me courage to have this baby. I feared I would ne'er see thee more, after thou and thy martial players marched to war. I feared thou wouldst never know of thy child, for surely I would die with my grave illness."

"And now?"

"Only one thing more to fear." She was shaking, the double cloaks notwithstanding. I wrapped her in mine arms and tried to comfort her, though I knew not then what was the matter. "Will, this place is called the Jews' Garden, as being the only place appointed them in England, wherein to bury their dead, till the time of their final banishment out of England. I have shown thee these relics tonight for one reason chiefly: that thou wouldst know thy child, soon to come into this world, will share my Jewish blood."

To that time, I had given little thought to the Hebrew tribe, beyond what thou hast said pertaining to thy father's trade in lending at interest. Thou knowest more than I, that the Hebrews were once great traders and money lenders, but were punished for charging Christians more than two pence a week for the loan of twenty shillings. I recall thy father saying they had all been banished from England, nor have I ever met a Jew, that I knew of. If Rosalind was saying now that she was one, there was no outward appearance. Does that change when they are at worship? I studied the deep green pools of her eyes for clues and, to be honest, held my breath for whatever would come next.

"O God, please help me explain all to my beloved, and grant him patience with me to hear it." She grasped my hands as tight as a child holds to its mother at a hanging, waiting not a moment for my reply. "In the time of Henry III, the king had seven Jews brought from Norwich, accusing them of stealing a Christian child that they minded to circumcise and crucify at Easter. Aaron, the son of Abraham, a Jew then living in London, was constrained to pay twenty thousand marks ransom, or else to be hanged with these other Jews. Before he could pay for their release, along with others of their tribe imprisoned at Newgate, their old rabbi fell into a privy on a Saturday and would not that day be taken out, for reverence of his Sabbath, wherefore his jailer kept him there till Monday, but by then he was dead. With no one to lead them and secure the money, the King thereafter hanged Aaron and eighteen more."

Thou knowest coz that there are no truer faces than those washed with tears. At that moment, Rosalind's was the truest face I had seen in my life. I dabbed her cheeks with my sleeve and bid her continue, though I could not imagine how this winding path would bring me to an understanding of her part in all of this. In brief, I was dumb-struck.

"Aaron had a daughter called Jessica, whom he gave to the care of a Christian baker's wife at the prison. This Christian woman had shown the prisoners many courtesies and she thereafter raised the child as her own, as a Christian, to protect her from further annoyances. Moreover, she gave the child a small silver cross, that she said should ever be a sign of her Jewish heritage, leastways in her mind, for on the back thereof she caused to be graven the single letter J, meaning either Jessica or Jew. Time out of mind erased the purpose, though not the letter itself on the metal relic. Only she should know the true meaning of the cross and she should pass it to her daughter, if God granted her such fortune. Indeed, Jessica married a mercer and had two sons and one daughter. Many generations passed, many now forgotten, but each daughter was told the truth of her ancestors and given the silver cross - - even this one that I wear now - - and sworn to secrecy with a pledge to pass it on from each generation to the next."

"Then thou art Christian? Thy bloodline has long since been diluted of any Hebrew." I bit my tongue at saying so, for the cross on her neck testified that these ancestors, no matter how vilified or distant, still meant something of value to her.

"Aye Will, I love God as much as any soul in Christendom and know nothing of Jewish ritual or superstition. But I know my people lay buried 'neath our feet on this plot of ground and, though only God knows their names and can recall their faces, I find comfort here."

By now, we shared the larger cloak, draped around our bodies that were so close together as to be indistinguishable in any wise. I fed her a piece of the licorice and assured her of my love, for I care not whether she be of this faith or that, having seen my father suffer from such questions and many die in wars about the same. Could God want his creations to behave in this manner when his son preached love and forgiveness? And who was I to pass judgments in His stead? I said as much to her as I painted a silly beard on her chin with the juice of the licorice. I felt her body, and her spirit, unwind as we laughed.

Rosalind unfolded more to me of what she had learned from Heather's books. The Jews' Garden had emptied now and we knew the time had come to also take our leave. We prayed for the souls therein and pledged to return to do them honour, one day with our own son or daughter. As we walked back down Wood street, we concluded one important duty: if a girl, she would be called Jessica; if a boy, we would honour the long-forgotten people of the garden at St. Giles yard, and call him Giles.

Our joy was complete, there being no more secrets between us; both in good health; and with some means to keep meat on our table through the winter. But the next day, being the 25th of November, God or Fate changed course most abruptly.

The Queen that day proclaimed Leicester's lands and goods forfeit, declaring the need of the Crown was greater than those who might claim his fortune and that there would never be another Earl of Leicester as long as she lived. His servants, including those who played under his former protection, were now formally without master and we were ordered to surrender his colours. Johnson thought the Queen could no longer afford spies in the land, her treasury exhausted by war and, with her victory, Spain was chastised. Those recusants who might help Phillip and the Pope were now either executed or under watchful eyes of local bishops, who are empowered to levy fines and gross humiliation (in London, ministers and churchwardens are ordered to observe who does not attend service once a quarter, their names then to be reported to the bishop and, if they did not reform, the bishop is to pronounce the offenders excommunicate!). Is it also thus in Stratford now? Moreover, all family and private meetings for preaching, reading, catechizing, and other such exercises are to be completely forbidden if attended by outsiders, there being so many foreigners in the City.

Even common players are now enforced to attend church in the City, each of us making his peace with this parish or that one. Bibles are now in every learned man's hand and passed around the tables in taverns. We read from one at the Mermaid that bore an inscription 'Out of dear love for my country after surviving the invasion, this bible to be chained to the church wall for the edification of those that shall read therein.' The benefactor had been better rewarded by supplying therewith a stronger chain.

Burbage secured employment for each of us as occasion allowed in other Companies in great need of skilled players after losing so many to wars, Plague, and old age. Imagine my surprise when my first part came with Lord Strange's Men, their playing of 'Jew of Malta' a new play by Marlowe. Nor could that Company perform this new play often enough to satisfy the multitude at the Rose or those nobles at Court who demanded to see it many times.

Wilson and I therefore returned our attention to writing some matter that would capture as much money as this great success by the men of Lord Strange. I again urged Wilson to gruesome scenes with battles and blood, seeing the crowd react to the barbarity of Barabas the Jew, cheering when he proclaims 'I walk abroad o' nights and kill sick people groaning under walls. Sometimes I poison wells and, with young orphans, fill up entire hospitals.' At length Wilson agreed, if we would set the play in ancient Rome, there being lately such excitement by the Queen and Court as conquerors in chariots and robes and wreaths. But we were only briefly in this endeavour when more urgent employment for our pens was thrust upon us, again delaying any new play.

Hast thou read the scurrilous pamphlet, distributed throughout the City, perhaps the whole country by now, signed by one 'Martin Marprelate, Gentleman'? Many lords and ladies and other great and wealthy personages now have copies, offending even some Puritans like Johnson, proving prescient those who have long feared the Puritans more than the Catholics.

The author, who says he writes in both mirth and gravity (but the Queen is not laughing), calls upon the church in England to embrace Puritan values by eliminating arrogant clerical 'royalty', those being the bishops, and wicked priests, all of whom Marprelate calls 'proud, popish, presumptuous, profane, paltry, petulant and pernicious leeches!' He names Bishop Aylmer of London for playing at bowls of a Sunday and for cutting down the elms at Fulham to fill his own purse therefrom. He calls the Archbishop Whitgift a sodden-headed ass, favoring papistry.

The Queen issued a proclamation calling this a lewd and seditious pamphlet, secretly dispersed by persons of unquiet spirit, and ordering the Archbishop Whitgift to use all means of force to find the authors, printers, and distributors, then to apprehend and commit them to prison. And once again, I am thrust together with the impenetrable vicar in this manner: Whitgift commissioned certain poets to write pamphlets in defense of the clergy, by that I mean some well-known to thee, John Lyly, and Robert Greene, and their new fellow Thomas Nashe (though he would by no means admit Marlowe, who is feared as himself seditious).[123] These produced some satire, keen and critical, but not sorting with a church led by our Queen, such as 'Almond for a Parrot', which was meant to show the thrift of a Puritan. Speaking few words at the grave of his dead wife, the Puritan tumbled her naked into the earth, without sheet or shroud to cover her shame, proclaiming over her 'naked camest thou out of thy mother's womb and naked shall thee return again.'

Whitgift was not amused and asked his man Bancroft, who is oft in our playhouses, to find writers to swiftly mend the work. Bancroft came to Burbage; Burbage turned to me. I am paid a gold sovereign therefore (and Bancroft says more may come). Wanting for a way to support Rosalind and send money home to Stratford, this seems a gift from Heaven, and I accepted the duty. I wanted to ask him why the Archbishop takes such interest in me, but he was not at leisure to answer those inquiries. In the mean season, the money was most welcome, and that same gold piece is conveyed to thee herewith for the comfort of my kin thither.

Upon the fifteenth day of December, I received thy letter, joyed to know Giddy hath safely arrived thither and our humble gifts for the holiday season delivered (the confection was made by Dick's good wife Elizabeth), yet pained to hear that my father still finds no remedy for consumption of his mind and his purse. In truth, that seems of little consequence to me now, given the matter I must describe to thee, if there is a God to grant me strength enough to write the words.

I have now reported to thee all events in recent memory, of any importance, and that brings me to the eve of Christmas, yesterday. 'Twas early, afore the cock crew, and in my swinish sleep I was again visited by that selfsame dream (the one I had the night before I first entered the City), yet again, an oracle of nothing good.

Once more in the dream, I stood upon the roofs of the buildings that line the bridge, but this time in the company of Rosalind, who tempted me to walk thereupon, repeating those selfsame steps I had taken in the dream before with Giddy. This time it was she that stumbled, knocking me overboard into the tumbling billows of the river. Again, I lived the grievous pain of drowning and the dreadful noise of rushing waters in mine ears. Again, I beheld the thousand fearful wrecks and ten thousand men that fishes gnawed upon. This time, there were no golden anchors, no jewels or pearls, only the empty skulls of the dead. As before, I found myself striving to yield the ghost up, but still the envious flood would not let it forth. And then began the tempest to my soul as I sought to cross the river Styx: first there to greet me was my good master Perkin. He tried, but could not speak, nor could I understand the meaning of his dumbshow, and so he vanished. Then, as before, a legion of foul fiends environed me about and howled in mine ears. But this time, the howls were not in dreams alone.

The great scream came from Rosalind, who ere then had slept peacefully beside me. To be brief, for I cannot write these words without weeping, she was in sudden pains for yielding up the child. Heather came to our aid.

Some hours later, a boy was delivered.

Giles: our unimaginable joy.

Still-born: our unimaginable grief.

The baby was washed and swaddled in a shroud. I held him and lifted the sheet to gaze, at least once, upon my son. He was asleep merely, I thought. His cheeks had the rosy red hue of the quick, not the pale cold gray of the dead. His visage was pinched slightly, not in pain, but rather the appearance of a wrinkled old man who is trying in vain to recall the name he gave to his first puppy; or to re-live the sweet taste of marchpane [*marzipan*] on Christmas morning. Never will our Giles know those simple joys. Or will he live them in Heaven? Will he grow older in Heaven, or remain always new-born?

Rosalind was spent, barely audible, but together we wept. Together we wondered why a dog, a rat, a murderer have life, and Giles no breath at all. She fell into a fevered sleep. I curst God for being the thief that robbed her of a child, that took this jewel so cruelly away.

I thought to let her rest, but would not leave her side, even when Kempe and Dick came calling. I looked into their faces, but none of us found words, nor were any truly needed on this occasion. Kempe thought it meet that we convey her to St. Mary of Bethelem hospital in Bishopsgate nearby, but Mr. Stow said it is mainly for distracted people, by the suit of their friends, and not without charges to their bringers in. Some streets farther, stands the late dissolved priory commonly called St. Mary Spittle, now a hospital well furnished for receipt of the poor and dedicated to the honour of Jesus Christ and his mother. Dick said the Virgin Mary might especially take her pity on Rosalind, owing to that her only child had even now perished, but none of us thought Rosalind could survive the conveyance thither. Heather next thought it good to call for the doctor, saying she thought Rosalind's blood had congealed from too much sadness, and further melancholy could pitch her into a frenzy. The doctor that conquered mine own fever last year was not at leisure to attend, but sent instead a man called Naper, but as Fate would have it, he came too late.

I cannot recall when the sun rose or set, nor how much time had passed on this most lamentable day, but at some length, Rosalind awoke and called out. I laid a hand on her fiery forehead. What a look she gave me then! A rueful eye she fixed steadfast upon my face, which to my death will never part from my mind's eye. She so loves the delicate fragrance of a rose, which cannot live in winter, but the water thereof we had from Heather, who had dipped a napkin therein, the which I now gave Rosalind to inhale. A moment it seemed to cheer her, she fumbled with the cloth and my fingers all at once. Then she cried out to God, twice or thrice, and I told her not to think on him yet, for Heaven was many years hence, at which she smiled and closed her eyes. She bid me lay more blankets on her and let forth a deep felt sigh, clasping my hands, casting her sight to Heaven. Then straightaway, pale Death pressed in upon her face and her fleeting soul forsook her mortal coil.

O coz, I pray thou wilt never know such pain, never live to see such a double tragedy within the space of a single, damned day. In that instant, alone with her in the dark, I could only think of chasing after her and Giles. Why should I live, linger forth my time in longer life, to double my distress? Think on it: were my bones already now in peace, long since lain within the ground, I would never have felt this present pain. But if I live, what of Rosalind? Will she stay forever young, while I grow old and decrepit, such that, if we are reunited in Heaven, she might not recognize me? Or want to?

I pressed the rose-scent against my face and prayed for tears or death, but could summon neither. O, that this too solid flesh would melt and resolve itself into a dew! If children die first, we are their offspring, and they none of ours. When old bees die, the young possess their hive: then live, sweet Giles, live again and see thy father die, but not thy father thee! I would cut out my heart in the instant if that would breathe life back into thee, but as I write these words, I know that a rose plucked, cannot grow again. It needs must wither, it needs must die.

I know that God hath fixed His canon against self-slaughter, but is that merely to lengthen my life and torture me day by day for my sins? God is now the main Inquisitor: His every petty action toys with me, His voice reprimands me in every sound, be it ever so mean, such as the creaking I hear now in these rafters. And why should I expect greater love, than those thousand souls He sent to Hell, because they loved him better in London or in Rome?

Coz, I know not yet which way I'll go in this weedy garden that seems now so stale, flat, and unprofitable, but will try to gather some peace from knowing that Rosalind and Giles are now secure from worldly chances and mishaps. For them, there lurks no treason; no envy swells; no damned grudges fester and grow; there are no storms, no noise. Only silence and eternal sleep. O my sweet loves, may flights of angels sing ye to that peaceful rest. If I can pluck the courage from my sorrow, I will fly soon after thee.[124] O John, my fairest friend, as I have always endeavoured to be faithful and just to thee, forgive me, when now I set this pen to rest, if all that follows is silence. I know thou wilt care for my family, as thou hast done in such great measure already. Heaven may reward thee: God knows I can never adequately do so. Thy very assured loving friend and kinsman, Will.

LETTER SIXTEEN
April 23, 1589

Wherein two loved ones are laid to rest, but from a tragedy played upon a stage, the new playwright discovers the power and solace of the pen.

Of all the nights I spent in conversation and exchanging packets of letters with Miss B, one that stands out vividly in my memory after all these years was when I told her that Shakespeare had fathered a son out of wedlock. I had hesitated to do so, unsure if discussing such topics about anyone, let alone William Shakespeare, might offend her sensibilities. She is British after all

When I shared that revelation, and the fact that Shakespeare also wrote that the mother and child both died and were buried in a secret Jewish cemetery next to a Protestant church in London, her reaction was not what I expected.

"Was she beautiful?"

I told her that my understanding of the letters was still very incomplete, but if I was reading them right so far, yes.

"Then the boy must have been beautiful too."

I don't recall what interrupted us that night, but the conversation ended there and that subject was never resumed. Miss B had a very precise way of saying things, such that if a word has two meanings, her inflection immediately made clear which one she intended. Thinking back on it, she may not have been asking about Rosalind's physical appearance, but whether she was an enlightened, exceptional person, as in the phrase "a beautiful mind." That may have been what Shakespeare was thinking of too, when he buried Rosalind in the Jews Garden.

Letter Sixteen is written on Shakespeare's birthday, April 23rd 1589, four months after the death of his beloved Rosalind, a period of intense mourning, but surprising triumphs. He relates how Will Kempe and Dick Cowley helped him carry the bodies of Rosalind and Giles to the garden near St. Giles Church and helped bury them in an unmarked grave under cover of night. Shakespeare keeps Rosalind's cross (which will appear again prominently in later letters) and leaves a sonnet in her grave (another poem that started life for one purpose, but was bequeathed to eternity in the published collection as Sonnet 50). Shakespeare then bids Kempe and Cowley to meet him in a nearby tavern and, to their amazement, explains that the building was originally a Jewish synagogue. They bow their heads in silent prayer for Rosalind and Giles.

Shakespeare finds work mending religious pamphlets that defend the Church of England against Puritan attacks on its clergy, but in so doing so, alienates his fellow writers, whose work he is altering. Shakespeare is simply trying to earn a living, but now ostracized, he is forced to try to write a play on his own, without the help of the intended co-authors. He can no longer bear to go back to his former lodging with Mr. Stow (too many memories of Rosalind), but he is granted leave to stay in the great barn near The Theatre. He finds inspiration from the elderly caretaker, Vernon, who excavates the Roman artifacts beneath the stage while conversing with their ghosts.

Shakespeare resolves to write a play that takes place in Roman times and Heather Burberry supplies the books that help him fill in the gaps of his imperfect knowledge of that time. *Titus Andronicus* draws plot points and characters from Ovid's *Metamorphoses*; Seneca's tragedy *Thyestes*; *Gesta Romanorum*, a book of popular Roman stories; and more contemporary fare including Marlowe's *Jew of Malta.*

The writing comes easily, and as his imagination is rekindled, Shakespeare's gloom eases. He wanders among the Roman ruins of London and tries to imagine the hearts and minds of people he knows, as if they were characters of the ancient time of the play. Shakespeare presents the play to Burbage and his fellows, cleverly flattering each man's vanity with the importance of their particular part. It is a story filled with honor, betrayal, horror and retribution. Master Burbage's verdict is: "We have a play."

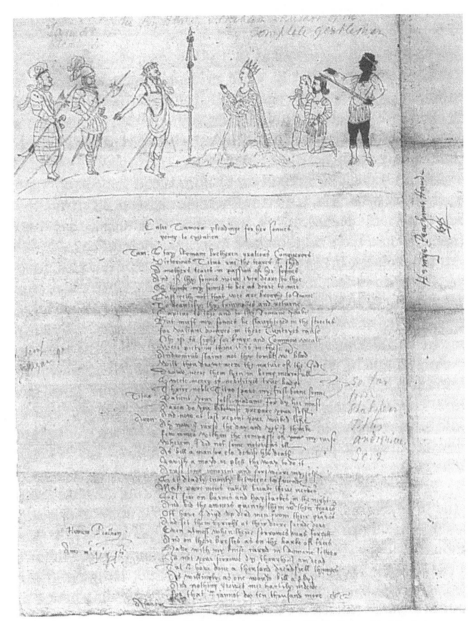

23. 1595 sketch of a scene from Titus Andronicus depicting how Elizabethan actors blended contemporary garments with period costumes.

The play premieres in the pouring rain and the only performance fizzles. The players are about to abandon Shakespeare's work, when Lord Ferdinando Strange comes to The Theatre unexpectedly (accompanied by the "girl-boy" Earl of Southampton). A fan of the play, Lord Strange entreats Burbage and his company to play Shakespeare's *Titus Andronicus* at the neighboring theatre, The Rose, together with Lord Strange's own players (Illustration 23 on page 413 is a sketch made by Henry Peacham, an audience member at a performance of the play in 1595, depicting how Elizabethan actors blended contemporary garments with period costumes to set the look and feel of the play). The theatre companies combine talents and execute the play to wild and thunderous applause.

We don't see many productions of *Titus Andronicus* these days, probably because of what seems to modern audiences as over-the-top blood and gore. A recent production I attended at the Globe Playhouse in London proved that, despite extravagant depictions of the brutality, the play can still focus the audience's attention on the politics (which would seem very familiar in our Left-Right politically divided world); the passions (who would not plot some awful revenge on an enemy that had needlessly slaughtered your child?); the racism; and what some will do under the guise of "love of country."

Shakespeare now has a profession and, at age 25, has grown somewhat older than when he first left his Stratford home and family and certainly wiser, as he contemplates the reflection of his receding hairline in the mirror (Illustration 24, opposite, shows portraits of Shakespeare and his contemporaries over time). He is writing sonnets for courtiers to give the Queen and is now able to send money home to Stratford and settle some debts. He even tries to repay the mapmaker he once stole from, but the man has disappeared and Shakespeare worries that he was in some way responsible.

When Shakespeare first began writing plays, the action onstage flowed continuously, characters coming and going, locations changing, but without intermission or any artificial division into acts and scenes. As his letters and numerous examples from late Renaissance theatre reveal, those divisons were added when plays were performed indoors at night and some Johannes factotum needed a break in the action to come onstage and replace the candles or

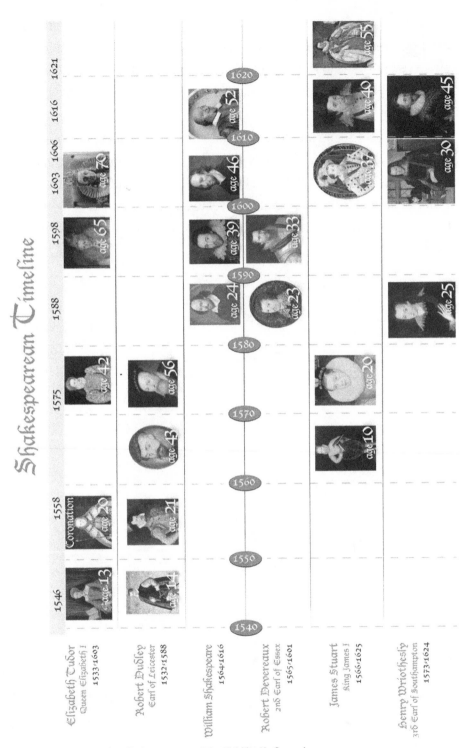

24. Timeline of Portraits: Shakespeare and the Nobility He Served

trim the tapers to keep the lights shining and the sooty smoke to a minimum. Indoor theatres were initially the province of the wealthy, who wanted then, as now, to visit the bar and kibbitz with other attendees, to see and be seen. Plays also became popular reading material around 1600 and the divisions created logical "chapters."

More than a scene has concluded with this letter, at least Act One of the definable chapters of Shakespeare's life, so it seemed an appropriate place to end Book One. But like the fifteen letters that precede it, Letter Sixteen leaves us with many mysteries and conundrums yet to unravel. Fortunately, the dozens of letters Shakespeare writes hereafter, that will be compiled in Books Two and Three, provide us with the tools to do just that.

St. George's Day, April 23, 1589, London

Coz,

As this letter will testify, I am not dead: neither by mine own hand nor any other, but never will my heart beat with the soaring hope it once felt. Thinking on how thou wouldst someday show my letters to Hamnet, that he might know his father unvarnished and full of human frailty, I imagined myself in his place, reading that the sorrow of a dead son outweighed the joys of a living one; that the love of a dead mistress meant more than the sincere affections of a living wife, his mother. What should Hamnet think then of his father?

Hamnet, look at what thy soul today holds dear: imagine it to be gone, for only then canst thou see how best to keep it living still, and gnarling sorrows, when they come, may be eased by such remembrance. I hold thee dearest, Hamnet, and though a father will ever mourn the loss of a child, so too will he, when the darkest clouds part, revive in the happiness of the ones yet living, as I do now in thee and thy sisters. Therefore son, please forgive thy sometimes foolish father: the darkest clouds having parted, thy light shines upon me now, and will ever grant me strength.

And coz, in gratitude for thy letter, I am reminded that Death is ever recompensed anew by Life: I mean the sad tidings that my cousin is dead against such joyful news that thy nephew hath now a new brother. I will write to mine uncle (for thou knowest I can now imagine his grief) but even as I take comfort in my son that lives, I will counsel him to find succor in his Lettice, who I trust is ever in good health.[125]

Now will I commit to these pages the events that I recall since Christmas Day, some of which seem to me frozen, as if trapped inside a great block of ice, visible yet unreachable, counterfeiting life, but cold and motionless, December bareness everywhere. These then, are the few glimpses of life through the ice, those that remain visible to my mind's eye. If you have tears, prepare to shed them now.

I can still see the hoary frost on the beards of Kempe and Dick, in streets yet darkened and drunk from celebrations on the day after Christmas, as we transported Rosalind and Giles to the Jews' Garden before dawn.

I can still feel the shovel in the receiving earth as we dug their graves in the only place she would have wanted our son, and her, to lie in final peace. I could feel her warmth, I swear, our hearts beating in unison one last time, as I bid my companions to hold off the earth awhile, till I had caught her once more in mine arms, before I lay her down, with Giles cradled in beside her.

I can still hear the dirt spilling over their shrouds and, from their fair and unpolluted flesh, my hope that violets would burst forth with life in the spring. I had thought to have decked thy bed with such posies, sweet Rosalind, and not to have strewn thy grave withal.[126] A grave that shall never have a monument, save God's memory and, I trust, His mercy.

I took from her the cross, though no issue of her body would carry its Jewish secret longer into the future, but promised to honour her ancestors therewith in some manner; and her handkerchief, that smells yet of rosewater and her own sweet breath.

I meant to leave her with some thing of me, but have no earthly possessions that could convey my love, and now, my grief. I thought to dedicate some verse, but who will believe a poem in time to come, if it were filled with her most high deserts? Any words would only serve as a tomb that hid her true life, never adequate to show the greater woman she had become. And if I wrote of her beauty, aye numbered all her graces, the Age to come would say 'This poet lies: such heavenly touches never touched an earthly soul.' Yet in her grave I did at last leave a verse, although I cannot say for certain when or how I wrote it, a memory now locked deep within that imagined block of ice:

> How heavy is my journey on the way,
> When what I seek (my weary travel's end),
> Doth teach such ease, and all repose, to say:
> 'Thus far the miles are measured from my friend!'
>
> The beast that bears me, tired with my woe,
> Plods dully on, to bear the weight of me,
> As if by some instinct the wretch did know
> His rider loved not speed, if farther off from thee.

The bloody spur cannot provoke him on,
That sometimes anger thrust into his hide,
Which heavily he answers with a groan:
More sharp to me, than spurring to his side.

For that same groan doth put this in my mind:
My grief lies onward; and all joy behind.

Neither Kempe nor Dick demanded to know of me why we buried them in secret, with no obsequies, lodged in ground unsanctified, until two days later, when at last I could summon up the courage to satisfy their honourable entreaties and bid them meet me at the sign of the windmill in Lothbury street opposite the Grocer's hall.

This street is possessed for the most part by founders, that cast candlesticks and such like copper or leaden works, and do afterward make them smooth and bright with turning and scrating (as some do term it), making a loathsome noise to the by-passers, and therefore by them disdainfully called Loathe-bury. Before that the Jews were from England expelled entirely, this was a house in which they did worship, called in their custom a 'synagogue'. If any man doubt this heritage, he need only ask about the street which intersects thereat, called Old Jury street, which is a confounding of the original name: Old Jewry. To Dick and Kempe, I told all that I knew of Rosalind and of the Jews' Garden and forgave them if they considered me now out of wits, visited by odd ghosts or other powers of Hell, ranting about old Jews and such:

"King Edward banished the Jews, but they are still here, so to say, and tonight ye shall know them, as I have, through Rosalind. The King was greatly enriched by confiscating their wealth and houses, but this Jews' synagogue was later obtained by a Londoner of great wealth, because it was then adjoining the mansion he had built. Hugh Clopton, a mercer, once mayor of London and benefactor of the stone bridge over the Avon, dwelt in this house, and kept his mayoralty here."

"In a tavern? Was that not Clopton Bridge our Company crossed over to make our way into Stratford? Why would such a great man live in a tavern?" I could see Dick look to Kempe for some hopeful explanation of my fantastical claims.

Kempe had lived a life more rough-hewn, so found the matter less amazing than Dick and conned my purpose without further cue. He called for wine, that we might drink to Rosalind and to Giles, 'that they may enter Heaven well-remembered', as he said. Across the tavern, some soldiers caroused and cursed that they had no further work at arms, nor had they yet been paid for the wounds received in service, their song providing an unexpected accompaniment to our solemnities:

"O' let the canakin clink, clink," sang the man with a purse, seeming he that was once an ancient in charge of the others. "Aye let the canakin clink … a soldier's a man … a life's but a span … why, then, let an old soldier drink!"[127]

"'Fore God, an excellent song," quoth a toothless lean and hungry looking beggar at his side, his other followers in sudden agreement that the song deserved more ale.

"Thinkst thou so? I learned it in Denmark, where, indeed, they are most potent in potting. Your Englishman, your German, and your swag-bellied Hollander are nothing to your Dane in the matter of revelry."

"To think my days of such happiness are now but a misty dream," I whispered to my fellows, hard-pressed to find humour in the sense-dulling fumes of the wine, the which now served as my physic.

"What, art thou both in shape and mind transformed and weakened?" Kempe had as much to drink as I, but showed none of the rust that covers a common man's brain thereafter. "Hath Death deposed thine intellect and taken up residence in thy heart? Even the dying lion thrusts forth his paw with rage and wounds the earth, if nothing else. Thou art not the only man ever to have suffered, but lived long after in goodly purpose."

"Is not your Englishman so expert in his drinking?" Although the lout was laughing loud and Kempe but whispering to me, I perceived the one as distant thunder and the other as a blade in mine ear.

"Nay, fool," quoth the ancient, spinning a coin on the table for the host to fill cups again. "The Dane drinks your Englishman, with facility, under this table and he laughs at your Hollander a-vomiting, ere the next cup is filled and drained and can be filled again."

"To the health of our English!" To which the three dozen souls in the tavern all roused up and shouted some manner of agreement.

"O sweet England! Will you hear my song again?"

Was I the only man ever to have suffered? No, not a jot. But what does a man with such grief? I gave Kempe what reply I could:

"Others have known grief, aye, that they have. But in tedious nights, I'll sit with others who have suffered and let them tell me their woeful tales, then to make their griefs seem pale, I'll tell the lamentable tale of Rosalind, and send them weeping to their beds."

"Will, I think thou cam'st hither to pray for her soul, in that place where once her ancestors sent their tidings and biddings, happy or sad, unto their God." Dick took away my cup and drew us three into closer conference, that no man other would overhear us. "I know not the prayers of Hebrews, but let us bid our God, on her behalf, to now find mercy enow for one of that tribe."

"Aye, and the unsullied Giles, whose tiny blameless soul was not long enough on this earth to sin, so who now must be with God." I think Kempe shed a tear as he bid us bow our heads in silence, the which we did for some long time. I suspect he had wept for more than a few babies, and the hard-bitten lives of their mothers, but rarely to comfort the fathers thereof.

More of that night I cannot recall. But what transpired next, as winter thawed into spring, I can relate in every particular, for I conclude my life is changed entirely. These most astonishing events will also satisfy thee, I trust, for why I am not at liberty to return home (though it pains me mightily to hear that my father's hands can cut and stitch no longer). I bid thee read these further pages before rendering harsh judgment on me, although Heaven knows I am an unworthy son, husband, father, or friend. Those first steps, on a much-changed journey that Fate has determined I must now follow, are these:

I have writ to thee about the matter of the scurrilous pamphlets against the church and also how I am paid to mend some broadsides in defense of the English religion. I thought little of the matter, excepting the chinks in my purse from the rector Bancroft, who brought me both pages and payment and has lately compelled me, in the name of the Archbishop himself, to attend the church of St. Helens at the Bishopsgate and thither to make note of any who speak of the Marprelate writings, for or against him, either way.

I swear not a week went by, but that every man and woman there in attendance knew me for a spy and stood farther apart, nor would anyone speak above a whisper when I came near, but Bancroft seems to know of my father's troubles with the church in Stratford and makes various assurances that these will be overlooked if I am faithful to my duties in London. In truth, 'tis no hard labour to sit at sermon and earn money therefor, but this battle of pamphlets soon turned into one between authors of plays.

It was the third Sunday in February, the cold making close pew-fellows of every soul in the church, the Vicar Smith oddly reasoning that talk of death would somehow warm his congregation, thus:

"Medicine may prolong thy earthly life, yet will not Death seize thee one day, aye and thy doctor too? Aye, and even Kings and mightiest potentates must die, for that's the end of human misery. But fear not: if death were but a sleep, no man would fear it at all, for who feareth to take his rest when the night approacheth?"

Such like he continued for nearly an hour, barely audible over wind-rattled planks on the roof, a dozen consumptives coughing, a baby protesting, and a drunk in the alley calling for his Kate. At length, the vicar came then to the true matter of his sermon:

"Then who is it that FEARS Death? Ah the SINNER, that's who! For 'tis a sure sign of an evil life where Death's approach is seen as something fearful and terrible! I mean such like those foul serpents whose tongues sting the body of the church with their spiteful, sinful prose and whose pens would hack down the state ecclesiastical, surely come from Hell, or the miserable church in Scotland. Has not Her Majesty, the sovereign of our land and our church, called them a railing sort and beyond the bounds of good humanity? And who dare says they are NOT just so!"

Bancroft has so fired up the Puritans against Catholic Spain, that now they will not be silenced on any matter. The very church in England seems to crumble under the weight of their demands to reform the bishops, calling any who disagrees to be 'wicked to think that Christ could leave behind him on earth an unperfect and maimed church', meaning that none should interfere with its governance (this latter, I take it, meaning the Queen herself). Catholics never posed such a threat as these rabid dogs, but once unleashed, they are not to be easily heeled.[128]

These then, are the themes that Kit Marlowe and his university fellows have taken up at Bancroft's behest, in their defense against the scurrilous writings of Marprelate.[129] But any man or woman on a London street going about their business finds these arguments dull with little purpose in their own lives. Therefore, did Bancroft call upon me to trim the fat; that the reader might see the cause more plainly; that he might be stirred to love his church and our Queen, who stands royally at the head thereof. But those authors were much offended to know I had changed so much as a comma of their authorship.

Who was I, an unlearned country lout, to think he might know better how to touch the hearts of a true Englishman? I replied that this was merely salary and hire, and Bancroft was the father of these matters, but no amount of apology or explanation would soothe these fellows, who congregate nightly to applaud their own cleverness, bestowed on 'an unpolished, uneducated, unpruned, untrained, unlettered multitude, which we have sought to enlighten'. I will not say more, but even mine own safety was at risk and I dared not show my face at the Mermaid for a goodly time.

But the effect of this distemper was that Wilson was then persuaded to abandon our labours to write a play together; Kyd, who had shown me some courtesies, now spat when I passed him by; and Marlowe refused to accept mine apologies or emissaries (although himself is in hiding, owing to his closest friend, Francis Kett, having been newly burned at the stake for declaring there is no God!). But 'twas Vernon who then restored my boldness, who gave me leave and heart to attempt the graver work that would soon surpass these petty jealous toads:

"Why should thy birth keep down thy mounting spirit? There's legions now of beggars on the earth, that their origins did spring from kings; and many monarchs in time, whose fathers were the riff-raff of their age." Vernon's eyes have dimmed, so when he wagged a brush at me, the paint thereon splattered the hindquarters of the horse and not my last good shirt. I lodge now at the Theatre, by leave of Burbage, so long as I aid Vernon with various repairs thereto, sleep-walking through a daily ritual of hammering, lifting, painting, and hauling (I can no longer rest at Stow's, whereat such memories of Rosalind linger and prick at me too sharply). My greater recompense is that Vernon is a second father to me and proves how great floods might flow from simple sources.

"Aye, and doth not Time wear out a king's estate to beggary? Why the Thames himself began life as a small and shallow stream, but grew to the life-blood through the heart and body of London and powers mighty ships now to the sea without limit. And what of powerful lords, like Francis Walsingham, the arm and sword of the Queen herself: was not his birth as mean as thine or mine, a son of a Foots Cray lawyer, no better, but now higher than any man in all of Christendom? Then, William, cheer thee up, and tell thy soul, that thou may'st live to flourish too!"

"Thou speak'st aright Vernon. Thy Roman ghosts feared not, whilst they lived, to dare greatness: else they had stayed in Rome."

"Aye lad, thou hast it now."

"To write a play is to put ink on paper merely, the which can be consigned to flames if it please not the many."

"Aye, lad, thou art mighty now."

"Nothing ventured..."

"Nothing gained. Now thou art the William my Romans think so highly on."

"The ghosts know aught of me?"

"And often speak of nothing else. From thy first entrance hither have their eyes been keenly bent on thee and marked thee for greater glories, numbered more than the biting fleas on this horse's arse."

I knew not whether Vernon, in his November years, wove stories of ghosts and triumphs on the stage in earnest or for jest, but he managed always to restore a vigour to my veins with both. For some days thereafter, we imagined ancient Romans striding across the stage of the Theatre, across the centuries from their time to this. At times, he would lift one skull from out of the dust and confer therewith. I could hear only his half of any such conversation, but the ghost he spoke withal must have been cheered to be so suddenly employed. Names, ranks, battles, arms, the habits of his kinsmen, all flowed freely day after day and made their way onto my pages. Our play would be called Titus the Great and center on a mighty general in victorious battles against the enemies of the Empire.[130]

Heather brought me books that filled the gaps in my imperfect knowledge of those times and further fleshed out the matter of the play. She had no patience for my slow and faulty translation and instead read to us aloud from her books, first in Latin, then in the most fluid English tongue, making ancients therefrom live again and join with the likes of Vernon's Roman ghost to populate our stage. Dick's wife Bess brought her spicy cabbage and a pasty, while he read aloud from Seneca, I from mine Ovid, taking up this story or shedding that manner, like parrots that steal and mimic their master's speech (Bess thought the enterprise was better left to others and missed no opportunity to bid Dick come quickly home, but otherwise it seemed all the world was fixated upon our labours).

In this wise, I did hammer out some semblance of a play and restore some semblance of a life (though Sorrow yet held my heart a prisoner), but though my words on the pages rang true and the parts were most excellent, the story lacked some spark of life and I would end each day tearing up more pages than I saved. Vernon chastised me, for paper is dear and time, quoth he, more valuable than gold or silver, but he gave me then a key that unlocked a hidden store of treasure, a source of words and feelings that breathed life into my hollow creations.

These are Romans in dress and time only, Vernon said, so he bid me give them the hearts and minds of people around me now. Imagine each part played by one of our fellows and then would I know their joy and pain. Think on Titus not as any father, but as my father: for what could ring truer than hearing the fate of a man that lives in my family, in the flesh, not one who lives in my imagination merely. Now I could see in Titus as the man who sacrificed his sons and treasure in service to his state and how that drove him to a kind of madness. Now I could hear the cold, haughty, and imperious Emperor who schemed to steal away a family's rightful heritage. Now I could feel the abject pain of a woman wronged, left alive a time to suffer in silence after being brutally cut off from that which she loved, that which she lived for.

From that time hence, the Romans on my pages spoke the lines to me almost without pause, not ghosts, like those that communed with Vernon, but living souls whispering conversations in my head. The Theatre seemed now to be a cage, and I the cat, aching to roam and sniff new airs. By day I haunted the places of the City known to have been occupied by Romans, to wit the conduit at Clerkenwell, frequented since Caesar's day by scholars and youths of the city in evenings when they walk forth to take in the air. Interludes are still played thither, of Terence and Seneca, and at times the reading aloud of Caesar's speeches. I walked around the walls of the Tower, to imagine the Romans building it as their fortress, for it hath been the common opinion that Julius Caesar, the first conqueror of the Britons, was the original builder thereof. Did he think his citadel would one day be the City's chiefest defense against its enemies? Or a royal palace for assemblies and treaties? Or even a prison of state, for the most dangerous offenders, and the place where dread executions of such villains would be levied? Would he take pride that it now serves as the place of coinage for all England and the treasury of the ornaments and jewels of the crown?

One of the days I was musing thither, viewing those public regions of the castle that house strange beasts since Roman times, I met a man who confirmed the magical properties of the place. William Foxley, who claimed he had been the potmaker for the Mint in the Tower, and told me the most fantastical story, that in the year 1546, on Tuesday in Easter week, he fell asleep, and so continued sleeping, and could not be wakened with pricking or burning whatsoever, until full fourteen days and fifteen nights later. The cause of his sleeping could not be known, but in this time, he said he walked abroad with Caesar and other Roman notables, and for these forty years since he has been given leave to reside in the Tower and convey the speeches of the ghosts to the learned astrologer to the Queen, that she might be forewarned of danger to her kingdom. Like Vernon, Foxley conveyed to me the Roman manner of speech and the ways they organized their war-like government.

Once did Vernon accompany me to seek the ghosts of Rome together, or perhaps owing to the fact I had money enough for us to take a ha'penny worth of strained milk at one stall he favours in the west end of Hog Street, wherein he claims the Romans took their meat and bread on feast days. He may have added this custom of his own making to encourage my liberality, but no matter, for it warmed my heart to see the old player weep with joy that my pen dipped into the inkpot of his stories and knowledge of such matters, bestowing them again with life upon a page. Vernon brought me to market at Leadenhall, where foreigners sell their wools and felts and strange cheeses and wines, the like he said contained the blood of animals or humans in Roman times. At one stall, with the most pungent cheese, he compelled me to spend my last on a morsel of 'Caesar's bacon' that was offered us, as he poked at the carcass of the slender hog that hung there and told me this tale:

"In my youth, the officers charged with oversight of this market did divers times take therefrom certain pigs, that were starved or otherwise unwholesome for man's sustenance, and these they notched in the ear saying 'Hail Caesar', a practice even unto this day. I know not why the Emperor of Rome is honoured in the practice, but one of the proctors tied a bell about the neck of just such a swine and let it feed on the dunghills, allowing that no man would hurt or take it up. But look you, if any person gave bread to this pig, that person forever thereafter did the swine watch for and follow, whining till he had something given him again, whereupon was raised a proverb: after any man delivers an unexpected kindness 'he will follow you now and whine as it were Caesar's pig.' But if such a pig grew to be fat, and came to good liking, as oft times they did, then the proctor would take him up for slaughter and serve his meat to the good use of the hospital adjacent, whereat thanks were given for Caesar's bacon."

I wanted to ask the serving woman if her bacon came from such a pig, but the bells of the parish church of St. Michael the Archangel rang, prompting Vernon to report to me another fantastical tale of a Roman presence:

"This hath been a fair and beautiful church in my youth, but of late years greatly blemished by the building of yonder tenements, whereby the church is now darkened and other ways annoyed." Vernon led me to the entrance, but would not enter this church, resting a hand against the stone foundation and closing his eyes, leaning back his head as if hearing again some distant sound. "I have heard that while ringing a peal of the bells a tempest of lightning and thunder did arise, when an ugly shapen sight appeared. A Roman soldier it was: cleaven by a sword, from shoulder to breast, gaping wounds weeping blood, for fear whereof the ringer-men all fell down, and lay as dead for the time, letting the bells ring and cease of their own accord. When the ringers came to themselves, they found certain stones of the north window to be razed and scratched, as if they had been so much butter, printed with a lion's claw, and so remain to this day. I have seen them myself, and have put a feather into the holes to measure that these Roman claws had entered three or four inches deep."

Such were mine introductions by day, to the many Romans who haunt the City since time out of mind, but when darkness fell and Vernon retired again back to the Theatre, I moved to the Windmill, aided there by free candles and a privacy I had not enjoyed at the Mermaid (whereat so many players gather and interfere, each in the other's affairs). By the last day of February, Burbage bid our fellows come to the Theatre to hear my play: and then for me to know whether it would ever be heard by anyone else.

"The Roman emperor is dead. So begins our scene." I had thought I might tremble when first presenting the matter to my fellows, and did somewhat, for the February cold was held back only by a little brazier that Vernon had set upon the floor where groundlings more commonly stood, some of the men nearby, others draped in various repose on the stage or first gallery. But God saw fit to steady my nerves and made me bold, as if I had done the like an hundred times before.

"His two sons, Saturninus and Bassianus, dispute who should succeed him, their followers ready to take up arms. A Tribune, Marcus Andronicus, hails his brother Titus as the people's choice instead, who returns now to Rome victorious over the Goths and leading a solemn funeral procession for his slain sons and other noble Roman dead."

"A good beginning and we shall play it to remind our spectators of the glorious procession witnessed lately for Sir Phillip Sidney," quoth Burbage, marking that Cuthbert should make a note thereof. "What next?"

"Enter Titus, to fanfare, bearing as prisoners the Queen of the Goths, called Tamora, her three sons, together with a scheming Moor called Aaron. Titus greets the people of Rome and instantly slays Tamora's eldest son to avenge the deaths of his own sons during the war, the which causes Tamora and her sons yet living, Demetrius and Chiron, to vow bloody revenge on Titus and all his kin. This business finished, Titus now refuses the throne, preferring a life in private after so many years service to his city, and supports Saturninus' claim. All are satisfied by the loving and loyal Titus, in recognition of which Saturninus, who crowns himself Emperor, vows then to marry Titus' daughter Lavinia. I see Johnson as the Emperor Saturninus and thou, Phillips, as his brother Bassianus. Clarke shall play Titus and Burbage thy brother, Marcus. The Goths, Demetrius and Chiron, are for Kempe and Pope, for those are villains but, as ye shall see, are sometimes antic and comical."

To my great good fortune, all nodded, save Dick, who protested: "O Will, let me play some part other than Lavinia, for my beard will not be forsworn."

"It can be shaved," quoth Burbage. "And who otherwise shall play the lady?"

"Fear not Dick, Lavinia is a woman, aye, but one whose tragedy requires tears and thy fine skill at dumbshow. Thou shalt see, soon enough, why such skills are important, such that will arrest all men's eyes. Bryan shall play Tamora, the fierce Goth woman-warrior, who shall also not soon be forgot." I paused to know if any man would question my distribution of the parts, but hearing none, continued bravely.

"Hear this then: Lavinia is already betrothed to Bassianus and she will have no other. Titus' son Mutius defends his sister and her rights under Roman law, to which Titus slays the insolent youth for thereby dishonouring the Andronicus name. Indeed, Saturninus now denounces all Andronici, for their effrontery to an Emperor in such violent quarreling, and instead takes Tamora as his bride. She then advises Saturninus to pardon Bassianus and the Andronicus clan, her guile meant to hide her true intent on revenge."

"Saturninus is a goodly name for this Emperor, for men born under the influence of Saturn are false, envious and malicious," quoth Johnson reading the opening speech I had writ for his part. Although the play was still only on foul papers, I had written out, in steadier hand, one speech for each part, therewith to beguile each player that his was the role best suited to him and certain to hold attention. "I like it well."

"Is there no part for me?" Richard asked, fearing he may yet again play a dozen minor parts and none that move the multitude to repeat his name, as they do again and again for Ned Alleyn when he plays Tamburlaine. We two were hired players lately, for an interlude in service with Pembroke's Men on Twelfth Night, whereat he showed more courtesy than he hath used towards me in all of our playing together these two years and odd. The festivities at the great Cecil House on Strand were some celebration for the Earl of Southampton, that boy of sixteen, as passionate about plays and spectacle as thou art about thy fees and interest. I digress a moment to report the particulars, in proof of Richard's warming heart:

"The most exquisite gloves I have ever worn, most exquisite." Countess Southampton graciously remembered me as the brother to the maker of her favourite gloves, using the matter to make idle chatter while we all waited for her tardy son that night.

"Your ladyship, as the brother is to such adornments, Will Shakespeare is to plays and poetry," quoth Richard to mine amazement. "He hath writ speeches for our players that thrill the senses and transport the imagination."

"Doth he so?" She turned back to meet mine eye, examining, like one about to buy a horse. "Wilt thou fill our waiting time with such a treasure?"

"Please excuse me, your ladyship, for I am not a tenth the player of my fellow, Richard Burbage here. Richard, wilt grant us a few lines from that matter of King Henry we played for Her Majesty?" With no further encouragement, and with no small amount of blushing from my praise, Richard spoke the speech, pertaining to the eve of battle, that I had amended into an old play about our late sovereign.

The hall where we played was cleverly ablaze with lanterns that resembled a hundred fiery glow-worm's eyes, dancing from mirrors and glancing off the jewels on the milky throats of the gathered ladies, as so many shooting stars around the room when they danced. But all eyes, lords and ladies, servants and soldiers, were steely-fixed, and every voice went silent when Richard spilled forth a rhapsody of words, my words, to which Heaven's face itself did then glow in the night.

His oration lasted not above three minutes, but when it ended, not a soul present thought anything else, but that they had just been rallied by their young monarch to join the fray against the enemy, against great odds but for greater glory. A moment of silence, which to me seemed an eternity, fearing we had somehow offended, but instead followed by the loudest roar of approbation I had ever heard in a theatre. Enter Lord Burghley with the young Earl, neither of which could understand the commotion, but impressed by the loving looks that showered on the figure of Richard Burbage.

Before that night ended, the Countess asked if I might undertake to craft a sonnet, which she would present to the Queen, in tribute of Her Majesty's great victory over Spain. When some days later I delivered to her the sonnet (which I will append in the main at the end of this letter), she approved my labours and hinted that she was in need of just such a 'persuading poet' (her words!) for a more lofty purpose. I have been in her company not more than three times ere this, but find her ten times more gentle than her late husband was crabbed (and he was said to be composed of naught but harshness) and think there's nothing ill can dwell in such a temple.

Returning now to the events in the Theatre and the presentment of Titus Andronicus to my fellows, I was able then to reply to Richard thus:

"Aye Richard, thou shalt play the most arresting villain that ever strode across our stage: Aaron the Moor. Our scene now moves to the day following and a royal hunt in celebration of the nuptials. Aaron has induced Demetrius and Chiron, with wild prophecies, libels and dreams, to slay Bassianus and rape Lavinia. This they do, casting the corpse of Bassianus' into a pit and dragging Lavinia, who begs Tamora in vain for mercy, into the woods to rape her and thereafter to cut out her tongue and lop off her hands that she may never betray who committed these heinous and barbarous assaults. Aaron has laid plots with a forged letter and hidden gold to cast blame for the murder on Titus's only living sons, Martius and Quintus. The Emperor is outraged by the death of his brother Bassanius and instantly sentences Martius and Quintus to death."

"Ah, I see a telling merely of Philomel from Ovid," quoth Cuthbert. "Will we not be laughed to scorn for such an obvious theft?"

"Nay, I think it not, for many have heard her tale, but who has ever shown it in a play?" Burbage knew the multitude would greedily drink up the gore of murders, rapes, and the cutting out of tongues and chopping off of hands. "Let them be clad in Spanish garments, the better to inspire rage at their filthy deeds."

"Did not the Queen's Men play some version thereof?" Cuthbert seemed to dust cobwebs from his brain to recall if he had heard of this or no.

"If they had, not more than once or twice, and never in London, else we had heard thereof."

"Or they played it so poorly, as they have done with other fare, that it was not favoured for the Court or City playhouses."

"Was it too violent for the ladies?"

The men debated the matter for a time, which gave me leisure to think on how my few lines had already sparked life into a Company newly laid low by the loss of our patron and the death of Perkin. Johnson draped his cloak about himself, like an antique Roman, and bestrode the stage to feel the part of an Emperor. Burbage sat on the first gallery with Cuthbert, who turned his father's vision of the stage to notations in the playbook. Dick remained below, kicking at some shells in the dirt, unsure if Lavinia would equal his hopes for more manly parts. Every man scanned his page to see the length of the speech, mouthing his lines and nodding or rolling an eye, but each seemed satisfied, to my greater relief.

"Not long after, Marcus discovers his mutilated niece Lavinia and brings her to Titus, who is instantly overcome with grief, as what father would not go mad to see his pretty bird so mangled? Enter Aaron, who says that the Emperor Saturninus will spare Martius and Quintus if Titus cuts off a hand and sends it to him in recompense. Titus asks Aaron's help to cut off his hand, the which is done and sent then to the Emperor. Aaron returns laughing, with Titus' severed hand, and thereto the severed heads of Martius and Quintus. Now enraged to furious revenge, Titus sends Lucius to raise an army among the Goths and presently invade Rome and unseat the traitorous Emperor. During this, Lavinia scratches the names of her attackers in the dirt: Titus knows he must now have his revenge on Aaron, Tamora and her sons."

"Will, since this is the story of Philomel, what thinkst thou to use the first book of that same work of Ovid," quoth Dick eagerly, at last hoping he might make some part of the story more compelling. "Wherein Zeus rapes a girl and turns her into a cow that she may not betray him for committing the act. Recall that, encountering her father, she scratches her name in the dirt using her hoof." The Theatre fell silent of a sudden and each man looked up from his lines to know if he heard aright, or no.

"Turn Lavinia into a cow, Dick?" quoth Richard, most amazed. "Silence fool, and let our poet finish this brave tale." Richard Burbage taking my side in any argument? My Lord, I thought, I am surely in a dream! Richard nodded to me, that I might return again to the matter of the play.

"We need no cow, Dick, for now will Richard and thee amaze the spectators more than if Zeus himself had appeared and turned you both into beasts. Thus more then: enter a midwife with a black baby, delivered of the adulterous Tamora, stamped that colour by the lascivious Aaron. He then kills the midwife and flees with the baby to save it from discovery and certain death, but Lucius, returning to Rome with his army of Goths, captures Aaron and offers to hang the baby unless Aaron admits his guilt and betrays Tamora and her sons, the which he does without hesitation."

"I like it well," quoth Richard, having read over his speech. He smiled and nodded approval. "And who shall play Lucius?"

"That will I do," quoth I. "For it is brief and becomes the chronicle of the play. But now our scene returns to Titus, who seems to have gone mad at his many indignities and savage losses. Thinking he is mad, Tamora and her sons come to him dressed as Revenge, Murder, and Rape.[131] Tamora offers to grant Titus revenge on his enemies if he will dissuade Lucius from attacking the Emperor. Titus agrees and invites the Emperor to a feast of reconciliation. Tamora, as Revenge, thinks herself successful and departs, but Titus insists that Rape and Murder, Chiron and Demetrius, remain behind. Titus then slays her sons, drains their blood into a basin held by Lavinia, and says he will play the cook and bake them into a pie."

"But have not many seen Thyestes, wherein villains are slain and baked into a pie?"

"Aye, but have the masses seen this, or only those who study ancient texts and spend some years at the law or university?" Clarke had been silent until now, but rose to the stage and imagined the scene to come at a great table. "I like it well, for we will be the first to bring such horrors to the many and tongues will wag for a year." A great weight evaporated from my back: I knew now my play had persuaded the masters.

"Thou'rt right, Thomas, for the final scene is the feast, wherein Titus asks Saturninus if a father should kill his daughter, if that she had been raped. Saturninus affirms this duty, so Titus slays Lavinia, telling Saturninus how she was raped by Tamora's sons."

Clarke, who had all the while acted the scenes as I described them, as a man working to fit a newly styled doublet with his tailor, now thrust Titus' imaginary dagger into the bowels of Dick's Lavinia, who himself practiced the shriek of surprise and agony that any daughter would unleash, seeing her father perform such a deed. As I whipped the story to its end, the others too played out their parts in dumbshow.

"He reveals next that these same villains have been baked in the pie that Tamora is, even now, so wolvishly devouring. Titus then slays Tamora, but is himself then slain by the offended Saturninus, who lives not a minute longer neither, for now Lucius slays the Emperor to avenge his father's death."

"Aaron is the father of these treacheries and tragedies, but he remains alive?" Richard turned over the single page in his hand as if some further scene were writ thereupon with a conclusion more satisfying.

"Nay, nay Richard: Lucius commands that Aaron be buried up to his neck to die of thirst and starvation. Thou wilt end the play with the icy speech of Aaron that thou holdest now in thy hand: unrepentant, regretting only that thou hadst not done more evil in thy life."

The brazier cracked of a sudden, like a lone spectator applauding the end of an epic tale. Did my fellows find fault with it? Or had it pleased? I gleaned naught from their faces, but their silence seemed to condemn.

"'Twill require some skill in a comic or bawdy jig to bring joy back to the spectators after such a bloody end." The men agreed generally with Kempe. "But I can manage that feat even while baked into a pie!"

"Some special music will I compose, to brighten the mood," quoth Phillips, who had been trying out various new melodies on a lute all morning as we laid out the play and its parts.

"Will not Tilney forbid such gore to be seen upon the stage?" Dick was troubled that he might not, after all, be given leave to portray so tragic a figure and to con the likeness of a woman with no hands or tongue.

"These may be horrors, but who has not seen the like in the 'Spanish Tragedy' and at Marlowe's plays?" I saw now that Burbage liked it well, having said we needed some such spectacle to steal away the crowd from our competitors. "And who has not seen worse in the flesh? Think on the hangings and quarterings, the beheadings and public burning of witches." Richard and Cuthbert, always quick to agree with their father, muttered some consent. Johnson and Clarke nodded too.

"Think, for that matter, on poor John Stubbs, whose hand was of late struck from his arm before the unwashed mob for writing ill of Her Majesty," quoth Johnson.

"A fine argument NOT to be a poet, eh?" Kempe aimed that barb at me.

"A man may lose a hand for the offense of his pen?" I had not heard of this and, if my means to earn a living was with a pen, I had best know more of these matters.

"O, who has not heard of poor old Stubbs?" Pope was now pricking me too, in league with Kempe. "Aye. Stubbs declared the Queen's proposed marriage to a Frenchman would be an immoral union, an uneven yoking of the clean ox to the unclean ass. There's a goodly line - - 'yoking' his clean 'ox' to her unclean 'ass.' Ha!"

"Hardly seems worth losing a hand," quoth I, unsure if this was some means to say that I should lose the hand that wrote this play.

"True, Will, but he did not protest when the sentence was meted out," quoth Johnson in a more serious demeanour, giving me to believe the story true. "He said merely something to the effect of 'pray for me now my calamity is at hand' - - a goodly jest, if true - - and after that his right hand was indeed struck off his arm, he politely removed his hat with his left hand, and cried 'God Save the Queen!' before fainting. Nor was his publisher spared, who lost also his right hand, but lifted it up and said 'This be a true Englishman's hand.'"

"Stubbs - - a fitting name, eh Will?" Pope pricked me again for Kempe's amusement, but now I feared mine own words on paper, what if they should offend the powerful? Might I too lose a limb? What foul service is this! Well, none so bold as those who know not the penalty for failure: the Company approved, and little else mattered to me.

"We have a play," quoth Burbage simply, his kind of verdict from which there is no appeal, once uttered aloud by him.

I took the pages next to a scribe of mine acquaintance near Gray's Inn. Turning them into a fair copy (for three shillings) was like turning dross into silver: for so modest an investment, I would be paid four pounds by Burbage upon delivery thereof! When he finished the task and I collected this treasure, I paused a moment, to think that this would have been a task that Rosalind might have joyously performed for me. I wept that the clean lines on each page were not in her sweet mellifluous hand. I felt such pain in my heart that she would never hear these lines spoken, never share in whatever bounty they might bring after so much uncertain hope, so many vigils at nights alone, so much waiting and wondering about our future. But the fate of Titus Andronicus would yet require more patience and waiting: no playhouse would see it played without one approval more.

The fair copy was next delivered to the Master of the Revels in Clerken-well to receive his stamp. I recall Marlowe saying his yeoman could be bribed to see that Master Tilney spent only a little time scrutinizing the play, but no such expense was needed when Burbage aided my presentment, for he is a familiar face to Tilney's man, (a black-fingered agent, counting pages so that he might not be later challenged over what a hopeful author had left in his care):

"Thy testament is valued here, Master Burbage. But thou knowest how 'tis that COMMON players, none like your men of Leicester have played, but I mean varlets showing of interludes and plays that, for the most part, contain matter tending to SEDITION. And in contempt of sundry good orders and laws, whereupon are grown much disquiet, division, tumult and I say to thee, UPROARS in the Realm."

In two days, and for the official nine shillings the stamp, we had the royal red mark that allowed the matter to be played anywhere in the king-dom. Thereafter the scribe committed each man's role to a scroll, that we might rehearse (and though the paper was dear, six more shillings, I paid some over, to lengthen the scroll for Johnson to make his part appear as long as those of Burbage and Clarke).

In truth, the added cost was superfluous, for Johnson, imperious as ever, more than adequate to the part of the Emperor Saturninus, he himself caused some forty lines to be cut from the first scene, it being too long in his opinion and the matter already stated. Nor could I disagree, for much of this first scene was borne of my fruitless partnering with Wilson, who himself brought lines from other authors and other joint labours, the which I liked not in any wise.[132]

We began on the first day of March and Burbage pronounced us ready on the first day of spring. Writing this letter today, St. George's own day with the Queen's procession passing nearby as if in celebration of my birth-day, I feel me something festive: but after we gave this play its first public showing, our mood was nothing of the like. Herewith a catalogue of our errors and those events most pertinent for thy better understanding:

Without a patron, there was little money for staging or playbills or the like. Burbage entered therefore into contract with a strange and suspicious fellow, one Jerome Savage (aptly named), a very lewd fellow who lives by no other trade than showing of other men's plays in his rotten carcass of a playhouse, without the City and south of the Thames, in Newington Butts. Savage had been at times a player for the Earl of Warwick's Men, but had presented such lascivious matters that they were forced from the City, and even a mile more south of Southwarke, to escape those beadles who might have chastened them. Therein was our first error, for many from the City that knew the Earl of Leicester's Men might have ventured to see us elsewhere, but not an hour's forced march across muddy fields towards hostile ground where picklocks and begging vagrants outnumbered honourable spectators.

Nor did we heed his neighbors, who demanded that all such noisesome activity cease, which they said brought villains and scoundrels and low women to their environs. Burbage heeded the money only and mine eyes were dazzled by holding a playbill that proclaimed the playing of my fiction. Savage wanted Marlowe's name thereon, the more to attract a crowd looking for another Tamburlaine, but Burbage would have none of it. Nor did my name appear, for it would have availed us nothing, but I felt evenso a swelling pride to see 'Titus Andronicus' pasted to a wall at the Mermaid.

The night before we played, we took up lodging at the south suburbs, at the sign of the Elephant, wherein we heard it was best to lodge. This was another of our many errors, for who could sleep when doors were banging the night long, every quarter hour, as patrons went and came again to the whores thereat.

When the day came, we fastened our laces and brightest faces, but steady rain bogged even the strongest horses from reaching Newington Butts. By three of the clock, already delayed, we began the matter, for some two hundred souls, sodden and shivering, which may have been not above fifty by the time Tamora was slain. Kempe tried desperately to rescue our fortunes, demanding of those brave few remaining 'if my tongue cannot entreat you to acquit me, will you command me to use my legs?' That they did, with one calling out for this bawdy jig or that one, and all our Company then joining in, which at the least warmed our joints and earned a few coins that were tossed at our feet.

Nor did we better fare the next day, under sunshine, the fields around now decorated with a clean, hoary frost and our Romans' steaming breath clouding their faces when they spoke. Marlowe and his foppish fellows, still angered from mine interference with their pamphlets and Savage's false rumour that they had writ 'Titus' at the Queen's command, had committed such disparagements upon our labours that many of our City friends came neither, although they later claimed no other reason excepting of the tediousness of the way to reach the Butts. Burbage bid us pack our goods after this second playing. Our mood was then sour and somber, but Fate had not yet finished with the honourable Roman, Titus Andronicus.

The first day of April, some warmth showing in buds on trees, we gathered in the barn next to the Theatre, the playhouse now occupied by the Lord Admiral's Men, whose payments for its use 'always good and welcome for our maintenance', so says Burbage. But laughter and cheerful songs, from the overflowing crowd, stood in harsh measure against our foul tempers in a barn with only King Arthur and three dogs to hear any matter from our Company. Enter Lord Strange.

Ferdinando Lord Strange, son and heir to the Earl of Derby, had himself a Company of tumblers and players of certain interludes, the which were said to amuse him and his peers, but which I had never witnessed. His messenger came to say he would come to us, if we were at leisure, and Burbage hastened to assure the Earl that we were even thus. Before dark, Dick saw this same Lord Strange come from the Theatre, with a boy, following his messenger to our meeting hall.

"Ah, the fair Lavinia," Lord Strange greeted Dick at the door, bowing and kissing his hand as if he were the Queen herself, to the great amusement of his companion. Before we might offer some honourable greeting and obsequies in return, he astonished us by tapping each man on the shoulder and greeting him by the name of that part he had played, making some further comment to his boy about the lines that such and such a player had spoken. When he came to Richard, he stopped and bid us all gather closer.

"Now this fellow, who I would recognize even without the face covered in soot, the selfsame colour as his soul on the stage, this fellow I admire the most, for so wholly transforming himself into the villainous Aaron, as he never assumed himself again, until the play was done, never failing in his part when he had done speaking, but with his looks and gestures maintaining still the most convincing Moor, the most soul-scorching demeanour."

"Aye, your lordship, this is my son Richard Burbage, and I'll warrant you, he kept that demeanour even in the tiring house, the better to play the part when again he might be called to the stage." Burbage was pleased for his son, but was hoping his intercession might suddenly command and reveal the purpose of this audience with Lord Strange.

"Who is the author of this play?" I now saw clearly that the boy with Lord Strange was none other than the Earl of Southampton, the girl-boy we had seen twice before at Court in the presence of the Earl of Essex, and whose mother, the Countess, brought players to their estates.

"I apologize for mine offence, your lordship. Will Shakespeare, at your service." What else could I say? I bowed, but he bid me stand straight and closer, the better to meet mine eyes with his lone raised brow, lips pursed to one side, as if mildly surprised or amused. Lord Strange was not more than two or three years mine elder and indeed we might have been brothers, for his face and beard were carved in like fashion, but our garments betrayed our very unlike stations. His garments were plain, yet of the finest silk, lace, and velvet, but it was his billowing hat of black felt and fur, trimmed with gold braid and buckle and one pearl pendant, that made him a striking and unique figure, almost comical if he were a commoner, but something stylish to be copied, owing to him being a lord.

"Nay, good poet, 'tis I that must beg thy forgiveness," quoth he. "I love the playhouses and have paid for Marlowe and Greene to give me their best. They so riotously spoke of thy play, that I braved the mud of Newington myself for comic amusement, but left in honest admiration. Canst forgive a fool for judging the quality of a matter, before he examines the goods?"

I stood mightily amazed and cannot recall what I may have said in reply, unsure if he was in jest or no, but Burbage took command and kept the lord in conversation for yet an hour apart, after which he took most gracious leave of us all. In sum then, we would play 'Titus Andronicus' at the Rose with Lord Strange's Men together, the latter giving notice that they would display new feats of tumbling and fair dances to music following the play. A new playbill would proclaim certain scenes wherein blood was shed, certain to please the many, and advertise the playing by those men in former service to the late Lord Leicester, 'the hero of Tilbury'.

Nor did our Company sit upon this seeming laurel victory: we trimmed some lines that now appeared superfluous and which might slow the march of action; Burbage bid Kempe repeat those lusty lines that he had added extempore, which sparked much laughter at 'mothers on their backs' and the like; and Johnson devised the brightest spectacle for the procession, wherein we would enter on our horses and pull behind the funeral bier into the theatre.

On Maundy Thursday had we our first look inside the Rose and by Saturday we did hazard our first re-playing of Titus Andronicus.[133] The weather mild, the ranks of spectators soon swelled, added thereto by those customers coming or going from Winchester stew next door. Every patch of ground, seat, stair, or cushion now filled, thanks no doubt to the encouragement of Lord Strange and his men, I resolved this time to leave no item, no matter how meager, to chance or Fate. Mine own parts onstage being minor, I made of me a major presence in the tiring house to prompt aloud where needed, to stamp at the bookholder, to swear for our properties, to curse the tardy tireman, to rail at any music out of tune, and to swear at every venial trespass we committed. My fellows quickly found me tedious, but I daresay not one ignored my double and treble admonitions! Nor did we wait long to be rewarded for our pains by the restless multitude, as followeth:

Johnson led our procession, not merely across the stage as was the custom, but from outside the playhouse, slicing a path through the crowd of groundlings that we might make our way inside, even unto the scaffold. Polite applause greeted our first fellows entering, especially Phillips playing his lively lute most enticingly, but once all present saw the seeming endless train, owing to our two Companies playing together, applause became a rumble; the rumble became roar. London has never seen the like!

Nor could the Theatre or Curtain or any of your inns hold such a mob of players and spectators together. The Rose is half again in bigness, the stage broader and deeper, each gallery holding rows stacked upon each other, such that twice the spectators could fill the place and each would have his view unobstructed. Lord Strange had caused the rails and posts to be festooned with silks and gold chains, the better to convey the pomp of Rome and the grandeur of our joint Companies' labours, himself seated in a space above the stage, together with that same boy Earl of Southampton and his Countess-mother, all dressed as Roman nobility. Though greater in size and stuffed, as it were, with more humanity, when the first words were spoken, they climbed to every corner and indeed to the very heavens in sweetest, clearest orations.

First Johnson's Saturninus regally commanded those spectators to the left to join his cause and acclaim him emperor; Phillips' Bassianus commanded those to the right to join his cause and take up arms against the former. Then did Burbage's Marcus Andronicus silence them all:

"Princes, that strive by factions and by friends, ambitiously for rule and empery, know that the PEOPLE of Rome have, by common voice chosen TITUS! A nobler man ... a braver warrior ... lives not this day within the city walls! Home from weary wars against the barbarous Goths. Returned bleeeeeeding to Rome ... bearing his valiant sons in COFFINS from the field, laden with horror's spoils, returns to Rome flourishing in arms!"

All was quiet. Though Burbage spoke of Roman sacrifices and ancient victories, did anyone present not see, in their mind's eye, our own valiant and victorious English Queen and her general, Leicester, marching home from confronting the mighty Spain? Whose heart did not swell in common cause after years of strife within the kingdom, eager for peace and unity? So convincing were our players, that both halves of the house were chastened, even groundlings played their part, calling aloud upon our Saturninus and Bassianus to unite in loving harmony.

This was my first leisure to take full measure of the Rose and those who breathed new life within her. Think on the paint that leaps from the brush when first applied to the head of a wall, but how it fades and struggles to impart any colour at all when the stroke reaches the bottom, vainly seeking to cover the gross clay of meaner sort. So it seemed as I gazed to the highest gallery, the gilded peacocks roosted thither, with gold embroidery and white lace nosegays; then coarser garments (and those who wear them) as the eye brushed lower, until the streaks of muddy gray are all that's left when such an audit reaches the floor of the playhouse, beholding the garlic-breathed many, jostling to gain the better view. Every part of our English society was there, each maintaining his station above the other, in an order invented by God and enforced by centuries of practice.

Equally so, out of sight, in the tiring house behind. I mean that I have never seen the guts of a clock, but it would now seem familiar to me having witnessed, over and over again, like the daily winding and unwinding there-of, those mechanisms, gears, and jewels within the playhouse. In truth, I had no need to fret or to oversee the great march of time thither. Every man his task, every garment, stool, bow-string, drumbeat, and flapping banner an essential part of the living whole, dividing divers functions, setting endeavour in continual motion. But it was the roar of a thousand voices that suddenly dispelled my vapourous observations and returned me in the instant to the house out front.

As we had planned, next came in the funeral procession, with pomp and ceremony, Clarke's Titus on a white charger, prancing and carving a path through the amazed groundlings. There followed six more horses, each dressed in rich furniture provided by Lord Strange from his own livery, making a fine impression (although King Arthur came last and limped from side to side more than what could be called proud prancing). Two players blasted trumpets in time to the drums; two more called for honest Romans to kneel, which the groundlings took to mean them, so they instantly obeyed. The rest of our Company clanged swords on bucklers and chanted in Latin.

All fell silent when the coffins reached the stage and Burbage held his hand aloft, declaring 'Hail Rome, victorious in thy mourning weeds!'

And when he opened the door behind, calling forth the imagining of a noble tomb, who among us did not shed a tear, thinking on sons lost in recent battles, even as he bid his dead sons to 'sleep in peace, slain in your country's wars! O sacred receptacle of my joys, sweet cell of virtue and nobility, how many sons of mine hast thou in store, that thou wilt never render to me more!'

As this scene played out its shifting tides, I could see that one amendment made since the Butts, at the behest of Burbage, rewarded handsomely. As friends become foes, the better to signify this to the spectators, Burbage had Saturninus go up in the balcony above our stage, together with the witch Tamora, her sons and the Moor. More than dividing good from evil, the emperor on high, declaiming to his inferiors and subjects below, his voice booming above all others throughout the rafters and closer to Heaven, made a marvelous effect. And though Richard had not yet spoken a word, his Aaron leered, when that Saturninus claimed Tamora for his bride, and appeared idly to clean blood from his sword, to chilling effect, as each man spoke his part and the scene then ended. Nor did the house wait long to know Aaron's true mind and purpose in the play.

The scene shifting next to a place before the palace, wherein only our spectators might hear Aaron speak his vile intentions: herein let Richard loose the reins. All men in London live in fear of he who looks not like his neighbor, perhaps made manifest by war with Spain and so many foreigners more, who daily flow into the City. Richard's Aaron had spoken barely a dozen lines, when a powdered youth in the upper gallery shouted 'villain', but with evil oozing from the Moor's lascivious tongue, it took not ten lines more before several others joined in; and hundreds more when Aaron showed how deep his villainy might plunge, cuckolding the emperor ere the marriage sheets were stained, as:[134]

"Then, Aaron, arm thy heart, and fit thy thoughts,
To mount aloft with thine imperial mistress,
And mount her pitch, whom thou in triumph long
Hast prisoner held, fetter'd in amorous chains.
Away with slavish weeds and servile thoughts!
I will be bright, and shine in pearl and gold,
To wait upon this new-made empress.

To wait, said I? To wanton with this queen,
This goddess, this Semiramis, this nymph,
This siren, that will charm Rome's Saturnine,
And see his shipwreck and his commonweal's."

Nor did Kempe's Demetrius and Pope's Chiron, oafish sons of Tamora, fail to cast a comic spell over the house with their own antic manners.
Would that I might convey to thee how they worked such a trick, turning
the anger and loathing, that but one minute earlier was aimed at Aaron, into
such extreme comedy that, were laughter water, so much then washed over
the Rose that we had all been swept into the Thames in an instant. Then, as
quickly, the flow of good cheer was stopped up again, when Aaron gave this
pair leave to rape Titus' daughter in the lonely wilds of dark and untamed
woods:

"The palace is full of tongues, of eyes, and ears:
But the woods are ruthless, dreadful, deaf, and dull!
There speak, and strike, brave boys, and take your turns;
There serve your lusts, shadow'd from heaven's eye,
And revel in Lavinia's treasury."

Again the common cry swelled, even from the hardest heart who had
survived a thousand tiny deaths, as if so many tongues might warn the guile-
less virgin. Now even the cushion riders in the higher galleries partook,
though mostly in more polite indignation with each other. Now I saw the
change this made in Richard: no longer the plaintive boy, jealous of attention his father gave to me, quick in quarrel at any slight provocation. I swear
he returned behind scene to the tiring house a foot taller, a chest half again
as wide and brave, as once it was, huffing, not in fear, but like a sly black
Hermes, astonished at his own persuasive powers and eager to repeat such
rough magic.[135]

Truly, his Aaron beguiled every living soul in our trembling wooden O.
Leaning forward in the first row of the first gallery was Mr. Stow and Heather, mouths agape; behind them sat Pug, comforting his new bride, perhaps
assuring her that they witnessed an actor merely; Giddy had been with
them, but preferred now to stand at the very edge of the stage, right in the
center, the better, quoth he afterwards, 'to feel every footfall and hear every
line wrought by my brother' (standing next to him, shoulder to shoulder,

was a woman with red curls under a white cap, who put me in the mind of Rosalind, a momentary hope, quickly erased the instant I thought thereon).

There swiftly followed the many murders, treacheries, and dismemberments, each soliciting some fresh outrage from the crowd, and these were yet more swiftly followed by tears as Titus and Lavinia suffered one injustice heaped upon another, Dick playing the slaughtered maiden with such delicate passion that we all thought we saw a ghost, no corporeal flesh and blood. It may have been mine imagination, but I swear I saw, in Dick's Lavinia, many of those selfsame faded hopes I note in the visage of his wife, Bess, here infused into the antique Roman girl he played upon our stage.

But this day belonged entirely to Richard and his Devil incarnate, Aaron, played with such a fealty not seen on a stage before. When Tamora is delivered of a black baby, he toyed with the spectators, turning their rage to laughter and back again to fury, as when Demetrius sees the babe and demands to know what he has done. Richard pauses to incite the groundlings to shout their own outraged demands, then says:

"That … which THOU canst not … UNDO!"

"Thou hast undone our mother," quoth Chiron. Even to the highest gallery now, every chattering tongue expressed their several shock at such an affront to Nature, whereupon Richard skillfully unlit the fuse, turning fury to lascivious laughter, saying:

"Fool, I have DONE thy mother!" Then, as the scene played out, he did re-ignite that fuse a thousand fold with: "Now, by the burning tapers of the sky, that shone so brightly when this boy was got, any man dies upon my scimitar's sharp point, if he touches this, my first-born son and heir!"

At length, when all played out and the pie was served to that Tamora, wherein her sons' flesh was baked, mild-pleasing Bryan showed me a stomach for acting a certain subtle fury that I had not before seen in him. But even the grisly death of the scheming Queen of the Goths could not distract a single spectator in the Rose from gaping open-mouth and chilled-spine when Aaron croaked out this final litany, savouring each line as if recalling in his mind's eye the very evil deeds incarnate, of which he did so cruelly take inventory:

"Even now I curse the day
Wherein I did not do some notorious ill:
As kill a man, or else devise his death;
Ravish a maid, or plot the way to do it;

Accuse some innocent and forswear myself;
Set deadly enmity between two friends;
Make poor men's cattle break their necks;
Set fire on barns and hay-stacks in the night,
And bid the owners quench them with their tears.
Oft have I digg'd up dead men from their graves,
And set them upright at their dear friends' doors,
Even when their sorrows almost were forgot;
And on their skins, as on the bark of trees,
Have with my knife carved in Roman letters,
'Let not your sorrow die, though I am dead.'
Tut, I have done a thousand dreadful things
As willingly as one would kill a fly,
And nothing grieves me heartily indeed . . .
But that I cannot do ten thousand more!"

Honest coz and dearest Hamnet: O how I wish ye had been witness to these events! As the Rose disgorged her human traffic, the talk was of Titus, of Lavinia, of Aaron and Tamora as if they had, for the two hours just past, seen them all quite alive. One man and his wife were inconsolable at the rough treatment of Lavinia, but their own daughter, no more than eight or ten, comforted them how she herself would grow as strong as our Queen and remain ever vigilant against such evils. Such a spell has our Company wrought this day.

I pray that one day thou shalt meet and know my fellows as I have come to know and love them, for if my life is to be a player, even a poet for players, I see clearly now the stages through which I shall pass: the apprentice, like Dick, that I have been. Surely next comes the fool, seeking the bubble of reputation, like Richard, Kempe and Pope. Perhaps, one day, like Burbage and Johnson, the leaders of men, with a fair round belly and eyes severe, beard more formal cut, respected, renowned, and rewarded handsomely for my pains. And perhaps, like Clarke and Perkin (would that God has granted him peace), when youthful hose has grown a world too wide for a shrunk shank, my manly voice a childish treble of pipes and whistles, I will be content to play the lean and slippered Pantaloon [*old man*], that ends this strange eventful journey.[136] Short tale to make, I mean that, here in the Rose, I may have discovered a New World that is not distant leagues across a tempest sea.

That Rose now void of its multitude, nothing left to signify that Titus Andronicus had ever marched across her stage, the men then hastened about their several duties and debates of the labours just ended. Each man hoped another would praise his achievement, but even when no friends are by, men praise themselves. I will admit to the sin of Pride and hoped some idle compliment would come from Burbage, but it was Vernon who took me apart and spake thus:

"Is it not brave, William? Truly, they will all remember my Sempronius, kinsman to Titus, will they not? His lines shall be repeated to the highest heavens and in every lowly tavern in Christendom, will they not?" As he poked me playfully in the ribs, his teeth nearly fell from his mouth, so wide was his smile in jest. "Nay, in truth THY creations, THY words that soared with eagles and gave the Rose it's sweetest fragrance, THOU wilt be called for, in places high and low alike, I'll warrant thee!"

At length, every man gave me some courteous thanks and Burbage counted more money than Leicester's Men had ever taken in one day, giving me four pounds for my pen-and-ink labours. But it was the day following, when Richard and I, together with Kempe and Dick, entered the Mermaid and several called out 'let Aaron dig up a dead man from his grave and set him upright at their dear friends' door', then did we understand that 'Titus Andronicus' would not soon be forgot. Then too did Richard seem to melt away all past unkindness and treat me as a brother.

Since then, we have played Titus no less than fifteen times and now, owing to Lord Strange's encouragement, will play it for the Queen in honour of St. George's Day. Nor have I said all of how Titus has both made and marred me.

Coz, I have read thy last letter every day, every night before I close mine eyes, such that I might dream my way to escape the chains that I myself have wrought, those that bind me here and that keep me longer from coming home to aid my father. I am sorely grieved to learn that he was seized for his debts, and had no thing of value to exchange therefore, but I am not allowed to leave London, nor could I do aught that might change his station from any other place than here.

My reason? That the Archbishop Whitgift's man, Bancroft I mean, has come at his behest demanding that I produce some plays of patriotic demeanour which might inspire the many to further defend their Queen, first from greater attack by Spain and Rome, but also from those Puritans who threaten the nobility of the church in England. Bancroft is a vile man who wasted no speech in these demands, saying that Whitgift will not soon forget my father's connection to the Ardens and the traitor Somerville, and that I may show his loyalty, and mine, by writing such matters and seeing that they are shown in London playhouses. Besides, quoth he, I will be richly rewarded by the Queen's loyal lords for such plays at Court and at their country estates. Yet this can nothing recompense for vile servitude and threats to my father, whatsoever his transgressions. I pledge to thee that I will omit no opportunity to turn the tables on these plotters (and the chiefest architect thereof) and restore the Shakespeares anon with honours so great that none can now imagine them.

I am something comforted to think I might send more money home and that, at the least, Giddy will work with father to make gloves, to which our brother Richard can also help, and that I can sell these to friends of Lord Strange with my newly-minted gloss (although Giddy must heed the styles that have changed here since the Armada was defeated). Pug says he might print and sell poems of my writing, with the aid of a well-esteemed patron. Did'st hear how he advanced from his indentures at Vautrollier's printery, after his master suddenly died and Pug married the widow? I will write to thee more thereof when next I am at leisure to do so.

O coz, my hand and eye grow weary, but surely I have emptied the vessel of my brain of all those contents of any import to thee or to my son. Yet now, being night, I am afeard all I have writ is but a dream. In my dreams, I am still a boy in Stratford, though the glass testifies already to the unfeeling passage of Time, lines added, hair lost. Gone too is the unsullied joy of our youth, lost when I think on sweet Rosalind and tender Giles.

Thus, I commit thee and all at home to God's good protection, and prithee, let not that thief, Time, take any measure of happiness from my son, leastways until I might return and take him once again into mine own protection.

In the mean season, I ask that thou kiss my boy and maids in my name and omit nothing else which thine honour deems best for their tender need. I am thine ever-loving servant in all else, Will.

PS: Herewith, 6 pounds real money, which I had first meant to settle my debt with the mapmaker Westerbeke, thinking it an honourable sum for so dishonourable a deed. My factor returned, saying the shop now stands vacant and none nearby can say what became of him. I remember hearing how the sailor Doughty, his life spared by Westerbeke in their youth, pledged that he would repay that kindness one day, even if it were in another life. I too must now pay my debt to him in another life, but regret my sin as long as I occupy this one. I recall how Johnson was most fascinated by my description of popish crosses and Hail Mary's that were much in evidence around the dingy shop: did he report this to Perkin? Was Westerbeke then taken away as a recusant? And did I thereby steal more than a map from a harmless old man? I prithee deliver this money now unto Anne, such as I earned from the play and the sum earned from that sonnet sold to the Countess for Her Majesty, herewith presented for thy honest censure:

> Not mine own fears, nor the prophetic soul
> Of the wide world dreaming on things to come,
> Can yet the lease of my true love control,
> Supposed as forfeit to a confined doom.
>
> The mortal Moon hath Her eclipse endured
> And the sad augurs mock their own presage;
> Uncertainties now crown themselves assured
> And Peace proclaims olives of an Endless Age.
>
> Now, with the drops of this most balmy time,
> My love looks fresh, and Death to me subscribes,
> Since, spite of him, I'll live in this poor rhyme,
> While he insults o'er dull and speechless tribes:
>
> And thou, in this, shalt find thy monument,
> When tyrants' crests and tombs of brass are spent.[137]

GLOSSARY

Abaft Toward the back, or the stern of a ship.

Ablutions Washing or bathing oneself.

Accouter Equip, array.

Acheron In Greek mythology, a river in Hades over which Charon ferried the souls of the dead.

Adamantine Resembling a diamond in hardness or luster.

Agincourt Village in northern France and site of a major English victory under King Henry V over the French in 1415.

Ague Illness involving fever and shivering.

Albion The oldest name for the island of Great Britain.

Amazon Member of a race of female warriors in Greek mythology.

Andalusia Southernmost region of Spain.

An't Abbreviation of "and if it."

Ancient An ensign, an officer of an army or ship's crew.

Angels Generally a slang term for coins. In the 16th century, it was one of the most common gold coins. This ten shilling coin depicted Michael the Archangel.

ANNO Anno Domini, in the year of our Lord, i.e. the years since the traditionally recognized date of the birth of Jesus.

Anon Soon, or immediately.

An't Abbreviation of "and it."

Apple Johns Baked apples.

Appurtenances Accessories

Arbitrement Settling a dispute.

Argosy A large merchant ship.

Armourers Makers of weapons and armor.

Arquebus An early type of portable long-barreled gun supported on a tripod.

Arrah Arrow

Arras Flemish tapestry used as a wall hanging or backdrop.

Ascension Day The Feast of the Ascension commemorates the ascension of Jesus into heaven 40 days after Easter. It is celebrated as one of the great feasts in the Christian calendar.

Assay To try or test. An analysis or examination of characteristics. "Taking assay" of a wounded animal was to kill it with a sharp knife.

Auditor A member of the audience.

Auditory Audience

Augury An omen, sign of what will happen in the future.

Bacchus A Greek god of wine.

Backsword A single-edged sword, the first European sword to have a knuckle guard. Also, a sword-like stick used in fencing practice.

Bailiff Equal to a town mayor. Shakespeare's father had served as bailiff of Stratford.

Barks Ships or boats. The earliest barks had oars and square sails but by the mid-1400's, some had three masts and triangular sails. Bark, or barque, could refer to a variety of ships.

Bawdry Obscenity

Bawds Brothels

Beadles Minor parish officers dealing with petty offenders.

Beard To boldly confront or challenge someone formidable.

Begnaw Chew, gnaw.

Besotted Drunken

Bill A placard or sign worn around the neck by itinerant tradesmen to indicate their trade or what they were selling.

Bishop A mixture of ale and honey served hot.

Black Friars Dominican friars.

Boatswain Ship's officer, or leading seaman, in charge of deck crew, hull maintenance, and equipment.

Bod-kin Dagger, stiletto.

Boils of Mars The medical faculty at the University of Paris informed the Pope and the King of France that the Plague was the result of corruption of the atmosphere due to the alignment of Saturn, Mars and Jupiter on March 20, 1345. Sores and boils caused by the Plague were sometimes named for this celestial event.

Bolts Iron shackles.

Bombast Puffed up, impressive sounding speech with little meaning.

Bootless Useless, ineffectual.

Bo'sun See boatswain.

Brace To clasp or fasten tightly. To grab firm hold on someone or something.

Brakes Thickets, ferns or bracken.

Brawn Jellied pig's meat, or headcheese. A pig's head (and sometimes the tail and feet) is cooked a long time, then strained and the meat is chopped and placed with herbs and the cooking broth into a bowl. It gels as it cools and is then sliced and eaten.

Breeches Short pants fitting snugly at the knee, upper hose.

Brook Tolerate

Brown bill See Halberd.

Buck basket Laundry basket.

Buckler A shield worn on the arm and held to protect the body. It often had spikes that could be used as a weapon if the bearer lost his sword.

Buff Dull yellow leather with a velvety surface.

Buggers of sheep Those who have anal intercourse with sheep.

Bumbastings Padding

Bung A stopper to close a hole.

Butt Straw bale archery target.

By'r By your.

Cadiz A port city in southwest Spain which served as a base for exploration and trade.

Caitiff A contemptible or cowardly person.

Caliver An infantryman's musket, a predecessor to the rifle.

Canakin A small vessel for drinking, literally a small can.

Candlemas February 2, church festival commemorating the presentation of Jesus in the Temple and the purification of the Virgin Mary. Candles were blessed at the festival.

Cape of Buena Esperanza Cape of Good Hope.

Capon Castrated male chicken fattened for eating.

Capuchins An offshoot of Franciscan friars. The name of the religious order derives from "cappuccio" or the hood which was part of their habit.

Carbuncle Painful cluster of boils under the skin. Also, refers to round red gems.

Carded Wool or other fibers that have been cleaned and disentangled using fine-toothed instruments, making them ready for spinning.

Carouse To drink the entire cup in one draught.

Carriage (v) Removal, carrying away.

Cassock Uniform

Castigo Literally, punishment. Gestures or expressions used by an actor to convey chastisement or punishment.

Catarrhs Excessive build-up of mucus in the airways or other bodily cavities.

Chain mail Metal armor composed of small metal rings forming a mesh.

Charon In Greek mythology, the ferryman of Hades who carries souls of the newly deceased across the rivers Styx and Acheron from the world of the living to the world of the dead.

Charnel House A building or chamber in which bodies or bones are deposited.

Chev'ril Cheveril, a soft, pliable skin used to make fine gloves.

Chinks Coins, money.

Chits A voucher or recording of sum owed.

Choler Anger

Choleric Angry, ill-tempered, touchy, irritable.

Choughs A type of crow.

Chronicles Histories, written records or archives.

Chuff A noisy exhalation.

Clefts Pieces of wood made by splitting.

Clink Jail cell, prison.

Closet A small room, private chamber.

Cocos Coconuts

Codpiece A decorative pouch worn to cover a man's genitals.

Cods Testicles

Coil Mortal life of the body.

Colbrand A Danish giant that, according to legend, was killed by Guy of Warwick.

Commonweal Commonweath or nation.

Compass To understand.

Con Understand

Conceit (v) Imitate, in this instance, imitating the sound of a bird warbling. Also, in other archaic usage, it can mean to imagine.
(n) Trinket, bauble.

Conceited Fancy. "Conceited characters," in this instance, fancy letters or other décor usually embroidered on a handkerchief.

Confido Literally to confide in, unbosom. Gestures or expressions used by an actor to convey taking someone into their confidence, or telling them a secret.

Conned Imitated

Cope A large ceremonial cloak worn by some clergy during solemn religious functions.

Cordwainer A shoemaker who makes fine, soft leather shoes. The leather from Cordova, Spain was used for luxury footwear and favored by the upper classes.

Coy Disdainful, distant.

Cozenage Cheat, deceit.

Cozen'd Cozened, cheated, conned, swindled.

Crabbed Irritable or easy to anger.

Cuckolding Dishonoring the husband by having sexual relations with his wife.

Cuirass A piece of armor consisting of a breastplate and backplate fastened together.

Cur Dog

Cutpurse Pickpocket or robber.

Dearths Scarcity, famines.

Declaim Speak in an impassioned way.

Descant To talk tediously or at length.

Dines Abbreviation for gabardine, a durable tightly woven fabric, often made from wool, cotton, silk or mixed fibers, twilled with diagonal ribs on the right side. Originally used for raincoats and other outerwear because it repelled water.

Dismasted To break off the mast(s) of a ship.

Disport Amusement

Disposition Direction, management, control.

Distemper Bad humor, unsettled.

Divers Various

Diverse Different, e.g. Divers gentlemen were born of diverse backgrounds.

Doublet A waist-length padded jacket.

Dock The enclosure where the defendant stood in a criminal court.

Down-gyved Hanging down about the ankles like leg shackles.

Draper A seller of cloth and dry goods.

Ducat A Venetian ducat was equal to a crown, or five shillings.

Ducked at the Yardarm An early form of naval punishment. Rope was tied around the offender and over the yardarm, a horizontal timber from which sails were hung. The offender was hoisted up to the top of the yardarm and then let fall into the sea, sometimes several times.

Duke of Parma Alessandro Farnese, Duke of the small Italian state of Parma, and Governor of the Spanish Netherlands.

Dug Nipple

Dulcet Sweet, soothing.

Dumbshow or Dumb-show A story told in mime.

Earthwort Wort can be a sweet infusion of barley or grain used to make beer, but is also an old English word for an herb or plant used as a medicine. In this context, it most likely was an herbal remedy perhaps made of many plants; he used "all manner of earthwort." Wort is part of the name of many herbs such as mugwort, butterwort, St. John's wort, and others.

Elysian Green or Fields In classical mythology, the final resting place for heroes and virtuous souls.

Empery Sovereignty

Enow Enough

Ensigns Emblems, flags used to indicate nationality.

Ere Before

Expired Slang, orgasm.

Factor Representative, broker.

Fagot A bundle of sticks bound together.

Fain Gladly

Farthing One fourth of a penny.

Farthingale Padding or a hooped petticoat worn around the hips, to extend women's skirts out from the hips.

Fealty Loyalty

Feast of the Ass Celebrated on January 14th to commemorate the flight into Egypt of Joseph, Mary and baby Jesus.

Feckless Worthless, irresponsible.

Fen Marsh, low or frequently flooded area.

Fenced Protected

Fencible Able to be protected or defended.

Fife A small, high-pitched flute usually with six to eight finger holes. By the 16th century, it was a common instrument in European infantries.

Frigate A light, fast ship with sails or oars.

Fluxes Dysentery

Foeman Foe, enemy.

Foil A light sword with a squared off point but without cutting edges.

Foists Pickpockets, see also nips. A nip would cut any cord attaching a money pouch to the clothing while the foist removed it.

Footman A servant who admits visitors, runs errands, and waits on those at the table. Also a servant who ran in front of his master's carriage or tended to a rider.

Fop A dandy; a vain man obsessed with appearance. A foolish person.

Forcier While no reference to this word can be found today, it appears to be some type of hand pump or gravity feed forcing the water through pipes.

Forfeit Defeated and in mortal danger.

Freestone-coloured Brownish-yellow, as the color of sandstone or limestone.

French Pox Syphilis

Fribble Fritter away.

Fustian Pompous, pretentious, especially in speech.

Fusty Stale, musty, moldy.

Gage Exchange

Gallants Ladies' men, flirts.

Galleasses Large fast galleys used especially as warships and having both sails and oars but usually propelled chiefly by rowing.

Galleys Early warships with sails and banks of oars.

Galliard A lively dance in triple time for two people, including complicated turns and steps.

Gallimaufry Confused jumble or medley of things.

Galli-skin breeches Loose knee length pants tied with garters below the knee. Also known as gallyhosen or galligaskins.

Gambol, Gamboling Run or jump playfully.

Garters Bands worn around the leg or thigh to hold socks or hose.

Gelosi troupe One of the most famous commedia del arte companies of 16th century Italy.

Gentlemen of the Chamber (Bedchamber) Gentlemen who waited on the Earl, assisting him in dressing, guarding access to him in the bedchamber, and serving him when he ate in private. They did not necessarily all serve at the same time but may have rotated schedules.

Gibbet Form of a cross used to hang a person.

Gibe Derisive or taunting word(s).

Gilt Gold coated.

Girdle Belt or cord worn around the waist.

Glass Looking glass or mirror.

God den Shortened form of the greeting Good Day.

Gold Sovereign Gold coin worth one pound, or 20 shillings.

Golden Age In classical mythology, the first and best age of mankind, an ideal, untroubled and prosperous time.

Goths An ancient Germanic people who played an important role in the fall of the Roman Empire in medieval Europe.

Grave (v) To caulk the seams and refasten planks to make a wooden ship more watertight.

Gray Friars Franciscan friars.

Gray's Inn One of the four Inns of Court, professional associations for barristers and judges. To be called to the Bar and practice as a barrister in England, an individual must belong to one of these Inns.

Groaning board A wooden table laden with so much food that it could presumably make the wood groan under its weight.

Groat an English silver coin worth four old pence, issued between 1351 and 1662.

Grograin or Grosgrain A heavy, ribbed silk fabric.

Groundlings Audience members in the theatre who stood around the edge of the stage on the bare ground.

Guildhall A town hall or building used for guild or organization meetings.

Gun'l Gunnel or gunwale. The upper edge of the side of a ship.

Haberdasher A dealer in men's clothing and accessories.

Habiliments Clothes, garments.

Halberd A weapon that combined a spear and ax on a pole about 6 feet long. Brown bills were a painted type of halberd.

Haled Dragged forcibly.

Halters Ropes placed around the head used to secure and lead animals, or in this case, prisoners.

Ha'penny Half penny.

Harbinger A herald who went ahead to find lodging for a nobleman and his entourage.

Hautboy An archaic type of oboe.

Haven Harbor

Hawking Noisily clearing the throat.

Hector A hero of Troy killed by Achilles who tied Hector's body to a chariot, dragged him around the city and left his body on the ground. Depicted in Homer's Iliad.

Hempen Made from hemp, a fiber used to make rope.

Hermes In Greek mythology, a guide of dead souls to the underworld. Also known as a prankster and a swiftly moving messenger of the gods (winged Mercury in Roman mythology).

Hock Tuesday The second Tuesday after Easter when women would tie up passersby with ropes demanding money for charity.

Hogshead A large cask or barrel.

Hose A form of pants worn by Elizabethan men consisting of upper hose, or breeches, and lower or nether hose, a knee-high stocking.

Huggle To hug.

Huzzah Expression of approval or delight, hurrah.

Incapable Unconscious

Imposthume An abcess.

Ixion In Greek mythology, Zeus bound Ixion to a winged, sometimes flaming, wheel which revolved in the air in all directions.

Jack A serving man, or an ill-mannered man.

Jack Cade Leader of a major rebellion (1450) against the government of King Henry VI of England. The rebellion was suppressed and Cade was wounded and died, but the challenge to royal authority led to the War of Roses, 1455-1485.

Jade An old, worn out horse.

Jaunce Prance

Jerkin Man's close-fitting jacket, typically leather.

Jocund Cheerful, lighthearted.

Joiner One who makes wooden furniture or wooden parts of a building such as stairs, window and door frames.

Joint-stool A four-legged stool made by a joiner with pegs holding the joints together. The most common form of seating at that time.

Jordan Chamber pot.

Jove Another name for Jupiter, supreme god in Roman mythology, god of the heavens and sky.

Keel The longitudinal structure running along the center at the bottom of a vessel's hull.

Keel-raked A punishment; the offender was hauled under the bottom of a ship and up the other side. Also called keel-hauling.

Ken Understanding, awareness, to know.

Kern A soldier of Ireland.

Kersey boot-hose Plain, coarsely woven wool stocking worn over the lower leg.

Kirtle A woman's gown or outer petticoat.

Knight of the Carpet A ladies' man.

Knight of the Golden Fleece Order of knighthood founded in 1430 to defend the Roman Catholic religion and to uphold chivalry.

Knights of the Garter The highest, and oldest order of British knighthood.

Knights Templar Skilled Christian military order that fought during the Crusades, from the 12th to the 14th century. They wore distinctive white mantles with a red cross.

Lackey Uniformed footman or servant.

Lady Day The holiday in honor of the Virgin Mary, observed on March 25th. It was also the official New Year's Day in England until 1752. Queen Elizabeth had issued a proclamation forbidding the making of malt from Lady Day to Michaelmas (September 29th) so there would be more grain on the market for food, and to keep prices from rising too high.

Lammastide August 1st, formerly observed in Britain as a harvest festival. Bread baked from the first crop of wheat was blessed.

Larked Engaged in playful fun or mischief.

Lasts Wooden models of the foot for shaping shoes or boots.

Lazzi A term used by traveling commedia del arte players for a bit of stage business, usually comic, that becomes a trademark of a character or actor. Lazzi are often ad lib; e.g. one famous Italian actor pretended to be bothered by a fly, then would chase it across the stage and eat it.

League An old measure of length that changed during the centuries, ranging from 2.4 to 4.6 statue miles (3.9 to 7.4 kilometers); but commonly a league was about 3 miles.

Lee side The side sheltered from the wind.

Leif Readily

Limbeck A conical device used to distill herbs for herbal remedies, perfumes and waters such as rose water. Also known as an alembic or helm, it had a spout on the lower edge to drain off the condensed liquid. The device was placed on a heat source or left in the warmth of the sun to create a distillate that contained the benefits of the herbs or other substances placed in the limbeck.

Line The equator, an imaginary line around the earth dividing the northern and southern hemispheres.

Lineaments Distinctive features or details of the face or body.

Liquamen A sauce made from the fermented intestines of small fishes.

List Cloth edging or border. Also, means "like," e.g. "take as they list."

Liveried Uniformed

Liveries Servants' uniforms.

Long in the tooth Old. Although they wear down, horse's teeth continue to grow with age and the phrase, "long in the tooth," referred to the age of people as well as horses.

Lord Chancellor A cabinet minister who traditionally served as the head of the judiciary.

Lout A clumsy ill-mannered person, uncouth oaf.

Maces Official scepters.

Maio The easternmost island of the Sotavento islands of Cape Verde, off the coast of West Africa.

Maltbarn A barn for drying and storing barley or other grains.

Mange A skin disease resulting in loss of hair.

Marchpane Marzipan, a sweet paste of almonds, and sugar or honey.

Market Cross A stone cross situated in the marketplace.

Marry An expression of surprised agreement, or indignation.

Mart A market or fair; a place to buy and sell.

Martinmas November 11ᵗʰ Feast of St. Martin of Tours. A harvest festival, especially of the grape harvest in France. St. Martin was the patron saint of vintners.

Master of Her Majesty's Horse The third Great Officer of the Royal Household, after the Lord Chamberlain and the Lord Steward. He is responsible for the Queens horses and carriages and the Royal Mews (stables).

Master of Revels Deputy to the Lord Chamberlain, responsible for theatrical entertainment. He wielded a great deal of authority as he selected the plays to be performed, as well as the costumes, and scenery, both at Court and for public performances. Plays often carried a political message so the Master of Revels not only controlled which plays would be seen, but also changed dialogue and scenes to suit the purposes of the monarch.

Mastic Aromatic resin or gum from a Mediterranean evergreen tree.

Mastiff A breed of large, powerful dogs with drooping ears, often used as guard dogs.

Matrix Uterus

Maylike conceits Trinkets or baubles seen at May Day festivities.

Mean season In the meantime.

Mellifluous Smooth, flowing.

Men o'war A man o' war was the term applied to any ship used in the Navy for battle.

Mercer A dealer in fine fabrics such as silk and velvet.

Mewling Crying feebly or querulously.

Michaelmas Setpember 29ᵗʰ, Feast of St. Michael the Archangel.

Milche-kine Milk cows.

Milliner One who makes, designs, or sells women's hats.

Minos, Eacus, and Rhadamant In Greek mythology, three brothers, sons of Zeus and Europa, who judge the heart of each person who enters the underworld at death.

Minotaurs Mythological monsters, half man and half bull, confined to a labyrinth in Crete and fed human flesh.

Moors Muslims living in northern Africa of mixed Berber and Arab descent.

Morris Dancers Dancers performing, on May Day and other festivals, a lively rhythmic dance. It was performed by men wearing costumes, often with bells attached, and carrying sticks or handkerchiefs.

Mountebank Magician or charlatan.

Mystery Trade, or occupation.

Napkin Handkerchief

Nemean Lion In Greek mythology, a large lion whose golden fur was impervious to weapons. Hercules choked the Nemean Lion to death.

Neptune Roman god of water or the sea.

Nether Lower in position.

Nether hose A stocking worn on the lower leg.

Nettles Prickly or stinging plants.

Nips Pickpockets, also see foists. The nip would cut any cord attaching a money pouch to the person's clothing while the foist quickly removed it.

Nosegay Small bouquet of flowers, usually sweet-smelling and held in the hand.

Nova Tabula New Map.

Offal Entrails and internal organs of an animal.

Ordnance Military supplies such as weapons, ammunition, and armor.

Ostler A man who cares for horses at an inn.

Packthread Thick thread for sewing or tying up packages.

Pages Young male servants.

Pallas Titan god of warcraft.

Palsies Tremors and paralysis often accompanied with uncontrollable shaking.

Pantaloon A character from the Italian commedia del arte troops of the period who played a foolish old man dressed in pantaloons.

Parley To talk to an enemy, especially to discuss terms of an agreement.

Parlous Great or excessive.

Passado In fencing, a forward thrust of a sword with one foot advanced.

Pasty A folded pastry filled with meat and vegetables.

Patents Official documents granting certain rights.

Pendent Hanging down.

Periwigs Man's wig of long hair drawn back at nape of the neck. Also called a peruke.

Phibbus' car The chariot of the sun god Phoebus.

Philomela In Greek mythology, daughter of the King of Athens. She was raped by King Tereus of Thrace who then cut out her tongue, but she wove her story in a tapestry to ensure it would be told.

Pike An infantry weapon with a pointed steel or iron head on a long wooden shaft, "twice as long as a man is tall."

Pikemen Infantrymen with pikes as their weapons.

Pinnace a light boat propelled by oars or sails.

Pipe A medium-sized barrel containing approximately 120 gallons.

Pizzle An animal's penis.

Plaits Braids, interlaced hair or fibers.

Platted Braided, variant spelling of plaited. "Platted hive of straw," a straw hat.

Pleasance A feeling of pleasure.

Pluto The Roman god of the underworld and the judge of the dead. Pluto is another name for the Greek god Hades.

Pommel A knob at the end of the hilt on a sword.

Popinjay A vain or conceited person, especially one who dresses or behaves extravagantly.

Potting Drinking alcoholic beverages.

Pouncet-box A box for carrying pomander, i.e. a mixture of aromatic substances enclosed in a perforated box and used to scent clothes and linens, or formerly carried as a guard against infection.

Power An armed force, troops.

Prating Chattering, talking foolishly.

Presage Intuition or feeling about what might happen in the future.

Presentment Indictment, or presentation of a viewpoint.

Prithee "I pray thee," or please.

Privateer An armed ship owned by private individuals and commissioned by the government used to attack and capture enemy ships.

Privy Outhouse

Proserpine In Roman mythology, the daughter of Ceres, goddess of corn and the harvest. Pluto fell in love with Proserpine, and abducted and dragged her to the underworld.

Puissance Great power, influence, prowess.

Puissant Powerful

Purvey To supply or provide.

Puttock Buzzard, a derogatory term for someone who is greedy or vain.

Pyrrhic A victory won at too great a cost (after King Pyrrhus who defeated the Romans in 279 A.D. but sustained heavy losses).

Queen's Bench The court that dealt with matters affecting the Crown and with criminal cases. Known as the King's Bench during the reign of a male monarch.

Quicksilver Liquid mercury.

Quiddities Pecularities

Quillets a subtle distinction, quibble.

Quintal A unit of weight with a base of 100. At this time, one quintal equaled approximately 100 pounds.

Quit Freed from, relieved of.

Quoit A ring of iron, rope, or rubber thrown in a game to encircle an upright peg.

Rack A form of torture and punishment where the ankles were fastened to rollers on one end of a rectangular wooden frame, and the wrists to the other end. The rollers were turned, pulling the body in opposing directions, causing intense pain, joint dislocation and, with prolonged use, limbs torn from their sockets.

Rapier A light, sharp-pointed sword.

Rawly Very young.

Rebato Wires Framework for the starched high lace collars worn by both men and women.

Recognizance A bond recognizing a debt.

Recovery A legal procedure for transferring property.

Recusant A Roman Catholic who refused to attend services of the Church of England or submit to other religious laws of that time.

Rhenish White wine from the Rhine region in Germany.

Rose Whore

Rother Cattle

Royals of Plate A large quantity of precious metal coins, usually silver.

Rue An evergreen shrub with bitter, strong smelling leaves used in herbal medicine.

Ruff A wide, starched pleated collar that forced the wearer to keep their chin up and assume a proud pose. A ruff was a symbol of status and wealth.

Rumbustiousness Loudness

Rush candle A candle made from a dried, partly peeled rush that has been dipped in grease.

Sack Fortified wine or sherry.

Saint Andrew's Day The Feast of St. Andrew was celebrated on November 30th. Andrew was a fisherman like his brother, Peter. Both were called by Jesus to be His disciples. Andrew is a patron saint of fishermen.

Saint Barnaby's Day June 11th is the Feast of St. Barnabas. Barnabas, a Jew from Cyprus, worked closely with St. Paul preaching the Gospel. He was a mediator between St. Paul (who had persecuted Christians) and the Jewish Christians who at times distrusted him.

Saint Elizabeth's Day The Feast of St. Elizabeth, the mother of John the Baptist, is celebrated on November 5th.

Saint George's Day April 23rd, St. George is the patron saint of England and was a Roman soldier born around 280. According to legend, he killed a dragon and saved the life of a princess. Shakespeare was born on this day in 1564.

Saint James' Day July 25th, James was the brother of St. John, both called by Jesus to be His disciples.

Saint Luke's Day October 18th is the Feast of St. Luke, a physician to St. Paul. St. Paul wrote the book of Luke and the Acts of the Apostles, and used more medical terms than any other New Testament writer. He is the patron saint of physicians.

Saint Swithin's Day July 15th, named for St. Swithin, Bishop of Winchester 852 - 862. If it rained on this day, it was said that 40 days of rain would follow, but if it was fair, then 40 days of fair weather would follow.

Saturnine Pertaining to the Roman god, Saturn. People at the time thought the planet Saturn was very cold, and the word came to mean morose, dull, or gloomy.

S'blood An exclamation or oath; abbreviation of "God's blood," so as not to take God's name in vain and thereby violate the third commandment. See also S'truth.

Scape Extremely harsh lye soap.

Scimitar A short sword with a curved blade that broadens at the point.

Scrating Scratching or scraping.

Scrivener A notary or professional scribe.

Scouring Diarrhea

Scow A flat-bottomed boat used to transport cargo between ships in harbor.

Scut Vagina

Scythian A person from Scythia, an ancient region of southeastern Europe and Asia.

Semiramis Wife of Nimrod, Queen of Babylon, worshipped as a fertility goddess.

Senna A laxative made from dried pods of the cassia tree.

Shearing Cutting corn with a scythe. Women were commonly added to the workforce to ensure a timely harvest and to employ single women and unmarried mothers.

Shire A county.

Shod carts Carts with iron wheels.

Shyte Shit

Skyey Ethereal

Slaver Saliva, spittle.

Sod "Sod thee," a sexual expletive.

Sodden Boiled, e.g. boiled meat.

Sophy of Persia The sovereign of Persia, now Iran.

Spits Long, thin, pointed metal rods such as those used to spear and hold meat while roasting.

Stale A cheap prostitute.

Star Court An ancient high court of England, controlled by the monarch, which was abolished in 1641 by Parliament for abuses of power.

Staves Shafts, vertical wooden posts.

Stay Support, e.g. "whose strengthless stay is numb."

Stews Brothels

Stock A stocking, e.g. "linen stock on one leg."

Stockish Dull, stupid.

Stocks Wooden structure with a bench where the accused sat while ankles, wrists and sometimes the neck were immobilized by thrusting them through holes in the boards. Passersby would mock and throw things at the victim.

Stool Ball Cricket played with a stool instead of a wicket.

S'truth Abbreviation of God's truth. See also, S'blood.

Strumpet Prostitute

Styx In Greek mythology, the river between earth and the underworld.

Sudden Temporary or makeshift; also the modern usage meaning abrupt.

Suffer'd Suffered, i.e. sustained or continued to endure.

Swan Protestant A patron of the Swan alehouse in Stratford known as a gathering place of Protestants. Recusant Catholics who wanted authorities to accept them as Protestants often patronized the Swan.

Swinged Beaten

Tackle A ship's rigging.

Taffety or Taffeta A stiff, shiny fabric used especially to make skirts and dresses.

Tagus River The longest river running through Spain and Portugal, emptying into the Atlantic Ocean at Lisbon.

Take assay Administering the kill of a wounded animal with a sharp knife.

Tallow Solid fat from cattle or sheep used to make candles, soap and lubricants.

Tawe To soften hides without tanning them by soaking and rubbing them with alum and salt. Often, other substances such as flour and egg yolks were added to the mixture. Tawed skins are soft and flexible, and usually white or yellowish. See also Glover.

Termagant Violent, imaginary diety often appearing in morality plays.

Terra Nova New Land or New World.

Tewkesbury mustard A thick, pungent mustard made since medieval times in Tewkesbury, UK. Made from mustard flour and horseradish root.

Thebes A Greek city prominent in Greek mythology.

Tick Tack A 16th century backgammon game.

Tinkers Itinerant menders of metal utensils.

Tipplers Those who drink alcohol, especially in excess.

Tire Abbreviation for attire.

Tireman Manager of the attire, i.e. the actor's costumes.

Tiring House Abbreviation of "attiring," meaning the dressing area.

Thraldom Servitude

Traffic Trade, buy and sell.

Tribune A Roman officer chosen by commoners to protect their interests.

Troth Truth, oath, or pledge of loyalty.

Tun A large barrel holding about 240 gallons.

Twelfth Night The last night of the twelve days after Christmas.

Unbraced Unfastened, loose.

Varlets Unprincipled, dishonest men.

Ventages The holes of a musical instrument covered with the fingers to change the notes when playing.

Via Off with you!

Viol Or Viola da Gamba, a six stringed musical instrument played with a bow and held between the legs similar to a cello.

Visage Face, countenance.

Vizard Visor or mask.

Voucher A legal proof of someone's right to property.

Walloons People living in southern and eastern Belgium and neighboring part of France.

Wanton (n) A lascivious person.

Water spaniel Breed of dog used to flush and retrieve waterfowl.

Wherries Various light boats used for carrying cargo or passengers.

White Friars Carmelite monks.

Whoreson Bastard, a greatly disliked person. Also a term of coarse familiarity.

Winchester Geese Prostitutes. Also a groin swelling caused by venereal disease.

Withal Expresses various kinds of additive meaning such as "in addition to," "as well," "besides." May also mean "nevertheless" when used to contrast something with a previous comment.

Withers The highest part of a horse's back above the shoulders at the base of the neck.

Wittawer One who tawes skins into soft, supple white skins, also called "alum leather" (although not technically leather since the hides are not tanned). See also, Tawe.

Wont Accustomed to.

Worsted Woolen yarn. A worsted stocking was inferior to a silk stocking.

Yare Moving lightly and easily.

Yeoman A sheriff's officer. In the royal household, a petty officer.

Yerd Penis

Zed The last letter of the alphabet. An ending.

Zeeland The westernmost province of the Netherlands.

DRAMATIS PERSONAE

Shakespeare's published plays included a list of the characters under the Latin phrase "Dramatis Personae" or "people of the drama". Here are the personalities that feature most prominently in the dramas described throughout the *Lost Letters*.

Alleyn, Edward "Ned" – (1566-1626) Considered one of the greatest actors of his time. Played leading roles such as Tamburlaine and in 1600, in partnership with Phillip Henslowe, built the Fortune Theatre and headed the Lord Admiral's Men.

Arden, Edward – (1542-1583) Head of a prominent Warwickshire Catholic family. His father, William, was a second cousin of Shakespeare's mother, Mary Arden. He had antagonized the Earl of Leicester and in 1583 he, his son-in-law John Somerville, and others were indicted for plotting against Queen Elizabeth. Edward was hanged December 30, 1583 and his head was displayed on London Bridge as a warning to others.

Babington, Anthony – (1561-1586) Devoted to Mary Queen of Scots, Babington plotted with of a group of conspirators to assassinate Queen Elizabeth and install Mary as queen. Walsingham and his spies uncovered the plot and in 1586 Babington and the others were executed.

Burbage, Cuthbert – (1565-1636) Eldest son of James Burbage and member of the Earl of Leicester's Men. Practical and matter-of-fact, he handled the acting company's monies and attire (costumes).

Burbage, James – (1531-1597) Head of the Earl of Leicester's Men, he was a joiner (carpenter) who erected the first building specifically for theatrical performances in London. He called it simply "The Theatre" and the year before his death, opened the first indoor theatre, Blackfriars. Besides being a theatre manager, he was an actor, often playing the role of a king. After his death, when the lease on land for The Theatre expired, his sons Richard and Cuthbert, along with Shakespeare and fellow players dismantled The Theatre and rebuilt it as The Globe in Bankside, Southwark.

Burbage, Richard – (1567-1619) An apprentice in the Earl of Leicester's Men, the younger son of James Burbage was initially often churlish toward Shakespeare although they later became friends. He became a great, well-known actor and played many of the lead roles of his day including Shakespeare's Richard III.

Burberry, Heather – A kind, talented woman who, although born without arms, was adept at using her feet to write and perform daily tasks. Her parents taught her to read and write and gave her many books. Throughout her life she spent much time studying. She was John Stow's housekeeper while Shakespeare was a lodger there and helped nurse him back to health when he had scurvy. She provided Shakespeare with helpful insights and books as he wrote plays.

Bryan, George – (1556-?) An actor in Leicester's Men who often played women's parts.

Burghley, Lord William Cecil – (1520-1598) Queen Elizabeth's main advisor who held many of the chief political posts of the land including Secretary of State and Lord High Treasurer.

Cade, Jack – (d. 1450) A notorious rebel who led an uprising in the time of King Henry VI and was depicted in Shakespeare's play of that name (part 2). Although the uprising was suppressed, it led to a weakening of royal authority and the War of the Roses (1455-1485).

Clarke, Thomas – (1542-?) Actor and one of the early members of Leicester's Men. He took Dick Cowley as his apprentice. A Catholic, he protected Shakespeare (known to be from a Catholic family) from some who might have accused him as a traitor.

Combe, John – (1561-1614) Shakespeare's close friend, "Coz," in Stratford-Upon-Avon to whom he addressed his letters.

Cowley, Dick – (1568-1619) The youngest actor in Leicester's Men, he played women's parts. He was Shakespeare's first friend in the acting troupe.

Devereux, Robert, 2nd Earl of Essex – (1566-1601) Stepson of the Earl of Leicester (Robert Dudley), he became, at the age of 20, Queen Elizabeth's favorite courtier. Rash and vain, he went off on an unsuccessful campaign to Ireland in 1599, and in 1601 plotted an uprising with the Earl of Southampton and other nobles. The Earl of Essex was captured, accused of treason and beheaded in 1601.

Drake, Sir Francis – (c.1540-1596) The first Englishman to circumnavigate the globe, 1577-1580. He plundered Spanish ports, returning to England with much Spanish treasure. In 1585 he sailed to the West Indies and to Florida, again plundering Spanish settlements. He was Vice-Admiral and helped defeat the Spanish Armada in 1588.

Dudley, Lord Robert, Earl of Leicester – (1532-1588) A favorite courtier of Queen Elizabeth I who richly rewarded him with lands including Kenilworth castle. She created him Earl of Leicester in 1564. His hopes to marry the Queen were never realized, but he married Lady Essex and became the step-father of Robert Devereux, the Second Earl of Essex who soon became the Queen's new favorite. Despite incompetence when sent with the English army to the Netherlands in 1585, the Queen put Dudley in charge of her troops at Tilbury in 1588 during the invasion by the Spanish Armada. He died shortly afterward.

Elizabeth I, Queen – (1533-1603) Daughter of King Henry VIII and Anne Boleyn, Elizabeth was queen of England and Ireland from 1558 until her death in 1603. Her reign is often referred to as the Golden Age and although religious persecution and turmoil were common, it was also a time of exploration of the New World, flourishing of the theatre, and the defeat of the Spanish Armada.

Essex, 2nd Earl of – See Devereux, Robert.

Farnese, Allessandro, Duke of Parma and Piacenza (aka Alejandro Farnesio) – (1545-1592) Appointed by King Philip II as the Governor of the Spanish Netherlands from 1578-1592. Philip ordered him to take his troops to the coast where they were to join the Armada and then invade England. Parma went to Dunkirk but, immersed in preparations, was not ready and proved no help to the battered Armada.

Grenville, Sir Richard – Like Sir Francis Drake, Grenville was an English sailor and privateer, though far less famous (then or now). He sailed to the New World and supported efforts to colonize it for England. He served in the fleet that defended England against the Spanish Armada in 1588 and died in 1591 in a sea battle against Spain's ongoing efforts to conquer England.

Guzman, Don Alonso Perez de, **7ᵗʰ Duke of Medina-Sidonia** – (1550-1619) Headed the Spanish Armada's invasion of England. Earlier in 1588, the original Commander of the Armada died and Medina-Sidonia was given the position despite his protests.

Hatton, Sir Christopher – (1540-1591) Appointed Lord Chancellor in 1587, he was a favorite of Queen Elizabeth's and a strong supporter of John Whitgift, Archbishop of Canterbury, in actions against overzealous Puritans.

Henry VIII, King – (1491-1547) King of England from 1509-1547. When the Pope refused to annul Henry's marriage to Catherine of Aragon, Henry divorced her and married Anne Bolyen. Their child, Elizabeth, ascended the throne in 1558. The break with Rome led to the formation of the Church of England with Henry as its Supreme Head. Years of religious turmoil and persecution ensued.

Howard, Lord Charles – (1536-1624) Lord High Admiral, commanded the English fleet against the Spanish Armada in 1588 and, in 1601, helped suppress the Earl of Essex's plot against Queen Elizabeth.

Jaggard, Vernon – Caretaker of The Theatre who befriended Shakespeare.

Johnson, William – (1545-?) One of the masters, or leading actors, in Leicester's Men. Imperious, with piercing blue eyes, he mostly played parts of nobles and brave soldiers. For a time, many thought he was a spy for the Crown.

Kempe Will – (1560-1608) A burly clown who performed bawdy jigs and other roles as an actor in Leicester's Men and who was a model for Shakespeare's character, Sir John Falstaff. His sister, Kathleen, sailed with her husband to what became known as the Lost Colony and was never heard from again.

Kett, Francis – (c.1547-1589) A physician and clergyman who was burned to death for his denial of Jesus' divinity and other views considered heretical. Many thought he influenced Marlowe's unorthodox beliefs.

Kyd, Thomas – (1558-1594) Playwright with the Admiral's Men best known for the "Spanish Tragedy" (or Heironimo). Kyd lodged with Christopher Marlowe and was arrested and tortured in 1593, suspected of treason. He was later released but died the next year.

Leicester, 1ˢᵗ Earl of – See Dudley, Lord Robert.

Leicester's Men – Robert Dudley, 1st Earl of Leicester, kept a company of actors that was granted the first royal patent of any acting company. As the Earl's household servants, they could travel freely in England. The Queen authorized them to perform throughout the realm and, with the Master of Revels' approval, their works were free from local censorship. Leicester's Men was headed by James Burbage and included Thomas Clarke, Will Johnson, Thomas Pope, Richard and Cuthbert Burbage, Will Kempe, John Perkin, Augustine Phillips, George Bryan, Dick Cowley and William Shakespeare.

Manteo – Native American brought to England during one of the 16th century voyages to the New World.

Marlowe, Christopher ("Kit") – (1564-1593) Leading Elizabethan playwright who wrote "Doctor Faustus," "Jew of Malta," "Tamburlaine," and other plays, but was thought by many to be involved in Walsingham's spy network. He died under mysterious circumstances after being stabbed in the forehead in what was called a "tavern dispute."

Marprelate, Martin – Pseudonym for the author(s) of Puritan religious tracts critical of Archbishop Whitgift and the Church of England.

Mary Queen of Scots, (Mary Stuart) – (1542-1587) Daughter of James V of Scotland and Marie de Guise, and a cousin of Queen Elizabeth I. Catholic Mary sought refuge in England from Scottish Protestants, but she was imprisoned for 19 years and the center of numerous plots to depose Queen Elizabeth and reinstate the Catholic faith in England. At the urging of her advisors, Elizabeth reluctantly agreed to Mary's execution and she was beheaded at Fotheringhay Castle.

Mary I, Queen (Mary Tudor) – (1516-1588) Daughter of King Henry VIII and his first wife, Catherine of Aragon. Queen Mary I restored Catholicism to England and burned hundreds of Protestants, adding to her unpopularity. She married the Catholic King Philip II of Spain but was childless, leaving her half sister, Elizabeth, to succeed her.

Medina-Sidonia, 7th Duke of – See Guzman, Don Alonso Perez de.

Munday, Rosalind – Shakespeare's mistress in London; she pretended to be his wife in an attempt to gain passage to the New World.

Parma and Piacenza, Duke of – See Farnese, Allessandro.

Perkin, John – (1542-?) Actor and company physician for Leicester's Men. He took Shakespeare as his apprentice and encouraged his skill as a writer.

Philip II, King of Spain – (1527-1598) King of Spain from 1556-1598, and while married to Queen Mary I, was also King of England and Ireland from 1554-1558. A devout Catholic, he ordered the invasion of Protestant England in 1588 by his "invincible" Spanish Armada, which was soundly defeated by the English forces.

Phillips, Augustine – (1556-1605) Master of Music for Leicester's Men and half brother to Thomas Pope.

Phillips, Kathleen – Sister of Will Kempe. Kempe asked Shakespeare to protect his sister when she went on the voyage to the New World with her husband, Miles.

Phillips, Miles – (1551-?) With his wife, Kathleen, went on Governor John White's voyage to the New World to help found a colony, which later became known as The Lost Colony of Roanoke.

Pope, Thomas – (1546-1603) Actor with Leicester's Men who played comic parts. Despite serious injuries from an accident in his youth, he still performed jigs and tumbling. Pope despised Catholicism although his half-brother, Augustine Phillips, defended that faith.

Raleigh, Sir Walter – (1552-1618) Explorer who sailed to the Americas and founded a colony in what is now Virginia. However, the colonists on the 1587 voyage struggled to survive and became what is known as the Lost Colony of Roanoke, never to be heard from again. Efforts in 1588 to resupply them were thwarted because all resources in England were needed to fend off the invasion by the Spanish Armada. As Vice Admiral, Sir Walter unleashed an attack of fire ships against the Spanish, turning the tide of the invasion and defeating Spain.

Shakespeare, Anne, Gilbert, John, Mary, etc. – See Shakespeare Family Tree.

Sidney, Sir Phillip – (1554-1586) A popular poet and statesman, who was interested in the new American colonies and hoped to go on an expedition with Sir Francis Drake. When the Queen sent a force under the Earl of Leicester to assist the Dutch against Spain, Sidney was shot while commanding a cavalry company and died a few weeks later from an infected wound. He was greatly admired, given an elaborate funeral and buried at St. Paul's Cathedral.

Souhthampton, Countess of – See Wriothesley, Mary

Southampton, 3rd Earl of – See Wriothesley, Henry

Stow, John – (1525-1605) A tailor in his youth, he became an historian who wrote a number of books, but is best known for his "Survey of London" published in 1598. Shakespeare lodged in his home and Stow gave him use of his extensive library. He provided vital information about the geography around London to Leicester's Men as they prepared for battle against the Spanish in 1588.

Tarlton, Richard – (1530-1588) Actor with the Queen's Men and most famous clown of his time. Upon his death, the Queen's Men lost one of its best players and the acting company fell into disrepair for a time.

Throckmorton, Francis (aka Throgmorton) – (1554-1584) From a devout Catholic family, Throckmorton conspired with English exiles in Europe, and with Catholics in England, to restore Catholicism, overthrow Queen Elizabeth and bring Mary Queen of Scots to the throne. Walsingham uncovered the plot and Throckmorton confessed after being tortured on the rack. He was executed in 1584.

Walsingham, Sir Francis – (1532-1590) A principal policy advisor to the Queen, Lord Burghley hired him in 1568 to spy on those in London who might be a potential threat. He organized an efficient spy network to protect Elizabeth and English interests. He had studied in Europe and was a talented linguist. Walsingham used double agents, propaganda and disinformation, and other techniques to uncover plots at home and abroad. He was pivotal in the trial and execution of Mary Queen of Scots.

Wanchese – Native American brought to England during one of the 16th century voyages to the New World.

White, Governor John–(1540-1593) An English explorer and artist, White went to Roanoke Island in 1585 and made sketches and paintings of the region and the Native Americans there. That colony was abandoned and he returned to England. In 1587 he sailed for Roanoke again, as Governor of what Raleigh hoped would become a permanent colony. At the end of the year, White returned to England for food and supplies but was denied, as all vessels were being pressed into service to defend against the Spanish Armada. He was not able to return until 1590, only to find the colony was long deserted. It became known as the "Lost Colony." White returned to England, devastated by the loss of the colony that included his own daughter and granddaughter.

Whitgift, John, Archbishop of Canterbury – (1530-1604) Elizabeth's chaplain in 1563, he became Archbishop from 1583 until his death. Whitgift strove for religious conformity to the Anglican church and suppressed Puritan writings.

Wriothesley, Henry, 3rd Earl of Southampton – (1573-1624) Henry's father died just before his eighth birthday and he became a royal ward of Lord Burghley. He was presented at Court when he was 17 and became friends with Robert Devereux, Earl of Essex. He loved literature and was a patron of a number of writers including Shakespeare.

Wriothesley, Mary, Countess of Southampton (nee Browne) – (1552-1607) At the age of thirteen, she married the 2nd Earl of Southampton and bore him a son, Henry. She was widowed in 1581 and married Sir Thomas Heneage in 1594, widowed again and married lastly to Sir William Hervey in 1598. The Countess bought gloves made by John Shakespeare and, as later letters describe, William Shakespeare came to know her well and wrote a play to celebrate her second marriage.

ENDNOTES

SCRIBE'S NOTES

1. *The Life of Henry, Third Earl of Southampton: Shakespeare's Patron.* Charlotte Carmichael Stopes. University Press, Cambridge, 1922

LETTER ONE

2. In one of my first clues that Shakespeare was indeed the author of these letters, I recognized the dialogue that follows as apparently the source of similar witty banter that he wrote in Act III, scene 1 of *Two Gentlemen of Verona*. In the scene he now describes, we learn more about customs and his traveling companion. For example, throwing partially eaten food at someone was a typical insult, so Shakespeare is making a point about the way Boy Burbage treats Dick Cowley.

3. I could find no famous character named Lenore in contemporary plays or poems, but considering how Shakespeare refers to her here, she must have been well-known.

4. Biting the thumbnail or clicking it against the teeth while flicking the thumb in someone's direction was taken as an insult.

5. I discovered that a scene in Shakespeare's *Henry IV part 1*, Act II, scene 1, has very similar dialogue among carriers to what follows. An "ostler" is a man who cares for horses at an inn. I have retained Shakespeare's capitalization here, since it may also be the man's surname.

6. According to *Shakespeare's England* (Clarendon Press Oxford, 1916, vol. 1 p201-3) horses were hired in London for 3 pence/hour, so this tidbit is consistent with known pricing of goods and services, especially for a horse that the carrier admits is worn out.

7. There are numerous references to the Combe family in Stratford, but no source I could find that describes division over religion, so Shakespeare's reference here remains obscure. As subsequent letters explain, England was in great danger from

Catholic monarchies trying to overturn the Protestant faith, which indeed divided families, friends, and would soon divide the men of Leicester's theatre troupe.

8. I found a similar list of ailments in Shakespeare's *Troilus & Cressida* Act V, scene 1.

9. My research found references to both of these plays, but no extant copies or references to authorship or performance history other than Shakespeare's mention here.

10. This scolding is a very interesting passage. A similar diatribe appears in *Two Noble Kinsmen*, a play that some attribute to Shakespeare, which may strengthen the case of those who believe he was the author.

11. Shakespeare's younger siblings were Gilbert, Joan, Anne, Richard, and Edmund.

LETTER TWO

12. Shakespeare wrote "years" and crossed this out, replacing it with "months".

13. In *Merchant of Venice*, Shakespeare employs a similar device for Portia to determine a man's character, having her suitors choose among casks of gold, silver, and lead.

14. The way Shakespeare refers to *Widow's Debt*, it appears to be a well-known play, at least to him and John Combe. I found only one obscure reference to a play called *A Lonely Widow and Her Debt* and no other information about its authorship or playing history.

15. Mr. Field was a tanner in Stratford. The 'drying barn' must have been a large structure for preparing animal skins.

16. Pope was renowned for mixing up names (often reflected in his letters). That may account for the use of 'John', especially since he would have met William's father in Stratford. As the witty clown in Leicester's Men, it may also have been his way of referring to the Company's "johannes (John) factotum" or jack-of-all-trades, which Shakespeare was, and may explain why Shakespeare repeats the apparent error in recounting the incident.

17. 'Hose' refers to the form of pants (not just socks, as that term would mean today) worn by Elizabethan men. The separate leggings were held together by a codpiece over the genitals, so Pope means Shakespeare's pants came apart and exposed his backside and privates. I found an expanded version of this poem that was published in 1597 in English in an obscure German publication about book fairs, so it apparently became quite famous and often repeated.

18. Bears were put in a ring with numerous dogs or other wild beasts that would attack and often kill the bear. The best bears took a beating, but killed their assailants and lived to fight another day.

19. Colbrand was a legendary giant (and people of the period generally believed giants of ten feet or more existed).

LETTER THREE

20. *The Life of Henry, Third Earl of Southampton: Shakespeare's Patron*. Charlotte Carmichael Stopes. University Press, Cambridge, 1922.

21. The religious holiday of Lammas was celebrated each year on August 1st.

22. Was this an original observation by Shakespeare or a common adage? Either way, he repeats it in Henry IV part 1, Act I, scene 2.

23. Thomas Jenkins was the schoolmaster in Stratford when Shakespeare and Combe were boys.

24. 'Dinner' refers to the midday meal; supper the evening meal. To "sup" is to eat supper.

25. Literally translated, "I Gelosi" means "the jealous ones" (there is no consensus in the literature why that name would be chosen for a troupe of acrobats and comic players) and apparently refers to a Milan-based playing company that is thought by some scholars to be the first one patronized by nobility in Europe, although as we have seen, there were already many such troupes in England at this time. Performances were recorded of I Gelosi in France, Spain, Germany, and England in the late 1570s, so Pope's account appears to coincide with this company, which must have been famous for Shakespeare to refer to it without further explanation to John Combe in this letter.

26. Shakespeare appears to have recalled Pope's description of his handicaps when writing *Richard III*, wherein the future king similarly laments his deformities in Act I, scene 1.

27. The contemporary historian Richard Hakluyt records the following events, of John Fox and Peter Unticaro, in at least two of his histories, which were published in 1582 and later, so Pope may have read or heard them from those sources. I have used those accounts to clarify names and to fill gaps in Shakespeare's re-telling.

28. Thursday was market day in Stratford, a time when many strangers came to town to sell their services or wares.

29. In 1584, Captain Mary Ambree was among those who liberated the city of Ghent from Spanish occupation, becoming the subject of a famous English ballad (which Rudyard Kipling later used for the title of his novel, 'Captains Courageous'). William Elderton was renowned as a poet, actor, and author of ballads set to music and may have written 'Captains Courageous'. Historians have not generally agreed on his date of death, so it is interesting to note that Boarwhistle speaks of him as already deceased.

30. Interesting to note that in Act IV, scene 1 of *Titus Andronicus*, Shakespeare's character Young Lucius says "Grandsire, 'tis Ovid's Metamorphoses; My mother gave it me." The mention that "she herself can make little use thereof" may refer to the fact she could neither read nor write.

31. I was thrilled to read this sonnet on the old paper, in cramped ink-blotted letters spelling out barely legible old English words, because with slight changes, this poem appears as number 30 in the collection of Shakespeare's sonnets published in 1609. Although most scholars accept the attribution of those sonnets to Shakespeare, later letters confirm he did not authorize the publication of them; that some were altered and the order they are presented in the book is not the order in which they were written (as this letter demonstrates); and that there are some very surprising reasons why many of them were written at all.

LETTER FOUR

32. A religious holiday celebrated September 29th.

33. Ale was often served with an egg in it.

34. "Dark lady" in this context seems to refer to anal sex. "Scut" is slang for vagina.

35. Gerrard was another legendary giant.

36. Maio is one of the Cape Verde islands off the coast of Senegal, Africa.

37. Drake was not knighted until 1581, so Westerbeke's tale reflects his contemporary knowledge, not just the facts at the time of the 1577 voyage he describes to Shakespeare.

38. Westerbeke's account, casting himself as a savior of his shipmate, may have been inaccurate or self-serving. I found another account set down by an officer on the voyage, including the mutiny, that ended with Doughty's execution.

39. They sailed around the tip of South America and into the Pacific Ocean.

40. Interesting to note that despite Shakespeare's solid Stratford grammar school education, he had never heard of penguins and did not understand that the seasons in the northern and southern hemispheres are reversed.

41. Most likely what is today San Francisco Bay in California.

42. The Miwok tribe was dominant in the area at the time and Westerbeke's descriptions are similar to anthropological studies as described in *Handbook of North American Indians* Vol. 8 (Smithsonian Institution, 1978).

LETTER FIVE

43. "Lord Robert" is a reference to Robert Dudley, Earl of Leicester, presumably said this way to demean his honor.

44. I found a similar rhyme in a play that some scholars believe Shakespeare wrote, but which was not included in the First Folio or any other contemporary publication associated with his name, suggesting either he did write *The Life & Death of Thomas Lord Cromwell* or the author heard and used Shakespeare's little bit of doggerel in that play.

45. In Virgil's *Aeneid*, King Priam's slaughter is described by Aeneas and would have been familiar to boys with an Elizabethan grammar school education.

46. This was not the Golden Hind, originally named the Pelican, which Francis Drake renamed to honor Sir Christopher Hatton in the middle of his voyage of circumnavigation (which, coincidentally, Shakespeare heard about and reported in a previous letter). All contemporary accounts report that the Golden Hind was retired after Drake's voyage, becoming a tourist attraction, which features prominently in a later letter from Shakespeare. Moreover, Drake's vessel displaced 300 tons and the sailor in this account refers to a vessel of only 40 tons.

47. My best guess is that Pidge is speaking of the Orinoco and Amazon Rivers in South America.

48. Shakespeare presumably means Prichard here, but the letter says Pilchard, a popular type of fish.

LETTER SIX

49. The Catholic tradition of eating only fish on Fridays was retained by the Church of England, in part to support the nation's fishing industry.

50. A bell was rung in towns, when the bodies of Plague victims were being collected, to alert families to bring out their dead.

51. Kempe was reciting a familiar passage from the Common Book of Prayer that was mandatory for use in English churches at the time.

52. Elizabethans counted dates in numerals (1,2,3, etc.), but money in Roman numerals. For easier reading, I have converted all numbers in Shakespeare's texts to standard numerals. Unskilled laborers earned about a shilling per day, so Shakespeare's nineteen shillings had little buying power.

53. April 23rd is St. George's Day. Shakespeare was born on that date in 1564.

54. Susanna Shakespeare was born in 1583, so these events took place three years before this letter was written.

55. Arden was executed at the end of December 1583.

56. Giddy is the nickname he gives to his brother Gilbert.

LETTER SEVEN

57. In the letter, Shakespeare identifies the pickpocket as John Gabriel Ratsey. There was a notorious highwayman, thief, and murderer named John Gamaliel Ratsey, who was caught and hung in 1605. The similarity of names seems too close to be coincidental (although Ratsey the thief wasn't known to have started his crime spree before 1600), but the differences could be explained by Ratsey intentionally using an alias or Shakespeare mis-remembering what he was told. Either way, Shakespeare was lucky to have escaped with his life (although a lighter purse, to be sure).

58. I found a similar debate over a letter that takes place in *King Lear* Act I, scene 2.

59. Shakespeare uses almost this exact quote about the evils of big cities in *Comedy of Errors*, Act 1, scene 2

60. I have not been able to determine the meaning of 'cretes' in this context, although one obscure reference suggests a card game, so Shakespeare may have been alluding to cards stacked one upon the other. He may have meant 'crates', but that is not a word I find anywhere else in his writing.

61. Burbage's partner in the Theatre was John Brayne, so either Shakespeare was misinformed of the man's name or mangles it here for the sake of the pun.

62. Vernon made quite an impression on Shakespeare, who applies a similar description for a character in *Taming of the Shrew* (Act III, scene 2).

63. Burbage attributes Vernon's oration to a play about King Edward, but we find similar lines in Shakespeare's Henry VI part one, Act II, scene 5. This highlights the way players and playwrights borrowed from each other's work.

64. Crab was the name of Shakespeare's dog (as he reports in other letters).

LETTER EIGHT

65. In Hamlet (Act IV scene 3) Shakespeare writes a similar description about commoners and kings.

66. A similar comparison of "tongue against tongue" appears in Shakespeare's King John (Act III, scene 1).

67. This must have been a familiar bit of doggerel from an old play (Pyramus & Thisbe), because Shakespeare quotes it again in Midsummer Night's Dream (Act I, scene 2).

68. I have found no evidence that Tilney had been knighted, so either Cuthbert was misinformed or being sarcastic here.

69. Rebato wires are the framework for the starched lace high collars worn by both men and women. Fashionable codpieces had grown larger over the years, such that by this time they included pockets.

70. The Saracen's Head and the Red Lion have been well documented as being near Aldgate, in east London, not near Ludgate in the west. It must be presumed that Shakespeare mixed up the many inns, or their locations, he had been visiting.

LETTER NINE

71. A "Swan Protestant" refers to a patron of the Swan alehouse in Stratford, known as a gathering place of Protestants. Recusant Catholics who wanted local authorities to accept them as Protestants often patronized the Swan. The reference to Perrott's daughter is likely a misunderstanding (although Perrott was known to disinherit heirs over trifles), because it was the wealthy Stratfordian's granddaughter who was disinherited for marrying Shakespeare's childhood classmate, Richard Tyler, without

approval and warning her sisters not to "match themselves without consent of their parents."

72. I can find no book with this title, but a Bible reference is somewhat relevant: "And ought not this woman, being a daughter of Abraham, whom Satan hath bound, lo, these eighteen years, be loosed from this bond on the Sabbath day?" Luke 13:16

73. There is no definition of 'dines' in the literature that is linked to clothmaking, so it is unclear what machinery or tool this might be. One possibility is that it is an abbreviation of 'gabardines', a cloth which Shakespeare knew (Shylock in *Merchant of Venice* refers to gabardine, for example).

74. Grograin = apparently from "gros grain", a wool or silk fabric characterized by its distinctive ribbed appearance woven in the same manner as taffeta.

75. Shakespeare repeats parts of this musical philosophy in *Taming of the Shrew* (Act III, scene 1) and again in *Measure for Measure* (Act IV, scene 1).

76. Jack Cade was a notorious rebel who led an uprising in the time of King Henry VI and was depicted in Shakespeare's play of that name (part 2).

77. Shakespeare refers to the main church in Stratford, Holy Trinity, which still stands today, and is the place of his tomb.

78. Nothing in the entire correspondence helps me make sense of this reference. It may be a response to something in the letter that Shakespeare received from Combe.

LETTER TEN

79. Shakespeare makes a very similar point in *Othello* (Act II, scene 3)

80. Shakespeare talks of the stages of love, like stairs, in *As You Like It* (Act V, scene 2)

81. There are records of an early version of *Hamlet* and some scholars believe Shakespeare wrote all or parts of it, updating it many years later as his writing skills improved into the version we have today, although he takes no credit for it in this letter.

82. Richard "Pug" Field was apprenticed to a printer at this time. In later letters, Shakespeare describes him becoming a licensed printer in his own right and establishing himself in business in a very unique manner.

83. I can find no other contemporary reference or definition for "waiting rooms".

84. Liquamen was a sauce made from the fermented intestines of small fishes. It is unclear how this would be interchangeable with butter, but that is how the recipe is presented here.

LETTER ELEVEN

85. Church and civic records show that Shakespeare (aged 18) and Anne Hathaway (aged 26) were married on November 27th 1582 without the multiple "reading of the banns" (the customary announcement of the impending wedding for weeks in advance). Susanna Shakespeare was born six months later on May 26th 1583.

86. "He takes false shadows for true substances" seems like a common saying of the period, but it is worth noting that Shakespeare uses it again in *Titus Andronicus* (Act III, scene 2), which he writes a few months later. I found it fascinating to see quite a few of these bromides in the letters, which must then have been in his mind when he came to write the play.

87. Shakespeare writes a similar dialogue between husband and wife in *Macbeth* (Act I, scene 5).

88. Richard Quiney was Shakespeare's contemporary and attended grammar school in Stratford at the same time.

89. If Shakespeare considered the rat a Spaniard, he would have been a "Senor", not the Italian version "Signor", but I left the word as he wrote it in this case.

90. At the time Elizabeth appointed the Earl of Essex as her Master of Horse, she also awarded him licenses over the importation of certain goods, which earned him substantial annual fees.

91. Fish Street is east of Gracechurch Street near the river, while the Mermaid was west of there and near Westcheap ("Cheapside"). Shakespeare may have seen Spanish wines poured out near the Mermaid or the ale houses of Fish Street, but the two were not close together.

LETTER TWELVE

92. Shakespeare uses a similar line in *Coriolanus* (Act I, scene 1) when people are bemoaning the lack of affordable corn, something we now know he witnessed in person.

93. There were no letters describing how a man held Kempe aloft for this jig and previous correspondence suggests Shakespeare had not seen John Combe in person since

he first left Stratford in 1586, so this must be a reference to a letter that is no longer extant.

94. Shakespeare uses equine references frequently in his work, but a similar bawdy banter as this one about horses is in found *Henry V* (Act III, scene 7).

95. Shakespeare must have been impressed by these nobles. He describes a similar gathering in *Henry IV Part 1* (Act I, scene 3)

96. Shakespeare gives similar mystical healing attributes to the doctor attending Lady Macbeth in Macbeth (Act IV, scene 3).

97. Shakespeare repeats that rhyming couplet in *Romeo & Juliet* (Act II, scene 2), which made me suspect it was a common phrase in praise of beauty, not something he originated. However other sentiments exchanged on the night he is describing in this letter seem to form the theme of that scene in the play, so clearly he drew upon his own experience with Rosalind when the time came to write his masterpiece of love.

LETTER THIRTEEN

98. Two brothers in the play are named Ferrex and Porrex, so Pope was making a pun.

99. The legal terms Shakespeare reports in this letter are repeated in several of his plays, including in Hamlet (Act V, scene 1), leading some scholars to suggest he may have had legal training himself.

100. He is apparently referring to Pope's half-brother, Augustine Phillips, who volunteered with George Bryan to fight in the troops gathered by the Earl of Leicester, and apparently left the Company, some months earlier.

101. In Marlowe's 'Jew of Malta', he expresses similar views about religion, but that play was not staged until the winter of 1588-89, raising interesting questions about the cross-pollination of ideas among players.

102. Shakespeare engages in a similar philosophical debate in *Henry V* (Act IV, scene 1).

103. As with Shakespeare's descriptions of Rosalind in other letters, he seems to have remembered the emotions and expressions of love when he later wrote *Romeo & Juliet* (especially Act II, scene 2), but nothing in his plays describe love-making as he does in this letter!

104. Shakespeare may mean Phillip Henslowe, well known theatre manager, but the record is unclear if he had anything to do with Pembroke's Men at this time. It is also

confusing that earlier in this letter. Shakespeare refers to a commission to write a play about King Henry the Fifth, but here he refers to already having done so (and to a performance of his scenes at Court). I could find no records of a performance in England or at Court of a play dealing with the English King Henry V before 1590.

LETTER FOURTEEN

105. The Queen's grandfather on her mother's side was Geoffrey Boleyn, a wealthy London merchant. A monument was erected to him in the St. Lawrence church in Shakespeare's day.

106. By contrast, the English seaman got a gallon of beer a day, a pound of biscuit and 2 pounds of beef or pork on 4 days a week; and the other 3 days butter, fish, peas or cheese.

107. This is the same Duke of Parma who Leicester so notoriously allowed to take back provinces entrusted to him by the Queen during his Governorship of those lands.

108. I can find no contemporary definition of "cruzado" but it seems to come from the word crusade and in this context means dispensation or automatic forgiveness for sins, such as killing someone in war.

109. Drake did more than diminish Spain's naval fleet at Cadiz. After that raid, he proceeded up the coast, pillaging coastal merchant vessels and destroying the Andalusian fishing industry, including burning the staves and stealing the iron hoops needed for making barrels. When the Armada sailed a few months later, their stocks of salt fish were meager and old; the number of barrels for water and food greatly diminished. This proved decisive in the war when the Spanish ships were unable to land and replenish their supplies.

110. Shakespeare refers here to Ascension Day, the celebration of Jesus' ascension to Heaven, typically celebrated forty days after Easter. In 1588, this would have been in mid-May.

111. I can find no definition of "Welsh style" for horse grooming, but assume from Shakespeare's reference and the Elizabethan view of Welshmen as "wild" that it was some method of leaving the hair, mane, and tail uncut and unbraided. It is also noteworthy that Leicester was bestowed lands in Wales and had the Bible translated into Welsh, so he had some familiarity with and affinity for the customs there.

112. Shakespeare refers to the fact that Robert Dudley's (the Earl of Leicester) father was the Duke of Northumberland, but the family was condemned to death for backing Lady Jane Gray's claim to the throne over Henry VIII's daughter (and Elizabeth's half sister) Mary. As queen, Mary, a Catholic known as 'bloody Mary" for her persecution of Protestants, married King Philip of Spain, essentially making him King of England. Ironically, Dudley regained favor by fighting for Philip in his wars to regain French territories, but now had the opportunity to revenge the treatment of his father and family—much as Shakespeare had to fight now for Leicester while looking for revenge for the treatment of his father and family.

113. Flooding was common in southern England that July. The Avon overflowed its banks in Stratford and damaged Clopton Bridge, stranding several in the middle of the river and sweeping one woman to her death.

114. The Queen received a letter he wrote from where he was taking treatments and wrote on it 'his last letter', placed it in a jewel box and kept it beside her bed until her own death.

LETTER FIFTEEN

115. Horatio has similar views on natural events as warnings in Hamlet (Act I, scene 1), so this may be an inspiration for those lines, however, as we have seen in other letters, Vernon quotes familiar plays and may have been doing so in this case. If so, Shakespeare may have used another playwright's speeches as the basis for at least some of the lines in his masterpiece.

116. Shakespeare means *The Spanish Tragedy*, whose central character is Heironimo.

117. As in Letter 14, the reference to this play is obscure. In any case, it is not Shakespeare's version of King Henry V, which he wrote a decade later. My best guess is that the times called for patriotic plays and Henry V was an inspiration to the English, so there were likely numerous attempts to bring him to life on the stage.

118. Sir Richard Grenville was an English sailor and privateer comparable to Sir Francis Drake, though far less famous (then or now). Like Sir Walter Raleigh, he sailed to the New World and supported efforts to colonize it for England. He served in the fleet that defended England against the Spanish Armada in 1588 and died in 1591 in a sea battle against Spain's ongoing efforts to conquer England.

119. A ship's clock strike's once to mark the passage of every half hour, beginning at half past midnight. At eight bells (4AM) sailors know it is time to change the watch (crew). The cycle of eight bells repeats every four hours, so six bells in the afternoon would have been 3PM.

120. As an example of how plays of this period were collaborative efforts, Phillips reprises his song ten years later in As You Like It (Act II scene 7).

121. Mary Wriothesley, (nee Browne) was the Countess of Southampton through her marriage at age thirteen to Sir Thomas Heneage. As later letters describe, Shakespeare came to know her well and wrote a play to celebrate her second marriage.

122. Richard I was coronated on September 3, 1189 in Westminster Abbey.

123. There was a group of poets and playwrights who had attended Oxford or Cambridge universities, including Thomas Kyd is sometimes included in the group, though he did not apparently attend university. They were noted for a disdain of authors who were not classically trained. In the 19th century, a historian called them the 'university wits', although that term was not used in Shakespeare's day in any reference I can find.

124. Similar sentiments appear in the funeral scene, Act I, scene 1, of Titus Andronicus, the play that Shakespeare was about to write.

LETTER SIXTEEN

125. Thomas Combe, brother of Shakespeare's friend John Combe, had a son, Thomas, about this time. He already had a son named William (born 1586), so John Combe now had two nephews. Shakespeare's uncle Henry (his father's brother) had a daughter (Lettice, aged 7 at this time) and a son (James, aged 4,who died at this time).

126. In Hamlet (Act V, scene 1) Shakespeare recreates a similar scene, as Hamlet mourns the death of Ophelia.

127. Shakespeare had witnessed the drinking songs and habits of foreigners on his travels before this, but he captures the song and observations of these old soldiers in Othello (Act II, scene 3).

128. In essence, the Puritans behind the Martin Marprelate pamphlets demanded a Presbyterian church hierarchy based on the will of the people in the congregation and merit of the clergy, not the episcopal approach of royal appointment of bishops that mimicked the nobility of the Court.

129. In Letter 15, Shakespeare mentions the pamphlets of these authors, but notes that the authorities would not commission Marlowe (most likely, because of his scandalous beliefs about religion in general). It is interesting to note that in this letter Shakespeare suggests Marlowe was the leader of the group writing for the church. Either he mis-remembers at this point, or things have changed since the first Marprelate letters were written and the church hired more authors to defend it, including the very popular and famous Marlowe.

130. Although *Titus Andronicus* would evolve from what Shakespeare was apparently considering at this point, it is interesting to note his obvious initial attempt to copy the success of Marlowe's *Tamburlaine the Great*, a story of a war-mongering general.

131. Interesting that Revenge personified is also used by Kyd in *The Spanish Tragedy*, which Richard Burbage described to Shakespeare and the other players just before the war (see Letter 13).

132. Many scholars have concluded that the first act and other portions of *Titus Andronicus* were written by Robert Greene, but this comment by Shakespeare could explain how such contributions were added or deleted from the play that was finally performed.

133. The Thursday before Easter, which was April 5th in 1589 (the Queen typically washed the feet of the poor on this day), meaning the first successful staging of a play by William Shakespeare was April 7, 1589.

134. A cuckold is a spouse who is the victim of adultery.

135. Hermes is the Greek god associated with being a swiftly moving messenger (winged Mercury in the Roman mythology).

136. Shakespeare's maturation since leaving Stratford is nicely summarized in this observation about his fellows. The emotions stuck with him, as he uses similar metaphors in his famous "seven ages of man" speech in *As You Like It* (Act II, scene 7).

137. In the published version of Shakespeares sonnets, a similar version of this appears as number 107. Scholars have long thought enduring the 'eclipse' refers to surviving the Spanish invasion and other contemporary honors refer to the dawn of a golden, Endless Age of peace and prosperity thanks to Queen Elizabeth (the 'mortal moon').

ABOUT THE AUTHOR: TERRY TAMMINEN

From his youth in Australia to career experiences in Europe, Africa, China and across the United States, Terry has developed expertise in business, farming, education, non-profit, the environment, the arts, and government. He studied Theatre Arts at California State University Northridge and served as the resident Shakespeare lecturer for the Los Angeles Music Center Education Division. In 1989, while performing his stage play "Will Power" on the life of William Shakespeare in England, he discovered the lost letters of William Shakespeare.

Terry's public service career began when he founded the non-profit Santa Monica BayKeeper in 1993 and later served as the Executive Director of the Environment Now Foundation. In 2003, he was appointed as the Secretary of the California Environmental Protection Agency and later appointed Cabinet Secretary, the Chief Policy Advisor to the Governor. During his service in state government, Terry was the architect of many groundbreaking sustainability policies, including the Hydrogen Highway Network, the Million Solar Roofs initiative, California's landmark Global Warming Solutions Act, and the creation of over a million acres of "ocean parks" along California's coastline, resulting in The Guardian listing Terry No. 1 of its "Top 50 People Who Can Save the Planet." Terry founded the non-profit Seventh Generation Advisors in 2007 to help world governments adopt clean energy and sustainability polices based on California's successes and was named the Cullman Senior Fellow for climate policy at The New America Foundation. In 2016, Terry was appointed CEO of the Leonardo DiCaprio

Foundation, which is dedicated to the long-term health and well-being of all Earth's inhabitants.

In business, Terry managed a large multi-family housing company in the U.S.; owned a successful recreational services business; and assisted the West African nation of Nigeria with the creation of their first solid waste recycling program. He has also advised global companies and institutional investors on sustainability, including Walmart, Proctor & Gamble, and Pegasus Capital Advisors.

An accomplished author, Terry's book, *Lives Per Gallon: The True Cost of Our Oil Addiction* (Island Press), is a timely examination of our dependence on oil and a strategy to evolve to more sustainable energy sources and *Cracking the Carbon Code: The Keys to Sustainable Profits in the New Economy* (Palgrave) shows how to find the low carbon products and services that save money and preserve resources for generations to come. He has also authored a series of best-selling *Ultimate Guides* to pools and spas (McGraw-Hill) and *Watercolors: How JJ the Whale Saved Us* (Seventh Generation Press).